THE SWAN BOOK

Also by Alexis Wright

Plains of Promise
Grog War
Croire en l'incroyable
Le pacte du serpent
Take Power (as editor)
Carpentaria

THE SWAN BOOK

Alexis Wright

Constable ● London

CONSTABLE

First published in Australia by
The Giramondo Publishing Company, 2013

This edition published in Great Britain in 2015 by Constable

A CIP catalogue record for this book
is available from the British Library.

ISBN 978-1-47212-055-7 (hardback)
ISBN 978-1-47212-056-4 (ebook)

Typeset in 10/17 pt Baskerville by Andrew Davies
Designed by Harry Williamson
Printed and bound in Great Britain by Clays Ltd

Constable
is an imprint of
Constable & Robinson Ltd
100 Victoria Embankment
London EC4Y 0DY

An Hachette UK Company
www.hachette.co.uk

www.constablerobinson.com

FOR TOLY

All those travelling black swans
Gone to desert lagoons after big rains
In the Todd River next to Schultz Crossing
And thirty flying north along Larapinta Drive
in Alice Springs on the 14 January 2010

And in memory of Yari Tjampitjinpa
(Kumantjayi Zimran)

A wild black swan in a cage
Puts all of heaven in a rage

Robert Adamson, 'After William Blake'

CONTENTS

Prelude
Ignis Fatuus

Upstairs in my brain, there lives this kind of cut snake virus in its doll's house. Little stars shining over the moonscape garden twinkle endlessly in a crisp sky. The crazy virus just sits there on the couch and keeps a good old *qui vive* out the window for intruders. It ignores all of the eviction notices stacked on the door. The virus thinks it is the only pure full-blood virus left in the land. Everything else is just half-caste. Worth nothing! Not even a property owner. Hell yes! it thinks, worse than the swarms of rednecks hanging around the neighbourhood. Hard to believe a brain could get sucked into vomiting bad history over the beautiful sunburnt plains.

Inside the doll's house the virus manufactures really dangerous ideas as arsenal, and if it sees a white flag unfurling, it fires missiles from a bazooka through the window into the flat, space, field or whatever else you want to call life. The really worrying thing about missile-launching fenestrae is what will be left standing in the end, and which splattering of truths running around in my head about a story about a swan with a bone will last on this ground.

So my brain is as stuffed as some old broken-down Commodore you see left dumped in the bush. But I manage. I stumble around through the rubble. See! There I go – zigzagging like a snake over hot tarmac through the endless traffic. Here I am – ducking for cover from screeching helicopters flying around the massive fire-plume storms. And then, I recognise a voice droning from far away, and coming closer.

Oblivia! The old swan woman's ghost voice jumps right out of the ground in front of me, even though she has been dead for years. White woman still yelling out that name! *Where's that little Aboriginal kid I found?* No name. Mudunyi? Oblivion Ethyl(ene) officially. She asks: *What are you doing girl? I never taught you to go around looking like that.* Her hard eyes look me up and down. The skin and bone. My hair cut clean to the scalp with a knife. I am burnt the same colour as the ground. She takes in the view of the burnt earth, and says, *I never expected you to come back here.* The ghost says she still recognises the child she had once pulled from the bowels of an old eucalyptus tree that had looked as though it could have been a thousand years old. But this is no place for ghosts that don't belong here, and the virus barks continuously, as though he was some kind of watchdog barking, *Oooba, booblah, booblah!* The old woman's ghost is as spooked as a frightened cat in flight by the virus's sick laughter carrying across the charred land-scape. It frightens the living daylights out of her, although she still manages to say, *I know who you are*, before swiftly backing off across the landscape until she disappears over the horizon.

If you want to extract a virus like this from your head – you can't come to the door of its little old-fashion prairie house with passé kinds of thinking, because the little king will not answer someone knocking, will not come out of the door to glare into the sunlight, won't talk about anything in level terms, or jump around to appease you like some Chubby Checker impersonator bent over backwards under a limbo stick. Nor will it offer any hospitality – swart summers or not – no matter how much knocking, trick-ortreating, ceremonial presents, or tantrums about why the door was kept closed.

I can prove that I have this virus. I have kept the bit of crumpled-up paper, the proper results of medical tests completed by top doctors of the scientific world. They claimed I had a remarkable brain. Bush doctors, some of the best in the world, said this kind of virus wasn't any miracle; it was just one of those poor lost assimilated spirits that thought about things that had originated somewhere else on the planet and got bogged in my brain. Just like assimilation of the grog or flagon, or just any *kamukamu*, which was not theirs to cure.

The virus was nostalgia for foreign things, they said, or what the French say, *nostalgie de la boue*; a sickness developed from channelling every scrap of energy towards an imaginary, ideal world with songs of solidarity, like *We Shall Overcome*. My virus sings with a special slow drawling voice, like an Australian with *closed door syndrome* – just singing its heart out about cricket or football without a piece of thought, like Harry Belafonte's *Banana Boat Song – Day oh! Oh! Day a day oh! Daylight come and I want to go home*, etc. Well! There was nothing wrong with that. It could sing its homesick head off to the universe of viruses living in the polluted microscopic cities of the backwater swamp etched in my brain.

The extreme loser, not happy with having trapped itself in my brain, was acting like it had driven a brand new Ferrari into the biggest slum of a *dirty* desert in one of the loneliest places in the world, and there had to fit high culture into a hovel. The doctors said it was a remarkable thing, an absolute miracle that nobody else had ended up with a virus like this freak lost in my head, after testing thousands of fundamentalists of one kind or another. They called medical testing a waste of public money and drank polluted swamp water to prove it.

Having learnt how to escape the reality about this place, I have created illusionary ancient homelands to encroach on and destroy the wide-open vista of the virus's real-estate. The prairie house is now surrounded with mountainous foreign countries that dwarf the plains and flatlands in their shadows, and between the mountains, there are deserts where a million thirsty people have travelled, and to the coastlines, seas that are stirred by King Kong waves that are like monsters roaring at the front door. Without meeting any resistance whatsoever, I have become a gypsy, addicted to journeys into these distant illusionary homelands, to try to lure the virus hidden somewhere in its own crowded globe to open the door. This is where it begins as far as I am concerned. This is the quest to regain sovereignty over my own brain.

So I lie in the brochures that I send the virus, saying I must come and visit, saying that I have blood ties in homelands to die for in the continents across the world of my imagination, and a family tree growing in dreams of distant lands. The fact, I say, is that my homeland has grown into such a big spread that it has become a nightmare of constant journeying further and further out. I am like Santa Claus riding the skies in one single *mungamba* night to reach umpteen addresses, and why? Just to deliver the good of myself, whether the receiver wants it or not. The virus was quite interested in my idea of belonging everywhere, and asked why I took these journeys that bring in more places to crowd up its little world. I say that I begin locally, navigating yellow-watered floods that grow into even greater inland sea-crossings, to reach a rich alluvial plain that feeds shaded gardens, where the people who live there say they do not know me and ask why have I come. Always, I move on.

And so I travel, fired up with the fuel of inquiry about what it means to have a homeland, to travel further into strange and unknown lands covered with holy dust and orchards of precious small, sun-ripened fruit that are sometimes half-destroyed by war, and at other times, slapped hard in the face by famine. But still, even when I bring gifts to their door, the local people, although hungry and tired, find the courage to reject a person from their paradise no matter how far they have travelled, simply for not belonging.

I tell the virus that I have felt more at home with the cool air flowing on my face from a wild Whistling Swan's easy wings sweeping over snow-capped mountains in its grand migration across continents, than in those vast ghostly terrains of indescribable beauty that have given me no joy. I must continue on, to reach that one last place in a tinder-dry nimbus where I once felt a sense of belonging.

The virus thinks I want what it wants – to hide in a dark corner of its lolly pink bed, where it dreams, in my diseased mind.

Dust Cycle

And I hear the clang of their leader crying.
To a lagging mate in the rearward flying...

When the world changed, people were different. Towns closed, cities were boarded up, communities abandoned, their governments collapsed. They seemed to have no qualms that were obvious to you or me about walking away from what they called a useless pile of rubbish, and never looking back.

Mother Nature? Hah! Who knows how many hearts she could rip out? She never got tired of it. Who knows where on Earth you would find your heart again? People on the road called her the Mother Catastrophe of flood, fire, drought and blizzard. These were the four seasons which she threw around the world whenever she liked.

In every neck of the woods people walked in the imagination of doomsayers and talked the language of extinction.

They talked about surviving a continuous dust storm under the old rain shadow, or they talked about living out the best part of their lives with floods lapping around their bellies; or they talked about tsunamis and dealing with nuclear fallout on their shores and fields forever. Elsewhere on the planet, people didn't talk much at all while crawling through blizzards to save themselves from being buried alive in snow. You could bet your life on it – they hardly talked while all around the world governments fell as quickly as they rose in one extinction event after another. You be the judge. Believe it or not.

Ignis Fatuus = Foolish Fire. That's you Oblivion! You're just like that old Rip Van Winkle fella of the fairytale time. They were always calling out to him: 'Wake up coma man.' That man who slept like a log, more than an old dog, and kept on sleeping for so many years that when he woke up and went home, his house was gone – just scrub there, and nobody knew who he was anymore. He was empty – like a mystery man. Nobody remembered him. He could have been anyone. They kept poking him in his bony ribs wanting to know, 'Who do you reckon you are?', what his name was, and why he kept saying that his house had disappeared and all that. It is very hard to lose a house. Why would anyone want to do that? So bloody good job. Serves him right. You should always know where to find your home.

'It was here! It was here!' That was what the Rip Van Winkle man kept saying. He was just like you for making up stories like that, Oblivion. Nobody liked him either.

Some say that there was an accident before the drought. A little girl was lost. She had fallen into the deep underground bowel of a giant eucalyptus tree. In a silent world, the girl slept for a very long time among the tree's huge woven roots. Everyone had forgotten that she even existed – although, apparently, that did not take long.

Locked in the world of sleep, only the little girl's fingers were constantly moving, in slow swirls like music. She was writing stanzas in ancient symbols wherever she could touch – on the palms of her hands, and all over the tree root's dust-covered surfaces. Whatever she was writing, dredged from the soup of primordial memory in these ancient lands, it was either the oldest language coming to birth again instinctively, or through some strange coincidence, the

7

fingers of the unconscious child forming words that resembled the twittering of bird song speaking about the daylight: but the little girl could not understand the old ghost language of warbling and chortling remembered by the ancient river gum.

Her fingers traced the movements of the ghost language to write about the dead trees scattered through the swamp, where *dikili* ghost gums old as the hills once grew next to a deepwater lake fed by an old spring-spirit relative, until they had all slowly died. This happened during the massive sand storms that cursed the place after the arrival of the strangers from the sea. Their voices were heard arching across the heavy waves in the middle of the night. All their shouting ended up on ribbons of salt mist that went idling from the sea along an ancient breezeway – travelling with sand flies and tumbling bats through kilometres of inlet, along a serpentine track, dumped where it could dig into the resting place of the old story that lived inside the ancestral people of the lake.

The beetles blanketing the lake shook the night in a millisecond that shattered its surface, like precious old Venetian glass crashing onto a pavement. The roar of those harsh-sounding voices from the sea startled the ghosts which rose from beneath the lake's water – from hearing those men calling out – *half past midnight, half past two,* echoing from inside several brackets of reeds.

Sleepy children from the little dwellings around the lake heard voices speaking from large leafy fields of waterlilies. They felt words chasing after them, surrounding their feet like rope trying to pull them back as they ran away. Anyone daring to look back into the lake's echoes heard voices like dogs barking out of the mouths of fish skimming across the surface as they chased after the hordes of mosquitoes – *around four o'clock.*

Those echoes of voices which originated far out at sea were coming from the Armed Forces men involved in a large-scale sweep-up of the ocean's salty junk, floating about, bobbing and buoyant across the horizon.

The men from the Army were taunting these haunts of ghosts and outlaws to surrender themselves by dawn because they shouted: *Grab your liberation! Freedom! Called ghosts, you what?* It was a tragic demand to abandoned steel, planks of timber, brass lanterns and fittings, whose ghost sailors were unable to respond to military voices. But surprisingly, the empty wreckage obeyed. Vessel after vessel crawling out from behind the waves gleamed with the light of the stars dancing with the moonlight.

A parade of tugs towing the collected ruins churned across the breakers and headed towards land, and while the voices giving orders rose and fell, the flotilla began motoring through the deepwater channel towards the vast lake where the caretakers lived – the Aboriginal people who were responsible for this land. *First Contact* Whatever the men from the Army had been saying to each other on that night of bringing the junk to the lake was quickly forgotten, since around here, the words of strangers meant nothing.

Up to that point in time, the people of the lake had felt secluded in their isolation, even invisible to the outside world. They were more interested in singing in praise to the ancient spirits for the seasons lived alongside eels, fresh-water mussels, turtles and other aquatic life. Now they were truly startled by voices that resembled angry animals fighting over a few scraps of food.

It was freakish, yet they were frightened for no reason except instinct, from having their invisibility exposed by a simple little *scared* thing – lit up in the night as though it was the middle of the day by the beams from the Army's high-powered search lights swivelling on the tug boats – eyeballing along the shoreline for witnesses.

Their instinct for invisibility caused the entire population to slink away from its homes and slip into the bush, but in this inglorious fleeing for safety, something more sensational was noticed by one of these so-called nouveau-journalists of the event.

Somebody had eye-witnessed the lake bubbling from tug boats mix-mastering the water with their propellers, whisking it like a spritzer and putrefying all the dead ancient things rising to the surface, spraying it around like the smell of eternity. No wonder the local people, the traditional owners and all that, were too frightened to go back to the lake anymore. They had heard stories – bad stories about what happened to anyone who went back there.

Oblivia's fingers kept on writing the swirl language over the dust that fell on what the tree had witnessed in its lifetime, and the history of the stories that continued to be told by the locals about the years of fighting like a bunch of battle-axes – for umpteen friggen decades, without success, to get back what was theirs in the first place, and of years later again before these old families quit their tourism of other peoples' lands by saying they had had enough of wandering around homelessly for years worse than a pack of overseas gypsies, and returned to their rightful place of belonging, their ancestral domain.

Then, to top it off, they had no sooner set foot on the place, when they were told that Australians now recognised the law of Native Title after two plus centuries of illegal occupation, but unfortunately, on the day that they had left their land, their Native Title had been lost irredeemably and disappeared from the face of the planet.

The first thing they saw on their arrival at the lake that no longer belonged to them was the audacity of the floating junk. Even the tugboats had been left there to rot unfettered and untethered. Undeterred, the traditional owners ignored the view, and acted as though the lake was still the same tranquil place that it had always been from time *immemorial,* before the day that their people had been frightened away.

They took up their lives with the eyesore view of rust amongst the lilies, and very soon, everyone felt as though they had never left. But, it was strange what a view can do to how people think. The rotting junk clung to its secrets and in turn, the local people who did not really know what they were staring at or why the junk was staring back at them, also became secretive.

They wished and dreamed for this emotional eyesore to be removed and gone from their lands forever. It was foreign history sinking there that could not be allowed to rot into the sacredness of the ground. Their conscience flatly refused to have junk buried among the ancestral spirits.

These were really stubborn people sticking to the earth of the ancestors, even though they knew well enough that the contaminated lake caused bellyaches, having to eye each cup of tainted water they drank from the lake, but drinking it anyway.

There was not much choice about pure and pristine anymore. It was no good thinking about contaminated water leading to deformity in their culture for an eternity.

These people were hardened to the legendary stuff of fortune and ill fortune. They saw many children being born without any evidence of contamination. All children in living memory of the lake people's history, and regardless of the Army intervening in their parenthood, were deeply loved by their families, until this girl came along who was so different to any child ever born in their world, it made everyone think about why Oblivia had been born at all after this dumb girl was dragged out of the eucalyptus tree by old Bella Donna after years – a decade of being missing – and who disowned her people by acting as though she had by-passed human history, by being directly descended from their ancestral tree. Time would tell if this was true or false. Who was anyone to judge anything?

The junk on the lake was used as regular target practice for bombs falling from the warplanes that appeared unpredictably, flying low across the water from time to time throughout the year. Surprised at first, the local owners soon realised that their homeland was really a secret locality for Defence Force scheduled training manoeuvres. What a blast was that? Things getting blown up, up and down, in the isolated northern part of the nation.

Only heaven knows, there were millions of people throughout the world who either offered pigs as sacrifices to their Gods, or flowers, or the first grain of the new season's crop. There were even others who offered their own people to the Gods. Now the day had come when modern man had become the new face of God, and simply sacrificed the whole Earth. The swamp locals were not experiencing any terrific friendship with this new God. It was hell to pay to be living the warfare of modernity like dogs fighting over the lineage of progress against their own quiet whorls of time. Well! That just about summed up the lake people, sitting for all times in one place.

These were anti-halcyon times for the lake people, where the same old festering drains and degraded lands were struck hard and fast by a string of bad luck, which all in all, amounts to the same thing happening with the surprise of being struck once, or twice, or a hundred more times as though it were a chosen place.

Sand storms continued pouring over the lake and turned it into a swamp. The sand flew about in this freak weather until it banked up into a mountain with a pointy peak reaching into the sky. The mountain blocked the channel leading from the sea to the swamp.

Then an elder, a healer for the country arrived to examine the devastation, which he called, *a total ugly bitch of an annihilation*. He turned up like a bogeyman. A *kadawala*. *Dadarrba-barri nyulu jalwa-kudulu.* He claimed that he was feeling pain in his heavy heart. Turns up from nowhere like an aeroplane. *Bala-kanyi nyulu.*

He just flies where he wants to. This old *wululuku* was an Aboriginal man with an Asian heritage, the kind of person all sorts of people liked to call a half caste, yellow fella, or *mixed blood urban* Aboriginal. Half caste. Thinking! Thinking! Mixture. Mixed up. Not straight this or that. Extract! Lost purity. Not purely trustworthy. Exactly! No matter! He liked to call people a lot of names too, but he called himself the Harbour Master. He favoured calling himself by his own *worldly acquired* bona fides: a bony man with sun-darkened brown skin and sunglasses, a slack shaver with stubbly growth on his face – someone who resembled Mick Jagger. Someone with special healing powers who travelled anywhere he was needed, just by thinking himself into a sick person's mind. His was *wanami*, like fuel, and *wakubaji* – goes like anything. He started to live like a *persona non grata* sitting up there like a motionless exile on the sand mountain's summit. Japanese type. Something *sage-guru-expert* turnout. He became simple, like a snail-eating dune hermit. Somebody short on detail about what else he was going to feed himself with, and no tap water either to boot. Still, only kings live above everyone else, watching everybody else like this. So, maybe, he was a bit of a king too.

Oblivia remembered thinking that dust had a way of displacing destiny the first time she saw a swan. A red ghost was rolling in the sky when a lone, grey-black swan suddenly appeared at lunchtime over the riparian rook of this northern world. General swamp people sitting around as slack as you please, were shovelling freshly sautéed fish fillets into their mouths when they heard the strange song of the swan. The whole place went silent. Nobody said a word. Everyone stopped eating. Half-raised forks froze mid-stream above the dinner plates. The dinner went cold while everyone stared at the first swan ever seen on this country. Only their thoughts wild with noise were asking why this strange bird stilted the heat of the day with song where there was no song for swans. The locals asked the storming almighty red dust spirit relation, *What's that bro?*

In all of this vast quietness where the summer sun was warming the dust spirit's mind, the swan looked like a paragon of anxious premonitions, rather than the arrival of a miracle for saving the world. Seeing the huge bird flying through the common dusty day like this, disturbed whatever peace of mind the stick-like Oblivia possessed. Everyone watched a swan's feather float down from the sky and land on her head. Oblivia's skin instantly turned to a darker shade of red-brown. What about her frizzy hair then? Well! There was no change in that. It was always sprayed out in fright. *Ngirriki*! Messy! Always looking like tossed winter straw that needed rope to tie it down. She was *psychological*. *Warraku*. Mad. Even madder than ever. That was the most noticeable change. She did what was expected. She nose-dived like a pitchfork into the unbearable, through broiling dust vats, to countless flashbacks of what was over-the-top and dangerous. Everything in her mind became mucked up. This is the kind of harm the accumulated experience of an exile will do to you, to anyone who believes that they had slept away half their life in the bowel of a eucalyptus tree. Well! Utopian dreaming was either too much or too little, but at least she recognised that the swan was an exile too.

Suddenly, the swan dropped down from the sky, flew low over the swamp, almost touching the water, just slow enough to have a closer look at the girl. The sight of the swan's cold eye staring straight into hers, made the girl feel exposed, hunted and found, while all those who had suddenly stopped eating fish, watched this big black thing look straight at the only person that nobody had ever bothered having a close look at. Her breathing went AWOL while her mind stitched row after row of fretting to strangle her breath: *What are they thinking about me now? What did the swan have to single me out for and not anyone else standing around? What kind of premonition is this?* Heart-thump thinking was really tricky for her. She feasted on a plague of *outsidedness*. It was always better never to have to think about what other people thought of her.

It was through this narrow prism of viewing something strange and unfamiliar, that the girl decided the swan wasn't an ordinary swan and had not been waylaid from its determined path. She knew as a fact that the swan had been banished from wherever it should be singing its stories and was searching for its soul in her.

The black swan continued travelling low, then flew upwards with its long neck stretched taut, as though it was being pulled away by invisible strings as fine as a spider's web held in its beak. She saw a troupe of frost-face monkeys holding the strings at the other end of the world. They were riding on a herd of reindeer crushing through ice particles in those faraway skies. Those taut strands of string twanged the chords of swan music called the *Hansdhwani* that the old gypsy woman Bella Donna would play on her swan-bone flute while you could watch the blood flowing to the pulse of the music through the old white lady's translucent skin. It was the swan raga the girl heard now coming down from the sky, the music of migratory travelling cycles, of unravelling and intensifying, of flying over the highest snow-capped mountains, along the rivers of Gods and Goddesses, crossing seas with spanned wings pulsing to the rhythm of relaxed heartbeats.

This was when the girl realised that she could hear the winnowing wings from other swans coming from far away. Their murmurings to one another were like angels whispering from the heavens. She wondered where they were coming from as they entered her dreams in this country, this first time she saw a swan. She could not have known anything of how long it had taken the huge black birds to make the migratory flight from so far away, to where they had no storyline for taking them back.

The swans had become gypsies, searching the deserts for vast sheets of storm water soaking the centuries-old dried lakes when their own habitats had dried from prolonged drought. They had become nomads, migratory like the white swans of the northern world, with their established seasonal routes taking them back and forth, but unlike them, the black swans were following the rainwaters of cyclones deeper and deeper into the continent.

Bevies of swans crossed the man-made catchments and cubby dams on pastoral lands, and flew down to the tailing dams of mines, and the sewerage ponds of inland towns, where story after story was laid in the earth again before the dust rose, and on they went, forging into territory that had been previously unknown to these southern birds except perhaps, for their ancestors of long ago, when great flocks might have travelled their law stories over the land through many parts of the continent. The local people thought, *They must have become the old gypsy woman's swans!*

So it was really true. The old *badibadi* woman had always said she could call swans, but it was a white swan she wanted most of all, not these black ones. Bella Donna and the girl that she had adopted after years of searching for her and pulling her out of a hollow in the trunk of a tree, lived together on one of the old rusty hulks stuck out there in the middle of the swamp where the black swan was flying. The girl remembered how the old woman was always talking about how she owed her life to a swan. Telling Oblivia about how much she missed seeing the swans from her world. It was a foreigner's *Dreaming* she had.

She came beginning of dust time, some of the old dust-covered people claimed, remembering the drought and the turtles that had lived there for thousands of years crawling away into the bush to die. They had studied her bones that could be clearly seen under her thin translucent skin. This they claimed was caused from eating too much fish from her life at sea, and said that Bella

Donna was a very good example of how other people were always fiddling around with their laws. These were people old enough to still remember things about the rest of the world, whereas most of the younger generations with a gutful of their own wars to fight were not interested in thinking any further afield than to the boundary of the swamp. All of these big law people thought tribal people across the world would be doing the same, and much like themselves, could also tell you about the consequences of breaking the laws of nature by trespassing on other people's land. They were very big on the law stories about the natural world.

The girl was full of the old woman's stories about swans before she had seen one, and even if words did not pass through her lips, she would imitate Bella Donna's old European accent in her mind: *I have seen swans all my life. I have watched them in many different countries myself. Some of them have big wings like the Trumpeter Swan of North America, and when the dust smudges the fresh breath of these guardian angels, they navigate through the never-ending dust storms by correcting their bearings and flying higher in the sky, from where they glide like Whistling Swans whistling softly to each other, then beating their wings harder they fly away. I know because I am the storyteller of the swans.*

Where I came from, whole herds of deer were left standing like statues of yellow ice while blizzards stormed. Mute Swans sheltered in ice-covered reeds. The rich people were flying off in armadas of planes like packs of migratory birds. The poverty people like myself had to walk herdlike, cursed from one border to another through foreign lands and seas.

You know girl? I owe the fact that I am alive today to a swan. But anyhow, my story of luck is only a part of the concinnity of dead stories tossed by the sides of roads and gathering dust. In time, the mutterings of millions will be heard in the dirt...I am only telling you my story about swans.

Could an ancient hand be responsible for this? The parched paper country looking as though the continent's weather systems had been rolled like an ancient scroll from its top and bottom ends, and *ping*, sprung shut over the Tropic of Capricorn. The weather then flipped sides, swapping southern weather with that of the north, and this unique event of unrolling the climate upside down, left the entire continent covered in dust. When the weather patterns began levelling out after some years, both ends of the country looked as though normal weather was being generated from the previously dry centre of Australia. With the heart of the country locked into a tempestuous affair, hot and sticky, what was once the south's cool temperate climate mixed with the north's tropical humidity until the whole country was shrouded in days of dust – *Jundurr! Jundurr!* – or, all the time in heavy cyclonic rain.

Its journey took the black swan over the place where hungry *warrki* dingos, foxes and *dara kurrijbi buju* wild dogs had dug out shelters away from the dust, and lay in over-crowded burrows in the soil; and in the grasses, up in the rooftops, in the forests of dead trees, all the fine and fancy birds that had once lived in stories of marsh country, migrating swallows and plains-dancing brolgas, were busy shelving the passing years into a lacy webbed labyrinth of mud-caked stickling nests brimmed by knick-knacks, and waves of flimsy old plastic threads dancing the wind's crazy dance with their faded partners of silvery-white lolly cellophane, that crowded the shores of the overused swamp.

Up you too, Oblivia snarls under her breath after being reminded of the people she suspected were keeping an eye on her, after they saw the swan looking at her.

The swan had swung into shock-locked wings when human voices interrupted its nostalgia, but still it kept flying over the dust-covered landscape. This child! The swan could not take its eyes away from the little girl far down on the red earth. The music broke as if the strings had been broken, and the swan fell earthwards through the air for several moments. Maybe, it was in those moments of falling, that the big bird placed itself within the stories of this country, before it restored the rhythm of its flapping wings, and continued on its flight.

Oblivia gave the swan no greater thought after it had disappeared, other than to think that it was heading in the right direction – towards water, to reach the sea, the place that she knew existed from stories she had heard of what was beyond the northern horizon. She thinks people are talking about her and glares unkindly towards the multitude of residential shacks jammed cheek to jowl like a sleeping snake ringing the swamp: a multi-coloured spectacle in the bright glare of sunlight, of over-crowding and over-use, confusion in love, happiness, sorrow and rage, in this slice of humanity living the life of the overcome. All about, birds squabbled noisily, chasing one another over the rooftops for space in air thick with the high cost of living for a view of a dead lake.

These people keep looking at me, the girl mouths the words – *read my lips*, centimetres from Bella Donna's face. No sound comes out of her mouth since she had decided not to speak, that it was not worth speaking. She would rather be silent since the last word she had spoken when scared out of her wits, the day when her tongue had screeched to a halt with dust flying everywhere, and was left screaming *Ahhhhhh!* throughout the bushland, when she fell down the hollow of the tree.

Bella Donna felt invaded by Oblivia's hot breath striking her face. In an instant, her sense of privacy diminishes into the spoils of war flattened over the barren field of herself, even though she recognises the girl's clumsy attempts to communicate with her. That the girl has never recovered from being raped. But feeling and knowing are two different things: she retaliates all the same, and like any other long-standing conflict around the world, one act of violation becomes a story of another. *Remember who it was who rescued you with her bare hands. Did you see anyone else digging you out of that tree? Out there in the heat? Sun pouring down on my head in the middle of the day? Did you hear anyone else calling out for someone to come and help me to pull you out before you died out there? No! There was nobody else coming along and helping an old woman. Nobody else spent years looking for you. It was only me who was walking and walking in the bush and calling you girlie – you remember that. Even your own parents had forgotten who you were. Dead! They thought you were dead. It was only me who looked for you.*

Try as she might to rectify the problem of the speechless child, Bella Donna knew that the girl would only manage to make certain sounds that did not even closely resemble vowels. It seemed as though the child's last spoken word had been left orbiting unfinished, astray, irredeemable and forsaken. The only sounds she heard emanating from the girl's mouth were of such low frequency that the old woman strained to distinguish what usually fell within the range of bushland humming, such as leaves caught up in gusts of wind, or the rustling of the *wiyarr* spinifex grasses in the surrounding landscape as the wind flew over them, or sometimes the flattened whine of distant bird song, or a raging bush-fire crackling and hissing from *jujuu jungku bayungu*, a long way off, which the old woman heard coming out of Oblivia's angry mouth.

The girl did not actually care whether the old gypsy lady from the land of floribunda roses was listening or not, nor did she care that the old woman kept saying she was in charge of caring for her until she was covered with dirt in her grave, and even from the grave itself, she would still rise to cook, and wash and what not, because she was a saint who took on responsibilities like this. *I told you these people keep looking at me.*

What for girl? My sweet Lord, they only see what they want to see. They are blind, not stupid. They see, but they are blind, the old voice did not feel like answering the girl – never understanding the speechlessness, making it up as she talked.

Oblivia! The startled old woman, believing she understood whatever the girl was saying or thinking, having cracked the code of the language of windstorms or wind gusts, spoke in a pitched tone of voice that implied she held a high status in this poor community. She had given the girl a fancy name and everything. Oblivia, short for Oblivion Ethyl(ene), was her unconsciously inspired, synonymously paralleling sentiment for a girl perhaps best suited dead, instead of returning like a bad smell from the grave. She continued with pride in hearing herself saying the name again, *Oblivia! You have become a very cynical person for someone of your age.*

The old woman was trying to make good use of her burden, whose aim in life was to get the girl to act normal: behave and sit up straight at the table and use a knife and fork properly, learn table manners, talk nicely, walk as a butterfly flies, dress like a normal person, learn something marvellous on a daily basis, and show some resilience. Over and over, Oblivia sings in her head: *Nah! Sporadically all the time. Be full of useful facilities.* And, this: *Treat people decent.*

It seemed as though Oblivia had learnt nothing in years of living with the old woman except how to stay bent and rake thin, but not even she could prevent the force of nature. She could not go around in a perpetual state of warring with the obvious, by forever imagining herself to be like a piece of rotten fruit peel curled up inside the tree. Bones straightened out. She grew taller, and her skin darkened from the nondescript amber honey of a tree's heartwood, to radiant antique gold – darkened, like a tarnished red-yellow ochre pit blazing in the sun after rain.

In this world of the swamp, people had good ears for picking up every word that went skimming across the surface of the water, and vice versa, from the old lady's hull and back. You could almost reach out and grab each word with your hand. They were listening to what was considered to be some general crap coming out of the old lady's kitchen. The girl copycats those nicely spoken words, but prefers the tempo of the local dialect, to interpret like a local, and with her tongue tapping around behind closed lips, echoes soundlessly the homilies of her home life: *Toughen up. Get out there. Make a difference. Don't be like the rest of the people around here. And have a good day.*

The old lady's speech was considered quite charming but inspired nothing in the local Indigenous people's summation, where it was generally thought to be, *Very good English for sure, and would go far for the language betterment of Australia, but not here.* Naturally! Out on the swamp where life was lived on the breeze, her tongue was considered to be too soft, like a cat's purr. It could not adapt to the common old rough way in the normal state of affairs, *cross-cultural-naturally*, where all English language was spoken for political use only. Whatever was decent about English speech in the way she spoke it, was better for chatting a long way away, in its homeland. Maybe, while taking a leisurely walk with ladies and gentlemen through the environs of a finely constructed English garden, with those whose day delighted in the sight of every fresh rose, or were surprised by a squirrel scampering across the path with a plump autumn acorn in its teeth.

Swamp people were not ignorant of white people who, after all, had not turned up yesterday. Having lived it all, they claimed to have at least ten, or possibly more generations of knowledge, packed up tight in their mentality about white people doing good for them. Seasonal crop farmers, harvesters of potatoes, cabbages, fields of beans, yellow pears, wheat for whisky, wine grapes, dairy cattle or pigs, truffles and olives, death feuds, imprisonment, domination, the differences between rich and poor, slaves, war and terror – whatever celebrated their faraway ancestral districts. Still! Why worry about the old woman's voice going – *Blah! Blah!* Or jumping – *Ting! Thang! Thing! Ting! Thang! What!* – it was only the needle of her compass spinning back to the north from any radius of her wanderings of the Earth. Opera! It was only opera. This was how the local population living packed up and down in the great distance around the swamp described her kind of talk.

The old woman spoke loudly to the girl while feeding flocks of black swans gathering around the hull. She was fed up. She had always gotten on well with people everywhere in her life before being rudely treated by a child. *Not just from this swamp. Yes,* she said, *I have used my opportunities for influencing people across the world. You must use the voice.* The girl thought that she should be silent if words were just a geographical device to be transplanted anywhere on earth. Then if that was possible: *Was it possible for her voice to be heard by imaginary people too?*

Wanymarri white woman was from one of those nationalities on Earth lost to climate change wars. The new gypsies of the world, but swamp people said that as far as they were concerned, even though she was a white lady, they were luckier than her. They had a home. Yes, that was true enough. Black people like themselves had somewhere, whereas everywhere else, probably millions of white people were drifting among the other countless stateless millions of sea gypsies looking for somewhere to live.

Bella Donna of the Champions claimed that she was the descendent of a listener of Hoffmeister's Quartet in F. This music was cherished throughout the whole world she boasted: *But not here.* That was true enough! The swamp people had never heard of such music. She said on the other hand, whilst living happily enough among the Aborigines of Australia now, she was from many other countries equally and felt *not really here and not really there*. When you had travelled so far and wide in a lifetime as she had, of course you would be heard anywhere on Earth if you had left your tongue everywhere. She had often told the girl that all of humanity's past and present had locations stored in her head. *That was what the head was for – storing knowledge about the world that you might want to use one day.*

Right! As if!

As all stories begin with once upon a time, so the old woman always began her story, while looking into the levitating crystal balls she juggled, as though all stories that ever existed originated from these objects. Anything was possible when her snowy hair seemed charged with electricity and flew about wildly in the wind. All about her tall lean frame, the faded red hibiscus flowers of her old dress billowed as if caught in a cyclone. Her hundred-year-old face creased into a hundred more wrinkles. White lines of fog filled the fractured lines in one ball. Red dust swarmed inside the other.

With eyes the colour of the oceans, she continued staring absentmindedly, perhaps from habits formed on journeys over listless seas, but the scary thing was this gave the impression that she was releasing the words she spoke from inside the mesmerising glass, struck golden by the sun. So transfixing was the power of these objects, it did not occur to anyone that she might be fiddling with their minds, cursing them perhaps with overseas magic. Her trick made people stare straight into each spinning ball as it hung in midair like a miracle, the pivot reached before each slow ascension, while haphazardly heaping into their brains whatever they liked to remember about her story.

For all anyone in the swamp knew, she might have been Aine, the sun goddess of Ireland. An old woman, mortified from having

been dredged out of her lake in haste, and then, having to suffer
the indignities of being dragged around the world in stinking
boats. The swamp had become the place for reincarnation for all
sorts living around the place. For sure, she was grand enough,
enticing people, tricking their dreams, and juggling things around
the edges of their minds. A goddess who had dragged herself out
of the ocean then become an ordinary old woman.

Her country of origin, Bella Donna had claimed, was where
people of the modern world once lived happily by doing more or
less nothing, other than looking after themselves from one day to
the next to fuel the stories of their life, but they were *finished now*.
Always she returned to the memory of a single white swan feather
resting on the spider web outside a window of her childhood home
next to a forest where deer lived. She would recite a line from a
poet from Hungary, *Snow, fog, fingerprints sprouting swans' feathers on
the windowpanes…It was just a childhood memory*, she always snapped
abruptly on reaching this point of her story, as if her most treasured
melancholy thought was not fit enough for *this* place.

She claimed that one day, some devil, not a person, but a freak
of nature, went to war on her people. *Old woman what kind of freak
was that?* Well! Swamp people wanted to know. Had a right to know.
She looked startled, as though she had been asked to describe the
inexplicable, of what happened to people affected by the climate
changing in wild weather storms, or the culmination of years of
droughts, high temperature and winds in some countries, or in
others, the freezing depths of prolonged winters. *Peace*, she said,
it was called peace by the governments that called on their people
to fight land wars. She had seen its kind rampaging across the
gentle lands of her country, destroying everything in its path, and
leaving those who survived with a terrible story to tell.

Listen to what I say: cities, towns, homes, land, as well as
animals and crops, were flattened and could be no more. It was bad

weather that made fanatics like this. Her voice thrilled as though her tongue was on fire while she listed her foes: *Dictators! Bandits! People bashers!* She could spend all day listing the world's villains who had destroyed her people's land. Those willing to push the world into an unstoppable catastrophic slide of destruction and hatred with nuclear fallout, she shouted, as though swamp people were deaf to the sound of the outside world. *Everybody looking twice at his neighbour's property. One land-grabbing country fighting another land-grabbing country, and on it went with any people excess to requirement killed, or they left on their own accord by throwing themselves into the ocean.* Her voice fell into lady-like pretty-garden reminiscences now, quavering with the memory of a lifetime enmeshed with sea waves in a volatile shifting world that was irreconcilably changed. *With their country completely destroyed and radioactive, who could return? Which millennium, this one or next? What would her people be then?* Her words were caustic and frightening, but beguiling too in the minds of the overwhelmed swamp people trying to imagine this ghost country where nobody goes.

Then, without country, imagine that? Imagining! Can't imagine. For country never leaves its people. This was what the swamp people claimed while seeing some sort of country in her, and dragging it out of her by listening, like scavenging rubbish out of a bin, rubbish lying everywhere – hard to imagine where it all came from. She asked them to think about the people of her nation as they joined a trail of misery forged by those who were walking before them.

What about them? These people owned nothing but the clothes they wore and whatever could be carried away on their backs, handy things like: *television, computers, mobile phones?* Whoosh! Splat! Bang! They were the sounds you heard all day long when technology was being thrown over the side of mountains in the search for food and water. The story of her people, she claimed, was like the chapters in a nightmarish book. What would come next? The people of the swamp knew about stories. Stories had value. Could buy trust. Could buy lots of things. Even silence. This story was new cash among people full of suspicion of one another.

Helter skelter, running away, fleeing people became refugees marching onwards just like deer would through winter steppes to nowhere. Hunger was constant. Waves of vermin, rats disguised as men, drove the moving chains of humanity into traps. The killing of people was without reason, fruitless and endless. This was Bella Donna's life when her people were being forced off their land. Eventually, beyond breaking point, there in the mountains under some spirit-charged rowan trees that were thousands of years old, they reached another summit of hopelessness. Bewildered, and staring down from above the clouds clinging to the sides of the mountains, they tried to locate holes in the scrims of mist to the fells, to see if the face of so much inhumanity was resting somewhere among the rivers and forests with smoke pluming from camp fires, but eventually, even those who had survived to this point resigned themselves to a fate of total annihilation.

So be it! Miserably, but almost bizarrely joyous too for such a final realisation that they were at the gates of their Maker, Bella Donna said those who were standing on the mountaintop ready to die, now turned their fragile gaze upwards to Heaven. If there was a bigger picture than the landscape, they were acknowledging the existence of a much mightier hand inflicting this enormous punishment on their depravity, even though they had once felt that their lives were normal enough. Then, as they knelt on the frozen ground to pray silently for the end to come quickly, something very unusual happened.

They heard God approaching in the fog. Music, so sweet as though nature was singing, it was just like hearing *Spiegel im Spiegel* played lightly on a cello. A single white swan flew by: its wings beating with music. *The bell-beat of wings above our heads,* the old lady whispered, a line that an Irish bard had once crafted with ink on paper to sweeten the world. They saw a Mute Swan, one of the biggest of the eight known types of swans in the world. It circled above, and then flew down and landed amongst them. It whispered a greeting of good day and good fortune. Its hot breath formed a little cloud in the cold air.

Listen closely: *Our thoughts were not brave. Should this fat bird, the only one seen for days, appearing like an angel in response to our final prayers to Heaven, be eaten? Should angels ever be eaten, even one, by so many hungry people?*

The swan had dirty feathers, ingrained with the ash spread through blackened snow on the burnt plains of low lands where it had walked under the clouds. It did not stay long. Swanlike, it ran heavily, carrying away the past, present and future on its webbed feet, slapping along the sodden, mossy, alpine swamp until it was treading water then air in its wake.

But unlike a wild creature, the swan returned. It flew in swooping circles around the people gathered on the mountain, forcing them to get up off the cold ground they had been kneeling on, and move. The freezing temperature, already sourer than a hoar wind, threatened to turn them into statues of ice. Several thousand people began walking in circles through biting wind and rain, their spirits lifting in the talk circulating about a swan that had once landed at the feet of a saint. The sinking into the well of memory about swans on that day was remarkable. Back! Back! And even further back, remembering how this very creature was descended from a Knight Swan, which of course convinced them of their own relationships to the swan's *descendency*. Someone yelled to the swan flying above – *Lohengrin.* A chorus, remembering Wagner's opera, replied – *The knight Lohengrin arrived in a boat drawn by a swan.* History! Swan history! Quicker! Quicker! Remembering this, and remembering that; and there it was, the swans loved and hated through the ages in stories laid bare by this huddling melee of the doomed trying to find warmth on frozen moss. They grabbed a trillion swans in their imagination, dragged them back from the suppressed backwoods of the mind. *So! God help us,* Bella Donna said, they all sang – *live and let live,* until the throng sang for their life to keep warm, then decided to head back down the mountain.

They followed the swan quickly, breathlessly, and down they went, becoming strong again simply from believing there was goodness left in the world. From remembering God and words, and lines of poetry, *Upon the brimming water among the stones, are nine and fifty swans.* The old woman looked as though she was back on the mountain that day years before, reciting lines they sang, quicker and more quickly, as their feet hit the stony path, *And scatter wheeling in great broken rings, upon their clamorous wings.*

Through the swan, they had put their faith back in life as routinely as though they had been watching a favourite weekly television program. They knew without reason that the swan would always be there on the land, would always return, and always be remembered. They were like their ancestors of the Dark Ages who once followed swans up and down imaginary paths with the single-mindedness of saving themselves – from what? *A similar misfortune?* The swan flew above the gushing bluish-white torrents coursing down the mountains. *We followed the idea of living,* she said, believing that this swan was a guide that had reached out from our past.

The swan flew on and on while every man, woman and child followed, tumbling in their own stream down rocky slopes and slippery moss to take up their flight, until finally before nightfall, the big white bird flew over the coastline through wild winds out to a grey sea, guiding Bella Donna's people to safety from wars.

Severely deluded into believing that they could be saved from whatever calamity chased them, the people went clambering after the swan even though the winds butting against their faces tried to push them back from the sea. But in the terror of having nowhere else to go, somehow the miracle of the white swan continued urging them onwards. They stumbled through the darkness, and they ran along a river covered with solid ice until they reached the shore. They ran straight on into the freezing water, towards the abandoned, unseaworthy fishing boats still bobbing in the bay.

They set sail; following the swan's own long migratory flight out of the country, heading towards the moon squatting on the horizon. Bella Donna lamented to the swamp people, the swan disappearing across the sea was like the myth of Icarus whose wings fell off for not heeding the warning of his father. But, people running away do not always remember precisely what was in any old text locked away in the library. Instead! *Let's sail.* She sighed, and nodding her head, looked as though she was back on that same rough sea crashing on to the foreshore and revisiting the scrambling scene of their chaotic departure. She claimed it was an angel with swan wings pushing them out to sea that night; hands of the angel holding the masthead, covering the sails that should have been torn apart in the wind.

Gladdened to be nestling under moonlight and safely afloat, Bella Donna of the Champions said, *We wanted to relinquish our lands, their memories and stories, and after a little reflection and the buoyancy from being so far out on the water, we said we wanted to be exonerated from history.* Soon, indeed on the morning of the following day and every day afterwards as they headed further out across the ocean, only the inconsequentiality of the day before lingered in the memory of their new identity as boat people. They believed they had become mythical oarsmen with gilded paddles rowing sedately to beating drums, in time to the rolling wave of a chanter waving outstretched batons, with long white horse hair flying in sea wind. It was as though they were on a flying swan the size of a ship flying smoothly over the tops of waves. *We imagined ourselves sailing on the magnificently crafted Subanahongsa swan barge. Our swan's feathers shining like gold and precious jewels in the sunlight, and the pearl that hung from its neck, the size of a huge ball, shining in the moonlight.* And so she claimed: *We called ourselves the people who could call swans.*

Aunty Bella Donna of the Champions travelled the seas as wretchedly as any other among the banished people of the world, but as luck would have it, she came to live out her last days among the poorest people in a rich land. A hidden place. Another Eden. A place where hunger and death were commonplace to its elders, the landowners who knew that they were a social-science experiment with a very big cemetery. A small place where sometimes things got so bad when the swamp's little gang of brain-damaged, toxic-fume-sniffing addicted kids ruled, that parents asked only for one moment of peace. Where any silence was considered heaven-sent. People were gambling the cards and playing like ghosts. They were gambling about the Messiah. Made bets to see who was the luckiest. Well! Song sung true! Messiahs come and go, usually in the form of academic researchers, or a few chosen blacks and one-hit wonders pretending to speak for Aboriginal people and sucking-dry government money bureaucrats. They were the only Messiahs sent with answers. You got to practise what you preach. Pray God, waste not.

It was unimaginably miserable to be languishing at sea, moving from one ghost ship to another as the last living soul of the armadas, when finally, by simply saying enough was enough, this old woman invaded Australia. She saw the Australian beach lined with pandanus, smelt bush fires, caught the dust in the breeze laden with the aroma of over-ripe mangoes, *gidgee kadawala* woodlands and bloodwood *corymbia capricornia*, and she would listen no more to the law of breaking waves slapping against the shores of a forbidden land. She gathered up into a bag her old swan flute, a pile of books about swans, and those crystal balls. Then she walked straight across the Australian coastline and headed into the bush.

Anyone there? she called.

A bullfrog sitting in the *janja*, the mud, a lone tiny creature guarding the closed-gap entrance to the security fence of government transparency erected by the Army around the entire swamp answered, *baji* – maybe. It was happy enough to grant her asylum when she asked for a look.

She turned up on an Indigenous doorstep, and the children called out: A Viking! A Viking! An old, raggedy Viking!

All covered with dirt, grass and sticks, she looked as though she had forgotten how to walk or comb her hair and had swum through the scrub. Two laws, one in the head, the other worthless on paper in the swamp, said she was an invader. But! What could you do? Poor Bella Donna of the Champions! The sight of her made you cry. She was like a big angel, who called herself the patroness of World Rejection. She wasn't some renegade redneck from Cammoweal or Canberra. This was the place for rejection: there was no hotter topic in the mind than rejection in this swamp, so to prove that they were not assimilated into the Australian way of life, the ancient laws of good manners about welcoming strangers were bestowed – Here! Stay! Have a go! We don't mind.

The old woman was terrified that she would be taken back down to the beach and thrown into the sea, and struggled to explain her lengthy and extraordinary ordeal. The crystal balls, her swan books and swan-bone flute in a canvas bag were all that she possessed, and these she tried to bargain for her life by pushing them into the hands of the elders. No one would touch them. Everyone backed away, fearing contamination from what were plainly the sacred objects that locked in her story. In quick gulps, she mentioned secrets – an important message about how she had been saved to tell the tale.

She was quizzed by the old people with the ancient wisdom. They asked if her secrets were in their national interest, by which they only implied their own big swamp of a nation, not the shebangs of anybody else's business. Well! Those hearts almost jumped straight from their chests from seeing so much horror in her eyes as she levitated the crystal balls, which created another illusion altogether, as though her world had once been like these balls, momentarily able to float in space.

All of this kind of thing happening out of the blue like that was not the message from a Messiah that the Government in Canberra had told the swamp people to expect, but still, none could deny that she had been a sort of answer to prayers, even though she looked more like the local soil covering the roots of trees. She answered their inquiry by saying that her stories were of the utmost interest to the world. Well! they thought, why not. Our nation was small. Our boundaries not very large. It was very nice land. A bit flat. A bit hot. What they liked best, the kinsmen told her, was that they had nothing to do with the rest of Australia. They thought that they might like to have a bit of a holiday from some ancient responsibilities, and told her: So stay. Have the floor old one. Tell stories.

The maddest person on Earth told her stories of exile endlessly, but who listened? The swamp people were not interested in being conquered by other peoples' stories. Aunty Bella Donna of the Champions knew times when no one listened to the inconsequential stories she sung to herself: when hungry people feed themselves fat on voices droning from the radio, and repeat what they hear, they are like canaries. The girl replaced any dream of a big audience.

But Oblivia stared into space, not listening. It was just music. Wave after wave of it rippling through the swamp. The score of a long concerto in gibberish and old principles cemented in language that ears had never heard before in that swamp.

First off! There was fright. Hell's people were naturally jumping around with Bella Donna's prolonged talking in this silent place of worship. She liked talking about surviving, intervention, closing the gap, moving forward as the way to become re-empowered, learning 'lifestyle', of aesthetically pleasing houses and gardens. This confused the swamp. They thought she was really a local-bred redneck after all. The old people asked her: *Weren't you supposed to be some kind of a holy orator who remembered each epoch-making episode and emotional upheaval of the Planet's nomadic boat people?* Heads spun with all the fires and violins endured in oceans as barren as a desert when she got back to the facts. She told it all: Feast and famine. Flutes of bewilderment. Drowning cellos. The voices of lovers. Crying births. Storms screaming. Wailing loss, abandonment, silence. Rejection. Bombing. Prayers. Theft. Beseeching. War. Puzzlement. Starvation. Staring at death. Organs from all over the world were playing in the swamp now. Thieving pirates. Robbers. Bandits. Murderers. And, somehow, more survival until: Glory of migrating swan birds filling the skies.

Her poetry was about the grind. A treadmill recalling unlaurelled bravery. Notes for those dead at sea. Men, women and children captured forever in the ghost nets of zero geography. She floated on the calm of swamp brine like the halcyon bird that sung the myths of wind and waves for the polyglotic nations of the sea. The uncharted floating countries of condemned humanity. Twenty-first-century cast-outs ploughing the wilderness of oceans. But that was long ago she said. When the years passed and the floating worlds of refugees had grown white-haired, become weak and old of heart from waiting for any welcoming country on earth that was either big or small enough to let them in, all but one of those tens of thousands of obsolete people, the rejected of the world, had died.

The swamp people said her stories were lies. The sovereign facts lying on their table said that there was nothing worth hearing about from anywhere else on earth that was like her stories. Their sun hissed down and crackled on tin roofs. They did not need more heroes. Their own healer of country was already sitting up on top of the sand mountain trying to figure out what to do with it. And they knew what it meant to be sweltering in the heat, and dirt poor. Politely, they asked the *wambu wanymari* sick white lady to speak elsewhere about the snow, frost and chill. They had never seen any of that. *Go tell China! Africa! Bundaberg! Istanbul! Don't come here with stories sounding like some kind of doomsaying prophet. We need our own practical measures to safeguard our culture. It is after all factual that terribly, terribly dry stories that flip, flop seven times in one hour straight are dangerous to the health of the mind.* No worries. What if times were blind and tight? *We were dead in the water in a dirty world,* she claimed while wiggling her fingers at the locals. Forget the raving. Forget the ranting. *We will not give away our rich provenance to the rest of the world, just to be like madamba – joined together like friends, no way,* the local broadcasters replied in song sung blue, and weeping like a willow.

Lesson over and another begins. *Oblivia! You must always remember eyes and ears are everywhere.* The old woman still spoke from a mind that lived elsewhere, with her speech that ran off to thoughts of hearing twinkling bells like the sound of a swan flying away. Oblivia listened to Bella Donna from a corner of the kitchen in the hull where she usually sat on the floor, without saying a word, imagining no one could see her. The old lady was retelling for the millionth time, the story of spending years in a row-boat far out in the sea with only a ghost swan sitting beside her for company, while passing old houses and dead trees stuck out from the water. *I called out to see if anyone was there,* she said, *but only seagulls answered – laughing. Yes! Fancy that! Laughing at me. And kicking rats around the water for fun.*

Every now and then, every day in fact, the Harbour Master would come down from the sand mountain and row across the swamp, passing the rotting hulls, all the swans now living on the swamp that he called the wildlife, and anything else – decaying plastic, unwanted clothes, rotting vegetable matter or slime that bobbed, *wanami* diesel slick – on his way to visit the old woman who was looking after the girl he called The Human Rat. The stupid thing that got under his skin, who he was convinced was too lazy to speak, and was always sitting on the floor like a dog in the corner where she thought nobody could see her. Why did a thing like this land on her feet? Big question. This very thing made him wild enough to want to kill her because he thought she should be sitting up on a chair properly, if she was lucky enough to have one. He knew plenty of people who wished they had a chair to sit on. Why he even thought of himself, and he did not own a chair. If the white lady sat on a chair then the girl ought to be made to sit on a chair too, instead of acting like a white woman's black dog by sitting around on the floor, and the old woman beaming, *Oh! That's Oblivia for you.* These visits usually caused his mind to spew a bag of dead peace doves as soon as his eyes caught sight of Oblivia, and the more he saw her, and dwelled on all of her not-talking pretentiousness, and watched the old white lady struggling to teach the thing to talk, he was convinced that he had the girl pegged. *Git up off the floor and show some backbone like the rest of our people,* he snapped quick smart out of the corner of his mouth whenever he had the opportunity, behind Bella Donna's back, and added for good measure, *you make me sick.* Usually Oblivia ignored him, or else she shot him one of her several nasty expressions – eyes down, eyes blaring, screwed up or blanked face looking blacker than black, or more generally she spat on the floor between them, and with a bit of spit dividing their mutual disgust of one another, quite frankly, that's where the matter rested.

But Oblivia watched the Harbour Master who she thought ought to be doing something more about the sand mountain – unblocking the swamp for instance – he was taking long enough, and he should be more involved in fixing and healing like a real healer, instead of swooning about like some stupid cringing dog after Bella Donna. He splattered his soul that was fat with complaints all over the kitchen table for the old woman to see what the world had come to, of how difficult it was to heal anything these days in a place controlled by the Army like the swamp was. He was not superman was he? How could he take the love of Aboriginal children the Army men had stolen from parents and return it to them? And moreso, he thought that instead of Bella Donna wasting her time on the useless girl, she should be consoling him and giving him some excellent full-bodied strength platitudes about how everything would work itself out for the best in the end.

The Harbour Master could not help himself, even though he sincerely believed Bella Donna was really a spy working for the Army and telling them lies about the swamp people. Why did he believe this? He told himself it was because he believed that he could spot a spy from a mile off, and he had. He could spot spies anywhere, and they were everywhere, even ones as small as an ant racing about and minding other people's business, or somebody obviously white and conspicuous like Bella Donna, although she just about knocked his socks off.

Like! Like! Oblivia overheard his whispering, and her guts had groaned and moaned while her stomach muscles tried to shove a jumble of dog vomit words up her windpipe, although always in the nick of time, any of those screaming words that made it up to her mouth, crashed like rocks landing on enamel at the back of her clenched teeth. So, by remaining silent, saying nothing and stewing with hate and spitefulness in her guts, she reminded herself with a shiver down her spine that she would rather be dead, than waste her breath speaking to an idiot.

The Harbour Master was oblivious to that tongueless thing Oblivia's attempts to communicate through a piece of spit and continued on with what he had come for – his total intoxication with the blissful Bella Donna who he claimed was on par with a saint, even if she was a spy and a traitor of the Aboriginal people. She was too much in his heart, so he kept telling himself, *Don't chase her away. Balyanga Jakajba. She's staying here. Jungku nyulu nayi.* She became his soul mate. She made his heart beat faster. Why ignore somebody who could wind his motor up? He was intrigued with Bella Donna's mission to kill off any strength and sign of leadership in the Aboriginal world by running straight to the Army with tales of Black insurgents, Black uprisings, Black takeovers etcetera around the swamp to keep his people in control, under the thumb and weak, but at the same time, needing with every ounce of her being to nurture a sickly, damaged and most obvious to everyone else, crazy, *warraku* Aboriginal child who would never be cured no matter how much the old white lady tried to change the girl's attitude by showering her with compassion, do-gooding, saviouring and so forth. A complete useless waste of time. But, he thought, what was the use of him being a fanbelt spinning around, that was always intervening and arguing with Bella Donna about her spying for the Army against any sign of Aboriginal strength, while mothering Aboriginal weakness, if that was the whole idea of racism. No! the Harbour Master reasoned. Who on earth was he to think that he could intervene in a white lady's prerogative to think the thoughts of racial fanaticism? A plain man like himself only had simple thoughts on offer. He was not the anti-racist God almighty, and he almost drooled down both sides of his mouth while listening to each of her nicely spoken well-rounded vowels as she gave a total list of her acts of compassion as though it was her penance for having sinned, for having survived the horrendous boat journey of her life. Whatever she spoke of, he believed that he could easily have listened to her talking all day long, if he did not have to be constantly busy minding the sand.

The Harbour Master was missing his monkey friend who lived in an overseas country and who he claimed was a genius of world politics. He was always sorry about leaving the monkey eating grapevines, or where wolves hide out in forests of chestnut, or conifers, or larch trees that he claimed were like Bella Donna's rowan trees, a thousand years old. He missed not being on the scenery of world politics and speaking the monkey's language, and often complained, *I should be looking after all of my responsibilities instead of being caught up here having to guard the sand.*

But the joy of his pre-dawn *gloriosus* rowing, was to glide among the dumped military ships and vessels that had once been used by commandos, militants, militia, pirates, people sellers, cults, refugees and what have you: everything dumped there by the Army and a very good place for a spy to hide.

This particular huge dark hull where he climbed up the rusty steel steps to come on board was the home of the old woman and the girl. He was their only visitor because he and the old woman had comparable memories of times when the countries in the world were different and, once he got Oblivia stirred up enough to spit on the floor, he got on with the job of reminiscing with Bella Donna about the world's geographies and analysing the old maps they carried around in their heads. Some countries they remembered had even disappeared. They enjoyed a lamenting conversation of, *Oh! How I wonder what happened to that country! No. Did that little country disappear? Nobody lives there anymore. It just does not exist. You really mean that old place no longer exists, it can't be true but I guess it must have disappeared by sea rising, or wars. Had to happen.* Talk like that. Lead-poison brains kind of talk. Conversations that meant nothing to overwhelmed swamp people who had always been told to forget the past by anyone thinking that they were born conquerors. They already knew what it was like to lose Country. Still, it did not pay to fret about the world when you were imprisoned. They were already the overcrowded kind of people living in the world's most unknown detention camp right in Australia that still liked to call itself a first world country. The traditional owners of the land locked up forever. Key thrown away. They were sick to death of those two going on about what it was like having – *Been there!* And, *Been there too.* And, *You should have been there before the whole place turned to nothing.*

I wonder why you never see a white swan landing on the swamp? The old woman was always asking the famous Harbour Master this question, ignoring many large flocks of black swans that now already lived on the swamp, and he in turn was always singing and talking about the Rolling Stones songs that his genius of a pet monkey once sang. Yes, for sure, he missed the monkey he called Rigoletto. Sorry he had abandoned it after the monkey kept making a nuisance of itself by predicting colossal wars that started to frighten the life out of everyone. Sorry he thought the monkey was mad. *How does this swan look in your dreams?* He seemed to have been waiting for the swan to arrive too. No! She had never seen it in her dreams. These two had travelled to so many places in the world, surely, one of them had seen it somewhere, from viewing the land in a boat of banishment.

They looked for her lost white swan down in the chasms of gullies and valleys wrinkling the world, tramped through mill ponds, listened to the Mute Swans ringing the food bell in a Somerset moat, gone along the flaggy shore of County Clare and searched among the Liffey Swans dipping for weed. It was like a giant séance for gathering the thoughts of at least half a million swans from Europe to Central Asia.

Bella Donna talked of having walked the stoney shores among the Iceland Whooper Swans of Lake Myvatn to Reykjavik, of having skated along-side swans taking off on a frozen lake surrounded by icicle trees in Sweden, of having lived among migrating swans rushing to fly from snow on the mountains in Russia. She spoke to the *oo-hakucho* wintering in Japan's Akkesi-Ko, descendents of the great Kugui flocks that came from the olden times of the *Nihonshoki* in the eighth century and now sleeping on ice in the mist of Lake Kussharo. She had slid across the ice on Estonia's Matsalu Bay among sleeping Bewick Swans, still like statues, escaping wolves on their long migration. In her imagination, she had flown among the thousands of black-beaked Whistling Swans lifting into the Alaskan skies and in flight to the Samish Flats of the State of Washington, and far off, she had heard the bugling of the royal swans owned for centuries by monarchs, gliding along the Thames. Did she look around China for her swan? She had sat silently in a small boat under a Chinese moon where the Shao Hao people's winter angels live among kelp swishing in the sea of Yandun Jiao Bay. Long were the distances travelled, and all lonely! And all of them slow from too much hope in the heart, expectation, and the yearning to return.

The two old people's stories fly on through storming specks of ice, where the air had frozen into crystals that danced around the swan as it struggled to fly over the peaks of Himalayan mountains. They searched every abandoned, broken-down and flattened nest in the Eastern Kingdom on the Mongolian Nurs, and then hiked, wet and wretched across grassy plains, while a migratory procession of white Whooper Swans flew over Hulun Nur, to Cheng Shanwei's Swan Lake. On lonely roads the old woman ransacked the nesting material of sweet swans running away from her over the ice on Dalinor Lake.

The old man and woman daydreamed themselves into every swan image on earth, and off they went again. *There they go – la, la, la,* the wild girl Oblivia whinged under her breath, excluded from entering their world of knowledge. So fair enough to travel in talk, about what it was like being among a pandemonium of snakes while wading barefoot and broke into old desert ponds covered with tumbleweed, to find a black-beak Whistling Swan with its head curled under its wing asleep, frozen to death. In the end it was always the same. No swan. Not the one she was expecting. Flat broke from renting hire cars, driving them until they become rust buckets. Finally! Their journey ended at the river where a poet carried a black-necked swan in his arms that was too weak to breathe. *Yes, ode indeed, lost swan.* Then the old woman and the Harbour Master each crawled back into their own separate, quiet dry caves dug somewhere deep in their minds. A silent place where each had their own swan blessed with flowers and fruit carved into granite grey brains.

He has the best intuition, the old woman said. Bella Donna was often full of her own gloating and fandangoing about geography and reminded the girl that she and the Harbour Master were very much alike. They were peas in the same pod. Exactly similar! Both had fled countries. Identical. He had always known the time to go too, uncanny, just like swans. *Which goes to show that Aboriginal people who put their minds to it, can track anywhere.* She could not praise him enough. She even continued rejoicing about the Harbour Master in her sleep, high praising the likes of him for his natural intuition about migratory routes, immigrating cycles and so on. It was for these reasons she had found a friend to talk to out here in a swamp that was in the middle of nowhere. *This is why he is very famous. He's the full packet, you betcha.* And all that...

Well! Nothing much comes marching in on thin air, even though the old woman was relentless in her belief that somewhere over the vast oceans lying between her and the old world, the grandest white bird of all laboured in flight to reach her. But what did its continued absence mean? She could not understand it. Or why she was being denied her only wish. The only legacy she had left. Had she lost the ability to call her dead country's swan? Bella Donna offered the only possible explanation: *Because it was dead too.* The Harbour Master had to agree: *Died on its way. Fallen from the sky.*

Like a proper English-speaking child, the voiceless Oblivia learnt to sit straight-backed at the dinner table and chew fish, while contemplating the adult world talking themselves silly with their stories. In her mind she mused, *Brain rust rent-a-car mouths. Car dead. Brain dead. Aren't there enough black swans here, all nesting in rusted car bodies dumped amongst the reeds? And together they go: Toot! Toot!*

It took her no trouble to imagine the bird falling from the sky. She could see its body floating in any stretch of ocean that lay beyond the horizon – even though she had never seen the sea herself. She skipped a heartbeat. Any thought of distance did that. Her heart almost stopped beating every time she had to listen to their talk about travelling overseas to see swans. She was more comfortable with closer geography, with what lay in front of the horizon, as far as the top of the sand mountain, and into the ocean of the Harbour Master's stomach. She smiled at the gargoyle with a small white down feather sticking out from the corner of his mouth.

Bella Donna's world of exhausted journeying continued to shrink until it became so small, there was only space left for her one lost white swan. It loomed ever larger in her mind, until finally, her mind contained nothing else but the swan. She would not believe it was dead. How could anything so special, that was celebrated by hemispheric legends on both sides of the equator, be dead? She gifted the swan with eternal life. She quoted Hans Christian Andersen. Hadn't he written about a swan sitting on a nest of fledglings that perpetually flew off to populate the world with poetry inspired by their own beauty? Now her swan was the Denmark swan, and she wanted to know why it had not come to the swamp to create poetry. *Well! Why not?* How could a resurrecting swan, with the strongest pair of wings for flying half way around the world, be lost? Perhaps it was always shot dead on arrival? Fallen in sediment. Its poetry condemned. Evading its final splash down in front of her eyes.

Oblivia thought about the invisible swan whose stories occupied every centimetre of their hull. Was it real? Sure! Acts of *descendency* were important ideas in the swamp; and even, whether it was right to think about stories of birds like a white swan in the swamp.

One day Bella Donna's old storytelling voice told the girl: *A black swan flies slowly across the country, holding a small slither of bone in its beak.* But then she hesitated, perhaps realising she was deviating from the white swan she had been longing for. Her voice stalled, tapered off into whispers that even the girl, now the perfect mimic of the old woman, could not understand. It was as though the old woman had become so old, she was unable to continue either to dither or to go thither in a fantastical story that began not at the beginning, nor at the end, but centrally, in ether. *What was it? Ah?* Was she unable to comprehend progress? Did she now doubt the white swan's ability to navigate its journey? Or perhaps, she just told stories the way swans fly.

Obediently, Oblivia listened. She had become more interested than ever in the old woman's stories, even though she thought old Aunty was just facing another storm, and this made it difficult for her to speak. Where was it this time? She wondered if it had always been like this for old *wanymarri* white woman Aunty. All beginnings, wherever begun, lost? Perhaps even, that the old woman was neither life, dreams, or stories. Just air. The girl looked away and whispered into the steel wall of the hull: *She was nothing*. It might have been so! *Fat plague of loss*. The girl accused the old woman of being a victim by telling the wall, *You dream like a refugee – of never being able to return. Being lost all the time. That's all you think about. Think about that.* The girl had turned examiner of other people's consciences. But what would you expect? She knew old Bella Donna like her own thumb, knew exactly what it was like to be unable to realise one single idea without falling over a multitude of anxieties. In numerous conversations with the wall, she explained the crux of the matter – *The old woman was a victim of her own mathematics*. She had become lost in senseless tangles. An eternity of trying to calculate the exact weight of a swan travelling from so far away through such a long period of time. How long would it take to reach its destination? *There are endless, infinite possibilities, you know.* When she thought more kindly, the girl softened her image of the old woman flying around in *etherland*. *Might be as good a place as any to be with her swan.*

You could see that the old woman had become a little bit *day-dreamy*, but she often tried to impress on the girl one single thing of importance: *A love story can be about swans, but the swan looks more like death with a bone in its beak. It could be a human bone, or a bone from another swan. Its mate, maybe.*

The old lady's fearful whisperings like this at night lulled the swamp people in their cradles, cocooning them like machinery rattling away, like swarming bees, and sea gulls squalling for hours on end in the distance, or else remembering hawks piercing the hot air with their cries all day long. But it was different for birds. The seagulls and hawks flew around the swamp, absorbed in their own business of surviving in a peaceful and orderly manner. The birds disregarded the monologue of northern hemisphere *outsidedness* humming like the engine of a boat, trying to move their relevance to their native country further away in the fog.

When the girl whispered, the old woman interpreted – guessed what she wanted to know – and spoke for her, why *can't I see that swan with the bone if you can see it?* Something dropped into the water. Plop! Was this a fact that had slipped from her hypothetical love stories? The girl thought that she could hear ghost music. A string of musical notes gob-smacked in bubbles broke through the surface of the swamp. Even the old woman noticed the music, but she continued on her merry way with her story, regardless: *I have become an expert on music made from old bones, and I say it could be from swan bones, or bones of drowned people, or of drought-stricken cattle, imitating the scores of Mozart's fingers racing across the ivory.*

The greatest love story this country has ever known began somewhere around here, the old lady said while sniffling back at the bubbling water, speaking only to herself, or to somewhere way past the girl, that could have been the Harbour Master listening from the top of his hill.

A large flock of black swans whispering to each other in their rusted car-body bedrooms all over the swamp whistle, glide and bump over the waves driven along by the sudden arrival of gusty winds, while the old woman sings more: *I got to roll you over, roll over, rolling bones.*

Far into the night, the swamp music continued telling the old woman's love story through the girl's dreams where, in the underwater shadows, she looked like a cygnet transformed into two people entwining and unwinding back and forth in the bubbling swamp, in waves scattered by a relic dropped from the beak of the black swan imagined by the old woman.

Black swans kept arriving from nowhere, more and more of them, from the first one that had arrived unexpectedly and spoiled the swamp people's dinner.

After black swans came to the swamp something else happened... A soft yellow beam of light fell over the polluted swamp at night. It was the torchlight of armed men flying in the skies like Marvin Gaye's ghost looking about the place, to see what was going on. *Yes! Well! You tell me what was going on?* The Army men sent by the Government in Canberra to save babies from their parents said that they were guarding the sleep of little children now.

The swamp bristled.

This was the history of the swamp ever since the wave of conservative thinking began spreading like wildfire across the twenty-first century, when among the mix of political theories and arguments about how to preserve and care for the world's environment and people, the Army was being used in this country to intervene and control the will, mind and soul of the Aboriginal people. The military intervention was seen as such an overwhelming success in controlling the Aboriginal world it blinded awareness of the practical failures to make anyone's life better in the swamp. This 'closed ear' dictatorial practice was extended over the decades to suit all shades of grey-coloured politics far-away in Canberra, and by tweaking it ever so little this way and that, the intervention of the Army never ended for the swamp people, and for other Aboriginal people like themselves who were sent to detention camps like the swamp to live in until the end of their lives. The internment excluded the swamp people from the United Nations' Universal Declaration of Human Rights, and the control proliferated until there was full traction over what these people believed and permeance over their ability to win back their souls and even to define what it meant to be human, without somebody else making that decision for them.

Now the swamp people's voices were talking in the girl's dreams, telling her: *Your tree did not exist.* Screamed: *TELL HER. No strong tree like that ever existed here.* The girl panicked, would wake up in fright from not remembering anymore about how she came to be asleep in the tree. She started to believe what other people believed: *She was telling lies.*

The light quickly travels across water, twice over buildings, through the football oval, and along streets, then swirling around, the Army men on the boundaries go through the exit gates, before turning around, locking the gates, and the lights march off again.

The girl watched the other children. They play a game of pretending they are from another life – from the *space age*, living on Mars or some other planet, and run to be saved by the passing light.

When the old woman was not watching, Oblivia studied the running rays of light reflected on the surface of the swamp, unsettling a black swan that lifted, tail splashing, into garnishes of serendipity. There were bones rattling like loose change when the torchlight hit flocks of white cockatoos, causing them to screech from the rooftops where they sat roosting – *Sweet Lord*. A light ran again across the water saying, say again: *What's going on?*

Humpies! Hundreds sprung up all along the banks of the swamp like nobody's business now. Well! The dominant voices around the country and western bloc of the country's politics had not balked for a second about Aborigines when saying, *'Why not?'* This was what happens when you put the Army in charge of the swamp, long after it had become one of those Australian Government growth communities for corralling Aboriginal peoples into compounds. These were past times for kicking Aboriginal people around the head with more and more interventionist policies that were charmingly called, *Closing the Gap.* But, so what? The very sight of the place was vilified up and down the country for being like dogs in the pound begging for food.

Well! So what if it was just another moment in a repetitious black and white history repeated one more time for Aboriginal people from wherever about the place, after having their lives classified and reassigned yet again? Anybody's politics was a winner these days, so long as they were not blackfellas caring about their culture. So it was nothing for Australians to get excited about when Aboriginal people started being divided into lots and graded on whether anything could be done for them. Upper scale – if they could actually be educated. Lower scale – just needed some *dying pillow* place to die. Many Indigenous populations began to be separated regardless of family or regional ties. In growth centres like the swamp, thousands of Aboriginal people became common freight as they were consigned by the busload, then more conveniently, by the truckload. The swamp now renamed Swan Lake was nothing special. It was the same as dozens of fenced and locked Aboriginal detention centres.

Only starving skin-and-bone people with hollow-eye children who refused to speak came off those trucks and Army buses. Their clothes were stiffened with dried sweat and dirt from the journey. These strangers looked here and there initially, as though trying to avoid the heavy spirit of bad luck swooping down to sit on their backs. They got spite eyes from the local people. A little dull blue butterfly flew through one of the buses to have a look around and sat down on a young boy's head. He would commit suicide this poor little *juka*. Everyone knew. More boys and girls would die like this.

The swamp people, the big time protesters, rocked to their foundations from three centuries of dealing with injustices already, will probably feel the same way in two centuries more – who's speculating on the likely projection of this tragedy? Now they were yelling and screaming, *Weren't we supposed to be the traditional owners? Doesn't that count for anything?* Serious! Well! They were right about that. So! *Alright.* An Army general put in charge from the Government said they were the traditional owners of a convenient dumping ground for unwanted people now.

What were unwanted people? Well! They were little people who can't fight a big thing like the Army in charge of all the Aboriginal children – little pets owned by the Mothers of Government who claimed to love them more than their own 'inhumane' families. *Disgraceful business?* So inter-racially intolerant Australia was still the same old, same old. Aunty Bella Donna, now old as the hills, said that she felt like a thief, even a kidnapper, and she went around the place like a mad woman trying to mop up any insinuating words she thought were generating from out of thin air – *I told you myself, that I found her...in a tree.* If she had saved the girl or not – what did it matter? The girl could answer anyone herself about what it was like to be saved if she thought about pillaging a few words from somewhere in her mind to speak. She could have said that she did not know who she was. Or that she was so damaged that she could not speak. She was under a spell. But she felt nothing about pain or joy, night or day. She thought no life was worth saving if it was no longer your own.

I think that girl caused all of this Army business coming here. Holy smoke why had the swamp people forgotten? The Army had come a long time ago. But this swamp was plaguing for revenge and pumped itself with so many compelling ideas of fear they were now far beyond the capacity to clean the floor off with a mop.

You should have left her where she was.

The cuckoos and cockatoos heard every single thing and, it might be, their nervous flinching and tapping of beaks on wood were imitating insecurities in the hearts of the children.

The light that came from the sky at night was relentless. It was the Army swinging around the searchlights. Where was the joy in this? Ungovernable thoughts unfurled into the atmosphere from the heads of people hiding beneath folded wings that might have belonged to the black swans that had died in the swamp. Yes, those grand old birds flying high into the greatness of life without paying a dollar for the flight could just be angels.

The swamp's murky water was littered with floating feathers, and it looked as though black angels had flown around in dreams of feeling something good about one another. *Well! Not around here when you were nobody, you don't feel like an angel,* Bella Donna said as though she read thoughts, but she was just passing traffic – generalising about what was going on in the girl's brain. She had no idea of how the girl saw those wasted grey-black feathers.

Ah! All these feathers were just sweet decoration. Feathers floating on fading dreams, obscuring the address that was difficult enough to remember for transporting the girl back to the tree, where in her mind the route she chased while sinking away into slithers of thoughts slipped silently in and out of the old threads woven through the forest of mangled tree roots. When she runs in these dreams, her footsteps crush the delicate crisscrossing patterns of the worn stories, that reached deep into sacred text, the first text, in saying, *We are who we are.* Fancy words, scrolling back and forth in the girl's mind, float like the feathers that stop her escaping back to the tree.

Rubbish stackings, tied with yellow clay-stained stockings – too many of these human nests encasing the swamp. The sand bank that had grown to mountainous heights still separated the brackish water from the sea, while a fast-growing population of Aboriginal people from far away places was settling, living the detention lifestyle right around the swamp.

The truck people kept on arriving. They were more like arriving cattle being segregated and locked up in 'growth centres', now called National Aboriginal Relocation Policy by some mind-dead politicians clap-trapping that they were dealing with rats. Suppose hard come, and easy go, for the traditional land of the swamp was snatched again. The real owners hidden in the throng could not count the number of times their land had been ripped from under their feet.

In this oasis of abandonment, home for thousands forcibly removed from other 'more visible' parts of Australia by the Government, the swamp became a well-known compound for legally interning *whoever* needed to be secluded far away behind a high, razor-edged fence from the decent people of mainstream civilization.

It was just a contemporary painting – a pastoral scene, the old lady surmised in the early days, while her eyes swung along the ever-increasingly crowded shoreline.

It's really insanity here, she told the Harbour Master about the people living all about the place. *It's not like it used to be, honest,* he replied, the magic lost from his voice. He was forgetting to sing his Mick Jagger songs. The girl sunk deeper into her thoughts: *So! What did I care? What about my story? Me! Different dollar please!*

Now while Bella Donna was carrying on like this, the population would peer out each day from package crates, donated cubbies from foreign aid, and rubbish that sprung up in the overcrowded slum now running around the entire shoreline. *What unimaginably difficult poverty-stricken circumstances,* Bella Donna cried, wiping up her tears with a bit of newspaper. She consoled herself with poetry, reciting lines like John Shaw Neilson's *I waded out to a swan's nest at night and heard them sing...*

The Harbour Master stayed on top of his mountain, too frightened to leave. He was just sitting like everyone else, and listening to all kinds of fruitless, high volume *megaphoning* protest from the minority landowners trying to reach inside the closed ears of the Army men protecting the swamp. *What do we want? We want you white bastards outta here.* Waste of breath. Their mantra was five or six words more or less which meant the same thing: *Nobody asked us for permission, moron.* Every day, hours were put aside for protesting. It was like listening to a continuous earthquake of hate from a stadium built out of the swamp itself.

Can you tell me why those Aboriginal people had to be relocated here for – from across the country, Aunty? The girl sometimes imagines herself speaking politely, in a pretty voice, while mouthing off her soundless words.

God knows it was only a swamp, of what a storm gives, or easily takes away.

A low-pressure weather system was unpredictable and nobody knew whether it would bring more dry storms or blue skies sulking through another year. Still, a flood of mythical proportions would be required to drive the sand back into the sea. The ceremonies sang on and on for majestic ancestral spirits to turn up out of the blue, to stir up the atmospheric pressure with their breath, to turn the skies black with themselves, to create such a deluge to unplug the swamp, to take the sand mountain back to the sea. But more was said than done. The ancestral sand spirits flew like a desert storm and backed themselves even further up against the mountain. Silt gathering in the swamp lapped against the dwellings of the increasing population and crept further inwards as the swamp decreased in size. This was the new story written in scrolls of intricate lacework formed by the salt crystals that the drought left behind.

The swamp's natural sounds of protest were often mixed with lamenting ceremonies. Haunting chants rose and fell on the water like a beating drum, and sounds of clap sticks oriented thoughts, while the droning didgeridoos blended all sounds into the surreal experience of a background listening, which had become normal listening. Listen! That's what music sounds like! The woman once explained to the girl that the music of epic stories normally sounded like this.

This is the world itself, disassembling its thoughts.

It was just the new ceremony of swamp dreaming, the girl thought, for what she called, Nowhere Special. She thought it suited the wind-swept surroundings of the dead swamp, where children played with sovereign minds, just by standing out in the wind to fill their cups with dust given to them by their ancestors.

Dust covered the roads and nobody knew where they were anymore, and the old woman claimed that even the bitumen highways were disappearing. Soon, no one would have any idea about how to reach this part of the world.

If you leave here, you know what is going to happen don't you? People are going to stop and stare at you the very instant they see the colour of your skin, and they will say: She is one of those wild Aboriginals from up North, a terrorist; they will say you are one of those faces kept in the Federal Government's *Book of Suspects*.

Bella Donna said that even though she had never seen this book for herself, she had heard that it had the Australian Government's embossed crest on the cover, and was kept at the Post Office where anyone could study it. What was a post office? The girl had listened.

This was the place where they kept faces plucked from the World Wide Web by Army intelligence looking at computers all day long, searching for brown- and black-coloured criminals, un-assimilables, illegal immigrants, terrorists – all the undesirables; those kind of people.

Never ever leave the swamp, she said, adding that her own skin did not matter, but the girl was the colour of a terrorist, and terrorism was against the law.

Bella Donna's home was camouflaged in the middle of the flotilla of junk littering what she called the vision splendid. The hull jutted out of the swamp like a war monument saluting in grey-coloured steel. This joyless, rusting hull with a long war record of stalking oceans looked like a traitor imprisoned away from the sea, but it was not alone in this polluting junkyard choked up with so-called 'lost' Army property. Its neighbours were the remains of all the *muwada* – cargo boats, trawlers, tugboats, fighter boats and rickety old fishing boats. These phantom vessels were either falling apart at the seams from decades of bobbing themselves into oblivion, or had become dilapidating wrecks.

While the hull was slowly sinking its huge belly in the yellow mud, the old foreign woman chopped carrots in the galley. She sang her premonitions as she chopped. *The hull was burying itself at its own funeral.* It was a kind of simple theory, as far as theories went. All kinds of conspiracies poured out of her old lips to the sound of the knife clipping the wood, chopping vegetables for another stew. *Was this going to be the unrecorded record of the world's longest suicide attempt?* The longest pause! You could feel the slide, slipping and dipping further into the mud, by a few millimetres a day.

The bounty the old white aunty business brought from overseas was about reading the signs of the unsaid and speaking about what was not obvious. Well! Why not listen? The resident Queen of the manufacturing and boat-building industry did reigning well. She knew what you needed to feel in your bones about nautical living, boat steel and planks of wood. Even her bones could feel how the hull was reorienting itself towards the fanfare of East Coast cities. She asked any passing spirit bystander she noticed hanging around her kitchen, *How else was the hull going to capture the glory from which it had been robbed?*

Sounds were destroying the memory of the girl who only wanted to be living in her tree again. She felt as though she was locked inside a suitcase that the old woman dragged along and pussy-footed about on noisy gravel. It was the *walk of life*, old Aunty claimed. How it felt to be living inside the steel of a battling war hero robbed of the hullabaloos, feeding off the fanfare of pomp and ceremony, had it not been dishonoured. Sabotaged by traitorous telltale words, *Welcome Boat People*, which protesters had once sprawled in white paint across its side.

These words, decrypted many times by the old woman, had almost faded away from years of sitting in the swamp, just like the memory of most of those protesters of good causes, once they scrubbed up and rejoined their conservative Australian upbringings. The old woman said that she had often heard the hull moaning, crying out as though it had lost heart in the idea of achieving perfection through one last salute. Let there be Death! The girl walked around with the hull's colossal lament impaled in her heart. *What could I do?* She demanded. There was nothing she could do about glory.

So! Bad luck and so forth, Aunty said, because anyone could dream like fish on the other side of the sand mountain, where shifting winds were funnelling the outgoing tide back to the sea.

The swamp people were really frightened of the flotilla. Some would not even look at the decaying boats. Some claimed that they could not see any dumped boats out there on their pristine swamp. *Ya only see what you want to see and that's that.* They did not go around looking for things outside of the *sanctum* of traditional knowledge. They said old scrap boats were dumped in the Congo, in real swamps, among the boa constrictors. Well! You learn a lot of things like that from looking at too many of those old movies.

Nor did it take much from a separatist-thinking swamp person to believe that Bella Donna was a real ghost even before she was dead, or that girl *whatsherface* too – for turning up years after she was supposed to be dead. Rah! Rah! Everything was vapour. There were plenty of people around who said that they would rather be dead than sniffing old fat hissing from a frypan where ghosts were frying up their fish. Exactly right! *Whitefella ghosts, seasonal plagues of grey rat ghosts, other vermin ghosts like swarming cockroaches, march flies and infestations of hornet nests.*

So floating junk, if seen in the light of having too many foreigners circulating in one's own spiritual world, could always be ignored for what it was – other people's useless business. Of course it was infuriating for all of the witnesses of the swamp world to see so much waste not being put to some proper use. After all, anyone could see that foreign ghosts were not particularly harmful if you got past the innocuous cunning way that they could steal a whole country, kill your people, and still not pay all those centuries' worth of rent. It was just that all those men, women and children in the detention camp living cheek to jowl in broken-down shacks, crates and cardboard boxes had no affinity with dead strangers. Cramp was better. So much preferable to being haunted when you did not feel like being frightened by other people's ghosts.

Only the old woman had decided to be radical by taking up a grandiose lifestyle on one of the flotilla's rust buckets, and in the end, when she had claimed responsibility for the girl, she had taken her out there on the water to live. She said that the hull was part of the Australian way of life. She was helping to make Australia a great country. *I am not a separatist from Australia*, she claimed.

The detention camp was now a settled population of traditional owners from kingdoms near and far, and swamped with a big philosophy about the meaning of home. Why do they do it? *They could also seek asylum and permanent Australian residency by living on navy junk*, the old woman claimed, referring to her hull as a solid piece of Australia that was immune to traditional land ownership laws. She liked being part of mass Australia and owning her own home. It gave her a sense of authority when it suited her. *You think that they would want to grab the chance to become fully Australian. A chance to live like everyone else.*

It was easy, and eerie, to see bleeding-heart, rust-staining yellow water. It gave you the shivers. If you looked closely at the flotilla for long enough you saw people at war. Saw military parades. Dead men marching up and down on the decks, and in your sleep you dreamt of people screaming and running for their lives from the explosions. The girl did not say much about that, or the ghosts screaming in her sleep about the wars they had never left.

The rotten and broken-down vessels were a jarring sight, but the old queen marvelled over the slicks of pollution – the strange panorama of toxic waste swimming on the surface of the water. The water gleamed with blue and purple oxidising colours, and if you were to look long enough at the sun hitting the swamp from 1400 to 1600 hours in the winter months, this polluted glare became even more dazzling – where the water was broken into trails of rainbows made by the movement of swimming swans.

Swamp people regarded this particular sight as something

evil, created by devils, easy, easy now, and in this respect the swans coming to the swamp with no story for themselves generated a lot of talk. They were suspected of being contaminated with radioactivity leaking from some of the hulls. Of course it was mentioned, considered, even nurtured by the swamp-dwellers' constituency, now permanently submerged and half-drowning in open wounds, by asking forlornly any question that would not be answered such as, *Was this the silent killer then, the Army's final weapon of mass destruction?*

No more! It was easier for the swamp people to shift unanswered questions to somebody else – *Here! Chuck it over to him,* passing the buck, and end up blaming the old Harbour Master for the pollution. They complained of not seeing him remove one speck of sand, and that the situation had gotten worse, and whinged, *He was supposed to be a healer for the country. That's what he came here for when he could have just arrived in a dream and blasted the mountain like that, like an email, and finished the job off like we asked him to do. Just get rid of the sand mountain, that's all we wanted, and he could have done that from anywhere, instead of ending up coming here personally. We can't look after him forever. Well! Pronto. We are waiting…and he should finish the job off straight away, not taking years to do something.*

The sand mountain that the Harbour Master lived on seemed to be growing even further towards the sky, while its shadow now rested over the swamp for a good part of the day. Anyone would have thought that the Harbour Master was actually shovelling the sand up to the sky himself. The shadow spread uncertainty as to where it would all end, as much as being a feast to be devoured by the swamp's full-time philosophers, soothsayers and fortune-tellers emerging at the crack of dawn from their homes of cardboard and similar stuff – like worms crawling out of a hole, to look way up the mountain where they could see for themselves how it had grown a couple of centimetres higher during the night.

All the great holy and wise people of the swamp would come and stand around on the shoreline looking across the water towards the hull, and while deep in whispered conversation with each other, you could tell by their sour facial expressions that they were not happy at all about what was happening to their land. The girl thought that they were accusing the old woman of upsetting the Harbour Master and jumping in with the status quo. It was during this time that Oblivia began to understand that nobody noticed her on the hull. It was obvious that the locals acted as though she never existed, was too unimaginable, unable to be recognised and named.

Traitors! Bella Donna's voice rang like a big tower bell over the water to any assembly on the foreshore looking her way whom she accused of not being patriots to the Australian flag. She had good communication skills for throngs. The whole riled swamp now ate each other's venom for breakfast. They yelled at her: *Yea! That's your story.* Patriotism! *Ha! We'll show you what bloody patriotism means.* A blaze of colour of Aboriginal flags unfurled in the wind, some intact, some tattered, or just bits of faded material, even paper coloured black, yellow or red, were hoisted up on sticks of makeshift flagpoles in her face.

Boat person! Loser! Terrorist!

As the worldwide know-all of everything, the old woman claimed that most of the rotting boats dotting the lake had belonged to an army of textbook terrorists who invaded other countries. She had once chopped carrots for terrorists and claimed: *I am recognised in all the seas of the world.* She waved her stick at the sea-wrecks bobbing up and down or stuck in mud, noting with sage-like authority which of the old boats had carried people she knew, which had run from wars in far away countries and which had fled over dangerous seas trying to reach this unwelcoming land. She knew millions of people, shouting it around, *I knew all those people who didn't even make it. Those left behind to suffer the hand of fate. Those millions of refugees out there somewhere who were still dreaming of coming to your paradise,* she yelled.

Water levels went up and down, and during the winter months many wrecks were left squatting in the mud.

What became of their owners? The girl mouthed this question as many times as Bella Donna spoke the words for her, hoping to coach Oblivia to ask more about her sea journeys.

The earth buries the dead. Lovers to Lovers. Dust to Dust. Their families hate all of us, Bella Donna said, giving the same answer every time.

Far off behind the dwellings on the other side of the swamp, on the top of the sand dune mountain that blocked the channel between the swamp and the sea, now that the Army had taken over the Harbour Mastering responsibilities, the old Harbour Master had become even more reclusive. His mind felt strange. Useless. He felt unable to control what was happening any more. He hardly ever scrambled down the sand ghost, or longed for the pleasure of brushing past the swans guarding the hulls in the middle of the night, and those old sailor spirits crying down in the mud, while rowing the stagnant waters to visit Bella Donna of the Champions.

His worries grew proportionally with the sand mountain steadily reaching towards its zenith, knowing undeniably it would eventually be vanquished by its own weight. He fretted about this final collapse. What would he do? This was the reason that he could hardly risk leaving the mountain, yet he had to see the old woman to tell her of his dreams.

He frequently dreamt that he would leave the swamp by clinging to a ghost flying like a huge Zeppelin of sand through the atmosphere, as the drought moved somewhere else. Culture was such a formidable thing to him now. He did not know how to hold on to such a thing anymore. This idea of the sand taking him away from his country was his constant concern – the thing he had to tell her – to be calmed. Only she knew how to look at him straight in the eye and tell him he was wrong, and when she smiled, it was as though she had looked through music – a pleasing melody, that had come out of his mouth.

Whatever she heard reflected through the filter of foreign musical manuscripts nestled in her brain of tonally lifeless melodies, he could have been playing a shakuhachi in Japan, or whistling like an Asian songster, or seducing the world through a bamboo flute. How would she hear him? She was still attached to the libraries and archives left behind in the western part of the world. It was as though she had never left.

Sorry! Really sorry! About the sand! We will both go together, he warned, turning away, and with a further thousand apologies, forced his rowboat through the league of hungry swans packed around the hull. Until finally, he ran back up the mountain to wait, too anxious of missing the moment when the ghost would decide to collapse and be gone with the wind.

The girl felt the anticipation of change creeping towards the swamp. She already saw the old man as streamers of sand blowing their own *espressivo andante* of an exodus-song for homeland.

Him sand – every grain is sacred. The Harbour Master was desperate to inform others to be prepared to leave on the big journey, calling on the locals, even the alienated and stigmatised truck people from the cities, and whoever went up to the top of the mountain to ask him why he lived his lonely life, separate and unsociable and isolated in this outstation from the swamp's growth town.

Well! It was truly something strange to do, the old woman even thought that, although she was also living apart from the rest of the community. But unlike the Harbour Master who everyone seemed to care about, nobody came over to the hull and asked her what her responsibility was.

You should leave and the sand might follow you instead, she had suggested, and he laughed.

She told him that people were wishing on a falling star for bulldozers to come and destroy the sand mountain.

They say it was foreign people thinking in a pristine environment that was making this trouble etcetera! The sand got no mind himself. Nothing to do with it.

The Harbour Master was insulted to be called a foreign person who did not know his own culture. He stomped around on the mountain. Sand rolled through the air, teasing the whole swamp before flying off somewhere. He could not get the insult out of his head.

Old Aunty ignored it all. At times like this, she just played Hoffmeister type of music on her swan-bone flute to the swans.

Pythons and lizards, the fattest catfish from the swamp, bats and marsupials, were thrown like flower petals up the sand mountain as offerings. All of it landed with a thud. Taipan snakes shimmering about, danced amongst dead catfish with bodies coiled and heads raised off the ground.

Don't expect me to drive it away, the defunct Harbour Master called down to the gathered people below who thought he, an old man, just an old *malbu*, could have so much power in his body that he could snarl like some unidentifiable animal throwing poisonous snakes around in the sand and move a mountain away with his bare hands. But! He said his sand was welcome to stay regardless of all the inconveniences. *It will go away when it wants.* Well! Anyone could be a genius about drought saying something like that.

Bella Donna was sulking because the Harbour Master had

become too tied up in matters that did not concern her and preoccupied with arguing with the community now doubting his powers as a healing man for their country. These days she even tended to ignore Oblivia, and the girl felt neglected, a bit miffed, and renewed her vow never to speak again. Who was she kidding? The truth of the matter was that Oblivia had long forgotten how to speak, and did not know she could speak, and had no confidence to speak. She was glad that the Harbour Master had stopped coming to the hull. She was happy to hear him arguing with everyone thinking he was a fake, because he probably was as far as she was concerned. The reason she thought so was because she knew the Harbour Master only had a big mouth and that was not going to move the sand mountain. No. The Harbour Master was not even a big-shot character from one of the old woman's many treasured books. And certainly, Bella Donna had not incorporated him in the long self-edifying narratives about her journey to this, the concluding triumphant chapter of her life.

It particularly annoyed Oblivia that Bella Donna remained fascinated by her ugly-face ghost-man the Harbour Master and that the old woman had stopped telling her stories. In particular, one obscure and favourite story about a little *juka* who was called God's Gift. The old woman claimed she had seen the boy many times. She was always looking out for him and wondering when she would see him again. His home was the world itself because he was a special gift from God. She had heard about this boy people had been waiting for to care for their deer on the other side of the planet. His aura was seen standing among rays of sunlight shining through a dark misty forest next to snow-capped mountains where God lived. Or, she told of people having seen a vision of the boy living in the swamps throughout the world where swans lived, and also where God lived. She told stories of how the boy was thought to live in the houses of ancient cities where fig trees grew out of cracks in the walls and from the rooftops and, only rarely, could you get past the troupe of monkeys who were guarding him, to see him more closely. It seemed as though she had seen this boy all over the world, or wherever you found God.

The old woman often saw him visiting family along the swamp. He was always visiting she claimed. *Oh! You should meet him one day. He is a proper good boy. A boy the whole world would love.* The girl scanned all the shack houses around the shore of the swamp hoping to locate the ones where monkeys lived and where fig trees grew from the rooftops, among the din of ghetto blasters and loud television.

The old woman claimed that she had just seen him running around the swamp with his pet monkeys and even with a fox in his arms. God was here. *Did you see him too?* She thought anyone would have noticed somebody like that – a gift from God. Bella Donna would sigh and resign herself to failure, knowing that telling stories to the child was pure waste. The little girl had no imagination: *Never sees a thing.*

Look out! Taipan snakes dancing all over the ground.

It was impossible for Aunty Bella Donna of the Champions to conduct herself like normal people, like those who did not call out for all manner of things to be brought to them – calling to the skies to bring her swans. In that *la la* voice of hers, she snorted about the swamp's negativity, *Why be like other people calling all these trillions and zillions of flies to come here, dragonflies, sandflies, march flies, blowflies to swim in their tea cup?*

Believe it or not, everyone thought that the old white lady was one of those people who had invented climate change and that she really had brought the swans to the North to live on the swamp. The old black swans had heard her voice running along streams of dust floating in the breezes, that dropped in and out of the skies, and back and forth along telegraph wires, and through kilometres of pipelines, and on bitumen roads of state highways, until reaching the droughts in the South, where great colonies of swans normally lived. A flock of swans deranged by drought, then another, and another, laboured the distance, flew the same path to the swamp when it stopped raining, no *janja* for what seemed for ever, when the wetlands dried up. No one cared for the swans coming to the swamp's detention camp. Nobody knew what it meant. The very presence of those swans living with Aunty Bella Donna of the Champions on a swamp that belonged to a few brolgas, linked them very firmly with what they called, *some other kind of madness.*

In yellow froth and feather waters covered by films of dust, the swans led mottled brown and grey cygnets to the old lady whenever she appeared on her raft. They whistled soft music while gliding alongside their swan caller's floating platform. Her raft, constructed of Melaleuca paperbark trunks, was tied together with randomly found wire and rope, and that it floated at all was thanks to a little bit of starlight for luck. She looked awkward – juggernauting long poles that moved the platform. It was like looking at a brightly dressed, long-legged water bird walking through the muddy water. All along the foreshore, the swamp dwellers watched through the permanent haze of insects at what was happening to their lot. The old loved weeping spring was now the stagnant water among sad old lilies and long wriggling serpents.

Those black swans would glide from all corners of the swamp to the old woman. They moved through the water with their long straight necks held high and their fine black-feathered heads slightly cocked to one side to listen to her stories about the world she had known. Drops of water would fall from their red beaks, with the signature white bar above the nostril, while they listened to her. Continuously quavering, their beaks dipped slightly into the surface of the water, testing the level, sensing the evaporating moisture running away into the atmosphere. Suddenly, a swan would orate the reply by arching its neck towards the sky and trumpeting a long, mournful call. Soon all that could be heard for kilometres around were swan bugles heralded skywards in prayers for rain.

In those days of graceful gliding swans, swirling around in loops in settled softness, there was often a serene calmness that ran throughout the swamp. The swans stayed all seasons, even until the swamp almost dried up when the old loved spring did not flow. Sometimes, the whole mass would suddenly disappear in the middle of the night and the swamp would seem empty and silent – as though they had never been there – then unexpectedly, they returned, homing to the old woman. Perhaps it was her stories. Or, she really could call swans.

Among the miracles of over-crowding, conjuring more, praying for more – more swans arrived instead of rain on the swamp. Though they were previously unknown in this environment, the swamp people thought that the swans had returned to a home of ancient times, by following stories for country that had been always known to them. Swans had Law too. But now, the trouble was, nobody in the North remembered the stories in the oldest Law scriptures of these big wetland birds.

The southern swans kept descending in never-ending ribbons from the sky, and some said it was because they had noticed their kinsfolk below, detained and locked up. Their migrating journeys to follow their people across the continent had already taken many months. The swans were gathering into flocks of thousands, crowded in the swamp in black clouds that the old woman poled her raft through as she fed them.

Throngs of people gathered on the shoreline to throw nets, to catch one or two fingerling fish – and watch Bella Donna. It gave them something to talk about. They laughed. It was fun to watch the floating contraption with pole sticks moving abruptly through the choppy waters where the swans swam idly up and down in the turbulence. But seriously, no one had ever hoped or prayed for swans to come into their lives. Why would they? Swan eggs. Cygnets. Good things. But not for eating in this place! These were Law birds with no custodians in their rightful place. No one was that far down on their luck.

And to see the swans swimming about was considered a bit of luck for softening the look of the polluted mess of the place, staring at persistent drought, or having an accidental bomb fall in your face on a regular basis from the Army, or your spiritual ancestors dug up by miners and turning spiteful on you, or Army surveillances protecting your little children as though they were the parents who loved them. Everything had its impact. And bugger it all, apart from the things that were supposed to happen to close the gap of disadvantage in all of those makeshift dwelling places, a swan lake had emerged in the chaos. So that was one good story for local folk to say: *Wasn't that lucky?*

Yet what was the real lexicon about swans in this swamp? The swamp people, tight-lipped though they were about the presence of swans, really feared any ancient business that was not easily translatable in the local environment. There was total agreement on that. Old wise folk were talking strongly about it too, saying: *We do have our own local birds. Can't you see them everywhere if you bothered to look? All kinds.* Of course they had. Currawongs abounded. Noisy miners ran through the place. Thousands of brolgas were standing around, *tall and proud,* and living happily with the swamp people for aeons thank you very much. The grey-feathered cranes with long stick-legs were the emblematic bird of the local environs.

Brolga! *Kudalku*! Brolga! A bird of a big dreaming; a bird with a bare red-skinned head sitting on top of a long skinny neck joining a large body covered in grey feathers.

These birds crowded the lake too. They were the guardian angels roosting on every rooftop of the shanty shacks to watch over families – all of their kinfolk living inside. These homeland brolgas casually walked into any house without fear, gently prancing off the ground with spread wings, and stealing food they plucked straight from the kitchen table in a casual leap. No one cared less about what brolgas did as creatures that belonged there, with every right to have a bit of food – and who would harm a brolga anyway?

The girl fed the swans. She ran through the water with the fledging cygnets. She started to believe that by helping them to survive on the polluted swamp, she might learn how to escape as freely as they had been able to take flight. She wanted to fly. Dreams of stick wings attached to her arms that possibly grew feathers filled her mind with flights to escape. A great space in her mind played with words – *disappearance*, and *invisible*. She never thought that escaping a life of living with Bella Donna of the Champions was impossible. She was often flying like a swan. She watched the old woman obsessively, and decided to learn how to talk to swans too. Yes, she would be fluent in swan talk. She could feel the miracle of leaving every time swans lifted themselves off the water, the lightness of being airborne, in watching them fly until they disappeared through the dusty haze, and leaving her to dream about all of those invisible places she had heard the old woman talking about, that lay outside the swamp.

She watched the swans growing fatter and heavier, each a little battleship, that could still run in a rush across the water to take off, and fly back in to grab food thrown into the air. They swarmed in packs of hundreds for the food that the old woman threw at them. Other people's food! Piles of it in plastic bags and buckets, dumped like daily offerings to spirits on her floating platform. Old Bella Donna even had the audacity to swan around, humpy to humpy, counselling the greedy, and then collecting all the food scraps that anyone could have eaten themselves. She took everything: a pile of finely chopped yellowing cabbage, egg shells, old bread, wilting lettuce leaves, potato peels, fish bones, orange skins, a shrivelled apple core. She poured the lot onto the water and watched the frenzy of swans and brolgas devour every piece of scrap in moments. Then the swans drifted off, and resumed an endless activity of sifting waters stuffed with algal blooms, scum on the surface, and slime-covered waterweeds.

As time passed, the swamp people grew skinnier than any normal person sweating it out in the Tropics, while the swans became fatter on their food. The old woman, ancient now, did not have a guilty thought in her head. She prowled about on moonless nights to steal food right from the arms of children. Little things sound asleep from the exhaustion of clinging to their own special watermelon, from watermelon day, army fruit, good fruit given to them to treasure by the protecting armed forces. Such hot summer nights. Very easy being dead to the world. Deaf to the feral cat jumping out of the way when the door creaked, the breeze tinkling chime bells, or a thousand things moving, banging and clapping, while the ghostly old woman with thieving household brolgas walked straight in to snatch food right out of their little fingers.

The girl followed the old woman wading amongst the swans floating on their fat bellies, their red beaks preening themselves right next to their old benefactor's bright floral-patterned dress billowing in the water. Silently, the girl was a shadow that listened to the stories and secrets whispered into swan ears, and whatever she remembered, it was mostly poetry for swans.

Swamp people said the swans were frightening them. They

accused the swans of looking right into their souls and stealing the traditional culture. Bella Donna said she did not know why a swan would want to look into somebody's empty soul. Just an insult a minute. She had already looked inside their souls herself and said that she had found nothing there. *Just thin bits of weak weeds lying on the bottom of your guts trying to stay alive.* Perhaps swamp people had empty souls, but they did have pride. They jumped around a lot and told her, *Enough's enough now, don't you go talking like that.* Anyway, she retaliated: *What could there possibly be for a swan to see except these little bits of weeds lying on a tin plate in a tiny pile at the bottom of your soul?*

Guess there was no answer for that.

But red-ringed, black-eye swans dipping their beaks like fortune-tellers swilling and swirling old tea dregs around while swimming by the girl could create beautiful thoughts, staring straight into her eyes. The girl in turn thought she might read their fortunes in the language nature had written in the blackish-grey-tipped curled tail feathers scalloped across their backs. It was how swans read each other when choosing a mate. She was determined to solve the mystery of why they had left the most beautiful lakes in the country – a vision created in her head by the old woman's stories of other places. Her existence revolved around learning the route they took, how they had crossed the interior country, the old woman's geography of featureless sand dunes stretching to kingdom come, just to reach a North country polluted swamp. *It was the love stories,* the old woman chuckled to herself. She was amused at the girl's addiction to bolt holes. In the muddy waters the old woman went on feeding squads of cygnets volumes of a tangled, twisted love story about the Gods only knew what, which they soaked up like pieces of wet bread.

All children wanted were answers to universal questions about how people should live, and strangely, the girl thought she would find these answers by tossing herself in the old woman's madness of singing to swans. Just as she believed there was a secret route back to the tree – she believed there had to be a secret route that had brought the swans up to the top of the country. The mysteries were running away from her. Her mind too tied up in a jungle of tracks to run. Another way. Hidden passages. Places to hide. Always running. She had to become Aunty Bella Donna of the Champions who knew how to call swans, and time became desperate. But Oblivia remained out of kilter with the old lady's shadow, never quite fitting the cast of the sun, while the old woman sung her stories slowly, moving more and more slowly those days.

This story that began across the ocean, in a far-away land of a country which had already lost its name. In this place people were often telling common stories about themselves as they looked out at the awfulness of their land. The stories were never about history, or science, or technology. They talked about a useless landscape that grew nothing and which most of them could not see anyhow because of their blindness. These people spent ages comparing better times before who can tell what happened, except saying: We were already late when the God of the world said Git.

Ice-covered lakes dried up where the swans once lived. Beautiful creatures of snow-white feathers with yellow beaks had flown half-dead, half-way around the globe to reach extraordinary destinations in faraway lands.

Here, dead clumps of grasses by the sea billowed until whisked from the earth and into highways of dry wind crossing the continent that went round the world and back again. Trees stopped measuring the season and died slowly in ground bone dry several metres deep. Finches had been the first to swarm into jerking clouds hightailing it out of their hemisphere. In winter or summer, only the old-fashion homely birds scratched the ground for moisture from long ago.

You could see the white eyes of the old fishermen watching the flowing rivers in their memories, listening to them go on and on, it was like listening to the poetry of a canary's song dancing in those minds to sweeten the drought...

Draw breath, Aunty. Frequently the girl would interrupt her by laying her hand on the old woman's arm. Life was short. The old woman spoke faster, and was short of breath. The girl was greedy to know exactly what the old woman had to say and nodded repeatedly at her, asking Bella Donna the questions about what makes the world go around. Oblivia needed explanations quickly, not blind fishermen. How do you fly solo? Which way should you run to escape this world? Where do the swans go? No one else knew how to tell her how to shuffle the cards, so what harm was there in believing a mad person? The old woman finally leant forward and whispered into the girl's ear that the best journey she had taken in all of her travels in the world was with a swan in a sampan. The girl convinced herself that only the mad people in the world would tell you the truth when madness was the truth, when the truth itself was mad. Then the old woman began a new love story, *All rivers flow to the sea*, and its breath finished when Aunty Bella Donna of the Champions of the earth, who might have been an angel, died.

The Dust Ends

The night Bella Donna of the Champions died, boobooks called at her passing spirit, and when a swift wind swept through the distant woodlands of eucalypts, the rattling gumnuts could be heard as she travelled away. All night long, butcher-birds flew in circles and sung through the swamp. That was the parish! Traditional. Even first class. The country, finishing off the dead woman's broken serenade to the swans while the humidity wrapped itself in a heavy haze over the swamp and caught all of the leaves falling from the trees.

Around the swamp, the air was charged up like an electrified cat, always stifling and crowded. Oblivia dreamt the old woman was in the kitchen talking about her life, but her voice was jumping simultaneously between stories about times and places in the world that no longer existed. *All dead, just like me now. Extinct. Uninhabitable.* She was breathless with excitement. It was as though the old woman still wanted to breathe life into the stories of all those people in her life that she had seen escaping from their lost countries, taken to sea by a swan.

But then, what of her life in the swamp? *Our life here*, the girl uttered in her sleep. And the reply came out of nowhere. *Existence!*

Just a word echoed from faraway by old Bella Donna – a woman who was too worldly, too immersed; too spread everywhere, and she cried to the girl, *I don't know what is happening to me.*

Only the girl felt the sadness of losing the old woman forever, whose voice became less afflicted the more distant she became, *Well! Can you believe this?* Old Bella Donna had just been to the cloud house of a white swan in a Zhongguo city glowing with stars shining like antique lanterns, where the swan was still writing about itself with a quill in its beak, the same poem of missing its home, that it had been writing many centuries ago.

I feel so light now. It was the feeling of sunlight falling through dark stormy clouds embracing the giant granite swans placed all about the Indonesian village of stone carvers. And off she goes again, but instantly returns and tells of falling down through the dusty rays of light that form a sea around the ceiling of an ancient temple. It was where the golden swan boat of an Indian Goddess swings from waves stirred by thousands of chanting devotees.

Finally, the old woman's home was in sight, the country that was once covered with fir trees, where wild deer with bells in their antlers had run through fog snaking over the snow-covered floor of forests.

The white swans dipping for weeds in the river.

A crescent moon moved so low across the swamp that its reflection over rippling water looked like the wings of a magnificent white swan. It looked like the type of swan from other parts of the world where it might be called Hong, or Cigne, Kugui, Svane, Zwaan, Svanr, Svan, or Schwan. Its light glowed over the houses in the slum. Waterlily leaves shone in the moonlight. The light rode silver saddles on the back of hundreds of black swans huddling around the hull with necks tucked under their wings, where they dream their own names, Goolyen, Connewerre, Kungorong, Muru-kutchi,

Kuluin, Mulgoa, Kungari, Koonwaarra, Byahmul, and the recital continues, collecting all of the country's swans. Then waterlily leaves were blown over the water. Swarming insects backed away.

While circling in the skies, the swans dived endlessly through invisible crevices to other worlds. They were still searching for the old lady, always catching sight of her spirit, not letting her go. It seemed that the entire flock would not stop mourning for her. Everywhere, all over the swamp, there were swans behaving strangely, continuously sifting the water with agitated beaks, as though they were trying to find a way to reach the old woman's spirit, sepulchred beneath.

Then one day their behaviour changed. The entire population emerged from the reeds where it usually built its nests to join bevies of others swimming in from distant reaches of the swamp, until they eventually formed one massive flotilla that skirted around the floating dumps. The formation moved in a tight huddle with curled wing feathers that rose aggressively, an armada of thousands that floated slowly, around the swamp, to follow a threat that was visible only to their eyes.

Suddenly, on necks held high, and feathers vertically angled like black fins reaching for the sky, a sea of hissing red beaks pointed towards what threatened it from above the swamp. It was all action after that. In a spear-like dash across the water, the shadow was pursued until the long drawn-out choreography of swans finished with downward pointing beaks nestled into their necks. The flotilla often changed directions in this pursuit without the slightest hint of any confusion in its vast numbers. They turned as one living presence that shared the same vein of nervousness. At any moment, just like a sudden change in the direction of the wind, the mass would retreat then, just as rapidly, swing back across the water into another attack, always watching whatever was menacing the swamp through the single eye of the flotilla, gauging its movement, so that their mass would slow down, speed up, or turn sharply, to match the wings hovering above and create gusts of wind rippling across the swamp.

Oblivia slept so soundly, she missed the dawn spectacle: the sand went berserk and smothered the whole swamp before shifting, and flying off. The Harbour Master was about, saying his farewells. He said he was heading northeast, maybe riding on the cloud of sand somewhere out into the sea first, flying to where winds build ferociously. That was the story. Then, just like that, the mother of all sand mountains disappeared.

The official people of the local Aboriginal Government came and tore the hull apart. Books, papers, the lot were tossed all over the floor as though they did not want their hands contaminated by the devil, while the girl huddled in a corner. They were searching for the crystal balls because they might be worth something – you never know.

They had rolled away in the dust storm. She stared into the direction to where the sand mountain had flown.

The officials thought the girl was a liar – were convinced of it, but there was no point in arguing with her so they took the old woman's body away to be buried. Oblivia freaked, with the question burning in her mind: *What if they come back?* With the old woman's body gone, she felt unprotected and alone. She waited for something else to happen, something bad, expecting more people to barge into the hull at any moment. At nightfall, she felt as though her body had disappeared into the slate-grey wall of the hull and she was drowning, gasping for air under the surface, then she heard Bella Donna walking around in the hull and reciting poetry about a slate-grey lake lit by the earthed lightning of a flock of swans...Oblivia felt her life slipping away with the words, as though the old woman was lulling her away. It would have been easy. But suddenly the mood changed to storm winds spun in the darkness, and Oblivia left so fast it was as though she had been picked up and thrown head first out of the hull, and was already rowing away from it. She ran off into the wasteland at the end of the swamp to search for the tree that she now doubted ever existed.

The swamp people watched her searching among the dead reeds from their homes. *Who's that down there?* They couldn't believe it. Don't look. *Can this madness ever end? I want to look.* She scratched the ground with her fingers, searching for some evidence that would prove the tree had once existed. She needed to confirm what was in her head, of having lived inside the darkened hollow. She was digging holes like a mad dog. *Don't look. I want to look.* There was nothing but dirt where she scratched more and more frantically, with her head screaming, over and over, *I want to know*, as though she was asking the ground to ask the people she knew were watching, but nobody went over to the park to tell the girl what had happened to the trees, whether the wood had been chopped up for firewood, or sawn for timber.

Nobody said: *See child, the timber of the trees was used in that house over there. Nobody said: Look here is a chiselled digging stick whittled from the last slither of wood of the trees that had grown here.* Either the tree never existed as far as anyone knew, or it was a sacred tree in a story only remembered through the ages by people who had earned the right to hold the story. Who speaks for the ancestors? Who speaks for a child wandering around alone? What was the problem?

There was a story about a sacred tree where all the stories of the swamp were stored like doctrines of Law left by the spiritual ancestors, of a place so sacred, it was unthinkable that it should be violated. Old people said that tree was like all of the holiest places in the world rolled into one for us, *no wonder she went straight to it*. Funny thing that. The tree watching everything, calling out to her when it saw some people had broken the Law. Something will happen to them. This ancestor was our oldest living relative for looking after the memories, so it had to take her. When the girl was found though, the tree was destroyed by the Army on the premise that this nexus of dangerous beliefs had to be broken, to close the gap between Aboriginal people and white people. Those stories scattered into the winds were still about, but where, that was the problem now. It made us strong and gave us hope that tree. The kinspeople of the tree had believed this since time immemorial. Really all that was left behind of the story were elders and their families whose ancestors had once cared for the old dried and withered, bush-fire burnt-out trunk of a giant eucalyptus tree through the eons of their existence. They were too speechless to talk about a loss that was so great, it made them feel unhinged from their own bodies, unmoored, vulnerable, separated from eternity. They had been cut off. They called themselves damned people who felt like strangers walking around on their country. The reciprocal bond of responsibility that existed between themselves and the ancestors had always strengthened them. This was what held all times together. Now we are sick of it. Sick of that girl bringing up that memory to make us feel bad. All these people could think about while watching Oblivia dig the bare earth that day, was being reminded of the tree exploding in front of their eyes and there was not a thing anyone could do about it. Nothing at all. Couldn't bring any of it back. That girl is doing this to keep reminding us. Something must be wrong in her head if she can't even think straight. Watching the girl was one thing. They could not go out there and explain to this child what it meant to lose that ancestral tree.

Nevermind! Nobody forgets. You sprog, the old woman had once explained, fell over the escarpment of an invisible plateau.

Its geology was composed of stories much bigger than a little girl getting lost like you. Now the girl searched beneath the cracked parchments of clay where the dun beetles and ants lived, hoping to find a nest of termites feasting underground on the root system of the tree. The ants and skinks slink away. She leaves after a while, still wondering how termites could have devoured every scrap of evidence of the huge tree's existence.

Finally, the girl returns to the hull where the ghost of the old woman could still be heard talking to herself. The swamp people could never stay silent for long about her ghost either. Their voices swung bittersweet all over the swamp, and they were not just talking about each passing breath of their momentous lives. No! They were talking like the old woman. Her voice was triumphing over death. It made your blood run cold the way she returned like a witch inside of other people's voices. But what did she mean, swinging her mantra in some foreign antique language, the one the old sea explorers used when they saw a black swan for the first time, *Rara avis in terris nigroque simillima cygno.*

The girl listened while people around the swamp repeated the mantra to each other. She heard the same phrase sung every night because someone would start calling out the Latin words from a nightmare. Then, suddenly a very strange thing happened. Everyone spoke a few words of Latin in every conversation, and for a while after the old lady died and kept haunting the place, the swamp people started claiming that they were Latino Aboriginals.

It appeared that the old ghost had colonised the minds of the swamp people so completely with the laws of Latin, it terminated their ability to speak good English anymore, and to teach their children to speak English properly so that the gap could finally be closed between Aboriginal people and Australia. You could call it stupidity, naivety, logical, to allow oneself to become so integrated into the world of the old ghost woman, where all sorts were telling each other that speaking Latin made them feel holy. The swamp people, the eels, moths and butterflies, all wanted to go to Rome to live with the Pope. Some people even claimed that the swamp was Rome.

In the eyes of the beholder, all the architecture around the swamp had become the *relics of the greatest city in the world*. Old swamp people were becoming the greatest Romans of all times, even greater than the Romans themselves. The swamp had become a colosseum.

How bold to mix the Dreamings. Those laws of the two sides of the local world were always clashing. She decided to ignore the old ghost woman sitting in the kitchen of the hull speaking in Latin all night. She would simply remember the living Aunty Bella Donna of the Champions claiming that she had not inherited myths from purists, and not believing that the black swan belonged to the night dreams of some of her ancestors. *The facts girl. Here are the facts. It was the Feast of the Epiphany in 1697 when the crew of Willem de Vlamingh's Dutch ship claimed to have seen superstition come to life, when they saw alive, two black swans – a beautiful pair, swimming off the coast of Western Australia, and called it 'the epiphany of the black swan' – a celebration for science, a fact stripped from myth.*

When the swans scattered, the sailors randomly ran down four swans, and once caught, they were taken on board the sailing ship. When they were taken out to sea, the swans became morose from their own stories being pulled away from them, but they were kept alive anyway, the birds of nightmare specimens in the hands of science, exhibits in Indonesia's old Batavia, where the devil swan feathers could be touched by anyone in order to defy their superstition.

The girl lived in a limbo world. The directions of its map spread out like a peacock's tail. Who created it? Well! There were these boys who once chased a little girl down. They kept roaming in her wilderness. Which little girl? What poor little girl? Talk is talk. Costs nothing. Oblivia hears it everywhere now: *You remember Aunty. She was one of those failure-to-thrive babies. Had FASD. Foetal Alcohol Spectrum Disorder or something like that. You should not believe all the talk going around. You don't know if any of that is true or not. Aunty, it's true, as true as I am standing here. It's the truth of what you get with white government social engineering intervention mucking up more blackfella lives. She was a closing the gap baby. Us? Us left with the responsibility for looking after her.* Oblivia hears voices all the time, and thinks a lot about how stories are made, considering which words would be used down the centuries to describe herself, and representing what? Swanee! Like a devil's swan! The old woman had always claimed that she knew how to find the peculiar if she went looking for it. Destiny itself discovered the girl, and the old woman had explained: *You child, are really peculiar.* She once told Oblivia that she was joined with the *undoable*. It was the principle, she said, of the haphazard way sanity and madness were reaped from her having been gang-raped physically, emotionally, psychologically, statistically, randomly, historically, so fully in fact: *Your time stands still.*

Gang-raped. The girl hardly knew what these two words meant as she thought about herself in the sameness of passing time while sitting on the floor of the hull, pulling her head apart trying to remember what had happened to her, or perhaps whatever it was, it just happened to some other little girl that everyone was talking about and maybe it was not her either, or herself neither, but all girls. While trying to decide whether she was sane or mad like the girl she had heard about from listening to people telling their stories – whispering on and on about rape in a form of speechlessness, it was hard to hold everything back in her chest about the velocity of the things that she could not remember, about what those boys did to the girl she heard people talking about! Poor little girl! Which little girl? She did not know, and wished she had never been born. *It was not your fault.* Those were the old woman's final words on the matter, after explaining in general terms the cause and effect of an outrageous history that had created a destiny, to avoid speaking of a shame that was so overwhelmingly connected to the girl's experiences of life, and from her own shame of having to say to the girl that she had been raped by a group of boys, the plain raw truth of the matter being that this one boy, and that one over there walking about etcetera, were the ones who did it, and not speaking of what Oblivia could not remember from her childhood of something happening to her, where bits of truth were never enough while visiting her recurring nightmares, and not being able to speak of why she was waking up screaming and frightened of the darkness, and of being so petrified that she would be eternally connected to the age she had been just before she had been raped by holding on, and guarding that little girl before something bad happened to her, or even, explaining why she was found in the tree.

The girl continued to hear the hushed word *gang-raped* frequently, escaping through the cracks of the gossipy swamp – said without soul about an incident that had been forgotten, had to be forgotten, tucked away and hidden, but had returned. It was funny how some words can always be heard in whatever vicinity, no matter how softly they have been spoken. Just like eyesore words, standing out in normal conversations that attract everyone's attention by bringing back the memory of a little girl who had once disappeared from the face of the earth for a very long time.

A gang of boys who thought they were men were wracked out of their minds on fumes from an endless supply of petrol, glue, or whatever else they played with when they had chased the girl down. They were given a fresh start by a youth worker who coaxed them from the rooftops of the houses where they hung out, hiding under tee-shirts pulled over their heads and sniffing petrol from Coca-Cola bottles. They were taken to an entertainment centre where they could practice snooker and blackjack, and this was followed up with more largesse to close the gap of failed policies for Aboriginal advancement from the Government in Canberra.

A grand football oval, a state-of-the-art stadium, was built by the Army so fast it was considered to be a miracle. This monument, a grand design in the landscape, overshadowed the slum, the shanty houses where those brain-damaged petrol sniffers ended up crawling around on the floor, along with whatever else was blown in by the wind. There was nothing wrong with grandness-emitting hyper rays of positivism to build muscle and brawn, sinew and bone, to breathe hot breath and punch the air. Life went on. Money well spent. Football carnival days were definitely the rage. Families cheered their boys. The floodlights poured gold on the big crowds.

The swamp people would not need to speak about anything else really except football, and they spoke it in ghost Latin that nobody else understood, when the swamp became Rome for a while, because the Army said, *Rome was not built in a day. So let the Government do all the talking, all the planning, and the thinking and the controlling*, and tell old *Jacky Jacky* what to do in Rome.

People tell stories all the time: The stories they want told, where any story could be changed or warped this way or that. You see, the people of the swamp always claimed that the girl in the hull was a little foundling child, not the one who went missing – who was once lost in the bush. Yes! She had run far, far away, they said, and they said it was no good doing something like that. It only made people worry all the time. They did not fancy that she had hid in a hollow at the base of any old *eucalypti* tree. Yes! Fancy that.

The police and army search went on for days when the little girl they knew had disappeared. A line of emotionally charged people searched through every dwelling – pulling everything apart, then beyond, thrashing through the dried-up bush for five kilometres, working clockwise out from the swamp.

The thrashers told stories to occupy themselves: tales upon tales not to be taken lightly about things like this. In the unearthing of those sad old stories they found no lost child. All they found were new tracks of possibilities for things that had once happened and should stay buried with the past. These new versions of old stories did not fit the ground, because you know, old Law forms its own footpaths. A very bad feeling had spread among the thrashers. Soon they were saying quite frankly, *Why can't she stay lost? All this searching and searching*, they claimed, *and the only thing discovered was shame*. It was decided to let sleeping dogs lie. The search was called off. The girl's own heartbroken father was *manngurru nyulu*, and being so ashamed he felt weak, *mayamayada*, and now thought others saw him as being *warrakujbu* or mad, failing to take notice of his child, and had made a sudden request to all the *lungkaji* policemen, asking them to give up hope.

That was the moment when someone decided to make a nuisance of themselves, when that old bat Aunty Bella Donna of the Champions had decided to step in, to plough the ground with her own eyes, and to be totally ignorant of the ins and outs of family histories – their ground. She went on searching for the lost girl, losing all sense of time, and oblivious of how she was riling up spite and hatred from people watching what they did not want to watch – someone searching for a needle in a haystack. *Hey! Old dear. What? What? What did you say? You got to give up that ting you are doing.*

Those old ears of hers, delicate white with networks of red veins, that had no trouble hearing everything else, decided to be stone deaf to all the sneering, the abuse yelling anonymously behind her back, the *ins* and *outs* of what people thought about what she was doing on their land: *Why can't she stay lost?* She went on raking the ground, and continued ignoring those who said she ought to mind her own business.

She boasted obviously, not just round the hull, nor just to the swans, and expected eternal gratefulness from the entire swamp for finding the missing girl. *The triumph of good eyesight.* Who would have thought to look into the hollow of a tree? Evidently, no one!

In fact months passed after she found the girl before the old woman had thought of telling the parents she had found the missing child. Her little *bujiji nyulu*. The orphan. She had taken herself ashore from the hull on the Harbour Master's advice – *you got to tell the parents, her nganja, her kin, ngada, murriba, haven't you heard of the stolen generations? Janyii ngawu ninya jawikajba, I am asking you with my own mouth* – so she went over to the place where the parents lived, where she called out to them from the street, *I found that kid of yours.*

Now very old people with minds crippled by dementia, the bewildered parents were not interested in mysteries at that stage in their life, and were still fearful of welfare people like the Army coming back to plague them over their failure-to-thrive baby, and poking around with accusing fingers at their families' histories for evidence of grog harm on the little girl's brain – as if they didn't already know what happens to the inheritors of oppression and dispossession. It's not that shit happens as other people have said; it's the eternal reality of a legacy in brokenness that was the problem to them. They came out of their little shelter, fearful that people would start accusing them of being drinkers again when they had never touched grog, that *kamukamu-yaa*, and whispered to Bella Donna to *shut up. Budangku*. No. They had long since finished, *windijbi* with grieving after accepting a plausible inquest report and had never expected to see their missing daughter again. *Don't you know? Don't you remember?* It was a story that created a lot of sad havoc about the place. Word spread of Bella Donna troubling the old couple without anyone really believing a girl was found in a tree, and since nobody was missing a child, a consensus was reached. They said: *Tell her if she wants, she should keep that stray girl. Her business. Not ours.*

Why am I lucky? This was how the girl was lucky. Lucky, that the old woman had not found a skeleton. Lucky, the girl remembered being told by the old woman, when there were women and girls around the swamp who had gone missing forever, although some of them might call up eventually on the one payphone, just to say that they were *somebody calling someone,* to let their families know they are doing fine, living somewhere else. *We have escaped you know.* But on the other hand, some don't bother to contact anyone, and as far as anyone knows, nobody knew whether those women and girls who went missing were dead or alive. Nobody knows. Nobody knows if their bodies, still dressed in their best going-away dresses, were laying out there in the bush somewhere, buried in sand, or whether their skeleton was standing up against a dead tree, or they were looking towards the road to heaven, or towards the way to go home, or were just waiting to be found. You might see some of them out there sometimes. Who knows anything about the truth? There were many homes waiting for the public telephone to ring with news, or hating to hear any news, or yelling over each other in the night when the lonely public payphone rang, shouting for somebody to go out there and king hit the phone with an axe, or piss on it, or bowl the thing over, or fire a shotgun right into its guts. Lucky, that some people would say anything for silence.

Lucky that Oblivia did not know why she was lucky. Lucky that she never told the old woman she was lucky.

The girl had a different version of the events that led to Aunty Bella Donna of the Champions finding her asleep in the tree. The old woman had always claimed it was in the nick of time: *Child! Minutes! Otherwise! Otherwise it would have been a disaster*, what would normally be expected – *You would have been dead*.

Oblivia frequently dreamt of a child like herself running for the hole at the base of a tree – a little girl in so many different forests, timber lots, old stands of ancient trees, that now, it was difficult to remember any sequences of geographies stored in her mind. There were dreams where the child flees through densely overgrown chestnut trees. Sometimes she runs away in forests that smelt of resin, walnut forests, olive groves, mountain bamboo forests and cherry blossom trees. She still felt the cold wind on her face in alpine valleys of bare limb larch trees while running beside deer being chased by wolves. It was geography that was constantly shifting, for sometimes she runs by huge sea turtles stranded high in the branches of trees of the tropics, where there had been floods.

Quite often, Oblivia remembered a child running in the middle of a bush fire, to where it had been deliberately lit at the base of a eucalypt and left smouldering over several months until a large, charred hollow had been created into which a girl would eventually fall. On her shoulders, the child always carried long thin burnt branches like wings, but she balked, pulled away before reaching the hole in the tree.

Yet no matter how hard the girl tried to stop before reaching the hole, she was pushed along until squeezed into the hollow, no matter how small it became in her mind, and it breaks her wings. Once inside, she would fall through heavy air, plunging into darkness and weightlessness, as if she had been swallowed alive.

The girl had seen many versions of this charred stomach, where the floor inside the tree was overgrown with large, sprawling grey roots that grew down the shaft and on the way down were covered here and there with the initials of previous visitors.

The child in the dream looked as though she was no older than eight or ten years old, maybe she was younger, five or six, and very different to the story the old woman had always maintained – that the girl she had found was much older. Maybe, life stands still in a Rip Van Winkle way of sleeping. The girl that had eventually come out of the bowel of the tree had no memory of the swamp. Did not recognise it. Had no memory of the past. Her memory was created by what the old woman had chosen to tell her. *People only heard the swans calling. Nobody heard you running away.*

Oh! Yes! And I worked my skin to the bone looking after you for a very long time until you woke up from a coma.

There were many lost girls. In the old woman's stories, the girl was recreated in many lost childhoods. The ancient lost child of a Mountain Ash forest. The lost girl who had spent days running through a forest path of fairies where swan lovers flew one after the other, while circling above the swan poet's lake. A little girl became lost while travelling old tracks through the marshes to hunt where swans built nests near underground rivers. *You choose,* the old woman had said.

It was difficult for Oblivia to believe that the old woman had been capable of looking after an unconscious child, feeding her stories for nourishment, more than food. She kept dreaming those stories like a child, even when she could see and feel the strangeness of an adult's face reflecting back at her from the mirrored stillness of swamp water. She once remembered the old woman saying it was possible to hibernate underground in the drought, like frogs and swamp turtles, but Bella Donna was adamant in her discussions with the Harbour Master that it was impossible for a human being to shut down like a burrowing frog with cold blood. He did not like to admit it, but agreed. She would not be able to sleep through the drought like a frog, or like a swamp turtle, by conserving energy from living on a single heartbeat for whatever time was necessary to survive through hibernation. And Bella Donna had smiled at Oblivia, sitting on the floor, while the Harbour Master's flashbulb eyes were burning at the girl with disgust: *You were different. You were in a coma.*

The tumultuous universe of lost girls could still be heard from old Bella Donna's voice speaking through the walls of the hull. She must have left her voice behind after she died. Well! It was best not to argue with steel walls Oblivia thought, since the swans were milling around the hull, still waiting to hear the old woman's stories. She had more to think about. The swans were hungrier than ever now.

In this winter the swans only produced one egg. This precious egg, their ode to the swamp, sat in a nest marvellously constructed with thousands of sticks, dried algae and leaves individually chosen and carefully placed. The two swans had worked for weeks in its construction before the egg was laid. It polarised other swans, glancing, idling the day at the nest, as though admiring the egg's possibilities. The swan lovers constantly uncovered, cradled, and re-hid the egg under the leaf litter of their perfect nest where snakes slept for warmth. As time passed, the brooding pair looked as though they would stay forever protecting the dead egg, wishing it would hatch. Then one day, a group of haughty swans swarmed over to the nest and forced them to give up. More half-hearted nests were built crooked with randomly placed sticks and old bits of plastic rubbish, then all too briefly, only admired as foolish work of swans unable to predict what height the water levels would become with the uncertainty of rain. Whatever vague ideas of procreation had been in the initial motivation, these were abandoned for a different kind of infatuation – a love affair with the northern skies.

When swans mourned, their long necks hung with their heads almost touching the ground. It seemed as though the swans were now glued to the shores of the swamp where they looked dolefully towards the hull, waiting for the old woman's world of stories to appear, hoping for the hot air of the mirage to be filled with a cooling sweetness.

Instead of the swans saving themselves from swamp people's dogs, they continued staring like statues at the broken forms of silver reflections, shimmering over the water. It was like watching suicide – witnessing, the swans' refusal to swim away. Black feathers lay scattered over the ground and were blown over the water. Seagulls flew in from the coast many kilometres away and joined the nightly attacks. The swan frenzy raged on and on with blood-stained dogs and seagulls, while bleeding swans mingled with the red haze of sunrise, still sitting on the ground, heads tucked under their wings.

The swans kept dying in their eerie pact, leaving Oblivia to crawl over dead birds, and having to bury them under piles of broken reeds. Swamp people watched. *Will you look at the girl out there? Why? What is she doing now? She's burying the swans.* Pause. *What for? Because they are dead stupid?* So, so on, *manija* and so forth.

White smoke rises quickly in a breeze. It created a haze over the swamp from the bonfires the girl lit for the pyre of dead swans, and pushing the raft into the water and using the long sticks to poke down into the mud below, she carefully manoeuvred it back over to the hull to be closer to the stories from old Aunty's swan books.

She is reading through the old woman's collection of books about swans to find a way of bringing the swans back to the remaining waters in the swamp.

Swans swimming correctly and sedately in swanlike fashion, screamed in her head, *good news*, but the mud-caked flocks remained in sync with their perpetual north-south swaying, plodding through puddles, beaks sifting through mud searching for non-existent food.

The girl read about the many lives of swans flying around mystical, mist-covered palaces of princes who also become white swans. Curly wing feathers of black swans became the black curly heads of warriors in epic hunts, in places where the fearless steps of the bravest of heroes stalking along the banks of a coal-black river to kill a swan prince, might just as easily end in the hunter's death, or a swan that became a prince, or dead princes lying beneath waters flowing with green-grey algae.

When the rains finally came, all of the *winngil*, big rain – the bush dripped from clouds sitting on the land, until finally, with so much water flowing over grasslands and running through gullies leading into the swamp, the old lake reappeared again. The swans safe now from the dogs, were cleansed by months of preening from rain pouring over their feathers. The breeding nests were full with half grown cygnets. Their packs again swarmed through the water where constant winds flowing across sheets of floodwater rippled each pulse of the country's heartbeat. The air was electrified by the sun disappearing behind the *madarri*, clouds that packed the sky, and reappearing like a fiery pearl in the mouth of the creature formed by clouds that looked like an enormous swan.

The News from the Sea

Somewhere else, far away by the headwaters of a wide river, where another arm of the same Indigenous Nation as the swamp people lived, that belongs to other people – *maninja nayi jamba* – there was a young boy, a *juka* becoming a man named Warren Finch. He also stared at the future. The boy had just finished reading an article from a local people's community newspaper that he had been carrying around forever, that he had read as soon as he had hurdled over the big national benchmark for Indigenous people, to be literate in English.

This newspaper article was his only possession, and he had read it so many times each word was etched in his brain. Long ago, he had stolen the newspaper from his family when they had tried to hide it from him, snatched it out of his hands in fact, after he had asked them to read the story to him. He had kept it folded neatly in a rusted *Log Cabin* tobacco tin. He believed he owned the story, which was about the rape of a young girl in an Aboriginal community by members of a gang of petrol-sniffing children.

His elders, the old grandfathers, had told the young boy the story about a very important little girl who was raped by boys. Promised one for their country. His promised one. They said a terrible thing had happened on their country, at that *poisonous no good place* they called Swan Lake, which was polluted by all of the rubbish from the sea that had been carted into the place, turning good pristine water into rust. They described the journey they had taken to get to that place after the terrible incident to deal with the matter as the big bosses of country, a journey which along the way, had taken them over all the stories for this one, that one and other ancestral rivers, and a long way across from the old sleeping man range, and a long way from all that good porcupine spinifex flatland country, mulga spirit country, gidgee tree, black soil sacred country. They said, with fists thumping their hearts, that they had reached utter badness at the end of the journey, the only blight in all of their homelands, the place where the Harbour Master was looking after that sand mountain on the other side of their own Aboriginal Nation's territory that spread through hundreds of square kilometres across all their old song story country – mother country, father country, grandparents country, and so on through family closeness and feelings towards all things on their land. They claimed that those people *over there* had been paying for what happened to the country they were responsible for long before that thing happened to the little girl. They told the story of having felt radioactivity running about in the air *in that place*, and saw with their own eyes the Army in charge of the place – bossing everyone around inside a big fence, saying they were looking after all of the children, so all of the poison was already charging around inside the head *from a long time ago and still going on*. They even had to stop *dangerous thoughts* from getting inside their own brain, like a cut letting in the poison, and trying to steal the controls, and steering them around to do bad things to each other. *Boys should not play rough with little girls*, they said very quietly. It was no good for their whole nation. *You will see in time what we are talking about.* Then they told him never to talk about it, *never mention it again*.

The story about what had happened to the girl who was found in a tree became common knowledge through this large tribal nation. The story became a wild story. Everyone had an idea of what really happened. Some people were saying firstly that the girl was taken, kidnapped by the tree from her people as punishment. Others said that she was really the tree itself. She had become the tree's knowledge. Or, possibly she was related to the tree through Law, and the tree took her away from her people.

These elders, seasoned orators with centuries of reading Australian racial politics behind them, the AM to PM news aficionados, and track masters in how to skin a cat, or kill off a lame duck, had partly decided that it would be a good idea for this boy Warren Finch, already the joy of his people, to be brought up their way – the old way – away from the hustle and bustle of intra and extra racial Australian politics, a tyranny that they claimed was like a lice infestation in the mind.

Everyone in Warren Finch's world was full of gusto for the child and wore their pride on the outside. They already expected this finely built boy who shone like the rising sun, and was already as fearless at their greatest ancestral spirits, would one day become the best man that ever breathed air on this planet. His education was to be undertaken in isolation, out bush away from everyone. The story of the girl who was found in a tree was so polluting, it could only be resolved by feelings of resentment at the swamp people's spite for allowing something like this to happen when they knew that the destiny of the girl belonged elsewhere, to the clans-country on the other side of the hills, in the homeland of their boy, more wondrous then the air itself, like a bit of a sweetheart that sonny boy Warren Finch.

This whole thing about the girl would never do for the direct relatives of Warren Finch who saw themselves as the antithesis of those other people, their over-the-hills so-called kinspeople in the swamp, mixed up, undone people and what have you, who had thrown too much around of their brains and were germinating seed all over the flat, so that they ended up having to be guarded night and day by the Army. People in other words, who were so unlike their good selves, it was any wonder that they were related to one another. You have to weigh up the price of principle, of what it was worth, that was what Warren Finch's people believed, who reckoned that they owed their success to historical savvy, inherited from a line of hard nosed, hard hitting bosses you might call idiosyncratic, even mavericks, but real go-getter people, with the good sense for standing up and saying 'Yes Sir', or, 'No Sir, Madam (as the case may be, and conveniently so) Australian Government'. They prided themselves as being the anti-brigade, take what you want people, of having their own unexpected orthodoxies to what was expected of them. They even kept full-time cheer squads, everyone in fact speaking the anti-talk, to spruik the river of a special crawling language from their mouths at any professional white or black designer of black people's lives.

Warren Finch's people were good at it and taught the next and the next generation to behave accordingly. For instance, and it was only poking a twig at the tight-fisted ball of their status quo, for whatever it took to deal with people from the outside world coming along with great ideas for fixing up the lives of Aboriginal people, or wanting to take something else from them, mostly in the form of traditional land and resources, they agreed by presenting themselves as being well and truly yes people who were against arguing the toss about Aboriginal rights. They could rock the grey matter – like a peloton riding in the slip-stream of the agreeable – just like the majority of Australia, while at the same time be just like anyone else – as anti-culture, anti-sovereignty, anti-human rights, anti-black-armband-history for remembering the past, anti-United Nations, or Amnesty International, as much as being anti-pornography, anti-paedophiles, anti-grog, anti-dope, anti-littering, anti having too many dogs and pussycats, anti any kind of diseases or ill health, anti-welfare, anti-poverty, anti-anyone not living like a white person in their houses, anti having their own people building their proper houses unless the white government says it's okay – they can do it for a bit of training money. They wanted to be good black people, not seen as troublemakers, radicals, or people who made Australians feel uneasy, thinking Aboriginal people were useless, wasting Australian government money, and if it meant being anti all these things to prove that they loved their children, and could get on, and if this is what it meant to be reconciled – Well! So be it. What else? What else did they have to say to make things okay so that they could get on with everyone else? Well! They were also anti-truancy, anti-consultation, anti-others, anti-urban, city blacks, mix-bloods etc, just as much as they were anti-racists, anti-anyone black, white, or whatever and from wherever else speaking on their behalf, and anti anyone who opposed their human and personal rights, or their land rights, or their native title, anti never having enough heat in the weather, or anyone who got in the way of what they said was Aboriginal-defined self-determination, and they were just about anti any dissenting hindrances from Federal government of what they wanted, or any hindrances to hindrances in themselves, and anti whatever else was somebody else's reality, or what any other people said about black people no matter if it was right or wrong, and they were anti about whatever there was to be anti about if white people say so, and even if they seemed to be just a bunch of negative people, or uncle Toms, or coconuts, the upshot was that their highly successful and self-defined Aboriginal Nation Government was designed from such, and was as much.

A whirlwind blew the bit of newspaper out of young Warren Finch's hand. It landed in the river. That question, the young boy thought of what people thought of what happened to that little girl, as he watched the paper floating away, would now be carried off to the ocean. He was not sure who would answer the question. But somewhere, as the paper floats out to sea, he sees that a small group of hermit crabs have turned it into a raft. They are riding on the floating paper, and working to keep it afloat until eventually he imagines, after riding ten thousand waves, their little ship would moor in a harbour. He dreams that as luck would have it, the raft paper arrives safely in the busy shipping port under the cover of night. By early morning, a local fisherman in his fishing boat has dragged the newspaper in with his grappling hook, or perhaps it was dropped at his feet from the full-bellied seagull that flew overhead.

This man, Warren believed, would carefully dry the paper with his hardened fisherman's hands, because he honoured the sea that had given him this piece of news. What he read when the paper dried made him feel like crying, and he asked the sea why it had sent him such news. He made it his business to show the newspaper that fate had brought to him to all manner of people who lived there, because they honoured the sea too, and were interested in the news from other countries that the Gods brought to them.

Warren Finch thought about the law of a whorl wind for a story that wanted to go all over the world, and continued on his way...

Warren Finch could grab another person's luck, and dream it into a ghost story. He went back to his favourite fishing hole where there had been a hatching of blue butterflies. Thousands were springing off the paperbark trees, and spilling through the wind like a quivering evanescent blue river flooding towards the sky. The river fell apart, and the butterflies flew about the wild banana vines which grew rampantly over and under old growth, before winding around and through the bushland trees.

A hundred swallows hunting the insects flittered about, flying up and down from the skies above Warren's head. He had thought the girl in the story was weak, he had often dreamed about visiting her, and always the dreams were about how he tried to incite her to come out of her hiding place in the tree as though he was frogmarching an insect out from the darkness and into the sunlight of his world. He was a child, but his mind was already laden like a museum, where old and new specimens, facts and figures, lived together as evidence of his own personal history.

On this warm to meddling hot day, Warren Finch started to conjure up the circus that had taken place in his life. He could remember how it annoyed him so long ago, when everyone said that he was uncommonly wise for someone so young. Now, the same as back then, he would throw his fishing line into the water, neither caring whether he caught fish or not because he always caught fish, even while he was planning the content of speeches he would be giving, or not giving later in his life. He was flicking the line in the direction of the blue butterflies, staring at trees, and he stared straight though the country, to the place he had carried around in his mind most of his life, until he finds the little girl again inside the tree, where he speaks to her, asking her to listen to the love song he has composed for her.

So! Hold on to your seat real tight, hold your breath, keep your eyes in your head, and go on, don't be frightened.

Please! Calmness! Peacefulness!

Silence costs nothing just as silence means nothing.

Cheer up like loud people and clap your hands and stomp your feet about this. Louder.

I don't think I can hear you.

Oh! Come on! Don't be a sooky baby.

You have to be better than that.

Your little mad girl's world is a bit shy you know.

You are frightened of what people will think of you.

You do not want people to think bad things about you.

But I got to tell you to come out.

I insist. I want you to.

You have a story to tell.

So, clap louder!

Quickly!

Tell everyone you have a few home truths to say to them.

And plans?

Yes! Yes! Really! Let's think. You will have plans.

You have to listen to your plans.

I'm part of it.

He could still feel the way she had always moved back, flinching at the warmth of his breath filling the dark space as he reached inside the tree to find what he already thought he possessed, as though he could reach across any space of time and distance in his thoughts. She was embarrassed and confronted by the way he travelled with his imaginary crowds of ancestral spirits that proudly followed him over the land, and who were watching, as he came down to where she was sleeping cradled in the spirit of the tree. The girl kept slinking further away from the strange boy who came through the darkness to talk to her about his frightening ideas, using words he had heard running out of the mouths of old men and women, and from families calling to one another from one scrap of dirt to the next, about people who trespassed on their native land.

Warren Finch's boy heart thumped like an animal mapping its own way down through the roads it ought to travel, like migrating birds reaching their destination before embarking on the journey.

He was at his own concert and hoarse from screaming for a ghost to leave the tree.

Warren Finch was travelling on the flat ground above the river, leaving the butterflies, to go where the grey-feathered brolgas were dancing ahead. The tall slender birds were performing a legendary fight in the Dreamtime story – one that the old law had marked on them forever with a wattle of flaming red skin on the back of their heads. He was studying this brolga dance which was being performed with the accompaniment of a whirly haze of dust sprayed from the rusty wrecks of car bodies strewn over the flats behind them. A coy wind rushed by, picking up and blowing their soft grey chest feathers, and a fine yellow dust that closed him in the atmospheric stench, and drew him further into the brolgas' traditional, well-worn, and danced-about roosting ground.

His elders had come by earlier as they did regularly, to check on Warren, the boy who brought only joy, and who was commonly called, *the gift from God*. He lit up their hearts. Even though he was a half-caste. They said he was the incarnate miracle. He even lit Heaven at night. They agreed wholeheartedly with the ancestors, and with any new gods if they cared to be about in the country of the traditional owners, and with all the insurmountable riffraff bothering them in modern times. *This boy pumps up our hearts with proper pride and it feels good. What we say again, and again, and again is this, isn't it a mighty proud day wouldn't you say to be seeing this boy of ours out here on country?*

You could say that Warren Finch was a pretty special child. He was living alone, in the crowded space of the breeding colony of the brolgas, as he had done for several years of his schooling, away from his parents' outstation where they were etching out a living with cattle and growing forests of wild plum trees for carbon trading. In this isolated place, it was clear that his schoolroom and teacher were the land itself. He was watched over every night in his dream travels by the elders who brought him lessons. They could not have cared less, or given two hoots about the fact that in the wider circles of Australian opinion, his education was typically called 'special treatment', or perhaps even wasteful, by *somebody* following them around like a big shadow in the many guises of omnipresent Australia.

A colonial omnipresence looked like the daggers sticking out of the heads of elders these days. All fired by Australia. All conveniently rolled up nice and personal into one person called *Official Observer.* That official *who thinks himself,* from the Capital of Australia, Canberra, to ask *a bloody squillion and a half* questions about education, by ramrodding with his own valued opinions into the minds of Aboriginal people. The elders refused to answer anything. They offered only their big sighs of resignation. That that was good enough to give anybody who they thought was not their business, as these elders claimed with solemn faces: *We are doing our own business here.*

The boy could not have possibly known how scrutiny works, or that he was a special test case for the curriculum of education devised by his elders. These were ancient-looking men and women – six of them – keepers of Country, who kept on living as though they were immortals. They were the bosses of this Aboriginal Government. Boss! That's all they were called. No other name suited people who wholly belonged to the old Laws of Country. They were Country and they looked like it, and you don't argue with Country.

The Observer was always reminding the old people just how many Australians, whether they knew anything or not, and not to mention the big national media governing Aboriginal opinion in the country, just loved being judge of Aboriginal failure. The elders always replied with heads together – better than one: *Well! Doesn't inward darkness like to latch on to some other darkness?*

But how can birds in the bush educate him? He should be in school. The National Observer literally pulled out his hair to get this so-called Aboriginal Government to listen to him properly, and it was not unusual to see him storming off from the Brolga colony until somebody ran after him and persuaded the white man to *please Mister* come back, to try to be more reasonable in his understanding. He knew what they were doing but he was not going to say it. He was not going to sacrifice his career by mouthing off his theories about the kind of education Aboriginal Government was creating, but he knew the boy would be dangerous in the end. He just wanted to know how he was going to big note himself to his peers, the Australian Government, and to the United Nations watchdog about honouring the rights of Indigenous peoples.

This trial with the boy's education since early childhood was just a little periwinkle of an experiment, with a *let's see how it goes* attitude for a right to educate, begrudgingly gifted by Australia while maintaining the perception that Aboriginal Self Determination was unworkable, and after two plus centuries of jumping up and down about this very thing being non-existent by Indigenous peoples.

Weren't the Indigenous People's Rights embedded in that 2020 Constitutional Agreement thing that Australia signed, sealed and delivered to me here right into this hand of the old man? What was that about? The oldest local Indigenous man, a white-haired wise man regarded in the highest esteem by his people, had excused himself forever from answering any undermining question posed about an absolute. He had his right on a piece of paper and that was what mattered as far as he was concerned. Long time we been fight for that. What? Three hundred years maybe fighting over me being Black and you being White? Like mangy, maggoty dog fight.

Can't fight properly. Always having to scratch for fleas. Rubbish tings like that. Always floating around. Always. Can't ever get rid of it. The old man was told to be quiet by the Observer who was sick of listening to him talk about politics and his rights. *Hold your tongue old man. You are talking too much politics. You are obsessed.*

So what was that treaty I signed? older man asked again, while endlessly rolling the treaty word around the roof of his mouth with his tongue, just to feel how satisfying it sounded in his head, and it still pleased him to hear the word which he would keep saying a million times more perhaps, before he died. He had the right to feel pleased. He had forged the only treaty of its kind in Australia after three centuries of denial about original land theft that lead to the creation of Australia. He had gone to the World Court as mad as a run-over dog to do that. This old man got his treaty between Australia and the traditional owners of this piece of Brolga country alright, and pinned the bloody thing up on the door of his house. The words on the paper were faded by the sun, but that did not matter because the old man could recite what had been written on it, word for hard-forged word – one for every man, woman and child of his kind. This treaty was for the rights of Indigenous people over the traditional country that Warren would one day inherit as one of its senior caretakers.

Traditional responsibility. That was what these elders were training him for with their educational system that prickled the nerves of the 'official observer', who was a man who had been one of the masterminds behind decades of failed Australian government policies, but somehow, because of all of his experiences, Canberra had judged him worthy of this position. Yep! No trouble at all. He was still king of his patch.

Thank climate change and even the wars such a catastrophe created, and thank the millions of refugees around the world being sick and tired of how they were treated, that had cleaved the opportunity for this one nation of Indigenous people deemed worthy enough, to force Australia to sign a treaty by bringing the country to its illegal colonising knees in the World Court.

But Brolga people had been opportunistic. They had made sure that they were in the right place at the right time. They blamed themselves and others like the swamp people for their troubles so that rich people would give them plenty of money. Luck was involved too with being anti-people, when they found themselves caught up in a mix of new thinking throughout the world about how to treat poor people, oppressed people, Indigenous people and whatnot! Things like that! Not normally done for have-nots. They had a long tradition of knowing how to say *yes, yes enough*, and that was fair enough too, while agreeing to a heart-breaking trade-off – only done they believed for the long-term survival of their nation – along with the shame they would carry forever, a perpetual sadness and melancholy of the heart starting with the old white-hair man, to have the swamp people's part of their traditional estate, the Army's property and dumping ground, deleted from the treaty.

Well! Canberra bosses wanted to see treaties given like Christmas presents – they really did, because they wanted to explore the better angels of their nature, to explore what ideas of fairness and justice for all meant – right down to the last child sitting in the dirt with nothing. Usually in this tiny era of history, it was common in the Brolga Country and right down to Canberra to see people sitting around all day long thinking about what was utopia and what was peace. And to question what could have been the most peaceful era known in the existence of the world. Where had it all gone wrong? Were they already experiencing the greatest era of peace in the world but could not recognise it? Questions raised up more questions for goggling around in the mind. Can angels strike others in violence? Can lightning strikes be equated to genocide?

Meanwhile overseas people flocked to talk to the frail old spiritual man of the Brolga Nation Government who had lived forever on nothing but his own sustainability, the ancient intelligence passed down the generations that he said was his religion. Easy words, but he just called it, looking after Country. He was proud that he had seen his people at last recognised as real people, not just a second-hand, shit-cheap humanity. He was happy now that this oldest culture on Earth was recognised as being fit to govern itself through its own laws, and to live on its traditional land. And, this boy, Warren Finch. This was what made his heart feel good.

The Brolga Nation was chosen by an international fact-finding delegation to be their showpiece of what a future humane world was all about. A UN sign was erected at the entrance to the Brolga Nation. It read, *Peace and goodwill to all peoples*. This modern Brolga Nation was just the kind of place that International Justice could promote to bring an end to the wars of homelessness across the world. This high law said it was the showpiece, the example for the future, the hope for kindness to reign over the world for the next marvellous century.

So, these elders, now traditional leaders of the modern world, who already knew that they were high class, were hailed for sitting on their land since the beginning of time, and for having fought very quietly for three centuries the war of oppression. They joined the ranks of other peaceful men in the world like the Mahatma Gandhi, or the Dalai Lama. They were properly cashed up for Rights of Culture, Land, Government, Language, Law, Song, Dance, Story – everything. It was under these circumstances, necessary to explain, that they had hand-picked their brightest child – a gift from God even though he was a half-caste – and had gone so far as to have bequeathed him to their vision of the new world.

This was how he became the chosen one, singled out from all the others in this Australian warzone of torn people, and was hailed in vows under the Brolga Country moon as the truest gift from ancestral heroes, and having a bit each way, not just from God, but any other gods on the planet too.

The education Warren received at his Aboriginal Government's authorised school was a mixed marriage of traditional and scientific knowledge. In a curriculum that the elders had personally composed with all of the reverence of their traditional law, they watched over his education like hawks. In fact, they were like hawks with all progeny, teaching the young to survive in tough new environments. *We are swapping band-aid education for brand new education, sealing the cracks – all the holes in the broken-down fences of Australian education policy for Indigenous peoples.* Yes, they continued the *better education, we know what is best* rhetoric in their on-going war with the *sceptic observer* whom they continually accused *was pass em this and not pass em that – always out to destroy Aboriginal people like a record still stuck in the same grove.* Anyway. Whatever. Agree or not. This was the hammer, even in officially recognised Aboriginal Government, pulping confidence. The hammer that knocked away the small gains through any slip of vigilance. The faulty hammer that created weak ladders to heaven.

So there it was. Warren had been taught, from the day he entered his people's Aboriginal Government School of Brolga Nation as their *sweetest* boy of six years of age, that he would fulfil a vision primed for their own survival, that above all else, he would connect Brolga values with the future of the world.

This was how Warren Finch had been able to live on his traditional land as a practising pupil out on his Country. The official words about this education were described as being: *culturally holistic in all its philosophical, political and environmentally sustainable economic approaches for a school's curriculum which honoured traditional law and the art of sustainability for culture and land.* A lot of thought and hard work had been put into a boy like Warren Finch to create *New Light*. But everybody in his world already thought he would inherit the world after he learnt how to make laws by studying the dance and life cycle of the brolga.

There was another time Warren Finch remembers from when he was still a boy learning how to be a man. He had stopped somewhere along the fisherman's track above the high reddish-grey earth bank of the river, and was listening to the silence of the middle of the day. He reflected on the pleasure of his thoughts about what the future held, where one day in another place and time, he would recall this time. And he wondered what he would feel then, as he danced to a fiddler's tune with the dragonflies above the river affectionately known as the Pearl – a traditional breeding place for local river turtles. He found it difficult to see through the large flat leaves and flowers along the way, but he was sure the river was not dry like it had been in the winter, when the lily bulbs lay dormant, hidden in the cool ground with the turtles, deep below the surface.

In the middle-of-the-day sun that showered the land with bright light, he walked further up the river in search of the black angel he had already seen flying low just metres above his head, the previous night, having been awakened from his dreams by droning wings far off, that he could not see. He had called out: *Who are you, flying there?* The thing he had seen flying close above his eyes looked like a very large woman. A twinkling bell-like voice had also awoken him from his sleep. Warren Finch lived in a world of bells, where birds like *willy wagtail* and magpies sang like bells even throughout the night, and beetles and geckos cried bell-like, and grazing cattle wore bells that rang in their night foraging over stubbly grasses. His elders often reminisced about the days when their people did everything to the sound of a bell on the Mission, rung by a white manager who ordered them about. *Ding! Dong! Ding! Dong! Bell! Or: Ding-a-ling. Or, did it sound like: Dang! Dang?* They inherited bell clanging, whatever the variance in sound. It was stitched in the brain.

A black angel cloud flying in a starry night and playing harp music should be easy enough to find. But the moonlight shining sporadically through cloud cover only returned fragments of his dream by just revealing slithers of a woman's naked body that looked enormous in the sky. She had come to him like a promise, from moving slow along the river that flowed as slowly as his blood. He felt her presence bonding with his own, slowly flowing like the river did, in his blood.

Again and again he tried to recapture the woman's shadow passing over his thighs under the light of the moon. She aroused a desire he had never known before, and with sudden urgency, he tried to force the images of the woman to return, but her fly-about hair, breasts, arms, legs slipped quicksilver through him, and in an instant, the memory of her had faded away into nothing. He was as before, always alone, and although he tried with great difficulty to recall this dream of dreams, others more mundane reminded him of the practical side of his life, where his responsibilities lay.

His frustrating efforts to bring her back revealed nothing, except confusion whenever the dream suddenly surrendered a small memory, bringing him a small victory of being millimetres apart from the dark skin of the woman's body above him, before it again became a cloud passing quickly across the landscape, travelling away through terrains he had never known. He was never sure when these images would reappear, or whether he even delighted in the idea of travelling further to find a glimpse of what had already died.

Brolga and Swan

Vignettes of flying grass seeds spiralling into columns on colliding paths, though neither a girl who hibernates and is kept alive through dreams inside the trunk of a tree, nor a boy who grows on his dreams of looking down on the world, could understand how destiny works. This was so: the girl refusing to have visitors walk into her dreams; the boy trading reality for dreams where he thinks he is a saviour. How children relegate fate as though it was a toy – something to pitch against their repulsion of each other while playing with a vague knowledge of the future they had watched in a dream. Their story was unfolding dangerously through the complex design of children growing up in untidy times. Of times inscribed in the warped, dull state of a publicly determined fate. Or Law that stretched back to the beginning of time.

Oh! helplessness of helplessness, there were pirates of high places rattling knitting needles with the skills of an idiot, and measuring the overload of historical repetitiveness, where children like leaves into the wind were seriously jeopardising each other's existence.

In this breeding season, thousands upon thousands of brolgas of the crane genus *Grus rubicundus* congregated noisily across the plains. They hovered in the sky above Warren Finch. Masses of brolgas danced before the boy by mimicking his movements and endlessly paraded in the dry cracked clay pan all along the horizon of yellow flattened grasses. As this supreme ceremony of Country continued there were many groups of hundreds of cranes lining up, to prance springlike off the ground, to bow long thin necks at each other, lift heads to the greatest height possible to toss sprigs of grass, and to stretch grey chests skyward, wings still arched, while other troupes bounced with light grace a metre high up into the air and landed just as lightly, as though their bodies were pieces of floating paper. The sky was turning grey as thousands lifted and flew high into the atmosphere, passing others descending on ribbons, each hovering, waiting to find space to land.

The boy went down to the river where the yellow water was flowing. He thought of himself as being a human raft while he floated through the shimmering haze at the hottest part of the day and stared upwards to the sky where the old brolgas, some said were at least eighty years old, were gliding in the thermals of hot air.

On this day, the tantalising movements of the old brolgas were stealing his thoughts away, lifting his daydreams up a thousand metres, and floating them there, all his secret splendours of the night suspended in the sky, chanting *Swans beat their wings into the height*. Too bad! Serves him right. He should have been paying attention to what was happening right down around his own two feet.

His mind sailed on and on into the thermals until he was in a trance floating along the river, so captivated in his thoughts now, he was almost touching the flying woman he had seen in his dreams. He felt good. He was in amidst the teeming brolgas searching across the landscape for the distant music of the night-time minstrels, those black wings whooshing through a dry breeze, and remembering how he had once heard a traveller, a travelling Indian woman's voice swaying like that through a slow Hindustani raga.

His head was high, lost in the vastness of the clear blue sky, when he saw in the corner of his eye a flash of black, of last night's dream, now down-stream in the river. His thoughts crashed in one swift jolt into the water, and only the brolgas were spinning alone in the ghostly quiet of the thermals.

He let himself be carried down the river, half-walking waist deep, half-swimming, not noticing the riverbank owls, *julujulu*, in the trees, because he was thinking that his dreams were starting to come true. He was very young. How could he understand that his dreams belonged to the future? Again, he glimpsed what he chased, a small object up-stream that was still too far away. Curiously, the object did not appear to be moving, although it always maintained a safe distance from him. Once out of the water, he walked along the bank towards the small, insignificant dot until he reached a point, past the owls roosting in the canopy of paperbark trees reaching across the river, to where he could see a black swan, visible only whenever the sunlight found its way through cracks in the shadows.

Warren Finch, who had never seen a real live swan before, could hardly believe his eyes. He was impressed with the sight of this magnificent creature, a Whispering Swan, sunning itself on the river. He could not understand how the swan could be in his country, or why he was glorying in this creature of more temperate regions.

The swan was gliding away, more interested in its surroundings, a sea of lily pads in a garden of long-stemmed purple waterlilies. Warren was already claiming the mysterious swan as his own, for it had appeared in his dream of the previous night. Could there be two realities? Bird of the daytime; woman of the night? He moved carefully towards the bird, but the riverbank felt unstable and he was unable to concentrate. He did not want to listen to reason from the old brolgas above, that the swan did not belong to him at all. He was whispering words he had heard, *sweetheart swan of sweethearts*, and hoping that if he could pacify the swan with the power of his voice, it would not fly away. He knew where it belonged. Its home was right across the country in the South, thousands of kilometres away. He thought it might die.

He moved to find the quickest way up the river, taking great care not to snap the twigs on the ground, and all the while, almost believing that he was flying. He was up in the skies. The rhythm of his breathing was like a tabla beating to crush the occasional alarm calls of those soaring old brolgas. There was no stopping his desire: he wanted to touch the swan. Some old excitable fool that lived dormant in his heart was up and about. A rogue spirit that had become as transfixed as the boy had of seeing a swan.

Quite possibly the bird was injured. Absolutely! Rogue spirit agreed. *Let's go. Let's get closer. Quick! Quick! I will race you there.* Warren could justify trying to aid an injured swan. It was an act of compassion, condoned. *Cause. Cause it's true.* Any human on Earth would have thought so. But the swan seemed content to stay where it was so the boy could not be sure, and of course he thought, it would be best to capture it. There was nobody around except his rogue spirit to tell him to leave it alone. He forced his way through the brambles growing densely beside the river and up and down the river gums. He ignored the thorny vines lacerating his body which could have been the country trying to teach him to stay away – if he had been thinking about education. Finally, he reached the closest point of the bank to the swan, but still, the bird was far from his reach, idling about on the other side of the river.

His eyes rested on a levee, some floating monument of sticks higher than the bank itself, all of the *yimbirra* refuse that was slowly on the move from up the river. It groaned up to where he was standing. He could see the inflammation banking right back up the river until it was out of sight, and it surprised him that he had not noticed it before. He thought of the big woman's nest as he leaped straight onto the summit of sticks, branches and rubbish stacked no less whimsically than a million flimsy thoughts describing the nature of the world in his head at that particular moment. The old fool in his heart steered while the boy walked over the top to the edge and leant over, arms stretched towards the swan.

Now he could see that there was something troubling the swan; its wings flapped frantically at the water while its feet ran on the spot, tangled in a bundle of fishing line knotted in the roots and tree branches. The sodden and limp swan now sensing its end was certain, was pulled helplessly through the waters.

A wall of floodwater exploded through the piles of sticks, branches, tree trunks, old tyres and broken down motorcars, that went flying through the air behind the boy, and you know what he had? *Only that old fool at a steering wheel.*

The swan was drowning for Warren Finch, and all the boy saw were pictures of Aboriginal spirits with halos of light, just like Van Gogh had painted. The boy had not known what struck him. He had been so excited about the swan that he had not heard the river shouting behind him.

Twenty Years of Swans

I t was more than twenty years since the day Warren Finch had nearly killed himself for a swan, when he arrived in the Army-run detention camp of the swamp in a flash car – a triumphant long-anticipated homecoming to his traditional homelands, with enough petrol for driving up and down the dusty streets for nothing.

Around he drove with his friends, down every street, the back roads and by-roads, sizing up everybody who was a *Black* thank you – checking out the despair, mentally *adding up the figures and checking it twice*, and deciding like he was White – that it was *all* hopeless, nothing would help, and driving on.

He was sure going to miss the pride of the place. The swamp had become truly wondrous in the eyes of the benefactors. These locals, along with the other detained people from God knows where, all jelly-soft now from years of inter-generational interventionist Australian policies of domination, were true beholders of wonder and fervour-ridden with the beauty of home. They had no say about anything important in their lives. This had been an Army-controlled Aboriginal detention camp for decades. Whereas Warren Finch's Aboriginal Government Nation that was just down the road, had grown prosperous with flukes of luck here and there called mining, and saying yes, yes, yes to anything on offer – a bit of assimilation, a bit of integration, a bit of giving up your own sovereignty, a bit of closing the gap – and was always paraded as Australia's international showcase of human rights. The swamp people had seen life triumph. Hadn't they witnessed the growth of an enormous flock of swans on their country? The swans had thought it was okay to live there. Well! This, and the loveliness of their children and country, traditional or adopted, gushed like a permanent flowing river through their hearts. Hearts must have it sometimes, for after a lot of bureaucratic argy-bargy with Canberra for around two hundred years – but who's counting the cost of crime? – the community had been successful in giving the swamp the far perkier name of *Swan Lake*. It was the only thing they had ever achieved in a fight with Canberra. Their name received official status from Australia and that was a beautiful thing in the eyes of the locals.

But nope! Not Warren. He saw nothing for the sake of sentimentality. He drove right around the watery expanse for a bit of sightseeing, an excuse for intensifying and exercising his cynicism while describing what he was looking at to people he was *mobiling* back down *South*. Finally, he snapped the mobile phone shut in disgust and parked his dust-covered white government Commodore thing in the shade of the Memorial. The twin, giant, concrete-grey, crossed boomerangs. He stepped out of the car, into the full force of a north country summer's day, and glanced at the block at the base of the boomerangs – the sign inscribing a dedication to all those who had fallen in the long Indigenous war against colonisation with the State of Australia – *And continue to fall*.

Who knows if Warren Finch paid much attention to the Memorial, but he would have agreed on one thing at least, that it was a pretty ingenious idea to erect this traditional icon, so symbolically embedded with psychological power. Nothing was going to beat clapping boomerangs calling the stories and songs – not even Warren Finch standing around the base tapping his song into the concrete, just to check that the whole darn thing was not crumbling from shonky trainee workmanship, and likely to collapse on his car.

He would not have known the local stories about what they thought was pride. The boomerangs belonged to the old people. They had devised an image of themselves as super mythical beings – giants of the afterlife clapping these boomerangs all day long. These were their longed-for days. They said they would be better off dead. *More powerful.* They would telepathically stream their stories forever through any time of the day they said: *We will haunt Australia good and proper, just like the spirits of the Anzacs living in war monuments all around the country, and just like the ghosts of wars living in all of that rust dumped in the swamp away from white people because they thought they were too powerful.*

Warren Finch was not some *random* person, someone who had come to look at Aboriginal people for the day as part of their job so that they could make up stories about what they had seen, and even though he did not have much respect for the sacred monument, he was convinced that those two grey swellings of cultural pride illuminated at least one fact – *that nothing easily slid into oblivion.* He gazed beyond the monument and zeroed in on the polluting junk that lay around in the swampy lake.

The vista seemed to excite him, and he started muttering on about some of his important theories of colonial occupation, but whatever personal conversations he was having with himself, those who overheard him said they could not understand what he was talking about, and dreamingly claimed, *No! Nah, nah. Whatever!* Of course the junk in the swamp was not a glorious sight, and well may this be true, but this man's time was in no way infinite.

Warren was very conscious about how much the world beckoned for its few important people. He strode about life in his natural state of beckoning overload – *one, two, three, that's all the time I've got for you*. These days he spared only a minute or two on most things that crossed his path, and this was what he did while spending sixty seconds flat intellectualising the swamp full of war fossils. *Tis this sight alone,* he chanted in a flat, bored voice, almost as though he was still speaking on the mobile, *that justifies many thoughts I can't get out of my head about dumped people.*

It's a mighty slow crawl from ancient lineage. That's why you can't fast-track extinction, he claimed, murmuring to his fellow travellers, although to them – recognising the fact of their being Black, and his being Black – it was hard to understand why he was talking like that about himself. They did not want to become extinct through assimilation, if that was what he meant, while assuming it was. But, just what else would a man see? Someone like Warren Finch who was touched by all of the cultures of the world was now seeing the poorer side of his own traditional estate for the first time.

In the swamp there was a long-held belief and everyone knew what it was. The whole place believed that one day prayers would be answered, and it would happen like this: there would be an archangel sent down from heaven to help them – a true gift from God. Not like all the previous rubbish stuff. Then so it was. It was heard through the grapevine that the gift had been delivered. This would have to be the boy genius that everyone had heard about from those other people of their vast homelands – the ones who were much better off than they were themselves. The ones they were not talking to. Those rich sell-out Aboriginal people with mining royalties and a treaty.

So when the archangel Warren Finch arrived, sure they were supposed to know because it was supposed to be a miraculous occasion. A gift from God was supposed to be incredulous. Perhaps there would be more stars in the sky. Or, perhaps, beams of sunlight shining from him would dazzle all over the swamp. They had always imagined what this occasion would be like, and most had even prophesied how the archangel would hover over the lake indefinitely so that everybody could get a chance to see him up there doing his business by spreading his protective wings over them, and all would be well after that. Not like all those other so-called miracles for assimilation that had been endured and considered God-given failures. However, Warren Finch deceived everybody. He really looked no different in appearance to anybody else living in the swamp.

For a few moments, the archangel glanced over the lake, and he thought naming the ugly swamp Swan Lake was a really stupid thing to do. He started to interpret the name in traditional languages, and then in the many foreign languages in which he had fluency. He said the name was common enough, but what's in a name? It was not going to save people from heading towards their own train-wreck.

What was more, he thought the name was only a deceitful attempt to stretch the largesse of anyone's imagination. He would not be tempted to pity the place. Instead, he took pleasure in picturing the atlas of the world and dotting all of the places he knew that were named Swan Lake. So he had to ask himself: *What was one less Swan Lake on the face of the world?* He considered the possibility of having a quiet word with the world-leading astronomy centre of which he was the patron, to see if they could rename a hole of some obscure outer-space nebulae *Swan Lake*. Yep! Why not? Once he was down the road which would not be long now, he would make a point of doing exactly that on his way back to Heaven.

This was the era of unflinching infallibility, claimed Warren, the postmodernist, deconstructionist champion, affirming from the bottom of his heart that any view of a glitch in the modern world could be reshaped and resolved. He laughed, saying that he felt like a foreigner standing on these shores that represented nothing more than the swamp of old government welfare policies. He looked like he knew exactly what to do. Someone who believed as most people believed of him, that he owned the key to the place where political visions for the entire world were being fashioned. *And where was that?* This was his question to himself, his concern, as he turned back for a second glance at the swamp, and his answer was also to himself: *Brains! In the brains of the men on top.*

The late afternoon shadow of the monument ran like a dark road across the entire lake, and Warren Finch's eyes were led along it straight to the old Army hull in the centre of the water, the largest vessel amongst all of the wrecks. He had only parked in the broadest part of the shadow next to the monument because across the road he could stroll over to what he called – *their 'so-called' Aboriginal Government building.*

As he looked at the hull, he thought about how ideas of *flightlessness* occupying his recent dreams were mostly about his childhood, and for a moment he once again felt the gravitating seductiveness of the swan woman's shadow. He was flying with her towards the realisation of the journey his dreams had always evaded. Then he looked straight past the vision, and all he saw was the sun reflecting the shadow of the flotilla's rust and wreckage on the watery expanse, before a whisper of wind dissolved into a nothingness the muted hues of rippling gold.

The girl thought old Aunty and the Harbour Master had returned and were outside, their spirits walking over the swamp. Whispering on the water. It made her blood run cold. She wanted it to be old Aunty and the Harbour Master talking about raising the evening mist together, and already mist was blanketing the water, covering it like a shield. The voices continued a whispering conversation, where old Aunty was saying that lingering reservations kept occurring in people's lives, and were always holding them back from what they should be doing. Harbour Master was more specific. More grounded. He said someone was tapping the concrete boomerangs up in the park and arguing with the old people. The Harbour Master said that person thought that he was living in a big ship populated by castaways – a bunch of scavengers, he claimed. *A big captain shouting orders from the decks of the destroyer that gave people berth – if they liked the way he was single-handedly shipping and trading the world.* The Harbour Master said he just watched and was keeping his own particular mouth shut.

Up in the middle of the memorial park of Swan Lake, several swans had scattered from puddle to puddle under a sprinkler watering what remained of a lawn. A plague of grasshoppers, *jibaja*, bloated from eating everything green, chirruped, jumped up and down, and rose away in a wave when the swans scattered. But dozens of the town's thousands of pet brolgas with the quickest eyes around the place suddenly remembered something from the past. This was their old friend Warren from their former colony near his own community. These ageing brolgas also regularly sat under the park's creaking set of sprinklers, while enjoying the spurting jets of water, falling into deep sleep as water rolled off their grey feathered bodies. The brolgas went haywire and immediately leapt up from the mud to run over and greet their old friend from days gone by.

The old brolgas had led the flocks from the abandoned rookeries after the brolga boy had deserted his country. These brolgas had become *half urbans* from living at Swan Lake. They were flourishing in the rookeries that they had built all around the swamp. Nests stacked on the rooftops of houses. Look out in bits of backyard and you would see a grey throng sitting there in a day-dream of devising methods to steal food from the township that they too thought was wondrous.

Earlier in the day when Warren Finch was driving around, the old brolgas had been taking a majestic stroll up and down the streets to knock over the rubbish bins, and to squabble in D minor about all the useless rubbish they saw lying on the ground. Everything was going along fine until the flash car beeped the horn at them wherever they were spotted. They had retreated back to the lawn in the park, to continue examining the exposed roots of the lawn struggling to replace each green shaft of leaf repeatedly plucked clean and eaten by insects, until finally, they sank into their deep peaceful sleep.

Disturbed again. The bright red and featherless heads crowned with buzzing flies watched Warren stepping out of his car, and looked very puzzled. It took them some time to gather up a distant memory of a boy dancing their dance. But once they recognised him, their excited trumpeting called in more brolgas, dogs and people. The bugling went on and on, and the ballet of brolgas prancing lightly off the ground followed each other up, up, up and down while trampling the excuse of a lawn into a feculent pool of mud.

Warren smiled slightly, but he did not dance with the brolgas. These days he was far more excited about how the world danced for him from way up high, or in the couch-grass backyards of every Australian city, its towns, and right down to any far-flung, buffel-grass infested corner of the country where people watched a battery-operated television in their rusty water-tank home, cardboard box, or packing crate, and looked out for fire, flood, or tempest coming up the track. All people liked to dance for a gift from God. The Warren Finch dance. He was the lost key. He was post-racial. Possibly even post-Indigenous. His sophistication had been far-flung and heaven-sent. Internationally Warren. Post-tyranny politics kind of man. True thing! He was long gone from cardboard box and packing crate humpies in the remote forgotten worlds like this swamp.

Warren Finch's name was saturated in the hot and humid air of climate change. He had a solid, strong face to stare at the world, like a modern Moses – same colour, but in an Italian suit, and with the same intent of saving the world from the destructive paths carved from its own history. His whole body bent from carrying the world on his shoulders, and from lurching forward on the staff of responsibility to reach too much of heaven.

But look! To be frank, Swan Lake did not have arms wide enough to catch the troubles of the world, so what was he now doing in a place like this? What would he find out about himself from coming back to his *so-called* roots? Why would he call on his lost people now that he was the Deputy President of the Government of Australia, and basking in the parliamentary system of a powerful political dynasty that was long skilled in the mechanisms for overturning any of the commonly understood rules of democracy? It was true that who spoke the loudest received the most justice, consensus, transparency – all that kind of talk about being decent. If you wanted to take a swipe, you could say that he only got as far as he had, not because he had clawed his way to the top, but because the colour of his skin was like Moses', and everybody wanted skin like that these days.

There was nobody around, Warren noticed. Nobody there to greet him! The whole place looked abandoned, except for some homeless loners watching the brolgas dance. He was not used to being ignored when he arrived somewhere. Shouldn't there be an official welcome? He was not just anybody. Even the lowest of the lowest politician should expect to be greeted in an Aboriginal community out of respect, and here he was with supposedly his own people ignoring his first (kind-of official) visit to his own traditional country. One of his minders mused, *You must have been jilted bro.*

Most of the swamp people (those approved by the Army to watch television) were in front of a television, and watching a good documentary about Warren Finch. They always kept up with the news about Warren. This documentary explained why Australia needed an original inhabitant on top of the political ladder and they liked that. They liked the idea that Australia needed a blackfella to hide behind. Warren was no lame-duck party man of the old guard political parties that had dominated Australian politics forever.

Only remnant racism stopped him from taking his final place on the top of Paradise Hill. Even so, *Warren Finch*, the documentary on television explained, *held more power than the Right Honourable Mr Horse Ryder. Was that so?* That piss-dog Ryder, as he was locally known, was just that old nationalistic politician who (even though the country had changed its constitutional governing powers) continued calling himself a Prime Minister, and who was from the big bush electorate that included half of Warren's traditional country. The man was clinging to power by the slenderest of straws, and said that he loved Warren Finch like a son.

Well! It turned out that politics was just the same old caliginous turnout it had always been, but everyone knew Warren Finch was waiting it out. He knew he would lead the country in the end because in fact, he already did. The swamp people finished watching the documentary and gave it their usual thumbs up, before getting on with dinner with plenty of Canberra politics to talk about. And there was: you had to give it to Warren Finch for being a survivor of deadly times, sitting it out with a string of rat-faced men and women back-stabbers ruling Australia who had knifed him in the back.

But Swan Lake? Why break the progress of the claw on its way to the top by being seen in a small place that had no power at all?

The unexpected news of Warren Finch turning up in their Army-run Aboriginal Government territory was not only as incomprehensible as divine intervention, it was just plain inconvenient. He was right in the middle of Friday night's fish dinner. It was *kamu*. Suppertime. There was a lot of swearing amidst the sizzling and splattering fat flying out of frying pans cooking fish too quickly, about a slapped-down dinner having to be gulped half-raw like a pelican eating fish. And just because nobody had bothered telling somebody that there was a visitor who looked like Warren Finch – the bloody Deputy President of Australia – waiting up at the boomerangs like a complete *Nigel* for someone to get their arse up to the office to greet him.

So then! Now the local hierarchy of the Aboriginal House Government for Swan Lake were smudging over the recent brolgas' tracks with their own footprints, hurrying on the way up to the office to meet this Warren Finch if it was really Warren Finch, and wanting to get to the bottom of this mystery of why no one had shown common courtesy by forewarning them about his visit, because for one thing, someone could have cooked him a supper. They blamed the Army men, and the white controller for being the racists that they were.

This journey of racism was long, and all the way, the conversations they shouted to each other across the dog tracks went like this: *Why do we have to be continually gutted by these people making their punitive raids on this community?*

The schoolchildren sitting at home with stomachs full of fish and chips were quickly told by departing parents who had just glimpsed him again on the 5 O'Clock News, to watch something educational for closing the gap between black and white, like the serialised exploits of Warren Finch while they were gone. Adults were out of homes with departing words: *What is wrong with you children?*

Their children had no shame. They had bailed up and decided that they would not go up to the office to welcome their hero and, good go! present him with some flowers or something. They announced, *we are staying home*, and seriously gloated that the reason why they were not going to the monument to see if it was him or not, was number one, because it was too cold outside.

The temperature had already plummeted from 44 to 33.5 degrees Celsius, and number two, they announced that they were sick of hearing about Warren Finch, the role model for how Aboriginal children could become good Australians. *Why was the whole country telling us to become another Warren Finch?* His life story was centre stage of compulsory Indigenous education policies from Canberra where the saga of the brolga boy becoming number one Australian hero was constantly drummed into their ears. They were sick of hearing how he rose out of Aboriginal disadvantage, and how the whole country wanted other brolga boys to be just like him. Only that day, this new generation had learnt that Warren Finch was a cultural man of high degree. His first doctorate, although he had numerous doctorates, was the first to be achieved through a University of Aboriginal Government. They mocked him on the television series, saying, *Yep! That's right. We know those old brolgas outside taught you how to knock em down rubbish bins.*

The race was on, with more officials of the Swan Lake Aboriginal Government leaving their homes as the news spread, and running towards their office with hearts banging flat chat against rib bones in the heat of *furthermores* and whatnot speculations of what had sent Finch like some maniac to their office on a Friday night of all days. And how could he have travelled so fast to get there?

They had just seen him on the television news and he was supposed to be somewhere else, with people who looked like polar bears – where it was snowing, on the other side of the world.

How could he also be at Swan Lake when they had just seen him talking to more old *tribals* in a European village with one of those unpronounceable names, and Warren Finch actually speaking the same language as those people. They were all standing around in the snow and it looked cold. Maybe it was minus 20 or 40 degrees Celsius. Who knows? Nobody would know at Swan Lake. They had never been in snow like that. Not any snow.

He had been speaking like this on the television news for weeks in daily reports as he moved from one country to the next, each time with ancient law holders by his side in his role (one of many) as the special old-law rapporteur to the world's highest authority of elders for ancient laws, ancient scriptures, and modern Indigenous law-making. He was wearing yet another hat from his home hat, or his national hat, who knew these days. He had too many hats. They say he was leading the development of new laws for the world on the protection of the Earth and its peoples, after centuries of destruction on the planet.

The little world of Swan Lake though, and many others like it, were speechless, glued to the television, to watch Warren's fingers running down the pages of centuries-old documents containing ancient laws, and they were convinced that one day he would actually find secret information in these documents about how to save the planet, just like he was saving just about everything else. They knew he lived on an Indigenous high plateau. But somehow, perhaps another miracle was needed to understand how it happened, but he had left his important work with these polar bear snow people, and travelled halfway around the world since doing the news, and driven hundreds of kilometres from an airport, to be at Swan Lake on a Friday night.

Warren Finch would find it hard to communicate with people such as those who were running to meet him, working their way up the winding tracks towards the Government building. Why didn't he know that they only wanted normal things on Friday evening, why wasn't Warren Finch at home in Canberra relaxing, or at the Casino in one of the cities of Heaven, and having the time of his life?

What was he going to open his mouth to say? But! On the other hand, this man they were running to meet was one of the most important men in the world who knew the world's cultures backwards. He was Warren Finch. He had come from their country. What could they say when they were introduced to all this embodied in one man who was really their own? The only news they had to tell him was how good their country's fish was, that they had just eaten for dinner.

What would you offer a world leader for dinner when something lavish like a lobster or a frozen chicken should have been carefully prepared, or even flown in especially with a chef from the city? If only they had known. So, while *Australian political hero* easily rolled over the tongue, and put brains on fire, Swan Lake-ian people could only run proudly and empty-handed to meet Warren Finch. They had no food to give him. Many cheered his government's election song – *We are not war makers and poor makers.* Now they – *the little people trying to climb the life of snakes and ladders* – were finally going to meet him at last, their true gift from God. They had voted for him in every election. They were the master race of politics in a thousand-kilometre homeland that had pushed and shoved him, like a rocket, all the way to the top.

The Swan Lake Government officers were exhausted from shifting about their thinking, and moving through their humid tracks, and yet they still had some way to walk their carbon-neutral pace through the short cuts. Could you believe that this was Friday night? No one believed in using their own vehicles just to drive over to the office, and especially not when the world's foremost environmentalist was visiting – and if anyone needed to know, they had some of the world's true environmentalists living at Swan Lake. They could bet a million dollars that they were not using much of the world's resources. It was exciting to think that they would soon be on television surrounding Warren Finch. No one was to know that down at the war monument Warren did not have his media throng, even though he was still wearing his familiar grey suit seen on television that night, the style of suit that made him look 1950s quintessentially Australian.

Warren took deep breaths because he had to, had to find within himself a memory of home, but nothing sprung to mind. He only caught the faint aroma of eucalyptus oil, an old memory past its use-by date sprinkled for luck on his suit. The fetid smell of swamp and fried fish was truly awesome and off-putting, and all he could think about were better memories of his life, and having closer familiarity with other places buzzing non-stop in his head.

Very seriously though, he looked like a composed bouncer standing outside a Docklands nightclub, while the breathless local leaders clambered to introduce themselves. With a blank face, he lightly shook hands. An awkward silence followed. What had he to say to these people?

This first sighting of Warren was surprising for some. He was not really as handsome in the refined way they had expected from someone who lived in the city. He looked different on television. But all the same, they saw themselves in him, even though he wore a designer-labelled suit of the Menzies era, and they did not. Much was said: *Welcome! Welcome! Complete grovel! Voice of the nation! Face of Australia. Three cheers for Warren. Go Warren. Go Finchy. Go us.* They cheered him wholesomely, like they generally did for football heroes.

Quiet! Listen! He was signalling with his little left-hand finger, indicating: *Watch the brolgas dancing.* His gesture made the local crowd feel as though he was no different than anyone else. They were just ordinary people together.

The brolgas danced chapters of the story they had produced out of their life at Swan Lake. It was an unusually frenzied repertoire, perhaps connected to the frustration they felt at losing their leisurely evening walk from house to house to snatch the bits of fish they had to gobble instead in the excitement of meeting Warren.

He gave a little speech, although it was pointless trying to listen to him, when all eyes were on the transfixing sight of excited brolgas leaping madly, as though hallucinating to the smell of fried fish hanging in the air. Warren had to speak louder, until finally, he was speaking loudly enough that his voice was carried across the swamp and into the hull, where, *Oh! Dear,* Ethyl(ene) (Oblivia) Oblivion or whatever her name was, was still cooking fish in a frying pan hot with crackling oil. She was not listening to anyone, but she was the only person who heard every word he said.

Warren claimed to be one of those people who used the voice given to him by the spiritual ancestors of the land for its only useful purpose, to uplift Aboriginal thought to its rightful place of efficaciousness, to be fit in mind and body, and residing in thought and action alongside the land. A high-pitched cockatoo squawked: *Gone were the days where the Aboriginal people's culture was being strangled in the sewer of the white man's government.*

Nobody listened. Poor buggers in poor people's clothes were not the ideal crowd for the voice from Heaven. Perhaps the brolgas' dance was more mesmerising, or swamp people preferred to muddle through life in silence after eating fish. Perhaps it was the point of view.

Anyone else would have been a dead dog though, if anyone else had spoken like Warren, saying that he thought they were: *Unable to change. Unable to experience the depths of self-analysis. Hell was hell. No point sinking any lower than that.* This was a talking surgeon cutting with precision, but then, quickly stitching all of the infections back into the wounds, covered with a couple of band-aids: *You need to expand yourself beyond personal selfishness. Bite the bullet if you want to make a life for yourselves. Don't get stuck on your whacko solutions if you don't want to live in whacko land.*

Well! Bravo. Great lame duck applause! *Arrr!* After an uncomfortable pause, then came the automatic practised cheerful roaring that could be heard a kilometre away, like that usually roared all afternoon at local football matches.

Now, the brolgas' long performance, locally interpreted for Warren as being about the law of freedom and life, was finished, and the birds walked off, leaving the razzamatazz of political mindlessness to the dancing tongue of Warren Finch.

The fish-eating people literally bent over backwards into a dancing, circling mob ingratiating themselves all over Warren Finch, to take it in turns to sing his praises, and in chorus thundering: *Oh! We just want to congratulate you because what you said just now made our hearts feel really good.* They embraced him as though he walked the same dirt roads as they did.

They sung more bird music. *This was really good that you have come here finally, so far out of the way, to speak to the littlest people of Australia. Oh! You are really the true way.*

In her hull home, Oblivia Ethylene was thinking about a group of butterflies with pretty wings that had flown around her in the moonlight once, when she had seen a wild boy from the ruby saltbush plains in the glow of a night lantern. He was singing nursery-rhyme speeches to the stars in a parliament house constructed of dry winds and decorated by dust storms.

The Yellow Chat's Story

Whaay? Whaay? Why? And early may? A lone, brightly coloured yellow chat whistled from the top of the Crossed Boomerang Memorial, its longing song about ancestral ties went wafting down into the ears of the poverty people standing around below, who looked as though the sky was about to fall on top of them.

In the crowd, little Aboriginal flags held up in the breeze danced to a nervous low whistling of *Stand By Me,* while the shock-stricken, distant relatives of Warren Finch were busy amongst themselves, obsessing about all of their shared origins no matter how distant or close they were to *good boy,* who was once the child prodigy of their large sprawling Indigenous nation. *Shouldn't you tell him how you are related?* You could hear the warbling chat feeling sick with shame that nobody really knew the answer to that question, that they all shared the same genes – *Shouldn't he know how...Shouldn't he?* Although in reality, Warren Finch was honestly acting as though he was nothing more than a complete stranger.

He yawned and stretched with his arms wide open. He was weary of listening to his own preachings and speeches, and what was more, totally oblivious of the yellow chat's song – a rant, a rave, pointless to him. Homeland? What did it mean any more? After the experience of being cooped up in his Government car for endless hours of travelling across plain after treeless plain, he had reached – whatever the term meant, and what others called – *his people*. The world was in fact his home, homeland, place of abode, and where his people lived. There were no childhood memories in his mind. His nostalgia had been the pull of movement, but movement had drained life from him, and he was ashen-faced, like the grey feathers of the brolgas standing outside of the crowd replicating his every gesture, stretching their wings too.

Still his relatives were excited with the belief of finally quelling his restlessness, and where they were breathing the same exalted air as he exhaled, they could not help realising too, that the taste of his breath was so much sweeter than theirs. Fine! They had lost their fish dinner. Didn't matter. This closeness to the *gift* was exciting. His relatives felt complete to be so close to his flesh and blood, and could breathe at last for having a precious belonging returned to the ordinariness of Country. But there was one cold hard fact, for in reality he did not resemble any of them at all.

Slowly, the crowd started to feel let down. They began to feel normal again. A natural suspicion snuck back into the picture of life, the larger landscape, what was painted in the framework of life. They began to think that he looked more like one of those outsiders – the complete strangers. Those Aboriginal people from other places the Army had trucked in and who were now tucked up in their lives through marriage, family, living under the one roof.

Even the *outsiders* resembled his people more in the flesh and blood than Warren Finch, where on this night of wasted fish, each enlightened revelation like this was just another kick in the head. With these thoughts in mind, poison from their hearts swept to their brains, which asked further questions: *How could he look like a gift from God at all?* He now looked like the devil. Just a half-caste!

It was insulting that Warren Finch thought they were his relatives. Nobody was related to him. They had never seen this man singing to the birds in this country. *His skin is not permeated with the dust of our plains. Where is his language? Where is the salt of our swamps on this man?* Now he was a total stranger. Nobody knew him at all. A familiar question popped out about heritage: *Where was his family among any of them?* It was a bit déjà vu, reminiscent of those old Native Title stories that ended up as laws to include or exclude families.

A bit of analysis would reveal that the genesis of Warren Finch lay with the elders who authored his childhood. Hadn't they perceived the era of colonialism continuing longer than their lives? They created movement in him that was like the travelling ancestral spirits. Now in his early thirties, it was true that he had little attachment for people, least of all his barely surviving, flag-waving relatives who noticed the difference. They could see that Warren Finch's feelings were nothing more than weightless dust, particles of responsibility from their own Brolga plains he had scattered across the globe.

Warren Finch's life could be simplified in an instant, by sitting in the seat of an aeroplane soaring through the thermals over his own homelands, flying him off to those cities and towns located thousands of kilometres away from them. There was no point sulking about it. If he did not have it to be local, then he did not have any affinity to his own humanity, and he only thought of a moving world, which he epitomised by *imagine what you will?*

Perhaps, you could imagine that he swam in the ponds of an ultimate paradise, where continuous cool sea breezes kept on working to distil any traces left of the North from the face of the rough boy who had once lived among the brolgas.

Perhaps you might find him at home in a foreign place that could carve regal, fine-bone men – those who grow older with carefully smoothed grey-black hair from a brown forehead.

How could any of the swamp people explain this comfortable face they saw on television that held a universal magic capable of mirroring the faces of countless millions of ordinary people, who like themselves, had been duped by their own sense of community into recognising some uncanny likeness and affinity between themselves and Warren Finch?

Warren had not travelled alone. The vehicle was packed with his entourage of three tall and well-dressed, sinewy-bodied men. His friends looked like Indigenous football stars – the ones seen advertising high-end fashion gear on city billboards. In those brown stubbled faces, each wore the fine chiselled lines of what was commonly termed by *neo-colonists* who study race, as nice inter-racial breeding.

These men were Warren Finch's minders, or security men for the Night Lantern – his global name. They viewed everything casually, through sun-reflecting sunglasses, like justice men, free and tolerant, comfortable wearing handguns strapped to their chests, and being wired for constant communications with the central security headquarters back in Heaven. The general perspective in Warren's world was that these were good men – the best you could get, barely in their thirties, but tougher than most. For their trip to the north end of the country, they had exchanged their expensive southern city suits for slick Italian casual clothes.

After the speech-making, they hastened Warren away from old crying relatives, talking to him about oblique kinship ties, and all those grey birds. The locals called the haste, *Manhattan finesse.* Enough time had been wasted, especially the over-performing brolgas homage that they agreed had taken longer than *Swan Lake* performed back to back by every ballet company of the world, and quoted Auden, *Lion, fish and swan/ Act, and are gone/ Upon Time's toppling wave.* The entourage moved towards the office of the Aboriginal Government of Swan Lake.

The general swamp people stood back and gawked with pride. They rejoiced to see these smoothed, supple-muscled, dark-skinned men of action, their own people in fact, moving around as though they owned the place, although on the other hand, they took the trouble to reassure each other that only white people behaved like this. Even the atmosphere had turned excitable. Heavy clouds bearing an electrical storm were now overhead, but the swamp crowd hardly noticed that, and you could tell they were dying to call out to the poster guys that they were exactly what a black brother should look like.

Warren disappeared into the office, leaving most of the spectators to stroll home in the storm to eat cold fish.

In the humidity of the hot, airless building, before all the members were present, Warren Finch opened the meeting of the Swan Lake Aboriginal Nation Government. He announced matter-of-factly: *I am looking for my wife.*

His *mangkarri!* His wife! Listen. *Manku!* He's speaking, making his *jangkurr* speech about something. *Jangkurr-kanyi nyulu ngambalangi.* Let him talk to us. Don't start a fire. *Balyangka ninji jadimbi-kanyi jangu.* Be silent. *Kudarrijbi.*

He might start getting cheeky like lightning making the ground explode, *dumijbi jamba, malba-malbaa kijibajii,* like dynamite-*waya,* maybe. *Kudarrijbi* now. *Kuujbu nyulu kiji-anyi.* He's looking for a fight. Because of his wife. *Mangkarri-wunyi.* We'll see if he talks straight. *Diindi jangkurr nyulu ngambalanya.*

In this building where *truth* was the motto, the Canberra-imposed controller of the Swan Lake Aboriginal Government turned Army-controlled asylum was a real *weisenheimer,* the name by which the *mandaki* white man was commonly known around the swamp. *Miyarrka-nangka mandaki*. Whiteman can't understand. He was supposed to implement white ways of loving children as being better than theirs. These people of the Aboriginal Government looked him over, and thought as they normally did, *We turned our back on him*. They had turned their backs on a lot of people. They had issues with showing tolerance for any outside government policy people especially. No! Of course they were not tolerant people. Tolerance was not their forte. They either liked something, or didn't like it. Simple! It was one or the other, and nothing in-between. No maybes crippled up in the heart. Or this or that prolonging nothing thought in the head. You don't survive on grey areas. This was what having sovereign thinking meant in the time immemorial law of the land. That was how their people had survived the aeons. The controller chose not to hear what Warren Finch had said about looking for his wife. The assumption was that he never burdened anyone about his personal life, so why should he have his Friday evening disturbed by listening to someone else talk about what ought to be – *their own business*.

Mr Weisenheimer looked around the room at *his people* – the worst basket case he ever had to work with in a long, distinguished career in Aboriginal affairs. All he could see were the innocent faces of the Aboriginal Government representatives who were his charges, still arriving late and sitting down at the table whenever they were ready. They were doing what he had already assumed they would do – just sitting there and staring at the table and not saying a word. He knew this because he was an experienced career man of Aboriginal Affairs. He had seen this happen heaps of times.

Weisenheimer knew Aboriginal people better than they knew themselves, but that was okay. That was how he earned his bread and butter. He was a learned man about Aboriginal people. An academic. He had a national reputation that set the benchmark for Aboriginals to achieve results in Indigenous policy, which he had influenced in its development for numerous years with the Government in Canberra.

These people though? He believed that the people he looked at around the room were *had it*. Did not have what the policy required of them. Did not share the dream of Australianness. This was the reason why they had to be in servitude. It was the only hope if he was to shape the next generation on his human farm. And quite frankly, he thought it was hard work, almost impossible to save the children. He expected that they would continue to have nothing to say, and it would take several generations – more than his lifetime of assimilating them – even if it all started tomorrow, to eventually one day see a good, decent Australian citizen from any of these people.

While the entire meeting remained silent, Weisenheimer was expert enough to instantly fetch to the surface something from somewhere deep within himself – the whim-wham thing called the goodness in his heart. He prattled on about his programs – about how well everything was progressing (now that he was in charge). In doing so, he chose to adore Warren for being Aboriginal, by instantly ignoring the statement of marital intention that was no business of his, but all the same it confirmed in his mind that all Indigenous people were the same, since even the great Warren Finch could just come straight out and voice his personal business to all and sundry – to anyone at all.

Good old financial controller! He raised his grey eyebrows and remembered he had visitors in the room, which prompted him to get back into the saddle of managing the social, political, economic and cultural life of these people. You could trust him on this. He averted the staring at hands and the silence in the room with the appearance of busy work, pulling out of his white plastic shopping bag the remote control for the overhead fans, which instantly from a flick of his finger, spun a cool breeze on sweat-dampened skins.

Looking for my wife! The assembling representatives of Swan Lake's Aboriginal Nation Government were very surprised by what Warren Finch had just said. But they waited until everyone had sat down at the table dedicated to the ancestors, after they had greeted each other in their own languages, and an ancestral anthem song had been sung to the mighty ones, plus an obligatory *Advance Australia Fair* to show some interest in closing the gap. A few words were said about what Warren wanted, then the oldest one they called *No One At All* – who would rather be speaking in his own language, but spoke in old time blackfella English to Warren Finch to affirm the controller's beliefs – simply said in a few reluctant grunts that no one had seen a woman arrive in that piece of rubbish car they saw Warren Finch cruising around in without even thinking of coming into his place to say *hello*. *Her spirit must be living inside his head, that's what I think. His wife's spirit was either controlling him, or he had lost her himself – must have, inside all of that rubbish overseas knowledge stuff he got cutting loose in his brains.*

The Aboriginal Government seemed to agree since they were being cordial, they were practised people in governing too, just like the government in Canberra he was more used to dealing with. They commonly sat around this table being nice and eternally grateful, patting the table, or looking at it. It was the table of expectation, like an empty plate. They did what was expected with the expectation that, after he had delivered the berating that they usually received from politicians about their mismanagement, and the lack of transparency that was always how Australians regarded Indigenous people in remote places whom they could not see anyhow, Warren would announce some good news. It was to be expected, since no one important enough had ever travelled to the swamp, without giving them news of extra funding – a relief to save the little housing program once again, or a few biscuits to carry them over a few more weeks with essential services like fuel for the generator, or sewerage disposal.

What else could politicians do with the enormous, gigantic mess that they had created? *No One At All* explained, by concluding what he always needed to say, *We are all living in the age of anxiety here, Mr Sir whatever-your-name, what's your sustainability for us?*

Welcome to the dystopia of dysfunction. The controller Weisenheimer again reclaimed the meeting by dismissing, or not hearing this local speech by the most important and most senior man still alive at Swan Lake. He was keen to have the first word about the business that needed to be completed in this impromptu meeting. He needed to bring proceedings back to a professional standing, and he made his stand, by saying that he was not interested in *loose change from Canberra*. He deliberately spoke in terms that he thought Warren Finch would know exactly what he was talking about, while at the same time knowing that his words would be full of mystery to these uneducated, local people. It was his place to speak to Warren on behalf of the meeting, and he gave this address:

We have been waiting for a long time, Warren, for a bit of action. Isn't that right that we have been waiting for somebody to turn up here and tell us how we are going to fix this crisis? We need someone to tell us how to run the community store, the health centre, get the bums on seats at the school, fix up all the violence, alcohol, petrol-sniffing, criminality, over-housing, maintenance, tell mothers how to have babies, healthy babies, pretty babies, clean babies, immunised babies, and to implement Canberra's policy to teach these people how to love their children, and while I am mentioning health, to rid the place of diabetes, heart disease, kidney disease, mental health, eye, ear, nose disease and dogs; not to mention training people for work, to go out and be useful to society, to drive a bulldozer, build houses, be electricians and plumbers, grow and cook their own food, feed it to the children, and then to lift a box and bury themselves in a box. To have a choice! We really need we-can-do people, that other old black man Barack Obama-type people who become Presidents and leaders of some sort or other – of their people. Warren! We will need money to do that.

How do you do? When the controller stopped speaking, each of the councillors got up from his or her seat like sovereign kings and queens of the place, and went and shook Warren's hand, and his minders' hands, and returned to their seats.

My associates, Warren said briskly. *This is Dr Snip Hart. Dr Edgar Mail. And Dr Bones Doom.* Then Warren paused, to check whether his audience was still listening, and continued slowly. *Dr Hart here has a doctorate in hagiology, mythology and oneirology. Dr Edgar Mail holds a PhD of palaeontology, palaeoecology and ontology. Dr Doom has many doctorates too, of ornithology and oology. Mystagogy. Musicology. In other words, you might say between them, they are pulsatory omni-scientific, very scientific! Scientists in the laws of two ways, in all of the things a black man needs to know about today's world in the bush up here, down in Heaven, or Paris whatnot, to make music.*

All hands gripped the tear-stained table, though not the sceptic Weisenheimer. Only his eyes had not glazed over from Warren's music about Black science, but it did not seem to matter for the whole room was experiencing bedazzlement. How it felt to feel grand. These people agreed that they felt close to God! *Real close actually.* They smiled to be amidst so much omnipresence – the omelette of *ology* words floating gaily in the breeze of the noisy fans, and then dissipating featherlike, over and over in the ear en route to the brain cells.

Play something nice Edgar, Warren said quietly, when no one could break from the word net that had been thrown over their heads; and now even furthering the sense of amazement and pure wonderment, the one called Edgar it turned out, was a musician as well. The Swan Lake Government men and women looked like statues under the appraisal of those soft, pale brown eagle eyes of Warren Finch studying everyone in the room.

Sure, Boss, Edgar said. *I'd love to play.*

Edgar was a tall and beautifully proportioned, strong-boned, golden-brown-skinned man with a face so flat and smooth, it made him look like the brother of an owl. He cradled an old wattle-wood violin in his arms as though it was a spirit creature and then, the silence in the room was broken by a long melody. The music softened his smoothly shaven face, and the sounds floated away like moths flying off softly to clear away any residue of hardness in the room, and with their little hair-coated legs, to coax gentleness back on the faces of those gazing on the musician angel. The music flowed outside, past the boomerang monument clapping thunder and lightning, and over the swamp and into the hull where the girl and the circling swans outside were listening to the sounds from faraway, like the murmurings of owls spreading across the distant range country of ancient cypress trees and coming up through the stillness of a freezing night.

This music of far-away places poured through the building and the call of owls seemed to come from every angle over the swamp. The swans swarmed into a giant serpent formation on the water. The brolgas rose in skittish, frenzied flights up into higher altitudes to escape the owl-like sounds floating below them. The music drowned the sounds of barking dogs, and inside homes there were small children imagining it was flowing from the pumpkin flowers on the rampant vines which interlaced the buildings and covered them with large green leaves. In the Swan Lake Government chambers, the men and women of the government saw themselves swimming in medicines with the thought of the three doctors. They had never had a real doctor visit before. Never had a real doctor stationed there.

The sweet violin music kept blurring the here and now, and more of the fantastical escaped from minds usually locked in despair, even bringing back memories of the Harbour Master whose responsibility he now chanted to all the black consciousnesses sitting around the table, telling them to continue keeping a watchful eye on the sewers of thought.

The heads of the old spirits popped up from the manholes in their minds to see the travelling music passing by the cornerstones of memory. Lights were switched on. The despaired room spun with too many thoughts! But only thoughts, after all, of oodles of money from Shangri-La! Fancy that! Fancy sending three doctors to the swamp on fish and chip night. Oh! Man! Hear the gratefulness rising. Thank you! Thank you! Now black consciousness could see fat cattle everywhere in the room. Who mentioned cattle? The feast of music stopped suddenly. Warren Finch's voice had a way of slamming the door on any more thoughts about poor health, and people needing to eat a bit of fat steak, and having doctors galore arriving way out here in the sticks to do some good. *Forget the cattle!*

I am looking for my wife, Warren said it once more in plain English, and since no one spoke, he sat back with a slight smile on his face and continued to sift the room with his eyes.

Warren knew he had shocked these simple people to the core, by talking about a wife when no one thought he had one. The noise from the fans now paralysed anyone's ability to think in the room, but quite honestly, there was nobody in Swan Lake who would even resemble the wife of someone as important as Warren Finch. Swan Lake Government now thought outside of their own beloved homeland, something they rarely did, and tried to imagine

Warren Finch's big life elsewhere – overseas, looking for his lost wife in a European café – at another Swan Lake in a Mozart setting in Austria, or a beautiful model wife in Paris swanning around as she should, because these were places they thought any wife of his would belong.

He kept checking his watch to quicken the thinking in the room about how to respond to his demand to find his wife. *Now think fast*, and forget the cattle. There will be no cattle for you.

The financial controller Weisenheimer was not easily intimidated. He did not care for Warren's attitude and asked several pointed questions.

Why would your wife be here? Where did she come from? You can see for yourself that this Swan Lake Government is highly managed, and we know all the people living here. After all, and as you know yourself, this is an isolated community controlled by the Army. Everyone knows who comes here. Don't you? Weisenheimer only expected nods from his people. He intended to keep the meeting from entering into the known nightmares of bad terrain and talk about cattle. He had had a gutful of Aboriginal whingeing and complaining.

But a discussion erupted. It turned into genuine interest about the lost wife. Everyone tried in vain to remember anyone who might be his wife – names of famous women, movie actresses she might look like, as well as trying to recall whoever had recently turned up. No! Not Really! There had been no ladies leaving or arriving for many, many months. *Only dead people leave. Only babies arriving. That's all, if we are lucky!*

Still! It is really hard to remember everyone who turned up on our doorstops, who was looking for someone else by running away from who they should be living with, and taking care of, like they are supposed to do. Or something. You know, my Sir, said Mr No One At All, as the delegated speaker of the Swan Lake House.

The discussion took a strange exploratory route, analysing

the blocked tributaries of Western matrimony, and being a distinct Nation themselves and people of the longest surviving culture in the world, they had become world-wise at studying such marriages. They favoured a cynical critique, where each member of the Swan Lake Government had their own peculiar but excellent first-hand knowledge about other people's relationships; the warring spouses, neighbours, or adult children, and numerous family dealings with bad marriages in countless Western soap operas. They presumed the right to ask questions, *when a husband comes looking for his wife, you have to think whether there is anything good in marriage?*

Was this the bloody butcher's shop? The abattoirs? Nobody hesitated or blinked an eye at the fact that Warren Finch wanted to collect a piece of meat. He hardly noticed the fakery in the cynicism in their enquiring about his personal affairs. *Mr God Sir. Well! Who didn't suffer in marriage?* Mr No One At All asked. If Warren worried about his wife, so what was the mystery in that? He could join the club of broken marriages in Swan Lake. There was a bad smell in the room circulating with the fans, as if a very fat rat had died in the ceiling. The smell reached down the nostrils and mixed with the fish dinner into a nauseating retch but the Ministers for Government seemed unaffected, used to problems like that, and asked if the putrid smell was still there to avoid Warren Finch glaring at them. And someone, probably the controller, changed the subject by bluntly asking: *What wife?*

So what does your wife look like? It was insulting for the minders to hear anyone speaking to Warren Finch as though they were talking to a piece of scrap. The retorts came thick and fast. *What was wrong with you people? Don't you know who you are talking to? You are speaking to the Deputy President of Australia here. This man is so highly respected abroad, they call him Deputy Right Excellency, Deputy Mr President of Australia. Show a bit of respect!*

Warren held up a gracile hand in a gesture that was like a blessing given by a holy man. This was the hand frequently seen on television news from countries throughout the world. It was the very hand that had stopped atrocities and made peace amongst war-torn peoples. The hand was loved throughout the world. Here though, it simply meant, *enough was enough!* The ghostly Harbour Master panicked in his ethereal heaven somewhere up where the rat smelt in the ceiling, and stirred-up extra doubt in the room: *Does he really stop destruction?*

The question about his wife was a difficult one to answer without resolving what residual similarities lay between him and the people of Swan Lake. They could only answer him by asking what old bridge still existed between them and this top Australian? Did it mean if they spoke plainly to him that they were Australian too? Or, were they really invisible in anyone's language no matter what they said, and would remain un-Australian for loving ancient beliefs of their traditional lands too much. All history had to be tested in these questions. Why? All history needed to be addressed in their answers. So what wife was he looking for?

A wife, a wife, in any case, might end up being a piece of meat. Someone who might have been called *Does it matter*, then asked a simple question really, and very politely, *What's her name then – your wife?*

I sent you people a letter, Warren snapped, while checking the time once more on his watch, and blimey, he kicked his brain for wasting time.

Honestly, nobody remembered receiving a letter: *Can you tell us what was in the letter?* Weisenheimer asked.

It was explained in the letter. Warren Finch said – full stop. He was in no mood to explain what should have been read in a letter.

Was it that impossible to read a simple letter? He was clearly annoyed that these people were trying to force him into talking about what was really, after all, a delicate matter. His minders thought so too. A man of his position expected to have things organised properly. It happened that way everywhere else on the planet, so what was the trouble with this place? Why could one simple thing not be done right in this place of all places – his homeland? *You want to tell me if someone wants to play around with me here?* He suspected the financial controller was lying. *If you are running the show you must have seen the letter.*

The meeting waited while some clerk was called up to the office to find the letter. Meanwhile, Warren looked miserably around the building at paper piled and paper strewn, and then blankly at one of his minders who immediately left the building to make a call on his mobile phone to an office so far away from everything abysmally slack-assed that he could see in the dismal swamp, and cheerfully spoke to the real world of Heaven, where things happened with a single snap of one's fingers, where people could not run fast enough to do things properly. When he returned, the minder reported that the letter had been sent a long time ago and there had been no reply. The two-line, three-short-sentenced letter was now emailed to the mobile phone that was passed around the room, so everyone could read the contents of Warren's letter.

Well! Wasn't that just typical, just typical.

At this point the electricity suddenly stopped flowing from the malfunctioning power station down the road, and the fans rumbled to a halt. There was sweat in the room. The Army mechanic, who had gone away fishing for the weekend with 'neglected' children, would not be able to fix the problem, Weisenheimer announced. He was uncontactable. Finch had now clearly had it up to his eyeballs. *What use was a mechanic if you can't even contact the bugger when you haven't got any power?*

Well! You tell me? Who is the boss? You, or the flaming mechanic? Finch glared at the controller. *Or who the parents are around here?*

He was now counting the bad vibes, all falling like dominos. All the ammunition! He was a master at pinpointing incompetence. Unlike beef cattle, this was what fed the belly of Canberra, the paradise hungry to shut down the Indigenous world. A bloody lost letter, and the lost wife, now the lost power, plus the smell of a dead rat in the ceiling, who could dream of what was coming next? The question of Warren's lost wife quickly became a lengthy *in camera* discussion in the full-blown humidity of the tropics in the closed room where swarming mosquitos were playing noughts and crosses on exposed skin.

So it was in this inner sanctum of the swamp's Aboriginal Governmental Nation, which was trying to find a pleasing resolution, while Warren Finch was simply wondering if they were even worth saving at all. Then, the last-straw cold tea circulated to the meeting by a young girl – long after she had responded without much enthusiasm to repeated loud, clicking fingers by Weisenheimer, because she was too busy ear-dropping at the closed door and dreaming that *she* was Warren Finch's wife – blasted the lid off politeness. No tea tipped the balance.

She was a promised wife. *A promised wife? Ah!* Now that was different. *This is very different to what we were thinking. Sorry, but we didn't think about that, because we don't do that kind of thing here anymore. It died out years ago. Nobody wanted to continue with this old law.* The old elder said this straight out because he said he was nobody, and not just because everyone knew that a discussion of a highly contentious issue like this might end badly by the end of the night.

One of the older women said she had been a promised wife. Another woman said that she was more concerned about how the township kept moving by itself, and if this moving around of people kept going on, soon there would be so many of them, they would be living off their traditional country, and something needed to be done about this. The controller urged the meeting to think very carefully about what Mr Finch was talking about. He too wanted to hear the truth about the lost letter that might explain the reason for such a highly prominent person in the Australian community behaving this way – like what the locals would gleefully think was a deranged hobgoblin sent by Canberra to personally annoy him, so of course he asked: *What age would this 'so-called' promised wife be?* He wanted to know if Warren required a child. Was it a virgin? What hymn sheet were they to sing?

The Aboriginal Government men and women saw all kinds of awful ramifications for Swan Lake and stayed quiet. Actually, they knew the reality of his request, but Weisenheimer was on a roll, becoming emotional – nothing would stop him. Now he lost the plot by asking a lot of questions on behalf of his people's welfare:

Why did you come here like this, making these demands of us?

Why didn't you just come here with good intent?

What about those doctors? Why were doctors being wasted as bodyguards? We need doctors here to look after the sick people. We've got plenty of sick people here.

Yes, Warren Finch could have gone anywhere he liked while he was busy out saving the world, other than visiting the people who needed him most, his own people in Swan Lake. And! Gosh! A man like Warren Finch was too busy, he did not need a wife.

So why come here and bother the little people on a Friday evening when people needed to be home relaxing after a hard week and eating their dinner while it was hot?

Warren Finch had obviously thought the whole thing through – start to finish – beforehand. He had come to collect his wife and expected a wall of silence, but he knew he would push on through the night if he had too, and he was digging in. He was prepared to get no sleep for days to get a result, and knew the ramifications of naming his mission.

Dr Hart, Dr Doom and Dr Mail, his long-time minders, who always thought that they knew everything there was to know about Warren as his closest confidantes, now exchanged questioning looks. Warren Finch already had all the women he could ever want. Didn't he have some sort of long-term relationship with somebody in Canberra? What about Marcella of Milan? Wasn't he seeing a Maria in Warsaw? It was hard to keep track of the women in his life. Why would he want to do this? What kind of wife was he thinking of?

Names, names, names, Warren continued, clicking his fingers impatiently. It was only a simple name that a person needed. *This was a reciprocal agreement and it must be honoured,* said one of the ex-boxer-type minders. His minders were quick to take up the thread of what was news to them, while not knowing how a promise wife fitted into Warren's grand plan, in which he had always been honest enough to admit that he had no time for wives. The painful issue was prolonged further by excuses from the Swan Lake Government suggesting it would be happy for *the promise* to be annulled. *It was time to go home. Time for bed.* But it was up to him to make the final decision since they knew the families involved in the first place were now deceased.

Weisenheimer pushed on.

Warren, I can guarantee you as real as I am sitting here that we do not have anyone around here who would even remember this promise wife arrangement.

He encouraged others to say something to end the matter, and they did.

You do not have to go through with it, Mr Your Highness. You should feel free to marry someone else and we give you our full blessing our boy.

Yes. This is what people do now because the Army is in control here for the Australian Government punishing us people. We still live in punitive raid times. They do not worry about the promise. We just get married with the controller's permission.

No! No! No! The minder called Dr Doom fired the shots in a deep operatic voice of the likes you would hear in the *Teatro la Fenice* in Venice; a soaring ghostly phoenix roaring, that as sure as hell did not belong in this swamp. The boom killed free speech in an instant. Meandering *talkathons* were pronounced dead. There were no other cards to play except Warren's, and he had placed those squarely on the table. Men like Doom made many people wonder whether there were other Aboriginal people coming up through the education system who could use their voices like that.

Still, what was pretty much the *vox populi* of wishes in Swan Lake became grist for eyeballs bouncing back and forth, where they looked up from the bottom of a Rio Grande chasm between one of these super humans and the next. Warren Finch's eyebrows rose, and he transformed himself into television Warren with legs stretched out under the table, but nobody copied his behaviour. It did not matter to them how much Warren Finch was relaxing because it just felt like intimidation. They knew that feigning to be relaxed was one thing for the champion peacekeeper of the world, but this type of person does not travel out of his way, just to reach a swamp and settle for rejection, be bluffed by diversions, or just plain mucked around. His relaxed state only emphasised his intransigence and he casually restated what he wanted, with a smile: *The law is the law.* He simply wanted what was his to claim from an agreement made between families, of *Our nations,* he said.

It should not be that hard to understand.

But nobody told us, somebody nervously chanted.

But nobody told us? Warren's sauna-soaked minders whispered, in mocked shock. The pressure-cooker room was not to everyone's taste.

You had to give it to the bosses of this swamp for being true masters of their own game. They were not going to be duped by anyone walking in off the street so to speak, or more factually, coming in off the road like some unannounced hobo Black fellow, and aiming to rip the dirt from beneath their feet. They knew what people like this try to do. He was making a claim on their traditional land. They dug their heels in. Claimed no knowledge of the letter. Claimed there was no misunderstanding, and the reason being, they were always kept in the dark. Nobody could blame people who were kept ignorant to whatever was going on behind their backs. A few words on a mobile phone? *Blah! Meant nothing.* It was not a letter they received. *You can't receive letters on a telephone. Never heard of such a thing.* They accused the financial controller: Ask him! *He never spoke to any of us Aboriginal people.*

The fuming controller's many freckles looked like a nest of redback spiders about to burst as he shouted that if anyone wanted to make an appointment to get information about themselves, his office door was always open. *Wasn't that true?* He yelled at each of the people he pointed to around the table. In the end, a mumbler spoke into his chin and called the controller a rude man. The controller was uncontrollable. He had lost the letter, but it was plainly obvious that no harm had been intended, so the meeting agreed on the spot that such an agreement might have been cemented between two families, and the good news was that the misunderstanding could be put right. A likely name was whispered, that matched Warren's information about a family promise he received a long time ago at the bedside of his dying father.

The financial controller took Warren aside, outside the building, over on the lawn, far from the meeting, to be discreet. *The girl you are looking for is called Oblivion Ethyl(son), Ether(son), something or other like that.* The Aboriginal Government was betrayed by Weisenheimer who could not keep his mouth shut for a minute about anything. They always knew that she had been promised to

Warren Finch so they had banned promised marriages. She lived down on the hull. And everyone knew why she was there.

Very unfortunate business they say. She was interfered with. (Sigh). *But that happened a long time ago mind you. Long before I arrived here.*

I already know about that. Warren Finch snapped – his words slamming against each other. Back inside the office, he saw the flinching and twitching, but he smiled like he had hit the jackpot, and the meeting resumed admirably, with everyone getting on with polite letting bygones be bygones.

The financial controller finished the meeting by limply saying. *She shouldn't be down there all by herself anyway.*

You got our backing Warren. We vote for you all the time here. There was a line formed and everyone took their turn to clearly state their allegiance to Warren. Whatever he thought was good enough for them – anything would be okay – a few cattle? And just like that – they personally acquiesced as though the girl had never existed.

The brolgas outside wished to dance all day, but the day was gone and now they too were walking away into the night. The swans overhead sent a few peals of their toy trumpet calls through the dust, and continued flying down the swamp to the hull.

Swan Maiden

The moon was hidden behind the cloud of swans swarming over the swampy lake, where in the darkness, thousands hissed as they dived at the water and stabbed their beaks around Warren Finch in a rowing boat heading towards the hull. Battalions of swans swooped at the boat. Warren Finch could feel the warmth of their soft bellies as he brushed through their barricade.

One thing leads to another, and before the girl could really understand how to think like an adult, a complete stranger had boarded the hull. The man said he was looking for her.

The girl was fearful of the oars moving through the water and the noisy ruckus from the swans. She thought it was the owls she had heard earlier calling across the water. Now her invisible life had been split apart by a strange man's presence in her home, and in that moment of visibility she felt ashamed of how she looked.

You must be the swan maiden. His voice teased. She met him with a knife in her hand. He was still excited about how he had been challenged by the swans. *How romantic!* It amused him to cast himself into the story found across the northern hemisphere of the hunter who captures a mythical swan maiden in a marsh.

He removed the knife in an instant, simply by reaching out and taking it from her hand while she was still in shock. *Don't hesitate if you want to kill somebody*, he said. *You want to do it straight – Pow! Slam! Into the heart. Get it over and done with – just like that.*

She looked away, but remembered hearing a voice once that was similar, and tried to understand the circumstances of how she had heard it. She could not remember because a flood of stories, swollen and submerging under their own weight rolled into waves that pushed her further away from its memory, until finally, the whole heavy weight of remembering collapsed, and she felt as though she was suffocating in her own life.

In these images returned from the past, there was the face of a small girl urging her to run, to become once more the story of when she was alone, sleeping inside the tree. But Warren Finch's gaze was like ice. A wall of ice in the way of running! His eyes held its glare. She heard him saying that her solitary life on the hull had now finished – *a girl should not be living alone in this place.* She did not want to hear him. *It was not safe,* he said. He looked her up and down like a cattle buyer. *Not right.* She was running away through the path made in her thoughts to the tree that stood clear in her mind. But stories were switching themselves around like rope thrown out in a crisis, and in the midst of trying to grab a story to save herself, the reality of swans called from outside in the sea of blackness around the hull. They reminded her that the tree was destroyed, there was nowhere to run. The swans' clamorous trumpeting made her realise that nobody ran from Warren Finch. Already, he possessed her life.

He liked to view people like an X-ray machine – technical, and without emotion, as though this was the way to examine the function of an asset. *She looks deranged. Unhinged. She still acts like a child. But she must be about eighteen, nineteen, even twenty. What's wrong with her. She can't always be like this.* The girl felt sick in the stomach. She was like a lizard trying to disappear down a blocked bolthole. Was it worth opening her eyes to see if she had succeeded, if neither he nor she existed? Working quickly, she installed the spirit of Aunty Bella Donna of the Champions, but the loud-mouthed Harbour Master returned too. He said she must be joking. He laughed: *How can her memory rescue you, girlie?* He warned her to get away from the past. The girl fought back by reciting, in Bella Donna's high-tilting voice, the many swan maiden fantasies that have vanquished men who hunt swans. She screamed the story of the hunter, that of a fisherman, another of the man in the woods – of their capturing swan women that always eventually escape. Stories she knew well about escaping. Screams these into Finch's face to cover the sound of his voice.

He was trying to put aside his thoughts, the reality telling him to walk away, his ego telling him everything would be fine. *She's fine. She's okay really. It is all this. This place. How would anyone feel? Nothing that can't be handled with a bit of care. It will be fine.*

He would make it so.

The thing about a levee is the way that it breaks apart with too much flooding. This was the type of thing that excited the Harbour Master about taking over the scene. He had to come into Oblivia's mind and see what was happening, to sort it out, and he burst in and asked the girl what the hell was going on. *What on earth are you thinking?* He was in full swing for musings, and told her to stop digging into the ground. *Your roots are piss weak! Won't grow in this soil. It's got no seed. Can't grow it.* His voice invaded every crevice in her mind, from knowing the girl did not know anything about God or the spirits or the Holy Ghost, and knowing she was too exhausted to dig around for any more old stories.

What is his name? Warren asked about the swan hunter in

the story she was trying to concentrate on. *She does not know, shit!* The Harbour Master was the boss and she was trying to hear what he was saying. Warren interjected constantly. Then he asked kindly: *Would the hunter ever return the swanskin?* The question puzzled her. She did not know if the swan wife would survive without her magical swan cloak in a place where her kind of story about swans belonged.

Either the girl escapes or not! The words jam in her head. Drum beat to erase the existence of Warren Finch from her mind. But droning wings from clouds of swans drum fear louder, insisting that she *Get him out of the hull.* The breeze caught by their frenzied wings flowed along the soft-feathered breasts and bellies of these boats that glide in the sky until finally, the wind rushed inside the hull and whooshed the girl into its embrace.

Are you awake? he asks, speaking loudly. His fingers click – *Ethyl! Is your name Emily, or is it really Ethyl?* He casually walks around the hull home, still with the knife in his hand, while glancing at the shabby books stacked on top of each other, or lined up in shelves, others that lay open on the pages of treasured passages, on which he reads a few lines to discover something of the girl's intimacy with the swans. He flips pages with the knife and reads at whim wherever his finger rests on a page, and in the silent room, only the sound of flicking pages is heard as he moves to another passage.

He continued reading and the girl looked away. She was ashamed. Her head screamed for this invasion of privacy. There was a complete casualness in his approach as he moved on, *And they fade away in the darkness dying.* Chinese poetry of swans, Baudelaire's swan poem, and those on the floor in foreign languages he casually moved aside with his shoe. Then he looked at her as though she would tell him why these books were on the floor and why she had chosen others to read.

Finally, he looked at the messy room and saw that she conducted her daily life like a child. They exchanged looks as though each was vermin. She was a frizzy-haired, stick-like kid – ought to be a young woman, but dressed in a rainbow-coloured T-shirt and baggy, grey shorts. The girl thought of escaping but under his gaze she was petrified, and incapable of lunging past him and out the door.

You are Em-i-ly Wake, or are you somebody else? he asked, looking at her again as though she could be of mild interest to him. She did not know the name. Never heard of it before. It occurred to her that this stranger could tell her who she was, the identity she had sought by searching through words written on a page. Em-i-owake. She tried to say that her name was Oblivia Ethylene Oblivion, although generally, she thought Em-u-awake was something someone had said to her once.

Go slow Warren, he said quietly to himself, while simultaneously checking the time on his watch. *Do you know who I am? My name is Warren Finch.* He asked if he could sit down, and sat down anyway on the only other chair, on Aunty Bella Donna of the Champions' side of the table. This surprised her. She never used the chair. It still held the essence of the old woman's authority. He told her to sit down too if she wanted. There was no warmth in his voice but the girl slid sideways onto her chair. Her gaze travelled over the floor and out the door to the swans calling and thrashing and rushing through the water. She did not hear a word he was saying.

The swans swarmed in their panicky flight around the hull – great wings flapping wildly, as when they were alarmed by predators on their territory, and the great white swan that had haunted the swamp for old Aunty's spirit.

Already she felt the swans becoming disconnected from her. They were marooned in flight, unable to break apart from their fear. She saw in their erratic and chaotic struggle their desperation to flee, and understood the very same nervousness running through her own body. They were trying to persuade her to leap from the hull and fly with them. No, they would not leave without her. She wanted to run but she faltered, kept hesitating, not fully comprehending the extent of the swans' electrified sense of danger, the sudden readiness to lift in one synthesised movement greater than that of their predator from the first sense of a deadly strike in the water. But the eagle was already in the hull, and ready to swoop.

I suppose you don't know who I am, do you? he asked again, his eyes steady, ignoring the upheaval around the hull.

Sit there. You and I have got some things to talk about. And bloody relax. I am not going to eat you.

This was the first time she had looked a person straight in the face. She recognised his clothes. They belonged to rich people like the ones Aunty Bella Donna of the Champions had described. The people she had chopped carrots for while they protested about the state of the world and all that. He caught her glance and his face softened momentarily, as though it amused him to catch the rat girl off guard. She looked away quickly.

We are married already, equally co-joined through Country, Law, story. Our marriage marks a new epoch in our culture. Our challenge will be the lying reality. Something to overcome, Warren Finch told Ethyl(ene) (Em, ya, I, or u awake) Oblivion(a), soon to become Finch.

The girl did not think so. She leapt the plank he had laid with words and dived into the sea tide in her mind – that big deep sea, where she struggled to hold her head above the surface. Around her swarmed old Aunty's stories of thousands of drowning people blowing swan whistles, and the boys of long ago with their faces covered by white masks. They pushed her aside as they jostled in some kind of game, reaching up with their arms to snatch from the air a face, Warren's face, so that he became one of them. The memories splashed everywhere, suffocating the air in a jostle of whistles. She saw the boys laugh from the blank space of their mouths. She felt relieved by hands pushing her down into the bowels of the giant eucalyptus tree where it was just stillness.

Stupid to take nothing. Somehow, in his struggle to overpower any of her attempts to escape him, Warren Finch had gathered up many of the books in an old fishing net she used to scoop up tiny silver fish bait that swam beside the hull. Apart from books, the only other things she took from the hull as he forced her over the side of the vessel were those tangled memories that filled her mind.

The swans swam all around the dinghy, cooing to be pacified by her. When she did not speak to the quizzing eyes that needed to understand the stranger and her odd behaviour, their grey, black and white-tipped wings flapped frantically and they lunged with their long necks into the boat and bit Warren's arms as he rowed.

She would hear the swans in the swamp for the last time from where she sat in the back seat as the car drove off, hemmed in between two of his minders. Swans ran along the water in the swamp, and flew in a cloud that looked like a black angel lit by lightning, but receded into the distance and their bugling faded into the thunder and the skies dark with midnight storms.

You can take it away, and with that, Warren Finch switched off his mobile phone. There was no need to speak. There was the journey ahead. He had just ordered the total evacuation of Swan Lake. The Army would do it. The whole shebang would be bulldozed that night. He imagined total annihilation. The swamp dredged. The unpredictability of seasons passing, weaving the light as he fell asleep.

The girl watched from the road as the kilometres passed, noticed the vegetation changing from one geographical region to the next, while stacking objects in her mind. The woman's voice on the radio was singing...*Pick me up on my way back.* How would anyone sing the particularities of 3003-4-5 cans, 51-2-3 abandoned car bodies, 600 road signs, 86 carcasses of dead animals where wedgetail eagles swooped down and soared upwards, 182 old car tyres? There were lowland territories of emus, swarms of budgerigars, twisting green clouds over spinifex *kinkarra* plains, isolated groves of old eucalypts, river crossings with ghost gums *dikili*, solitary *murrinji* coolibah trees around dry dips in the landscape, salt pans, salt lakes, forest stands of gidgee in dry grass, lone bottle trees and fig trees growing out of rocky hills, salt plains, landscape blackened from bush fires, *kulangunya* blue tongue lizards, or frog calls, diamond doves, runs of spinifex pigeons. She would remember it all, by repeating the list over and over again, as the number of sightings increased, until she succumbed to exhaustion and sleep.

In her dreams she struggled to find a lifeline to grip. No safe anchor in the exploding water, where the chaos was so terrifying, the girl jumped out of her sleep. The car was still travelling, and it startled her before she remembered where she was.

The headlights flashed over telegraph poles beside the road, an endless line running behind them, which in her mind began forming a swan map of the country. She could imagine the swans flying above the wires strung across the poles in their slow migration along the Dreaming track from another age, while heading the journey up to the swamp. Now, she began fretting for them. Occasionally, the lightning lit up a landscape wild with wind and she remembered how the swamp drummed with rain in nights of storm.

In the relentless movement of travelling through a rain that had captured the country, her world became shrunken, pieces of memory flew off, became eradicated, until even the polluted slicks running across the swamp had disappeared into nothingness. She sensed everything known to her had disappeared and blamed herself. Had she really negated her responsibility for the greater things in her care? She could not ask what had happened to the swans. Would not ask to be taken back just to see whether they were safe. Her stomach had no momentum for pushing words into her mouth so that she could speak to anybody. She would have no words sophisticated enough to say to high-up kind of people like these men. Outside the claustrophobic car, the never-ending rain was falling heavily, so even if she had spoken, nobody would have heard.

Warren Finch slept in the front seat. He had fallen asleep from the moment they started out, but the three bodyguards talked on through the journey. A thick haze of cigarette smoke danced around in the car, and they sat in this smoke like genies squashed in a lantern. The three men talked non-stop about how things happened a lot to them while working for Warren Finch, and listening to them, you would think that they had never known any other life. They had never been born. Never had a home. Never had a family.

The girl fought the sound of these voices that talked on and on about things she did not understand. It became more and more difficult to stay awake, to remember the road, to count the signposts, her only way of finding the way back. She lost track of her calculations – the categories slipped into lesser numbers, and were forgotten. Now, she thought she was becoming delirious from imagining devils monotonously speaking in the talk of the bodyguards.

In lightning strikes their faces looked freaky. Nobody looked real with their skin replaced by a watery substance trapped in opaque layers of silicon. The lightning convinced the girl that these silicon remnants of ancient waters must be spirit genies that had decided to dress like men and were now working for Warren Finch, and pleasing his every wish. The girl wondered whether he knew of their true identity. It was no wonder that his pugilist scholars could do all manner of tasks, far more than any normal men. This was why Warren Finch was not sitting up awake in the front seat wishing to be rich and powerful and a genius. He already had his three wishes.

Who uses up their three wishes? A wish for this and a wish for that in each puff of cigarette smoke filling the car! The girl thought the sleeping man was running out of wishes, and she tried to imagine where the genies would live after he set them free. When that happened she would get her wish too. She would steal the magic lantern car and drive it straight back to the swamp to calm the swans swimming aimlessly around the hull. She would arouse the paralysed huddle on the foreshore with heads tucked under wings, waiting for death.

In her dream, a migrating swan moved rhythmically through the night as it passed across the changing landscape while following the lights of the car below. It glimpses Warren Finch sleeping in the front seat, and caught off guard hits the power lines and flips in flight. With wings faltering it ascends disoriented higher into the sky and spins off towards the stars while struggling to breathe. Oblivia was slowing down her own breathing too. Hardly breathes at all now, she is in a flight to death. She slips into unconsciousness while following the broken swan flying off through the darkness. Then the swan is pushed aside by the Harbour Master walking towards the car from a long way off and suddenly he is in the back seat of the car, where he squashes himself on top of the two men and the girl. Oblivia wakes up in fright, opening her mouth wide as the Harbour Master punches her hard in the chest. He is pushing air through her lungs, while squeezing the wrist of each of Warren Finch's men in turn, until they are in so much pain, they are forced to wind down the windows to let in some fresh air, allowing the rain to belt into the car. *Stupid girl*, he says, and he remains in the car throughout the journey, watching the rain and taking note of the country, making it almost impossible for anyone to move in the back seat, especially Oblivia, who remains calm. Warren Finch kept sleeping, but the genies felt spooked by a foreboding in the car, a heaviness that stopped the talk, and made them think seriously about why they had bothered taking this journey right now, at this time of year, the stupidity of the whole trip really, and why they were not somewhere else instead.

Owls in the Grass

The Grass Owl has always been regarded as one of Australia's scarcest owls, rarely seen and with only a handful of nest records, yet here was a concentration of birds, with evidence of multiple nesting.

The girl finally discovered where the three genies lived. After travelling many hours they reached a night world where men in singlets ruled lonely roads. Sweaty men yelling out over radio and satellite phones to each other to dig out the rulebook: *That one written in hell.* From then on it was hell on earth on this lonely single road, a highway stretching a thousand kilometres over the heart of the country.

This was the place where the mind of the nation practised warfare and fought nightly for supremacy, by exercising its power over another people's land – the night-world of the multi-nationals, the money-makers and players of big business, the asserters of sovereignty, who governed the strip called *Desperado*; men with hands glued to the wheel charging through the dust in howling road trains packed with brown cattle with terrified eyes, mobile warehouses, fuel tankers, heavy haulage steel and chrome arsenals named *Bulk Haul, Outback, Down Under, Century, The Isa, The Curry, Tanami Lassie,* metal workhorses for carrying a mountain of mining equipment and the country's ore.

A crescendo of dead – the carcasses of splattered or bloated bullocks and native animals lay over the sealed or unsealed corrugated roads, where the eyes of dingoes and curlews gleamed in the headlights.

The genies stopped frequently to check the road kill. Hunger filled the car. The girl watched as they collected those still with a trace of life: small rodents, mangled rabbits, various marsupials, broken-back snakes, a bush turkey, a smashed echidna. All of these bloodied, broken creatures still warm, were thrown in the back seat of the car. Along the way, the Harbour Master decided he could no longer be bothered staying in a car loaded with road kill, so he got out, and walked off somewhere out there on the open road.

You could only expect to arrive in the most isolated destinations like this after midnight, one of the genies murmured to the others in the car, after driving hour after hour through flat and wide country to reach a place where the winds collided and spun the soil into clouds of dust. Home at last. The genies walked off into the bush. They spoke to the country. Let the country know they had come home. Who the sleeping man and the girl were in the car.

The genies constructed a campsite on ground thick with rats, and smiled whenever they passed the terrified girl sitting in the car watching the earth move with their footsteps. *Child! Pretty rats. Ratus vilosissimus. Bush rats!* The air was dry and smelt of dust, rats and the heat of many days that had stayed in the ground. The rats scattered in rolling waves at every movement while scurrying in and away for all the fur and offal thrown to them by the genies preparing the road kill for the fire. Doom, Mail and Hart could not put aside something that had been niggling them ever since they had arrived on their country with the girl. None of them knew the stories from her country. They did not know anything about her, nothing of what she held within her, or the spirits of the law stories that she now brought onto their own territory. How would they know how these stories connected both countries? What other questions should they be considering if her stories did not connect with their country, not even one story-line connecting their lands together, if that was possible? They did not know. And the girl? She had not spoken a word and as far as they knew, she was not able to speak.

These questions started to haunt them, and it seemed as though the ancestors were already asking them to consider the consequences of trespassing spirits, and how they connected themselves to land and to her, and what knowledge they would turn to on this country. They were not senior story-men, nor in positions of authority as elders holding the law of the country on which they stood. Not like Warren, still asleep in the car, who was a senior lawman with much authority on his own country.

Well! It was pretty serious stuff to worry about, and they thought Warren was stupid for bringing her along in the first place with the excuse of using all of that promise marriage stuff – where did that come from? And simply by glancing from the girl and at each other, they agreed being back on their country was going to be one hell of a sobering-up exercise for each of them.

Since they were already calculating the cost of having her on their country, each man instinctively understood how these things work; of being responsible for looking after the girl. It was pretty obvious to them that there was something different about her – not because of Warren, but her strangeness made them feel uneasy, and convinced them that she had spirits looking after her. This was the thing that they had felt in the car, and now the whole mess of not knowing what to do about her continually bothered them. It was because of their foreboding about what they did not know about her, that they were already thinking about leaving, and realising if they continued thinking like this, it would get to the situation where it would be impossible to leave, because if not today or tomorrow, any one of them could suddenly be seized, and driven into that state of impossibility. Leaving would become a rock hanging around their necks. Leaving would become tied to a sense of foreboding, seen as being riddled with bad luck, where anything could go wrong with the whole situation of watching, caring, and thinking while they went about their scientific work on the environment – the annual task, the one small important thing that they had been asked to perform by their own nation. Now, instead of the work being a joy, with a sense of respect, and honouring their country, they would always be waiting...watching and waiting while nothing happened, until their own berserk, cartwheeling prophesying was fulfilled.

The dust rose like shadowy priests wandering through the darkness. A celestial haze stirred up by the cattle. The cattle called to one another in response to their leaders, collars swaying around their necks ringing their bells. The girl was too frightened to leave the car, but Doom ordered her to get out. *Don't be stupid. Nobody is going to hurt you.* Blood boils in her face as she stands back in the shadows, too afraid of becoming lost and disoriented as rats scurry in and out of the ghost bush, where *darraku* was everywhere, and feeling that *kundukundu* scrub devil reaching out with the wind, and she feels him scratch, *kurrijbi* all over her body, scratching along her arms and legs, he ensnarls her into the foliage.

The cattle bells roll, and remind her of Aunty Bella Donna of the Champions singing sacred texts to unlock the terrifying memories of her people. Again and again, by ringing the bells she brought them to life, legendary heroes that stretched right back through the ages to the time when wisdom-singers like *Wainamoinen* of the *Kalevala* were walking their land, *swans came gliding from the marshes...came in myriads to listen...*

The same old oracle was everywhere, even in the dust of rats. This time, Bella Donna was quietly singing the poetry of Ludwig Rellstab's *In der Ferne – In the distance – of fleeing one's home broken-*

hearted, from Franz Schubert's *Schwanengesang D.957.* Hovering! Somewhere up in the sky! Asking the breezes to send greetings to a time when women stitched those white and golden swans in treasured embroidery that became heirlooms, before they fled along broad rivers towards the sea where white soot-stained swans were nesting in the burnt marshes.

Warren Finch did not stay asleep for long. The genies were too full of enthusiasm, divined more song and talked of seeing so fine a starry night. *Hey! Girl, look at that,* they called Oblivia frequently, constantly checking to see where she was as she stood in the darkness. They kicked rats away, and their laughter swirled about with the wind. *Hey! Girl, did you see that?* The car produced bounty – food, cooking utensils and bedding, more than anyone could have imagined would fit in its boot. A campfire was lit. Meals were cooked. Aromas filled the air. Wine and water appeared as though they had been divined from the windy earth itself. *You will feel pretty good while you are on this country, Boss,* they reassured him. He was on their land. *It fills you up with life. All the energy you need. You'll see.* The men exchange knowing looks. There is no need to speak. They all belong to the same game. They know what Warren Finch has to work out before they go back to the city.

Let's go, jila nungka, Finch said flatly to Oblivia, after he had eaten every piece of meat on his plate. She had not eaten, or as Warren guessed, refused to eat. He could see hatred in her eyes, and felt how tense she was, but he took her by the hand, pulled her to her feet from the ground where she had been sitting near the fire, and led her back to the car. In this moment of pulling her away from herself, she knew he would overpower her life. Even the sensation of his hand touching her had sent her back into the tree in her mind.

Once Warren had left with the girl, the genies chatted lightly about city women, international woman who called him up night and day. Now therein lay the mystery: She was not in the same league. They had seen enough of her on this journey to know that he must be regretting his mistake. She was just a kid. Well! She certainly looked and behaved like one. *What did he think was going to happen once they got back home?* Anyone could have told him not to go around picking up 'damaged goods' girls from dysfunctional Army-controlled communities like the swamp. Main thing being that bloody place was her homeland. *The man's got enough troubles.* What was he thinking? The girl was overcome with shyness and here they were, a thousand kilometres away, and she would not even look at them, let alone speak. *What he went and done now is a wrong thing.* They knew how lightly he treated women, but thought he understood which women had any chance of standing up to him. Well! That was too late now. He had laid the idea of 'worldliness' at the feet of a recluse. Who knew what was the matter with him? *He's gone too far.* They did not have to say what each of them already knew, that they could not fix this problem. It would not be like having a 'small smart chat' to one of the city women he was tired of, who he wanted to go and get lost.

I am so tired, Warren told her, after he had driven a short distance from the camp the genies had made for themselves, and threw his swag on the dirt.

Come here and let's get some sleep, he said, pulling the trembling girl towards him, onto the swag, and into the blanket of dust swirling over them. The surrounding bush smelt of the rats that were rushing through the grass whining for food, which made her believe they would attack once she fell asleep. She felt nauseated by the closeness of this other person, but surveying the surrounding darkness, she saw that there was nowhere to escape in the dryness of the strange country that frightened her. Forced to lie together in the cold, locked for warmth like sheltering animals against a windbreak he had erected with the canvas of the swag against the car, his arms wrapped around her made her feel that she was in the grip of a snake. She listened closely to the dry grass and shadows of scrub being rustled by the wind, singing stories and laws that she would never know, and knowing this single thing about being its stranger was like having the weight of the world on her shoulders. This was the kind of weight she carried to stop her from sleeping in this country. Whenever she drifted off to sleep, she would instantly be re-awakened; just by the simple fact of knowing she should not be there, and knowing that rats crept all over the ground searching for food. She felt the country's power. Knew it could kill her.

Every sound convinced her that his bodyguards, the genies, were in the bush waiting for her to run. She does not trust any of them. But how could they be lurking around, when from further away, she could hear them singing the country through the night, their voices resounding in the wind gusts, and echoing through the landscape, as though there were many others singing with them. Her instincts keep telling her to run, she cannot stand being near him, feels like death to her, but fearing he would kill her, she remains frozen, barely able to move. Whenever she moved slightly, even to breathe deeply, his grip tightened. But he slept easily: the songs travel with him, and he carries the spirits of homelands inside him. It makes him strong: the hands of the ancestors are in his own, acting in unison.

She lay very still in the hope that he would stay sleeping even though she did not want to be left awake to listen to the sounds of the country. She hears the sharp cry from a rat and imagines that a snake is killing it, and this convinces her that she is sleeping on *miya-jamba*, snake ground. She imagines snakes are everywhere and hates the place, and is hot from panicking to be off the ground. The thought of rats and snakes infested through every centimetre of this piece of country makes her growing hatred for Warren Finch grate that little bit harder, and she is desperate to move, but just when she wishes to kill him and reaches around to find a rock to slam into his head, forgetting to fear she might touch a rat or a snake instead because she can't see a thing in the darkness, or that he will wake up and see what she is doing and kill her instead, something happens. She forgets to act – either to run off, or to kill him. She has changed her mind? No, that was not it. Her mind changes itself. It is at war with action. Fights decisions. She forgets to act when memories quickly regain control of her brain, and instead of fighting, she escapes with a flood of thoughts running back along the song-lines to the swamp, and the language inside her goes bolting down the tree with all the swans in the swamp following her.

He knew her terror. It was the fear of a child that even the rats sensed and were scattering in frenzy. What was he to do with her world? This was when he realised that he would never be able to reach her. Hadn't he given her a fair go? He had built a dream as complex and ingrained as her own, but where he knew that his would keep pushing him out in the world, she would always dig a hole to hide in. She was still the girl in the tree. Untouchable. Rolled up in a tight ball like a frightened echidna. Yes, it was easy to decide not to touch her. Perhaps he never would. What did it matter? Nobody would accuse him of being a paedophile or a rapist. Number one rule of his forefathers. What could he do? He drifted off into half-sleep like he always did, while thinking about a mountain of crises in any country that sprung to his mind, and through the wee hours of the night, he would spin by the world's troubles, resolving crises one by one, intervening step by step in other people's fortunes or misfortunes, in his dreams.

When the wind dropped, all she could hear was his breathing resounding through the sounds of owl fights, and screaming rats. Above them, she thought she saw spider webs being spun on fine threads that ran down from the power lines and across to the low-growing mulga trees. These enormous webs were being woven thicker and thicker and spiders were flying through the air in search of places to anchor their threads, as though setting a trap to encase them during the night. She lay flat beside him as he slept, and drifted into sleep with the thought of touching the walls inside her tree, and dreamed of a struggling swan enclosed by Warren's icy body while Old Bella Donna sang from afar – *A swan with a slither of bone in its beak.*

The dawn landscape was grey and solemn as it revealed a silent vista of mostly grass and sparsely scattered scrub, until the baying of cattle echoed in a chain reaction that sallied back and forth from the distant horizons. When the sun rose, the cattle had already broken through spider webs and gathered around the two sleeping figures. She was in a cathedral of Law where marriages were always honoured but she would not honour hers. The morning air felt cold. So were her thoughts, vowing that nothing would spring from the dirt of this ground.

You will learn that you and I are going to stand for each other as the only ones we can trust, so never forget that I am your best friend, and only friend, Warren said, preparing to leave, and added – always serious – *You remember that, and that will be the main thing I will want from you as a wife.*

She looked at the landscape – a vista of sameness in every direction – and knew that this was why women went missing on journeys with their husbands. They were lost forever. This country would devour anyone walking in it that did not know it. Only local people would know how to move through it. A voice she recognised was surfacing: *Look around here.* She thought this wedding country was the home of stories about women thrown overboard, cast out, abandoned, those bodies lost in *wiyarr* spinifex waves.

Isn't it a great country, Warren said, already flowing into the day ahead, and pushing aside the troubling dreams that had come to him during the night, where he had met himself as a dead man, disoriented, weak, and his ghostly face full of disbelief, while being supported by the genies through the streets of the city, and he had watched as they walked on, to a grave he would be buried in.

Swans mate for life: that was what she thought. And if a swan loved its mate, then what would make one kill its mate as she had seen once in a sudden and vicious attack, alongside the hull? It was a silent death. There was no such thing as the dying swan call. It died without sound. She had no sound either, and knew what it was like to be without sound. This country would never hear her voice, or the language she spoke.

The genies' camp was a mess. Their smart clothes were abandoned over the ground, their pots, pans, and swags spread in a chaotic palette. Encircling it all, dead rats in their hundreds lined the periphery. Swarms of blue *Lycaenidae* butterflies, unusually massing in one spot, flew above the heads of Drs Hart, Mail and Doom who were now dressed in their oldest bush clothes, that might have been buried for years under clumps of spinifex. The three men were busy with the fire, creating breakfast, and totally oblivious to the blot they had created on the landscape. *Welcome home*, smiled Mail. Oblivia looked around at their camp. It looked as though they had not moved from their position around the fireplace from the previous night. They were listening intently to a distant magpie, just *jarrburruru* absorbed in its song.

Hear it? A Thessalian maiden no doubt, Doom said. A slight smile of appreciation spread across his face as he spoke to Warren Finch.

Warren nodded casually. He began poking the fire with a stick to send up the flames. His mind was set on the black billycan steaming with the aroma of tea and with pushing away the shock of seeing his dead face in a dream, which was still clear in his mind. Oblivia noticed Dr Doom's face softening, the hardness of the day before had disappeared. He looked like a boy staring into the distance, locked into studying the structure of the magpie's tune. After a while he stood up, and faced the direction of the songster. He whistled the song perfectly. The bird replied. A song war continued until the bird flew from twig to twig across the ground to investigate, and seeing how it had been tricked, flew off.

Would you like to have some owl's eggs? Snip Hart asked her. He had been squatting beside the fire, stirring a large fry pan amidst the smoke, but had come over and spoken quietly while handing her a plate of food. She looked away in disgust. She was not eating owl eggs. *Eat it,* Warren demanded in a voice that made her wince at the ferocity of it. Her eyes rested on the wanderings of a rat daintily sniffing over each corpse of its dead friends. It touched the tips of grey bloodied fur with its nose as though it was searching for a faint breath of life or a ticking heart, before moving on.

The girl could not understand what the genies thought the reason was for spending most of the night killing rats. They told Warren that these were plague rats, *were attracted to the light of the fire.* There was blood on thick sticks of wood resting on the ground beside the fireplace, right next to the king-sized frying pan filled with bright yellow scrambled eggs. She tried to guess how many owls' eggs had been taken from their nests and looked at the landscape of spinifex *kinkarra* and grasslands, where nothing much grew higher than a metre off the ground. The girl tried to locate where owls would nest in those plains where there were no significant trees, except mulga. She remembers owls nesting in the ghost ships on the swamp and she gets up and feels that she is starting to walk off towards home, which feels very close in her mind, but Warren makes her sit on the ground. The plate of food is placed in her lap. He repeats this exercise a number of times before she realises that she is not going anywhere.

Well! So many rats, so many owls, and all night, 'The tremulous sob of the complaining owl...' Bones remarked excitedly, his face covered with grey dust. In an authoritative voice, he explained that they were sitting in the best place in the world right now to see owls. *Man! We are right in the middle of a plague of rats that are multiplying in droves. Never seen anything like it before.* He explained that the rats had migrated in strands of millions flowing inland through the desert. In their wake, large flocks of native grassy owls had followed them, and the *Tyto capensis grass owls*, he explained, were also quadrupling in numbers each time they bred. The food supply was so good – *different, unusual, changed weather patterns are causing it. Well! It was like sitting in the middle of a feast*, said Doom, speaking knowledgeably about the extraordinary phenomena – a million to one chance they were lucky to witness. He had been visiting places like this for years, waiting for this to happen.

Yep, Snip added, *Don't forget the owls were attacking the moths attracted to the fire as well and I think...*

Yes, of course, Doom interjected with science talk, *But I don't think the fire was a consideration in the mind of swarming rats being chased by owls.*

My friend! Who knows the workings of a rat's mind, Snip replied.

I thought that was our expertise: to know a rat when we see one, Doom laughed, but Mail took a more serious analogy about predation in a natural feast or famine occurrence.

Vigilance! My friend. It was only sheer vigilance – the nature of our ancestors, that had saved us from a storm of vermin.

Snip said he agreed because he felt Mail really possessed the mind of a genius, and laughed. *In a way*, he said, *I really equate that brain of yours Mail with a high tech microscope. Someone, who could without hesitation, and with the least bit of prompting, easily cast his mind back through time in a matter of moments, to situate himself inside the brain of the first man and recreate his prophecy.*

And the reason? Ancestry. It all boils down to the connective tissue of heredity. A miracle that is not restricted to time. The brain is a marvellous organ.

You are one of a kind, brother, Mail laughed.

This whole thing was one of a kind.

One continuously ponders the puzzle of life, Warren said with a deep sigh.

Of course, genius is always hard to ignore, Snip said, with a wink.

Exactly. The reason why *Tyto capensis* and *Tyto alba* were nesting like flies around the spinifex.

The souls of women, Warren reminded them, and looked at the girl who was still staring at her plate, unwilling to eat strange food.

You had better eat. It will be another long day.

The return to the highway commenced with a greeting from a blue-eye crow. It was crying next to its squashed-in-half mate left in the middle of the road. Warren stopped the car. The bird tried to defend itself as Warren sought to befriend it. Quietly, he moved closer, holding out his arm, then the bird did a very strange thing. It leaped onto his outstretched hand and onto his shoulder, while crying *aah-aah-aah*, and began chuckling its secrets into his ear. He asked questions, calling it a wise bird, for wise it was with age from the colour of its eyes, and then, he consoled it for its loss. The bird responded well to his voice, for it did another strange thing to demonstrate its ability to communicate its feelings to human beings. It began to mimic lines from that famous old ABBA song – *Money, money, money, it's a rich man's world* – which its ancestors perhaps learnt from listening to a truckies' roadhouse jukebox where they had spent decades pilfering scraps, and which the bird now sung repeatedly in so many *Aahs*. He sang, and the genies sang, and the bird was almost beside itself.

The girl wanted to keep this lonely bird. Warren saw her

moment of vulnerability and in that instant, she received his first lesson about what he meant by friendship. He sent the raven back off to where it belonged, into the northerly wind.

The day was spent examining owls' nests. Their vehicle had been left beside the road covered with Army-issued camouflage netting. Warren and the genies took great care to ensure that the vehicle would remain undetected, and had walked back along their wheel tracks off the main dirt road to buff up the grass.

They travelled on foot, walking into the vastness of low vegetation plains surrounded by smooth, tussocky hills. The work was hard. Dust rose with each step, filled the air with each breath of wind, and fell to settle in their hair, over their skin and in their clothes. They looked as though they had crawled in it, but they had blended into the country, and were indistinguishable from it.

The task of locating the nests of the grass owl was not easy. The nests were concealed at the end of tunnels constructed through the thick *kinkarra* spinifex grasslands. The genies walked in circles between each nest. Warren trailed behind. Oblivia always felt that he was watching her, just in case she tried to escape. She was seething with anger. She hated being watched, of knowing he was staring into her back, getting into her mind. She thought of ways of killing him once she had the chance. His phone rang. He was always busy on what the girl learnt was a mobile phone, capable of making calls from where they were, in one of the remotest places on the planet. Each time it rang and abruptly broke the silence of the bush, he would fall further back, while he talked into it. *Sure! Not now. Speak to you later.* Warren Finch, important or not, was determined to have this time on Country. He silently indicated *five days tops* with a show of his open palm to the genies when they looked back at him speaking on the mobile. They smiled. Agreed. He continued talking. Somebody else. *You will have to cope. You can cope for a few days can't you?* A lot of hard talking had to be done to keep the world busy while he was away. How to finally topple that old goat Ryder once and for all? Take the reigns as the new President? March right up to what the country needed. It was time. He was saying how he wanted time to think, to prepare, to be ready for what was coming. How was he going being married and all? He repeats the question each time it's asked. Fine! Right!

Keep hitting if it makes you happy, he said, whenever Oblivia decided to run back to take another slog at his face.

The genies always tried to mask the conversations Warren was having by talking about owls to the disinterested or disconnected girl – they could not decide which – by naming and describing the two-hundred odd species in the world. It became an endless conversation between the three men about the twenty or so types that included different barn owls, fishing owls, burrowing owls, wood owls, little owls like the one Picasso had as his sad pet. They discussed the Latin family names like *Tyto, Megascaps, Bubo, Otus,* but only *Ninox* and *Tyto* represented the nine different owls found in Australia. She learnt that barn owls could be used by farmers to control plagues of rodents as these owls were now doing out in the desert country. *I am in rodent country,* she thought while she turned and spat towards Warren. The three genies talked a great deal about why the owls had come from the east. What this meant. The ecology of the country had changed. Was this the Law doing something to the country? Then something changed. Words trampling her into the ground could also pick her up. She looked surprised to be told that each family of owls consumed several thousand mice and rats in a breeding season. *Yep!* Bones Doom commented, as though speaking for the girl's silences. She glared at him. She did not want to know these things. *These fellas will keep on breeding out here until they have consumed all the rodents, and then their own numbers will decrease, because most owls will not live more than a couple of years.*

Such a large bird, very unlike the Sulphur-crested Cockatoo which might live for eighty or ninety years, explained the gentle Bones.

There was no owl's nest passed before it received a thorough examination. The men never tired of their interest in how an owl had constructed its nest. With each clutch of eggs discovered, the find was welcomed by the genies as though a miracle had taken place, and chorusing, *Doom, how do you do it man, you are a fucking genius. How many is that now? 12,001? 12,002?*

The eggs were examined for number and weight, and each egg created serious discussion to judge its particular shape and age, held up like a diamond against the sun to examine the embryo forming inside, and then finally, enthusiastic thought was given to how each egg felt as though it was the first marvellous thing they had ever held in the hand. Oblivia thought all the nests were the same. Whenever she was the first to see a nest she did not volunteer the information. What did it matter? She could not be bothered that each nest consisted of six or eight eggs with a displeased sitting owl. Who cared? She wanted to go home. The urge to bolt through the spinifex overpowered her. Only the swamp loomed large in her mind. A vision now contaminated with the ghostly sight of Warren walking like a dead man. A vision that would not leave his mind either.

The information about the owls' nests, including the level of anxiety to the disturbed owl, was recorded on pocket-sized computers. Doom was constantly reminded how painfully slow and tedious he was in his search to locate each nest in a fixed area, before the group could move on. *It's for science. Nobody knows anything about why these birds come to this place, or why the rats are driven here.* The girl was desperate to go. Warren catches up with her each time she walks away. She knows that she slows them down even further. The work becomes slower. Always Doom gives the same answer, while sometimes glancing conspiratorially at Warren, the man on top of the nation who has up to this point, always been in a hurry. Warren nods: *Sure! Who hasn't got time for science?*

We were doing this all last night, Edgar Mail told the girl in a voice that was like an echo from distant spinifex groves, but there were other words burning inside of her: *Stupid girls get into trouble.* It was Aunty Bella Donna of the Champions' voice. *Stupid girls deserve to get what is coming to them.* The Harbour Master was dancing across the plain, stopping every now and again to stare quizzically at the owl hunters whom he repeatedly called, *stupid people.* He and the old woman were both shouting over the distance to reach one another, reminiscing about the bad luck of the girls with weather-beaten bones that lay scattered in places exactly like this. The Harbour Master called it *kinkarra nayi.* The desert. Spinifex. *Wiyarr! Wiyarr!* Everywhere. What next?

They said their bones were like white chalk. *Odd, how these bones were scattered around the ground throughout the spinifex.* The girl's stomach nods, rolls, and nods again. She saw prowling dingos with white bones in their mouths wherever the sun's glare struck the horizon. The dead lady's voice reminded her that all men wanted was sex, *so how do you like that? It happened on the refugee boats. It can happen in the mulga too.* The girl remembered there was an owl, a *julujulu* that once lived in the darkened hole in the roots of the tree. She had felt its soft feathers with her fingers. Now she was reminded of its softness.

Edgar Mail continued talking, *You should remember that anyone can be a habitual colonist perpetually in search of difference to demystify myths, always trying to create new myths to claim as their own.* The girl could hear the old woman and the Harbour Master chuckling somewhere in the air above them, telling her to forget about what that man was saying. *What would he know about the Feast of the Epiphany, the twelfth day of Christmas back in 1697 when a white man first saw your mythical black swan swimming about over there in Western Australia, who had always thought black swans were evil and never really existed? Did he stand back and not touch, believing he would be doomed on a shipwreck for taking a black swan?*

You know, most of these eggs will hatch but when the food runs out in the summer, the rats will perish, and so too will most of the owls, Edgar Mail said lamely, while looking at Snip, who looked at Doom. The girl began to think about how she was going to disappear into ghost country, just like the girls who never returned. She looked out over the ocean of grey-green grasses and thought of how Aunty Bella Donna of the Champions had spent years looking across oceans to stop herself from dying at sea. The Harbour Master reminded the girl that it was very difficult, impossible really, to survive if you never existed.

The genies kept talking about Oblivia's name.

Immya Wake. You are kidding me. Nobody has a name like that.

No. No way man.

You tell them, Warren laughed, looking at her. The girl felt as though she had been stripped in broad daylight. She looked away while trying to decide where to run, but there was no place to run. The plains country was already a coffin for brides.

That's not a good joke comrade, Snip snapped.

Yes! You are right, Warren replied. *Swan girl, I know your name is Ethyl. Will always be Ethyl. I don't know who gave you that other name. But from now on it's going to be Ethyl, short they tell me for Ethylene Oblivion. A beautiful name really, Ethyl.*

The genies wanted to know where that name originated.

The girl stalked off, spitting all over the ground as she went.

Warren Finch liked her spirit. *She was a good hater.* He smiled as though he was pleased with his new possession. The girl did not go far before she realised that she wanted to live, and this dead face Warren Finch was bloody well it, so when Snip commanded, *Stop.*

Stay dead still until I come to you, she froze on the spot. All she hears is Warren's voice, talking again on the mobile phone.

Snip Hart charmed snakes. *Snakes are my thing,* he laughed as he appeared without a sound beside her: *Not yours I can see.* He urged her to pick up the snake coiled on the ground directly beneath them. She remained glued to the spot, full of hate for the man's continual speaking, leaning back and forth, taunting the snake to lunge.

Come on. I am right here, he urged. The girl felt the serpent eyes staring right into her mind. She felt the sensation of its glare and the immediacy of her fear travelling back through its nervous system, pushing its strength down though the muscles of its body, and from there her fear sat like a spring in readiness, as the snake prepared to strike. Snip waited. *Shh!* he whispered. Perspiration ran from her forehead onto the snake's shiny head and over the black beads of its eyes. The snake lunged. Her blood raced to the spot where it would bite before Snip Hart swung the snake up off the ground and into the air by the tail. It hung from the top of his up-stretched arm, struggling for freedom.

He smiled: *See how simple it is?* He gave her a pat on the shoulder as he walked past to show the others. Snip was an expert on desert snakes. It was his country. The girl thought that the snake had not seen him because he was invisible to it. He was already inside the snake. It had only concentrated on striking her. *Snakes were also numerous,* Edgar Mail explained to Oblivia as they walked, *because all the unusual climatic changes which were creating plagues of insects and rodents, also increased the numbers of species that fed on them.*

You just have to be quick, Snip claimed, as if snake-catching was an ordinary skill that people needed to know to be able to walk in a country like Australia. Oblivia continued watching him as he walked ahead while trying to discover whether he really was invisible to snakes. In the sun, she was soon hypnotised by thoughts of hands that moved from running down the body of a snake and examining owl eggs, to hands she pushed away at night.

Snip Hart was fast. He plunged his arm straight down a hole in the ground, or a spinifex tunnel, and grabbed a snake. He announced the measurements and weight in breaking news, while noisily tapping the results into his computer with one hand, and with the other holding the snake. Afterwards, when he finished with each snake, and before releasing the writhing creature, he stared into its eyes to speak lovingly to it in simple words describing its numerous points of beauty, its measurements, and stroking it, he successfully seduced the creature into limp submission in his hand. In its hypnotic trance, he said, it only dreamed of loving this land. How many sexual encounters he wondered, had this snake experienced. *Ten?* Edgar Mail guessed, fingering the length of stubble on his face while studying the size of the creature. *Twenty, by its size,* reasoned Snip. Then he laid the creature on the ground, where it stayed motionless, and walked away.

There is a lot to learn about owls, Mail claimed dreamily in camp at night. He was singing his curiosity to the country and asking the ancestors for their reasoning, as he built his thesis on the plague of rats. *Not the type of thing you could learn in one day in a place where samples of the biosphere in a vast stretch of the country were being carried through some of these creatures we were examining. How do you explain their special stories of origins and creation, return and renewal, which are as new as they are old?*

No! Don't tell them anything. Wait until I get back. Warren on the other hand, had spent most of his day ignoring the world of rats, owls and snakes, and was still answering and making calls on his mobile phone's secure link. He spoke to people across the world in their own languages. He chatted to all of the policy-makers he was interested in, and lastly, told his men that there were people trying to find their location, and continued to speak calmly, while fetching Oblivia back from another attempt to walk off in a half-awake dream, or having to duck from her sudden outbursts of arms swinging to either punch or scratch him, or avoiding another round of aeroplane spitting. *Ah! Janybijbi nyulu julaki jabula! Naah!*

Well! People will be looking for you, Edgar Mail said, already knowing. It was always understood that Warren Finch's life was lived in danger. He was simply a wanted man. Everyone wanted a part of him. To put it mildly he was a saviour, and we know what happens to saviours. Threats were continuously being made on his life. This time, the threats were so serious, he was advised to think about his future security by old untrustworthy, O.K. Corral Horse Ryder, if he wanted to stay alive. Yet Warren and his men believed that this was simply how he had to live. In their world, it was hard to know what was sound advice, or what contained a threat, or what was just someone crapping on in their mind. It could not have been any different, and Warren relished each challenge, where he would constantly be dealing with trouble, and out-smarting anyone in the world who wanted to take a shot at him. It was these threats to his life that became the reason, the *modus operandi* for Warren's elusiveness, where nobody really knew or understood where he was. He led people into believing what he wanted them to believe. So routinely exercised was this art of illusion in fact, in a puff of the genies' smoky haze, Warren Finch could will himself to be anywhere in the world, instantly in flight to another country, instantly appearing in another part of the continent, or regularly popping up on the television all over the place, while all the time, it was assumed that he was still living normally, like other people. His artfulness in disappearing and reappearing was so strange, that as the swamp people had believed he was somewhere else, he could still make you feel that you had never seen him – that he was never there at all. This was why they were out on the genies' country. A bushland so vast in its sameness, that only the traditional owner could read the subtle stories of its contours. This was where they always took Warren to work out strategies to fend off the latest round of would be assassins.

Let them wait. I am having a break. Want a bit of time to think things through.

Warren kept a lot of the information he had received to himself. Business. Policy. His security. The seriousness of new threats to his life. It concerned him after all. He would deal with the waiting game for others to strike first. Keep punching – just like he had told the girl.

Stay as long as you want, Edgar agreed. *You are in charge. But you better keep it in mind that the longer you are away, the more difficult it is going to be to take control when you get back.*

Nothing to worry about, Warren said. *There is nothing they can do without me. I am not even back in the country as far as anyone knows.*

I am just saying there are things happening in the country right now, Mail warned. *Might do better with your presence, that's all.*

I know that, Warren said in a tone of voice that made it clear that he did not want to be reminded of having other responsibilities: *What we are doing here. Finding out what is going on in the country. This is more important right now.*

The genies smiled and continued relaxing on the ground next to the fire well into the night, drinking tea, their eyes upwards, searching the star world. Nothing Warren said was of any consequence to them. His fingers rang up and down the girl's hand while she froze for what felt like a dead man touching her, and he thought of his own death march to the grave. The onset of owls screeching aroused quiet academic discussion which grew into an argument about a single pitch once heard, the purest of sounds, and whether this was an owl signalling its territory, or something else altogether – a voice from the spirit country.

Edgar Mail took the violin out of its case. He tuned it slowly as his fingers worked on the yellow wood instrument shining from the light of the fire. It softly responded to his touch while he listened, until suddenly, he began playing the melancholy tune of owls calling through the stillness of night. The music created ripples in the rhythm of the owl calls as he replied to their sound with his own composition. Near and far, the owls replied. The music was theirs. Edgar was almost in a trance as he walked around the camp with his violin and drifted away into the darkness of the surrounding spinifex with rats parting in haste to create a path, and his music calling and responding to the instructions of the owls.

He was playing like the old powerful chants of bringing up the country. Law music. The music was unearthly, but belonged to this land in the same way as the chanting of ancient songs and the sound of clap sticks beating through the night. The music now contained joyfulness, sometimes dropping suddenly into a barely audible lullaby, then out of this calm, it would suddenly grow again in pitch and rhythm until another and another crescendo was reached. Finally and abruptly, Edgar stopped playing, too exhausted to continue. He would have to remember the music. He said what they had listened to was the beginning of the first movement of music to grass owls in D flat major.

The nights in this windy landscape were spent with the law spirits who were travelling the country to scrutinise the marriage of plagues – keeping the balance where insects, rodents, snakes and owls were breeding. Warren Finch wanted the ancestral world to create the balance in his marriage. He whispered into her ear that this was the way he wanted the land to see them. Oblivia moved away as though he was already a ghost. She saw the infestations of the day were still exactly the same at night. She was back in the tree in her mind. Safe there. Worse than ever: scribbling that silent language in the air. In truth, Warren was becoming convinced that for whatever reason he had taken the girl in the first place, it was not going to work. Even the act of consummating it seemed a waste of time. When he looked at her all he saw was a child. You can't have sex – make love with a kid. She was scared stiff of the sight of him. Terrified when he touched her. His face, to her, was contorted with death. That was how she dreamed at night beside him. He saw clearly that it was beyond his power to change her, but by morning he would see the day afresh as a challenge to be met to make his marriage work, just like he tried to make everything else work, whatever the challenge, because to him, that was what life was all about.

He kept reminding her that they would become friends. *In the end you will trust me.* That he should succeed in gaining her trust was important to him. The first goal he wanted to achieve. She was his last real link to a world he had severed, the attachment he had planned to keep. Sometimes she thought he was right. She would trust him.

During the day whatever else he thought, he kept his distance, walking behind, always speaking to someone on the mobile phone. He knew that she had overheard some of these conversations. He said that these were just people he loved. People that he trusted. He depended on them for their safety. *Yours too now,* he added.

Warren Finch did not sleep at night. In fact, the death dream returned the moment he dozed off on this country. He lay awake with their future – his future – weighing heavily on his mind. He had decisions to make, and he wondered whether it was worth taking the risk of continuing his political life. His death seemed to be the only future from it, and he kept revisiting the scene of being led to his grave.

Could he bring her into that world? He tossed the question over and over, although he knew that it was not a safe decision to take her any further. She would need a lot of looking after that was for sure. He tried to push aside any imagining of what his life would be like with her. Couldn't form a vision of it. Somehow, thinking about the future did not seem to make any sense as the night wore on. He was more familiar with having a rough ride in politics and doing it alone. Never thought about his own personal future before. Just the country's future. It was his speciality. The only dream he felt that he could make real. This was the best way he knew of dealing with his enemies. As though making enemies was his life. He looked at Oblivia pretending to be asleep. Wondered how much longer he could stay, but confirmed in his own mind, that until he knew where the new threats were coming from, he would keep stalling his return. There were government security people on to it. They kept updating him. Getting closer, he had been told. He only trusted his own bodyguards: Hart, Doom, and Mail. They had been close for years. If they thought his life was in so much danger, so be it. They had agreed: *We will take as long as it takes to deal with it.*

Tomorrow they would be out of this death country, and it couldn't be quick enough. But what to do about her? It almost did not matter to him which way the wind blew. He was always ready to fall. Yet he knew she would not be able to take the blows, although she had given him a few, and continued to lie awake until dawn, knowing he would have to do something about it. She would struggle. For the first time in his life he had to admit that he really felt jinxed.

The vehicle was left far behind covered with spinifex, where it melted into the landscape on the edge of the salt lake country through which they were travelling. The whole country could burn behind them if disaster struck, but the genies were not interested. They were born and raised on the land and they knew how to walk in it.

Don't look back, Edgar Mail said, surprising the girl as he whispered into her ear. *We wouldn't want to see you being turned into a pillar of salt.*

In the days that followed, they continued travelling further across the white sea. The defining landmarks of this salt lake country were small crags that jutted out here and there in the salt. These were the possession of spirit guardians travelling on a journey far away to important story places. The salt crust broke underneath them with each footstep. There was even more solitude in this place than in the spinifex country they had just left behind. They felt the presence of the enormous white glistening body that contained the quietness of a resting serpent spirit fellow who was listening deeply to hear even an insect perching on its skin, come there to recite its song. The landing of butterflies. The feet of a lizard pounding on crystals of salt.

There were battalions of stink beetles crawling over each other and the salt. Plague grasshoppers jumped away at the coming of strangers. Moth storms swept across the lake. Crimson and orange chats whistled from the heath of spinifex, pittosporums, mulga and eremophila scrubs growing along the sides of the lake. The girl saw green twisting clouds of budgerigars crossing their paths at various times throughout the day. Up high, harriers and kites cried out as they glided in the thermals. To look back was to see fine salt crystals dusting over their tracks as little storms of salty filaments gurgled about in the desert air.

That was during the day. The salt glowed at night, and the body of the lake moved differently when the ancestral winds lowered themselves from the skies and whistled eerily across its surface. The night spoke in dreams which took the wandering thinker far below the surface, to be jostled in a spirit sea populated with the salt-encrusted bodies of millions of grasshoppers, shoals of tiny fish bones, brine shrimps, larval fish like splinters of glass, colourless moths, seeds and stalks; grotesque bloated grunters, bony herrings, frogs, tadpoles and water birds that had perished in the increasingly saline waters, and been entombed when the water evaporated.

The girl dreamt of swans, chaotically misshapen creatures frozen in death that were forcing their spirits through films of salt to reach her during the night. Had they come searching for truth, but found encasement? She awoke from dreams where her fingers were red raw from trying to peel away the salt to straighten the pinion feathers of the swans and let them fly.

They passed through old times, coming through hillock after hillock covered in spinifex, of Country that had a serious Law story for every place, and of everything belonging to that place like family. The genies kept calling the names of these places which were thousands of years old, and which joined the Law stories of naming, titles of belonging, maps of exclusiveness that ran like this, throughout the continent. Oblivia kept quiet. Listened to the names. Tried not to think in case the spirits heard her and dragged her into their realm. She would not die on this country.

While the genies were drifting even further back into ancient times with their name calling, Warren Finch was making the equivalent leap into the future, and impatient to get a move on and back to his job of bloody well running the country, he told the genies to speed it up. They were getting out of here. Before the bloody country got fucked up good and proper by Horse. *That cunt of a man. Can't turn your back on him for a second.* The genies looked concerned, but not overly bothered, having seen it all before, on other occasions when they had to get him out of a jam. Tops! They might make him last another few days out in the bush. Yep! The boss! Too right! Power crawled like a pack of cut snakes through his body. He was an addict to it. Addiction? They knew he wouldn't last long. Couldn't. They had seen the man explode if he was not in control. They knew that what was left for him was time. But, like the man said, he had work to do, and everyone knew how toey Warren could be if he didn't get a fix from being in charge, and feel the power surging through his blood. He would chase it down anywhere. Do anything to assert power. *Why couldn't he just chase that girl around a bit more? Crazy thing had his measure already.* Warren always thought it was a waste of time to hold up the entire country just for the sake of a few people getting in his way. Well! Bring it on. He knew it. They knew it. Impatience was a fact of life. Yep! Everything will be fine. *I will be fine. The girl will be fine.* He convinced himself of it. *She would grow up. Why wouldn't she? What else could she do?* He was bored of marriage already.

Doom, Mail and Hart understood the deal: they could only hold him up for as long as they could possibly get away with it. Already he had imbued every molecule of air with the stench of Horse Ryder. Rah! Rah! Rah! Can't keep still for a minute. *Can't stop talking about Horse Ryder.* But, even they thought he would maintain some interest in the girl he had taken. His keepsake. This little challenge he had set himself – a promise wife. They knew the threats on his life were real this time. *Why can't he take it seriously instead of worrying about what Horse is doing?* The girl saw an endless journey ahead in an unchanging landscape that they would continue walking forever. Just like ghosts! Perhaps they had already crossed over into that world. Would she escape? Do ghosts escape?

A day passed of counting the fluffy fledglings transforming into orange wash and white feathers that were hidden in the grasslands by the shores of saltpans while waiting to fly. The country was consuming the girl's memory. She could not carry the past and had to let some of it go. A few of her old messages to her swans had returned from places that no longer existed – address unknown. The Harbour Master had come along and saw the burden she was carrying, and for a while, he walked beside her while trying to persuade her to give up some of her treasured nightmares. He sat around in the salt sorting out which thoughts should stay, which should go, telling her off for sending away anything he thought was really valuable. He was the kingmaker of policy too. *You always need a few of those bad thoughts to chuck around.* He kept telling her how he could not stand the sight of Warren Finch. *Look at him. Stalking along. Planning and scheming some other stupid thing – probably how he is going to kill you off since he is sorry he bothered with someone like you in the first place?* And the genies? *Mate! I know a ghost from the Middle East when I see one.*

Maybe you are from the Middle East yourself, the girl growled and walked away from the Harbour Master who was piling up her thoughts into salt columns of what was to be kept, and what cut loose.

This is not all we do, Doom said, feeling that he ought to prepare the girl for their departure – once the owls left the desert after the rats perished in these hottest months.

There was a shop he owned, he said, in the city where she would live. She did not understand what he meant. *Cities are where people die.* That was what old Aunty always said about cities. *Illness places. You will be arrested for being a terrorist.* She wondered about what he said, and thought: *But I like it here now.* He looked at her sadly. *You could ask Warren about the city.* Could she ask him what would happen to her? Why would she do that? Speak! *To terrorists from the city?* The salt lands now became unreliable, temporary in her mind. *I specialise in many things. Birds. People. Books. I am not always there. Travel with the boss a lot. Love to spend time at the shop though,* Doom said.

He explained that he, Edgar and Snip were all involved in specialist trade and had the most beautiful shop in the city. It was the place where you could feel the country: *This place. I made a place in the city to hold my heart. Like this place.* He said that they sold birds, old butterflies from all over the world, exhibited rare eggs and feathers, bird books, snake books, musical instruments, traditional maps of routes and footpaths, maps for following foxes and bees, old instruments for finding dreams, stars, or fossils. This was the place to seek professional advice on cultural law, societies, myths and almost anything anyone needed to know of the human condition from Edgar, Snip or him – *the filler of ears, the purveyors of information.*

She was to learn that Snip loved nothing more than selling his customers gadgets to find stars, and that Edgar Mail specialised in selling old sheet music he had collected from elderly men and women in the inner laneways of ancient cities. He also recorded and spent tireless hours publishing the music from these works. His own music was printed on the old printing press in this shop. They believed in their enterprise. *Our customers are people seeking knowledge about the world. Mostly from the Middle East, Europe and Asia. Australians? Not too many. We are specialists you know. You will probably want to visit us from time to time.*

Oblivia tried to anchor these new pictures of the genies in her mind, but she had no idea of how to hold the details of what she had never seen. Their words died as soon as they were spoken and buried in her mind. She squinted in the sun, had to blink to see what lay ahead in the endless story of yellow lofty crags in salt lakes, owls, rats, snakes, when she saw a speck in the horizon of blue skies. Yellow! White! Blue! Black!

A Lake of White Water

A lake of white water, not a mirage, lay far ahead. This was where she saw the swans. Black wings swirled down from the clear blue skies to skid across the water. The girl thought it was her dreams catching up with her, coming back in the daytime. She needed to run to see if these were her swans but knew not to, to watch from a distance the swans gliding on the white water, *while I glide swanlike...I glide and glide.* From the sides of her eyes she saw the hurdles. Warren Finch would see she had not forgotten the swamp. She never knew how the genies would react.

Questions surfacing in her mind about leaving ran from the girl, and disappeared into the vista of the white sea. She felt homesick, a terrible yearning to go home. She ran towards the swamp that wasn't there. The swans saw her coming over the salt, and before she had a chance to come anywhere in reach, they snapped loose her spirit from theirs, and took to the air. She watched until they were out of sight, flying further ahead, in a south-easterly direction.

Warren watched her run. *Sure! Sure! I'll be there.* He spoke loudly into his mobile phone. *I am ready. Let's do it.* His words caught her, ran along the surface of her arms as she ran, and as though a net he threw had unfurled over her, she realised in this moment, that she was attached to him. She would never escape, even if she ran forever from a world that had fallen apart.

Doom tried to console the girl about the swans flying away. *They were not your swans. They are free birds.* They belong somewhere else. She felt residues of bad luck lurking inside of his voice. It was his bad luck that the swans had sensed, why they had flown. Around their feet, a little breeze picked up grains of salt with dead grass and carried these along, signalling the owls to start their retreat, back towards the east coast for the summer. *Most would not reach their destination,* Doom said sadly. *So much work done for nothing. Why breed?* He knew that they would all be gone that night.

Hare stew.

Meal fit for kings. And a queen. Eat before the lizards steal it.

The Milky Way lit the landscape, and Snip took the girl away from the campfire to give her a lesson about the night sky. *I think you will like it. There is something pretty special up there tonight.* She had learned a lot about the alignment of the planets from him. The genies often pointed to the path in the west where Venus would fall earlier each night, until in the winter nights it was Mars that was the first to fall. *Remember! Winter rains will fall on this land, and in the middle of the night, a cloud of mist will descend to touch the earth.*

Remember to come back here, Snip said, as they stood on a hill, staring at the sky.

The thought of returning seemed unlikely. She could not imagine how it would be possible.

These are the methods of positioning yourself for finding South, he said, explaining that they were in the galaxy of the Milky Way that rose like smoke from the horizon until its river of stars ran directly above them. Their light rebounded off the salt and it was this phenomenon that seemed to make the stars shine more brightly. He showed her how to position where she was by drawing a line through the Southern Cross and joining it to a line drawn to the halfway point from The Pointers. *This will form a V for you, and from there, if you draw a line down to the horizon, you will know where to find South.* Or another way, he explained, was by forming the same triangle by drawing an imaginary line down from the brightest star in the sky, *Canopus*, and across from the star *Achernar* which sits low in the southern sky.

However, this is not what I really want to show you, he said, taking her hand, and pointing her fingers along with his into the northern world of the sky, he drew along the stars the outline of a swan in full flight.

Do you see it?

She nodded, seeing the swan's long head arching down towards earth.

That is the constellation of Cygnus, the Swan. The star of its tail is a supergiant named Deneb. Look for it up along the Milky Way. If you can find it in the sky, you will be able to follow it North, until the weather becomes warm again.

She continued looking at the swan's changing position, wondering how she would remember to find it again.

Don't always look in the same place. He will move across the sky. Remember you will only see Cygnus at the onset of winter. Just like your swans I imagine.

In the darkness with a dying fire, they waited for the final moment when the earth opened the spinifex grassland abodes and the hands of the spiritual ancestors released the owls like pollen into the skies. The swooping waves of owls flew over their heads, the young travelling eastwards with their parents in a colony of thousands.

Men may do the same one day if they fear too much. Imagine it. Imagine a dust cloud travelling right through this country. Snip's voice was almost a whisper, and in that moment, the clouds heralding the cool change appeared from the east, travelling in a westerly direction.

While the girl and Warren slept, the genies were searching for a few stray owlets in the spinifex. Doom said there had to be one or two that had not fledged. He promised one for Oblivia to keep as a pet. *In the morning I will have one for you,* he said. She thought of this owl while sleeping in a low-lying valley filled with white flowering lilies that shone in the starlight breaking through the clouds.

But the valley became a box when clouds settled on the hills, and very quickly it was filled with an overpowering perfume pouring into the air from thousands of flowers. Sometime during the night her lungs ached for fresh air, and this was when she heard Warren moving away. Very silently, he was slipping away into the night, but she thought it was already morning and they would be going back to join the others.

Shh! he said, and left. Her tongue failed to form words to ask him where he was going, and she watched him walking further away into the night. He did not return, and she was unable to prevent herself from falling back to sleep as the heavy putrefied air swallowed her into a nightmarish dream. Those boys from long ago emerged from the ground. It had happened suddenly with the ground swelling and growing around her until she was covered in total darkness, but she knew them instantly, knew what they were doing – she had not killed them in her memory. She remembered their closeness to each other, in touch, smell, and breathing. Of being joined together with them as firmly as a ball of animals rolling over wet ground. She saw through them as they were falling in, over, above, coming through her in sepia-coloured waves of brown, grey and red. They rolled in desert wind over the surface of the land, and down the green and yellowing spinifex smothering the hillocks that rose and fell into valleys of lily-coloured skin, and over the distances of salt marshes.

The landscape had closed over with mist, and the perfume of the lilies under the mist was suffocating even the flowers. Her arms and hands pushed at the fumes but she was unable to reach fresh air higher up, and succumbing to the intoxication, she crawled away towards her memory of the tree. She reaches the tree in this state, and falls back into the safe darkness to hide. From the shadows of her dream she sees the swans lifting off again from white water, pushed upwards by vaporised hands reaching out of the lake. They have been rejected, pushed away by the country from her outstretched arms.

She was coiled inside the tree in a dream, and when she woke, she could see the valley surrounded by hillocks decked by clouds.

Better get ready. We will be leaving soon. Warren spoke slowly but firmly, as if to a child, and the way he watched her, she thought he had been in her dream. She felt violated by the way he continued to stare at her with his eyes moving over her. Perhaps he had watched. It seemed that he knew what had happened. Perhaps it had not been a dream. *You better eat something first,* he said, handing her a piece of damper.

She ate the brown bread that was made from seeds and bulbs. It had a sour bitter taste under the salt that had been added to the dough before it went into the ashes. *Take your time,* he said, after noticing how she was struggling to swallow each piece. She washed the lumps down quickly with cold tea. She watched him doing the same. They left empty-handed. Whatever had been brought in with them, the pannikins, swags, simple things like the tin billy, were left behind.

Soft light filled the lily plains with William Blake hues in the first light, which was like looking at the living museum of another time surviving in the arid landscape. Warren told her that some people saw these flowers as a fragment of life from another era, when there might have been a different language that once described the wetlands and rainforest in the heart of the country, before it disappeared. *This living fossil was all that was left of those times,* he explained. She knew it was a ghost place. Closer to the eye, groups of pale green, firm fluid-filled stemmed flowering plants luxuriating in their freshness opened their petals. Each stem had stormed through to the surface from a large swollen bulb that grew at least a metre deep in the red soil. This garden of lilies rose to the surface he explained, only if water lay long enough to soak through this dip in the landscape after heavy rain. The flowers open. She thinks the petals are like the wings of old Aunty's white swans. He asks her if she is all right. She nods. She can look after herself.

Warren Finch and the girl walked through hills, the ones that were called the great bodies of the spirit men moving through the land. *What about the others?* she tried but failed to ask Warren as she kept looking back to where the genies had been camping.

They have other things to do. We will see them later, he replied simply and to the point, no differently than how he normally spoke to her. He looked as though he had aged, grown old on this trip. She kept thinking something was not right, that something had happened to them, and she kept looking back with growing concern as the distance grew greater. But only the old voices of Aunty talking to the Harbour Master could be heard coming from behind her, through the sound of the ground breathing, casually talking behind Warren Finch's back. The Harbour Master said he was pretty sure the genies never existed. He had never recognised them as real people. They had come out of a brass lantern from the Middle East as far as he was concerned. The old woman crowed on about the men on the boats she had seen murdering each other out of rivalry and jealousy over women. *Oh! Yes! I saw it all. All the time you know. Did you cause this?* The old woman was talking loudly, starting to accuse Warren of every travesty, until she got around to what she really wanted to say, *you killed those nice boys*, and the girl looked away from Warren who was telling her to keep moving, because she was thinking that he had murdered the genies too. The Harbour Master became silent because the old dead woman's ghost was putting things in the girl's mind about Warren Finch. *Girls were always thrown overboard – I told you about that. Girls were left to die in the bush. You know the public payphone really only rang sometimes…Unwept girls, all killed by their husbands.*

The Harbour Master turned controversial, snubbing Bella Donna's ghost, which was raving on like a mad woman about how the Aboriginal killer husband Warren Finch would end up killing Oblivia too, *because he was already proving his true colours by killing the genies*. The Harbour Master swung away from the old woman's spirit every time she came close to him, calling her, *Liar. What you think all Aboriginal men are violent or something?* He poked his bony face in Oblivia's while walking backwards in front of her as she walked ahead of Warren Finch. In the end, the Harbour Master spurted out everything in his head through hissy spit: *You know something? Warren Finch only saw Doom, Mail and Hart, dead on the ground. He didn't kill them.* He makes a fist with his hand and with the index finger pointing from it like a pistol, he waves his arm around in the air, while calling over his shoulder to the old woman raving behind him to shut the fuck up about Warren Finch and warning her to stay away from them, and walking backwards quicker to stay in front of Oblivia's face he releases more spit-hissed words, and on he goes: *They were killed instantly – BANG! BANG! BANG! No mucking around. Just smack, smack, one shot each was enough.*

Knocked their lights straight out (clicks fingers) – *knocks them flat in their sleep.* Oblivia was really frightened now. She stared ahead and walked even faster as though she thought the only way to stop hearing the Harbour Master was to walk through his frightening face, and all the while she was looking around for old Aunty and old Aunty was calling from somewhere behind, *wait for me*, and all the while trying to convince herself to ignore the healing man's powers, for that's right, no man would take over her mind. But the old Harbour Master was relentless and was using his bony fingers to jab her in the chest, and on and on he went in his tirade about the deaths he witnessed – while telling the old woman to *git out of their country*, that nobody else saw what happened, not even that idiot-features Warren bloody Finch. *You want to know who did it? Not that gutless wonder Warren – he didn't do it – look at him? There's no way in the world that a slack-assed cunt like him could kill face-to-face. He gets other people to do his dirty work. You want to know what I saw? A mob of assassins who killed them! All of them came running, hooded, and disguised in Army fatigues through the scrub but I saw them.*

Oblivia looks side-on across the haze-covered spinifex as though she fully expected to see soldiers from the swamp following them, but all she sees through the *wiyarr* is Bella Donna's ghost straining to drag things out of the ground and calling for them to wait for her, and Oblivia thinks she must be digging up the genies, or she found some dead girls, and this makes her heart pound even harder and she walks faster and hears the old woman's voice reciting – *So mastered by the brute blood of the air...Before the indifferent beak could let her drop?* – and she tries to walk through the Harbour Master who looks where she looks, and he walks backwards quicker, but ignores what the old woman was doing and he continues talking right into Oblivia's face as though he is taunting her to use that half-dead tongue of hers to shout at him to get out of her way. *There must have been dozens of those blokes running amuck with their revolvers with silencers and whatnot, and sneaking through the spinifex with infra-red search-lights strapped onto their heads. Like combat soldiers. Yes, just like soldiers in some war zone, although who knows if they were soldiers or not – I just don't know for sure what they were, or if they were from the whiteman's hell. Could've been from the swamp. They could have been anyone, just like you or me, or more like me than you because you would be too gutless to kill anyone, just like you are too gutless to speak. Alright then! They didn't know 'someone' was looking at them through the darkness with my own infra-red night-vision binoculars eyes.*

Oblivia thinks he is tricking her and tries not to look at his eyes and continues to look around for Army men, although she cannot hear the old woman any more who she figures must be still trying to dig up bodies, but the Harbour Master goes on about how good his infra-red vision eyes were. *I saw the whole thing coming, just like silly Warren knew it was coming, only difference is a person like me can dream wherever I want to go, whereas Warren Finch, he's a dog! Well! Look at him. He has to call someone on that mobile of his to tell him what's going on and he hides somewhere else.* The Harbour Master paused to pay his respects to the genies, *I really and truly hope you good boys haunt the living daylights out of some of those buggers. Come back and haunt Warren Finch too if you like. Yea! That would be good.* And he continues berating Oblivia, *That's the reason why your-suppose-to-be-husband Warren bloody Finch was acting strange last night. I saw him sneaking around in the night too. He knew there were people wanting to assassinate him. He heard their vehicles. You better lay low, I am telling you girl, if you are going to keep hanging around with that idiot. He will get you killed before too long. You can bet on that. That's why you will never see those good fellas again. Really decent blokes too they were.* Oblivia was listening now and walking normally, so the Harbour Master slowed down, but continued talking, and whenever he spoke about Warren, pouted his lips in his direction. *The coward Warren disposes of the bodies quick smart. Buried his staff members in the bush. Hardly dug a hole deep enough for any of them. You would think he'd do something better for his mates. Shallow graves. Real shallow. Better get a rifle too if I were you. You are just another staff member. Remember that.* The Harbour Master blamed Bella Donna's ghost for killing the genies. He really had it in for her. *You know how she needs to kill off any strong black people. It gives her strength,* he claimed. *Yulurri! Murderer! Yulurri! She led the assassins right up to them like a bloody big road train heading through the bush with an arrowhead marking the spot just in the front of where those three boys were sleeping. Didn't know what struck them, it was strange seeing it happen – real quick like that. You don't want to think about her any more if she is going to cause trouble like this. Get rid of her from your mind. You don't need her now.* The Harbour Master looks back, and although the old woman's ghost was nowhere in sight, he tells her to git away from them. *Get away from Australia. Yulurri! We don't want you overseas ghosts here.*

At the end of the day of walking and the Harbour Master's tirade to Oblivia, they reached a sandy river overgrown with the vines of paddy melons laden with fresh yellow balls of fruit. A flock of white corellas stared with black beady eyes as Warren Finch and the girl passed by, then continued gnawing with sharp pointy beaks on the paddy melons held in their claws. Families of bush ducks flew from out of the reeds on the side of a dry riverbed, where there were still ponds of water from the flood after the rains of months ago.

Across the river the next morning, Oblivia was alarmed to see that there was a small rural township of less then a dozen unkempt houses painted in every combination of bright primary colours, flash blue, red, green, and yellow. All was quiet, and it seemed as though these houses had been willed to appear like a playful whim in amongst the spinifex, and if you turned your back, would disappear. Oblivia saw that they were close to the roughly cut airstrip that ran through the thickets of saltbush where, the evening before, Warren had taken an interest in walking along its length and kicking the dirt runway with his feet. She noticed that he did not use his mobile phone now, and this made her feel even more vulnerable, unsure of what was going to happen to her, and of the possibility they would be seen by strangers in this town without his genies to guard them.

She could not help staring at the houses.

Just people, Warren snapped, as though he knew she was wondering about who lived there.

What kind of people? People. People, who are more interested in talking to their white daddy and granddaddy graves about selling cattle, horses, or people for that matter; they work at the petrol and diesel service station over there. Mostly used by cattle trucks. He spoke impatiently as though speaking to a child. She knew that he did not want to speak to her. Did not want to answer questions. The town was silent. It looked deserted.

In the distant mirage beyond the houses, Oblivia saw the green and white service station. The sight of the green roof became a thought to reach, not of running away, but taking back her life. He knew her thought as she looked off in the distance, and said: *It won't pay to go over there. You will find that this is a pretty rough joint. We will wait here. The plane won't be long.* His mobile phone rang once, twice, and three times before he answered it. *Yep! Right!* He seemed relieved to be leaving. She could hear him talking about the plane's arrival time and then the droning off in the distance. She listened to the sky too – for the heartbeat of swans flying, and for a few moments of panic, caused by the thought of being forcibly pushed onto the plane by Warren, she was again standing on the shores of the empty salt lake. Only the warmth of the swans remained where they had rested on the ground covered with low-growing tussock grass and saltbush.

Within moments of the blue aeroplane landing they were gone. Only the deafening howl of the engine could be heard as it flew above the saltbush landscape, over the salt lakes, and into another world. There was nothing but clouds, and the frightened girl thought how the clouds would look around the mountaintop of the old woman's homeland, and thought she should have asked the old woman a question about clouds, because she did not know: *Who spoke of great seas of clouds where wind was eddying under the crevices?*

The Christmas House

After clouds, always mist, and another ghost story to tell.

Ah! Beautiful, isn't it. This is where we will be living from now on. Well! For you this will be your home for a little while at least. Look! Right down there, can you see it? Just there! That place! It will be your home from now on. Warren Finch sighed, his face marvellously at ease as he looked longingly through the small window of the plane. Below, the city she saw was a sea of stars twinkling from the base of mountains, and sprawling across flatlands to the ocean. The plane flew through dozens of searchlights splashing back and forth through the skies, and on to Warren's relaxed face while he was humming that old song, *Sea of Heartbreak, sea of dungkumini, malu of heartbreak...the lights in the harbour, don't shine for me*, and the relief was in his voice: *Yes! It is good to be home.*

There was no way Oblivia ever expected that she of all people would see the riches of paradise from a plane. *How come?* She thought about the Heaven people taken from the cities by the Army and dumped in the swamp. They prayed all the time for the chance to see their paradise again, *How did I lose you, where did I fail?* The lights he called home spun meaninglessly in her head. She searched for the distant light of the burial chamber he had pointed out, to show her where she would be living and from the sea of lights below, all she extracted was a single glow. She looked away to censure the old woman creeping from the clouds and into her head, forbidding her from asking the question about women and girls who have disappeared: *Can you see any left dead on the side of a road in that light?*

Ah! Don't worry, you are dead already, the Harbour Master answered on the girl's behalf. He was also somewhere on board the plane – said he was the bloody pilot. *That's right,* he laughed, *better remember to put the wheels down. Who was to know if she was dead or alive?* The plane bounced on the winds of *one pilot short,* in its descent to land.

Warren kept talking: *You are going to love it here. You'll see. It will take a little bit of time but it will be better for us if you give it a chance.* He spoke philosophically, *so it is equally important that you make an effort to do this for me and for yourself. You will find that life will be better if you see things like this.*

They stepped from the aircraft and into a world shrouded in fog and darkness. Warren Finch was immediately surrounded by a group of security people, and within moments, they were leaving in a shining black, chauffeur-driven limousine with a small Australian flag fluttering in the breeze. Several security cars, that had been discreetly parked, would also accompany them for the rest of their journey.

The limousine careered through a foggy maze of concrete industrial buildings, high-rise offices, factories and houses. In this closer glimpse of paradise, the girl could see that much of the city had cracked; the city was breaking up, as though the land beneath had collapsed under its weight. This had happened a long time ago and now, the natural landscape was quietly returning and reclaiming its original habitat. In its strange kind of way, the city was creating a garden. Through the cracks in the footpaths small trees had sprouted, and ferns and grasses became obstacles through which people were struggling to steer a clear path as they walked. She saw more mature trees with the orange fungi *Pycnoporus coccineus* growing from branches and tree-trunks, while ferns and grasses that swayed from mossy walls and roof tops caught her attention with each gust of wind. There were places on the roads not hit by heavy traffic where long grasses grew.

She saw no camp dogs hanging about these streets. No birds. There were only crowds of people moving quickly past one another with blank faces, and many others living in footpath ghettos, like people were in the swamp. They were begging for food. She heard frogs croaking in the drains where the rainwater poured in such profusion it was hard not to imagine an underground river flowing beneath the city.

Warren continued a running commentary like a tour guide. He spoke about why people were running, what they were doing, whether they went into restaurants, grocers, supermarkets, fish shops, meat shops, women's clothing shops of every description, shoes, pets, computers, furnishing, delicatessens, banks, office buildings that stood side by side reaching for the skies, down and up through narrow streets and onwards, while countless lights shone from the homes of families, single people, couples, and apartments where parties were held, and couples made homes, made love, grew children, cooked food or brought home takeaways, and new furniture, and spent all night discussing life or conspiring, or deceiving, or divorcing, or engaging in adultery, throwing out rubbish, playing computer games about war. He talked more or less about all of this while the girl was thinking about something else. She was trying to determine the natural sound of the wind through the distortion of sounds passing through the laneways between buildings.

The Christmas house of prehistoric green was lit up like the solar system. It stood in a garden of worse-for-wear Norwegian fairytale forest firs covered in glowing balls of coloured lights that swung madly on the wind-tossed branches. Owls were calling out to one another from the deep foliage like calls from the genies they had left on the salt lake. The girl looked at Warren but he was too occupied with the spectacle of Christmas lights, and what lay ahead. The journey they had taken was now clearly wiped clean from his mind. The first thing she noticed as they stepped from the car was the fragrance of the trees clutching the mist, and the house groaning in despair each time it was buffeted by winds coming in from the sea.

The Harbour Master and the old woman exiled amongst the clouds were both awestruck with the glamour of it all. Could this be the home that Warren had been pointing to from the plane? *It's bloody marvellous* the Harbour Master claimed, but the old woman scoffed at its cheap imitations, and described how pretensions made her feel nauseous by pretending to vomit on the bonnet of the shiny car.

The driveway was lined on either side by a parade of adult-size glowing snowmen. The people greeting them enthusiastically at the large door shone in the way that people usually greeted Warren Finch. He said they were his anonymous friends. This was a safe house, which immediately had the Harbour Master asking what he needed a safe house for. But before the girl could think of an answer, she became too wrapped up in being ashamed, and looked away. All she had seen looming at the doorway were giant-sized people with red hair blowing like fire in each gust of wind. They were not introduced. The man, the woman, and two children, one boy and one girl, became an avalanche of fiery white ghosts flying out of the house, and descended on Warren with non-stop pattering.

Don't tell me this is your E–thyl? Is this really her? The big woman squealed.

This was a safe house because it was typical, Warren had forewarned Oblivia. *Typical of what? Australia! Paradise?* Even she could believe it was a place that nobody of right mind would want to come to and she had been nowhere. Old Aunty squealed like the big woman. The Harbour Master pushed his way in front of them and yelled to the girl to keep away from the bunch of red-necks. This had the old woman and the Harbour Master arguing about how you could identify a red-neck. She insisted that they were only missionaries. *I know what a missionary looks like,* he claimed combatively: *How would you know anything? You think every white person is a missionary.* The girl wanted to disappear from hearing her name falling off everyone's lips. *Yes! It was true then?* They had been talking about her for days, practising that name, because they did not want to offend Warren's lady. *Why, she will be the first Indigenous lady of the country soon.*

E-thyl was a very pretty name the lady claimed, and said she insisted on knowing how she had been given such a name. *You sure you got it right? You sure it is not Ethel? That's a girl's name. I don't know where you get a name like E-thyl. Was it Aboriginal?*

The girl was covered in goose bumps every time she heard the name. She hated the name. Wondered where it had come from too and would have preferred to be called nothing, like normal. The girl wore filthy clothes – the ones that she had on when they left the swamp. Warren laughed at everything the red-haired people said. He had not stopped laughing since he had arrived. Should she laugh too?

She felt thinner and darker than normal people while standing next to this strange family that she thought were the typical Australian family, because Warren said so. And beside their snowy whiteness, she felt an out of place darkness, much darker than Warren even whose golden skin glowed in the soft yellow lights of the house. The more she saw, the more in awe she was of how white

Australians lived. Unconsciously, she edged herself up against the wall to keep out of the way of the endless movement of these big people scrambling and gushing with every footstep in welcoming Warren back into their home.

Hold on now! I have only been gone a few weeks, he joked and laughed loudly, and even the girl was surprised to see him competing to be more extraordinary in a plain, simple laugh. The din of laughter echoing throughout the house was deafening for someone who never laughed. She thought *Why laugh?* How do you laugh? To say continuously, *Ha! Ha!*

Oh! Boy! Our Warren, the woman and her husband beamed in satisfaction, and together they raced through the dark echoing wood-panelled house to see the Christmas decorations in the backyard, while calling back for the girl to follow.

Come on. You got to have a look, Eee-ah? Come on. It's better than last year even. Now Warren was speaking like these people, even forgetting how to pronounce her name. *What's wrong with you? Get going. You think that they are contagious or something? Might turn you white?* A voice that sounded like the Harbour Master echoed in her head.

The large garden was a forest of full-grown pine trees decorated with coloured lights. It stretched all the way to the edge of a rocky cliff where waves crashed, but the red-haired lady said it was a good thing they had planted the trees to muffle the sound of the ocean, *because you get sick of it roaring day and night. It was enough to give you a headache.* Underneath the dripping canopies of the trees a single seagull was lost somewhere in the needles, singing its airs to the seagulls gliding far away, over the sea.

The family ran breathless along curving paths, brushed against the wet foliage of the trees, and deep in the forest were greeted with Christmas carols sung by a glowing metre-high smiling robot snowman with a red carrot nose, and black top hat. *It's an extravaganza – a miracle,* Warren exclaimed, saying that he had never seen anything like it in his life. *It was first prize mind you, in the whole of the city,* the children and their mother said proudly.

Warren looked on warmly, his face flushed and glowing as the soft lights touched his skin. He said it reminded him of how great Christmas was in this house. And there, in a corner of the yard, sat many more second-hand Christmas trees of all shapes, sizes and condition in pots. The girl learnt that these were orphan trees. They had been dumped by people in the city, and were waiting to be planted one day – once space could be imagined for them. *Yea! We drove around and collected them all – couldn't bear to see them die senselessly,* the wife claimed. *It does not pay to take your eyes off them though,* the husband added with a wink, *otherwise their numbers would increase.* Then they ran from the mist in a jostling stampede back to the house just in time to experience a crinkling smell of smoke, as the electricity short-circuited the wet lights. *It was different in the old country, where you had to run around with a torch in the middle of the day to see where you were going.* The woman's voice filled the house.

Christmas! Christmas in the city was different now. The girl had to listen very hard, to keep up with the quick-speaking red-haired people racing through everything stockpiled in their heads for this moment, as if every precious second counted while Warren Finch was in their home. She watched words tumbling out of four mouths that never stopped moving – open and closed, up and down. Their voices shouted to be heard above each other to complain about power surges in the city, and the malfunctioning Christmas lights that were never like this before. They remembered a time when you could leave the lights burning all night without anyone batting an eyelid. *Bring back the good old days when we could even cover the whole yard, trees and all, with the snowflake machine.* The only good thing apparently, was that it had been another bumper season for the growth of the Christmas trees. The red-haired man was jubilant about this. Conifers loved the rain, and the perpetual mist, and did not seem to mind if the sun never shone.

Which is a good job with the way it has been raining all the time, the red-haired man said with a sigh.

That's right love, the wife replied with another happy peal of laughter.

All the trees must have grown approximately three metres, just since spring.

Whatever happened to the good, old, hot Australian Christmas, hey, Warren? It will be snowing next thing.

Warren said it was all to do with global warming and climate change, but his moving-mouth friends were more concerned with the failure of the electricity in the yard. Still there was great relief that they had been able to show him the lights, since the woman said, she could not remember when Warren had missed seeing the lights of Christmas in their house: Not since he had been sent by his elders to the city as a young man to complete some of his education.

The refrigerator was worshipped. Glorified like the supreme spirit of the city. The huge blue fridge dominating the kitchen was like a house within the house – bigger than a humpy. Coloured lights lit up the interior when you opened the door. Warren was told that it was a new fridge. That it had come from overseas. It had been the biggest in the shop, the biggest you could buy, and with Warren there for Christmas, they were pleased that they had gone ahead and bought it. Whenever they spoke now, it was about some item extracted from the fridge for consumption. Food had to be talked about while it was eaten like people do in Paris the lady said.

Warren Finch was in his element. He relished the conversation about food and talk of regional differences in dairy products, recipes and dishes he had tasted at various restaurants in countless countries he had visited since the last Christmas. Oblivia had only seen him eating with the genies, where he did not seem concerned about what he ate. He put anything in his mouth. She watched as they talked endlessly of things of no importance to anyone but themselves, and now about the brands of butter you could buy in places called the 'new' supermarkets, which was not like the old days, they claimed, when they had no butter at all during the long drought. They said it was almost as bad as the place where the girl had come from – *God! Blessed girl.*

Isn't that right E–thyl? The girl's failure to answer their questions stiffened the room. She did not know what these conversations were about. Warren, who had never stopped smiling, just shook his head in a familial gesture that the family understood, without wasting words, *don't bother, don't fuss, not worth the trouble.*

Well! Eee-thyl will have to know which butter to buy if she is going to be living in the big city now.

Why? The red-haired husband asked in mock astonishment. *E–thyl might not even like butter.*

Of course she likes butter. You like butter, don't you Eee-thyl? The girl nodded, but she had never tasted butter.

A woman can be good for other things – not just being knowledgeable of which butter to buy.

Warren laughed. Mentally, the girl noted the joke, thinking it might be useful to know how to make him laugh one day.

In this introduction of what gave peace and pleasure to Warren Finch, the girl had found hell. She wanted to scream. She hated everything about these people. Her mind left the room to look for the genies' camp among the owls and rats, and somehow, in a slim crevice of non-stop talk bouncing off the wood panelling, she heard an owl outside calling from a Christmas tree. She wanted to leave. Go outside. Disappear. Crawl away from this dead wood house that Warren had claimed would be her home. Her mind walked through its wooden cocoon where geography was lost, and where momentarily, she saw the ghosts of trees with branches swinging in the wind, that swung out and would hit her.

Noticing her silence, the woman said, *Ethyl, you just make yourself at home, love. This is your home now too, you know.* The girl's fingers ran along the wood panels which she visualised as tree trunks in some dense forest in her head. *Why could he not have been like other men?* asked Aunty Bella Donna of the Champions. She was standing in the back of the room trying to pull the girl from the tree roots and telling her to start acting polite and grateful, and stop that chatting to herself like an idiot. Harbour Master stood in the doorway. He just yelled at the girl that they were a pack of racists. *Couldn't he just have been like the men who killed their wives in the bush? Not go around bringing them to places like this. You would be better off dead. Skeletons left propped up against a tree somewhere. Sun bleaching bones with pieces of skin hardened to leather, and pieces of rag from their dresses fluttering in the wind. A bird picking about on her bones! Things like that!*

The girl escaped. She left the table where the continuous sound of voices grated like gravel thrown across the floor of her brain. In the corridor of that vast house she felt lost, although relieved in being alone, and tried to remember the route of the journey with Warren. No plan of escape came easily to mind, so she explored the Christmas house.

The voices faded as she followed a corridor lovingly decorated with festoons of pine branches that were tied with red ribbons in big bows, and large silver bells tinkling automatically from an inbuilt sonar detection device. Otherwise, it was a quiet house with empty rooms where only the sound of clocks could be heard ticking from walls, mantelpieces and cupboards. She was guided by an orange, grey, black and white marbled cat that ran ahead and led her into its favourite room. On entering the room, she discovered it had been permanently divided into more rooms, and these smaller rooms had been partitioned within, into strange, little alcoves on the Christmas theme that replicated in miniature scale nostalgic wintertime memories of foreign countries.

She felt as though the meowing cat was sweeping her along, urging her not to linger too long – *don't get sucked into other people's worlds. And don't knock anything over and spoil the dream.* They passed each elaborate world of dreams, where miniature winter people went about their business walking, stopping to talk to others, living lives among reindeers, tending baby deer, riding colourful sleighs, and looking at a cheerful Santa with elves, and grinning snowmen. There were carol singers that looked into rooms full of brightly wrapped presents, decorated Christmas trees, dinner tables laden with feasts, bowls of delicious apples and pears, and behind them, a countryside full of red robins singing in bare-branch trees, and miniaturised forests of pine trees laden with fake snow.

The girl examined each of the created worlds closely with a dark, morbid fascination, consciously searching for failure, proof of fault, in the perfect images of nostalgia. She heard herself saying: *Did not exist. Did not exist,* and drowned the old woman's delight in recognising all the places she had known once upon a time, and the Harbour Master mumbling in her other ear about all the racists running around and ruining the country. The cat protested. *Meow! Meow!* Insisting it knew the consequences of falling in love with constructed fairylands, *so mind you don't break anything because the red-haired people really love their memories.* But the girl had already become lost in the theatre of the remembered foreign lands. She did not want to be reminded of footsteps on gravel when Aunty Bella Donna of the Champions was already walking among

Christmas valleys, and pulling the girl back to a day long ago when up in the mountains they searched the vista for a house in a village that no longer existed.

They travelled to fields in the miniaturised scenery where saintly-looking people talked to birds, and small children lived in the care of swans while their fathers and mothers were away at war. These were lands where swans had been fed by a spring under a great ash tree where its three roots of fate kept spreading throughout the world to create the past, present and the future.

There, in another theatre, the old woman pointed to swan gods singing to swallows, *where the neck of the longlived swan is curving and winding;* and to the swan that swims on the river separating the living from the dead. She wanted to find a swan lifting off from a quiet lake and leading a people to their doom in the sea. Where had such a cruel swan come from? Was it living out Aristotle's death song of swans, and sung because it believed it was going to heaven, as Socrates assented, as it flew to sea to die? Heaven! The girl could hear an angel in the heavens above humming the swan waltz. Her swans might already be on their way back from heaven.

A globe contained disgruntled fishermen sitting around on the snow ice fishing in another winter, with lakes and seas frozen over, and birds in plight as snow fell. On icy waters, old Aunty showed the girl her cursed people who had been turned into swans. They dipped into freezing shallows to feed on the aquatic plants below. Some, the old woman said looking into the globe, were spirits condemned to live in the sea for centuries, while others would fly in a lonely sky forever. They were cursed like the children of Lir she said. They died because they were too old and decrepit when they had changed back to their human form, after living nine hundred years through an evil spell that had cast them as swans. Their fate twisted between Erin and Alba on the sea of Moyle.

The girl had spent hours searching for deception in these countless miniature scenes of Christmas, perhaps because she hoped that some tiny voice would reach up to her ear, but the more she leant into the little scenes, only their happy faces returned her gaze. And the more she searched, the more she found old Aunty's stories of swans really existed in other people's memories too. She even found the sailors aboard the East India ship in the year of 1698, and watched as they watched a black swan off *Hollandia Nova*. Sailors ran on the beach as they chased swans over great sheets of shallow water. Then, on a wooden ship on a Christmas sea, she discovered two black swans in a cage heading to Djakarta in 1746. And black swans in the Europe of 1791, at Knowsley, in England, where they were bred in the Earl of Derby's menagerie, and also in France – in the Empress Josephine's ponds at Malmaison – and the waters of Paris at Villeneuve L'Étang. She saw small graves of black swans with people standing around the little brown plots of earth, including Sir Winston Churchill, mourning his war gift from Australia before World War II.

After exploring all of these little scenes that had been created by months of labour, she had found no eucalyptus tree trunk with strange writing in the dust, no swamp lined with people guarded by the Army. She could not understand why this history did not exist in this world of creation. It was incomplete. Wrong. This was the flaw that she had searched for and found. There was no miniature black girl such as herself in any of these depictions of humanity, no swamp world of people quarrelling over food, not even Warren Finch among the black shepherds, or a black Wise King.

What became of the time when a young Bella Donna of the western world ran through the snow with her family and countless others as exiles? Where were they in the scenery of Christmas? Where were the escaping boat people who had placed their fate in a swan that led all the rickety boats that failed the decades adrift on the mercy of seas in that world of unwanted people? Where were the deserted boat people cities that had existed on the oceans of the world? She moved on with the knowledge that there was no link between her and Warren Finch's world.

City Swan

The fiery woman worked her fingers to the bone to get into the girl's brain, as though this was where one removed grime, salt, vegetation, blood of dead animals, lice, and whatever thoughts about having different origins she had brought into the house. Big Red, that was her name the woman said, after she had found the girl asleep in the corridor. With her sleeves rolled up, the woman joyfully prepared a more proper wife for Warren than what he had arrived with.

The girl had slept against a wall with the cat, and dreamt of a river walled up with knotted debris composed of words describing tree trunks, branches and leaves that had been washed away by previous floods. She knew it was not a safe place to stand against the wall breaking up in the flooded backwaters where volumes of words kept spilling over her head. Submerged and struggling, she bobbed up to surface every now and again, while swimming through schools of coppery red fish that were larger than whales jammed right to the steep banks of the river.

It was mid-morning when Big Red had transformed the girl with enough hot baths to convince herself that she had found the true colour of the girl's skin. She styled the girl's hair, contouring her wild golden-tipped brown curls to remain close to her head,

and coiled the rest into a bun at the base of her neck. She painted
her fingernails cream. The wedding gown was next. The girl was
thinner than expected and not as tall. She knew to expect her to be
dark, not that dark, but the colour was fine for the cream silk that
had been ordered. Now the dress itself did not fit.

She hissed between teeth filled with pins, cursing Warren for
having created a monumental problem by wanting so many things
to be done like this. *A wedding gown from Italy! What next?* It was the
bride's job to give her measurements. *How would he know?* And he
should have given more warning if he wanted to leave it to somebody else to organise everything for him. *Hold still! Don't move an
inch.* The girl dared not breathe. Yet! Yet! *My dear,* she sung finally,
saying she would build Rome with her bare hands in a day if she
had to. Why? *Because,* she explained, *Warren deserved to be happy for
all he has to put up with.* And with a pin she would stab the girl if she
did not make Warren a happy man.

*You are a very lucky girl. This is going to be the happiest day in your
life. I hope you know that. So, don't mind me. Who am I to complain over
a simple little thing like not having the dress as perfect as it should be?*

Finally, the dress clung to the girl's body and the cream silk
with embroidered lilies fell down to her ankles, and Big Red who
found it hard to believe in miracles, admitted Warren had chosen
the right dress. *Unbelievable! Who would have thought you could put
the bush where you come from into a frock.* The girl looked into an oval
mirror and saw herself like golden syrup in a cream dress with the
same colour arum lilies of the land of the owls, and gloved hands.
She looked grand, said the children applauding their mother who
was gushing with pride. Red said Ethyl looked exactly like a fashion
queen from a magazine. *A miracle,* she said to Warren. *And don't you
do this to me again.* Warren looked at the girl. He looked relieved.
He embraced the woman strongly. It was plain to see that she
meant the world to him.

Oblivia felt like she had been turned into a dolled-up camp dog and vaguely nodded to the question of whether she took Warren Finch as her husband to love and obey etcetera – since what did it matter whether she said, *I do* to Warren Finch, or fuck you arsehole if that was what she was supposed to think, and who was no less of a stranger in the room to her than anyone else there staring at her. Did it matter? Not the idea of marriage. This was the whole point with Oblivia, long after the house had filled with guests who greeted the red-headed dragon woman profusely as they entered. The man who officiated the marriage wore a tight black snake suit that could have been a boa constrictor strangling him. His face was sickly grey. He looked as though he had seen a ghost. Perhaps he was a ghost, Oblivia thought – she even thought it was funny, wondering whether she was really in some other reality, and if this was what the ghosts of white people did all the time, getting married, saying I do, promising the world and whatnot. She wasn't going to be anybody's slave. Whilst the marriage celebration proceeded with colour and glitz, the only strange person in the room was Oblivia with her girlish thoughts. *But, you have to understand,* said a woman-expert on Indigenous affairs in a small gathering of like-minded among the guests, *this marriage will cement bonds with these people. It is their law. He will need to keep his principles on his road to ultimate power.*

You need to understand something about Warren, Big Red confided in the girl. *His friends are important business people. Born rich. Men of old traditions lodged in other parts of the world. They give money to his work. They want a separate voice to hold sway in this country. Do you understand?* Only her eyes in degrees of openness indicated which of the cleanly shaven men embracing Warren mattered, while his own cleanly shaven face touched their own. They were either like people cast out in the desert or close-knit, like blood brothers. The girl followed Big Red's eyes, like a ribbon from her hair that had caught the wind and flew along an invisible current through the house.

These are all very close friendships. Big Red smiled even more stiltedly and self-knowingly at the wives who politely kissed both Warren's cheeks, fingers lingering suggestively as they slid a gloved hand across his cheek. She said nothing about those close friendships. Red said they were rolling in money. *Most of which is the laundered profits of exploiting natural resources which has wound every cent of its way around the globe many times before it lands in this multi-coloured fashion parade, my dear.*

The girl watched the kissing, hugging and laughter to congratulate Warren for marrying *his beautiful promise.* They glanced over to her, smiled, gave a small wave. *You see how they love Warren? They are also very important benefactors who will see to it that Warren becomes the head of this country. Do you know what a benefactor is? I suppose you don't. They give your husband a lot of money to help him become the most powerful man in the country. Not that he isn't already. I am not saying that.* Red looked at the girl strangely, and saw there was nothing one way or another disturbing her, so taking a deep breath and with a sigh of relief, ended the commentary: *Well! Whatever!*

Warren smiled amicably, briefly, politely to hear snippets of important news among these high-profile advocates of worthy causes, human rights, moral judgement, espousing correct answers for saving the lives of Aborigines, displaced people, freedom of speech, endangered species, the environment. And in fact, Red said, *Between them all, all of them have enough causes to cover the entire planet. You think they could bloody well save it.*

He drifted easily into careful quotes that one would expect from a happy groom, and to the varied questions of friendly media profilers. They smiled with great appreciation each time he spoke. He locked eye contact. It was impossible for the women journalists to break from his gaze until he freed them. The politicians, old hands at the artistry of seduction, cautioned a compromising situation, by ushering Warren aside. They spoke in hushed tones to fill the moment by clinking glasses to honour his peculiarly bizarre but honourable marriage whether they thought it was exploitation or not, the thing was, it was a novel idea indeed.

The matron Red eyed her special guests sarcastically, and was scathing in telling Oblivia about how they all wanted to know about customary law practices now: *See how they are staring at you? Look at them biting at the bit to say that they have always acknowledged arranged marriages. See how they are pulling Warren aside? Read their lips: Oh! Warren, What does it mean? Will this work? Last week they all wanted to outlaw it. You watch: They will be racing and falling over themselves to get back to Canberra in the morning to dust the cobwebs off that old 1970s customary law report and scratching their heads to figure out how to be first to bring all your old laws and practices into legislation which they had previously outlawed to death. That's what they are all whispering about over there. Trying to be honourable. Such hypocrites. All of them. Fancy trying to justify oblique practices from another culture they know nothing about and wanting to build it into the normal practice of Australian law. But what can you say? Men from the mountaintops will always come down to the molehill to conquer it. That will always be the vice of the conqueror.*

The tables were festooned with red fish, octopus, squid, oysters and silver urns overflowing with prawns, crayfish, salmon and all other things cooked red from the sea. A line of waiters queued at the door with platters of steaming roasts and vegetables under shining silver lids. It was a banquet, more food than the girl had seen in her entire life, and the sight of so much food for one meal made her nauseous, and unable to eat. Inside her loneliness, she felt the pangs of hunger the night she had raided the fishing nets in the swamp, and had not found a single fish. Then, she lost track of the number of cattle, pigs, sheep, and poultry slaughtered, and vegetable fields that had been raided, the sea emptied, and all of this – deteriorating into the guts of seagulls eating the rubbish.

She had no guests of her own. Even old Aunty and the Harbour Master had boycotted the wedding. The girl stared blankly into a world where hungry swans flew around the house in a frenzied flight of destruction. In the melee of crashing and swans' hisses, the huge birds strike at food off dinner plates and attack the banquet. Strangely, other things fall apart in her mind too, because somewhere far off beyond the house and wedding music and guests milling in talk she could hear the single cry of a swan gliding down a lonely river calling for its mate. She turned pale. This was old Bella Donna's story of the swan flying with a piece of bone in its beak.

The neck of a motionless swan lay limp on the bank of the river so far away. Its mate flew on and on, and the girl could hear the swan's wedding song coming closer as other things began to take shape before her eyes, and Warren's guests became swans. Their clothes were transforming into swanskin with feathers of glitter and shine.

It was a funny old world the girl thought, seeing people too preoccupied to notice their own metamorphosis. They were too busy thinking about the proper way to smile at a promised wife first lady who stared back at a room full of swans. Oh! My God! She smiled at the busy swans preening one another, and again, gliding across the glassy room to the music of Johann Strauss. Oh! My God! The girl had been captured in the blissfulness of being a bride. Look at her! She danced towards the swans flying through the air – and then, crying as they faded away, was unable to accept that they could have changed back suddenly into Warren's guests.

But the room danced with French champagne, chatter and music, and as guests were introduced to the girl, she found the sense of their humanity enticing. Warren's guests had learnt about poverty from not being poor themselves, in places where you did not hear the screams and yelling of help. Their words could stay on a flat horizontal plane from one end of the spectrum to the other in speaking about the emotions of the world. Well-fed speech was flexible, versatile, and heavily pregnant with a choice of words that could be tilted with enough inflection to win hearts regardless, so when she listened to Red, she had to remember they were actually oppressors, capable of slipping down to the bottom of a fetid well to destroy whoever got in the way of their success. She shook their hands just like they might have been swans.

In a room celebrating the glory of the country through political manoeuvres, there were no genies. This thought had struck her like lightning, and when Warren caught sight of her she froze. He patted the arm of the person he was speaking to, excusing himself to collect her. His arm guided her from one person to the next, circling the room in farewells, while she wanted to walk away. *You are supposed to be a trophy wife,* Warren whispered into her ear and capped it with a light kiss. He was obviously thrilled by what he overheard from his guests.

This is astonishing. He actually went ahead with it.

Married his promise wife.

Someone said he just went straight in and took her from a bush camp where she was living in squalor with ducks and what have you, and she had been raped and everything. A really violent place where children were neglected.

No!

Well! No one can be too surprised. That's the kind of thing Warren would do.

I agree. He has always been a man who will stand by a principle.

But she was half mad when he found her.

Was that when she was living in a tree or something?

They say she didn't even know her name.

Why? I never heard of someone not knowing their own name.

Well! It is true. Not all people are the same.

Bullshit! We are one country here. We are all Australians. All equal. No one is any different.

Well! If you don't believe it, go and ask her what her name is.

Oblivia overheard too. She felt strange, and could not understand why he had taken her away from her home either. *It is just games,* Warren said, squeezing her hand and smiling at his friends. *Why would people play these games?* Her head felt as though it was being whisked around inside a sphere tugged by swans circling the skies and narrowing in their search to find her.

Finally, they were back where they had begun, walking down through the pine trees where white mist rose through the foliage, and a violin was playing Edgar's grass owl rhapsody. She stopped to listen, and the music grew louder as it spread through all of the trees. Warren held her arm firmly. She pushed him away, trying to break free, she wanted to go back.

Where? Where do you want to go to, he said, while he maintained his grip on her arm.

Where is he? Edgar? she thought, trying to pull away.

Don't be stupid. Come on. Let's try to dignify the occasion. At least you should be capable of doing the few simple things you are supposed to do. Who put on that music? Listen! See! The music is being piped through the trees. That's all.

The girl struggled to look back, and strained to hear the music as it faded into the background of the farewells of guests crowding around them. Red's big lips smiled broadly. All eyes were on Warren as they wished him well, showering him with embraces in a wave that lifted the bride into the car while shadows flew overhead. But! Just when she thought the swans had arrived, the shadows disappeared from the curls in the mist, and then, it was sunshine. There was nothing but blue skies as the door closed, long before the violin finished playing its serenades.

Driving away, Warren happily chatted about the simply marvellous wedding to the driver he called mate, or to whoever else was on the other end of the mobile phone which was ringing constantly. *Wasn't it great, Ethyl?* Every call he included her, to back up what he thought about his marriage. *Yes, she loved it, didn't you Ethyl?* Warren's voice went on squashing her thoughts of salt lakes, spinifex and owls. She had lost the battle to preserve Edgar's music in her head.

The phone rang like an alarm bell interrupting her thoughts, to dominate the past, to insist the future be heard. She felt that the voice on the phone belonged to a snake. The marriage belonged to his viperous world. Then he was arguing with the phone. *It means nothing…Something! Something? Believe me it means nothing.* He looked out the window as he spoke, and she wanted to scream at him to stop robbing people of their thoughts. She hated how he killed silence.

She was certain that he had intentionally stopped her from hearing the music, just as he made certain that she would never reach the point from where her emotions would overtake his plans, to leave him somehow, to return to the swans. He reached across and touched her arm and she flinched in that instant as his voice drew her back into his world.

Warren smiled and said he had a little present.

Don't you want to know what it is?

He waited until she looked at him before he handed her a small red coral box. It was carved with tiny birds with fat bellies that were larger than their wings, and each bird looked up with golden eyes. *Go on, open it.* The slightest touch to the clasp on the side of the box released the lid which sprang open, and sounded a tune. *It is from Swan Lake the ballet. I thought you would like that.* Inside, on its bed of silk, lay a silver ring. She looked at her left hand with the gold wedding band that sat loosely on her finger.

Take it, he encouraged, and then put the ring on her finger.

This is for the right hand, he said, adding how he had had it made especially for this day. She looked at the design. Two thin bands were separated by crescent moons that encased a small silver brolga, and a swan.

Do you like it?

It is very nice. Thank you. She imagined that she had spoken politely, like Red, but said nothing. She wished the mobile phone would call so that the voice of the snake would sit between them.

I have another little present for you, he said. *In case you are thinking about where all of this is heading, you need to know one thing. You will never be going back to where you came from. I will tell you the reason why. It no longer exists.*

Oblivia looked straight at him.

His smile was victorious now, having conquered her indifference at last. *Simple! The place does not exist anymore. There is no time for places like that. So I did them a favour. I had the place closed down the day we left. Listen!*

He tapped the phone, held it to his ear, and spoke. *Is everything ready?* His voice was cold with authority. A shiver ran up her back. Then he placed the phone to her ear. She listened. The countdown finished, and then, a male voice said, *Do it: Now!* She heard the explosions whistling through the receiver and vibrating down her fingers. She had to hold the rattling phone away from her ear, but even over the noise of the moving car, could hear the piercing sounds of everything that had flown to the sky. Warren's face had hardened. She had only seen men around the swamp using their physical powers to destroy. How could this man destroy something so enormous that contained her world? All she saw was a very fine looking man in the suit he had chosen for his wedding day. His thumb silenced the mobile and after taking a deep breath, he placed it back in the pocket of his jacket.

That was for you, he said at last.

What is for me? That? What do you mean? The words did not surface, but the sound of her voice rose through a bottleneck as though gasping for air.

They had not protected you. Nobody did. You know it is true or deep down in your heart you do, just like I know it. Their job was to protect you. That was the law. He took her hand with the ring, and twisted it around her finger, and she saw a third bird, an owl, and she could not understand how she had missed seeing it before, but instantly, she felt calmer, emptied, as though nothing remained of herself which had been scattered far away.

So it's very simple. Really. Anyone would understand why places like that cannot exist. It is what the whole country was thinking – even if the Government was never prepared to do anything about it.

What will happen to them – those people? He asked the question for her. She imagined the swans agitated and frightened by the panic of people being cleared out of their homes. Flying off. Their flight shifting in clear blue skies from the sound of the explosions, the black columns of smoke chasing them away. What would happen if they had continued swimming around the hull, confused, waiting for her to return? Did he destroy the swamp and the swamp-people too?

They had two choices. Either being moved into the nearest town where they would have to learn to live just like everyone else. Or, being returned to homelands where their real laws and government exist. There will be no Army looking after anybody anymore. Stupid idea in the first place. Intervention! Safer futures! Can't for the life of me see why stupid thinking like that has lasted a century.

What if they don't like it there? What if they go back? Again, he felt the need to frame questions on her behalf, to explain his apocalyptic decision. She was still thinking about the swans and about what would happen to her, if she could go back, and if the swans were not living there anymore.

What if, what if? What does it matter to you, or us? They only have themselves to blame. But if you want to know: Everyone on earth is obliged to live a life without endangering somebody else's life. I work at trying to make people safe. Why do you think I went up there? I wanted to have a look. See what the place was like for myself. That was how I found out that I was right all along from the time when the old people told me about you. I had already known that you were to become my wife when I saw what had happened to you. I knew about the arrangement our families had made from a long time ago when I was a boy. You know, I could have closed them down a while back, but I just wanted to make sure, and I needed to go and collect you, and in any case, it was better to do it this way. You have a future ahead of you now. They were doing nothing to change things by themselves for the future so they had given up the right of sovereignty over their lives.

She only half listened, without having any idea of what he was talking about. His boring words went in one ear and straight out the other. *Bloody sell out!* There were two others in the car. The old woman. Old Harbour Master. Both sitting in the front seat with the driver. They were discussing this matter too. *Who does he think he is? God! Where did he learn about bombing people's homes? Where does he think he is? A war zone. In Afghanistan? That old war! How long has that been going on for? Does he still think he is in Europe or America? Doesn't he know this is Australia? Who gives him the right to decide on other people's sovereignty?* The old woman was saying how her bones would be blown up now, and she would have to go and find them, *Let me get out of this car,* then she disappeared.

The girl looked at the passing buildings – the black and grey concrete statues lining the footpaths. She could feel the cold dampness coming off each building as they drove on. It was the same feeling of fear she had had from the abandoned dogs savagely sniffing through the sedge grasses while circling the swamp, huddling the black-feathered chaos until the water was red and putrid from the smell of rotting flesh and wet feathers. Inside a small pocket of bravery hiding in the crevices of her brain, she imagined herself being united with the swan ghosts flying away from the massacre. It was the only way she could wish herself out of this place. The brolgas would just leave naturally and rejoin the masses further east – back in Warren's country – and dust off their old rookeries.

What about the genies? Haphazardly, she held up three fingers to his face, and waved her other hand around, and blew mouthfuls of air.

There are no genies. Genies don't exist. The things you see here are what exist. Nothing else. Trust me and I will show you everything you need to know.

Oblivia winced at Warren's denial, and stared at her three fingers while slamming them into her other hand.

Where are they then?

I told you they have been moved to town.

The owls? All the eggs we counted? Those men?

Very casually he lent over and covered her face with his. The Harbour Master raised his eyebrows and spat in disgust, *A kiss to seal a dream with…Look! Girl! He's got lips like Nat King Cole.* She started to disbelieve herself. Her memory was unreliable. Why would she have travelled over salt lakes? She had beaten the odds. Had not been left to die in the bush. She lived in this city with a rich man. The wedding seemed like a daydream. The red-headed family were just ghosts of people from storybooks that she thought of meeting one day.

She remembered Aunty Bella Donna of the Champions once saying that no story was worth telling if no one could remember the lesson in it. These were stories that have made no difference to anyone. Old Aunty was fading away forever. But…even true stories have to be invented sometimes to be remembered. Ah! The truth was always forgotten. She was in a car with a stranger.

Gypsy Swans

In amongst grey city buildings as solemn as each other, and at the end of silence, they reached a laneway of old and rundown buildings, to stop in front of what Warren Finch called his home.

He called it The People's Palace.

The first thing Oblivia noticed about the building was the iron bars lacing the windows and the single door of the shopfront. The building was a cage. It reached up to the sky like a giant finger that had come out of the ground to orchestrate the heavens. Cold winds flew down the street with sheets of rain. The building frightened her. Would she be locked inside its guts? Like the women locked in the guts of Country?

In the grinding rain there were many poor people in shapeless brolga-grey coats milling around the laneway, who stared sideways through the limp wet hair falling down over their faces. Some held out their hands for money, but then withdrew them quickly, and passed by without raising their heads. Underneath their hair, some stared at her from the corner of their eyes. Theirs was a primeval kind of surveillance, like wild dogs. She pretended not to notice how wet the people were who slept against walls, some standing, and others lying under pieces of cardboard while styrofoam and

plastic rolled over them in the wind. They lay on the concrete sideways with an ear to the ground, as if trying to hear the stories that
lay underneath. Oblivia did not understand then that what they
were really listening for was the hint of another tidal surge flooding in the sewers below the city. Harbour Master looked around,
then bent down and put his own ear to the concrete footpath and
said Warren Finch's home was a piece of shit. These people threw
venom from their souls at him. A woman walked by with a pink
towel wrapped around her nostrils and mouth, and stared at the
bride. *The air is bad here girlie,* she muffled.

They stood in the rain as Warren unlocked the cumbersome
gate and the heavy green door with apparent ease, giving the
impression that he knew the building well. *Welcome to my home,*
he said.

Is this a shop? she thought, picking up the voice of Dean Martin
singing along with the Harbour Master, *Well! It's lonesome in this old
town...I am going back to Houston, Houston, Houston.*

No, this is not a shop. It is a place. That was all he said.

They stepped inside a lantern-lit world of water gardens and
concrete ponds from which rose enormous antique fountains,
while overhead roaming in mist, were large and colourful puppets
of birds, dragons and people with wings that swayed from long
strings attached somewhere in the ceiling. In this idyll of constant
movement, jets of water spouted in the air from wrought iron
or brass horns carried by larger than life cupids, giant maidens
and young men, or spurted out of the beaks of enormous swans
and geese, and from lotus flowers, or from the mouths of frogs
and dragons. Whenever the water reached its zenith, it loosely
and noisily fell into a *Klangfarbenmelodie* of music, dropping into
the multitude of shallow ponds, from where it was sucked into
pipes, then spouted back up into the air again, taking with it Dean
Martin's song of what it was like to be going home, to *Houston...*

In this crowded space, where eyes swung hocus-pocused through the kaleidoscopically fantastic creation, there was even more drama unfolding, with statues of ancient Greek men and women watching on with faces of wondrous serenity over ibis, eagles, the imagined animals of fairytales, and giant lions with heavy manes that lay on the floor with heads upright, staring into the distance. Wherever there was space not taken up by the human ability to marvel in its imagination, ropey plants, palms, aloes drooping and stringy battled to survive in the atmosphere of wetness and dimness, by stretching half-starved stems towards whatever light came through the windows.

There were cats asleep on pedestals, mantlepieces, steps and shelves, and any place free from being sprayed by mist. The cats watched Warren Finch with yellow eyes as he led the way. A brighter light came on from somewhere above, and when the girl looked up, she saw a break in the clouds passing over the glass dome roof. He led her to a wire cage that belonged to another century. It surrounded the elevator that he explained was a masterpiece of engineering. *A bloody marvel that still works perfectly even after practically two-and-a-half centuries,* he claimed. *It must have been the pride of the city when it was first built.* He pressed the dirt-and-grease-coated brass button that shone on the mark where fingers had been pressing it forever. *Bloody impressive!* She saw him quiver momentarily, while they waited for what did seem like forever, for the lift to come. It slowly descended, whining with pain, until suddenly falling the last metre with a thud. A manlike creature like those she had just seen on the street outside, pushed open the concertina door, and said very slowly: *Hello, Mr Flinch. You're back.*

Hello Machine. How have you been? Pretty good? Meet the Missus. He did not mention her name.

The man grunted and said that he had nothing to complain about. He looked at Oblivia with old dog-type eyes for a split second, and then continued looking at the floor. By the time the lift had struggled several floors up to the top of the building, he had managed to say *Hello, Mrs Finch.* The fountain garden far below was bathed in yellow lights that reflected off the water, but looking down made her feel dizzy. Beside the lift were several flights of dimly lit steps. In the darkness, Warren placed a key into a door with the number 59 barely visible, screwed onto it. Inside, he switched on the lights and walked through the rooms.

Everything works, Warren said, while striding around the apartment that looked as though it was never used. She was given a quick demonstration of electric appliances: stove, fridge, jug, toaster, microwave, washing machine, television, radio. Rubbish: Left nightly outside the door. Water: Hot and cold shower, bath, basin, kitchen sink. Toilet: How to flush. Cleaning: Broom, mop, bucket, wipes. Cleaning liquids: Kitchen, Bathroom, Toilet, Laundry, Floors. Clothes: There were some spare clothes left in the wardrobe. He slid a glass door open and she could see a line of clothes hanging for her. Shoes on the floor. Underwear in the drawers. He continued on, and quickly explained what she could and could not do in the apartment, which he said was, *yours now.* Frequently, he called out lists of instructions with: *You must promise me that you will remember.* Then he emerged from the bedroom, bags packed, one in each hand. The mobile was calling but he did not answer.

Her eyes had been glued to the images changing on the television until it occurred to her that the mobile was still ringing.

I will call them back in a minute, he said, and looking at her for a moment as he tried to remember something he had to say, he continued: *I will try to get back on the weekend.*

Her eyes were now fixed on the bag in his hand. Warren could see her face locking into meltdown, another panic attack, and thought he better say something to her, before she destroyed the place, or stopped him from leaving. Yes, that would do it. He would explain his work to her – where he had to go.

Sometimes Canberra. That's the nation's capital. I am in government you know. Sometimes the world. Anywhere. My parish is the world. Wherever I am needed in the neighbourhoods of power. That is where I work: where I do business. Your business is to stay here and be my wife. Machine will look after you.

It was his words that described hugeness that helped her to realise how powerful he was, and her lack of power, in a place that she did not know.

Just ring the lift if you need anything. You can trust him so don't worry about asking. You will be good company for Machine. He is a good man and he does a good job. He broke the slight awkwardness in his voice by looking at his watch to confirm his departure.

Look! He said impatiently, *I have got to go right now to catch the flight. This is something you will have to get used to I am afraid. I have to go tonight because I have been away too long and I have a lot of very, very urgent work to do, starting first thing in the morning. Look! I will call you.*

Then he left. She heard him talking to the man he called Machine on the other side of the closed door, and shortly afterwards, the slamming concertina gates, then the rumbling noise of the lift wobbling back down its own neck, and the whining sound of creaking ropes fading further away.

She now belonged in the menagerie of exhibits artificially created by the weirdo named Machine. That was how the Harbour Master described the situation.

From that moment of silence, Oblivia would be waiting for Warren to come back.

Countless times, the girl stood in front of the large glass windows of the apartment, as she would do numerous times in the future. What did she watch? Cold rain mostly, that fell on the sun-deprived walls of the buildings across the laneway while she daydreamed about how she would escape through the mazes stacked in her mind – thousands of unknown city streets and distances across the country too great to be imagined, to return to the swamp – imaginary flights that always fizzled into a haze-land between the here and then that stopped her every time. She followed the routes of rainwater pouring through the moss and black lichen that grew in profusion down the shady walls, or dripping melodically like piano notes onto the drooping foliage of fig trees, banana trees, tropical trees and ferns growing from cracks in these buildings. She watched dark-hooded people drifting into the lane to sleep. Those who formed a huddle for security at night, then left in the morning. Sometimes, she would be awakened in the middle of the night when she heard people screaming *King Billy*, and she rushed to the window to watch dark shadows scattering though the waters flooding in the laneway, the old drought-buster spirit when tidal surges flooded through the sewers into the lower, poorer, and central parts of the city, usually at times when violent hail storms from cyclonic weather struck the coastline. She watched the people from the lane moving away, or sheltering from the rain and hailstones under pieces of cardboard and plastic, or standing around for hours in floodwater, holding their belongings to their chests, until the waters subsided.

Old Bella Donna's books about swans wrapped in fishing net were left on the table like a souvenir. Oblivia had found the package one night while roaming around the apartment after she had woken startled from a nightmare taking her to the brink of madness. Her common nightmare of being caught in the improbability of returning or leaving, of being locked in this moment forever, and there it was on the table. Had Warren come back? She froze, looked into the shadows, then started searching the place with the kitchen knife while the Harbour Master was winding her up so fast, urging her on to kill the useless prick if she found him, that she was racing around in a frenzy like a mad woman cut loose. The books could have been a wish come true. Washed up from the tracks of dry salt lakes. Hauled through the clouds outside the window. She had missed the genies tapping on the glass, to grant her wishes if she had any more to make.

The Harbour Master kept calling Warren Finch a fuckwit for leaving them all in this dump of a place. He was itching to leave. He said he had seen her bloody books in the vehicle where she had left them. *On the edge of the salt lakes.* The books smelt of the hull. If she touched one, or picked it up, images of being in the hull flashed through her mind.

Somehow, the books became good company. Pages were flicked over, and lines recited, and reflected upon: *The wild swan's death-hymn took the soul of that waste place with joy.* Was this wasteland the swamp? She left the books on the table, and touched them frequently as though they were her friends. She sang over and over, a chant, her lonely incantation to the swans flying over Country, *All the black swans sail together.* She moves on, finds another thought – *He who becomes a swan, instructs the world!* This swan could spread his wings and fly where his spirit takes him, and Oblivia imagines the past disappearing in this flight to a frightening anticipated unknown future. Shakespeare's *Sweet Swan of Avon! What a sight it were...*where a Mute Swan, or Whooper Swan, flying ten-thousand leagues, had taken the old swan woman's people across the sea. But her mind turns away from that vision, and returns to anticipate how her own black swans from the swamp were moving over the country she had travelled, and listens to them singing their ceremonies in flight, and she holds this thought in her mind because it soothes her, instructs her in endurance and perseverance.

Days passed and weeks turned into months of not knowing how she could continue reminding herself of the home she had been taken from, a place that no longer existed in the way she remembered – *Now, when you awaken, remember the swan's last dance.* As quickly as she tried to reconstruct the swamp in her mind, the quicker the images of watery slicks consumed the hull, capturing *the earthed lightning of a flock of swans*...and the rotting abandoned hulls flew away in the wind from a world fallen apart. It was not safe to have thoughts that were now wavering into forgetfulness until all that remained were vague memories too hard to hold. She no longer felt safe thinking about the hull. Slowly but surely, her life had become anything Warren Finch wanted it to be, *the Swan I tempted with a sense of shame*...and he was already doing that by not coming back.

In the middle of the day Oblivia watched the liftman from her window, when he was down in the narrow lane, right where the water was gushing out of the pipes carrying the water flooding from the top of the building. His shoes are wet from the windswept rain, but he continues emptying the rainwater from their bowls and feeding his cats. They follow his every move despite not liking the rain falling on their fur, because they are hungry. They are mainly orange marmalade cats; black and grey brindle cats; black and white cats. Soon, they are just wet cats. He judiciously supervises the feeding ritual to ensure that each cat manages to grab a bit of food.

Machine reminds her of Warren. The dominant, stronger cats are often discouraged from being too greedy with a swift kick from the tip of his boot. Other times, when in a hurry, he does not bother emptying water from the bowls. On these occasions, he just throws scraps of meat all over the laneway and wherever a bit lands, the cats rush towards it, and it all ends up in catfights. He watches for a moment or two as though he finds pleasure out of the spectacle of fur and claws, then he turns his back and saunters off towards the street entrance to the building. Other times he seems to be sick, and just empties tins of congealed cat food onto the ground in the running water. Then afterwards, he picks up all of the tins and carts them away in his rubbish bag.

Over rooftops where the crows wait, she would often see right out to the grey bay where the clouds were chopped by wind. She listened to the sound of ferry-boat engines whining in the rough, and the jets that flew continuously over the roof tops, and she wondered whether Warren might be on board, antlike, up in the sky. In the street below, in the constant sound of traffic, she saw delivery trucks travelling back and forth to feed the city, as if the entire population of the country existed only in this place.

Sometimes, when the weather eased, and if she looked closely, out into the shadows of the greyness, she would often find the dark form of a fisherman huddled in his secret fishing place among the rocks along the edge of the bay. She watched the small motorboats slowly churning over the choppy water, where hunchback fishermen went back and forth, then as night fell, the boats moving between lanes of flickering red, green and golden globes, and a seemingly never-ending trail of bats travelling from one abandoned park to another across the city. Then she moved away from the window. Her daily routine was completed.

Warren Finch still did not return, and she did not wish he would come back. She started to believe that one day the view from the window would change. A plane might fall from the skies, straight into the deepest part of the bay in front of her, with his body still strapped to its seat. She waited expectantly, anticipating the time when she would become one of the hunchbacked people on one of the little fishing boats, with eyes blinded by a stinging sea spray as they searched the crash site.

The rain never stopped falling. Sometimes it fell so hard it was impossible to see the bay. The telephone never rang. She had placed the receiver on the table and left it there.

Oblivia avoided Machine like the plague. Never wanted to see him. She did not even watch him feed the cats anymore. She feared that one day he would knock on the door and she would have to answer it. Yet, the liftman did his job of looking after her. He regularly left groceries and money outside the door in a box along with the household and personal things she hardly used. She stacked the things left by Machine into a mountain as high as the ceiling until the construction tumbled. She restacked bath soap, tins of food, laundry detergent into a higher pile. Most of the perishable food she did not eat, she left in the rubbish bin outside the door, where more food was left for her.

One night she woke up thinking that Machine was searching through her rubbish somewhere in the building, some place where she imagined he lived in a den like an animal, and where occasionally she thought she heard a phone ring. She felt disgusted and threw her rubbish from the window into the lane, but always quickly afterwards, she would see him picking up every single thing she had dropped with a pointed stick, and dropping it piece by piece, after he inspected it, into a large, green rubbish bag. It was these little incidents that fed her loathing of the ugly man. Her mind grew fat on it. But she could not leave. She depended on him. And still she did not wish that Warren would come back.

Sometimes, in the middle of the night, she would suddenly wake up to the sound of the concertina door of the lift slamming repeatedly in her head. She would run to her door and listen. Always watching the brass, hook-shaped door handle, waiting for it to turn. She thought Warren had come back. He had changed his mind. Then she heard slow, laboured breathing, and she wondered if each achievable breath would be the last. Instinctively, she knew it was the liftman on the other side with his ear to the door, listening to her – checking to see if she was still alive. She could hear Warren calling Machine on his mobile phone when the thought crossed his mind: *Keep checking just in case she tries to kill herself.* He could hear her heart pounding. The knife she slides across her hand is so sharp, that she often cuts herself. She tries not to breathe while waiting for the door handle to move. The blood falls from her hand. But he always leaves with his shoes dragging across the floor. The concertina doors open and slam shut. The lift begins whining back down to the lower floors.

It was only when the lift faded away that she would breathe normally again, but one night after he left she heard breathing coming back to her through the walls, in rhythm with her own breath. She now understood it was this sound that had brought Machine up to the top floor of the building. The sound flooded the apartment. She was too afraid to turn on a light, and went from room to room trying to find the sound, but it was coming from everywhere. It came from the air of her breath. The air was wrapping breath with breath.

Then she knew. She could feel the presence of their bodies, of beating wings from lean-chested birds, lightened from the long journey, with necks stretched in flight. The swans had arrived. Above the building they flew in a gyre that was lit intermittently by strobes of searchlights. All around, soft breast feathers fell lightly. The swans flew through the narrow lane outside the window, and upwards into the darkness, after their eyes had found hers. Their search had ended.

The swans flew around the building looking for a place to land. They tried to land on the roof then flew off towards the bay. Their numbers had grown. Along the way, the land had given up its swans from all the drying inland watercourses, swamps, man-made lakes and sewerage ponds, drains and cattle dams. The migration had assembled a black cloud that flew in the night on its long journey to find the girl.

But the swans were gone in the morning.

City of Refugees

Late at night gangs of street children heard the swans singing and followed them into the lane. Their world was the deep night while the city was in blackout to conserve energy. The swans were driven by nervousness, but their bond with the girl was greater than fear and held them to the lane. Hundreds of swans circled the building every night, flying in lines, sometimes coming so close their wings clipped the buildings and triggered a chain reaction of downward spiralling. Again and again they returned, and flew through the narrow corridor with even greater compositions of desperation than the previous night.

These aerobatics were how the swans communicated. With all of the nervousness generated at night, the swans kept away from the busy city during the day. Instead, they waited in the polluted waters of the bay, and in ponds in the ruined botanical gardens of the city, and any other abandoned flatlands with a sprinkling of water.

They returned in the quietness of the night and flew continuously through the lane, the closest they could get to the girl staring at them from her window. It was the flight of the obsessed. The continuous trumpeting of great numbers of swans joined harmoniously with their soft whistling to twist a melody that was sombre and grief-stricken, but this music was charming to the street kids. They barged into the lane and were ready to challenge any fear they had of being threatened by the roaming cardboard-box street dwellers that had claimed the lane as their own.

The life of the deepest part of the night in this pitch-black, power-starved city was always left to prowlers like the street kids looking for something to do. They roamed the shadows to feel alive. They were the sleepless of the world with no peace in their souls. They were the children of the homeless poor people of the city. Well! They were boys and girls of all ages and from all racial backgrounds mingling together like friends when they followed the swans through the city to the lane.

You know what they believed? That the lane was blessed. A filthy lane was the place to find Heaven. So! The kids arrived in hordes, groups of seven or eight that soon became hundreds. All the leaders had a bony *Staffy*, the dog of choice, Staffordshire Bull Terriers, with thick necks adorned with studded collars and led on rusty chains. It was miracles these children were after. And they felt closer to a miracle just from looking up to the sky and seeing the swans as they swarmed through the lane. They started calling the very ordinary lane a sacred site – *The holy place*.

They developed war games, firing non-stop rap songs in quick succession. Soon, they could not stop themselves from challenging one another to jump from the edges of buildings they had broken into, hanging out of windows on the higher levels to be at the height of swans in flight. They played a sound game by toying with the rhythms from the swans' beating wings. Their chants dared one another to fight for territory, or *to fly off, take off, fall to death, never come back*. In this cacophony echoing through the lane, they spent hours learning to replicate the glory of the city's cathedrals, as they swung between buildings on ropes worsted from rags of old clothes, trying to touch the swans.

The melee of sounds bounced back and forth along the walls, and exploded in the lane below so loudly, it could have woken the dead. The only ones disturbed though were the sleeping bodies inside the platforms of flattened cardboard boxes; the nests constructed by slow hands. This invisible world of the city, a place where decades of dampness, flooding and rain had ridden the lane with slimy algae, was now the street kids' cathedral.

Those who slept there in rubbish-bag coffins stuffed with newspaper to keep warm, while water leaked continuously from the rooftops, were unable to get a decent night's sleep. Nor could they die in a sweet dream. So, they just lay there, and cursed the fact that they were still alive.

The river of swans continued on, they flew trancelike through the gaps between the buildings. They circled and spiralled towards the moon, and gathered something in the air that had been locked out by the walls of the city. They were capturing from the skies the small packages of memory of the girl who was thousands of miles from her home. Perhaps this was what they sprinkled in the lane with feathers dropping, sprinkling dust down like magic so that her mind ran straight back to the swamp's ancient eucalypt, tangled in vines from countless seasons of bush banana.

You know it doesn't work like that, the Harbour Master often claimed while standing beside the girl in her apartment to watch the spectacle in the lane. Even the Harbour Master's small monkey, who thought it was Giuseppe Verdi's Rigoletto, and was always dressed magnificently in brocaded silk jackets, confirmed this was not like the real world whenever it was asked to throw in a bit of good advice. What a disappointment. It had no intentions of becoming the fortune-telling monkey of the lane.

The Harbour Master had brought his monkey friend back from overseas, after he had gone on a cruise ship around the world in search of Bella Donna's homeland. *Had no luck*, he said, *in finding the descendants of her swan leader.* He spat in disgust about his adventure. It was only a love boat he said. The ship had no idea where it was heading. It was full of gypsies searching for something to happen in their lives, their world had been like that from the day their ancestors had been expelled from the Garden of Eden. So he got off the stupid boat with the pie in the sky people and hitch-hiked the rest of the way like a real man, hopping along the floating islands of boat people until he found success.

What he found was that there were swans in most continents of the world and finally, he believed he had found the old woman's swans. There were not many left. The poor things had flown back to paradise, which was an oasis in the desert, just like *the Middle East.* He had watched these swans for a very long time while they stood around in dried-up marshland where decent people were reciting poetry, and for the hell of it, singing for rain, as though rain would open the gates of the most fantastic gardens of all times. All he learnt was that those swans were completely mad so he left them there. They were too blind to see that gardens were everywhere. The whole Earth was paradise in the eyes of its custodians.

Whereas, look at the monkey, he said. This creature had no illusions about paradise. *He carried his paradise inside himself like a little holy man. Flocks of pigeons followed him wherever he walked though the seas of humanity.* The Harbour Master said the monkey was his guru. He was better fun than trying to bring a swan across the world that was overweight with its own dooming prophecies.

The monkey and I flew back to Australia on a Qantas flagship – full of choir singers singing old Mamas and Papas songs over and over until you hated the sound, 'each night you go to bed my baby, whisper a little prayer for me etc, etc, and tell all the stars above this is dedicated to the one I love.'

Once the Harbour Master returned to The People's Palace and saw the large crowds forming in the lane for the coming night, he said that he would be staying around for a while. *This looks interesting*, he claimed. The little monkey thought so too even though he was really a serious creature that looked as if he belonged in an office where a lot of money was being made.

It was not long before the world of the lane did not intrigue the monkey. It silently chewed reused PK gum with its big brown teeth, and looked as though it was reflecting on its life so far thinking that all up, it could have been better. Still, nobody could say the monkey had a victim mentality because he was now a drifter, or because the world of the lane had overnight turned its fur grey, and before too long, the grey had turned white like a snow creature from the arctic circle, far snowier even than a Japanese Macaque.

The fact of the matter was that the snow monkey simply did not like Australia. It had turned ancient-looking with all of its yearning to go home, to go back to a city of millions, possibly a billion people, to some quiet little monkey house with a big rock in the front yard from where he could sit all day long and beg pistachio nuts from passing tourists. *Gee!* the creature said while shredding a lettuce into thousands of little pieces to resemble its own shattered mind, *the lane was not like the jungle – not a proper jungle.*

But that was not everything. There was much more to be said about what happened in the lane. Oblivia changed her mind about her nerves, and frequently, she left the building at night to rescue the fallen swans. Many fell in the *street-kid* game. The rescuing manoeuvres became a regular occurrence. Oblivia, the Harbour Master and the monkey would rush to the door as soon as they saw a swan falling.

In an instant they abandoned their fearfulness of the city, as well as the ongoing debates about whether they liked Australia or not, and stampeded into the crowded lane in the middle of the night. They would be off without a second thought, while hassling each other along the way to be the first one to open the door that kept out boogie men like Machine, so that they could *be bop a hula* down the gauntlet of at least a dozen flights of stairs – instead of taking the slower-than-death lift that still had an electricity supply attached to it, probably because only someone like Warren Finch could afford to pay the excessively expensive electricity charges in the city – then chase one another in circles to find the actual front door through the maze of fountains, cats and statues, while cold shivers rushed down their spines.

She knew Machine never slept and was always watching, but she did not hesitate in her hasty exit through the front door to the lane. Once outside, with the Harbour Master egging her to fight the people sleeping in the lane with her knife, and the monkey's little fingers raiding everyone's pockets for food, a Mars Bar or PK gum, she realised how easy it was to grab a swan under her arm and make a hasty retreat back to the building.

Whenever she found herself in the lane, Oblivia realised that she could move inconspicuously like any of the other darkened shapes covering the ground and no one would care less. This was so, even when the conglomerate of bodies huddled together under blankets, paper and cardboard frequently erupted and flew apart in waves of swearing and fights. They would settle again momentarily like a butterfly pausing to rest, when some old peace-keepers switched on the ghetto blasters roaring *Benedictus qui venit in nomine Domini*. She pushed and shoved people aside, all psyched to fight anybody that got in her way, but swans falling in the lane right on top of people did not exactly cause a world war. The multitudes sleeping in cardboard and newspaper bedding kept on snoring, having already anticipated a bit of night clubbing.

Before long, Warren Finch's apartment became a menagerie; a swannery for stunned, injured and recovering birds. Oblivia was a recluse but no Greta Garbo locking herself away and letting bygones be bygones forever. She could not get out of The People's Palace fast enough to save another swan.

Glass was a big problem. Swans in the swamps have no idea about glass. In each desperate attempt to reach the girl, some would crash head first into her window. Some would fall into the lane after being swiped by the street kids playing their game of hanging out the windows on the upper floors of the catastrophic city's abandoned apartments that smelt of decades of rose fragrance, impregnated aromas of herbs and spices – cumin, turmeric, cardamom, or of cat urine – and where old people lived in dank smelling rooms.

When absolute silence entered the lane during the early hours of the morning, and the swans began to disappear over the rooftops, the rain-soaked street kids with vacant eyes left too. They would come down from the buildings to wander off to crash on the busiest streets in the city where they slept. These bundles of rags were barely noticeable pushed up against shop windows, and were almost absorbed into the scenery of the most prestigious department stores. There they stayed, and you would never know if they were dead or alive. Their lullaby was the continuous sound of shoes clipping the pavement. The general public watched over them like guardian angels rushing by, while ignoring the dreams pervading the air, that sounded like trumpets from heaven calling for a shepherd to take the children home.

So far, Oblivia had avoided the police. While the sirens of police cars raced towards the lane, the door to The People's Palace would open immediately, and be slammed shut behind her after she returned with another rescued swan. The girl suspected Machine called the police. His turf war! Just as it was his door to open and close. His building. His dilemma of noticing that swans not only filled her apartment, but makeshift pens on the rooftop too, waiting to be returned to unknown places he had never set eyes on.

Oblivia could not understand how she kept seeing glimpses of herself on the television. The monkey had noticed her first because out of boredom it was flicking around with the control switch to find a nature documentary, preferably about monkey homelands or performing monkeys, and ended up watching an old sepia-coloured Marlene Dietrich movie. Everything was going along fine until the monkey yelled out in a startled squeal, *Who is that?*

This was when the Harbour Master began watching the movie to see what the monkey had seen, and he saw the same thing too. The girl was changed almost beyond recognition, as though Marlene Dietrich's spirit had jumped out of the television and into the girl and then appeared in a news flash where she was standing right beside – of all the people on Earth for goodness sake – Warren Finch. This person whoever she was only flashed across the television screen in a split second. But it was enough. Enough to see that the girl was dressed up like Marlene Dietrich in sepia and parading like the actress, and was actually beside Warren Finch. This same news flash was repeated many times through the Marlene Dietrich movie.

The Harbour Master was nursing a sick swan on his lap, and so was the monkey, and wondering why he was looking after these creatures in a squalid apartment. He asked Oblivia, *Where did you get clothes like that?* This was what the Harbour Master wanted to know, after seeing the pale sepia-coloured satin dress most of all, as she and Warren Finch walked off in the distance, and noticing the matching high-heel shoes. He said she looked unbelievable. *At first,* he exclaimed, *I told myself no way – I really couldn't recognise it was you.*

After this happened, all the Harbour Master wanted to do all day long was sit around waiting for a chance to see Warren Finch on the television, just to criticise him. Any news about the Australian Government was just grand. The Harbour Master believed that because of bloody Warren Finch, he had become a specialist in Australian politics – not that this was difficult to do, he claimed. They were all gutless wonders. He grumbled continuously about not being able to stand the sight of the man, so whenever he saw the new President of the country on television – because this was what Warren Finch had finally and seamlessly become (through an inspired shove of the exceedingly long-serving and unpopular Horse Ryder from Government during the course of one stormy night when so many trumped up and legit charges of conspiracy against the machinery of the party flew like a flippen maelstrom through the corridors of power in the country) – the Harbour Master and the monkey yelled at him for the complete sell-out that he was; a complete reprobate of the first order who had dumped his wife and turned against his own people. *Ya moron*, they screamed at the television.

The acclaimed monkey genius Rigoletto had become so obsessed with watching the news, he started to make specialised comparisons with how politics worked in the monkey world. He claimed that Warren Finch had stepped out of line with his own society. That he had left his people for dead. They were now joined to the throngs of banished people wandering aimlessly around the world, always searching and always lost, and who created more banished people wherever they went.

You give people no choice, the Harbour Master, sick of sitting in swan shit, shouted at the television. *You want them to be like you – a lost man. Like you did to this girl here. What is she now? Hey? Tell me that? Come here now. I want to fight you.*

Now Oblivia was left to rescue the fallen swans herself, because the Harbour Master and the monkey could not be bothered. They were too obsessed about having no real voice in the politics of Australia. Neither would leave the television for a minute. They were consumed in a running commentary about Warren Finch.

This massive consumption of electricity just for a television, and glut of injured or recuperating swans also consumed with television viewing, did not stop her from wanting to see herself on the television as well. Then finally – bingo! What a shock on the 7 O'Clock News. She quickly noticed the really small things that were totally opposed to how she thought about herself. Where were the downcast eyes for instance? Why the lack of self-consciousness? Where was the shame? How could she have agreed to allow people to stare at her like that? She had to adapt to the television picture of herself with fingernails painted red or pale pink, speaking through lipstick, looking from eyeliner and orderly designed hair, and how she moved with an air of confidence dressed in Marlene Dietrich clothes.

The Harbour Master said she looked beautiful but Warren Finch was an ugly man. These sightings of the President with his wife became more and more frequent the more that they watched the television together, so they had to surmise that Warren Finch was forcing the girl to go mad from seeing herself being paraded around as the wife he wanted her to learn to be. And equally alluring, they reasoned that these daily sightings of the Indigenous President of the newly created Australian Republic with his promise wife were intended to be very newsworthy to the viewing public that adored the country's first couple.

Yet there was more to think about. It had taken numerous glimpses of seeing herself masquerading around the place as Marlene Dietrich, for the girl to realise that Warren Finch was stealing parts of her life for his own purposes. *Yes, that was how he was covering up his mésalliance of a marriage with her.* She did not know how it happened, but somehow, a part of her life was being lived elsewhere with her husband. She came and went into a different life which Warren Finch returned through the television screen.

The Harbour Master and the monkey were deeply committed to their investigative arguments about this theft of her identity by an impostor – or not – and argued with Oblivia who believed it was her all right, and this gave them the excuse to be more or less glued to the television because why kill the dream, when otherwise they would have to be rescuing swans. They complained: *Wasn't the place crowded enough?* It was all they could think or speak about, including abusing that ugly man Warren Finch, saying *we are sick of you*, because they were stuck in an apartment with poultry swans. There were now so many of them nestled in the apartment it was hard to walk around the place without thinking you were in a stinking swannery. So the Harbour Master and Rigoletto, now covered in swan lice, sat tight in front of the television, unwilling to move unless it was absolutely necessary to feed themselves.

Oblivia had swans living on the rooftop where the cold wind whistled continuously, and now many needed to be released. She believed it was her job. It was the only reason why she was staying, and had not become a permanent television wife. Soon it would be the swan's breeding season and each swan would have to be reunited with the rest of the flock before their instincts to breed became too great, forcing them to panic on the rooftop and in the apartment, while attempting to escape.

Oblivia knew that she must take them to clear land, or to a large stretch of water so that they could have the space to run and take to the skies. She needed help to find this space in the city that sprawled like a maze in her mind, with neither the Harbour Master nor the monkey interested in helping her. They were more interested in Warren Finch than swans, or becoming lost in the city, and said if she wanted help: *Ask Warren Finch's Mr Machine to take you to the genie shop.*

Machine was sitting in an armchair on the ground floor with his favourite white cat wrapped around his neck like a scarf; it chewed the man's hair as though it was feathers. When Machine saw Oblivia standing in front of him with a piece of paper signed by Warren Finch, saying he should help her relocate the swans, he shouted in shock. *Well! Well! Well!* He was surrounded by misted water spurting several metres high from a colossal fish mouth and falling, but that he was damp did not worry him. He just kept swinging along to the amplified sound coming through the loud speakers of Dean Martin singing *Houston*, while a pile of damp cats purring and snarling at the white cat tumbled all over him. *What's the matter? You want a tour of dilapidation? Want to see the ruined city or something?*

Machine said he would need some time to study the street guide – an old disused book he pointed to on the table beside him that was half a metre thick. He thought it would be very difficult to work out the easiest directions to reach the magic shop she was talking about. *Okay.* This was a skewed dream of a city, he explained, with tidal surges at any time, and in saying he never liked people much, asked whether she realised that there were millions of them rushing around right outside their door – people doing anything to save themselves in the day to day? Mostly he grumbled about how the city was stuffed and nobody cared what it looked like anymore. *Everything is falling down around you. Nothing is getting fixed up. Pigeons are flying everywhere. The sky is full of them. I have seen thousands of the things circling around this building alone. Their shit – falling everywhere. They call this globalised depression. I call it shit. Subsistence life. The trouble of being micro-managed by the government with intervention this, and intervention that, until passivity breeds the life out of you and you may as well be dead. You want to become like that? It was an absolute disgrace. You are better off staying where you are – inside.* But still, because Warren Finch's signature was on the note, he agreed to take her there, but only at night for these reasons: hatred of sunlight, and because he did not like walking around in the city during the day when it was crowded, although even the Harbour Master had told her that in reality, he had only seen dribs and drabs. It was a ghost city. Hardly anyone lived there any more after the thousands of unemployed people had moved away and disappeared into thin air apparently. Machine patted his knee cat and said: *Be ready when you hear a knock on the door.*

After several hours of waiting that night and being scared out of her wits, there was a scratching sound on the other side of the door. *Quando! Quando?* The Harbour Master interrupted what he called, *another bloody quandary to deal with,* and told her straight to *F–N straighten up,* and that she had better get used to answering the door. The lice-scratching monkey agreed, and claimed the Harbour Master was a natural mastermind at getting things done in a timely fashion.

So! Olé! She answered the door and found an owl sitting there. The little bird busy scratching with its beak was disturbed by the door opening and flew off in fright. It descended slowly down the atrium. Instinctively, the girl knew the owl wanted to be followed, and even more than this, she thought that Machine had become the owl – the one that had been promised to her by the genies. She quickly looked at all of the swans jumbled into the apartment honking over the top of the sound of the television: *Take/me! Take/me!* She quickly grabbed the swan with the strongest wings flapping in readiness for flight, and left dressed in her darkest clothes with the hood of her jacket pulled down over her head as she entered the lane outside.

Out into the rainy night, and walking quickly through street after street and lanes and darkened alleyways with the swan in Warren Finch's napsack strapped over her back, with her mind swinging around in her head about why she had not been smart enough to see what was not visible to anyone else, such as the owl-like features in Machine's face, she followed the owl that could have been him.

The owl kept a hasty pace in its flight. There was no time for faint-hearted indifference about whether she should follow it or not, though she was being taken far away from The People's Palace. Any idea of how to return had not dawned on her yet, although she was keen to return as quickly as possible in case she had to be transformed into Warren Finch's television wife again – because she was forced to go everywhere with him. *In your dreams,* the monkey claimed, *Let's escape. Why not kill Warren if we ever see him again? Then we can all go back to the swamp.* How? How played over in her mind a thousand times a day. What a word *how* was. It could drive anyone mad. The owl flew on oblivious to any quandary she was having about needing to be somewhere else. Even if she had changed her mind and wished she had never left, it was too late. The owl kept her alert to its sudden shifts in direction, and often flew high to cross buildings while she had to run down and around them while lugging the heavy swan, to find a way to keep following. She was convinced that the creature wanted to lose her in the labyrinth.

The air was like ice. Massive clouds soared across the skies of the city. A hard wind blew the owl along until finally it landed on a lamp post in front of a long-abandoned, boarded and nailed-up shop where, on the business sign, painted monkeys and owls danced across faded yellowish words that she was barely able to read, *The World of Magicians and Genies.* The owl shook itself to end its flight, and then suddenly flew straight through a crack in the deserted building.

This was how the world stood in the darkness, but whenever a rouge neon light flickered brightly, it lit up the street, and she could see behind the boards and inside the shop. But genies were oblivious of time. A rose fragrance that had been sprayed in the shop for decades by those who had worked there, was still in the air of this otherworldly, something not of this time, unbridled to time perhaps, magic shop that brought it back into existence.

The first thing she noticed as light flashed into the building was movement on the floor. It was alive with the city's lizards and skinks that had gathered in the warmth of the room. Perhaps, she thought, they were participating in a historical conference about old homelands when lizards lived in trees. The desks where the genies had sat looked as though they had been gathering work for hundreds of years, while the books that they had written in had grown into tall mountains. She could see the notes and drawings they had left behind, notes about the measurements they had been taking of grass owls, seashells, seeds, feathers and odd things like that.

There were elderly owls in the room. Not local. These came from other wild places in the world. The old owls sat very still and civilised on perches, so as not to waste their breath on life's flippancies. Only the younger owls did that – flying soundlessly to and fro across the room – leaving and returning from the city streets. The room's other large bird life consisted of several old rare and valuable parrots that preserved the entire history of their species inside their heads. Who knows why the genies wanted them saved? What could anyone do with information about what no longer existed?

The girl heard the parrots chatting about the ordeal of travelling across the world aboard bankrupt ships with the genies. These vessels were now rotting down in the harbour. Permanently anchored. Saved up for a rainy day. She thought the parrots looked lucky to be living in perpetuity in this ageless room. They would always remain perched on their ornate bird stands studded with pearls, but deep inside their little ticking hearts, she knew they looked around their diminished world, and pondered where they had ended up.

Sometimes the homesick parrots' thoughts caught them in a nostalgic moment, and they would suddenly utter words from ancient languages. The girl watched the parrots waste their knowledge; their rare and valuable words disappearing into thin air. Never to be spoken again when the lost languages faded away.

Well! Holy! Holy! The swan flew in the dead of the night. Its faith was in itself. The great black bird had struggled to be free from the girl's arms and like a racehorse, ran in the direction of the neon sun where three strange men had appeared. They may have only been drunks, or spies sent by Warren Finch to keep an eye on her, but slunk away when noticed, and disappeared in the fog.

The great swan was soon in the air, wings spread in slow flight, just above Oblivia who was running after it down the street. The swan was completely savvy about directions in the city and took shortcuts, for within minutes she was back inside the lane. *Where you been?* Odd Machine was waiting at the door, angry but relieved that she had come back. He complained about how lonely he was, but she sped past him and ran back up to her apartment. The healed swan joined others outside in flight paths leading to the eel pond in the botanical gardens in the centre of the city where flocks of great numbers were assembled for the night.

Now swans were set free every night. Oblivia had faith in the owl with the Dean Martin *Houston* song stuck in its head, as it flew continually waving and gliding and twisting its body as it looked around, to suddenly change course over buildings. She followed its flight through the darkness on whatever route it took, keeping the bird in sight, and knew that the owl would always end up in front of the abandoned magic shop.

It did not matter that the owl's destination was just around the corner from The People's Palace and that she was pursuing the owl over vast distances for nothing. She told the Harbour Master and the monkey that an ordinary, logical route was not the point. If she had walked there herself in the most direct route possible, she would never have found the old genie's shop on the long abandoned street where the city's ghosts came at night, and which was best to release swans returning to flight. It was the desire she followed, of completing an arduous journey that allowed her to see the right perspective of the neon sun shining through cracks in the boarded-up frontage of the shop, and she grew stronger by imagining the genies still working in their workshop on the other side of the boards, and by believing that the spirits in this place – all of the ghosts that had never been taken home – also ran with the swan along the street, and helped it to fly. It was a ghost street. Very exciting: there were thousands of ghosts there. She had seen them herself, she claimed, although the Harbour Master and Rigoletto were not really convinced about her story. They knew a thing or two about ghosts.

Rigoletto sang his anthem, *questa o quella*. Badly sung opera was enough for the street kids to stop using the lane. They left, while shouting that whoever was singing like a monkey should stop. The gangs found something new to do, and gathered on the street corners waiting, to follow the owl leading the darkly clothed and hooded girl with a swan under her arm, or sometimes slung over her back.

The street kids kept their distance from Oblivia staring at the boarded-up building. They punched each other in the head to stand back to pay a bit of respect for the traditional owner of the land. They wondered whether she was just mad, you know, having gone crazy in the city, and crept in closer to see over her shoulder.

None had the girl's ability to visualise how the genie's shop had once been, of seeing the tiny birds buzzing inside an antique Chinese aviary constructed of wire that had once been forged into decorative swirls. She ignored their voices whispering in her ear, *What are you looken at, sis?*

Inside the aviary flew the smallest hummingbirds in the world – but only if you thought of them flying, flying from cone-like nests in which they slept. The more she stared at the stillness of the nests, the more the hummingbirds would become animated, and would begin darting around the fresh flowers inside the cage. The street children were oblivious to the ghosts of the street crowding around them to watch the hummingbirds, but they felt that there must be something special about the building, and were organising a break-in.

Oblivia knows that her nights on the streets will not last long and she ignores the owl flitting around the light poles to catch insects, and the street children breaking into the building. She has too many other things to think about. For instance, she never knows when she will have to dress up again to appear on television – and what if Warren was already at the apartment waiting to pick her up? Already she feels that she will not be living in the apartment much longer. Feels it in her bones. Even the Harbour Master was packing his things.

Ships' bells can be heard faraway in the harbour, and the black swan released from her arms stands alone and confused on the empty wet street. Each swan was the same; uncertain about its ability to fly again until the wind off the changing tide pushed it along, and its webbed feet would start running down the road with their heavy load. The wind gusting along this corridor grew in intensity, and soon picked up the running swan and pushed it into flight.

The neglected city had thousands of pigeons flying around the rooftops of buildings, and trees sprouting out of the sides of cathedrals, chestnuts growing from the alcoves; fig tree roots clung to the walls, and almond and apple trees grew from seeds that flourished in the damp cracks. In these trees while pigeons and pet budgerigars slept, down below the troupe of owl, girl and swans travelled with a multitude of ghosts. Their parade implied a pilgrimage, a dedication to their never forgone longing for what was and had been, a prolonged hurting, like the Portuguese word *saudades*, describing the deep yearning of those left in limbo, and the melancholy dream passing through every quiet street in the city. Then Oblivia would again feel an excitable urge exploding in her stomach, to rush back to the apartment in double-quick time before dawn, for she was always hoping to become the television wife, to see herself as greatly loved, with the jubilant political husband – Head of State world leader – to actually experience what it felt like to be beside someone like this, and which would prove once and for all it really was her in the picture, that she felt this love seen on television, and by establishing her authentically beyond any measure of doubt to the Harbour Master and the stupid monkey.

In those nightly pilgrimages they heard the *Monteverdi* vespers sung over the droning of ancestor country. The winds whistled through the buildings, and through the skies, she was able to see that many swans were gathering in each ancient breath, and their flight formed landscape through the perpetual rain.

Yes, the swans were multiplying, nesting among flooded trees, reeds and swan weed, and had already overfilled ponds in the abandoned botanical gardens and a small lake in the city's zoo, then the city's shallow lakes where they were breeding along the bays, gullies and inlets.

At night, squadrons of swans flew up and down the brown-coloured river that cut through the city, and Oblivia sensed they were in training for something even they had not quite anticipated. She thought that they were trying to tell her something. The thought shifted around in her mind – floated here and there while it grew, and then she was tossing it around something big, throwing it about, slamming it against the wall of her brain, until it became something ugly and angry, too hot to hold, too tough to manipulate and examine, the thing that she was too afraid to recognise – that not only was there was a lack of communication in her 'so called' marriage, feelings of betrayal, manipulation, and abandonment were the goal-posts where havoc scored inside her head.

The thought stuffing up her mind made her angry, and she tramped on in the nightly parade, unable to concentrate on the swans flying up and down the river. Well! What was the problem? Obsession. Television wife. She started to ask herself questions: Why was she always in a hurry for someone she only saw on television? Who she only knew through the television? Where each image was a portrait of a happy marriage? Even she believed it. And whenever she saw herself on television, she could only explain herself in sketches of what she appeared to be – the image presented, rather then remembering her actual presence as Warren Finch's wife, and always, forgetting the details of ever being with this man who was her husband. She could not remember him – had no idea, even what he looked like unless she saw him on the television. But none of these things mattered really. What really mattered was that she could not admit to herself that Warren was using an impostor. *Of course,* the Harbour Master kept explaining with the impact of discovering nuclear energy, *the big high and mighty Warren Finch doesn't want to be seen with some complete myall like you for a wife. She is the pretend wife. Not you at all.* But, Oblivia wouldn't believe it. Could feel it in her bones that she was the television wife. She promised herself, the Harbour Master and the monkey, she would prove it.

Of course they wanted to know how she was going to do that. But her mind slipped, went slack, played tricks on her and, without the steam to propel the thought, she again concentrated on the swans, following them with poetry running through her brain, *The swan has leaped into the desolate heaven: That image can bring wildness, bring a rage to end all things, to end...*The swans continued the circuit and she followed while she thought less about the apartment, and more about the need to keep up with flight. They were communicating with her about flight, long flight, not about Warren Finch who was living it up elsewhere – resuming life as usual as the head of state of a dilapidated country in a dilapidated world.

The monkey had changed too. It decided to move out of the apartment because it had become too dirty. He had heard the girl talk about seeing poor, neglected monkeys in the zoo. He became very excited and left quietly in the middle of the night when the Harbour Master was asleep in front of the television. He went to the zoo and unlocked the door to the monkey house. From then on, he was the head honcho of a dancing troupe of monkeys that went to live as fugitives in the cathedral in the city, amongst the almond and fig trees growing from crevices in its sandstone walls. Free at last, the monkeys were popular buskers in the city malls. Always cashed up to pay the street children for protection.

The Harbour Master stayed home sulking about the monkey becoming independent and the apartment being emptied of swans. He sat on the couch. He was in rough seas with the Panasonic television that blared old cricket games in the apartment night and day. Games that had been played years ago, and in-between the news, where he could watch Warren Finch's face growing older every day. But there was no great satisfaction in watching someone grow older. Well! Not the face that never reached the destination of fulfilment, where Warren's continuing triumphs – each seemingly more glorious than any before – were always sensed as personal failure.

Yes, the Harbour Master still preferred to glare at the television. It was as though he was trying to steer the whole darn spectacular life of Warren Finch from the couch, propelling him along blasphemously, while hollering over some invisible howling rain, *You know, people can talk and talk about how they are going to save the Aboriginal, world, ditto people…it goes on all the time, always wanting to save people who would rather talk about how they want to save themselves. When are you going to start thinking straight about that, Mr Warren Bloody Finch?*

Well! Let's end the bad vibes with the cricket bats and kneepads that were all flying about the room. Why be so unhappy? Any of Warren Finch's newest major concerns were challenging to the old Harbour Master. He always had to prove how he had seen better, or knew about something that was absolutely more amazing in some off-beaten track of the world to laugh about. Still! You could not avoid the fact that Warren's life was being lived at a higher percentage elsewhere with the glamorous 'promise' wife, the First Lady of whatnot, than being wasted in hanging around, and minding reality in a swan-filthy apartment.

The Street Serpent

This was not all you will see in the city, this junkyard from where swan flocks ascended into the heavens, and flew the brisk breeze amongst swallows and pigeons up where ghosts shouted down: *What a load of rubbish!* But the swans overcrowding in the botanical gardens were edgy with hunger. They searched for swampy waters and found nothing. These old luckless things could only return to the abandoned sprawl of overgrown gardens, to roam among the butterflies and insects. A place that served no purpose to city people who grew nothing, but ate their food from packets. They called this sprawling greenery *a flippen and friggen untidy mess!* And saw no point to having this old-fashioned, overgrown park in a city where there were people starving – better off living off the Government, and safer on the streets, like those living in the lane.

You could watch people like that walking by the old city's botanical gardens that made them think of a nursery rhyme for children, of still believing the city's legendary story that this tangled mess of brambles was the home of an overgrown *Lepus europaeus* called the hare king, but otherwise ignoring the place, applying the same sense of invisibility usually given to anything useless, obscure and made redundant. This landscape was once prized throughout the world as having the richest library of the most precious, rare and extinct flora on Earth.

The people in this city did not regularly use words like *once upon a time* for being nostalgic and remembering things, but once, when it was hoped that the bad weather would change back to normal climatic patterns, the city had also hoped that the historical richness of the site would never be lost. Whatever was within man's power to save his environment was done for the rare old trees, flowers and shrubs, but in the end the struggle to save greenery seemed meaningless. The long drought killed kindness in hardened hearts. Then, when the drought was replaced by soddening rains, year in and year out, the canopy grew into an impenetrable wilderness too dangerous to people, and the precinct was just another place locked up forever.

Oblivia ignored the rusty old signs. What were signs to her? These ones were wired all along the fence of wrought iron. She did not bother reading the warning of the dangers of entering, or notice what the penalties were for trespassing in neglected areas such as these old botanical gardens. The signs that might have once stopped homeless people squatting, now robbed the city's memory of the gardens. Who in the street life of the city would guess why such a wasteland had ever been created? It was as though places of antiquity had lost their usefulness to those who lived for the moment, the here and now, and where the gates were forced shut by boa-constrictor thick renegade vines, wound like a monster's woven carpet throughout the wrought iron lacework.

The swans circling in the sky above the neglected gardens guarded the green leafiness of their island in the city, while people who had come from other parts watched the phenomenon like it was a thing of wonder. The Chinese people, who had long lived in the city, praised each sighting of swan flight for its momentary beauty, and called the swans *hong* in their own language. A story floated around the Greek side of the city, of likening the swans circling the island of wilderness to a long ago belief of a mystical island surrounded by white swans where Apollo was born. These were all poor people's stories. A good feeling was left in the air from seeing swans, they said. The air felt lucky. Even – prosperous. Safe. Warren Finch was in the city. Everyone felt in a blood-tingling way that something big was about to happen.

All of the broken birds had been set free from the apartment in The People's Palace, and now, in the botanical gardens, Oblivia was watching the assembling swans swarm in numbers so vast they blocked the moonlight. But this freak of nature plagued her. When had her swans bred? Where had time gone? How many seasons of swans' breeding had passed by and she had not noticed? How long had she lived in the city?

This was the reason why she never went to the genies' magic shop any more. It was not just that the owl never returned once all of the swans had been released, or even that the owl's memory had receded from her mind as silently as its flight. It was how she had been kept captive, while time had been stolen from her in those long nocturnal journeys following the owl around the streets with a swan under her arm. Now she knew there had been many seasons of swan-egg cradling and cygnets reared which signalled above all else, that she had spent more time in the city then she had ever expected.

The girl had not even thought about saying *goodbye* or *sayonara* to Machine, nor said *yunngu*, that she was going away for good, nor a simple *ciao* to the Harbour Master. Leaving was leaving. Nothing more than a curious unemotional response – a flatness of spirit for the flight inward when being removed from places, as it had from being pulled off the hull and before that, from the tree. She left Machine to piss around in his own fairytale. Left him mooning over his cats. The Harbour Master? Left imagining why his monkey had just trucked off for nothing, and to blow his mind away with whatever took his fancy about Mr Fat Cat, Indigenous leader of the country, Warren Finch on television.

She had just kept walking, barely noticing the network of overgrown hedges reaching for the sky inside the wrought iron fence surrounding the botanical garden. When she was far away into the park steaming with early morning mist, she no longer heard the skin and bone dogs barking on the street outside. The street kids and their dogs still followed her from the lane as though she was some kind of reclusive ghost kid, just like an Aboriginal *tinkerbell* fairy. Would she lead them somewhere? That was the thrill of it all.

But now, outside the botanical gardens, they held back and just hung about on the footpath, too augured in dusty city mythologies of what lay beyond the gates – where they heard thousands of noisy myna birds pealing hotly at one another from orange aloe flowers growing all over the place like weeds, and flying aggressively through the dense undergrowth. Their dogs panted for water beside the legs of their owners, while all the while the ghosts from the park were out there in the street in broad daylight, whispering scary stories close into the ears of the children about this and that, but mostly about the troubles of dark nights in this wilderness, and scaring the dogs stupid too.

Where was the guidance from elders? It was the cruellest fate for children of bad weather times, whose brains had been clogged with mysteries of their own making, more than you could imagine – where would you believe? The skies were haunted with the ghosts of swallows and pigeons flying about. Among the throng of children out there on the footpath, their Mohawk-haired leaders of skin and bone were swearing black and blue at their mad dogs snapping at the air. These animals saw invisibility better than anything real, and everything untrustworthy, while all the while, they went on lurching madly about on their chains.

Well! What would you expect? This was not an ashram out on the street. Theirs was a city that bred the jumpiness of sissy-girl boys who normally saw ghosts flying about – right above the streets. They always pointed out the ghosts travelling through the mist and smoke rising over the city – and even travelling procession-like in the sky trains of diseased bats. Well! Lucky virus bats were asleep. They were dangling upside-down through several groves of trees in the old botanical gardens.

And what of the Aboriginal girl they followed? That skinny thing in dark trackies, hoodie covering her face with the swans flying around her? Well! If you think like a sissy-girl, then she was not real neither. They saw her as a spiritual ancestor because they knew what an Aboriginal looked like, since they were modelling their subsistence as it were, albeit only on junk food, on the country's original inhabitants. She was their backfill now.

Erratic, unexplainable weather makes you feel no good in the heart, and this was how they felt about Oblivia with the ghost swans that seemed to multiply into clouds when they flew in the night. They talked about how she was the first Aboriginal spirit they had ever seen, the only way any could return as far as they knew from the total cleansing of the city of all those people 'rounded up' and impounded in the North country in the old days, many years ago.

The dogs continued barking although Oblivia was now far away in the undergrowth with the fluttering butterflies, leaving the whole shebang kid-and-dog thing chasing one another up and down the footpath in the bedlam of yelling and dog howls. Those darn dogs, uncontrollable if not kept properly tethered to their chains. Dogs more wild for chasing ghosts than anything else, driven mad by the smell of swans and bats. Oblivia ignored the noise and kept going. Soon, she would not hear the little war with other gangs converging on the footpath.

Hey! What's happening sissy-girls? We were here a long time first.

What is a long while? Ten minutes?

There were rules about standing your own ground, even if you were a sissy-girl when anybody could be *hookin' em* and *trickin'* a good gang.

Hey! Wait youses.

Nah! Let that blackfella fairy go. She's ours. Not yours. We will fight you for her if you like.

Come on then…

The river of bats streamed over the battle on the footpath without noticing a thing, and kept flying towards the epicentre of the darkened parklands. The colony had come from city suburbs where it had flown the previous evening at dusk to find gardens with fig trees loaded with ripened fruit. Down below their roosting trees, Oblivia continued to crawl through tunnels in the undergrowth that foxes had once clawed apart to chase the aged hare king. She passed several grassy fields trampled by the swans, and finally arrived at the grasslands where the colonies of swans were gathered around a marshy lake infested with insects. Who knows the truth, but it was in these grasslands where swans had preened themselves and slept in waves with long necks curled s-shaped over their backs, that life seemed the cleanest, and where the air filled her mind with a sense of peace.

She ignored the bats snoring in skeleton trees, to listen to the conversation of the swans' agitated whistling, and swinging necks lunging and hissing, before falling into quietness, when suddenly, the cicadas roared from the treetops. The alarm radiated over the entire precinct of the abandoned jungle of undergrowth and sprawling treetops. The butterflies of blue, yellow and black jumped in midair. The swans scrambled, tumbling with quivering wings spread, fanning the rising mist to take off, and in a stormy rush, all were gone.

The Harbour Master was bone-idle, sitting up there in the apartment of The People's Palace, and actually minding his own business in his smelly old singlet and shorts when all of a sudden, a news flash appeared right there on the television, and he saw the assassination.

Those people in charge of television programs should think about what they are doing to an old man. Poor old thing was shaken. Who had been half asleep and dreaming about Rigoletto, and half watching an opera program on the ABC. When he saw the assassination he instantly felt sick. Soon, all there was to see on the television was news replayed a thousand times about the assassination. This was the fact of the matter. Warren Finch had been shot in the streets of the city, and his life was fading.

The old Harbour Master's face was concrete grey and motionless, but his head was spinning. He was like the rest of the world –' spellbound and compelled to watch hours of repeated footage about Warren Finch's life on news media television.

He thought that he saw the girl-wife, a glimpse of somebody that looked like her anyhow, running beside the ambulance trolley that was carrying the heaviest public life in the world as though he weighed nothing. Bodyguards he recognised as those genies threw themselves in front of cameras to shield anyone getting a proper view of Warren Finch. All seemed to be lost now. All lost. But somehow in all of those thoughts of loss that now blanketed the world, something extraordinary happened when a burst of energy filled the apartment. Could it possibly be? *Warren at last visiting…* The apartment felt as though it had become alive.

A sensation of phenomenal energy swishing around madly – horizontally bouncing from one wall to the other, and each time it passed, cold air slapped the Harbour Master across the face until he had been struck countless times.

It had to be Warren Finch who lay dying on a stretcher on television too lifeless to look at his watch or answer his mobile phone, but he had come back to the apartment like a crazy person with no time to spare, and acting like he could not find his favourite pair of socks. Well! He left everything in his path upturned and strewn, because sure enough, he would not be staying long. His voice was another matter: it was like a large ball at the end of a piece of rope being dragged into the ear of the Harbour Master, as well as Machine downstairs with his cats – *Where is she?*

Then the Harbour Master snapped. He felt very alone with the solemn television presenter who was trying to become his friend while he spoke intimately about the life of Warren Finch who lay covered in bloodied sheets on the stretcher, and as the journalist was trying to speak with the ambulance men frantically working with drips and life-saving equipment, they moved to take Finch to a hospital. But, the old man was no longer in the mood to know whether Warren Finch was dead or alive. He packed his bag in a jiffy, all his clothes (not much), found the monkey's exotic clothes of course, and after a quick, final glance around the apartment, he left very speedily, through the gushing fountains, and the mist settling on the mossy statues. He walked straight past the openly crying Machine who was hugging his wailing cats, and was all too occupied watching the television to notice the front door slamming and the Harbour Master screaming, *Where is the wife in grief?*

The swans have all gone to the sky, but the sound of their wings beating quickened every beat in the girl's heart. Swish! Swish! The sounds resonated, but she felt only the familiar claustrophobic sense of being trapped in a confined space, a place where her vision had been reduced to a keyhole view, of being slung back into the roots of the ancient eucalyptus tree. It was a view she had seen before, a blanket of swans forming into a giant bird in flight.

But this world was falling apart, and the girl's heart raced like a trapped animal looking for the fastest way out. There were voices everywhere now with the news spreading quicksilver through the dense population in the streets. Yes. The city itself was screaming for her, beckoning, beseeching, or if you like, crucially confronting her with its great pain by trying to pull her into its troubles. *Ahhh! Ahhh! NO! She's looking the other way. Is she actually doing that? Her husband is dying for pity's sake. Don't go. She is running away. Come quickly! Come back you somebody. Somebody! Stay!* The city people cried a million buckets of tears for their famous Warren Finch to live. But! But, this President's wife, she was a very good question indeed. What was she doing? Where was she? The problematic promise bride who had turned up from nowhere! Her name being just too plain forgettable and foreign – the real heart of the issue: who would remember such a fictitious, ridiculous name? *Where are you, you person?*

She barely heard the quibbling of thousands of people calling for her around the city. It was really more the memory evoked from long ago, that warned her to keep running from painful voices falling over the reeds in the swampland to reach her – bowling over the beauty of wild flowers that were kind of special, and crackling branches of trees where dozy fruit bats had fallen flat on the ground.

Now she could be seen by the swans in the sky as she ran around the marshy lake in the botanical gardens, and through the hare king's bramble tunnels where she sees the grey hare run off in front of her, and heads after it loping through paths that the foxes had dug. All the while she is looking skywards – trying to keep up with her swans flying overhead in the cloud, and needing not to lose them, she must stay under their shadow. It is as though she is running in somebody else's dream, where someone like Warren Finch is calling – *fly me to the moon*. She sees the three genies too. They are like giants standing in passing clouds, talking to one another while they struggle to steer the swans flying wildly away from the city. *Listen! Can't you hear? She's making a wish. She wants to fly with the swans so that they do not leave her behind.*

Swans were not the answer in times like this. The big birds were struggling up there in the sky. A changed wind blowing in from the opposite direction was so strong that the wings of the swans were being buffeted. The wind circled like a cyclone and carried everything in its path towards the centre of the city, including people hurtling through the streets who had wanted to see their visiting Head of State. The swan wings became sails that were being blown backwards in squalls moving towards the noise of thousands of screaming people caught in the storm in the streets where Warren Finch had just been assassinated.

Whether she ran or not in dreams of other things, nothing could change the fact about running against the wind, for she was back next to Warren Finch. Beside him, she felt strangely re-united to the moment when he had left the apartment on the day long ago when she had arrived in the city. She still feels the strength of his control even as he lies flat over her lap. She cannot move from his weight, but her mind switches uncontrollably in a futile struggle. She shivers with the shock of finding herself beside Warren, replacing the television wife, even though in her mind, she is still chasing after the hare king through raspberry brambles. Alone and exposed, she recognises the faces of the street kids placed here and there among the crowds falling over her, hears the approaching sounds of sirens of police cars and ambulances speeding through the city. She feels terrified because they will think that she has killed him. She does not remember, does not know what has happened anymore. Was she just chasing the hare king? Everywhere the voices of police on loud speakers rip apart both reality and dreams, and she focuses on the helicopters hovering haphazardly low, with rotor blades whirling where the swans are flying above her.

The pains of distance roar through her like a flood emptying into insignificance, that leaves behind, as in dry plains, a surreal indifference in the midst of chanting crowds that have become hundreds of thousands deep, and still throng on the streets, as police desperately try to force through an ambulance. Hemmed in by the cries and screams, she is stuck, unable to leave, and cowers into Warren's limpness. There is no chance of escaping, except when she looks upwards to the swans correcting their flight above the narrow street with the sudden disappearance of the wind. He is going now.

The doors of the ambulance were quickly pushed closed, but nothing can move through the outpouring of grief from the surging crowds blocking the road. In this bedlam, where there is no control over what is happening, the security people manage to create a barrier and have the body loaded into a helicopter precariously hovering above the buildings. The girl-wife is left behind while the helicopter makes its way to the hospital, but the crowds break through the barrier in efforts to express their grief to her. She is enveloped in a sea of hands. Strangers one after the other shake her hand, tearfully hug her, and pass her on to the next person in grief, and the next, until she is lost and drowning in the crowds. She is pulled by this tide of grief through the city streets, packed with people crying and praying, people determined to express their gratitude to her, for the man who had watched over the global security of all peoples, whom they had known as Warren Finch.

The long day slipped into evening and by this time there were the hands of the monkeys, street children, the Harbour Master, security guards, police, the genie minders – strangers steering her into the night.

A mother of all storms could grieve too, along with all those sad old country and western songs piped through the flooding city streets that carried, among other drifting things, an abandoned Chinese dragon that only yesterday had played a bamboo flute sweetly from its mouth to evoke a desert homeland, when the mythical creature danced a thousand-year-old ceremony through this foreign and soulless city as a welcome to the new President. Well! Its festival was over. So were the drums, and the clanging cymbals, the big brass band, the Scots Highland bagpipes, and all the jazz and gospel choirs, as well as the spinifex dancers with clapping sticks in front of the swans dancing with wings spread wide. These people had welcomed the President of Humanity they treated like a living God with death. They were all probably sleeping now.

Oblivia, the missing wife of the assassinated President, emerged through the large open mouth of the dragon. She looked around, still not knowing whether she had killed Warren Finch or not, and then stepped out into the ghost fog that rested its old body over the city. There had been another cyclone during the night and a tidal surge had flooded many of the city's streets. She held onto the golden tentacles that flowed along the side of the multi-coloured creature with mirrored scales, while it rocked and moved effortlessly through the darkness.

Only the monkey living in the main street's Cathedral was up this early. It was listening to the silence of traditional Country – the only sound it believed belonged to this city. The monkey was way up high, sitting in a small fig tree that grew out of the steepled roof of the sandstone cathedral. He began saying his morning prayers to his distant monkey God, this God and that God, the God of the church where he lived. Prayers that took forever, until he could no longer concentrate on what he was praying for, or even believing which God loved him equally with other Gods. He started looking down through the lonely fog spirit travelling through the city, hoping nostalgically for a dawn chorus of songbirds that no longer existed. Then the monkey had to remind itself that some old habits died hard. The white furry creature sung a religious hymn of joyous awesomeness about how he too had become invisible like the gods, and how he actually felt magician-like. He could disappear then return to life again without even knowing it had happened.

It is only Rigoletto, a flock of common myna birds squawked as they flew out of the cathedral's nave, *that religious monkey from Asia*. The monkey ignored bird chatter, particularly that of starlings, crows and myna birds. He believed that he was too good for screechy types of birds. He preferred to think of himself as an old gentlemanly monkey that looked down at life, like he was now looking down at fog ghosts, but this time was different. He saw the Chinese dragon floating along the street with a cold-looking bony girl clinging to the side.

From so far above, he was not sure whether it was the girl he was supposed to be looking after or not. Rigoletto's eyes were not like they used to be, even if he could clearly remember a time in his life that was spent snatching fruit, and stuffing his mouth with a whole peeled mandarin while performing multiple somersaults on the top of a stick all day long for tourists. You need good eyes for that. He often reflected about this magnificent feat, and about how this so-called land of opportunity had robbed him of his spontaneity and each point-zero-zero-zero-one-half-of-a-percent of a dollar he could have earned from performing the trick right throughout Asia. He doubted whether he had the heart for showing off this kind of trick now. He felt that a big devil in this country had gutted him of every bit of spontaneous happiness he had in his body. Now he casually looked down with an accusing eye at the fog ghosts just to show – he knew it was her.

Rigoletto sprung from his perch in a heavy free-falling fashion that felt as though his body was full of lead, and in no time at all, he had scaled down the wall of the cathedral and half swam, half ran through the storm-water, until he too was holding on to the dragon's golden tentacles to save himself. He worked his way along the dragon until he was behind Oblivia and peering over her shoulder and looking at her face, to make sure it was *her*. Lo and behold, it screeched. It was the Harbour Master's *gardée*.

This made the monkey very angry. He leapt in front of Oblivia, splashed about in what resembled a sort of dog paddle, and dealt with the crisis by thrusting himself as stiff as a board in and out of the water, and screamed his native language into her face to ask her what she was doing, which in Australian English meant: *You are crazy. What in the bloody hell's name are you thinking? Don't you know what you are doing? Haven't you got a clue in your head?* He swallowed a lot of water from screaming his lungs out for nothing in all forms of language. Swallowed language. Moral language. Peace and harmony language. Religious language. Angry language. Law language. Culture language. Political language. Enthusiastic language. Monkey language. The wings of language will never again fly so triumphantly in the soulless country. If the monkey wanted Oblivia to go back inside the dragon where she would be safe, she paid no attention to a single thing it said.

Instead, Oblivia looked straight through the monkey as though it never existed, and concentrated on the low fog shrouding the high-rise glass buildings on both sides of the street. Her eyes focussed on the darkened haze of a cloud of flying swans with steam flowing out of their nostrils, their wings labouring in flight from pulling the strings attached to the dragon, pulling it ahead.

She heard a voice coming from the water – coming all of this way from somebody's final resting place. Warren Finch's voice, teasing as he tried to hop on board the dragon of great hope and expectations, almost as mighty as the dawn swans flying Apollo's chariot while he pulled the sun across the sky. *Are you trying to escape?*

Then he was gone. Or it may have just been the monkey Rigoletto complaining as he swung himself behind her again, and when he had a good grip of some golden tentacles, he kicked her for all of his troubles, and as many times as he could to force her towards the dragon's mouth. But nobody feels the kicks of an invisible, oppressed, and foreign-to-boot monkey that did not like living in Australia. The defeated monkey ended up sitting on top of the dragon sulking, while nervously chewing bubble gum in its big teeth.

As he looked around the deserted and broken city, it was only a cheap form of advertising that managed to fly around his head. The flittering myna birds had spied an audience to spread their same old government propaganda about generous household assistance that they had been trained to sing for peanuts. Worthless incentives. The monkey had no need for a government. He stubbornly turned his flat face this way and that, looked into space, and was not buying any of it. He was more concerned about myna birds alerting the security people.

Rigoletto already knew that the flooded city was being scoured from top to bottom to find the girl-wife from a call he had received on his miniature mobile phone. The phone's ringtone went ding dong all night, until he answered it. It was the Harbour Master hollering into his ear that the girl was all there was left now for the people of the world that had gone into mourning after Warren Finch's assassination.

Listen! the absent Harbour Master chattered into the complaining monkey ear: *She was his wife so of course they want to find the only living thing that they think was close to their dead legend who they reckoned had championed peace for people across the world, even if he didn't, and was only a self-proclaimed Indigenous hero who had made it all the way to the top in a suit and haven't I told you before about the importance of looking well dressed in a suit, because it goes to show that even an Aboriginal man in Australia can get elected by the common Aboriginal-hating people to be the Head of State of Australia, and that was a very good thing, even if it was the best thing that ever happened to the flippen what have you country, and now some mongrel moron still had to come along and murder him out of jealous racist spite. So, don't groan – of course she has to be found, even if you and I KNOW she was not close to him, and she can't save them from themselves, but she still belongs to these people because she is still the First Lady of whatnot.*

Any little monkey could rattle off a litany of worse things happening in his world, but Rigoletto sat with steely red face on the dragon, and thought very seriously about prescribed responsibility as the worst kind of thing that could have happened to him. It was the only problem he had with being a pet monkey. He knew that he was supposed to step in like a man instead of just being a monkey and become the girl's guardian if the Harbour Master was not around, although very clearly, he recognised that the act of guardianship over others did not come naturally to him. He hated being trained to act responsibly. There was nothing in it. He was not the Harbour Master's pet monkey by any stretch of the imagination.

It was moments like these where a few guilty pangs forced Rigoletto to forget he was supposed to be a pet by acting like a wild animal. A wild animal was not supposed to look after people. It was supposed to be the other way around. Where was the beauty in a monkey worrying about people? His brain bolted from the reality of floating along a flooded city street on a magnificent but ruined dragon. His idea of beauty lay tens of thousands of kilometres away where long-necked swans foraged for insects in muddy rice fields with the swallows, in a world that enjoyed listening to exquisite plum-blossom music being played on a bamboo flute. He held this thought. He hummed through bubble gum sticking between his clicking teeth, and did not lose any sense of the flute's musicality in his own rendition of the plum- and cherry-blossom music that he had locked in his head.

These were only the delusional thoughts of a monkey that had enough troubles occupying his mind than to be bothered with fantasies being projected on him by the Harbour Master like, *You poor, old, good monkey.* He had the worries of a thousand monkeys. So *da, da, de, da, and la, la, la!* Presently, aloft on the dragon, his main worry was the soaking wet Rigoletto jacket. Would it shrink on his furry body and strangle him? A monkey sitting on a dragon in the middle of some common big-storms-of-climate-change-raising-sea-levels event was nothing to worry about. He hugged himself tight. Rigoletto had seen flooding on seaboard city streets all over the world. It was really just as natural as seeing water flooding in the lanes of Venice, Bangladesh or Pakistan.

Where are you Harbour Master? You got to come back. Rigoletto's experience of global warming was academic, not practical. He remained on guard while Oblivia continued to be dragged along with the dragon through the water, knowing that very soon she would be found. She was part of the most important story happening in the world right now. There could be no other way for the girl-wife. If she survived...

Travelling Road Show

I was a terrific funeral. Everyone was saying just how marvellous it was. Best speeches. Good old-people's songs like: *Through the ages I will remember blue eyes crying in the rain...someday when we meet up yonder, we will stroll hand in hand again.* Still the best bloke, that old Hank Williams, and others like him. But things took a turn for the worse after that.

The biggest cathedral in the country, where Warren Finch's body lay in state, kept overflowing with mourners. All sorts turned up to pay respects, including the everyday local mourners of the city. All those homeless people who would not go home. The poor from the streets and alleyway communes started elbowing for space with overseas dignitaries, Heads of State of other countries – many with fragile diplomatic relationships with Australia. The Earth's powerful demanded appeasement. They wanted their very own religious services. It all added up. No wonder the country was broke. Still, the country pulled together. It showed some respect and unity for the situation. Then other important people started filing through the door. World musicians wanted to play together for world peace. The world's most popular professional actors brought glitz and bling to mourning and paying respects to the big actor himself who had known them all. Even King Billy kept calling into the city more and more tidal surges flooding through the streets, and up the steps of the cathedral.

All services for the dearly beloved, the mourning, the last respects, country and western music, hymns and special foreign music, were heard continuously, and on a daily basis. In actual fact, nobody thought a thing about the consequences of unabated mourning. Certainly, no one questioned the excessiveness of sorrow, and whether there was going to be an end point of mourning for Warren Finch. That was until finally, one day in the middle of a lot of smoke, what looked like most of the countryman's wildflowers and gum leaves arrived with scores of his ceremonial elders from his Aboriginal Government, and they sung his world. They said that they were smoking his spirit back to their own traditional country. *His spirit was no longer in this place.* This was when the sky practically fell down, when they – these people (his own people) – wanted to remove the coffin from the cathedral.

Total pandemonium broke out between all the different types of mourners until officials one, two and three, with more to follow, told these cheeky people from the bush of some far-flung part of the country with an unpronounceable name that nobody had ever heard of, that Warren Finch's importance as a man far outweighed any of their cultural considerations, *and hum! Peace Brother! Go in peace. Let that be the end of the matter.* Yet it was a stalemate! Stalemate! These people from the bush would not listen to anybody. They would not leave the coffin, and they just stood there amongst the choir singing, and made even greater smoke with their leaves, even though anyone could see that a long queue was forming behind them with urgent people becoming very irate.

The bush people wanted to talk about culture. No! Ears were only listening to the church choir. Everyone wanted to get firm now about this disturbance. These Aboriginal people were told to stop being un-Australian, and to leave – their time was up. Did they not understand that everyone had to take equal turns to stand next to the coffin? Move on! *Why?* the Aboriginal elders asked, *His spirit is gone now. Up in Country.* But their explanation would never do. Even if Warren Finch lay dead in his coffin, he was still Head of State until someone else could take his place. *Was that possible? Yes.* He could still give advice and blessings to his government, just like he did when he was alive. And even though he was dead, he would always be one of the most loved world leaders that ever existed in the history of mankind. How could anyone argue about this? Who could replace him?

The more his Aboriginal people argued and argued, persisting it was their right to take his body home, as though his body was like that of a normal body of a kinsman and should be given a proper burial – the more they were treated like selfish people, and the more the idea of a final resting place became full of contention and attributed to the whole country's denial that Warren Finch was really dead, when they preferred to think of him as just sleeping like Sleeping Beauty.

Well! Grass grew. And the bush folk had made a permanent campsite beside the coffin.

Finally, in a nasty episode of aghast, there was a string of official and much publicised questions raised about who these Aboriginal people were – who did they think themselves, and why had they turned up in the first place, and who had given them room to do native things without permission in the most important cathedral in the country, making everything feel tainted in their sorrow? Were they really Aboriginal? Did they really belong to Warren Finch's ancestral country? Anthropologists, lawyers, and other experts like archaeologists, sociologists and historians were called to examine the genealogies of these people. An emergency legislation was bulldozed through parliament in the dead of night which claimed that Warren Finch was the blood relative of every Australian, which gave power to the government to decide where he was to be buried.

Ha! Ha! Ha! Roll in laughter, because it was funny, and thought inconceivable that Warren Finch could be buried in some wilderness place with no public access, where only a handful of Aboriginal people who knew the country would know how to get to his grave to say some prayers that they had made up themselves. There would be national prayers in time, legislated in a National Warren Finch Prayer Book. Would you trust Aboriginal people to stick to Australian law? The police were obliged under the regulations of emergency laws to intervene in the lives of all Aboriginal people, to throw the bush people out of the cathedral. Then, when there were no words left, and nowhere to live in a city that despised the presence of Aboriginal people, Warren Finch's clans-people went home.

The body remained in the cathedral, stuck there indefinitely in the smoky pall of burning coals – the incense of frankincense and myrrh, and emotional glue swelling in the broken-hearted city. The highly decorated coffin of the best black sassafras timber had been made by a master craftsman one hundred and fifty years before, who had willed the magnificent coffin to the nation for burying a great Australian man. This was the occasion, and the coffin was surrounded by burning candles, and adorned with the fresh bouquets of roses that kept arriving in the cathedral from rich people with enough money to keep sending roses grown on the plateaus of who knows where. The roses were piled into a mountain that mourners stumbled over, and spread like a range out into the frequently flooded streets.

There were no plans to bury the body. This was because no one in charge of the rare occasions of important world leader funerals seemed to consider it was necessary. It was not easy to make the final decision because as time kept passing with endless rows of grief callers parading by the coffin in the mass flowered cathedral, it was very easy to forget that the body had to be taken to a cemetery. Outside the cathedral, it was impossible to move through the city streets packed with fresh and decaying flowers and, every day, another round of mourners carrying *Farewell Warren* tributes on paper and cardboard signs held aloft on sticks.

And still more mourners came to see Warren Finch's coffin, pilgrim mourners weaving themselves through the country until they reached the country's most major cathedral, and kings and queens, counts and countesses, and other important overseas people who used up vast amounts of their country's wealth by emptying barrels of jet fuel to fly over vast distances and oceans to get to the cathedral. With the airport busy with flights, the tourist economy blossomed, so the Government kept welcoming visitors from the other side of the world. The mourners stood wherever they could in a slow line to the coffin.

As some more time passed, the infrastructure of the dilapidated city became an ever greater, uncontrollable mess. Rubbish everywhere. Power shortages. Infrastructure collapse. The sewerage system backing up and becoming clogged with nowhere to go. Stuff like that. Every foreign country dignitary expected to raise their own flag on the one flagpole outside the cathedral, have their own religious service, or the cathedral cleared of other nationals including Australians, or wanted a massive high-culture ceremony involving hundreds of their own nationals.

Whatever the homage, no-one cared less if nobody else understood their foreign language, since the internal affairs of Australia figured way down the scale of worldly matters after Warren Finch's mysterious assassination which appeared more like stupidity, something that would have been easily avoided even in the tiniest and war-torn poorest countries of the world.

It was a form of greed really with everyone wanting a share of the grief, lingering and dilly-dallying in their worship around the city while negotiating greater opportunities for migration into the country to save it from this anarchy, and some settling in as immigrants and asylum seekers themselves, as though they wanted to become local, and not wanting to return home. Their airplanes parked all over the place stayed at the airport. There were highbrow questions raised about this: What was the role of a griever? It was not clear because no one had had to think about something like this before. Not in this city, state, or country.

The glut of reverence seemed as though nothing was good enough for Warren Finch after his death, a fact verified by the girl-wife who agreed to these proceedings. The Government people kept her whereabouts top secret, but she was just sitting around under lock and key in The People's Palace apartment. The red-headed family marched in and took over the executorial role of Warren Finch's immediate family. The pathetic, mourning Machine who was full of excuses for the girl escaping to the botanical gardens was ignored. He was told by Big Red to mind his own business, shut down his fountains spraying water all over the place, stop playing Dean Martin music, and to remove his cats. *And to do it pronto.*

Every day the security people in charge of *the widow* moved through the quietened building, to take her to the cathedral. The girl-wife widow, First Lady of whatnot, perhaps Presidential killer, became the object of consultation about the mourning business, where she was to shake hands and nod to whatever dignitary mourners were saying in their own languages. *I am looking for the swans, they are leaving,* she often told these people, mouthing the words soundlessly as usual, and gesturing with her hands.

The diplomatic embassies looked puzzled as she tugged on their suit sleeves or ceremonial robes, yet they always followed her gaze around the nave in the cathedral, along the rafters, up in the hollow shell ceilings painted with frescos of angels with the wings of swans. *These are swans in a cage*, the French diplomat proclaimed to his people, and in the style of their old poet Baudelaire, they then murmured to each other, *And this swan, is castigating God.* The Harbour Master and the monkey Rigoletto always sat spellbound in a pew near the back of the cathedral. They were quite caught up with the razzamatazz surrounding the coffin, and the poetry the Frenchman recited, *A swan escaped its cage: and as its feet/ With finny palms on the harsh pavement scraped,/ Trailing white plumage on the stony street,/ In the dry gutter for fresh water gaped...*

But, here we are, the whole country still cried and fretted for the loss of the irreplaceable Warren Finch, and asked: *Is this the best we can do?* Anyone would think that he had been the only Aboriginal person on the planet. The only one who had a voice, and could voice his opinion. He had become the only public Aboriginal voice of the era. The only one Australians would listen to, and reported in the newspapers, or had given their airways to whenever he spoke publicly. It certainly seemed as though there was national deafness to hearing what other Aboriginal people had to say of themselves. Perhaps it was the tone of voice? Or the message that could be heard, or could not be heard? Or the fact that the entire Aboriginal population bar this one individual did not have enough of the evangelical in their voices for proclaiming themselves sinners of their own race, like Warren Finch did on their behalf? Whatever the case, it seemed that the country was locked up inside a curse of national fever-pitch dimensions in its grief for this one Aboriginal voice now dead, but still heard throughout the world. How can you describe such a tribute in sorrow? Imagine grief as art, where perfection above all else, was to be achieved. There was

no doubt about it, that Warren Finch's life of striving for perfection
had rubbed off on the nation that now emulated his life with
perfect grief in pondering and procrastination, *How perfect could
national grief be?*

A whole month more of silliness went by along with continual
efforts to embalm the body to prevent decay, and then another
month of flags continuing to fly at half-mast, until the major
shock-jock news commentators took control. It was a field day
of open slather about keeping an unburied body lying about in
a public structure. In their broadcasting studios, they governed
public opinion by plying paranoia into talk-back fever. The
communication networks grasped the country in a teary anguished
embrace of voices, crying for their opinions to be heard and
listened to: *Why wasn't Warren Finch good enough to receive one last lap
of honour? Wasn't an Aboriginal person good enough to be treated fairly
and given the respect Australia gives to all of its other citizens?*

The city responded to its own questions by creating workplace
strikes, protests, and rioting on the streets. The squatters burnt the
abandoned buildings they had been living in. In the lanes of the
city where the homeless lived, the grief found its own language.
This nocturnal world destroyed everything that resembled its
insular lifestyle by creating bonfires of every piece of cardboard
shack they owned. Embracing grief escalated into a stranglehold
of destruction and looting over the city. The streets overran with
picketing mourners spurred on by a bellyful of Government
conspiracies in their heads. The mouth-to-mouth talk rampaging
through the streets was very simply this: *Warren Finch was not dead.*
In the uprising that now demanded the government stand down,
it was as though the protesting city thought Warren Finch could
be found amongst the wanton destruction of public property,
or under barricades of trashed cars and buses, or beyond the lines
of soldiers that had been called in to deal with the troubles.

These were only normal people of the times. People who were struggling to keep up with what was happening around them, so hard to keep up with the memories – the missing, yearned-for things in life, which now included Warren Finch. They prayed for the people who had gone missing, those that had been snatched off the street, those that had had the life beaten out of them by thugs wearing balaclavas over their faces at the end of a lane, or those seen shot and fallen to the ground on a lonely wharf in the middle of the night, then disappearing without trace. In principle, it was normal to live in hope, to hope that loved ones would return to life in the lanes and squats of the abandoned buildings, or hope for luck through sprawling suburbs where fate was as slender as a spider's thread blowing in the breeze.

The Ghost Walk

Fresh food and the body of Warren Finch travelled together. The important public officials, passionately depicting themselves as unified people, were obsessed with imagination, narrow though it was in their minds. Well! Aesthetics was all. They were pretty tricky to wipe their hands of the rioting city, by finally deciding to get rid of the coffin-worshipping in the cathedral. It was a job that had to be done, and quite frankly, they finally agreed to be finished with hand-wringing over rioters. They were over it. So, while standing around in the cathedral like a cohesive *think tank*, assembled to argue and shout each other down about what to do with the coffin, they reached a brilliant decision in total ignorance of the havoc on the streets, where the Bishop of the Cathedral was spending most of his time amongst the rioting picketers and youths breaking glass windows with rocks, trying single-handedly to calm everyone down. *You are in the Lord's presence would you believe?* He was just told to get out of the way.

It was not the Bishop's fault that he could not bring peace to the city, so with hands clasped behind his back, he strolled back inside his glorious cathedral. Then, with a quick glance around the building he had known for decades for peace and tranquillity, he singled out the public servants amongst the people crowding through the roses to reach the coffin, and rightfully asked: *What brings you down here?* The most senior public servant, the Director, drew the clergyman aside, where he spoke to him in the abstract logic of public official language about *Closing The Gap.* The Bishop knew that this was the language of economic rationing but he could not reconcile it with the language of the Church, of creating or closing a gap to catch the sinners. There was no gap between God and the Church. Yet, all was not lost on him. He was able to surmise the Government had a strategy, and during the conversation of voices speaking hastily, he heard of an assembling plan that was frequently called, *Highway Dreaming Code.* Ah! It was high talk. Way above what a normal person could begin to understand. A hard-edged decision made on the spot.

The Bishop's question of *what are you going to do about this*, with hands gesturing at the enormity of the crisis, initiated a quicker decision than would have normally occurred in the realms of public sector abstract dialogue – as impersonal as can be expected when talking about a coffin rather than a dead person – and it rightly ended with the officials complimenting him for reaching this solution himself. *Dead right, Holiness. A last lap of honour. People need to see the coffin. This is exactly what the country has been calling out for. What could be more beneficial than respecting the voices of Australians right now? This would show all of those foreigners we are in charge in this city, and that is for sure. And they can all get their planes up in the skies and go home.*

Warren Finch would be taken on a final journey to farewell the nation, and the beauty of the thing was its giving the Government time to make a final decision about where to bury the coffin in the end. The lap of honour could take as long as needed, even forever, if the need arose.

Naturally, the widow had to be consulted first, and the decision was explained to her in simple terms to spell blind her with the obvious glamour in it all, flying up the highways in a magnificent hearse. She instantly agreed of course to have the coffin removed a-s-a-p, from the cathedral. *Okay.* She was more interested in the angel swans flying on the ceiling's frescoes, tethered with the ribbons of heaven, unable to fly off. She heard the angels breathing, their warm breath falling down onto her uplifted face, and she wondered if the angels would *fly the coffin home.*

In the streets outside the cathedral, the rioters were sleeping in the pall of campfire smoke, low fog, or was it just the mist of sleeping gas, when the big Mack truck arrived. Perhaps rioting was exhausting work, or perhaps the city's angels had been rocking the night watchers' cradle, but no one stirred from the haze, lifted a head to see what was happening, stood up and yelled *daylight robbery* when the semitrailer hearse crawled in with the stealth of a sneaky fox. Even King Billy was asleep.

The huge vehicle slowly made its way through the snakelike barricades along each side of the road. The three-metre high riot barriers had been set up before nightfall when riot police pushed and crushed people off the road. With the cordon up, a long chain of heavily-armed soldiers in gas masks moved in, and were stationed on each side of the road.

The coffin was soon popped into the deep freezer of the *Fresh Food People* long-haul semitrailer attached to the Mack's cab – now painted up in blue, red and white, as though draped with the nation's flag. The semi was fully loaded and ready to hit the road at a quarter past three in the morning. *Soon,* the driver claimed through his gas mask to the sleeping widow accompanying him on this journey, *when we get the hell out of this,* he would soon be going somewhere else. This was the first and last thing he said to her. He was more interested in the road and the schedule. He normally travelled by himself and now it did not matter who was in his truck or how important they were, he still worked alone. This looming giant gripping the driver's wheel never slept. He stared ahead through black sun-reflecting sunglasses that rested on his white block-out covered nose. He wore his Aboriginal flag-coloured cap down to his eyebrows to block out the sun that would stream in the driver's window, and to keep his personal world secret, beyond the reach of others.

The cab was over-crowded. Claustrophobic. As well as the driver with all the clothing he owned on earth shoved in a bag, his collection of holy beads hanging from the rear-view mirror, and leprechaun good luck charms all over the place, he had to share the cabin with the security, all big sweaty units squashed up against each other, and the recently widowed First Lady thing – although what room did a mere slip of a thing like her need?

Even the Harbour Master, reunited with the recalcitrant Rigoletto sulking on his lap, had invited himself along for the ride. They were both squashed in a corner of the back seat next to Oblivia and were whispering to one another about having seen the security men before. It was hard to place where, the Harbour Master said, but he knew them. The girl thought the genies had come back into her life disguised as middle-aged men who now suspected her of killing her husband. These security men sat around in the cab of the truck and acted like Supreme Court judges. They whinged about dragging a coffin around the country, which they said was a stupid idea. Their power radiated through the driver's cab like hot air and the unmistakable, uncontrolled yearning of a courtroom that was seeking the truth about Warren Finch's killer. Unquenched, uncontrolled yearning that lasted thousands of kilometres with Oblivia tormenting herself with the question – did she, or did she not kill her husband, and was she just chasing the hare king that day? The driver pulled his cap further down onto his eyebrows. It was academic to him. He was not wishing for anything. Didn't care if she had an alibi or not, or whether it was easier to believe that she killed her husband than to believe she was chasing a hare king. He became lead-footed to cure any urge for wishing, thinking or yearning, pressing harder on the accelerator and sending the semi flying along the road. On and on they flew, hundred of kilometres of gum trees quivering in their wake, and flatlands of sheep and cattle-filled grasslands wondering what had just happened, while she tossed and turned over her alibi, whether she had one or not.

The road train carted the body everywhere – up the Hume Highway, down the Stuart Highway, around the Monaro – eleven highways in all. Twenty thousand kilometres of the nation's highways had been split down the middle to divide the country like two giant lungs.

The *See You Around* journey was for all people who bothered to stand out in a chilly night, or in the midday sun, if they cared enough to line the streets just to watch the *Spirit of the Nation* roaring by. The whole thing was a rhapsody in motion and could not have been more successful, as the road train roared down the highways of country and western music – mostly legend music by the country's great singers like Slim Dusty, Rick and Thel, a bit of Chad Morgan – Camooweal, Mt Isa, Cloncurry, The Barkley, Wagga Wagga, Charleville, Cunnamulla, Yarrawonga, Plains of Peppimenarti, and the Three Rivers Hotel. But mostly, the clockwork nature of the thing was to keep to the *Fresh Food People's* schedule of deliveries to its supermarket chain throughout the country, picking up and delivering crates of fruit and vegetables such as asparagus, mangoes, pawpaw, bananas and pineapples; or the oranges, apples, potatoes, strawberries and peas from the packing sheds and cool rooms of its Northern or Southern growers.

Along the way, the coffin was paraded and displayed for all to see in this festival of grieving. The black sassafras heritage coffin was wheeled out of the semitrailer on a trolley and set down in the middle of a dead-grass flat, banana plantation, or salt bush plain, where speeches were made in the slow drawl of the North, or a fiddle played through amplifiers at each tinker-tailor gathering, in fiddlestick towns, depressed cities, cut-throat roadhouses, or else, the coffin was rested on a bench in a mine's mess room, in machinery, produce, wool and cattle sheds, or laid on the best linen table-cloth over the dining table of a cattleman's station home.

It was a hard schedule, and the silent driver drove that little bit faster to keep on track when memorials could just as spontaneously spring up out of the blue when influential, backblocks politicians at the end of a dusty road demanded their impromptu *See You Around* event with the *Spirit of the Nation*. The driver did not complain. He did his job. Dragged out the coffin. Wore the consequences for making up time after listening to another dozen pip-squeak speeches for a half-dozen people at another local church, football stadium, soccer oval, paddock, courtroom or meeting hall of the Country Women's Association, Boy Scout, or other local hall of fame.

The ghosts travelling in the road train were not complaining. The security guards enjoyed the view and started granting three wishes to whoever required them. Who were they to give two hoots if the coffin was continually being dragged out here or there in a journey that was endless? But the driver wished for nothing. He just kept growing older and driving on. He pushed the now less than splendid, soiled and chipped coffin out one more time, waited for the mourning to be done with and souvenir-hacking to be completed, and pushed the defaced coffin back up the ramp and into the freezer. There was no time any more for deliveries. It saved time to cut the words *delivery* or *pickup* off the list. He kicked the security men out. Said that they were weighing him down. They were too congenial to their ever-increasing queues of wish seekers. He could not sit around all day for other purposes. Everything in the big freezer began to rot. The driver's eyes grew teary from being glued to the dusty road ahead, and he kept singing the same old song, *Yea! Keep your eyes on the road, and your hands on the wheel, we're having fun etcetera whatever.* But when he sang, he only heard the transport; the roaring road train's engine, wheels rolling over the highways. The widow never heard a thing said about Warren Finch in the endless parade of speeches. She had left before the journey began.

Goodness poor heart, the ghost walk. There are those who will warn anyone making this strange solitary journey, and will say: *You have got to take enough to make it through.*

This was what happened. Oblivia disappeared from the hearse's spectacular schedule after the wind dusted off an icy night. What was the reason? And what was it about those prevailing dreams children have about life, that make them to go ghost walking like this? Away! Anywhere! That's what happened to them. Was there ever a right way of leaving?

In a panicky night off she went, entangled in the vortex of a thunderstorm dizzily spinning over many kilometres in the higher strata of the atmosphere. She just walked away without any thought of where she was going. Death, dying, or living had nothing to do with it. The truth of it was that wars do this to children. War children, like the torn world of Aboriginal children. Where were the kind crickets singing? Or, the big leaf under which to hide? The country's hearth! Ah! She just walked around the smudged lines of the circles the giants had sketched in another of their hell maps.

She walked away from the semitrailer hearse, and listened for heartbeats: the silent chilled voicelessness of swans you hear in the weakened old and the very young tossed from the heavens, and those struggling to stay airborne with their wings stretched wide, locked against the force of the wind.

In a place where footsteps crackled on frost-hardened grass, her dreams were askew. Still! Quiet! Nevermind! There were people approaching, shadows in the darkness that looked like old Aunty and the Harbour Master with the monkey twisting around on his hip. The old woman was talking to the Harbour Master but her voice broke with the chill in the air. *You'd be reaching for gold to find the place now.* You could hear her continuing to recite bits of her old poetry, although she and the Harbour Master had already disappeared, and were walking somewhere that was infinitely far away.

In the morning there were only blue skies where the girl widow had walked off to find a flock of swans. For her, the mad hearse journey had finished. Who cared? The driver shouted to the thin vapours of air rising from the cold earth all around him, when he discovered she had left. *You there? You there? Come back here.* But tell you what? What did he care about anyone disappearing from his cortege if they had no respect for the dead? He had not seen the said personage contributing much to the memorial anyway. There were appointments to keep. A heavy schedule raced through his mind. He had a stiff in the freezer to think about. The haul going overseas once they got through Australia. So, with his cap pulled down lower over his sunglasses – man, he was hitting the highway. The rubber burnt the bitumen. A trail of smoke was left behind. You would think he was raising Lazarus from the dead.

She watched the semitrailer roaring up the highway from the ghost town's park, amongst oak trees with exposed roots like the fingers of giants crossed for good luck. *There he goes,* she thought of Warren Finch, *he's still holding on to power, still searching for the ultimate paradise.* Yep! The same stories you hear about power. A dead man was still making people run after him. It was the first time she had really thought about Warren Finch for a very long time.

Alone in this quiet forest where only a blackbird's song rung out while the last stars disappeared, and the scream of the schedule became a dot on the awakening horizon, she suspected he was not dead at all. But who knows what thoughts will come right out of the bushland when you are alone? She saw for herself how Warren Finch could loom monumentally in the atmosphere like a gift from God. He was so indestructibly alive, just like the sky. Even in the middle of nowhere, he was still around, just as he was when she had watched the coffin absent-mindedly on the long journey, where he was being preserved as though he was some masterpiece in an art gallery. And just like famous paintings, he would never die as long as people looked at his dead body and appreciated the unique quality of his extraordinariness, and the propaganda of what he stood for in the world.

With leaves dropping from the oak trees at the slightest hint of a breeze, she thought about the frailty of perpetuity, and imagined she could still hear Warren talking on his mobile phone from the coffin in the semitrailer's freezer, where he was continuously calling the driver and complaining about her disappearance. His muffled voice now giving the orders and snapping at the driver, the mobile capped to his ear, *Where in the hell did she go?*

Yes, she knew something. Warren Finch's elaborate montage-self never intended to be buried. He was insisting that the glassy-eyed driver forget what he called the girl widow. She could look after herself. He was wondering why she was brought along in the first place. He yelled down his mobile from the sassafras coffin in the freezer. *Well! Let it roar. You are doing the right thing driver. Keep going man – you got no time to frig around.*

For what was death? It was just a matter of continuing on, keeping his ideas streaming out of centre stage in perpetual memorials. The fact of the matter was that it was hard to kill off someone who had gotten as big as the United Nations itself. Naturally, the gift from God would have to go around the world after this. No drama. Death was not an excuse for burying a person, and a bit of good history along with it. No – no drama at all.

Somewhere in this landscape, swans were stirring. It was a bright starry night. As the entire flock awakened, great hordes wove in and out of the tight pack with necks stretched high. These birds anticipated the movement of wind in the higher atmosphere. They gauged the speed of northerly flowing breezes caught in their neck feathers and across their red beaks and legs. The swans made no sound, but stood still while the wind intensified through the ruffling feathers on their breasts. Then suddenly from somewhere a startled swan flies up, and is followed by the roar of the lift off, and the sky is blanketed by black swans in the cold night, and Oblivia recalls the old Chinese monk Ch'i-chi's poem of the flight of swans in the night, like *a lone boat chasing the moon*. She watched, and knew she had found her swans. They had found each other's heartbeat, the pulse humming through the land from one to the other, like the sound of distant clap sticks beating through ceremony, connecting together the spirits, people and place of all times into one. These were her swans from the swamp. There was no going back. She would follow them. They were heading north, on the way home.

On this night, she travelled over hills of heavily-scented eucalypt forests, until she reached the shallow swamps of winter-time flowing through the scattered tea-tree country where most of the land was perpetually under water. The swans rest, but there will be days of walking through water to follow them.

She was not the only one who kept away from the heavy migration of travellers – poor families on foot, and those able to afford to travel in a vehicle like Big Red's family – who had been forced to leave the ruined city. They were the people with passports and not a threat to the national security. They were not like potential terrorists: this colourful procession of licensed travellers – those who had passed the rigid nationality test for maintaining a high level of security in the country, and could pay the tax that allowed them to pass through the numerous security checkpoints on the highways.

Oblivia joined those who were travelling incognito on unofficial and illegal crossings through the swamps. There were so many people moving through the country, she was never alone. They were all searching for the same shallow pathways, and dazed like her, all following each other, while trying to take their life somewhere else. There were people dressed in dark clothes across the landscape, trying not to look conspicuous. Some were former street people. Others were the homeless people who had slept on the footpaths with cardboard blankets, or in empty buildings. Now in hordes and all travelling north, they crowded the swampy lanes on pitch-black nights and nestled close to one another for safety. Most had white hair, even the children, and similar stories of what happened, *it was those snakes. It was the last straw.* A moment was all it had taken, many had claimed, to turn anyone prematurely white; that night when the rain and wind hit the city like a brick wall had been thrown at it after Warren Finch was killed.

The navigators at the top of the line of the people travelling through the water were continually arguing amongst themselves about their weapons – if a bread knife was better than a sugar-cane cutlass for cutting through, or whether the thickness of a long pole was better cut by an axe, but whether or not they were arguing, they had to decide which direction either left or right that any idiot would take through the shallows ahead. And then they continued yelping: Yep! *Good job I traded that bread knife.* Yep! *Good job I made that bamboo pole longer.*

These men claimed to be the policemen over this stretch of country, although in the real world, they were only a bunch of intergenerational environmentalists, turned greenies, turned *ferals*, turned strapped for cash to save a multitude of furry or feathered threatened species in international forums, or their favourite rare trees. They knew the swamps. Their families had grown up with rising waters. When the opportunity arose to make some money, who could blame them for becoming entrepreneurial? Human removalists, they called themselves. It sounded nice. Sure it was not legit or leftie, but what was? Their mantra while leading the incognitos was a list of challenging superiority-complex questions, such as, *what makes you people from southern cities think you can speak for us? What makes you think we can't speak for ourselves? What makes you think you are better than us?* Or, *How would you know this country better than us?*

They guided dirt-poor people through rough country, even though the plain and simple truth was that they were just people smugglers, not interested in public investment, or becoming security-conscious public servants. Whether they thought what had happened in the city was of any consequence, what did it matter? There were plenty of snakes around this neck of the woods too. *It was all of this mixed up weather,* they claimed. Anything was possible, but that was not their problem. Their job was simple enough. Ask no questions, and get enough people through expansive low-lying flood water in the flat lands in a transaction that implied: *We can show you a thing or two about hardship if that's what you want.*

The job was simply this: keep the line from falling into deep flowing water: *Stop anyone from being washed away.* It was easy enough. The environmentalists and their families lived rough along the water's edges like nesting swans or a colony of egrets, in makeshift rafts, or roughly-made reed huts. Even their babies knew how to cling to the watery nests, or the bosoms of their mothers. It helped to have lived numerous seasons with spreading water to remember how to stop being washed away. Still, it was always difficult to predict before a crossing began whether there was a likelihood of flash floods. The last-minute cancellation of a crossing was always imminent. Refugees would squat by the water's edge in the rain until conditions settled, while the water-navigators argued the toss in numerous committee meetings about whether the water's stability was a goer, so a journey could begin.

But it did not matter how adept these environmentalists were with the bush, or with travel through water, or whatever else they could do to save lives. They were not to be trusted in the least by the refugees of every nationality coalesced by flights from the ruined cities – young or old who were hardened fighters too. None of them wanted any extra favour for who they were or where they had originally come from, and being essentially numb about risk-taking, they asked no questions, and just told the people-smugglers to get on with it: *All we want to do is head north. We don't care what happens. Just do your job. Anything will be worth it. Just show us where the Aborigine people live.* So for days, sometimes weeks, the lines of humanity walked knee-deep in yellow billowing water, and if the predictions were wrong, waist-deep or up to the neck of children, which left each person to figure out how to keep carrying the burden of treasured belongings. The leaders called, *Say c'est la vie, or drown. Chuck it all.* The trail was littered with submerged electronics, cartons of beer, some huge paintings that had become completely transformed by the mud, as did the books about birds or the high country, or any treasured books of philosophy, music, Shakespeare's sonnets.

Usually, the only treasures that survived were animals. Many had brought along the family watchdog, their old *daras*, and these were left to swim alongside their owners or were carried, like those tagging along with the dog boys, hungry puppies stuffed under their jackets, among hundreds of street kids on the run. Someone had brought along their cow, the old beloved black and white *bulaka*. It was not like travelling on an aeroplane, or a catering bus. Forget that. Nobody had any food. No aeroplane. *Budangku yalu julaki-yaa*. It was more like a self-serve journey, which meant everyone was constantly hungry, always too *balika*, looking for something to eat. The mortified travellers, who had not killed anything before, killed the cow finally. It was difficult to think of anything else. It was butchered in a frenzy in the water, and eaten raw, with no fire, *budangku yalu jangu-yaa*. Afterwards they had nothing. Not anything. *Budangku yalu jumbala-yaa*. Still, what was hunger to these people? They had always known hunger, and about this alone they cheerfully narrated their stories, rather optimistically, about how they were surviving on nothing: *Yea! Who cares about hardship? It is just being cold and wet, that's all, and being rained on, but was worth it.*

The more enterprising street people who had pillaged poultry before leaving the city, had a ten out of ten chance of feeding themselves on the journey. These fowl thieves carried bantam roosters and treasured, egg-laying white silky hens stuffed inside their clothes, or a half dozen ducks, close to their hearts, and secretly hoarded the eggs.

The buskers of the city sung through hunger, and kept singing through the night to keep warm as the weary line walked on, while more water seeping out of distant hills and creeping along the crevices joined the flow of the flood on the flats. You could say that the country was a drain that wanted to drown strangers singing up its landscape.

Oblivia walked with her head down, but she also watched

elderly men and women, and children holding cats, *kinikini* stuffed inside their jackets, trying to shield their pets from the savage attacks of dogs sniffing out anything they could eat. The dogs were often attacked with bamboo poles, which quickly escalated into brawls with the dog owners. The water leaders often lost control of the line when tempers flared over dogs, and the fighting broke into splinter groups.

Whenever skirmishes broke out, the line needed to be brought down to earth. A meeting was held in the water to break people into groups that related to each other. But lawlessness was what it was. People walked wherever, fought whoever and however, and often ended by walking off in all directions. Of course, there were consequences for anyone who thought they could make the crossing by themselves. Many were forcibly returned to the line. For others, it was important that the people they had paid to take them across did not walk off the job, or get killed.

With the journey headed deeper into the swamps, Oblivia walked with dozens of people with cages of birds whose song was a reminder of their old lives while they travelled towards the uncertain future. Nanny goats. Billy goats. A sheep. Someone with about a dozen pussycats stuffed under his jacket. Oblivia thought of the Machine. Perhaps he was somewhere, or still in the city. She carried in her arms a heavy fledging swan, having to *mulamula* it around all the time, inside her hoodie windcheater next to her knife. This was a half-grown cygnet that she called *Stranger*. The cygnet, like Rilke's swan labouring with what could not be undone, had refused its destiny. It had no interest in swimming away, or to fly with its flock. The great flock of swans, wary of the dogs, kept a safe distance from the travellers, but Oblivia watched them swimming in the distance, or sometimes flying overhead, as though reassuring herself that she would not be abandoned.

Darkness would fall and the trails of bats, thousands flying overhead, heralded the worst time for the disintegrating line of people, calling to one another throughout the night, straying out of hearing range and becoming lost forever. Very soon, the weariness of the line became total exhaustion. Many felt there was no end, or way out. They became increasingly disoriented in the sea of water and began to hallucinate, many rushing towards the mirage of the Aboriginal people's heaven they saw in the distance.

Only a few refugees from the city finally managed to reach the other side. The feral policemen leading the line, who abandoned the refugees that remained in their care, would eventually be arrested and placed on trial for people smuggling, but not for genocide, or mass murder, which were crimes thought to be so morally un-Australian, it was officially denied that anything like it ever happened, like in the rhetoric of the history wars era – genocide, a horrendous crime against humanity that was unheard of. It never happened. Not in this country.

The swan girl's worry for the cygnet now hidden inside her clothes, under Warren Finch's old windcheater, probably saved her. She walked with her head bent forward, trying to be unnoticeable amidst the dwindling groups of people. The Harbour Master looked very fearful with the frightened Rigoletto on his hip. He always knew where she was and crept up beside her again, and again. *Get out*, he demanded. *You are First Lady, not bullock being led around.* The line was struggling to stay together after days and days of tiredness and hunger, many falling by the wayside, unable to go on, with no one to help them.

There were murmurings, whisperings, and she could feel the primeval fear closing in as the crossing verged on mutiny. Anyone hiding animals was attacked. Groups of bandits moved alongside, picking off people they suspected were hiding food. There were numerous beatings of people unwilling to hand over their pets.

The dogs roamed freely, sniffing for food, attacking those carrying animals. The Harbour Master arrived wet and flustered with sheer frustration written all over his face. *Why won't you just go,* he sneered at Oblivia, while adding, *I am not staying.* He pushed her, and she swayed to and fro, but held her ground. *You are an idiot,* he snarled in her face. *Go now.*

Oblivia feared that the dogs would eventually find the cygnet. All around, she heard the savage packs attacking people and their screams in splashing water. Even the swans overhead were terrified, and lost momentum in their flight. They swooped lopsidedly in terror. She felt fear with each step, expecting something to happen at any moment. It was too terrifying to be discovered escaping, she had seen other people being cast aside for not being obedient to the discipline of the crossing. But, when it was time to go, she disappeared quietly, in the moments when the black swan cloud flew across the line of travelling people, covering the moon-lit water. She closed her ears to the sounds of the collapsing world behind her, and kept walking under the cloud of swans moving slowly just above the water, their loud beating wings creating a mad turbulence in the water that kept her camouflaged. Never turning once, she would not look back.

The only person who lived on the water amongst the flooded trees where no one ever goes was an old Chinese hermit. He lived on an island of sticks that looked like an enormous swan's nest. His white hair and whiskers were filled with sticks too. As usual, he was hoping to catch a fish, singing that old 1960s song *Wishin' and Hopin'*, just like he always did to paint the sky gold with the memory of Dusty Springfield's voice. He was thoroughly besotted with the singer, and his feeling had only grown stronger since the first time he had seen her singing the song illegally in a dream of long ago, which hum! made him run from China.

The fish were still not biting when the wing beats of swans flying low across the water through the dawn fog were so close to his ears that he could feel the spirit of Dusty Springfield singing her *Wishin' and Hopin'* in the breeze coming straight from their straining wings, and her trumpeter bugling in their calls, and the drums rolling in their heartbeats. It was just another amazing all-bells-ringing kind of day living with his idol and it was all too joyous, but then! down in the fog something moved. He thought he had seen ghosts. These ghosts kept walking towards him through the fog and shaking up the water, so he waited, and kept on singing his *Wishin' and Hopin'* song. It was too late for obsessing, to make his cares fade away because these all jumped and rolled in his stomach. When he saw it was just an old man carrying a monkey he thought he was lucky, but when he saw a girl who was the First Lady of whatnot, and with a cygnet as well? Well! He thought he was just too plain luckless for words.

He called to the strangers, *This is where you must go to enter another country,* but they just kept walking with the ghost wind blowing them towards where he pointed. When he realised they were not going to stop to speak to him, he called after them about his secret love for Dusty Springfield and how he was remembering her voice forever out there on the water. He believed they were ghosts though, and watched them go on their way until they disappeared into the watery horizon.

Later when he caught a fairly medium-sized fish, unlike the tiddlers that he usually caught to feed himself, he believed that the only real ghosts he had ever seen in his life had brought him luck. So, he sent a bit of his luck their way too, wishing the ghosts heading into the desert reached wherever they were going, and hoping that the Harbour Master found a camel to ride on the long journey – *to show them that you care just for them, sing the songs they want to sing...*

The old Chinese man's singing to his songstress in the sky must have been a lucky thing, the Harbour Master told the wet and sorry Rigoletto after they were saved by the weather. The group was still walking in floodwater when the skies turned black with heavy clouds, and very soon afterwards they were walking through a mad storm. A torrential downpour flew like a wild river in the wind. The big cygnet refused to swim and Oblivia had to stuff it back under her shirt. She could feel its heart thumping with her heart, but kept walking as though nothing was unusual in calamity. Well! The monkey knew about monsoons, and clung to the neck of the Harbour Master who was salubriously humming the highs and lows, and speed and caution, of Weber's Op. 34 Clarinet Quintet in B flat – although he was packing it really. The wind and rain blew so hard onto their backs that they raced along in the direction the Chinese man had pointed to, and where, soon enough, they were thrown out of the water and at the two-toed feet of a big fat camel standing in mud.

Lo and behold! The Aboriginal man on the camel spoke wisely – because he was supposed to – as he welcomed the strangers to his country. His pet cicada chirruped a song from under the piece of canvas that covered its cage when the camel man asked his talking companion for long journeys, since the camel did not speak, *Will you carry the monkey man and his soggy looking pet, or will we let the old camel do the job?* The cicada did not appear to have a direct answer to such a stupid question, if you could interpret the melody that remained unchanged to an ordinary ear not trained in interpreting how insects speak.

The Harbour Master was very weak from his ordeal, but still protective of the girl, and being an important man of another place, he bluntly asked the camel man, *Which one are you mate? Gaspar, Balthazar or Melchior? And is this the gate of Heaven or what?* Perhaps the camel man did look like one of the three wise men.

He was dressed in a thick green cotton shirt and red trousers – clothes stained reddish brown from the bush, while over his shoulders fell a large animal-skin cloak that protected him from the rain. His eagle-feathered cap was also fashioned from animal skin but it was now soaked with the rain that washed down his face and through his black beard, and over the seed necklaces hanging over his shirt.

The camel man said he was neither wise man, nor in Heaven. Introducing himself, he said the name that people usually called him was Half Life, and he offered no other explanation. *I'm from blackfella land. My kingdom is right where you lot are standing. You got anybody else coming behind you?* When Oblivia glared at him as though he must have been mad, he sat the camel down and quickly slid off. The Harbour Master was the one he helped first. *Old man you ride on top. No more walking for you now,* he said. *Girl, you get up there too with that goose.* He threw the animal-skin cloak over them, and handed over his flask, as well as a large piece of wattle-seed damper from a bag kept around his waist. The camel, unhappy with having to be sat down in the mud in the twenty-first century, was fidgeting with its mouth harness, spitting and oozing snot from its nostrils, and turning its long neck around to sniff and fuss about having mud in its fur, but with a quietly spoken word from Half Life, the animal quietly rose to its feet.

We follow the track the ancestors of mine made. Look who is here, he told his country. There was nothing more spoken in the rain journey ahead. Half Life needed to sing to his kin people their country's songs with his cicada brother, as much as to the camel that seemed to enjoy ancestor music while it went sauntering on its way.

All journeys on the ghost walk are hard and long. There was no way around it. One can travel forty days and forty nights across deserts in bloom or drought, or a month of Sundays of eating nothing else but hares and rabbits roasted over a fire at night, but it was all the same.

Just be careful with my people though, or they will spook the bloody wind out of you. My theory about surviving a day with them is always take short breaths so you don't miss it if they try to floor the life out of you. This was how Half Life introduced his people. *You have to be related to people like this to love them.*

This is a real sacred place here, Half Life said as they came into view of their destination – a camp of his kin-people living in the ruins of concrete-block buildings and rusted car bodies that were half buried with red desert soil, and from which grew clumps of spinifex, salt bush, native herb bushes, or the odd bare bush tomato and leaf-eaten bush banana, and the scrappy coolibah tree here and there – nothing to build a door with. Burrs and prickles covered the ground like a dense lawn, as well as chewed-up pig weed and twig-like arid country plants for the bull ants to trail through. Only salt soakages lay beyond to every horizon.

This is big Law here. We always come back. Spirits of our people live here. Ghosts living in abandoned car bodies. Some of them inside those old crap houses. Built by that top of the country's last government of self-serving politicians before it chucked the dummy and went bust when nobody bothered voting for them anymore. Nah! You wouldn't be bothered voting for people like that. They were like a bloody soap opera. Well! It's entr'acte times now. Better enjoy it before the next comedy of errors, another era with another round of tragedians and thespians mouthing off, and traipsing around on our block again, dragging us backwards through another bloody century of destruction. Our elders bring everyone here so that we can hear the Law of our people from the country itself telling us a strong story about what happened to them. What they do. Oh! Sad alright, some of those stories. But good ones there too. You can hear children dancing in the moonlight, rock-n-roll and shake a leg. Laughing. Those were the days. Make you want to cry how memories come looking for you. We move on again in a few days time. Palace next time maybe.

What was the point of complaining about how life had become? If all that was left of your traditional lands were tailing dams and polluted pond life, and the place looking like a camel's cemetery? *Still! No need to go around complaining because there is nothing left running in your brains except your bare-ass country and a pack of scrub donkeys,* said Half Life. *This is how we see life. Look around. Those donkeys follow us wherever we go.* The ground looked as though it was crawling, but it wasn't a miracle. It was a catastrophe. These were cursed people. Their worldly companions were a plague of *Rattus villosissimus* – the long-haired ugly rat – crawling grasshoppers, *Locusta migratoria*, and the flying ants swarming in the soup.

Oblivia looked at the ground-crawling camp and saw it was nothing special to freak out about, if that was what you thought about rat- and insect-swatting nomads looking as weather-beaten and wind-blown as she was herself. All of them living with sandy-blight eyes among thousands of wild camels and feral donkeys surrounding the camp, which Half Life explained, just kept following them through life.

We are Aboriginal herds-people with bloodlines in us from all over the world, he added, and dreamily listed all the world's continents that he could remember being related to these days, *Arabian, African, Asian, Indian, European all sorts, pure Pacific Islander – anywhere else I didn't mention? Well! That as well! Whereever! Even if I haven't heard of it! No matter – we got em right here inside my blood. I am thick with the spirits from all over the world that I know nothing about. Nah! Man! We don't live on their tucker though. Here it's bush tucker all the way if we can yank it out of the mouths of these ferals running around and breeding up like plagues of rats, flies, insects whatever; no matter we got em, and that's why we are trying to eradicate all these mongrel hares and English rabbits from being one less of a plague on the face of the country by eating every chemically deranged single bugger of them. It's like their spirit will not go away unless we eat em. Of course that's some other country mob business but what can we do! What Law? Nothing! We are retarded people now because of the history of retardation policy mucking everyone up. Leaking radioactivity. Crap politics from long ago. Must have been a madhouse then. Glad to be rid of them. That we survive at all is just a bloody fluke of human nature. Got the picture, if so, then you are welcome, if not, I reckon you got no alternative really out here and whatnot for understanding surviving.*

Anyone could see that the community was one big, buzzing hive of activity where busy Aboriginal tribes-people never stopped working. They were as driven as the millions of flies that infested the camp, and you could *betcha* one thing: these people would strike an accord with the ghosts of a century or more worth of politicians and policy makers of Australian governments. It had been bigot country then. They would be smiling on these camel entrepreneurial people, and saying success at last. For here, every individual seemed totally obsessed with being some kind of economic independence human success story in an Australian-made hell. There were people bumping into each other all day long to discuss or argue about the plagues of feral animals. Who was looking after the barn owls? How the camels were penned or not penned, watered and fed, who could use which one or that one, or why one camel was more worthy or trustworthy than another. In short – worrying about every aspect of domesticating the animals once imported into the country by other people, that they were not eating.

Rigoletto hid under an iron bed and stayed well and truly out of the way while the mostly leather-skin-clothed women and children that looked more like animals to the monkey were endlessly chasing donkeys in the rain, or wrestling them like wet squawking sponges to the ground, or whipping them senseless to make them move away from the camp. Why these donkeys wanted to hang around these people was a complete mystery to the Harbour Master and he yelled out in vain, *Why don't you let the baby Jesus' donkeys alone?* So he was told to shut the fuck up. What tradition, the Harbour Master wanted to know, talked like that to old men? He ended up arguing constantly with the women who had been looking after him but now treated him like a donkey too.

The camp itself was strewn with carcasses of hares and rabbits or any other feral creatures thrown on the woodpile. It was hard to establish if there were enough people who would be able to eat all this food before the camp moved on. Then there were the pelts in various stages of being tanned or turned into items of clothing – cloaks and caps like Half Life wore, as well as shoes, saddles and ropes. At night it was no different, for no one slept a wink in the bevy of ceremonial singing and hunting, or packing up and moving camp. Why waste time sleeping when far into a wet rainy night, all the able-bodied huntsmen and women rode off on their camels, with each person carrying a pet owl as their night hunter, and only returning hours later loaded with a hundred and fifty or more rabbits and hares strung over the camels' backs? This was why the one big over-worked feral shebang was monotonously the same, routine and endless.

At least you got somewhere, and all we have to do is keep going, that's all, the Harbour Master explained to the emaciated girl, although he could see the bony thing was not listening to him. He felt she was dying, and admitted that she had been too high maintenance for him as he sang to the country's spirits, long, long songs, that went across the country to her homeland. There was nothing more he could do. She lived in her own world with the cygnet that had now grown into a swan. There was too much noise in the camel community, and it made it harder for her to hold her thoughts together before they were forgotten. She could hardly remember what happened on the day that Warren Finch was assassinated. The images were like those recalled from a dream that flashed in her mind and were instantly forgotten. Her life in the city seemed to have coalesced into a stream of forgetting, of what happened so far away, and of memories that seemed implausible, or too hideous, and almost irreverent to be thought about in this place. So Oblivia and the swan sat in their own little corner of this shifting world, out of the way of being trampled by the industrious people and their animals. The camel people were pursuing their own course, in its own order of mayhem and hassle, which was oblivious to having her, or any outsider in its midst.

Oblivia turned her head away when the groups of children came by all day long to touch the swan and to throw it some food, the bits of damper and grass seeds still attached to stems they had collected for it. They were full of questions, asking why she was looking after the swan, where she came from, what she was doing just sitting by herself for? *Why are you mental?* Irritably, she quickly shooed each group off one by one, with the language of a stick angrily prodded at them, only to end up with even larger groups of children whiling away the time by sitting in front of her and copying her every move, the hostile way she stared at them, and teasingly throwing stones over her head – giggling for the stick to be chucked around, until their parents called them off for more chores – *to hurry up and get going*, while leaving her to make her own decisions about life. It was up to her. Entirely. Everyone was free to have their own thoughts about where they belonged or what they needed to do. There were only two options: live or die. Make your own decision. They knew the girl's heart was faraway from them, and assumed she was thinking about her own country.

Whenever Half Life walked by, he glanced at the huddle on

the ground, noticed she was still there, and thought that perhaps he should see what was happening to her – whether her spirits were up or down. He thought she was crying. What would she cry about? Was she crying about that prick Warren Finch? Half Life had heard on the radio that the beloved missing First Lady, now hailed as the heart of the nation, had joined the *illegals* travelling through the country, and thought it could have been her, but he said nothing. Who needed the fuss? He thought that he could have done with a wife himself, but he was far too occupied with the work that needed to be done. They all were. He had no time for standing around talking about life, marriage, raising a family. This was sorry business. They were mourning here. And tomorrow, they would mourn somewhere else. No! He did not want any children. Would he have to guard them with his life on his own country, lest the government took them away from him?

All she did, other than burying her head inside her jacket under her arms folded around her knees, was to look at the skies becoming clearer, as though it was there where she had to search for a road out, the road that emerged half-heartedly before disappearing again, that would only become fully visible when the swans arrived. She had become more eager to leave, to continue the journey before it was too late. She grew impatient and weaker. Conjuring her journey back to the swamp was hard work. It exhausted her. She hardly ate, and could only think of herself as one of the swans flying towards her, while niggling voices in her mind kept reminding her the time had come if she and the swans were to make the journey north to the swamp before summer set in, otherwise they would all die on the way. *You want to die out here? Like all those other women?*

She thought about death. Visualised the journey towards dying, and thought this was how Warren had planned to abandon her after all – just like other men who had dumped their disappointing wives in the bush. Left them to die. Only their bones were leaning against a tree somewhere, and those poor things still waving towards home for an eternity. At this point, she thought Bella Donna's story must really be about the last swan arriving back at the swamp with one of her bones in its beak, bringing it home. If this was so, so be it. She would be dead, that would be the end of her grand old love story, a fable of what happened after Warren Finch was killed, when his 'promise wife' was so heart-broken, she ran off and died in the desert. The missing First Lady. The enigma. Her body never found. She would be like Lasseter's Reef. Adventurers would just about kill themselves in the desert while trekking around the place searching for her. She would become a legend in the bastions of Australian civil society interested in the anthropological studies of Aboriginal people, just as long as it appeased the dark theories of a discipline that kept on describing the social norms of Aboriginal men as dangerous and violent. They would speculate about her bones in absentia, and wonder whether she really was a child bride – just a little girl – so they could experience the sensation of charging Warren Finch posthumously with incest, pornography and raping a child; or whether or not the bones were of an ancient woman, or of an assimilated woman; or of somebody with sapwood-imbued bones who really could have slept for a very long time in a tree – just like that Rip Van Winkle fellow – yes, the bones of a girl who had never really matured, never fully grown. Well! How could you tell? It was hard to imagine. Why wouldn't she show Warren Finch who was the greatest? Yes, it was easy to think about dying. Would you call just lying down in the grass to die revenge, pay-back, or a suicidal act?

So she waited more and more impatiently for the swans to arrive, becoming more fearful, and feeling more dependent on them to guide her safely through the laws of the country, the spirits who were the country itself – if they were still alive, and flying towards this isolated camel people's camp, a speck in the vastness of an undetermined landscape for those unable to read it, frightened at the prospect of having to attempt the journey alone through unknown territories without a guide to clear the path to her country. Then one day, when the caravan of people, camels and donkeys finally realised its intention of leaving when the soakages dried out and actually left during a surprise rain shower and followed the rainbow, nobody noticed she had been left behind.

The Harbour Master was the first one you could blame for negligence when he left with the camel people. He was a ghost of a man too preoccupied with losing the magic of lightning-speed travel. He was old-fashioned. One of those types too overcome with disappointment for this new world. He had to reach his destination in God speed. How could he think of travelling an eternity with camels and donkeys for God knows how many days, months, or *friggen* years? Sweet Dreams Baby! His destination was what? thousands of kilometres away – think of Heaven. And Heaven was not the next waterhole up the road, which dying camels and old nomads thought was good enough to call it a day after walking all day long in the sun. His spiritual resting place was his own chosen place, where huge angels that were called something good like *Prosperity* and *Eternity* watched over monkey country. His eternal resting place was not going to be in any barren wasteland that kept being killed off by political stupidity.

Anyhow, you only had to take a look at little Rigoletto in the pelting rain for pity's sake. He was too wound up and frightened about being trampled by wet, frisky camels running about, to come out from his hidey-hole under the iron-frame bed. The little monkey sat motionless with his arms tightly folded around himself. He looked like a rock. He clutched his possessions to his chest.

What? The stories? Worried in case a camel or donkey would try to eat his stories?

Yes! The Harbour Master could only dream of getting away from the spinifex shrubbery, the claustrophobic way this landscape can close in, surround, ensnarl. He clung to the monkey hope of living the high life on the balconies of the eternal white marble palace. On the Taj Mahal, Rigoletto would move gracefully through time, shaking the hands of passing tourists with his lips stretched back and through baring teeth, telling a good story. This dream of escaping was worth...Millions! *Can you imagine Rigoletto?* Millions of people handing over peanuts, bananas, pomegranates, oranges and the whole apple cart to hear a little monkey snarling through one of his favourite stories about living a thousand and one nights of hell with the Harbour Master. *We will never go hungry if we live in a palace, would we,* Rigoletto? But to get there, they would have to survive the journey through a lot of country with the camels Half Life described were destined for the ships exporting them to foreign markets. It seemed like a bit of a plan.

Marsh Lake Swans

So holy and beautiful to behold this country where the swans flew hillock over hillock as far as the eye could see along a rolling landscape of saltbush, stubby plants, pittosporum, emu bush and flowering *eremophilas*.

Their flight having begun at the old abandoned botanical gardens in the city so long ago, it was a journey foretold, clear in the oldest swan to the youngest cygnet – the flight through thousands of kilometres from the southern coast to a northern swamp.

Bushfires came in walls across their path. As the grasslands burned, the swans flew high, sailing through winds gusting above the smoke in a journey a thousand metres up in their dreaming of home. Each kilometre was achieved by wing flapping and slow glide through floating ashes that flickered with fire and dazzle-danced the sky in the full-throated blizzard of heat flying over the hills, before falling on the country beneath. The swans, their strength crippled, breathed hot smoke-filled air, and the smell of their own singed feathers crawled into their lungs. Wrapped in fear, they whistle up the dead to see how they are going, before surrendering to the air, plummeting thousands of metres down into the fire. It tested the will of their wings flapping slower, almost unconsciously, instinctively remaining airborne.

It happened this way, until the remaining bony creatures find they are descending into the stagnant, blue-green algae blooms of a flooded plain where the trunks of dead trees are a reminder of what was once a forest. Then they continue, the swans flying through seasons and changes in the weather, and over travelling refugees, and the fence posts of flooded and then bone-dry lands. It was as if the ancestors had pulled the swans across the skies, passing them on to the spirits of gibber plains, ironstone flats, claypans, salt lakes and drifts, towards a sacred rendezvous – a tabula rasa place – where all of the world's winds come eventually and curl in ceremony, and where Oblivia waited at the camel camp amidst the drying soakages, to be cleansed for entering another country.

She whistled to them; tried to blow music from the flute, a swan tune that dances around the hills. It was old Bella Donna's swan-bone flute she had always worn around her neck just like the old woman did before she died. The flute was made from the wing bone of a Mute Swan and had been in Bella Donna's overseas family for generations. It could have been a thousand years old. Only the cygnet the girl had carried in the crossing had gently played with the bone in its beak, otherwise these days, the girl treated the small wing bone like a necklace, a *walkuwalku* hanging over her clothes or over her back – the only belonging left from her home on the hull. She knew the sound was known to be sacred to swans. *You can't use something like this for fun.* Her music danced on among the din of winds rustling through the grass and ruby saltbush; and the swans flew down to rest among the arum lilies on an insect-infested marsh lake.

Miracles are funny things. The Harbour Master looked around for his miracles every day, but only saw the reality of living rough as guts with the herds-people sipping tea in the rain with all those camels moving about them with a plague of stink beetles, and women and children slinging stones at the donkeys they said were *feral-ing* up the place. He said that those favourites of his the *Prosperity* and *Eternity* angels had lost their minds if they thought this was it. But what was life if you could not have hope? Maybe the angels had forgotten to bring his miracles in the way of first-class airline tickets so he and Rigoletto could fly off to the heavenly marble palace. Maybe they had lazed about and dropped the *bloomin'* requested miracles off at the wrong place. He blamed history for making him think these mongrelised depressing thoughts.

The swans welcomed into the country's song now spent days in the swamp while it never stopped raining. They danced the water, stirring it up, even at night with wings spread wide, lifting and dropping as they ran along the surface of the water, as though dancing in wing-exercising movements. In this way they communicate with each other – while the girl watches, knowing how she must read the country now as they do to follow them home. Then once more, the swans fly, and dance the rainy skies above the swampland, and return, skimming across the water to land.

This ceremony of swans continued, where together in mass blackness, they swam in circles. Reeds and water lilies become trampled. The swans pause, then lift themselves out of the water to stretch the white tipped wings that beat quicker, faster, as more circles are made with wings and tails splashing, and synchronising heads dipping under water, webbed feet kicking up water as they move, then the pulse is broken, and the huge body of swans breaks up and reforms.

Wings beat the water on one side, but when they switch sides, the beat of the other wing changes the tone of the music. They are almost prepared for flight. Oblivia follows them into the water and the swans observe her as though she is a newly-hatched cygnet. Hour by hour, after dipping deep in the water to forage for weeds, they glide towards her to drop their offerings with little bugling sounds, until they can see that she is surrounded by floating weeds. She sleeps on the wet land among the grass at night, while the majority of swans continue the unbroken ceremony, but there are always swans resting beside her, necks curled over their backs and asleep, raindrops falling over feathers, heads nestled under wings.

It was at night, after an icy wind had descended from out of nowhere in the middle of the day to push the temperature down to zero, and the ground had become frozen, that finally with the wind running along the ground like a spirit, the swans flew away from the leaf-littered water.

The night was alive with the sound of thousands of wings and noisy bugling when the swans were ready to go. From up high flying slowly, they were buffeted in the wind, looking down to the land stretched before them. Circling in the sky, the black cloud began diving, and swooping low over Oblivia, they pushed her to go.

Again the Gypsy Swans moved to be gone, but only if she was following them. There could be no going back through the face of a gale. No more circling in wind. It had to be now. Oblivia thought that she was in the sky, flying, and could not remember the journey. She and the swans were caught in the winds of a ghost net dragged forward by the spirits of the country. The long strands of hair flying among the swans, holding them together, and those long strands capturing her, made her fly too, close to the ground, across the country.

When dawn broke, the winds had disappeared, and the swans and the girl had arrived at another water-laden swamp land of water lilies and ant-covered grasses spilling in the air with a million flies and moths, and where only bird-infested coolibah trees dotted the landscape. It was land screaming with all of its life to the swans, *Welcome to our world*. All the spirits yelled to the girl to *eat the water lilies*. It was land where the swans would rest, then dance this country too, where the same frosty evening would take hold, before bringing the old wind people up, and again, the swans would have to leave, lifting off, circling and pulling the girl along, before the wind set the pace and blew them forward. The journey could only continue this way for the months it would take before the winds stopped coming at night.

Then the winds grow warmer and disappear in the atmosphere laden with dust. Without a breeze, the land becomes so still and lonely in the silence, you know that the spirits have left the skies. It does not rain any more. The land dries. Every living thing leaves in the seemingly never-ending journeys that migrating creatures take, just like those herds of deer that Bella Donna remembered for marching flat out across vast deserts and forsaken tundra, to where the swamp had perished.

All now shared the spirit of the drought, like the skin-and-bone swans still trying to fly until all that was left were the empty bags of feathers that fall from the sky. Most did not fly again. Oblivia thought she could call the swans away and continue on. Her thoughts were full of their stories. She stood in the mirage and recited the poets' lines to the swans' beauty – Keats, Baudelaire, Neruda, Heaney – but their poetry stayed in the stillness where she stood, recalling McAuley's swan flying to quit the shore... *That headed its desire no more.*

There were stranded swans scattered all over the open bush, among the spinifex, caught on power lines, on the edges of dried-up soaks and inland lakes. If you were there you would have seen them everywhere. But the main flock struggled on, continued flying during the night.

In hotter skies, their wings beat faster in desperation until finally, they become completely disoriented. They lose faith in their journey. They lose each other. The remaining swans fly in every direction in search of the last drying water holes. They stand on baked earth and hiss at the sky they cannot reach, then the time arrives when no more sound comes from their open beaks. The weak, feather-torn necks drop to the ground, and eventually, with wings spread they wait for the spirit flight.

Epilogue
The Swan Country

All the raspy-voice myna birds have come here, to this old swamp, where the ghost swans now dance the yellow dust song cycles of drought. Around and around the dry swamp they go with their webbed feet stomping up the earth in a cloud of dust, and all the bits and pieces of the past unravelled from parched soil.

A crew of myna birds foraging the waste toss useless trinkets this way and that. The prickly pear trees that had grown up, and all the rusted junk scattered across the bone-dry swamp, were the sort of places where only the myna birds lived.

From a safe distance, you could hear these birds swearing at the grass in throwback words of the traditional language for the country that was no longer spoken by any living human being on the Earth. While crowding the stillness the little linguists with yellow beaks sang songs about salvaging and saving things, rearranging sound in a jibber-jabbering loudness. All the old sounds were like machinery that rattled and shook while continuously being reworked into a junket of new pickings. In this mood – Well! You had to hear these soothsaying creatures creating glimpses of a new internationally dimensional language about global warming and changing climates for this land. Really listen hard to what they were saying.

One day, all that will be left of old languages will be what has been vaulted up in the brainwashed minds of myna birds. They listen to every single sound, but all that they will remember of the English language of these times, will be the most commonly used words you would have heard to try to defeat lies in this part of the world. Just short words like *Not true*.

Oblivia sat on the hull with her old Stranger swan dozing on her lap, and through the reddened haze of midday she gazed across the ravaged landscape that had once been a swamp. Trees that were long dead creaked sometimes, but after a while, only the dust-stained First Lady of whatnot spoke to the drought.

She was not surprised when the drought echoed her words in the North country's open space. Why wouldn't it speak back to her? It was a close relative who had always lived in the same house. They echoed each other: *Listen, Hard Up! No-hearted cruel thing! Lucky for me with no words left to come into my mouth that I got back.*

Having lived in the dry country for several thousands of years, the ghostly spectre of the drought woman had seen as many generations born and die and when those beautiful swans rose up one day to the skies and disappeared, it broke the water lilies and weed-covered lagoon, pulled itself out of its resting place, and filled the atmosphere from coastline to coastline of rotted tree stumps, flat plains, or solemn river bends across the country. Then it continued in the southerly direction that the birds had flown.

In its far-flung search for the swans, the slow-moving drought left behind smouldering ashes and soil baked by the dryness, and the whole country looking as though it had been turned over with a pick and flattened with a shovel. When the swans were found, the drought turned around on its hot heels and howling winds, while fires blew smoke across the lands on fast moving currents, and came back to the swamp.

Oblivia claimed that party time was over at dustbowl, and told the drought she was jack sick of it.

You got your old job back. I am giving this last black swan back to you, and to tell you the truth of the matter, I am done with carrying it around with me. You look after this swan, she ordered. *His name is Stranger. Thinks he doesn't belong in drought country. See if you can make more swans from this old pensioner.*

The drought woman seared the atmosphere like ancient chastising aunties anywhere across the world from the back of beyond, and screeched: *Don't drop the swan.*

A *jamuka* whirlwind jumped in Oblivia's face from out of nowhere, swung through the door of the abandoned hull of the warship still sitting in the dry clay, and stood in front of the First Lady thing nursing that black swan on her lap. Oblivia always sensed the way old fingers work, that were now invisibly examining the swan she was holding next to her chest.

Feathers ruffle across the bird's back, on its breast, along its neck – in a manner suggesting all was not well, of things not being done good enough, of things not being taken care of properly. A pondering turbulence circled in the hull, where pots and pans were slammed, creating an impression of foul nature for as long as it went on being a din, while another sound coming up from underneath, a jarring song, was being sung with words that were vaguely familiar to her. Strange melodies abruptly begin and end, as heavier things of her old abandoned home are slammed on the floor.

A creepy voice full of dust said exactly what Oblivia already thought about the old wreckage of scraps: *There and there for one thing! Feathers properly wind damaged, frayed, singed and all that – can't walk.* The drought woman told her of all people, *You have to carry the swan.* Oblivia thought she was being put upon by some proper big dependency that was now far too much for her, and she snapped at the swan, *That was the big problem about being a survivor swan – outliving your lifespan, getting too fond of gobbling up the muck in the sewerage ponds of life, and not laying down and dying like the others!*

The old swan leader kept throwing back his head over his wing, and his long neck flowed like a snake resting over his black plumed body. His eye canvassing the landscape like a stranger trying to find the quickest way out of the place. The huge bird was never the same after losing his flock. It found being alone unbearable. It never stopped looking for the other swans. It was the kind of creature that belonged in old Banjo Paterson's poem about black swans, perpetually straining for the sound of wings beating, of *lagging mates in the rearward flying.* The old swan's red beak clicked twice, then as time passed, as it does but not for nothing, it clicked three times, or perhaps, twice again. The swan had some strange equation going on in its head. This continuous clicking of his beak exaggerated even greater numbers of swans he anticipated would return in his ghostly rendition of what life once was.

Oblivia sensed that he was waiting for the equivalent of one thousand years of swans, an immense flock, one that was capable of overcoming all adversity, but she told him straight in the eye to give up. *They have all gone now and finished up, and none are coming back.* Talk like this grieved the swan. It swooned and dropped its neck to the ground. To see the swan like this made the girl feel sick of the virus thing talking in her head, and telling her that she and the swan were joined as companions, of being both caught up in a *mal de mer* from the yellow waves of dust spreading over the land. The old swan would have to fight to win back control, to settle the dust, and return the rain. He was old now, but the girl tells him: *If I could fly high up in the atmosphere like you instead of swilling around in dust storms, I'd make it rain.*

But how in the hell would I know? Its belligerence was unbelievable.

It was not interested in saving the world. Defying everything. How would she keep telling the swan another million times that the lake was gone, having to hold its beating heart closer to prevent its wings from spreading in a swim through the dust, treading it like water, and whispering the truth: *Deader than a doornail! Drier than Mars! Don't you see that it is all bulldust out there?*

Her mind was only a lonely mansion for the stories of extinction.

They say that the gift from God kept getting out of his grave after Warren Finch was finally buried in his country, beside the river of that time long ago when he first saw a swan. The story goes, *He wanted to give his promised wife some gift. Oh! Yes! He still had power of eating the brains of politicians. That was why there were no smart politicians in the country any more. It was really true.*

It was just fate that brought him back. On the face of it, his body could have been anywhere else on the planet by now, if the semitrailer's axle hadn't broken down on a bad day in the North, and the mad driver hadn't called it a day by dragging the heavy sassafras coffin out into the boiling heat that one last time, and telling Warren Finch, *I am going to bury you here you bastard, and be done with it, then I am going home.*

This might be the same story about some important person carrying a swan centuries ago, and it might be the same story in centuries to come when someone will carry a swan back to this ground where its story once lived. Well! Talk about acts of love. A place where white whirlwinds full of bits of dry grass and leaves blew in ashes from a tinder dry giant eucalypt, where a swan once flew in clouds of smoke from fire spreading through the bush land, with a small slither of bone in its beak.

It has been said by the few heart-broken-homes people,

mungkuji left for that *kala* country, who come back from time to time to visit the swamp after Warren Finch had the place destroyed, and they had seen the girl wife, First Lady of whatnot, Oblivion Ethyl(ene), that she always stayed like a *wulumbarra*, teenage girl. Well! She walks around the old dry swamp pretty regularly they say, and having seen her where there is a light moving over the marshes in the middle of the night, like a will-o'-the-wisp, they thought that they had heard her screaming, *kayi, kayi kala-wurru nganyi, your country is calling out for you,* which they described was just like listening to a sigh of a moth extending out over the landscape, or a whisper from the scrub ancestor catching a little stick falling from a dead tree, although nothing that could truly be heard – just a sensation of straining to hear something, which understandably, was how anyone should whisper on this spirit-broken place, from seeing their old homes scattered to kingdom come, of being where the Army owned everything, every centimetre of their traditional land, every line of buried song, stories, feelings, the sound of their voices, and every word spoken loudly on this place now.

There is a really big story of that ghost place: a really deadly love story about a girl who has a virus lover living in some lolly pink prairie house in her brain – that made the world seem too large and jittery for her, and it stuffed up her relationships with her own people, and made her unsociable, but they say that she loved swans all the same. Poor old swanee. You can see swans sometimes, but not around this place. It is a bit too hot and dry here. *Jungku ngamba, burrangkunu-barri. We're sitting down in the heat now.* It's really just sand-mountain country. Like desert! Maybe *Bujimala*, the Rainbow Serpent, will start bringing in those cyclones and funnelling sand mountains into the place. Swans might come back. Who knows what madness will be calling them in the end?

A Note on Sources

Quotations embedded in the text of *The Swan Book* are from the following sources: Robert Adamson, 'After William Blake' (p v); A.B. Paterson, 'Black Swans' (p 6); Bari Karoly, 'Winter Diary', in *Leopard V: An Island of Sound*, London, Harvill, 2004, (p 25); W.B. Yeats, 'The Wild Swans at Coole' (pp 28-29); Richard Wagner, *Lohengrin*, Act 1 (p 28); John Shaw Neilson, 'The Poor, Poor Country' (p 53); Seamus Heaney, 'Postscript', in *The Spirit Level*, London, Faber, 1996 (p 77); James McAuley, 'Canticle' in *Collected Poems 1936–1970*, Sydney, Angus & Robertson, 1971 (p 111); 'Song (March 1936)', in *Tell Me the Truth About Love: Fifteen Poems by W.H. Auden*, London, Faber, 1994 (p 135); Paterson, 'Black Swans' (p 157); David Hollands, *Owls, Frogmouths and Nightjars of Australia*, Melbourne, Bloomings Books, 2008 (p 165); *The Kalevala*, trans John Martin Crawford, Cincinnati, The Robert Blake Company, 1910 (p 168); William Wordsworth 'An Evening Walk' (p 175); E.B. White, *The Trumpet of the Swan*, New York, Harper Collins, 1970 (p 195); W.B. Yeats, 'Leda and the Swan' (p 202); Walt Whitman, 'Song of Myself, 33' *Leaves of Grass*, Book III (p 218); Alfred Lord Tennyson, 'Dying Swan' (p 239); Douglas Stewart, from *Images from the Monaro: For David Campbell*, in *Letters Lifted into Poetry – Selected correspondence between David Campbell and Douglas Stewart 1946–1979*, ed Jonathan Persse, Canberra, National Library of Australia, 2006, p 226, (p 239); Shivananda Goswami, Baul song, in Mimlu Sen, *The Honey Gatherers*, London, Rider Books, 2010 (p 239); Mahmoud Darwish, 'Now, When you Awaken, Remember', in *The Butterfly's Burden*, trans Fady Joudah, Washington, Copper Canyon Press, 2007 (p 240); Heaney, 'Postscript' (p 240); Leonard Cohen, 'The Traitor' from *Recent Songs*, Columbia, 1979 (p 240); W.B. Yeats, 'Nineteen Hundred and Nineteen' (p 264); Hank Williams, 'Blue Eyes Crying in the Rain', song by Fred Rose, recorded 1951 (p 284); Charles Baudelaire, 'The Swan, to Victor Hugo', trans Roy Campbell, in *Poems of Baudelaire*, New York, Pantheon, 1952 (p 290); Ch'i-chi, 'Stopping at night at Hsiang-Yin', trans Burton Watson, in *The Clouds Should Know Me By Now – Buddhist poet monks of China*, ed. Red Pine and Mike O'Connor, Boston, Wisdom Publications, 1990 (p 302); James McAuley, 'Nocturnal', in *Collected Poems 1936–1970*, Sydney, Angus & Robertson, 1971 (p 326).

Acknowledgements

I would like to express my gratitude and respect to my countryman Kevin Cairns, Chairman, and the Board of the Waanyi Nation Aboriginal Corporation, for your kind permission to use the Waanyi Language Dictionary.

Thank you to Aboriginal traditional landowners and elders of the Coorong, Ellen and Tom Trevorrow, for your generosity, friendship, and guidance.

My gratitude to Professor Raoul Mulder, Department of Zoology, University of Melbourne, for research material on the behavior and ecology of black swans; Ray Chatto, Parks, Wildlife and Conservation, Northern Territory, for invaluable information about brolgas in Northern Australia; Bernard Blood, Curator of Lake Wendoree in Ballarat, for your wonderful story of swans returning to the lake after the drought.

I have watched swans in many places, and learnt the best place to see swans on the Liffy in Dublin from a truly amused interviewer at RTÉ Raidió na Gaeltachta. I learnt from Seamus Heaney's poem 'Postscript', displayed at Dublin airport, that if I wanted to see swans, I should look on the Flaggy Shore in County Clare. Many friends, colleagues, and family members very kindly and thoughtfully told stories, sent information, and swan presents, including music inspired by swans, or poetry, photos, pictures, objects, books, and life size statues of swans. Thank you Hal Wolton, Sudha Ray, Forrest Holder, Jeff Hulcombe, Ann Davis, Murrandoo Yanner, Evelyn Juers, Andreas Campomar, Benoit and Christine Gruter, Steve Morwell, Kevin Rowley, Pip McManas, my sister Robyn and brother-in-law Bill, sister-in-law Larissa, brother- and sister-in-law George and Barbara Sawenko, Francis Bray, Kim Scott, Terry Whitebeach, Stewart Blackhall, Robert Adamson, Dimitris Vardoulakis, Steve Morwell and Karina Menkhorst. Thank you to Nicholas Jose for showing me the nesting swans along the Torrens River, and Bruce Sims who went on visits with me to the Melbourne Zoo.

My daughter Tate travelled with me on a special trip to the Coorong, and also came on many walks along the Torrens River to see nesting swans and find the man who nurses a wild swan on his lap. My daughter Lily enthusiastically found images of swans that she sent to my computer in the middle of the night, and we had several special trips to the Melbourne Zoo where we visited a lone Mute Swan befriended by goldfish. Thank you to my step-son Andre for telling me the story about the swan that lost its way on a busy highway in Melbourne.

I am indebted to many people who offered encouragement and support, including my former colleagues at RMIT, and especially Antoni Jach. Thank you most sincerely to Evelyn Juers and Alice Grundy for reading the final manuscript and offering invaluable feedback; and to Darren Gilbert for permission to use his wonderful image of the swan on the cover of this book.

I am very grateful for the support of Professor Wayne McKenna, the University of Western Sydney, and Professor Anthony Uhlmann and all of my colleagues in the Writing and Society Research Centre at the university.

Ivor Indyk, my publisher, editor and critic knows the work that went into this book. Thank you.

Thank you to my husband Toly for our trips to Lake Wendoree, and for many thoughtful references you found from the beginning of a journey that continued through many parts of the world.

Of course, all of those swans, and also our kelpies Jessie then Ruby, and our cats Pushkin then Luna, for the company.

This project has been assisted by the Australian Government through the Australia Council for the Arts, its arts funding and advisory body.

Australian Government

Australia Council for the Arts

D0687366

World Food Supply

This is a volume in the Arno Press collection

World Food Supply

Advisory Editor
D. Gale Johnson

Editorial Board
Charles M. Hardin
Kenneth H. Parsons

See last pages of this volume for a complete list of titles.

TECHNICAL CO-OPERATION
IN LATIN-AMERICAN AGRICULTURE

Arthur T. Mosher

ARNO PRESS
A New York Times Company
New York — 1976

Editorial Supervision: MARIE STARECK

———◆———

Reprint Edition 1976 by Arno Press Inc.

Copyright © 1957 by the University of Chicago
Reprinted by permission of
  The University of Chicago Press

Reprinted from a copy in
  The Princeton University Library

WORLD FOOD SUPPLY
ISBN for complete set: 0-405-07766-1
See last pages of this volume for titles.

Manufactured in the United States of America

———◆———

Library of Congress Cataloging in Publication Data

Mosher, Arthur Theodore, 1910-
    Technical co-operation in Latin-American agri-
culture.

    (World food supply)
    Reprint of the ed. published by the University
of Chicago Press, in series: National Planning
Association. Studies of technical co-operation in
Latin America.
    Includes bibliographical references.
    1. Agricultural assistance, American--Latin
America. 2. Agriculture--Latin America. 3. In-
ternational agricultural cooperation. I. Title.
II. Series. III. Series: National Planning Asso-
ciation. Technical cooperation in Latin America.
[S403.M75   1976]   309.2'233'7308   75-26310
ISBN 0-405-07788-2

TECHNICAL CO-OPERATION
IN LATIN-AMERICAN AGRICULTURE

NATIONAL PLANNING ASSOCIATION

STUDIES OF TECHNICAL CO-OPERATION IN LATIN AMERICA

Technical Assistance by Religious Agencies in Latin America

JAMES G. MADDOX

Technical Co-operation in Latin-American Agriculture

ARTHUR T. MOSHER

TECHNICAL CO-OPERATION
IN LATIN-AMERICAN AGRICULTURE

By Arthur T. Mosher

THE UNIVERSITY OF CHICAGO PRESS

Library of Congress Catalog Number: 56-11908

THE UNIVERSITY OF CHICAGO PRESS, CHICAGO 37
Cambridge University Press, London, N.W. 1, England
The University of Toronto Press, Toronto 5, Canada

FOREWORD

By 1953, a number of public agencies and private groups in the United States were sharing their knowledge and skills with the people and governments of other countries. Most of them, however, were working independently. Although it seemed likely that technical co-operation programs could become an increasingly constructive element in international co-operation, all too little was known about them. No thorough organized effort had been made to determine the extent to which this sharing of useful knowledge was helping the underdeveloped countries to help themselves or to see what its benefits—tangible and intangible—were to the United States.

Discussion with informed leaders in this field and with policy-makers, administrators, and technicians who were actively at work in public and private technical co-operation programs clearly indicated that a review and evaluation of the purposes, methods, and results of such programs would have wide usefulness, both in administering present programs and planning new ones. It was felt, further, that all concerned would have greater confidence in the findings if a critical analysis were made by an independent organization not involved with any of the public and private programs.

The National Planning Association's decision to undertake a far-reaching study of technical co-operation programs in order to gauge their potentialities and limitations in Latin America grew out of these discussions. The study was purposely concentrated on activities in Latin America—not because they were necessarily the most important or the best programs in the world, but because technical co-operation programs have been under way longer there than elsewhere and, until recent years, on a larger scale. Also, a great diversity of programs has been developed in Latin America. This diversity came about because the programs were created under a wide variety of auspices and conditions—sponsored by private foundations, the government of the United States, international organiza-

v

tions, religious groups, universities, trade unions, and business firms —each with somewhat different objectives. The programs also differ because the level and pace of development vary greatly from one Latin-American country to another, as do the political and social settings in which the programs operate. It was hoped that an intensive study of the rich experiences of the public agencies and private groups which have sponsored these programs under such diverse and complex circumstances would furnish important practical guides for technical co-operation.

The main objectives established for the NPA Project on Technical Co-operation in Latin America were:

1. To find out whether technical co-operation programs are making and can make a significant contribution to the long-range interests of the United States and of Latin-American countries in international understanding and growing international prosperity.
2. To identify the present objectives of public and private programs and judge their merits; to weigh results achieved in terms of such objectives; and to indicate standards for deciding which programs have greatest value for the future for the people both of Latin America and of the United States.
3. To clarify the role of public technical co-operation programs in relation to private programs.
4. To point out ways and means of increasing the effectiveness of technical co-operation programs, of improving their administration, and of attracting and training competent and dedicated personnel for the programs.

Early in 1953, the Ford Foundation made a grant of $440,000 to finance the NPA Project on Technical Co-operation in Latin America. The Ford Foundation is not, however, to be understood as approving by virtue of its grant any of the views expressed in the research studies or the policy statements growing out of the project.

In accordance with NPA's established procedures, a Special Policy Committee on Technical Co-operation was formed to help plan the project, to consider the products of staff research, and to make recommendations on policy issues that confront the United States and Latin America in the fields of technical co-operation. This committee is composed of United States and Latin-American leaders from agriculture, business, labor, education, health, and other fields, to ensure that its recommendations take into account the experience and views of such broadly based representative groups. Laird Bell, a senior partner of Bell, Boyd, Marshall and Lloyd in Chicago and a trustee of NPA, is chairman of the Special Policy Committee.

Theodore W. Schultz, of the University of Chicago and also a trustee of NPA, has organized the plan of study as director of research and has selected the research staff and consultants of the project. He and the research associates have done field work in twenty Latin-American Republics, where they have made surveys and examined the records. They have consulted with business firms, religious bodies, foundations, universities, and other private organizations, as well as with government officials both of Latin-American countries and of the United States and with representatives of the Organization of American States, the United Nations, and its specialized agencies. A number of staff reports, incorporating the findings of the research effort, are being prepared. This book is the second in a series of research reports that are being published at irregular intervals. The first of these was *Technical Assistance by Religious Agencies in Latin America,* by James G. Maddox. The subjects of other monographs to be published and their authors are: Philip M. Glick on the administration of technical co-operation; George I. Blanksten on the relationships between technical co-operation and foreign policy; Simon Rottenberg on how technology is transferred through private business firms; R. E. Buchanan on the role of university contracts in programs of technical co-operation; and Theodore W. Schultz on the distribution of technology and economic development. Several of the staff reports are case studies of particular programs illustrating a few of the problems that are common to many of the activities studied in the NPA Project. A case study by Arthur T. Mosher of ACAR's efforts to help stimulate better agricultural practices and rural living in Brazil was the first pamphlet of this type. Authors and subjects of others include James G. Maddox and Howard R. Tolley on the training of Latin Americans through technical co-operation and Armando Samper on technical co-operation in the renovation of secondary education in Chile.

These studies are the sole responsibility of the authors. They are building stones for the NPA Special Policy Committee in its efforts to resolve policy issues in the area of technical co-operation.

A major activity of the Special Policy Committee has been to correlate the findings of the research staff and to prepare an over-all policy report on technical co-operation, which was published by the National Planning Association in June 1956. Meanwhile, the committee has issued recommendations or policy statements on matters which in its opinion warranted special attention. (The committee's reports to date have been published in a special series of NPA pamphlets.)

The NPA is grateful for the Ford Foundation's financial support, and is deeply indebted to all who are contributing to this project: to the Special Policy Committee members; to the project's research staff; and to other individuals—too numerous to list—in Latin America and the United States, in the United Nations and its specialized agencies, and in the Organization of American States, for their invaluable co-operation and generosity with time and knowledge. Our special thanks go to Arthur T. Mosher for his careful study of technical co-operation in agriculture, and to the Special Policy Committee for an accompanying statement recommending its publication, which follows the report.

H. CHRISTIAN SONNE
Chairman, Board of Trustees

PREFACE

We gave major attention to agriculture in our studies of technical co-operation. We did this because of the overwhelming importance of agriculture in Latin America and because many of the technical co-operation programs serve agriculture. Most of the population in Latin America makes its living in agriculture. In the United States the farm population is only 12 per cent of the total, whereas in Latin America it is about 60 per cent.

There can be no doubt that Latin America has much at stake in the development of its agriculture. More food is required for the rapidly growing population. Additional food is needed also to improve diets that are far below par. Exports of agricultural products play an exceedingly important role in the economy. The earnings from foreign sales, which are mostly sales of agricultural products, are about four times as large relative to gross national product as they are in the United States. Coffee, cacao, bananas, sugar, and cotton make up about one-half of the exports of Latin America. Add to these wheat, corn, meat, hides, wool, and linseed oil, and one accounts for three-fifths of the exports of these countries.

The development of agriculture is important, however, in a still more basic sense. Agriculture at present lays claim to most of the labor force. Industry, the services, and other sectors will require increasingly more labor if they are to expand rapidly consistent with the usual patterns of economic development. Agriculture, however, will have to become much more efficient in production and in the use of labor if other sectors are to have enough labor to expand rapidly. In this sense, progress in agriculture is one of the necessary conditions for economic development.

It has become fashionable of late to think of agriculture in the less developed countries as having on tap a large reservoir of labor that would be readily available to other sectors without reducing agricultural production. The notion of "disguised unemployment" in agriculture with many farm workers making no contribution to production whatsoever is widely held. It is supposed to be self-evident, but it is not. Nor is it supported by evidence.[1]

Progress in agriculture makes progress possible in other sectors. As a rule, progress in agriculture must go hand in hand with programs and efforts to develop other major sectors of the economy. Unless they advance together, not enough labor will be released from agriculture to make possible economic development on a broad front. One should also stress in this context the fact that the output of labor leaving the farms to work in towns and cities depends largely upon their health, education, skills, and outlook upon modern production methods. At present, almost everywhere in Latin America more investment in technical co-operation in all of these is needed by rural communities.

Despite rich opportunities and the large stakes that they have in the development of agriculture, most Latin-American countries have been looking for greener pastures in their efforts to industrialize. In the process they have neglected agriculture. Argentina, especially, has paid dearly for its economic policies of this kind; but it has not been alone in overreaching for a few mouthfuls of green grass on the other side of the fence. Brazil saw fit to place heavy burdens on its agriculture. Chile, too, has neglected its agriculture, and so have other countries in Latin America. A notable exception in this respect has been Mexico, where agriculture has received as good treatment as industry and the other sectors. Mexico has benefited accordingly. The amount of food available has increased dramatically; in calories per day it appears to have risen as much as 50 per cent since the late thirties.[2] Throughout most of Latin America, by contrast, the additional food forthcoming has been only about enough to stay abreast of the growth in population.

The several Point 4 programs, however, have not neglected agriculture. On the contrary, the United Nations, the Organization of American States, and markedly so the technical co-operation program of the United States through the Institute of Inter-American Affairs have organized and supported major programs for agriculture from the outset. About one-third of the 155 million dollars which the government of the United States has contributed through IIAA for technical co-operation during the thirteen years from 1943 through fiscal 1955 supported programs in agriculture in Latin America. The Rockefeller Foundation has also contributed much, notably to the corn program in Mexico. The American International Association program is another that has concentrated on agriculture.[3]

In many ways Dr. Mosher came better prepared than did the rest of us to study technical co-operation. Organized programs in technical co-operation are a new kind of public venture, with few or no benchmarks. Knowledge about the technical components entering into a particular program was required. Knowledge about cultural considerations was also exceedingly important. In this area, Dr. Mosher had the advantages of drawing upon both his United States background in agriculture and fifteen years of experience in the agricultural field as educator and as head of the Allahabad Agricultural Institute in India. This bicultural experience stood him in good stead in getting his bearing on the development of agriculture in Latin America and in gauging the role that the several Point 4 programs have played and can perform in helping agriculture develop.

THEODORE W. SCHULTZ
Director of Research

TABLE OF CONTENTS

INTRODUCTION

This is a study of technical co-operation in agriculture in Latin America. It is primarily a survey and analysis of those programs of technical co-operation that were active in 1953 and 1954. But because the history of these programs is important to understanding and evaluating them, an attempt has been made to dig back to the beginnings of selected programs, to learn how they started, how they have evolved, and what they may have achieved prior to the two years during which most of this study was made.

Current programs have been examined by means of field studies and by means of interviews with administrators in the headquarters of agencies of technical co-operation and with farmers in areas served by the programs. The history of each program has had to be deduced from records, reports, and interviews, and from previous evaluative studies of programs in the few instances in which such studies are available. A few programs have been quite fully reported, and in ways which inspire respect for their objectivity and accuracy, but even such reports do not form a basis for comparisons between programs where those programs are themselves dissimilar. Other programs have been reported in ways meant to justify the program rather than to facilitate comparisons. Still other programs are not covered by adequate reports of any kind.

In retrospect it is difficult to decide whether the great diversity of programs (and of agricultural problems) in different parts of Latin America has been a liability or an asset from the standpoint of the purposes of this study. Certainly these diversities have increased the difficulty of comparing the results of programs; because of them it is virtually impossible to make a quantitative generalized assessment of the effects of these programs. At the same time, however, the differences among problems are an important factor in the situation with which programs of technical co-operation have to cope, and a careful study of the differences among programs can yield valu-

1

able insights as to the relative advantages and disadvantages of different policies, practices, and methods within technical co-operation.

Field Work

In the preliminary stages of this study a number of persons were consulted about the problem of sampling. It seemed obvious that in a study limited to two years, but with terms of reference covering all Latin-American countries except dependencies, some selection of countries and programs would have to be made. The consultants, without exception, insisted that the study would have to be based on a sample if adequate depth was to be achieved by the study. However, again without exception, they insisted that no sample would be representative, that Latin-American agriculture and programs of technical co-operation vary so much that a large number of countries ought to be included in the study.

The procedure actually followed represents a blending of this contradictory counsel, and was an attempt to proceed in such a way as to use in an optimum fashion the experience and the available records of experience. Three types of field work have been included: (1) intensive comprehensive team studies in three countries, (2) individual visits by the writer to twelve additional countries, and (3) standardized interviews by a field investigator in six countries.[1]

As this study of technical co-operation programs in agriculture is only one part of the broader investigation by the National Planning Association of all phases of technical co-operation in Latin America, three joint field studies were made by the entire research staff of the total NPA project. These joint field studies, each lasting about one month, were conducted in Peru, Mexico, and Brazil. In every case, each member of the NPA research staff studied primarily those programs of technical co-operation which were his own assignment. In addition, the group met frequently while in the field for consultation and cross-information. A few of the interviews of administrators in the field were joint interviews by two or more members of the team. These team studies provided much of the information about relationships between programs of various types—agriculture, health, public administration, education, etc. The intensive studies of these countries also resulted in three of the case studies included in Part II of this report.

The twelve additional countries visited by the writer, for periods varying from a few days to two weeks each, are the following: Bolivia, Colombia, Ecuador, Venezuela, Costa Rica, Cuba, Haiti, Chile, Uruguay, Paraguay, El Salvador, and Honduras. These visits fully justified the decision not to concentrate on only a few countries; for each country displays one or more facets of the problems of agricultural development and of technical co-operation which are not prominent elsewhere. Consequently, each additional country studied contributes either corroboration of, or reservations about, the degree to which generalizations about agricultural programs of technical co-operation are justifiable. With the exceptions of Chile, Uruguay, Paraguay, El Salvador, and Honduras, all countries listed were studied early enough in the period of investigation that a second visit could be made where considerations seemed to justify it.

About half the writer's time during the seven and one-half months he spent in Latin America in the course of this study was devoted to interviews in capital cities. The other half was spent in the countryside, where he visited farmers, extension agents, and experimental farms, and observed the agriculture of the regions.

The third type of field work utilized in this study was a series of standardized interviews by a field investigator[2] in six countries: Venezuela, Colombia, Ecuador, Peru, Bolivia, and Paraguay. These included interviews with (1) administrators of domestic governmental programs, (2) field administrators of programs of technical co-operation, (3) field extension agents of both domestic and technical co-operation programs, and (4) farmers in localities where these extension services are active.

Consultation and Critical Comment on Tentative Findings

It is unavoidable that a study covering such diverse programs with such dissimilar records must depend to a considerable extent on the understanding and judgment of the person or persons making the study. Although this factor cannot be eliminated, an effort has been made to reduce the number of errors of fact, and to reconsider the statements of judgment in this study, by subjecting its tentative findings to outside criticism as rapidly as these emerged. All members of the NPA research staff have read this report at various stages and have contributed to it. Sixteen consultants from six countries and from all the agencies of technical co-operation whose programs are discussed herein (except the American International Association) met in Costa Rica for three days in July, 1954, to discuss the first preliminary report. A semifinal draft was read and criticized by administrative officers of each agency of technical co-operation before the final draft was prepared.

This process does not absolve the writer from final responsibility for the study, and the report has been altered as a result of these interim criticisms only to the extent that the writer felt them to be justified. But this process of consultation and criticism has been an integral part of the method of the study and has provided an invaluable part of the data on which its conclusions are based.

Any report like this is subject to the criticism that some of its findings or observations are out of date by the time the report is published. There seems to be no way to avoid this, in view of the inevitable period of preparing the report and getting it published. In the case of the present report, a process of submitting tentative findings as rapidly as they emerged to field administrators for criticism made most of the suggestions contained herein known to administrators of technical co-operation for one to two and one-half years before the date of publication. Within that time changes have been made, many of them in line with the recommendations of this study. The writer desires no credit for having influenced these changes, but he would appreciate not being criticized too severely for presenting conditions as they were at the time the field studies were made.

Obviously, the writer is indebted to all of his colleagues within the NPA research staff and to the innumerable persons in Latin America who have had a part in this study. He is particularly indebted to Theodore W. Schultz, director of the NPA Study, both for his rigorous criticism and for the atmosphere of responsible freedom for each member of the staff which he created and maintained. Aníbal Buitrón, of the Organization of American States, collaborated with the writer in field studies in the Andean countries and Mexico. Clifton R. Wharton, Jr., helped with the field work in Brazil and Venezuela, and in editing the report. Marie Moe and Terry Barham have typed several successive drafts of every chapter and have contributed to the readability of the report.

PART I

THE PROBLEM

1 TECHNICAL CO-OPERATION IN AGRICULTURE: DEFINITION AND SETTING

A young agricultural scientist of Colombia is made dean of one of his country's two colleges of agriculture. He sees opportunities and responsibilities of his college which cannot be discharged without a better-trained staff and better buildings and equipment. Unable to get the full needed support from his government, he turns to a philanthropic foundation in the United States. The foundation agrees to provide fellowships for members of the staff to study abroad and to provide equipment for college laboratories if the government of Colombia will finance the new buildings; and the challenge is accepted.

This is technical co-operation.

The twenty republics in the Organization of American States (OAS), concerned with their mutual needs to develop agriculture and rural life, join together in a program of short-course training to strengthen the professional competence of the extension services which many of them have been developing. The organization places a trained technical staff in three strategically located centers throughout Latin America to carry out this project—at Havana (Cuba), Lima (Peru), and Montevideo (Uruguay). Individual countries select trainees and send them to these centers for training, often on scholarships provided by OAS.

This is technical co-operation.

The Institute of Inter-American Affairs offers to act with the government of Paraguay in developing public services to agriculture. The two parties agree jointly to staff and finance a special agency within the Paraguayan government. It is to be directed by a United States technician responsible to the Paraguayan Minister of Agri-

7

culture. This new agency, with its own budget and staff, can under-take any project related to agricultural development on which the two parties agree. It establishes an experimental farm, sets up a program of supervised credit, and later starts an agricultural extension service with a big 4-H club program.

This is technical co-operation.

The government of Brazil decides that it should do more to exploit and develop its forest resources in the Amazon Basin. It asks the Food and Agriculture Organization of the United Nations to provide forestry technicians who will advise and further train Brazilian technicians. FAO provides the experts and later makes a grant of equipment for a demonstration logging project.

This is technical co-operation.

"Technical co-operation in agriculture," as the term is used in this study, *means all of those activities (other than importations of capital) that aim primarily at developing a more productive agriculture in a country and in which a non-profit agency external to the country is a co-operating partner.*

There are three reasons for adopting this definition. One reason is that it corresponds fairly closely to popular usage. The second is that it leaves us with a reasonably uniform set of programs for consideration. The third reason is that it sets the subject of this study off from several other closely related studies, all of which were part of the same research program as this one.

Excluded from consideration here, by the definition, are importations of foreign capital for agricultural purposes.[1] Excluded also are the activities, in Latin America, of United States business firms dealing in agricultural requisites (implements, fertilizers, insecticides, etc.) or in agricultural products, since the development of agriculture is not the *primary* purpose of such firms.[2]

A borderline exclusion is that of international or binational programs for the control of plant and animal diseases. Among such programs are the United States–Mexican efforts to combat the Mexican fruit fly, the cotton boll weevil, and foot-and-mouth disease in cattle. The reason for not considering these programs in this study is that they pose a set of problems quite different from those common to the programs we include in technical co-operation.

A purely arbitrary exclusion is the agricultural activities in Latin

America of United States religious agencies. These are bypassed here because they are considered in another monograph of this series.[3]

Even after these limits to our study have been set, however, we are left with a wide variety of programs with which to deal.

These programs differ, first, in the kinds of projects they undertake within the field of agriculture. Some of them conduct agricultural research. Some set up, or advise with, programs of extension education. Some design (and sometimes construct) irrigation dams and canals and wells. Some operate mechanized farm equipment on hire. Some co-operate with agricultural colleges in their teaching programs. Some of them counsel with governments on agricultural policy.

These programs differ, second, in the ways in which they operate. Nearly all of them send technicians-from-abroad to work with local agricultural technicians. Some technicians-from-abroad operate singly, as advisers; in other cases, several such technicians operate as a team, but still as advisers; in still other cases, such technicians operate as a team and share the administrative responsibility for operating programs to serve agriculture. In some programs of technical co-operation, the external co-operating partner (agency of technical co-operation) makes cash appropriations to co-operative programs within the country, while in other cases it does not. One agency occasionally makes a financial grant-in-aid without providing foreign technicians. All agencies of technical co-operation grant fellowships for foreign study.

Finally, the programs studied here differ in that five separate agencies of technical co-operation have been the external co-operating partners in these programs over the past twelve years, and each of these agencies has policies or administrative necessities that result in significant program differences.

Thus the subject of this study is a group of quite varied programs held together by two common factors:

1. They are all directed at the instrumental objective of developing a more productive agriculture in one or another part of Latin America.

2. In each case a non-profit agency external to the country is a co-operating partner in the program.

"Latin America," as the term is used here, includes all of the independent countries of South America—except Argentina, where virtually no co-operative agricultural programs existed at the time of study—of Central America, and of the Caribbean Islands, and Mexico. A realization of the magnitude and the infinite variety of Latin-American agriculture is essential to any assessment of programs of technical co-operation; yet it is out of the question to try to describe this variety in these pages.

Latin America embraces practically every type of climate to be found anywhere in the inhabited parts of the world, and it has all of the kinds of agriculture associated with these. Its agriculture includes practically every type of farm organization, ranging from communally owned and operated village agriculture with tiny, fragmented fields, through small private subsistence farms, small to medium-sized commercial farms, large commercial farms, enormous feudal haciendas, and one-crop tropical plantations. In some parts of Latin America one of these types of farming prevails over a wide region, while in other parts several of them are found intermixed in a relatively small area.

The agricultural regions of Latin America include high-altitude plateaus devoted to livestock and the production of food crops (as in parts of Ecuador and Peru), intensive coffee, sugar, and banana regions (in Brazil, Colombia, Honduras, and Cuba), rolling prairie grasslands (in Uruguay), intensive crop and fruit culture in isolated narrow mountain valleys (all along the Andes), and undeveloped, potentially productive temperate to tropical regions (in Bolivia, Peru, Ecuador, Colombia, and Venezuela).

From the standpoints of population, government, and culture Latin America is equally diverse. Millions of descendants of the Aztecs and Incas still live in large parts of Mexico, Guatemala, Nicaragua, Ecuador, Peru, and Bolivia, with many traits and values and customs inherited from their ancient past. The European migration to these countries (and to other countries of Central America) was chiefly from Spain. But to Brazil, following the earlier colonization from Portugal, immigrants have come more recently from Italy and Germany and other European countries. Northern and central Europe have provided much of the European stock of Uruguay and Chile. In equatorial Brazil and on the islands of the Caribbean there are now millions of inhabitants much of whose ancestry is African. In most countries of Latin America there has been considerable mingling of these ancestral stocks, sometimes resulting in amalgamation into truly national cultures. In other cases, despite considerable blending, there still exist quite different cultures in single countries, with differing degrees of political power and influence.[4]

The persistence of primitive practices of cultivation and of low agricultural productivity in large regions of Latin America must not be allowed to obscure the fact that there has been a great deal of agricultural development in these countries, brought about primarily by domestic efforts.[5] While most of the highland region of Ecuador has continued relatively unchanged for decades, there has been a rapid development of agricultural production on the coast, and there are a number of modern, progressive ranches scattered about the sierra. While the state of Minas Gerais, in Brazil, was remaining about stationary in agricultural production, the coffee region of São Paulo was modernizing rapidly, and production was being greatly extended in the states of Paraná, Santa Caterina, and Rio Grande do Sul. For all the charges of exploitation and imperialism, the fruit and sugar plantations of many countries have been under management which reached out for new techniques, and these companies have conducted considerable research of their own.

While the pattern varies greatly, there have been numerous domestic public programs for agricultural development in many Latin-American countries. These have included "development corporations," agricultural banks, marketing associations, plant and animal protection services, "one-crop" associations, land-reform movements, and considerable public investments in irrigation, roads, and transportation.

These Latin-American domestic programs for agricultural development would be a fruitful field for study in themselves. A little indication of how numerous they are is given in connection with the case studies in Part II of this report.

These many variations, both in the agriculture of Latin America and in domestic public programs for agricultural development, are so great that generalizations about the setting of programs of technical co-operation hide as much as they reveal. Nevertheless, the following generalizations are helpful:

1. Latin America is big and varied, with widely differing agricultural problems.

2. Latin America's potential agricultural production is far greater than its present yield, although the percentage of cultivable land is lower than in North America or in Europe.

3. The major industry of Latin America is agriculture, despite rapid industrialization in recent years.

4. The problems of increasing agricultural production are partly technical, but they are also economic, social, and political.

5. Latin America has not been idle with respect to agricultural development, but with the rapidly rising population, a contemporary compulsion to industrialize, a human problem growing out of a complex colonial past, and agricultural problems sufficiently novel that they require fresh study and unique solutions, the problem is involved and difficult.

It is into such a setting that programs of technical co-operation come.

2 TECHNICAL CO-OPERATION IN AGRICULTURE: HISTORY AND EXTENT

By the definition of this study, technical co-operation in agriculture means those activities (other than importations of capital) that aim at *developing a more productive agriculture in a country and in which an agency external to the country is a co-operating partner.* Five such agencies have been the external partners in the programs of technical co-operation examined in this study.[1] Two of these are private foundations: the Rockefeller Foundation and the American International Association (AIA). Two others are international governmental agencies: the Food and Agricultural Organization of the United Nations (FAO) and the Organization of American States (OAS). The fifth is the Institute of Inter-American Affairs (IIAA), which is the agency of the United States government for bilateral technical co-operation in Latin America.[2]

The programs of all of these agencies are young. With the exception of the Rockefeller Foundation, the agencies are young also. The agricultural programs of the Rockefeller Foundation and of IIAA were launched in 1943. Those of AIA were started in 1948. The "Expanded Technical Assistance Program" of FAO began operations in 1950, and the Technical Cooperation Program of OAS was undertaken in the same year. Thus, at the time this study was made, the programs of the Rockefeller Foundation and of IIAA had been operating about ten years, that of the American International Association was in its fifth year, and those of FAO and OAS were about four years old.

The Rockefeller Foundation

The International Health Division of the Rockefeller Foundation has had large health programs in Latin America since the establishment of the foundation in 1913. Working chiefly in the field of the control of hookworm, malaria, and yellow fever, those programs made substantial contributions to the cause of agricultural development by greatly lowering the incidence of endemic disease in many agricultural regions, but they are not properly within the scope of this study.

Since 1943 the foundation has had a large program in the field of agriculture in several Latin-American countries. The major projects have been programs of agricultural research undertaken jointly with the governments of Mexico and Colombia. These have

TABLE 1

Rockefeller Foundation Grants for Agricultural Development in Latin America, 1943–54

Scholarships for graduates of Latin-American colleges of agriculture in connection with the foundation's Mexican Agricultural Program	$113,000
The Faculty of Veterinary Medicine, San Marcos University, Peru	80,000
Two technical symposiums, one on plant breeding and one on plant pests and diseases	27,500
Postgraduate research facilities at La Molina, Peru	30,000
Grants, chiefly for research equipment, to three Mexican agricultural colleges and to one agricultural school	160,000
Buildings, equipment, and faculty support for the colleges at Medellin and Palmira in Colombia	314,000
The general agricultural program (chiefly extension) of the State of Mexico	100,000
Total	$824,500

been very substantial and significant projects. The program in Mexico represented an investment of about $2,600,000 in the first ten years, and is presented in some detail in chapter vi.

In addition, the Rockefeller Foundation made additional financial grants for agricultural development in Latin America between 1943 and 1954, as shown in Table 1.

The American International Association

The American International Association for Economic and Social Development was organized in 1946 "to promote economic and social development in the underdeveloped areas of the world," and has had programs in Venezuela and Brazil. Its early projects were varied: fellowships, advisory missions, short-term research.

Beginning in 1948, the American International Association has conducted joint agricultural programs with the government of Venezuela and with the states of Minas Gerais and São Paulo in Brazil. The program in Venezuela has been a combination of general extension, education, supervised credit, rural child welfare, and special agricultural studies. The program in São Paulo has been a co-operative extension program. That in Minas Gerais has been a combination of general extension education, supervised credit, and rural health. It is the subject of another of our case studies (chap. viii).

The total expenditures of the American International Association on all of its programs in Venezuela (including a nation-wide nutrition education program in addition to the agricultural programs) from 1948 through 1953 were $2,607,000, of which four oil companies operating in Venezuela contributed a substantial share.[3] The government of Venezuela contributed about $4,000,000 to these programs during the same period.

For its programs in Brazil, the American International Association appropriated $595,000 in the period 1948–53, and the two Brazilian state governments appropriated just under $2,000,000.

The Institute of Inter-American Affairs (IIAA)

The largest group of programs of technical co-operation in agriculture operating today in Latin America is that of the Institute of Inter-American Affairs. The institute is a United States government corporation, established in 1942, initially to administer bilateral programs of technical co-operation in the fields of health and sanitation, agriculture, and education.

In the early years of IIAA, programs of health and sanitation were much larger and more numerous than programs in agriculture, and those in agriculture were larger and more numerous than those in education. Chart I depicts the shifting emphasis of IIAA over the years. Programs in agriculture received approximately the same percentage (15–22) of the resources of IIAA each year from 1943 through 1950, but they have increased in relative size since that time.

Chart II shows that, starting with agricultural programs in 9 countries in 1943, IIAA closed all but 4 of these when United States appropriations to IIAA dropped sharply after World War II. The number of programs began to increase again in 1951. There were agricultural programs in 19 countries by 1952, and the number stood at 18 in 1954. In that year, the last covered by this study, IIAA had 252 United States agricultural technicians at work in 18 Latin-American countries, and the total of United States contributions, in services and cash, to the programs in which these technicians were

CHART I

Shifting Program Emphasis (IIAA)

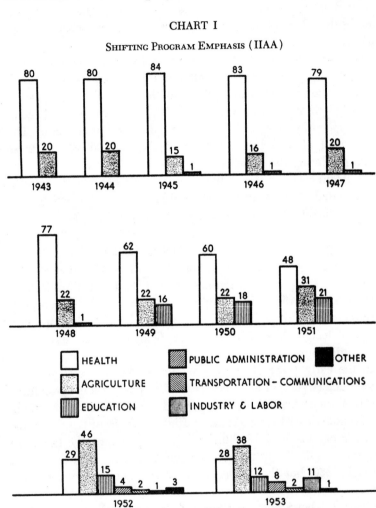

PERCENTAGES OF TOTAL U.S. CONTRIBUTIONS

serving, was $10,580,000 in fiscal year 1954. This amount constituted 44 per cent of all United States contributions for bilateral technical co-operation in Latin America for that year.[4]

Today, a wide variety of activities is being carried on within the agricultural programs of IIAA. Most, but not all, programs are developing projects of extension education. Many are doing some experimentation, and at least one program, in Cuba (see chap. vii),

CHART II

AGRICULTURAL PROGRAMS OF IIAA

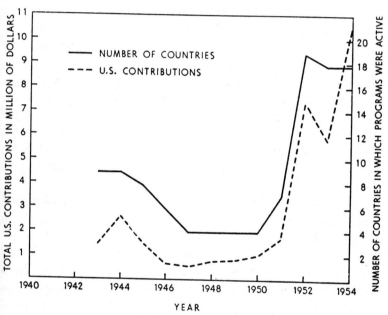

was solely research through 1954. Many of them have subsidiary projects devoted to importing and selling to farmers the seeds, fertilizers, and insecticides which they need but for which normal commercial channels are not yet adequate. A few are accelerating the mechanization of agriculture by operating "machinery pools" for land clearing and for large-scale cultivation. In several countries these programs provide engineering services to design irrigation systems, survey for land development, and design grain storage facilities. In Haiti (see chap. v) the bilateral program has constructed, and continued to operate, several small irrigation projects. In all countries these programs make grants enabling local technicians to increase their competence by study abroad.

Although IIAA has been the administrative agency for all bilateral programs in agriculture since 1950, other agencies of the United States government had programs in Latin America for many years prior to that time. These have not been reviewed in this study, but they are mentioned here to complete the record.

Probably the oldest examples of bilateral programs in the field of agriculture are the joint programs of the governments of Mexico and the United States for the control of plant and animal diseases: the cotton pink bollworm, the Mexican fruit fly and citrus fly, and *aftosa*, or foot-and-mouth disease, in cattle. These programs have been active for many years.

Next came the Rubber Development programs, launched about 1940, and administered by the Bureau of Plant Industry of the United States Department of Agriculture. These programs, which are still operating on a small scale in several countries, although under the administration of IIAA since 1950, were intended to explore the possibilities of more widespread and more efficient production of rubber in the Western Hemisphere.

The third United States bilateral program to be established was that of the Office of Foreign Agricultural Relations (OFAR) of the Department of Agriculture. This was a program, primarily of research, to stimulate the production in Latin America of those crops which were not then grown in quantity in the United States. From this fact, the program became known as the "Complementary Crops Program." It was set up to be a continuing program, with initial agreements with co-operating governments for a ten-year period (1943–53).

When, therefore, the Institute of Inter-American Affairs (IIAA) was organized and began to co-operate with Latin-American countries in 1943, it became the fourth United States agency simultaneously administering bilateral programs in the field of agriculture in Latin America. In that year, apart from disease-control programs, the Bureau of Plant Industry had active programs in ten countries, OFAR had programs in six countries, and IIAA started programs in nine countries. These were not the same countries in every case, and the programs were different, but OFAR and IIAA both had programs in four countries: Brazil, El Salvador, Nicaragua, and Peru. In Brazil and Peru, BPI also had a program of rubber development.

Having been set up under the Office of the Coordinator of Inter-American Affairs, IIAA gave first attention to programs felt to be important to the war effort. In Costa Rica, for example, IIAA first established a vegetable-purchase program to provide supplies for the Panama Canal Zone. Beginning with purchasing only, this program soon began educating growers in the use of fertilizers and insecticides and in grading their product. In Peru, likewise, the first program of IIAA was to stimulate the production of vegetables for a United States air base at Tulara, on the coast, maintained as part of the defenses of the Panama Canal.

From the standpoint of really becoming adjusted to the basic needs of each country for agricultural development, both OFAR and IIAA started with a substantial handicap. In the case of OFAR, the handicap was the necessity of dealing only with complementary crops, where they could in no way be accused of improving the competitive position of a Latin-American country with respect to the United States. In the case of IIAA, the handicap was a pressure for quick results directly related to the war effort. In addition, the two agencies became involved in an interagency rivalry in Washington which probably hurt the programs of both.[5] Though not limited to research by its legal authorization, OFAR argued the alleged superficiality of the IIAA approach and limited itself almost entirely to research.[6] IIAA, meanwhile, criticized OFAR programs for being isolated from national streams of agricultural development, and put a probably unwarranted emphasis in its programs on extension programs to get quick increases in production.

In any case, for a period of seven years (1943–50), there were two United States agencies carrying on programs with somewhat similar purposes in Latin-American countries. (The Rubber Development Program was quite separate and did not enter into the conflict between agencies.) In the years 1946 to 1950 (when IIAA appropriations were at a low ebb) IIAA had multi-project programs in four countries: Costa Rica, Peru, Haiti, and Paraguay. During the same years, OFAR had programs, chiefly research, in nine countries—

Bolivia, Colombia, Cuba, Ecuador, El Salvador, Guatemala, Nicaragua, Panama, and Peru—and sporadic, minor programs in other countries. As shown in Table 2, although the programs of OFAR were more numerous in this period, those of IIAA were much larger in terms of United States expenditures.

We shall have to return to some of the results of this history at a later point in this study.[7] For now, it must suffice to point out that

TABLE 2

EXPENDITURES ON UNITED STATES AGRICULTURAL
PROGRAMS IN LATIN AMERICA, 1946–50*

OFFICE OF FOREIGN AGRICULTURAL RELATIONS

Country	Average Annual Expenditure
Guatemala	$ 98,000
Peru	78,000
Ecuador	71,000
Nicaragua	40,000
Bolivia	31,000
Cuba	30,000
Panama	28,000
Colombia	24,500

INSTITUTE OF INTER-AMERICAN AFFAIRS

Country	Average Annual Expenditure
Peru	$237,000
Paraguay	200,000
Haiti	179,000
Costa Rica	138,000

* Excluding Rubber Development and Disease Control programs.

when the Technical Co-operation Administration was established in 1950, the OFAR programs were transferred to IIAA for administration. This brought on a final flurry of personal bitterness and program confusion on which we shall comment later, but at least since 1950 there has been only one United States public program of technical co-operation in Latin America: that administered by IIAA.

The Food and Agricultural Organization

The international Food and Agriculture Organization (FAO) was formally established in October, 1945, when thirty-two governments signed its constitution. Since that time, thirty-nine additional countries have become members, making the total seventy-one in 1955.

As initially conceived, FAO was established to provide, internationally, those services which many governments need in common in their separate attempts to increase food production and to adjust the production of specific crops to the current economic demand for each. In pursuit of this objective FAO established a varied program. One part of this program is an extensive reporting and publications program for world-wide agricultural statistics, in the form of a number of annual reports.[8] Other publications are in a series of monographs on "Agricultural Studies," summarizing information important to many countries, and a series of "Development Papers" on subjects important at the policy-making level to spur agricultural development in the less developed countries. Another phase of the FAO program consists of periodic international conferences on subjects of pressing policy importance to agriculture, forestry, fisheries, and human nutrition. FAO sponsors a number of regional organizations related to agricultural problems and supports several "working parties" of a continuing, consultative nature, each devoted to the problems of a particular crop. FAO also sponsors the initiation and negotiation of international conventions such as those for plant protection.

These basic activities of FAO are of great importance to world agriculture, and they provide many services which aid the less developed countries, but they are not programs of technical co-operation to accelerate agricultural development in specific regions of low agricultural productivity in the same sense as are other programs discussed in this monograph. They are, rather, services which all countries need in connection with agricultural development and in the determination of agricultural policies. With respect to these services, all countries are in a single category; there is no classification on the basis of the degree of development of national agricultural economies.

Three years after FAO was established, the United Nations Economic and Social Council, on August 15, 1949, set up what is called an "Expanded Technical Assistance Program" (ETAP) which brought to FAO a program of the type of technical co-operation which does fall within the field of this study.[9]

The purpose of the technical co-operation to be undertaken by

FAO under ETAP was stated in the "General Principles" adopted by the Economic and Social Council on August 15, 1949:

The participating organizations should, in extending technical assistance to economic development of under-developed countries: . . . Regard it as a primary objective to help those countries to strengthen their national economies through the development of their industries and agriculture, with a view to promoting their economic and political independence in the spirit of the Charter of the United Nations, and to ensure the attainment of higher levels of economic and social welfare for their entire populations. . . .

This is very similar to the statements of purpose of the programs of technical co-operation of the Organization of American States and of the United States government. There are differences of phraseology and mention of the "spirit of the Charter of the United Nations," but basically ETAP has the same purposes as other programs of technical co-operation.

The budget of FAO for its world-wide Regular Program was approximately $5,000,000 annually through 1951. It was increased to $5,250,000 for 1952 and 1953 and to $6,000,000 for 1954 and 1955. The Expanded Technical Assistance Program brought another $5,000,000 (approximately) to FAO, for "technical assistance to underdeveloped countries" throughout the world.

To administer this Expanded Technical Assistance Program, a new policy committee (Technical Assistance Committee), and a new administrative agency (Technical Assistance Board) were created at the request of the UN Economic and Security Council. Each specialized agency, including FAO, has one representative on the Technical Assistance Board. However, since the executive secretary of the TAB is appointed by the secretary-general of the UN, and the resident representatives are appointed by the executive secretary, there is considerable feeling in the specialized agencies that ETAP is in the hands of "co-ordinators" who do not understand the technical problems involved.

Thus FAO was given the administration of a program of technical co-operation with a budget of $5,000,000 per year, in addition to its Regular Program of similar size, and in the process had to accept the oversight for this program of technical co-operation of two co-ordinating bodies of the United Nations Organization.

Although the program of technical co-operation of the FAO has never been as prominent in Latin America as it has been in other parts of the world, it has been quite active there, and certain countries have made extensive use of its facilities. This program is discussed in chapter xi.

The Organization of American States

The formal drawing-together of the American republics may be said to have commenced with the founding of the Pan-American Union in 1890. This organization remained small for many years, but it did bring representatives of the American republics together at increasingly frequent intervals. By 1936 these conferences were discussing mutual problems related to the welfare of the American peoples, and at the conferences of 1936 and 1938 resolutions were passed urging co-operation and mutual assistance to raise living standards, to improve health, to increase food production, and to train technical personnel. In 1942 the Conference of the Pan-American Union, meeting in Rio de Janeiro, adopted another resolution calling for inter-American co-operation in health, food supplies, and education.

A significant step related to agriculture was taken in 1944, with the founding of the Interamerican Institute of Agricultural Sciences at Turrialba, Costa Rica. Then in 1948, at a Pan-American Conference in Bogotá, the Organization of American States was founded, the old Pan-American Union became its secretariat, and the Interamerican Institute of Agricultural Sciences at Turrialba, along with six other inter-American agencies, became specialized agencies of the OAS. Several of these agencies were already supplying technical assistance to member countries through direct technical services, consultation, exchange fellowships, seminars, and publications. They continued to do so as part of their regular programs that are financed separately through the provisions made in the international treaty under which each of the agencies was chartered.

Since 1950 the OAS has been operating its own program of technical co-operation. The purpose of this program was stated in Principles I and IV of the Resolution of April 10, 1950:

I. The purpose of the Program of Technical Cooperation is that through it, Member States may cooperate in the development of their economies, in order to improve the standard of living and to promote the social welfare of their peoples, in the broadest spirit of common benefit.

IV. The technical assistance rendered by inter-American agencies co-operating in this program should:

    (a) Contribute to the economic development of the interested Member Country or Countries or promote activities that will make this development possible:

    (b) Have as its purpose to provide training, instruction, and technical advice in such a way as to permit the earliest and broadest application of the acquired knowledge and techniques to the economic development of the Member States;

    (c) Contribute, in all cases deemed possible by the interested parties, to the earliest and most extensive preparation, improvement, or increase of technical groups and research institutions in each country.

OAS has pointed out that its program of technical co-operation "differs from other international and bilateral assistance programs in two ways: first, it is geared solely to technical education; and second, every American nation shares in its benefits, without expressly requesting aid." Of the validity of the first claim there can be no doubt; the projects undertaken within the program bear it out. As for the second, in reality those countries benefit which actually send trainees to participate in the training programs and which make good use of the trainees after they return.

The largest of the projects undertaken by OAS within its program of technical co-operation is its Project 39—Technical Education for the Improvement of Agriculture and Rural Life—administered by the Interamerican Institute of Agricultural Sciences through three regional centers in Havana, Lima, and Montevideo. This project is discussed in chapter x.

The other OAS agricultural project of technical co-operation is the Pan-American Aftosa Center, in Brazil, for the study and control of foot-and-mouth disease in cattle. The cost of this project is included in the figures for OAS in the following section of this chapter, but the Aftosa Center was not included in the study.

Comparative Scope of Public Programs

A very useful comparative summary of public programs of technical co-operation in Latin America is to be found in a memorandum prepared for the Fourth Extraordinary Meeting of the Inter-American Economic and Social Council, Rio De Janeiro, 1954.[10] In addition to giving a general review of all types of technical co-operation by public agencies, this report reproduces figures for the agricultural programs of the various public agencies for the year 1953/54.

Certain aspects of the report are summarized in Tables 3 and 4. The share of United States appropriations in the budgets of the two

TABLE 3

EXTENT OF PUBLIC PROGRAMS OF TECHNICAL
CO-OPERATION IN AGRICULTURE, FORESTRY,
AND FISHERIES IN LATIN AMERICA, BY PROJ-
ECT COSTS, 1953/54*

Agencies	Total Agricultural Project Appropriations	Percentage of Total Public Agency Appropriations
IIAA.........	$ 8,289,400	79.7
UN...........	1,198,100	11.5
OAS.........	914,900	8.8
Total......	$10,402,400	100.0

*Adapted from the table on p. 33 of the report cited in note 10.

TABLE 4

RELATIVE IMPORTANCE OF AGRICULTURE, FORESTRY, AND
FISHERIES IN PUBLIC PROGRAMS OF TECHNICAL
CO-OPERATION IN LATIN AMERICA, 1953/54*

Agencies	Total Project Costs of Technical Co-operation	Project Costs of Programs in Agriculture, Forestry, and Fisheries	Percentage of Agricultural Project Costs in Total Cost
IIAA...........	$23,175,000	$ 8,289,400	35.7
UN...........	4,253,300	1,198,100	28.2
OAS...........	1,808,100	914,900	50.6
Total.......	$29,236,400	$10,402,400	35.6

*Adapted from the table on pp. 33–34 of the report cited in note 10.

international agencies is indicated by the fact that the United States contributed 57 per cent of the total budget of the Expanded Technical Assistance Program of the UN and 70 per cent of the total budget of the Technical Cooperation Program of OAS. That portion, 64.3 per cent, of the total project costs of IIAA that did not go into programs in agriculture, forestry, or fisheries was devoted to programs in education, health, public administration, industry, transport, and communication.

As mentioned previously, the technical co-operation program of the OAS is devoted entirely to providing regional services to member countries—100 per cent of its agricultural project costs goes into regional programs—and it has no direct project with any one country. In the case of FAO and IIAA, a small percentage of the resources of each is devoted to regional projects, and the major portion of resources is committed to programs in co-operation with individual countries. FAO allots 15 per cent of its expenditures on technical co-operation in agriculture, forestry, and fisheries in Latin America to regional programs, with the remainder going into "country" programs.[11] For IIAA, the corresponding percentage for regional projects is 4.2 per cent.[12]

The country programs of FAO and IIAA in 1954 were to be found in eighteen Latin-American nations in both cases.[13] The relative sizes of the IIAA country programs are depicted in Chart III, and those for FAO country programs are shown in Chart IV.

Several significant facts about the programs of these two public agencies are revealed by the charts:

1. The programs of IIAA are much bigger than those of FAO, both in the number of technicians-from-abroad and in project costs. (In the number of technicians-from-abroad, IIAA had an estimated total of 252 in country programs in 1954, and FAO had about 50. In project costs, those of IIAA country programs total just about seven times those of FAO.)

2. IIAA makes cash appropriations to joint projects in co-operation with the government of each country in which it is active, in addition to supplying technicians-from-abroad, but such cash appropriations (plus the provision of supplies) vary widely from country to country. This is apparent from the fact that there is no constancy in the ratio of project costs to number of United States technicians (see Chart III). Apparently the criteria in determining cash contributions (and/or supplies) do not include any strong attempt to keep this ratio constant.

3. The percentage of the total Latin-American technical co-operation effort of FAO found in a few countries is larger than in

CHART III

Size and Distribution of
IIAA Agricultural Country Programs
(Estimated) Fiscal, 1954*

U.S. DOLLAR APPROPRIATIONS

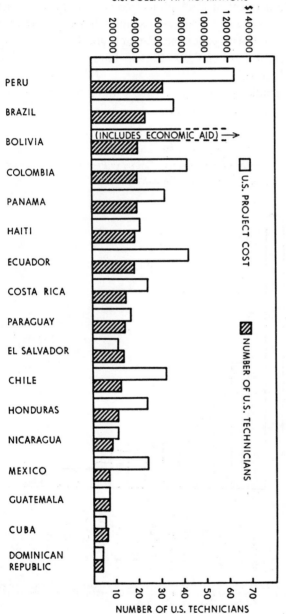

* From data supplied by IIAA to House Appropriations Committee.

the case of the IIAA programs. Some 70 per cent of FAO project costs (for country programs in Latin America) is devoted to five countries: Chile, Brazil, Ecuador, Mexico, and Honduras. By contrast, just 50 per cent of IIAA project costs (for country programs) went to the five country programs receiving the largest IIAA appropriations: Peru, Brazil, Colombia, Panama, and Ecuador. (This matter of the distribution of FAO effort in Latin America is discussed further in chap. xi.)

The case studies presented in Part II have been chosen both to

CHART IV

SIZE AND DISTRIBUTION OF
FAO AGRICULTURAL COUNTRY PROGRAMS
AMOUNTS "OBLIGATED," 1954*

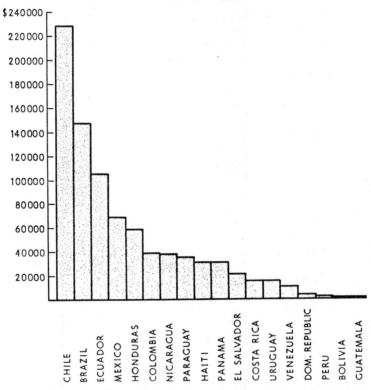

* *Source:* "Expanded Programme of Technical Assistance for Economic Development," *Seventh Report of Technical Assistance Board to Technical Assistance Committee, Economic and Social Council, United Nations, Official Records, 18th Session, New York.*

represent the variety of types of technical co-operation in agriculture and to correspond roughly to the relative size of the total programs of these various agencies of technical co-operation.

Summary

1. Technical co-operation in agriculture in Latin America is not one program but many programs. In these programs five different agencies have played the role of external co-operating partner. Two of these agencies are private foundations. Two are international governmental agencies. One is an agency of the United States government.

2. Technical co-operation in agriculture is an activity of considerable size in Latin America. As of 1954, the annual expenditures of the three public agencies alone totaled more than $10,000,000. These public programs employed about 335 technicians-from-abroad.[14] They included a number of regional programs (particularly sponsored by OAS and FAO) and country programs by both FAO and IIAA in nearly every country of Latin America. However, the programs of FAO and IIAA are quite different, as we shall see, both in their methods of operation and in the problems with which they chiefly deal.

3. Technical co-operation did not originate out of the desire of any one country or of governments alone. It has arisen in response to widely felt needs and has been proposed and supported by many governments.

4. Technical co-operation in agriculture in Latin America is young; yet the movement has grown very rapidly, and it ought to be possible, now that the programs have been in operation this long, to gauge their effectiveness and to learn from their experience.

3 OBJECTIVES AND STRUCTURE OF THE REPORT

The initial objectives of the series of studies of which this monograph is a part were evaluative in nature. It was hoped that the studies could answer such questions as the following: What contribution have programs of technical co-operation made to the productivity of agriculture in Latin-American countries? Have certain programs been more effective than others and if so, why? Is there a difference in effectiveness between the bilateral and international public programs? How do the public programs compare with those of private agencies? Are there certain types of activity in which a comparative advantage lies with a private program, or with a governmental bilateral program, or with the program of an international agency? These and similar questions were the terms of reference with which the study was undertaken.

Although it has been possible to go a considerable way toward answering these questions, two major problems of analysis have influenced the form of this report in such a way as to require comment. The first major problem to be encountered is the virtual impossibility of *quantitative* evaluation of these programs because of (*a*) their diversity, (*b*) their interrelationships with other programs, factors, and influences, and (*c*) the impossibility of estimating the indirect or delayed effects of educational programs. The second major problem is more basic: the process of agricultural development is imperfectly understood, and no agreed theory of agricultural development exists against which the effectiveness of programs of technical co-operation might be judged. This chapter is devoted to a brief examination of these two problems and to a statement of the procedure adopted in this study with respect to them.

Obstacles to Quantitative Evaluation

Programs of technical co-operation in agriculture being very diverse, criteria of evaluation relevant to one type are not appropriate for others. Some are programs of research. Some are programs of extension. Some include supervised credit as a technique. Some seek to provide commercial services without which other agricultural programs cannot go forward. Some rely mainly on international seminar-conferences related to specific agricultural problems.

It might be argued that different criteria can be applied to each type of program, and to a certain extent this is true. But the number of programs of each type is small, most programs are young, and the conditions under which they operate in Latin America make criteria already established in other cultures inadequate. And even if defensible criteria could be developed for each of these separately, there is no justifiable weighting technique by which achievement in one type of program could be compared with achievement in another in any quantitative fashion, allowing one to judge, for example, whether a research project in Peru has been more productive than an irrigation project of equal cost in Haiti.

A number of programs of technical co-operation pursue objectives that are simultaneously being served by other programs. For example, an extension program of an agency of technical co-operation may be operating in the same area as the extension service of a national ministry of agriculture. Our studies indicate that it is unsound to assume a priori that such a situation is bad; but where this situation exists, it is impossible to separate the effects of the two. Now add the complications: (*a*) that implement dealers and fertilizer salesmen are active in the same area and (*b*) that the program of each of these agencies keeps changing, often through the influence of each on the others. How can these factors be handled in evaluation, particularly where the number of instances of each combination of circumstances is small?

A seriously complicating factor in the case of the United States bilateral programs is the degree to which they are affected by political events in the United States and abroad. Every discussion in Congress of possible shifts in American trade policy, whether these discussions result in changed legislation or not, tends to affect programs of technical co-operation in the countries on which those trade policies would impinge. This happens because such discussions are widely reported in the world press and quickly affect public opinion in other countries. Similarly, when someone in a country in which a program operates raises the popular cry of "Yankee imperialism and interference," the effectiveness of technical co-operation may be seriously reduced. Such effects are entirely extraneous to the intra-agricultural methods of the program; yet they appreciably alter whatever objective data might exist for use in evaluation. If it is argued that such cases must be dropped from the sample, the reply must be, not that they are too numerous in statistical populations already small (although that would be true), but that such circumstances are inherent in intergovernmental programs. If such cases were dropped from our evaluation, we would no longer be examining part of the real world but would be altering it in order to be "quantitative" about a fictitious situation.

One of the popular characterizations of technical co-operation is that it is, or ought to be, education: helping people learn to help themselves, rather than "doing things for them." To the extent that this is true, it poses another problem for evaluation. One can measure whether people have mastered specific techniques through education, but it is difficult to determine the repercussions of these on agricultural production, and impossible to foresee, and assign a value to, the delayed but real effects of much of education.

A closely allied obstacle to quantitative evaluation is the difficulty of measuring the value of the concomitant effects of programs of technical co-operation. There are so many pressing needs within the task of agricultural development in Latin America that a by-product of a program may be as important as, or more important than, its announced objective. For example, a research program in plant breeding, in a country where government agricultural officials are so poorly paid that they have to seek other part-time employment, may, through its example of what better-paid, full-time technicians can accomplish, effectively alter the pattern of government agricultural services in the country. This may be more important than the specific research findings of the program; yet it is difficult to measure, and there is no way to aggregate such an achievement with achievement in the research field.

Even if dependable production statistics were available, they would be of only minor help in evaluation, in the early years, of programs of technical co-operation. It takes more time than most of these programs have had for their results to show up in production statistics for relatively large regions. Even after such programs have been running longer, obtaining dependable production statistics will seldom compensate for the inherent obstacles to quantitative evaluation. Nevertheless, fairly dependable yield estimates in Peru, Mexico, and Bolivia are of some help in evaluating programs of technical co-operation in those countries, and having more such statistics is to be desired.

Lack of a Theory of Agricultural Development

To increase agricultural production is a common goal expressed in every statement of objectives of programs of technical co-operation in agriculture,[1] but there are further objectives, stated or understood, beyond this goal in every program. These objectives are in the welfare field, in one way or another. Some have to do with the physical level of living of farm families. Some have to do with national levels of nutrition. Some are political, seeking to gain political favor through being helpful to farmers. Some are ideological, seeking greater agricultural production to provide a more solid economic base for free institutions. But common to all such programs is the instrumental objective of a more productive agriculture.

"Agricultural development," as the term is used in this monograph, *is the process by which agriculture becomes more productive.* In an exact economic sense, "more productive" denotes an increase of efficiency in the use of given resources. This means an increase in the output-input ratio. As used in this study, the term "more productive" includes such increases in efficiency, and it also includes increases in total production secured through the use of additional inputs, with or without a change in the output-input ratio. The inclusion of this second group of cases has particular importance in underdeveloped regions where there are unused resources of land which are not transferable to other productive uses, at least at present stages of development.

Although a considerable body of literature has developed on this topic of agricultural development, and on the broader subject of economic growth, there is no dependable consensus as to how such development or growth comes about; there is no accepted and defensible "theory" of agricultural development. The literature is by no means all new; it goes back to the primary concern of Adam Smith in *The Wealth of Nations*. Much of the literature, however, is quite recent and has arisen out of the many efforts being made in this century to accelerate economic growth in underdeveloped regions.

Without going to the extent of trying to review this entire literature, one can get some feeling of the variety of ideas with respect to agricultural development by reviewing the papers and discussion with respect to technical co-operation in the *Proceedings of the Eighth International Conference of Agricultural Economists*.[2] Within those discussions are to be found reflections of a *knowledge* theory of agricultural development: that what is primarily necessary is knowledge of agricultural techniques. Another train of thought follows a *capital* theory: that to become more productive the agriculture of a region primarily needs additional implements, fertilizers, insecticides, etc. A third implied theory puts the emphasis on *public administration:* since agricultural development depends on a variety of public programs, improving the administrative quality of these services deserves primary consideration. A fourth theory, implicit in Professor Ashby's discussion of the importance of transportation, might be called the *general economic climate* theory of agricultural development: this theory stresses the importance to agricultural development of factors outside of agriculture but in the total complex of the economic climate of the region: transportation, price policy, monetary policy, public education, public health, etc.[3]

It clearly was not a primary objective of the studies of which this monograph is a partial report to evolve a theory of agricultural development. Equally clear is the fact that the lack of such a theory constitutes a major obstacle to the execution of this study. If programs of technical co-operation in agriculture are meant to contribute to agricultural development, then one needs to understand agricultural development in order to be able to assess the programs. The task of this study is made much more difficult by the lack of an accepted theory.

Data accumulated in the course of this study support all of the foregoing theories, but without really giving any one of them a clear position of primacy. This information and its relevance to the problem of a theory of agricultural development are summarized in chapter xii.

Structure of This Report

Taking as given the task of trying to assess programs of technical co-operation in Latin America, and facing both the obstacles to quantitative evaluation of such programs and the lack of an accepted theory of agricultural development, what can be done?

The work of this study has been as follows:

1. To compile a series of case studies of selected programs of technical co-operation, sketching the circumstances within which they operate, how they have been organized, what they have done, and what appear to be the results.

2. To distil, both from individual programs and from the contrasts between them, what these programs seem to reveal about the process of agricultural development and about the role and potentialities of programs of technical co-operation.

3. To draw those inferences that seem justifiable with respect to the future administration of programs of technical co-operation.

These three steps are reported in Parts II, III, and IV of this report.

Part II presents six case studies of specific programs of technical co-operation in agriculture in Latin America, plus more general summaries of the Latin-American programs of the OAS and of the FAO. These case studies have been chosen from among a much larger number of existing programs in such a way as to represent a wide variety of types of programs, agencies of technical co-operation, and problems of agricultural development.

Part III presents a summary of what these case studies and less intensive investigation of other programs reveal about the process of agricultural development and about the process of technical co-operation. It also includes a chapter of conclusions with respect to domestic Latin-American programs of agricultural development.

Part IV builds both on the case studies and on the inferences of Part III in drawing conclusions with respect to the future administration of programs of technical co-operation in agriculture in Latin America.

Despite the difficulties of quantitative evaluation, decisions have to be made about the size and continuation of public programs of technical co-operation. Part V therefore presents the writer's own over-all assessment of technical co-operation in Latin-American agriculture.

Summary

Briefly summarized, then, the objectives of this study are three: (1) to advance understanding of the process of agricultural development in the Americas; (2) to define the appropriate functions of technical co-operation in agricultural development; and (3) to distil from past experience of technical co-operation in agriculture whatever insights can be gained for the conduct of future programs.

The initial objectives of the series of studies of which this is a partial report were evaluative in nature. It was hoped that answers could be found to such questions as: What contribution have programs of technical co-operation made to agricultural productivity? Have certain types of programs been more effective than others, and if so, why? Are there differences in the effectiveness of the programs of different agencies of technical co-operation? Should these programs be continued, and if so, how might they be improved?

Two major obstacles stand in the way of fully achieving these objectives. One is the virtual impossibility of quantitative evaluation of these programs, primarily because of their diversity; their interrelationships with other programs, factors, and influences; and the impossibility of estimating the indirect or delayed effects of educational programs. The other major obstacle is the lack of an accepted theory of how agricultural development comes about or may best be advanced.

In the face of these obstacles, the first procedure in this study has been to gather, within the limits of time and expense, as much information as possible about a wide variety of programs, conducted by a variety of agencies, in a number of different countries. The second procedure has been to try to interpret that information in such a way as to explain the role of technical co-operation in agricultural development and how it can be made more effective.

PART II

CASE STUDIES

4 THE BILATERAL PROGRAM OF SCIPA IN PERU

The program of Servicio Cooperativo Inter-Americano de Produccion de Alimentos (SCIPA) is a bilateral program of the government of Peru and the Institute of Inter-American Affairs. It was established in 1943 and is one of only three such programs that have operated continuously since that date. It is one of the better agricultural programs of IIAA; many United States technicians who have had experience in this program have later been transferred to other countries, taking with them the lessons they learned in Peru.

Background

THE LAND.—Peru is a country one-sixth the size of the United States, and it has a population of about 9,000,000 people. It extends for about 1,400 miles along the west coast of South America from its northern boundary 200 miles south of the Equator to its southern boundary with Chile.

Most of the country is mountainous, lying in and between the two ranges of the Andes. Peru has a narrow coastal plain 10 to 50 miles wide west of the Andes, and it has a third region, the *selva*, on the eastern slope of the east range of the Andes and down into the Amazon Basin. The coastal plain is all desert with almost no rainfall. Only in the narrow flood plains of seasonal rivers flowing across the desert to the sea is there cultivation,[1] and it is all based on irrigation. Until very recently the *selva* was virtually cut off from the rest of Peru and had little economic importance. In 1940 there were no roads on which automobiles could be driven across the Andes, and the normal route for infrequent travel between Lima and Iquitos was by sea from Lima around South America to the mouth of the Amazon, and then up the Amazon 3,000 miles to Iquitos.

It is the *sierra*, the Andean highlands, center of ancient Incan

39

civilization, that is still the chief agricultural region of Peru. In 1940, about 65 per cent of the population of Peru lived at altitudes above 5,250 feet. Another 25 per cent lived on the coast, along the rivers. The remaining 11 per cent lived in isolated settlements in the *selva*.

HISTORY.—The Peru of today is the historical product of two very distinct high civilizations. The Inca civilization, with its center in the vicinity of Cuzco, in the Andes, bound together most of the Indians of the whole Andean part of South America. It reached its highest development shortly before the Spaniards came in the sixteenth century. The other civilization antecedent to modern Peru was that of the Spanish colonial period, during which Peruvian silver rewarded the Spanish search for treasure, and the authoritarian pattern of Incan culture coupled with Spanish power provided plentiful slave labor once the Incan leadership had been displaced. The location of Lima near the sea gave easy access to and from Europe, and these factors together made Lima the foremost cultural and commercial center of Spanish civilization in the New World.

Although Peru has been an independent nation since 1821, the two parent civilizations still exert a strong influence. Today the two streams—European and Indian—are merging at the edges, but for the most part they are still distinct. The political elite has been strongly influenced by the European phase of its heritage. Until 1940 most of the sons and daughters of wealthy Peruvians went to Europe to study. The foreign commerce and nearly all of the large haciendas are in the hands of "Europeanized" Peruvians. Meanwhile, most of the Indians are only slowly emerging from the serfdom to which Spanish colonialism condemned them. Many of them have left their highland homes to work for wages in Lima and the other cities of the coast and on the large irrigated sugar and cotton plantations along coastal rivers. Most of them, however, retain the community customs of their ancestors and work on their own small farms or on the large haciendas of the *sierra*. Briefly, in the 1940's, a political movement to integrate Indians into the political life of the nation gained strength, but today there is little open agitation for higher-class citizenship, and the integration is only that brought about by increasing wage employment and increasing place mobility of population. Only to a relatively few persons is it an overt goal.

Modern Peru is changing rapidly. World War II accelerated the pace. Many people left their homes to work either in the mines or on the coast. Decreased shipping space stimulated manufacture of articles previously imported. The number of cotton mills has increased rapidly since 1940, and stood at 106 in 1954; this industry now employs more labor than any other non-agricultural industry in Peru.

CURRENT AGRICULTURE.—This current growth of Peru extends to agriculture. Within about five years prior to 1954, 35,000 additional hectares (87,500 acres) were brought under cultivation on the coast, entirely with Peruvian funds. While production statistics are scanty and not too dependable, a SCIPA estimate of the national net in-

TABLE 5

PERUVIAN NET INCOME FROM AGRI-
CULTURE AND LIVESTOCK

Year	Amount (Millions of U.S. Dollars)
1942	137
1944	145
1946	201
1948	441
1950	334
1951	409

come from agriculture and livestock showed a very substantial increase between 1942 and 1951, as shown in Table 5.[2]

Thus the technical co-operation program of SCIPA has grown up at a time when Peru has been undergoing considerable change and growth. SCIPA has contributed to this growth and it has also greatly benefited both from the spirit of change and progress by which it has been surrounded and from the supplementary services which industrial growth, the spread of education, and increasing commercial activity provide for a changing agriculture.

At the same time, it is important to recognize the differences within Peruvian agriculture as to levels of technology. Although the lines of division between them are indistinct, it is helpful to distinguish three general classes of farms: (1) large commercial farms, (2) large highland haciendas of (usually) absentee owners, and (3) small farms, many (but not nearly all) of the subsistence variety.

It is helpful to agricultural development that the medium- to large-sized commercial farms are as numerous as they are. Most of them are on the coast (where many small commercial farms are also to be found), but some of them are scattered through the *sierra,* thus offering a toe hold for demonstrations of improved practices in many parts of the country. There are many small commercial farms in the *sierra,* too, in addition to the 1,300 Indian communities in which a traditional primitive agriculture persists as part of a tight-knit community culture preserved through the centuries of Spanish domination.

There are an estimated 206,000 farms in Peru. Of these, 180,000 farms contain less than 5 hectares each; together they account for only 20 per cent of the total acreage in farms. There are 1,400 farms of more than 500 hectares each; together these account for 43 per cent of the total acreage in farms. There has been no effective demand for, or consideration of, a land reform that would change this pattern. Almost all of the owners of highland haciendas live in the cities, mainly in Lima and in Arequipa, and their interests lie chiefly where they live.

Peru has about 5,000,000 acres under cultivation. Something under 1,000,000 acres, all irrigated, are on the coast, mostly in river valleys where they widen near the sea. About 3,500,000 acres are cultivated in the *sierra,* mostly at altitudes between 8,000 and 12,000 feet. About 500,000 acres are under cultivation in the *selva,* the subtropical jungles along the upper tributaries of the Amazon.[3]

The most important crops, measured by the area devoted to each, in 1952, were as follows:

Crop	Acres
Potatoes	607,000
Corn	515,000
Cotton	477,000
Barley	457,000
Wheat	407,000

Sugar is important also, though occupying only 138,000 acres.

On the coast, the major crops are cotton and sugar, both of which are export crops and are extensively grown on large farms, many of which have capital to finance improvements in production. Cotton is grown on small coastal farms, as well.

Food crops are grown chiefly in the *sierra:* potatoes, wheat, barley, corn, *quinoa,* beans, and peas. In most parts of the *sierra,* farms are smaller than on the coast. In the vicinity of Huancayo, for example, there are few farms as large as 1,000 acres, many farms between 20 and 200 acres, and many more between 3 and 20 acres. In the *sierra,* also, there are communal Indian holdings, where a number of families hold land and cultivate it in common. These holdings average as little as 3 to 5 acres per family in many communities. However, in other parts of the *sierra,* the big farms are bigger and small farms smaller. Around Puno and Juliaca there are a few very large haciendas with hundreds of Indian communities in which the land per family does not amount to more than 1 to 2 acres.

The *selva* is least developed, and in it are many small settlements virtually isolated because of the great difficulties of transportation. The few new roads to the west over the Andes are exceedingly costly to build and to maintain. Lower in the *selva,* water transportation predominates, and the Amazon is the chief link between settlements and the outside world. Agriculture in the *selva* remains exploratory, and beef-cattle farming holds high promise.

On the larger farms of the coast and on some of those of the *sierra,* the availability of capital and the commercial outlook of large landowners account for considerable mechanization of cultivation. But the availability of labor at relatively low wages and the difficulty of servicing mechanized equipment where such is the exception rather than the rule have been retarding factors to mechanization.

On smaller farms, whether along the coast or in the *sierra,* the prevailing methods of cultivation are primitive. Thousands of wooden plows are still in use, and oxen are used for draft. Potatoes are dug by hand; grain is cut by hand; threshing is accomplished either with the flail or by the trampling of oxen or burros.

For the most part, agricultural laborers have had little or no formal schooling, and illiteracy is widespread. Agricultural laborers are considered literate if they have had only two to four years of school. The owners of large haciendas are usually well-educated men, but even so they, as a rule, have not been as inclined to scientific observation and experimentation in agriculture as were the large landowners of England in a similar early period.

Public concern about the productivity of agriculture in Peru stems chiefly from Peru's dependence on food imports. Farmers as a group have not shared this concern. Small farmers have not known that greater production is possible: they have assumed indefinite continuation of the status quo. Large farmers have not had any pressing incentives to change. Peru's need for sizable imports of wheat, fats and oils, and meat, coupled with the periodic balance of payment difficulties that beset the country, appear to have been the two key drives in the public motivation to agricultural improvement in Peru until very recently.

DOMESTIC AGRICULTURAL PROGRAMS.—Peru has a Ministry of Agriculture with six divisions: Agricultural (crop) Production, Livestock Production and Disease Control, Colonization and Jungle, Fisheries, Economics (statistics), and Administration. The field work of all divisions is supervised through the same fifteen regional offices. The strength of all these is that they are staffed by men trained at the reasonably good national agricultural college at La Molina. The weakness of them is that until recently they have had an inadequate concept of what field work can accomplish, inadequate means of transport to get out to farmers, inadequate supervision to upgrade their work, and they have been judged so largely by written reports that they have been tied to their desks. They share the disadvantages of all officials in a personalized government that initiative is not encouraged, not enough responsibility is delegated, and political favor enters too largely into appointments. The custom of having a new minister of agriculture each year makes both continuity of emphasis and skilled technical management of the ministry unlikely. The recent minister, Dr. Alberto Leon, 1952–54, is an exception to this: he is an agricultural graduate, principal of the agricultural college at La Molina, and he was reappointed for a second year as minister.

Peru has a good agricultural college at La Molina, about ten miles out of Lima. It has 1,000 students enrolled in a five-year course leading to the *Ingeniero Agrónomo* degree. Its faculty are nearly all part-time personnel who drive from Lima to meet their classes.

About $500,000 of the total budget of the ministry is spent on agricultural research. The main research station is at La Molina, also, adjacent to but administratively distinct from the college, which is autonomous. The station has twenty research workers on its staff; four of these teach about one-fifth time in the college. The regional research stations, of which there are eleven, operate as substations of La Molina but have very inadequate supervision. Three of these have three research officers each; the total budget of each of these three, including salaries, is $15,000. The other eight stations are smaller.

OBSTACLES TO AGRICULTURAL DEVELOPMENT.—Certain obstacles to agricultural development in Peru are mentioned by almost every observer. The five most frequently mentioned are: lack of level land, lack of water, poor communications, an unfavorable landownership pattern, and the prevalance of debilitating diseases in the *selva*. Other abstacles frequently mentioned are lack of agricultural credit and traditional social organization in the *selva*.

Lack of level land: The relatively restricted sections of the coastal plain flat enough for cultivation are desert, arable only by irrigation. Although in the *sierra* there are a few broad valley floors, like that of the Montaro River in Junin Department, the flat plain left by the recession of Lake Titicaca, and some fairly even high upland pastures, most of the land is steep slopes and mountain cliffs and ravines. The largest area of potentially cultivable land is in the *selva*, still in jungle, with other substantial obstacles to cultivation.

Lack of water: All cultivation on the coast is carried on with irrigation from rivers flowing across the arid coast to the sea. There is some possibility of increasing the irrigated area on the coast, both from rivers and by tapping the considerable ground-water resources of the region. In much of the *sierra* the limiting factor in moisture is not the total amount but its distribution. Almost all of the rain here falls during the months between October and March. Around Huancayo the average rainfall is about 40 inches. On the high plains (12,500 feet) around Puno, rainfall is less than 20 inches. Rainfall is all too plentiful in the *selva*, varying from 70 to 150 inches.

Poor communications: This is another effect of mountainous terrain. Road construction is difficult and costly. There are hundreds of potentially productive small valleys as yet unconnected with the outside world by roads that give access by motor vehicles. An example of the influence of this factor on agricultural development is the experience of the valley of the Huallaga at Tingo Maria. As colonization proceeded during the early 1940's, production was encouraged by high product prices resulting from transport costs of bringing competing products from the outside (partly war-induced local demands). As local production rose, so that the surplus product had to be transported over the Andes to the west, product prices fell to the outside price minus transportation costs; and although prices in Lima remained unchanged, local prices fell to a small fraction of their former level.

Unfavorable landownership pattern for agricultural development: This is an obstacle particularly in the *sierra*. On the coast, large landholdings are not necessarily adverse to increasing production of such export crops as cotton and sugar; but in the mountains, in many sections, large haciendas have used the reasonably level lands for grazing, kept large areas out of production because they were not needed in the livestock operations in which the haciendas specialized, and pushed the Indians onto small farms on steeply sloping hillsides.

Prevalence of debilitating diseases in the *selva:* Malaria is one of the more serious diseases. Some observers consider the control of these diseases, next to transportation, as the most important factor in opening up the *selva* to colonization and production. Actually, malaria is no more serious in the *selva* than in certain coastal valleys, but fear of disease, in the past, kept many people out of the *selva*.

It is highly significant that a very different list of obstacles to agricultural development is advanced by scientific agriculturalists. It is not that they deny the seriousness of the obstacles that have been mentioned, but they see so many possibilities for increasing production in spite of the physical and institutional limitations that they are impressed by what can be done in the face of the obstacles. It may also be significant that one gets different answers from the administrators of the Ministry of Agriculture and of SCIPA, and from their field agents.

Administrators stress the fact that there are many proved practices which lead to greater agricultural production: (1) the use of improved seed, particularly in the cases of potatoes, vegetables, wheat, and maize; (2) the use of insecticides and fungicides on potatoes, cotton, and fruit trees; (3) the use of appropriate fertilizers, particularly on cotton, wheat, and potatoes;[4] (4) the use of mechanized cultivation, with the dual effect of preparing a better seedbed and allowing more land to be brought into cultivation in the *sierra* than can be commanded by other methods of cultivation; (5) the possibility of greater productivity of upland pastures through the use of cultivated pastures and rotational grazing; and (6) the possibility of extensive beef-cattle farming in the *selva*.

It should be noted that each of the practices proposed by administrators is a result of the scientific study of agriculture. Another way of stating their conclusions would be to say that the limitations placed on Peruvian agricultural production by primitive methods of cultivation have held production far below the limits imposed by physical conditions. Those primitive methods consisted of plowing, sowing, and weed control but did not include adequate disease and insect control, or seed selection based on knowledge of genetics, or the application of non-animal power to the management of the soil or to the harvesting of mature crops. By applying to agricultural production in Peru the same methods of research and development commonplace in certain other countries, a tremendous increase in production is possible within the limitations set by topography and climate.

Field agents of the Ministry of Agriculture and SCIPA are almost unanimous in naming only two obstacles to agricultural development. They say, "We need more personnel in order to reach more people; and we need more equipment and supplies, so that we can respond to all of the requests we have from farmers for help." In other words, they are so confident of the measures available for increasing production that to them the only things lacking are more men and more equipment to carry to farmers the knowledge and the materials necessary to increase production. This attitude is an indication of major success in finding ways to make important improvements in agricultural production within Peru's natural limitations. At the same time, this attitude could be a danger signal if it were to distract administrators from the necessity for the additional research —more basic and more extensive—which will be continuously necessary to provide new and additional techniques to increase agricultural production.

Technical Co-operation: SCIPA[5]

AGREEMENTS AND PHILOSOPHY.—SCIPA was created in 1943 by a one-year agreement between the minister of agriculture of the government of Peru and the United States ambassador to Peru. It was renewed annually until a five-year agreement was signed on September 22, 1950. This agreement of 1950 set forth the objectives of SCIPA as follows:

A. To promote and strengthen friendship and understanding between the peoples of the Republic of Peru and the United States of America and to further their general welfare.
B. To facilitate the development of agriculture in Peru through cooperative action on the part of the parties to this agreement; and
C. To stimulate and increase the interchange between the two countries of knowledge, skill, and techniques in the field of agriculture.

These objectives are somewhat broader than those stated in earlier agreements but not sufficiently different to cause any marked shift in the program. Early in World War II two developments brought about the first agricultural co-operation between Peru and the United States: one was the need of personnel of the United States Army Air Base at Tulara and of the Rubber Development Commission staff at Iquitos for fresh vegetables and other foodstuffs; the second was the shortage of food for the Peruvian population on the coast, brought about by the decrease of shipping. Soon, however, the orientation of the program was altered, and the objectives of SCIPA were stated as follows in the agreement dated May 19, 1943:

SCIPA will submit and develop a program to increase the production of foodstuffs of vegetable and animal origin, or primary necessity, covering at least the following items:

a) Technical assistance for the increase and improvement of production of food products of animal and vegetable origin;
b) development of plans for crop adjustment;
c) development of new acreage including agricultural colonization, and plans for soil conservation works; dry farming; and soil survey for new irrigation areas;
d) supply of means, tools, equipment, insecticides, seeds, livestock, and other materials, for the increased production of food products of animal and vegetable origin;
e) assistance in the further development of extension work to promote the production of food products;
f) provision of loans or other assistance to small producers;
g) studies and related work in the fields of nutrition and diet.

The program of SCIPA has always been within, but has never been as broad as, these objectives. The selection of projects has been governed by a "philosophy"[6] embracing the principles: (1) that SCIPA projects are to be undertaken on the request of the minister of agriculture; (2) that SCIPA will not undertake regulatory functions; (3) that preference will be given to projects "that reach the greatest possible number of farmers in the most helpful personal manner"; and (4) that all SCIPA employees must abstain from partisan politics.

Resources and Projects.—The resources of SCIPA in 1953 consisted of twenty-four United States personnel, five special Peruvian personnel paid in dollars, eight full-time and eight part-time Peruvian personnel paid in soles from specially provided IIAA funds, and a budget of $600,000 (9,000,000 soles). Of this budget, $200,000 was provided by IIAA, and $400,000 by the government of Peru.

TABLE 6

SCIPA BUDGET ALLOCATION AND PERCENTAGE OF
TOTAL BUDGET, 1953

SCIPA Projects	Budget Allocation, 1953	Per Cent of Total SCIPA Budget
Economic studies..........	$ 21,000	3.5
Extension service..........	300,000	50.0
Reimbursable facilities and services for agriculturalists	170,000	28.3
Engineering services.......	31,000	5.2
Administration...........	78,000	13.0
Total...............	$600,000	100.0

In the terminology of the United States bilateral programs of technical co-operation administered by IIAA, a "project" is a specific field of activity entered into under a formal "project agreement" negotiated by the two co-operating governments after a comprehensive "Basic Agreement" has been signed. In SCIPA there are five projects, each quite broad, and each really constituting a division of the SCIPA organization. These five projects, and the budget allocations for each, are indicated in Table 6. The Administration Project handles the administration of the total program. Each of the other projects is described hereafter.

ECONOMIC STUDIES.—The Economic Studies Project, launched in 1943 and still active, is, like the Administration Project, primarily an internal staff project, its chief function being to conduct studies on topics related to current SCIPA activities or to new projects under consideration for the future. In addition to this, it has from time to time undertaken special studies for the minister of agriculture on matters related to other programs of the ministry. For example, when the ministry had a crop control program under consideration, the Economic Studies Project made a detailed survey of the problems involved and the probable benefits to be derived (on the basis of which study the proposal was dropped). Later the ministry engaged the services of this project to set up a crop and market reporting organization.

Altogether about one hundred studies have been undertaken by this project since it was established. As of 1953, the activities of the project were embraced in four subprojects: Statistical Study and Analysis; Crop and Market Reporting; Costs of Production and Community Surveys; and Studies on Industrial Development Related to Agriculture. This project is much smaller than the "operating projects" of SCIPA, but it is an important aid to program selection and planning.

EXTENSION SERVICE.—The backbone of the SCIPA program is an extension service, which represents about half of SCIPA's total yearly expenditures.[7] Operating through thirty-seven field offices staffed entirely by Peruvian technicians, this project consists of extension education carried out through farm visits, office calls, educational meetings, and field demonstrations.

A most important device of SCIPA's extension service is the Agricultural Community Committee plan whereby farmers are encouraged to form local committees with democratically elected officers. SCIPA's agents have organized 302 of these farmers' associations in Peru, and they remain a primary concern of the field agents. Specialists in the central office co-operate with the various committees as the agent has need for their services. Meanwhile, experience in such committees gives farmers both confidence and a new form of organization through which they can act together with their neighbors in dealing with local problems.

In the early days of SCIPA, when field agents visited as many individual farms as possible, it was found that such visits were often met by suspicion that the agent had some ulterior motive in proposing new practices. Consequently, the emphasis was changed and is now twofold: to respond to requests for aid by helping set up demonstrations so that farmers can see the effect of proposed practices, and to concentrate on organizing and servicing Agricultural Community Committees in which farmers can discuss their mutual problems and learn about scientific measures for meeting them. Agents still make many visits to individual farms on request (about 1,500 to 2,000 in a month), but the emphasis is on demonstrations and on organizing and strengthening local committees.

TABLE 7

RURAL AGENTS' ACTIVITIES

Type of Service	February	March
Bulletins distributed..................	315	479
Office calls........................	3,786	5,272
Farms visited......................	1,478	1,627
Farmer meetings held...............	181	188
Attendance.......................	2,475	7,397
Demonstrations given...............	242	289
Attendance.......................	1,508	1,910
Family garden packages distributed.....	128	32
Other vegetable seeds distributed (kg.)..	24	28
Other seeds distributed (kg.)...........	5,594	4,409
Insecticides distributed		
Powder (kg.)......................	2,399	4,086
Liquid (gal.)......................	33	126
Fertilizer distributed (kg.).............	208,314	833,191
Hand tools........................	3	67
Animals treated....................	4,493	2,480
Animals distributed..................	191	214
Fruit trees treated..................	5,025	2,934
Fruit trees distributed...............	924	722
New demonstration fields established....	6	7

The pattern and level of these activities are indicated by the summary reports of the extension service for February and March, 1953, as shown in Table 7. The distribution of seeds, insecticides, fertilizers, and hand tools referred to in Table 7 are part of Project D, "Facilities and Services for Farmers," discussed subsequently.

A recent development of great potential significance is the inclusion of Home Demonstration Agents in the SCIPA extension program. Three reasons have been given for bringing them slowly and relatively late into the program: (1) it was necessary first to establish an extension program that would help farmers increase their farm income, which work in agriculture would do but a program of home economics would not;[8] (2) since by tradition, women in Peru do not participate in public programs, organizing them in an extension program had to proceed slowly; and (3) with a limited budget, and in view of the other factors, it seemed wise to postpone an emphasis on home economics.

A dietitian from the United States began making food-consumption studies soon after SCIPA was organized in 1943 and her work was taken over in 1945 by a Peruvian who continued making such studies as the only home-economics technician in SCIPA until 1949. Data on the food habits, incomes, and needs of the families of small-farm operators and farm laborers were gathered in more than a hundred different communities in almost every department of Peru.

TABLE 8

HOME DEMONSTRATION AGENTS' ACTIVITIES

Type of Service	February	March
Bulletins distributed....	382	473
Office calls.............	75	73
Homes visited..........	178	149
Result demonstrations...	10	11
Women's meetings held..	81	99
Attendance...........	956	1,223
Girls' meetings held.....	15	13
Attendance...........	132	108
Other meetings.........	1	14
Attendance...........	6	1,064

The first SCIPA Women's Club was organized in Iquitos in 1947, on the same pattern as the Agricultural Committees for men. A second home economist was employed in 1949, and a third in 1950. The first Home Demonstration Agent was appointed in 1950, but the home demonstration program moved slowly until the spring of 1952. Late in 1952 there were ten Home Demonstration Agents, each working out of one of the SCIPA field offices. Three more were added late in 1953. The pattern of activities is indicated by statistics for February and March, 1953, as shown in Table 8.

REIMBURSABLE FACILITIES AND SERVICES.—This project, organized in 1944 as Reimbursable Facilities and Services for Agriculturalists, "includes all services of the SCIPA organization for which charges are made in accordance with work performed. Among these are operation and maintenance of machinery pools; purchase, importation, and distribution of livestock; purchase, distribution, and resale of selected seed and plant propagation material; distribution of insecticides; and similar services for assisting farmers in improving production."[9]

Each SCIPA extension agent has a revolving fund of $300 to $500 for stocking small amounts of seeds, fertilizers, etc., in his local office. Any farmer who wishes to try out a new method that he has seen demonstrated can purchase from the SCIPA office the materials that he needs for the trial. This service is made necessary by the temporary inadequacy of commercial sources of supply for new products. As more and more farmers build up a demand for a particular commodity, merchants begin to stock it, and the SCIPA extension agent can use his revolving fund for other, newer necessities. For several years, large quantities of insecticides and fertilizers were handled through this project. Demand for them has increased to the point where mixing plants have been established by commercial firms and fertilizers are now widely available in the market.

Farm machinery pools, another major activity under this project, have been an outstanding success in Peru. They were started as a project of SCIPA following a request of the Ministry of Agriculture of Peru in 1944. This activity has expanded since into two types of pools: commercial machinery pools scattered along the long coast of Peru to serve coastal agriculture, and demonstration pools located in the *sierra* to test the possibilities of farm machinery in the highlands. The pools provided new machinery and also a better use of that machinery at a time when the agricultural resources of Peru were being severely taxed during the war and during the early postwar years. They took advantage of the peculiar characteristics of the coastal agriculture of Peru with its climate that permits farmers to plow, prepare seed beds, plant, cultivate, and harvest over a comparatively long period—much longer than is the case in most agricultural regions. This makes possible the shifting of tractors and equipment as the season progresses, over a long stretch of about fourteen hundred miles. This, in turn, means that many more hours of work per year are realized in the use of tractors and of other equipment than is possible in United States agriculture or, for that matter, in most other parts of the world. The machinery pools recruit and train tractor mechanics and operators, and they provide an organization in which these men can be effectively employed.

An important element in the success of this program has been the method of paying tractor operators, coupled with the practice of assigning a particular tractor to each operator. Each operator is responsible for a particular tractor. He has an assistant operator to help him, and each of these men receives a basic wage that is the remuneration for operating the assigned tractor 48 hours per week. But each of them can draw overtime pay for operating the tractor up to 22 hours of any 24-hour period. (Two hours must be devoted to equipment maintenance and servicing.) If a tractor is immobilized for repairs, its operator and his assistant are denied the possibility of drawing this attractive overtime pay; therefore the system leads to excellent care of equipment. Moreover, equipping tractors for night work and allowing the operator and his assistant to take turns keeping it going have contributed to the unusually high average of 2,000 hours of field work per tractor per year.

In addition to the direct services they perform, the machinery pools also demonstrate to private entrepreneurs not only the need for, but the technique of, organizing this service for hire. Many farmers after seeing the value of machinery have acquired their own. In some communities after a machinery pool had operated for some time, private individuals bought machinery to do custom work for neighbors. When these private services became available, the machinery pool of SCIPA was withdrawn and moved to another locality.

There has been a shift in the kind of work undertaken by the machinery pools of SCIPA (see Chart V). In the beginning, pool equipment was employed in plowing and cultivation. As the value of such mechanization became established, farmers began to buy light tractors suitable for normal cultivation operations, and at most pools there was a shift away from cultivation to more plowing and to land clearing and leveling. As heavier tractors have more recently been purchased by farmers, the shift has been away from plowing to the leveling of land for irrigation, a kind of work that requires very heavy machinery. Private individuals are not yet prepared to offer machinery of this kind for hire, nor, of course, can an individual farmer afford to buy a large tractor and the expensive equipment required to move earth and to level it, just to work on his own farm.

From the beginning, the machinery pools have expanded through reinvestment of their own earnings, by additional contributions of funds from the Ministry of Agriculture, and by means of a loan of $1,300,000 from the International Bank for Reconstruction and Development.

CHART V

AGRICULTURAL MACHINERY POOLS*

SHIFT IN TYPE OF WORK, 1947–53

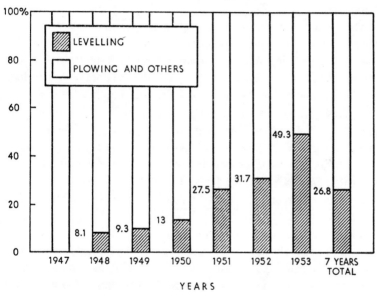

YEARS

* *Source:* Development of the SCIPA program. Mimeographed by SCIPA's Information Department (January, 1954), p. 58.

The *demonstration* machinery pools are in part subsidized because it is the purpose of these pools to determine to what extent it is possible to use such equipment economically under conditions of farming in the highlands. Some success has already been achieved. There are, however, a number of formidable obstacles to farm mechanization in the *sierra*.

In August, 1953, there were nine commercial machinery pools

and five demonstration pools in operation, with a total of 124 tractors working.

LIVESTOCK DEMONSTRATION FARMS.—Sheep and cattle are important in the agricultural economy of Peru. Sheep can utilize the high meadows of the Andes, and sheep grazing is an important occupation for Indian families and communities. Cattle grazing is the major enterprise on most highland haciendas in the mountain valleys, though the haciendas normally practice some cultivation as well. Peru had about 18,000,000 sheep and nearly 3,000,000 cattle in 1953. Wool production is low, only a little more than one pound per fleece; yet between a third and a half of the wool produced in Peru is exported. Beef production is also low, and Peru has recently been importing up to 36,000,000 pounds of beef per year.

The Peruvian government has taken several measures to improve the livestock industry. It has financed and organized several experimental farms. It has sought to improve breeding stocks by financing the importation of animals of high quality. It maintains a veterinary service primarily for the purpose of controlling livestock diseases.

In 1949 the government of Peru asked SCIPA to establish and operate two livestock demonstration farms and made a special appropriation of $260,000 for this purpose.[10] One of these farms is a sheep farm, Hacienda Porcon, in the northern highlands. The other is a cattle farm, Granja San Jorge, in the Amazon Basin.

Hacienda Porcon is a tract of 35,000 acres on a plateau at an average elevation of 13,000 feet. It is thus in a setting typical of the conditions under which much of Peru's sheep industry must be carried on. Before the farm was established, 300 Indian families were living on the tract, grazing their flocks and living as nomads, moving with the seasons and as pastures were depleted and renewed. There are two important results of the early years of work on Hacienda Porcon. The first is establishment of the principle of enclosure. The second is the increased wool production that has been achieved.

Because of the size (and the isolation) of Hacienda Porcon, SCIPA has been able to demonstrate what can be achieved by a radical change in land management. (This is a field of activity usually denied to programs of technical co-operation because it involves problems of land tenure, which usually can be tackled only by wholly domestic programs or legislation.) Existing patterns of land use in many parts of the *sierra* of Peru remind one of the conditions that prevailed in England prior to the enclosure movement or that prevailed on the "open range" of the Old West in the United States. Grazing lands in many regions, particularly on the higher meadows, are considered not privately owned but freely accessible to anyone's flocks. However, controlled grazing is one of the fundamentals of a scientific livestock industry, and this SCIPA introduced. One result was that 60 Indian families could man a sheep enterprise fully utilizing the land resources formerly shared by 300. To these families, although the prevailing wage rate in the region had been 1.50 soles per day, SCIPA paid 3.50 soles.[11] Of course, the principle of enclosure (and the controlled grazing which it makes possible) is only an instrumental objective: the effect of the change on agricultural productivity is the important thing.

What has happened to production on Hacienda Porcon in three years? In the first year of better stock and changed practices, 2,000 sheep were sheared, yielding an average clip of 2.6 pounds. In the second year 3,000 sheep yielded 4.7 pounds of wool each. In the third year over 5,000 sheep were being grazed on the hacienda. In prospect are more sheep and, once the breeding-stock requirements have been met, a substantial additional quantity of mutton.

Granja San Jorge is east of the Andes in the two-fifths of Peru that is thought of as jungle, an area having an annual rainfall of 70 to 150 inches. The Granja San Jorge consists of 20,000 acres typical of much of the Peruvian jungle where some cattle have been grown for many years. Consequently, the task of Granja San Jorge is not to prove that cattle can survive in the *selva* but to demonstrate what level of production can be achieved by scientific management.

The results in the first three years have been encouraging. Enough land has been cleared to carry 400 head of cattle, one-half of which are purebred animals. It has been found possible to replace normal jungle growth and grasses by improved pasture grasses. Two-year-old steers, fed only on grass, dress out at 400 to 450 pounds per carcass. A carrying capacity of one animal unit for every 2.5 to 4 acres is being achieved. Silos are being tried to preserve fodder for the annual dry season. The effects of supplementary feeds and minerals are being studied.

The serious obstacles encountered so far are cattle diseases and parasites, especially roundworms, which had not been reported elsewhere as parasites of ruminants. Effective controls for these have not yet been developed, but it is hoped that rotational grazing will help.

Other problems are on the horizon. The region is lightly populated, and it is hard to secure labor for the new tasks involved in disease control and in the management of rotational grazing. So far, there is a heavy demand for all the cattle produced on the farm from cattle-farmers who want them for breeding purposes. Once this demand has been satisfied, however, the problem of market outlets will arise, and this problem will be intensified as cattle production in the region increases. At that point, transportation west over the Andes or down the Amazon and out to markets on the Atlantic will become necessary. Even with such outlets, local cattle prices will fall because of the transportation costs involved in marketing.

These two farms operated by SCIPA are called demonstration farms, but at the same time they are experimental farms. There is no point in quibbling about the name, except that demonstration farms as an *extension* technique are frequently proposed, often tried, and almost uniformly unsuccessful (see chap. xv). These two farms are serving important functions. They are experimenting with total patterns of livestock farming for two important regions of Peru. Conducted much like commercial operations, they may have very important influence as demonstrations. But it is their experimental nature which gives them their validity within a program of technical co-operation.

The other comment that must be made in passing is that the success of these two farms is the result in no small measure of the practical experience of the SCIPA chief of field party as a practical livestock man before he shifted to a career in technical co-operation. His personal experience and his close supervision of these farms have been important factors in their success.

ENGINEERING SERVICES.—The Engineering Project of SCIPA has sections for irrigation and land rehabilitation, ground-water development, construction, and drafting. Since 1949 this project has undertaken about twenty surveys and reconnaissances for irrigation works covering an area of 46,500 acres; it has done soil conservation work on twenty-two projects covering 18,250 acres; and it has conducted topographic and miscellaneous work with respect to 81,500 acres. During this period it performed services in connection with the drilling of 114 wells, it completed 46 construction jobs, and its drafting section prepared plans for 223 irrigation, construction, and miscellaneous projects.

Land rehabilitation projects have included dams and irrigation canals, pumping, contour lines, intakes for canals, gradient lines, roads, hydrological studies, underground drainage, water regulation, soil-washing prevention, and water-distribution systems. The irrigation projects of SCIPA were too small to be handled by the Ministry of Public Works in its irrigation-development program or were otherwise outside the scope of the work of the regular ministries.

The Engineering Project has a dual objective: (1) to provide design and supervisory services in connection with the construction of facilities needed for projects of SCIPA itself or the Ministry of Agriculture of Peru and (2) to provide the technical services of irrigation and drainage engineers and soil rehabilitation specialists to farmers and communities who need assistance in land rehabilitation. These services are considered to be complementary to the work of the rural agents engaged in extension work.

There seems to be a genuine need for the kinds of services in which the engineering department of SCIPA is engaged. Competent architects and engineers, like all technical and professional personnel, are scarce in Peru. The price of their services is therefore high, and large projects, in which design and engineering fees are large, are victors over smaller projects in the competition for their services. Many of the structures required by SCIPA and by the Ministry of Agriculture are small and uncomplicated, and it is difficult to find well-trained architects who are willing to accept commissions for the design of these projects.

Since the coast of Peru is virtually rainless and only the valleys of some fifty rivers that flow down the Andean western slopes are cultivable, the search for underground water resources and the efficient use of underground and surface water are of great importance in raising agricultural output. More and better irrigation is also essential to enlarge the productivity of agriculture in some of the noncoastal regions.

SCIPA has engaged in construction engineering work because the right kind of services were not available from commercial sources. Land rehabilitation work has also been warranted for several reasons: Peruvian agriculturalists are not skilful in the arts of land and water conservation, and the rural agents of SCIPA needed expert help in these fields; yet the private sector of the Peruvian economy had not entered this field of activity.

Despite the need for it the Engineering Project has encountered substantial problems. In the early years irrigation and land rehabilitation engineering services were rendered by SCIPA to farmers free of charge. It was soon found that farmers were requesting services for the design of irrigation and drainage work never carried out; scarce skills were being put to work fruitlessly. Some of the projects were extensive and required the services of an engineer for as long as a month or two. Undesirable experiences were also encountered in connection with construction engineering work; sometimes a project planned and constructed by SCIPA at the request of one minister of agriculture was not accepted by his successor. The most prominent case of this kind was the Fish Terminal at Callao.

SCIPA now intends to resolve this problem by withdrawing from construction engineering work except where its own facilities are involved. It also intends to reorganize its land-rehabilitation engineering work. Some engineers will be attached to its extension staff to train rural agents in simple engineering tasks. The rural agents, in turn, will pass these skills on to farmers. Other engineers will be transferred to the Facilities and Services for Agriculturalists Project, where they will be available to perform engineering services (as distinguished from teaching others how to do them) on a pay-for-service basis. It is not anticipated that farmers or communities will be willing to pay for designs that they do not intend to utilize in construction, and wastage of time on unused designs will therefore be avoided.

Water surveying, however, will continue to be done without fee for any farmer or community asking for the service. This may result in a continuance of wastage, but in view of the importance of water in so much of Peruvian agriculture, it is deemed worthwhile to run this risk.

SCIPA has recognized the importance of ground-water development and has devoted some resources and ingenuity to work in this field. Actual well-drilling operations were not begun by SCIPA until 1949, when it came into possession of surplus United States Army well-drilling equipment. The purpose of the drilling program has been to locate underground water resources, to demonstrate methods for bringing it to the surface, and to stimulate the organization of private drilling ventures. The public interest generated by the drilling of successful wells justified the establishment of several private drilling firms. SCIPA assisted these firms by making available a drilling specialist and by selling drilling equipment to them. In addition to deep drilling, SCIPA has conducted a shallow drilling demonstration program to teach small farmers how to draw upon small supplies of water in strata close to the surface.

Evaluation of SCIPA

Is SCIPA achieving its objectives? When one looks at the three objectives of SCIPA as stated in the current five-year agreement,[12] and then asks how the achievements of SCIPA can be measured, it is obvious that the second of the three objectives is central: "to facilitate the development of agriculture in Peru through co-operative action on the part of the parties in this agreement." Whatever may be achieved with respect to the first and third objectives will be subsidiary to, or ancillary to, this process of developing the agriculture of Peru. Since SCIPA is a joint agency of Peru and the United States, the phrase "co-operative action" really imposes no limitation whatever.

Thus SCIPA does not fit neatly into any category of government agency in the United States. It is more than an extension service but could choose to be less. It is not a research organization but may, and does, conduct some research in its demonstration work. It is not primarily a credit agency but could, though it does not, lend money. It has a mandate to be and do anything mutually agreeable to the two governments, represented by the minister of agriculture (for Peru) and by the chief of field party (for the United States) that will "facilitate the development of agriculture in Peru."[13]

There are two basic questions involved in assessing the success or failure of SCIPA to contribute to agricultural development: Are agricultural products being produced with decreasing inputs of land, labor, and capital per unit of output? Is the total physical agricultural production of Peru increasing? Each of these questions is of independent importance. Each, however, can be answered only by inferences based on incomplete information at the present time; for there have not been specific surveys made to answer the first, and adequate statistics do not exist for answering the second. Nevertheless, there are indications in developments known to be connected with SCIPA that imply an affirmative answer to the two questions. These indications are the following:

1. There is a steady demand for the services of SCIPA's field agents. This is an indication that farmers find SCIPA useful and want to benefit from it. One of the more significant measures of this is the number of farmers coming unsolicited to SCIPA offices for help. During the three-month period January to March, 1953, a total of 13,500 calls of farmers are recorded at field offices of SCIPA, an average of 150 per day, or of slightly more than 4 calls per day for each of the 37 field offices. The number of calls per day varies considerably between different offices. The office in Huancayo had an average of 10 visitors per day throughout the three-month period, and of these, 46 per cent came from within a radius of 6 miles, 26 per cent came from a distance of 6 to 12 miles, 14 per cent came from a distance of 12 to 18 miles, and 14 per cent came from more than 20 miles. During the month of June, 1953, the office in Huacho had nine visitors per day, and the offices in Chincha and Puno each had three visitors per day.[14]

2. Farmers are purchasing considerable amounts of seeds, insecticides, and fertilizers through SCIPA. During the first three months of 1953 SCIPA field agents sold 16,000 kilograms of seeds (excluding vegetables), 11,000 kilograms of insecticide powder, 370 gallons of liquid insecticides, and 1,250 tons of fertilizers. Figures more significant than these would be the total of such purchases, whether through SCIPA or from a commercial source. It is the policy of SCIPA to recommend the use of improved seeds, insecticides, and fertilizers to all farmers, acting, however, as supplier for these commodities only where there are not adequate commercial sources. There is no question that SCIPA has greatly stimulated normal trade in insecticides and in fertilizers, but it is not clear whether appreciable amounts of improved seeds are available commercially.

3. The machinery pools of SCIPA are used to capacity. This is

apparent from the startling fact that SCIPA gets an average of about 2,000 hours of use per year from each of its tractors. It is also indicated by the total acreage cultivated or leveled by SCIPA implements, which jumped from 18,700 acres in 1947 to 58,500 in 1952.[15]

SCIPA has made a profit on most of its jobs, and this may be attributed partly to SCIPA's large-scale machinery pool operation, with central shops in Lima and with pools in many parts of the country, making it possible to increase greatly the annual hours of operation per machine by moving the machinery from place to place as seasonal demands fluctuate. This scale and efficient organization have not as yet been achieved in the operations of private custom operators. The profits accruing to SCIPA from these operations are used for two purposes: to finance demonstration pools in the *sierra* where operations in the beginning stage must operate at a loss, and to buy additional equipment.

4. SCIPA has demonstrated that considerable increases in production are possible on lands now under cultivation. This is most spectacular in the case of potatoes, a crop grown on perhaps 10 per cent of the cultivated acreage of Peru. By a combination of improved seed, insecticides, and fertilizers SCIPA has shown that the yield of potatoes can be increased from two- to fourfold. One measure of the importance of this development is to be seen in the work of the field agent at Cañete. Prior to the program of SCIPA in his area, only about 125 acres of potatoes were grown, with a yield of 106 to 120 bushels per acre. By 1953 there were between 1,125 and 1,250 acres of potatoes annually, yielding about 250 bushels per acre. Another indication is that 74 per cent of the visitors to the SCIPA office at Huancayo during January–March, 1953, came to inquire about, or to purchase, insecticides for use on potatoes.

Another example of SCIPA's success in demonstrating improved methods of production, this time in livestock, is in the use of rotational pasturage for sheep and cattle and the increase in production already reported from Hacienda Porcon and Granja San Jorge.

5. SCIPA has brought considerable additional land into cultivation. Although no exact figures were found on this point, there are several indications of this development and the engineering section is continually making surveys for projects to bring more land under cultivation.

The engineering section helps with numerous projects to extend or repair irrigation facilities. One such project is the Pampa de Ñoco project near Chincha where about 200 small farmers secured permission to buy 7,500 acres of land in the Ñoco Valley. To irrigate this land, they are digging a canal 9 miles long, doing all the work by hand. SCIPA has done the surveying work free of charge and has loaned equipment, including an air compressor and air drills, for making a tunnel over 900 feet long.

Another group of 500 farmers, high above Cerro de Pasco, irrigate their 1,250 acres of land from canals built by the Incas. They came to SCIPA for engineering help in repairing the canals. SCIPA made the necessary survey and a cost analysis for the job. Now the farmers are borrowing money from the Banco Agricola to buy materials. They will do the work themselves, and an engineer of SCIPA will check progress and insure that the work is well done.

SCIPA's report for February–May, 1953, tells of another engineering service:

> Two years ago, SCIPA assisted in the formation and development of a well-drilling company called ACISA which has stockholders from Peru, Switzerland, and the United States. This company has had notable success in drilling on the coast. So great has become the demand for wells and irrigation systems that recently the company increased its capital stock by $117,600 (s/. 2,000,000). Their plans are now to organize an irrigation development company as a subsidiary. They plan to drill wells and develop land on a share basis for people who have acquired dry land in coastal valleys but who have neither the equipment nor the money for developing irrigation systems and sources of water.[16]

SCIPA has drilled a number of irrigation wells itself, in addition to aiding in the establishment of this independent, commercial company. Ninety test wells were completed in 1953.

Quite a different way of SCIPA's extending the cultivated area is exemplified in the community of Huayao, in the Montaro Valley. Several years ago, a farmer of Huayao named Luis Delgado hired the use of a tractor from one of SCIPA's machinery pools to do his plowing. He was so impressed that the following year he borrowed money to buy a tractor of his own, while other members of the community used the machinery pool. By 1953, Señor Delgado had three tractors and a truck; in addition to his own work he was doing custom work for others; and five more tractors were owned by other members of the community, which numbers 80 families. Because farmers now have all the equipment they need, SCIPA's machinery pool no longer works in this area.

When asked what difference the tractors and implements have made in his and his neighbors' farming, Delgado said that yields have improved because of better seed-bed preparation and that much more land is now cultivated. Members of the community owned the land previously, but it went uncultivated until they learned the use of tractors.

Still another method of extending, as well as improving, cultivation is through the program of land leveling. This was begun in 1948 with only two machines and has expanded as funds became available for buying additional bulldozers, scrapers, carryalls, etc. In 1952 SCIPA's 15 machines worked a total of 36,283 hours on leveling projects. During the five-year period of its operation, this project fulfilled a total of 926 contracts averaging 75 hours each. It is estimated that about 10,000 acres of additional land have been brought into cultivation by the operations.

The preceding five points are sufficient to indicate that SCIPA is making progress in the direction of its central objective—the development of Peruvian agriculture. They also serve to indicate that SCIPA is not a single program but a holding company of those projects that the minister of agriculture and the chief of field party agree can well be co-operative projects of the two governments concerned.

There are two further questions to be posed: Are farmers in Peru taking an increasingly scientific attitude toward their occupation? Is the extension service of SCIPA soundly conceived and well organized? These questions, it will be noted, are significant more from the standpoint of future development than from that of past performance. It is conceivable that a poorly organized program, or one using methods of doubtful social effect, could yet result, at least in the short run, in increased agricultural production or efficiency or both.

Are farmers increasingly scientific? In the long run, an agricultural extension program should make individual farmers more resourceful in increasing their own efficiency. The available evidence indicates that the program of SCIPA is working in this direction.

One indication is the number of farmers who now take the initiative in coming to SCIPA for help. Another is the number who are purchasing their own equipment rather than continuing to rely on the services of SCIPA's machinery pools. Another is the vitality of the more than 300 SCIPA Agricultural Committees, which, although still in their infancy, give promise of developing into strong farmer organizations and of speeding the introduction of scientific practices.

Is SCIPA well organized? Two elements are essential to the effectiveness of an agency like SCIPA, and one is as important as the other. One is a pattern of organizational relationships that expedite "housekeeping," minimize friction, and secure efficient operation. The other is an atmosphere of confidence, mutual trust, and enthusiasm. The first without the second becomes caricatured "bureaucracy"; the second without the first may become chaotic. On both scores SCIPA rates well.

In organization the responsibilities of each person are definitely stated, and relationships between persons are clear. Field agents are able to get out of their offices because each field office has its own secretary and its own field assistant. The central office is kept informed through the daily field-office records summarized and sent to Lima monthly and through an adequate staff of subject-matter specialists. There is a full-time inspector-general visiting field offices and carrying out exhaustive standardized inspections; and there is a central-office clerical staff sufficient to keep up with administrative details. Although overstaffing and overorganization are always dangers, the writer has seen too many extension programs suffer from poor organization, and lag because of inadequate provision for administration, to feel that SCIPA is to be criticized at this point.

But SCIPA would be "succeeding" even if it were much less well organized: the staff radiates confidence and enthusiasm. On this score, Aníbal Buitron makes the following significant comments after interviewing field agents:

The interviews with Peruvian field agents show a high degree of loyalty to SCIPA. There is not a single case of complaint, dissatisfaction, or disagreement with the central office. They all seem to know what they have to do and are confident that the central office trusts and backs them.

SCIPA has selected its personnel well. The agents interviewed, and a few more with whom I had a chance to talk briefly, are well-trained, honest, responsible, very much interested in their jobs and in getting results. They show sympathy and understanding for the people they are trying to help.[17]

The most important "substantive result" of the Extension Service of SCIPA to date is this liberation of well-chosen staff into full use of its own powers in a profession new in Peru: an extension service free of political favor, with adequate financial provision of family incomes for members of the staff, with pride of professional achievement, and with confidence in farm men and women.[18] That kind of staff can liberate cultivators of the soil into self-respecting, scientific husbandmen and their wives into alert, perceptive, intelligent homemakers and mothers.

CRITICISMS OF THE EXTENSION SERVICE.—The extension service of SCIPA is good; yet there are two points at which it suffers by comparison with certain similar programs. One of these is in its geographical spread; the other is in its failure to utilize more Peruvians as subject-matter specialists.

Peru is a large country, and SCIPA's thirty-seven field offices are scattered across it. This has three unfortunate effects. The first is that supervision of the field agents is difficult. There is a Peruvian inspector-general of the extension service in addition to the Peruvian director of the service. The director travels assiduously, but of necessity he must spend most of his time in Lima. It is the responsibility of the inspector-general to visit the field agents, checking on their work and their office records. With such great distances between offices in a land where travel is not easy, he is unable to get to the various offices often enough. We found some offices that had not been visited for a year.

The second disadvantage of the geographical dispersion of the service is the difficulty of in-service training of extension agents. As it is, these agents do come together annually for a conference and somewhat more frequently in regional meetings, but a much better job of in-service training could be done if the agents were closer together. Spread so thinly, they cannot begin to cover their territories intensively. They could accomplish more if they were concentrated in groups with the agents of each group far enough apart to be kept fully occupied but close enough together to facilitate supervision and in-service training.

The third disadvantage of the wide distribution of offices is that it contributes to the appearance, and sometimes to the reality, of competition with the other agencies of the Ministry of Agriculture. For the most part, field agents of SCIPA and officers of other agencies with similar objectives are to be found in the same towns, sometimes in the same buildings. Informal divisions of labor are often arrived at by mutual agreement, but there is no part of the country where SCIPA by its absence leaves the field open for the development of a wholly domestic extension service. It would be better if there were. The other agencies of the Ministry of Agriculture have taken over several features of SCIPA administrative practice. They have given a number of their field officers vehicles enabling them to visit farmers, they have increased salaries so that better men can be recruited and retained, and they have begun using some of SCIPA's extension techniques. But there is no part of the country where they can build up a whole program that could some day absorb the extension project of SCIPA successfully.

Survey investigations, conducted as a part of the present study around selected towns where both SCIPA and other agencies of the ministry have offices,[19] reveal that in some places farmers consider SCIPA agents more competent and helpful, while in other regions other agents in the ministry appear to be more effective.[20]

If SCIPA were to confine its activities to selected areas, it could do a better job where it works, and other agencies would have a better chance to develop their own programs in the other regions.

The second criticism of SCIPA is that it seemingly could have moved faster in preparing Peruvians to act as subject-matter specialists for the extension service. SCIPA has a good staff of United States technicians for this purpose. One gets the impression, however, that they do not put enough emphasis on having well-trained Peruvian counterparts and on helping these men increase in competence so that they could take over this task.

The whole extension service except for subject-matter specialists is staffed by Peruvians. Although a few United States technicians should be retained in the project, it would seem that the time has come to make them training advisers to Peruvian subject-matter specialists and to give certain United States technicians a more intensive assignment for in-service training of field agents in extension methods. One gets the impression that field agents in SCIPA are successful more because they are able persons with basic agricultural training than because they are well trained in specific techniques of helping farmers help themselves.

SPECIAL FEATURES OF SCIPA.—Three special features of the program of SCIPA should be emphasized. The first is its conscious effort to help those farm families still living in Indian communities. The second is its effective public relations program. The third special feature is the policy of holding some resources in reserve in order to act quickly on new proposals.

As one looks back on SCIPA after studying programs in several other countries (SCIPA was the first program visited in the course of this study, in the summer of 1953), one is inclined to feel that some of its success has resulted from the fact that medium to large-sized commercial farms are to be found scattered throughout Peru. It is the managers of such farms who not only respond to improved practices but reach out for them. It is they who are most responsive to programs of general extension education. They have been so responsive that the field agents of SCIPA could have been completely absorbed in serving them. But SCIPA agents have made a particular point of rationing a considerable share of their attention to the less responsive small farmers, many of them living in Indian communities. The response is slower there, but in the interest of the future development of Peru it is imperative that these poorer people, living almost entirely by tradition, be helped to learn to live by making choices in a pattern of rural living that utilizes scientific knowledge. SCIPA has been strong at the point of giving attention to these people, though it may not yet have found the best methods of helping them. It is likely that broad community development programs would be more effective with the Indian communities than anything yet tried.[21]

The second special feature of SCIPA is its effective program of public relations. This program includes frequent news releases to newspapers, release of photographs about SCIPA projects, regular annual reports for distribution among influential citizens, and a quarterly magazine. Early in this study, the writer was inclined either to bypass programs of public relations as frills or to eye them with suspicion as unwise advertisement of the part played by United

States technicians in programs of technical co-operation. Both attitudes were wrong. Astute public relations is an important and integral part of technical co-operation. The purpose of such publicity is, or ought to be, not to blow a horn for the agency of technical co-operation, but to educate and enthuse the general public about agricultural development.

Although the fields of operation of any program of technical co-operation are limited, the factors which influence agricultural development are nation-wide. While SCIPA works with Peruvian government technicians in agriculture, and with farmers, the political support of wider programs of agricultural development and the badly needed improvement of practices of public administration wait on the support of the political elite, which in Peru is constantly expanding.

A good public relations program helps educate influential citizens of the whole country in the need for, and the imminent possibility of, agricultural development. It helps build a feeling of hope and enthusiasm for rural improvement. It helps build urban confidence in the innate capacity of all rural people, whether Indian or European, to solve many of their own problems when they have, not direction, but facilities for learning and for organization.

SCIPA has a program of public relations performing these functions well. Moreover, in SCIPA public relations plays a role in program planning, for an important element in the success of a new project is public readiness for it. When SCIPA is considering a new project, it publishes a "trial-balloon" article about it in its quarterly magazine. There are eighty-five newspapers in Peru. When ten of these newspapers respond with favorable editorials to such a SCIPA article, the time is judged to be ripe for the project.

The third special feature of SCIPA is its policy of always keeping some uncommitted resources in reserve. The purpose of this uncommitted reserve is to allow SCIPA to respond quickly to new requests coming from the minister of agriculture. This helps a great deal to bolster SCIPA's position as an agency within the Peruvian Ministry of Agriculture. It gives the minister an agency that can respond quickly without waiting for annual budgetary allocations. It allows SCIPA to capitalize on emergent enthusiasms and to strike while the iron is hot. Obviously, this valuable feature is one which can exist only when IIAA allows discretionary latitude to its field administrators, keeping the definition of those "projects" which have to have headquarters approval very broad, so that there is ample room within them to take on new projects quickly.[22]

NOTE ON AGRICULTURAL RESEARCH IN PERU.—It has been pointed out earlier that the Ministry of Agriculture conducts a substantial program of agricultural research at La Molina and at eleven substations throughout the country. Between a fifth and a sixth of the total ministry budget is devoted to research.

In addition, there have been three programs of agricultural research in Peru in which the United States has participated. One of these was the Rubber Development Program of the Bureau of Plant Industry, begun in 1943, never large, and now integrated with other projects of technical co-operation. The second was the program of the OFAR, inaugurated in 1942 and continued until 1952, when its program was absorbed by a *servicio* for agricultural research. This program of OFAR built and developed a well-equipped research station at Tingo Maria, in the Huallaga Valley, and had a marked effect on the development of that region, far removed from Lima and from other agricultural programs. Altogether, the United States put $664,000 into this program between 1942 and 1950. In 1952 a *servicio* was organized, the Programa Cooperativo de Experimentacion Agropecuario (PCEA) by the government of Peru and by IIAA. This *servicio* took over the operation of the research station at Tingo Maria and also co-operated in the central research station of the ministry at La Molina. After two years PCEA was absorbed into SCIPA as an autonomous unit for research. Then, in 1954, a contract was negotiated with the University of North Carolina to carry on a co-operative program with the Ministry of Agriculture at both La Molina and Tingo Maria.

This has been a rapidly shifting scene. It affords both a commentary on the differing emphasis of OFAR and IIAA and a hopeful example of evolution made possible by shifting attitudes within Peru itself. In its early years, and even to some extent until now, IIAA has emphasized extension activities on the theory that they can achieve results more quickly and that "enough is already known to make considerable progress." OFAR, on the other hand, put its emphasis on research and shrugged off the need for substantial technical co-operation in developing public programs to get improved practices into general use. Meanwhile, the Ministry of Agriculture was proud of its station at La Molina and did not welcome co-operation there.

The first break in this situation came when the Technical Cooperation Administration brought all United States programs in Latin America under IIAA. By that time SCIPA had become impressed with the need for new agricultural research, and the ministry, through its years of experience with SCIPA, had become less averse to co-operation in La Molina. The new research *servicio,* PCEA, brought Tingo Maria, La Molina, and the ministry together but was never very satisfactory as an operational device. The present arrangement gives hope for fruitful co-operation in the future and brings in the technical resources of the College of Agriculture of the University of North Carolina.

5 THE BILATERAL PROGRAM IN HAITI

Haiti is one of the most perplexing countries in Latin America from the standpoint of technical co-operation in agriculture, so perplexing that one is tempted to omit it from this group of illustrative sketches of programs. One reason for the omission would be that culturally Haiti is so different from the remainder of Latin America, being chiefly African and French rather than Indian and Spanish or Portuguese. Another would be that the complex of agricultural resources, density of population, and legal and commercial setting in Haiti makes its problems of agricultural development uniquely difficult.

However, neither of these criteria for ignoring Haiti in this study stands up under examination. Culturally Haiti is unique, without a doubt, but the differences between Haiti and Peru are probably no greater than those between Costa Rica and Bolivia or between Ecuador and Brazil. Haiti's problems of agricultural development are distinctive, but so are those of Cuba, Mexico, and Paraguay.

It is certain that Haiti needs agricultural development and needs whatever technical co-operation can contribute to that process. Her per capita annual income is among the lowest in the Western Hemisphere. Her resources other than agricultural are very meager. Her country is tiny (10,000 square miles), but she has more people (4,000,000) than Ecuador and more than any one of the republics of Central America. It is estimated that 97 per cent of her people gain their livelihood from agriculture or from agriculturally connected pursuits.

Background

The Republic of Haiti occupies the western one-third of the island of Hispaniola, the eastern two-thirds being the Dominican Republic. The division occurred in 1697, when, in the Treaty of Ryswyck, Spain ceded the part that is now Haiti to France. In the ensuing century, what is now Haiti developed into the most prosperous colony of France. By 1791 there were 36,000 whites, 28,000 free mulattoes and Negroes, and about 500,000 African slaves in the colony. The foreign trade of Haiti in this period exceeded that of the thirteen American colonies together, and it exceeded the combined foreign trade of the Spanish colonies. Sugar was the chief export, followed by coffee, indigo, cotton, and cocoa.

Under the laws of France, the whites and the free mulattoes and Negroes should have enjoyed equal rights. However, the whites used all the stratagems at their command to prevent this; and the bitterness thus engendered in the *gens de couleur* (mulattoes and Negroes), intensified by the slogans and spirit of the French Revolution of 1789, led to the revolts of 1791 and 1803 culminating in the independence of Haiti in 1804.

During the first half of the nineteenth century (her first half-century of independence) many of the seeds of Haiti's present agricultural problems were sown. The large colonial plantations were divided into smaller landholdings during this period. Few deeds were given for the land, and no land surveys existed; thus today the outstanding characteristic of Haiti's land system is vagueness of title. A great many occupants of land have no proof of ownership, and few farms have legal boundaries. With the division of the plantations, the trade in sugar collapsed, coffee trees went untended, and irrigation systems deteriorated until many of them could no longer be used.

Throughout the nineteenth century, Haiti was ruled by a succession of military leaders, mulattoes held all important government posts, and agriculture lapsed into a primitive subsistence economy. Today, the agricultural population of Haiti is almost entirely Negro. The people speak Creole, are mostly illiterate, and retain many cultural features from their African heritage.

In 1915 United States Marines landed at Port-au-Prince. Haiti had fallen badly into debt to foreign investors, both United States and European. The United States had both the pretext of protecting its own investors and the excuse of forestalling similar military action by Germany or France. The occupation, which lasted until 1934, left a mixed legacy. It left roads, bridges, hospitals, telephones, sewage systems, and water supplies. It left a considerable number of well-trained Haitians, many of whom had been sent to the United States to study in anticipation of the withdrawal. It left a "democratic" constitution, which under the first president after this new independence was drastically revised to strengthen the executive and reduce the power of the legislature. In subsequent years the government has taken on more and more of the characteristics of *personalismo,* so common among Latin-American countries. The occupation also left the bitterness that always follows in the wake of foreign domination, intensified by resentment against the United States for a number of stupid mistakes and senseless brutalities.

The submarine warfare of World War II cut off Haiti's trade with Europe and brought a kind of technical co-operation into the economy:

> American financial and technical assistance, unfortunately, took the form of a joint Haitian-American Development Corporation (SHADA), $4,000,000 of whose resources were devoted to the experimental growth of a rubber-substitute weed known as *cryptostegia.* SHADA became a political football. Haitians claimed that it threw peasants out of their homes without proper compensation, destroyed the best land and fruit-trees in the Republic, produced no rubber. Americans denied all charges except the last, but added that rubber or no rubber Haiti's economy would never have survived the War without this shot in the arm.[1]

Today the population of Haiti is sharply divided into a very small elite and a very large (more than 90 per cent) rural peasantry. Nearly all of the large landholdings today are in the hands of sugar and sisal corporations, owned partly by Haitians and partly by foreign (Cuban and United States) investors. One aspect of the situation is quite different from the usual Latin-American pattern and has great significance for agricultural development: Haiti's elite owns relatively little land. The income of the elite derives almost entirely from commerce and from government employment. One result of this weak connection between the elite and the land is that the ruling class little understands the problems of agricultural production or of agricultural development.[2]

The government of Haiti is financed chiefly by export taxes (the major export being coffee). Export and import taxes together make up 80 per cent of all government revenues. There are few non-agricultural resources in the country and relatively little manufacturing. Agriculture (and small-scale agricultural processing), therefore, is the one immediate hope in this heavily populated land, other than an increasing tourist business.

Technical Co-operation

It is out of this background of history that Haiti's agricultural problems have grown, and it is against this background that the bilateral program of technical co-operation in Haiti must operate. The first task of the bilateral program was to help get back into production an estimated 140,000 acres of land that had been devoted by SHADA to the unsuccessful effort to utilize *cryptostegia* as a source of rubber during World War II.

In 1944 an agreement was signed by which a Food Production Program was to be established by the United States government in Haiti. For the first year, the United States contributed $125,000, and Haiti $50,000. Each year thereafter until 1948, the United States contributed $50,000, while Haiti contributed $50,000 in the second year and $175,000 for the next 18 months, until the launching of SCIPA.

SCIPA (Service Cooperatif Interamericain Production Agricole) was established as a *servicio,* with the United States chief of field party as the director, responsible to the Haitian minister of agriculture, on July 1, 1948. In 1953/54 and in 1954/55, Haiti contributed $266,000 annually to SCIPA, and the IIAA contributed $177,000 and $180,000 in the two years, respectively, plus the cost of United States technicians. The authorized fields of activity for SCIPA are about the same as those of agricultural *servicios* in other countries. As in other countries, however, the actual fields of operation have been much narrower than this authorization. From its beginning in 1944, there have been two major emphases of this bilateral program. One has been to increase Haiti's agricultural resources through irrigation. The other has been to try to help develop an extension service, with this effort slipping over into fitful, short-lived research projects at irregular intervals.

Irrigation Projects

It is estimated that in all of Haiti there are only 2,500,000 acres of arable land, and that 1,000,000 acres are currently being cultivated. Another estimate, which gives a somewhat smaller potentially cultivable area, is that 80 per cent of Haiti is too mountainous for cultivation. Much of the gap between present cultivation and potentially cultivable land is due to lack of moisture. The rainfall in most of Haiti varies from 27 to 80 inches, but on most of the cultivable plains it is not above 40 inches. This rainfall is not evenly distributed through the year but comes in definite seasons that vary in different parts of the country. Moreover, much of the rain comes in sudden storms, with high run-off. Much of the potentially cultivable land can only be utilized effectively through irrigation, and this has led to high priority being given by programs of technical co-operation to developing irrigation facilities.

The activities of SCIPA in the field of irrigation fall into three groups: (1) The construction and operation of small-scale irrigation works, (2) participation in planning and executing the project in the Artibonite Valley, ultimately to irrigate about 100,000 acres, and (3) well-drilling. Two projects of the first type were visited in the course of this study.

FONDS PARISIEN.—The village of Fonds Parisien lies on a stony outwash plain at the edge of the Cul-de-Sac Plain, about 25 miles east of Port-au-Prince and only a few miles from the Dominican border. It is in a region almost completely cut over for charcoal. There had been little or no cultivation in the vicinity for forty years prior to this project.

To get water adequate for irrigating 1,200 acres, it was necessary to go about six miles up a mountain stream and to put an inlet in the bed of the stream at a point where the flow was adequate and dependable, not yet having been depleted by seepage in the porous outwash plain. The water was led by lined canal and pipe down the valley to the land around Fonds Parisien. Since irrigation was established by this project, 1,200 acres have been planted to Egyptian shallu, grain sorghum, sweet potatoes, red beans, avocados, and bananas. This project was constructed at a cost of $193,000 to irrigate 1,200 acres.

Once the water had been provided, SCIPA started an extension service for the people of the community, to help them utilize the water profitably. This program was not particularly good, but until catastrophe hit the project, agricultural production and the level of living rose very rapidly.

The whole program at Fonds Parisien has been badly upset by two developments. One was a natural catastrophe of a type which could be expected but of such magnitude that it was highly unlikely. The other was a foreseeable outcome of bringing irrigation water to a small, impoverished locality in a heavily populated country.

The natural catastrophe was the torrential rain and floods following a hurricane in October, 1954. In designing the irrigation installation the probability of floods was considered, and a substantial margin of safety was provided; but the sudden rainfall (forty inches) was so heavy that the ensuing flood lowered the bed of the stream at the point where the irrigation inlet had been constructed a full fifteen feet. This left the inlet hanging like a bridge across the gorge, eight feet above the new bed of the stream, and it washed out considerable sections of the canal and pipe, filling other sections with debris. Farmers of Fonds Parisien contributed thousands of hours of labor to cleaning sections of the canal to catch water from farther down the gorge, but this is only a temporary measure. In January, 1955, the engineers of SCIPA were trying to decide whether to rebuild the system along lines of the original design, or to look for ground-water sources on the outwash plain, or to abandon the project entirely.

The foreseeable outcome of bringing water to Fonds Parisien for which adequate preparation was not made was the rapid rise in population. When the project was initiated, 750 people lived in the vicinity of Fonds Parisien. Three years later there were 4,000 people in the same area, since the irrigation water so raised the productivity of the locality that people began moving to Fonds Parisien from the less favored sections roundabout. SCIPA was not prepared for this influx, nor were the laws and other public services of Haiti. With all land titles vague, and no cadastral survey, land-holdings were rapidly fragmented, with titles still as vague as ever. Because of a division of authority between ministries and because of SCIPA's binational character, SCIPA could not charge users for irrigation water. The fact that irrigation water was provided free compounded the confusion born of inadequate land titles. SCIPA is now working on a scheme for water-payment to assure that the funds it brings in will be used for maintenance of this system rather than reverting to general funds of the government.

A third complication, common to bilateral programs of technical co-operation, had to do with the location of the project. Fonds Parisien was chosen as the site for a SCIPA irrigation project at the insistence of the Haitian government. The government wanted a thriving community at Fonds Parisien because of its proximity to the Dominican border. Its reasons were both political and economic. It wanted a strong border community, and it wanted an enlarged means of livelihood for Haitians coming back across the border from the Dominican Republic, to reduce the influx of refugees into Port-au-Prince.

This government pressure, more than the suitability of the locality, dictated Fonds Parisien as an irrigation project of SCIPA. One may say that this pressure should have been resisted more strongly, but it would be foolish not to recognize the reality, and inevitability, of such pressures on binational programs. Private agencies engaged in technical co-operation are better able to resist such pressures than are governmental agencies.

It is interesting, in view of the vicissitudes of this project at Fonds Parisien, to study the "Plan of Work" proposed by the Haitian project director of SCIPA in that locality for 1955. His proposals reveal that he still does not understand how terrifyingly enormous is the problem of improving rural welfare in Fonds Parisien. At the same time, it is significant that he does not feel defeated and recognizes real grounds for encouragement in statements such as this:

It is true that on October 11, Hazel (the hurricane) washed out irrigation structures in many places over the country, and the irrigation system of Fonds Parisien has been very hard-hit, endangering the results of our efforts. *Still, the forces we have developed have given confidence in the future.* It is our responsibility to make an inventory of the available resources of the area—and one of those resources is the enlarged population itself—to study the conditions we have helped to create, to make decisions . . . and to execute them.

The project at Fonds Parisien may have been badly located. There was inadequate preparation for it. Important problems were ignored. Still, a change in people came about through the program that may make them more flexible and alert to new opportunities. This is added, not in justification of the project, but merely to complete the catalogue of its characteristics.

SAN RAPHAEL.—Another of the small-scale irrigation projects developed by SCIPA is at San Raphael, on the northern edge of the Central Plateau, fifty miles southeast of Cap Haitien. Prior to irrigation this was range country; it is still a major livestock region, but now many pastures are being plowed for irrigated cultivation. At an elevation of 1,200 feet above sea level, San Raphael has a pleasant climate, well suited to a variety of fruits and vegetables as well as to such crops as rice, sugar cane, and beans.

SCIPA provided irrigation water by constructing a small dam across a mountain stream and bringing the water ten miles by canal across the plateau. So far, water has been supplied to 1,000 acres; eventually 2,000 acres will be irrigated within the project. Here, SCIPA agents have been much more active in organizing farm families to utilize their new resources. A start has been made on getting fields consolidated into workable units. Farmers have been persuaded to pool some of their plots into a field of 125 acres where individual plots are marked by wooden posts. The first plowing was done on hire by SCIPA tractor equipment. The farmers agreed on a single crop for the field. After the first plowing, each farmer cultivates his own plots and harvests the crop. A contract has been signed to form a second such field. SCIPA operates a small demonstration farm for the entire project, trying out new varieties of crops, different methods of water application, measures for disease control, etc.

Farm families have been organized in five community groups each with elected officers, each meeting monthly to discuss common problems and plan joint projects. Three credit unions were organized in 1953 and 1954. The oldest has 150 members and now has $3,000 of capital, all saved by members. Only two members defaulted on loans in the first two years. Some of the farmers are building their own new homes, locating them just outside the irrigated area to avoid the malarial mosquitoes that have increased with the coming of the water. Here, as in Fonds Parisien, farmers do not pay for irrigation water, but they do join together three or four times a year to clean the canals and channels.

This project is more favorably located than that at Fonds Parisien in several respects. It is a more straightforward, conservative type of irrigation engineering. The soil is much better. It is in a part of the country less heavily populated, with fewer "hardship areas" from which the new prosperity might suck indigent emigrants. In addition, it has had more imaginative and more comprehensive leadership. The Haitian in charge, who is particularly able, had five years in Puerto Rico and a year at the Imperial College of Tropical Agriculture in Trinidad before joining SCIPA.

ARTIBONITE.—The largest river in Haiti, the Artibonite, crosses a large deltaic plain before flowing into the Gonave Gulf. Most of this plain is dry and has not been intensively cultivated; the lower part of it has been partially cultivated from an ancient French irrigation system using water from the Estere and Artibonite Rivers, but production has been limited by the salinity of the soil. Still, there are said to be upwards of 100,000 people living in the valley, chiefly by "patch" farming.

For many years, engineers have contemplated irrigating the plain. It is said that the French drew up extensive plans for such a system about 1748. In 1916–17 United States engineers in Haiti with the Marines surveyed the valley and outlined a plan. In 1946 President Estimé of Haiti, whose home was in the Artibonite Valley, asked the Food Production Mission (predecessor to SCIPA) to establish an irrigation project in the valley. A new chief of field party, who was an irrigation engineer, arrived to undertake a survey. The first result was the Villard Project, which irrigated 5,000 acres. The Food Production Mission established a well-equipped research station on 125 acres at Bois Dehors, using it for experimental work on agronomic problems involved in the Villard Project. The station was later operated by SCIPA but was then transferred to the Artibonite Valley Authority (ODVA) of the Haitian government. When the station was transferred, the Haitian technicians who had been trained by SCIPA went with it; but they were soon dismissed in favor of political appointees, with the consequence that the program has suffered badly.

Meanwhile, studies were begun for a much more ambitious scheme to irrigate 100,000 acres of the valley and also to generate 40,000 kilowatts of electricity. (The total present electric supply of Haiti is estimated to be 18,000 kilowatts, of which 6,000 kilowatts are generated by individual consumers.) The major installation of this project is the Peligre Dam, rising 190 feet above stream level, with a storage capacity of 265,000 acre-feet. On this larger Artibonite Scheme, SCIPA aided in the preliminary survey preparatory to a Haitian application for a loan from the Export-Import Bank. A loan of $14,000,000 was granted and two United States firms were employed, one to make the final engineering studies and designs and the other to construct the dam, canals, and other installations. At the present time, IIAA is responsible only for providing technicians to advise on the agricultural development of the newly irrigated lands and on project operation and maintenance.[3] This last is badly needed in connection with the project, but IIAA serves only in an advisory capacity, and the need is not being adequately met.

Altogether, aside from its work on the Artibonite Scheme, SCIPA has constructed irrigation projects serving about 4,000 acres to date, in addition to its well-drilling operations which allow irrigation of perhaps another 2,000 acres.

Agricultural Extension and Research

While the Food Production Plan and, later, SCIPA were building irigation projects with one hand, they engaged with the other in a number of projects called "agricultural." These have shifted from year to year, and one gets the impression that almost everything has been tried in the eleven years beginning in 1944. Only a few of the projects have lasted beyond a few years, and apparently only three of them have been taken over by the Haitian government. One is the farm at Damien; the second is the research farm at Bois Dehors; the third is a grain-storage scheme.[4] Several factors can now be discerned in this history, but a review of the projects is in order here.

DAMIEN FARM.—Haiti's agricultural college at Damien, just outside Port-au-Prince, has a four-year curriculum following secondary school. It admits a new class of about forty students once every four years. The students, coming from city families of the elite, have no rural background. They are not accustomed to working with their hands, and the curriculum at Damien includes very little practical work for them. They are trained at Damien ostensibly to be employed in the Ministry of Agriculture, but in recent years the ministry has not had places for nearly all of them. Each student receives a government scholarship covering the full cost of education and of living expenses for the four years.

Beginning in 1948, SCIPA took over the farm of the college at

Damien. The agency cleared forty acres and brought in new varieties of crops and new strains of livestock. It organized part of the farm into demonstrations and the remainder as a commercial operation. It took students of Damien into the program for practical training. But in 1950 the co-operative arrangement with respect to this farm was discontinued. One North American and one Haitian informant independently said that the reason was that "the experimental results did not agree with the textbooks." The North American felt there was some anti–United States feeling involved in the discontinuation also. Another Haitian claimed that SCIPA antagonized the Department of Agriculture by belittling it instead of building it up.

Of the purpose of operating this farm at Damien, a SCIPA report of 1949 states: "The objectives of our Damien farm are a demonstration of methods of cultivation and irrigation, of use of farm tools, machinery, and insecticides; the introduction of imported varieties of crops, the production of seed for distribution through our extension service; and [the provision of] training for SCIPA employees and the students of the National School of Agriculture."

EXTENSION SERVICES.—The Haitian Ministry of Agriculture has about a hundred field agents located throughout the country. They are regulatory officers for the most part, performing such tasks as granting permits to cut trees, to sell livestock and hides, to slaughter animals, and to feed cottonseed meal. They do some extension education, but they have not developed any systematized extension program. Only the district agronomists (regional supervisors) have vehicles. Until recently, some field agents carried guns to emphasize their governmental authority.

From the time of SCIPA's organization in 1948, a major part of its program has been in the field of extension. It had thirty-three Haitian extension agents in 1954. It has a Haitian director, and one United States technician, recently arrived, for extension methods. As of 1954, SCIPA was operating in twelve regions, each having three or four agents, and the Ministry of Agriculture was operating in twelve other regions, each with six to nine agents (excluding assistants with little training).

The method of operation of SCIPA in extension has been much the same in Haiti as in other United States bilateral programs: farm visits, demonstrations, youth clubs, and (since 1952) home demonstration agents. That is the extent of the similarity, however. The field agents have not been effectively backed by subject-matter specialists, who, in any case, would have little verified information to depend upon because of the total lack of research.

An activity not found in other such programs is the organization of credit unions. In the early years of the program considerable quantities of seeds and small tools were given free to farmers. Later

TABLE 9

EXTENSION ACTIVITIES (SELECTED MONTHS)*

ACTIVITIES	1949			1951			
	June	Sept.	Dec.	March	June	Sept.	Dec.
Visits to farmers........	254	817	736	444	529	192	619
Farmer visits to offices...	384	244	604	529	495	246	518
Group meetings.........	38	89	47	35	31	33	....
Attendance...........	919	2,209	1,884	1,609	1,497	611	....
Cash sales..............	$200	$135.36	$303	....	$59.60	$45.40	$73.50
Poultry vaccinated......	....	1,436	2,521	....	....	....	....
(fowl pox)............	....	....	....	90	97	220	806
Hogs vaccinated........	....	120	....	....	....	....	....
(cholera).............	....	....	....	....	....	....	....
Seeds distributed........	954	335	1,307	....	....	....	....
(in pounds)...........	....	....	....	....	....	....	....
Credit clubs............	....	....	....	42	44	44	44
Membership..........	....	....	....	1,794	1,834	1,834	1,834
Youth clubs............	....	....	....	57	59	59	60
Membership..........	....	....	....	1,303	1,403	1,403	1,445
Demonstrations.........	....	....	....	39	65	69	82
Attendance...........	....	....	....	1,254	641	305	615
Hours on horseback.....	....	....	....	674	333	289	909

* From monthly reports of SCIPA, Port-au-Prince.

this policy was changed, and such requisites were sold in the same way as in the reimbursable facilities projects of other countries.

Table 9 reproduces the SCIPA tabular report of extension activities in selected months of the second and fourth years of the program. This shows, in general, the same types of activity being carried on in other countries, but the *level* of activities is considerably below that in Peru,[5] for example, except in youth clubs and credit societies. There were approximately the same number of extension agents in the programs in Haiti and Peru, but agents in Haiti made only about a third as many farm visits, held fewer than a third as many meetings, and conducted fewer than a fourth as many demonstrations.

Prior to 1955 SCIPA carried on extension activities wherever it had an irrigation project but did not confine its extension to those areas. In preparation for supplying water in the Villard project in 1949, SCIPA conducted an agricultural survey, got farmers to dig the laterals, and distributed vegetable seeds and plants. At San Raphael, credit clubs and youth clubs were organized as part of a continuing extension program. At Bois Dehors, a Future Farmers Club of young men and women was started, and it flourished as long as SCIPA was operating the experiment station. At Fonds Parisien, a continuing extension program has been part of SCIPA's activity. At the beginning of 1955, SCIPA was considering concentrating its extension efforts in fewer spots, each around an irrigation project, combining agricultural extension with health activities and with a general educational program. Accordingly, IIAA has added a community development adviser to its staff, in the office of the country director.

CREDIT UNIONS.—Beginning in 1950, SCIPA undertook to organize study clubs that could develop into credit unions. Credit unions were introduced into Haiti by the Oblate Fathers of Canada, who still sponsor some of the bigger and stronger unions. One of their unions, at Camp Perrin, had 600 members in 1950 with $13,000 capital, all collected through dues.

The need for credit unions grows out of the fact that credit is only available to most rural people at high rates of interest, in some cases reaching 20 per cent per month. The credit unions have no outside capital, only their own savings, which they lend to members at 1 per cent per month.

This sponsoring of credit unions has gone through three stages. In the first few months only a few unions were organized, and the emphasis was more on the study clubs, more on helping people learn how to manage a credit union than on organizing new unions. The second phase saw rapid multiplication of unions launched without much time spent on the preliminary study clubs. Believing that it had been a mistake to slight existing unions in favor of new ones, SCIPA in the third phase quit organizing new unions and, from late 1953, worked only with the unions already established.

These unions are developing slowly. Being poor, the people cannot save much, and no outside capital is being put in. For this reason, some technicians of the SCIPA staff feel that the study clubs are the most important part of this activity. What people learn about thrift and credit appears to such technicians to be more significant than the small amount of credit which the unions can make available to their members.

In the SCIPA report for January, 1953, one finds this remark: "The typical rural credit union in Haiti has been organized fifteen months. It has 38 members, with a total capital of $170, an average capital investment per member of $4.48. A start has been made in teaching credit union officers how to make agricultural loans."

The country director feels that these clubs' chief function is education and hopes their demonstration of handling small funds well will result in their being given authority to manage outside capital, perhaps provided by the Industrial and Agricultural Institute of Haiti.

YOUTH CLUBS.—In 1950 SCIPA began organizing youth clubs. Most of these are built around home garden projects, but a few of the boys raise poultry, some care for livestock, and the clubs do some cleaning of irrigation channels. These clubs are an important activity, but not enough attention has been given them by SCIPA personnel to make them really effective. From sixty clubs in December, 1951, the number dropped to twenty-four by September, 1952.

IN-SERVICE TRAINING.—SCIPA does not have a good record for in-service training of its extension agents. Four times it has conducted a two-week summer course in extension methods. On at least two of these occasions, rural teachers were invited to participate with SCIPA agents. On at least one occasion, personnel from the Ministry of Agriculture joined in the course. An attempt at a fifth national training course was dropped in favor of regional training visits by the veterinarian, to save travel costs for ministry employees.

Conversation with SCIPA extension agents and with North American technicians reveals that contacts between the headquarters staff and the extension agents are occasional and irregular. At the time of this study, SCIPA extension agents had not all been together for a conference in the past two and one-half years. Thus in-service training, which experience shows is vital to such activities, has not had adequate attention in the Haitian program.

One exception to this general neglect of in-service training has been in the field of veterinary medicine. All agents have had field training in parasite control, dental care, hoof treatment, and care of simple wounds.

HOME DEMONSTRATION.—In home demonstration, the extension service is no better and no worse than most other such programs. The first Haitian home demonstration agent was employed by SCIPA in 1952. In 1953 six more were employed after a training course lasting six weeks. A competent North American home economist has been on the staff of SCIPA since early 1953, but the program has not been given the emphasis it deserves. Nowhere does such a program get adequate attention except at the insistence of the chief of field party, and such insistence is rare. Because it is a relatively new program all over Latin America, few people recognize the need for it, and only substantial changes from the North American pattern will make the program suitable for women in Latin-American culture.

MINOR PROJECTS.—Other minor activities have been undertaken by SCIPA at one time or another. Two small machinery pools, for example, have been established and continue to operate reasonably well, but they are too small to achieve anything like the operating efficiency of the project in Peru. The Food Production Program persuaded the Ministry of Agriculture to undertake a grain storage scheme—to buy grain from farmers at the average price for the previous year, then sell it back to them as needed at cost plus a handling charge—but this "faded away," apparently because of lack of supervision after being taken over by the government. Attempts have been made twice to introduce animal-drawn implements into the Haitian agriculture, which normally uses nothing between the hoe and the tractor. One attempt with animal-drawn implements was quickly abandoned; the second is still going on but without anyone seeming to know how to adapt implements designed for mules to use with Haitian bullocks and without sufficient attention being given to training farmers in adjustment and maintenance of the implements.[6]

Not all the failures among these projects constitute failures of

SCIPA. It cannot be emphasized too often that technical co-operation is called for at a time when experimentation in methods is necessary, and it is inevitable that many trials fail. However, some failures occur, not because the idea was wrong or even because it was ill-timed, but because of poor administration, of insufficient emphasis, or of quitting too soon. There is evidence that SCIPA has been weak at the point of follow-through. Some of SCIPA's failures were unnecessary, while others were almost inevitable at this period in Haiti.

HURRICANE HAZEL.—On October 11, 1954, Hurricane Hazel hit Haiti and left widespread destruction. Haiti's appeal to the United States for relief was granted, and the relief came in the form of food, medical supplies, and seeds, tools, insecticides, and other requisites necessary in re-establishing agricultural production.

SCIPA was pressed into service to help administer the distribution of food and supplies in rural areas. One result of this was that all regular activities of SCIPA were virtually stopped for a period of three months and seriously curtailed for five months more. Another result was that hundreds of thousands of rural Haitians had a new contact with SCIPA. On the whole, their reaction to SCIPA's role in relief was one of gratitude and appreciation; this followed partly from SCIPA's role in food relief and partly in some localities from elation at the extraordinarily fine crops that grew quickly from the seeds imported to be sown immediately after the disaster. A pinto bean, in particular, produced very well on many fields.[7]

Despite general appreciation, there were a few localities where quarrels about food relief resulted in the kind of resentment that any regulatory function often involves. To the extent that the reaction to SCIPA's role following the hurricane was one of appreciation, SCIPA gained an advantage of the same type that accrued to ACAR in Brazil through ant-control. SCIPA could return to its normal activities in early 1955 with a public reputation of helpfulness in difficult times. This public reputation is useful if SCIPA can live up to it.

On the whole, neither Haiti nor SCIPA has been happy about SCIPA's record in extension. Haitians tend to feel that SCIPA has squandered its resources by moving from project to project. They accuse United States technicians of sticking to their desks instead of getting out into the field. They say that SCIPA administrators have refused to undertake needed research, claiming that their instructions from Washington were to get increased food production quickly through extension. SCIPA personnel, meanwhile, seem to feel they have made little progress except in a few localities like San Raphael. They, too, mention the drift from project to project, ascribing it to the conclusion that nothing they try seems to work; thus they keep trying new approaches in the hope of finding a more successful program.

Observations and Conclusions

1. Haiti, of the countries visited during this study, is the most difficult one in which to bring about agricultural development. Four components of this difficulty can be identified.

a) Circumstances in the Haitian countryside make agricultural development difficult. Foremost among these is the limited quantity of arable land, on which a dense population must live with few non-agricultural resources to become the basis of substantial non-agricultural employment.[8] The fact that farms are small means that to change Haitian agriculture requires educating hundreds of thousands of farm operators to new practices.

These basic problems of rural Haiti are greatly aggravated by the lack of a cadastral survey, vagueness of land titles, uncertainty of tenure, and consequent disinterest in soil conservation or in "building for the future" in other ways. No one knows quite what he owns; no one has any certainty about what land he may be able to cultivate tomorrow.

This vagueness of status pertains to the family as well as to the land. It is common for a man to have several households in several villages, with the "wife" in each household working as overseer and labor-supplier for the land of the father of her children. This does not mean that the family is not important to Haitians—it is very important—but the farm-and-home planning and the emphasis on the farm family central to extension activities in the United States and to programs of supervised credit are based on the monogamous family. Thus they do not fit many of the household groupings of rural Haiti.

Despite the loose organization of many elements of rural Haiti which are important in agricultural development, there is a real culture in the countryside. The life of the agricultural population is rich in ceremonies and in everyday social intercourse. In few parts of the world does one find such lightheartedness (coupled with deep fears) or such outgoing friendliness.

b) Attitudes of the elite of Haiti and the status of governmental services make agricultural development especially difficult. For the most part, the urban elite,[9] based on ancestry and politics, ignores the rural masses. Members of the elite are concerned about commerce and government. They do not fear an uprising of the masses, and there appears to be little reason why they should. The administration of President Magloire and that of President Estimé before him have shown considerable interest in Haiti outside of Port-au-Prince, but this is chiefly in the other cities and towns of the country. These administrations have been interested in roads and irrigation, and these will benefit agriculture, but beyond these there is little concern for, or understanding of, the masses by the elite.

Governmental services are poorly prepared to serve rural Haiti. As in many other Latin-American countries, appointments to the Ministry of Agriculture are political, even down to subordinate employees. Seventy-five per cent of the budget of the ministry goes for salaries, and each post and its salary are designated by the Budget Bureau. For these reasons, any Minister of Agriculture who understands rural Haiti and really wants to spur agricultural development has very limited opportunity to improve his ministry.

In the above respect, the problem of government services in Haiti is similar to that in other countries. But there are two additional problems. One is that Haiti is not yet organized to administer irrigation projects well; the second is that her one gesture toward agricultural credit results chiefly in more hotels.

Except for those controlled by SCIPA or ODVA, the Ministry of Public Works administers the irrigation facilities of Haiti. In 1954 it managed projects totaling 125,000 acres in area, but data are not available on the total acreages irrigated. Although the ministry operates several large systems, a good picture of irrigation conditions can be had from the data for 26 small projects, totaling 24,826 acres. The ownership of cultivated lands varies from less than an acre to 125 acres, with a total of 8,025 water users, an average of 3.1 acres per user.[10] An irrigation tax formerly was imposed on water users, the proceeds being used "to maintain the canals." This tax law was repealed in 1946, allegedly because of widespread corruption in collecting the tax. There was no tax for irrigation water from 1946 until October 1, 1952, when a new law provided for a graduated tax, varying from $0.81 to $10.12 per acre, depending on the amount of water used. However, as no attempt is made to measure the water used by each farmer, every user pays the minimum tax of 81 cents per acre.

The point here is, not that Haiti is inherently incompetent to administer irrigation projects wisely, but simply that ability in this direction has not been shown to date in a democratic setting. There were extensive irrigation systems during the French colonial period, but they were maintained under a system of colonial domination and slavery. What must now be developed is a pattern of irrigation administration for present-day needs.

With the development of the Artibonite, better administration will be imperative, but the future of Haiti requires that there be better irrigation administration not only in the autonomous Artibonite Valley Authority, but throughout the country, where irrigation is under the Ministry of Public Works.

Within the current administration, Haiti has established an Institute for Agricultural and Industrial Credit. It is the responsibility of the institute to make loans to small farmers and businessmen. In practice, the loans go almost entirely to city businesses, the construction of hotels being the purpose of most loans. This building of hotels is wise for Haiti: the recent increase in tourist expenditures in the country has made tourism second only to coffee as a source of income from foreign trade, and further expansion of tourist facilities is probably Haiti's biggest opportunity to increase her income quickly. In this process, the fact that agricultural credit is supposed to be cared for by this same Institute for Agricultural and Industrial Credit that is financing urban development means that agriculture gets left out, and no adequate source of credit is available to small farmers.

c) There is neither a determination in Haiti's leaders for, nor mass agitation for, agricultural development in Haiti. This is the third, and possibly the greatest, factor in the difficulty of accelerating agricultural development in Haiti. Haiti has meager resources, a rural culture ill-adapted to the needs of progress, an elite cut off from interest in the land (other than speculation), and ineffective government organization. However, other countries of Latin America have faced similarly unpromising situations in the past, and certain countries elsewhere in the world face them today. If there were both intellectual and emotional determination in Haiti to change matters, or a mass demand for a re-orientation of national effort, all of Haiti's obstacles except meager resources could be removed, and even the meager resources could be substantially augmented. Reforestation could re-clothe the mountains. Crop rotation and other conservation practices could hold the cultivated soil. Reorganized irrigation administration could greatly increase efficiency in the use of water. Research could find better crops, develop controls for pests and diseases, analyze soil needs, etc. Education could help rural people begin to see the possibilities that lie within themselves. All of these, and other developments, could take place, *were there the will to make them happen.*

The thesis that the attitudes and institutions of any people are powerfully affected by their physical surroundings needs no proof, but history also reveals numerous occasions when a people has taken physical surroundings by the scruff of the neck and has shaken them into a more productive form. It is easy to catalogue the difficulties which face Haiti at this time, but it would be folly not also to recognize that a determined Haitian people could greatly improve the production and the level of living in her countryside. Determined peoples have done this in the past and are doing it today elsewhere in the world.

The critical importance of this national will to advance grows out of the number of obstacles to development which face Haiti today. These obstacles are so interlocking that no single program, no piecemeal effort, has a chance to succeed. Only a multiform program on a wide front can help, and only a national, emotionally charged crusade to succeed can make changes on such a wide front politically possible and socially acceptable. Of course, such a will to progress would be no substitute for painstaking research, carefully designed and constantly modified public programs, and scientific competence of many kinds; but with a will to advance these could be created.

d) There are no medium-sized or large-scale farms, under alert management, to offer a toe hold to a conventional extension service. This conclusion is more specific and less sweeping than the preceding three. It may, however, be crucial to an analysis of the impact of SCIPA on Haitian agriculture.

There are other countries in Latin America where many farms are quite small: Peru, Ecuador, Bolivia, and Mexico, for example. Agricultural development is proceeding much more slowly on the tiny farms than on the larger farms in those countries. We have inquired in each country to discover whether programs of technical cooperation are affecting the smallest farms. In some they are, but in every case administrators of programs speak in the following terms: "These small farmers need a different kind of program. They are too closely knit in their community culture to move quickly alone. Our methods of extension work much more quickly with larger farms; meanwhile, we experiment with new, broader programs which may be more effective on the smaller farms."

A country with many small farms is likely to develop agriculturally much more rapidly if there is a sprinkling of medium-sized farms throughout it. The medium-sized farms are organized and under single management, even when nearby small farms may be vague in boundary and their operators closely knit in community groups. Therefore, the farmers with more land are in a better position to try new methods, they are more likely to have a commercial attitude toward farming, and their innovations can demonstrate what is possible with the agricultural resources of the locality. At the same time, farmers of these larger holdings are likely to have some political influence; thus the success of an extension service with them leads to greater political support for the agricultural programs on which further improvement of all farms, both large and small, depends.

Haiti does not have this advantage of a sprinkling of larger farms. An extension service in Haiti must work almost exclusively with peasants possessing bits of land. Because conventional extension programs are not well-adapted to these, they are likely to fail, either through ineffectiveness in their own field or through being frustrated by obstacles to progress which are outside of their field of operations.

2. Overestimation of the role of conventional extension in agricultural development has characterized the program of SCIPA in Haiti. Because it is weak in so many of the elements of agricultural development, Haiti demonstrates the limitations of a program of agricultural extension standing virtually alone. The conventional methods of agricultural extension, which United States technicians take with them wherever they go, owe much of their validity in the United States to the conditions of security of tenure, adequate rainfall or good irrigation administration, general dispersion of elementary education, commercial availability of agricultural requisites, adequate research, and active participation by many farmers in the political process. Even in the United States, conventional extension made little headway among farmers with small resources and without access to credit; and programs of supervised credit had to be devised before this class of farmers began to move ahead.

SCIPA's personnel, like those in most other bilateral programs of technical co-operation, overestimated the role of extension activities and consequently felt frustrated and tempted to abandon projects when the shortcomings of this method, standing alone, became apparent.

3. While overestimating the role that conventional agricultural extension can play in agricultural development, SCIPA may have disproportionately emphasized irrigation projects.

Three questions have to be asked in discussing what the emphasis of a program of technical co-operation in a country should be:

a) What does the country *need* to accelerate agricultural development?

b) What does the country *want* through technical co-operation?

c) With limited resources for a program of technical co-operation, what emphasis will give the greatest returns in agricultural development in the sense that projects of technical co-operation should be "germinal," sowing seeds of greater achievement through domestic programs in the future?

As for what Haiti needs to spur agricultural development—almost everything. Irrigation certainly is one of her needs. Appropriate adult education for agricultural people is another.

As for what Haiti wants through technical co-operation, SCIPA's emphasis on irrigation has had the wholehearted support of, and has been encouraged by, the Haitian government. This may have been partly because Haiti overestimated what irrigation alone could accomplish, just as SCIPA overestimated what conventional extension methods could achieve under Haitian conditions. It may also be that Haiti favored irrigation projects because through them she could get not only the participation of experienced technicians but a substantial share of construction costs as well. SCIPA's records do not easily yield an estimate of the amount spent in constructing irrigation works, but it is certain that SCIPA spent over $200,000 on the Villard Project, at least $100,000 at San Raphael, and at least $193,000 at Fonds Parisien, not to mention other projects. Moreover, because no charge is made for irrigation water on a project operated by SCIPA, there is no repayment for the $40,000 to $50,000 which SCIPA spends annually on the maintenance of irrigation systems. (These figures, it must be understood, are SCIPA expenditures, not United States expenditures. Two-fifths of SCIPA's income is from United States funds, the remaining three-fifths being contributed by Haiti.) If there is a criticism of putting substantial amounts into irrigation construction, it is not that all of the funds come from the United States but that such expenditures greatly reduce the balance available for other projects within the SCIPA program. (A former IIAA official challenges this conclusion, holding that had IIAA not agreed to substantial projects in irrigation, Haiti would have appropriated much less for SCIPA. The argument would appear stronger had the IIAA chief of field party not been an irrigation engineer. Nevertheless, it is true that the choice in technical co-operation seems to lie frequently between doing nothing or undertaking projects that technicians-from-abroad judge to be second best.)

A generalized answer to the question of what emphasis will give the greatest returns in agricultural development is that irrigation projects are easier to execute, visible and definite in outcome, but not very high in reproduction value, while educating rural people to more productive agricultural practices is difficult, diffused in effect and hence difficult to measure, yet absolutely essential if Haitian agriculture is to move forward. The facts that irrigation projects are easier to execute and show more tangible results are inherent in the comment of two SCIPA technicians: "SCIPA got into irrigation projects because the Haitian government pushed us in, but one reason we have stayed in is that otherwise we would have very little to show for our work." To recognize this is not to deny that more irrigation is a valuable asset for Haitian agriculture; it does, however, indicate that the "germinal" characteristic of a project has not been the major criterion in SCIPA's choice of projects.

There is an additional valid justification for irrigation projects, closely allied to this often-maligned argument that "they get results which show." At this juncture Haiti desperately needs some agricultural projects that obviously succeed. These are needed to help create public confidence that Haitian agriculture can change markedly for the better. Many of her needs are in directions in which progress will be barely perceptible for a considerable time; yet it is precisely within this period that active enthusiasm for agricultural development must be created both among farmers and among those with political influence and power.

Irrigation projects can help engender public confidence in agricultural development, but to do this they must be really successful in subsequent years rather than merely well-engineered structures. For this reason, SCIPA should not abandon its irrigation projects but should intensify two efforts with respect to those it is now operating:

(1) SCIPA should seek an arrangement whereby water users pay for their water and should assist in other ways in developing a pattern of irrigation administration that will make these projects self-supporting with respect to maintenance and operation.

(2) SCIPA should intensify its effort to find a pattern of total community development adapted to the needs of the people served by these irrigation systems. Such a program can utilize many of the techniques of a conventional United States extension program but probably will have to be much broader than the needs of agriculture and family-living alone. While continuing with the irrigation projects it has under way, SCIPA should not start additional ones until it has made substantial progress toward irrigation administration and community development.[11]

Meanwhile, what of its other activities? Although far more difficult, and with results slow and hard to measure, an effective program through which to educate and otherwise aid rural people to greater production and to higher levels of living is of prime importance. Conventional United States patterns of extension are inadequate, but other patterns exist, and still better ones may be evolved through imaginative innovation. While harder to achieve, real progress in this direction would be truly "germinal" and might demonstrate a method that could spread across Haiti as a domestic program, meanwhile training Haitians in the operation of such a program.

This argues for a shift of major emphasis by SCIPA away from irrigation toward other phases of agricultural development. Such a shift is already apparent in the nature of recent appointments to SCIPA's staff. In late 1954 a community development officer was added to the staff of the country director. About the same time, a new *servicio* for rural education was established. Although so far not co-ordinated with the program of SCIPA, the existence of this new *servicio*, as well as of the much older *servicio* in health, provides some of the technical understanding out of which a broader, more effective program might be fashioned. In 1954 SCIPA was considering further concentration of its activities in fewer localities. The trend to fewer project localities is sound, in view of the resources available. This, however, should not be understood to validate small areas of work, lest the fate of Fonds Parisien (and of the UNESCO project at Marbial) befall future projects. With the high pressure of population on the land, substantial progress cannot be made in any small project "island" in Haiti, any more than it can result from one program emphasis (like extension) functioning as an island in a sea of inadequate public services and of other pressing needs. Haiti's present condition calls for a broad rural program embracing agriculture, health, and community organization over a contiguous area wide enough that rural people can feel that something widespread and significant is happening. Even such a program cannot go far without legislative actions which straighten out land titles, maintain irrigation installations, and lay the groundwork for full-time secure careers for Haitians in domestic public programs serving rural people and the needs of agriculture.

Obviously, this is a bigger, wider need than can be met through programs of technical co-operation alone. Haiti would be well advised to ask for technical co-operation, with one agency or another, in the field of public administration. She needs so many changes in public policy that it might be wise to secure counsel on public policy from more advanced agricultural countries. Meanwhile, within such a broad attack by Haiti on her rural programs, SCIPA would be wise to co-operate with all other agencies in developing a broad community development program, utilizing some of the techniques now being developed by the government of India.

4. Without much more adequate research, agriculture cannot advance very far. Even now, after ten years of United States participation, an extension program in Haiti has very little to "extend." Whatever the reasons, and there is much disagreement about them, IIAA has not succeeded in getting agricultural research well-established in Haiti. Haiti's problems are complex, and her need for agricultural research is great. Haiti needs a good, permanent agricultural experiment station, in which adequate attention is paid to research in agricultural economics and rural sociology as well as to the biological growth of crops and livestock. SCIPA should urge on the Haitian government the need for such a station, preferably in the Ministry of Agriculture, and should offer the co-operation of its technicians in getting the station established and its program under way. The pattern of SAI in Bolivia might well be followed, with United States technicians playing the dual role of research workers (along with Haitians) in the experiment station and of subject-matter specialists (along with Haitians) in the rural development program.

5. SCIPA has been weakened by lack of continuity of leadership, of United States technicians, and of policy. In the ten years 1944–54, the Food Production Program and SCIPA had five chiefs of field party. The longest any one man held the post was thirty-nine months. The average length of service of the seventeen United States technicians in the Food Production Program between 1944 and 1948 was fourteen months. Only three technicians were in Haiti longer than seventeen months. In recent years the record has been somewhat better, but only two technicians in January, 1955, had been with SCIPA in Haiti longer than two years. No foreigner can

make a substantial contribution under such circumstances in a country where problems are as difficult as they are in Haiti.

The way technical co-operation is organized and administered in Washington chiefly causes this discontinuity, and the harmful effects that lack of personnel stability impose on any country are aggravated in Haiti by the complexity of the problem. The inappropriateness of the agricultural projects as organized has been another reason for the lack of continuity. Technicians tended to be baffled by the problems they faced, and consequently many of them became discouraged and asked to be transferred.

But the fact that the severity of problems in Haiti has increased personnel turnover does not change the other fact that personnel turnover, both of administrators and of technicians, has greatly weakened the program of SCIPA.

6. Progress is bound to be slow, but the need to stimulate agricultural development in Haiti is imperative. There is no quick way to raise agricultural production and the level of rural living in Haiti. Haiti has more different obstacles to agricultural development than any other country visited during this study. Some of these obstacles can only be removed by the Haitian people themselves; in the case of a number of others, technical co-operation can help considerably.

While results will be slow, one of the greatest needs at the present time is for widespread Haitian enthusiasm for agricultural development. This will have to infuse both farmers and those with political power if the necessary steps are to be taken. A new breadth of rural program is called for. Only a program concentrated in one or two regions can reach the pitch necessary to transform attitudes; yet these one or two regions of concentration must be big enough that they are not swamped by problems outside the project area and big enough that the people in them feel they are part of a national movement rather than selected guinea pigs.

6 THE OFFICE OF SPECIAL STUDIES IN MEXICO

The Office of Special Studies of the Department of Agriculture of the federal government of Mexico is a co-operative enterprise of the Mexican government and the Rockefeller Foundation. There are three features of this program that warrant its inclusion among the case studies:

1. It is a very successful program of a type not encountered elsewhere.

2. It embodies personnel policies that contrast markedly to those of the United States bilateral programs.

3. It has succeeded in a country where United States bilateral attempts at technical co-operation in agriculture had not (at least until the advent of university contracts) been successfully established.

Background

Second in size and population (26,000,000) only to Brazil, the uniqueness of Mexico is in her institutions and spirit; it is not in the land. Physically, Mexico is similar to the Andean countries of South America, although it is larger and more varied in terrain. The mountains are not as high the Andes, but they are rugged. There are tropical coastal lowlands, but most of the people live on the central plateau, at elevations of 5,000 to 8,000 feet, where the climate is mild and rainfall moderate and limited to a single season. Fortunately, Mexico has considerable gently rolling land in the north which, though semiarid, can be irrigated. Culturally, Mexico has a Spanish and Indian history similar to that of the Andean countries, but a real revolution produced a national unity of which Mexicans are justifiably proud.[1] Before the Spanish came, Mexico was the center of a high Aztec civilization. Spanish colonization brought the same pattern as in Peru: large haciendas on which Indians toiled as serfs, some mines worked by the Indians for Spanish masters, authoritarian government closely allied with the Catholic church, and education—usually in Europe—only for the Spanish elite.

THE REVOLUTION.—But revolt against this pattern came early in Mexico, finally terminating in the revolution that erupted violently between 1910 and 1917, continued quite actively through the 1930's, and persists today. The political party in power continuously for two decades is the "revolutionary" party. True, the revolution has cooled off to a point at which Mexicans can begin to look critically at some of its products, notably the *ejido* system of land tenure, but the revolution nevertheless continues.

This revolution—against dictatorship, the clergy, the large estates, and for the Indian and widespread economic and social opportunity —has permeated most of Mexican life. It has achieved results sufficiently substantial to engender a strong self-reliance and national pride in governmental officials, in professional and business people, and in some farmers.

Because this revolution has affected all phases of Mexican life, and because agricultural development is determined by factors throughout the culture of a country, the revolution obviously affects agriculture in many ways. These need not be spelled out here, but the three aspects most directly affecting agriculture may be briefly described. They are land reform, agricultural banks, and public investment in roads and irrigation facilities.

The *Ejido* System: When, as a part of the revolution, Mexico sought to break up the many large haciendas, it chose as the new land-tenure system an adaptation of the precolonial *ejidos*. The ancient *ejidos* were lands belonging to a village and held in common. The *ejido* pattern as it is being re-established breaks up the former large haciendas into small holdings to which cultivators have heritable rights of tillage but no right of sale or mortgage. The tillage right can be forfeited by failure to utilize the holding for two successive years. In many *ejido* villages each cultivator manages his own holding individually; in many others a "production committee" is responsible for collective management of cultivation, assignment of tasks to *ejidetarios*, and division of the harvests. The size of each holding varies from place to place and with the character of the land, different limits being set for cultivable irrigated land, cultivable unirrigated land, and pasture land. There have been considerable misuses of the system, as well as considerable favorable effects of the system in widening social and political consciousness and participation in the national life of Mexico.

It is chiefly on the score of its effects on agricultural production that the *ejido* movement is being subjected to increasing criticism. In the attempt to give some land to as many *ejidetarios* as possible, the amount assigned to each person, particularly in the early years of the distribution, was too small to provide full employment and a "decent" income to farm families. Collective management has been an easy mark for abuse and misuse, but at the same time production seems to have held up, or even to have increased, better on collectively managed *ejidos* because fewer managers have to be educated in improved practices. On the individually managed *ejidos*, the area of each is too small for the introduction of mechanized cultivation. Finally, the qualified right of possession does not lead to the most thorough utilization of many holdings but restricts mobility of *ejidetarios*, inhibiting the movement of some of them into urban industrial employment.

Recently, a movement has developed to give title in fee simple in place of the qualified inalienable right to cultivate and to increase the size of each grant of land. A consequence is that today, while much of the cultivated area is still in *ejidos*, the number of "small proprietors" is increasing; and, partially due to illegal manipulations of *ejido* principles, there is an increasing number of commercial farms varying from twenty to five hundred acres each.

Apart from what it has done for the *ejidetarios*, there have been two important incidental effects of the land reform. One is the fact that the breaking-up of the large estates and the reduction of inherited wealth have caused people to value land on the basis of productivity. Landownership is no longer an uncontested basis of social prestige; nor is it highly valued as a "safe" investment, especially in view of the persisting possibility of further land distribution. The same attitude now pertains with respect to investments in land as with respect to other investments in anticipation of an economic return. The second incidental effect is that the sons of privileged families, who formerly could have lived on inherited wealth, now must find remunerative employment. They are consequently preparing themselves for careers as engineers, research scientists, trained agriculturalists, business managers, and government technicians. This gives the country a valuable new supply of competent, trained, and ambitious younger men.

The Agricultural Banks: Since the revolution, two agricultural banks have been established to serve the small farmer. Both banks have suffered loan defaults, and both have been reorganized frequently. A great deal of what was meant to be production credit has been used by borrowers as consumption credit.

The Bank of *Ejido* Credit was established in recognition of the fact that the possession of *ejido* rights in land would be of little value to hundreds of thousands of small farmers without adequate credit facilities. The bank, set up in 1925 with an initial capital of 200,000 gold pesos, suffered high defaults from the beginning. An article on agricultural credit in the *Review of the Economic Situation in Mexico* for February, 1953, reports that "ten years after its [reorganization in 1936] 50% of the portfolio of the Banco Nacional de Credito Ejidal was composed of loans long overdue." Moreover, while theoretically the loans it makes are for production credit, in practice a high percentage of them is used as consumption credit to tide families over until the harvest. One 1953 estimate by a bank official is that 50 per cent of the loan proceeds are used in this manner. This bank employs a number of agronomists whose primary duty is to recommend and recover loans, but they are encouraged to give general extension education as time permits.

The Agricultural Bank, also established in 1925, is a separate institution, designed particularly to serve small farmers who are not *ejidetarios* but own or rent their land. It is not as large as the other bank, and some observers believe that the percentage of its loans actually used as consumption credit runs perhaps to 80 per cent. Its record of loan recoveries is no better than that of the other bank, and it, also, has been frequently reorganized.

Roads and Irrigation: The third major governmental activity affecting agriculture is the program of investment in roads and in irrigation facilities, a program to which millions of pesos have been devoted since the end of World War II.

Until 1947, highways were constructed chiefly to connect the more important cities with Mexico City. Since 1947, the emphasis has been on the construction of feeder roads, with the federal government, the state governments, and "local citizens" all sharing the expense, each paying one-third. The federal government's share is paid from receipts from a 20 per cent tax on the sale of automobiles and trucks assembled in Mexico. By 1952, the annual expenditures of the National Committee of Rural Roads had reached 58,068,000 pesos, and 1,466 kilometers of roads had been completed under this co-operative arrangement since 1947.

Mexico has invested large sums in irrigation projects throughout recent years. The annual investment in irrigation projects reached 50,000,000 pesos in 1941, and increased annually to 450,000,000 pesos in 1952. The Ministry of Water Resources worked on 78 different projects in 1952, each of which will irrigate more than 1,000 hectares; during the year 8 of these were initiated, 42 were continued, and 28 were completed. With only a few of these current projects in the northeast and extreme south, most of them are concentrated along the Pacific coast and across the central plateau on a line slightly north of Mexico City. One figure of the total area commanded by irrigation facilities provided through this ministry up to and including 1952 is 1,567,221 hectares, or nearly 4,000,000 acres.

Although most irrigation projects are administered within the Ministry of Water Resources, Mexico also sets up special autonomous commissions for the administration of large projects. There are three such commissions operating now.

The Papaloapan Commission is responsible for a large, multipurpose project on the coastal plain south of Vera Cruz. Over 150,000 hectares will be irrigated from the Presidente Alemán Dam, the largest in a system of dams. This commission operates two agricultural experimental farms on two soil types typical of different parts of the region to be irrigated.

The Tepalcatepec Commission, headed by General Cárdenas, popular former president of Mexico, is a similarly autonomous, government-financed corporation responsible for developing the lands which can be irrigated from the Tepalcatepec River in west-central Mexico, chiefly in the southwestern corner of the state of Michoacán. This region of hundreds of dead volcanic cones rising above a level-to-gently-rolling plateau extends into mountain valleys above the plateau. The mountain valleys are the homes of Indians still fairly isolated from the mainstream of Mexican life, though Apatzingam, the chief town of the region, was the site of the signing by Morelos of the first Mexican constitution renouncing the Spanish connection. There is scattered cultivation on the plateau floor now, with spots of highly productive orchards and gardens, and this cultivated area will be greatly extended when irrigation being established now by the Tepalcatepec Commission is available. The presently cultivated lands are mostly in collective *ejidos*, and out on the plateau ten miles east of Apatzingam is the site of proposed construction of a model *"ejido* city."

The Lerma Commission is the autonomous irrigation-development corporation planning and executing irrigation schemes to utilize the waters of the Lerma River in, and to the northwest of, the Toluca Valley of the state of Mexico.

In addition to the previously mentioned programs, Mexico has a number of other public programs affecting agriculture in many ways. Rural elementary schools are by no means universal, but they are widespread, and the number is increasing rapidly. The Cultural Mission movement, an attempt at community education to bring Indians more into the stream of national life, is continuing, though without adequate support at the present time. Bienestar Social Rural is a rural social service program administered by the Ministry of Health. It had fourteen centers in 1953 and planned to add twenty more in 1954. The National School of Agriculture, at Chapingo, near Mexico City, is an old, fairly good college of agriculture. Four new colleges of agriculture have been started in the north of Mexico in recent years.

AGRICULTURAL DEVELOPMENT IN MEXICO.—As measured by national statistics of land in cultivation, labor employed in agriculture, selected capital instruments employed, and agricultural production, there has been very rapid development of Mexican agriculture in recent years. This is important in itself, but the factors responsible for it and the regional location of that development are more important.

This recent rapid development of Mexican agriculture has been analyzed by Clarence A. Moore in an unpublished paper, "Agricultural Development in Mexico."[2]

One of Moore's tables (reproduced as Table 10) shows that between the periods 1925–29 and 1945–49 agricultural output increased by 60 per cent. During this time the area of land under cultivation increased by 23 per cent, the inputs of selected capital equipment and supplies rose by 372 per cent, and the input of labor rose by 16 per cent. There are obvious qualifications to be applied to these calculations, such as the fact that changes in the quality of labor, if any, are ignored. Moore mentions the necessary qualifications in his paper. After all qualifications are made, however, it is obvious not only that production has increased remarkably but

TABLE 10

INDICES OF OUTPUTS AND INPUTS IN MEXICAN AGRICULTURAL
INDUSTRY BY FIVE-YEAR PERIODS

PERIODS	AGRICULTURAL OUTPUT		LAND INPUT		CAPITAL, EQUIPMENT, AND SUPPLIES	LABOR INPUT
	Index I	Index II	Index I	Index II		
	Per Cent					
1925–29.....	100.0	100.0	100.0	100.0	100.0	100.0
1930–34.....	94.8	91.3	96.1	98.2	53.7	103.3
1935–39.....	105.4	99.3	96.6	98.4	80.8	107.1
1940–44.....	132.7	127.9	113.6	114.1	139.7	110.1
1945–49.....	160.8	159.5	123.2	122.9	471.6	116.3

that there has been a greatly increased use of capital and that the relative contributions of land and labor have declined.

Another interesting table in Moore's paper summarizes the trend in the proportions in which the factors of production were combined in agriculture, over this same period. It shows the same trend toward the greater use of capital in agriculture (see Table 11).

Within this rapid agricultural development in Mexico in the past twenty years, it is important to note which crops and which parts of Mexico have been affected and which have not. The new lands brought into cultivation have been chiefly in the north and northwest, utilizing both new irrigation facilities and dry-land farming techniques. The greatest increase in a single crop has been in cotton, of which Mexico exported about 1,000,000 bales in 1953. Modern, productive farms are the exception on the central plateau, where most of the older agricultural population lives, and Mexico's major food crops of corn, beans, and potatoes underwent very little change before the program of the Office of Special Studies got under way in 1943. Much of agricultural Mexico is still relatively isolated in mountain valleys and plateau basins in central and southwestern Mexico where the old Indian culture persists to a considerable degree. Thus vast sections of Mexican agriculture are primitive and need and lack the same type of assistance and stimulation as the mountain areas of the Andean countries of South America.

There is still considerable possibility of bringing new lands into cultivation and of extending irrigation facilites but probably not to

TABLE 11

MEXICAN PERCENTAGE INDICES OF CHANGE IN THE
RATIO IN WHICH FACTORS ARE COMBINED

Years	Labor	Land	Capital
1925–29	100.0	100.0	100.0
1930–34	122.5	113.9	63.6
1935–39	112.9	101.9	85.2
1940–44	90.9	93.8	115.3
1945–49	49.0	52.0	199.0

the same extent as during the past thirty years. Mexico is a dry country where well over half of the nation has less than twenty inches of rainfall per year. The central plateau around Mexico City gets thirty to forty inches of rain annually, but all of it falls in about five months. There is considerable scope for many relatively small irrigation projects in the transitional slopes between the plateau and the coastal plains but little hope for substantial additional irrigation, except from wells, on the plateau itself.

The Office of Special Studies

In this Mexico of rapid change the Office of Special Studies (OEE)[3] was organized in 1943—a Mexico of rapid change in the cities and in the agriculture of the north and northwest. Although government interest in agricultural development was strong enough to bring about construction of numerous irrigation works, the land reform and the agricultural banks to go with them were more a part of a social revolution than of a narrowly economic program. It is also worth noting that substantial agricultural development has taken place without an extension service, without good agricultural research, and without high-quality agricultural education. Undoubtedly, a considerable amount of the development in the north and northwest was nourished by research results from north of the Rio Grande. Still, what has happened in Mexico is eloquent testimony to the contributions of private initiative and private business in contributing to agricultural progress. Farmers reaching out for new ideas and merchants seeking to increase sales of machinery, fertilizers, and insecticides played a large role in Mexico's rapid agricultural development.

What must be remembered is that Mexico's production of major food crops did not expand in the twenty years of rapid advance in the north, and the agriculture of the central plateau and of the mountain valleys did not greatly change.

In 1943 the Rockefeller Foundation joined with the Ministry of Agriculture in a program of agricultural research. This program has continued, it has grown from year to year, and it has no terminal date although it is based on a contact which must be renewed periodically. Its success encouraged the foundation to begin a similar program in Colombia in 1950, and the foundation is considering repeating the pattern in other countries.

It is particularly important that the reader realize the nature of this report on the OEE, which rather than discussing OEE's research methods sketches the program in broad outline with particular respect to three selected questions: (1) Is such a concentrated research program a *type* of program that might wisely be attempted elsewhere? (2) Are there elements in the personnel policy and other operating practices of the OEE which might well be copied? (3) Is there a connection between the success of this program and characteristics of Mexico? It is for this reason that we give only an outline of the program itself but dwell at greater length on selected characteristics of it.

OBJECTIVES.—The OEE program has two objectives. The first is "to raise the level of national food production." The second is "the training of Mexican agricultural scientists."[4] As will be evident from the following discussion, these are not separate programs. It is chiefly by the employment of young Mexicans (who are already graduates of agricultural colleges) in the actual research program devoted to raising the level of national food production that the second objective of the program is achieved.

ORGANIZATION.—The organization of the OEE is the same as that of the co-operative *servicios* set up in other countries to administer programs of technical co-operation except that in this case the foreign co-operating agency is a private foundation rather than a governmental organization. The director is an employee of the Rockefeller Foundation, and he is administratively responsible to the Mexican secretary of agriculture. OEE is not bound by the normal administrative procedures of Mexican governmental agencies but is free to determine its own procedures and its own employment and salary policies. Appropriations are made by the government and by the foundation. In general the government contributes the cost of buildings, land, and certain services.

PROGRAM CHARACTERISTICS.—It should be noted that the first step taken, even before entering into an agreement with the government of Mexico, was for the foundation to send three highly qualified agricultural scientists to Mexico to make a survey of possibilities. Two features of this survey are important. First, it was conducted by outstanding men. The members of the survey group were: Dr. E. C. Stakman, chief of the Division of Plant Pathology, University of Minnesota; Dr. Paul C. Mangelsdorf, director of the Botanical Museum, Harvard University; and Dr. Richard Bradfield, head of the Department of Agronomy, Cornell University. Second, it was a thorough survey. The members of the group spent over two months in Mexico. They traveled over 5,000 miles, visiting more than half of Mexico's twenty-eight states, observing agricultural methods and talking with agricultural scientists, government officials, and farmers. It was on the report of these three men that the program was based. Dr. J. G. Harrar, head of the Department of Plant Pathology at Washington State College, was appointed field director.

1. The central program of OEE is a highly integrated research program devoted to increasing the production of Mexico's chief food crops: corn, wheat, and beans.[5] From time to time OEE has been urged to give attention to non-food export crops—chiefly cotton—but these proposals have been successfully resisted; the organiza-

tion has chosen to stay within its self-imposed limits, believing that a concentrated approach would be more productive.

How highly integrated this program is can be seen from the organization and physical layout of the central research station at Chapingo, twenty miles from Mexico City and adjacent to the National School of Agriculture. The United States staff of OEE consists of first-class specialists in plant breeding, plant pathology, soils, and entomology. Their laboratories and workrooms are side by side around a central patio in which much of the seed treatment and preparation is carried on. By keeping the field of operation very limited (corn, wheat, and beans), by restricting activities to research and experimentation (leaving seed multiplication and extension to others), and by emphasizing field experimental work under the direct supervision of the top scientists of the staff, the day-by-day interplay between geneticists, pathologists, entomologists, and soils scientists is much greater than in research programs with more diversified projects. Moreover, the use of trainees to do personally most of the field operations such as planting and hand pollination serves both to make their training really practical and to give the top scientists a corps of assistants who understand the scientific nature of what is being done. They are therefore less subject to the unintentional mistakes that unskilled laborers are likely to make.

Corn: To date, the major emphasis of the program has been on the improvement of corn, which occupies slightly over one-half of all the cropland of Mexico. Corn is grown in all parts of Mexico, under widely varying conditions of soil, topography, climate, and altitude; therefore, no single variety can be adequate. To facilitate the development of improved varieties suitable for the many sets of conditions, OEE operates, or co-operates with, many experimental farms throughout Mexico, including its own two substations, one in the state of Morelos and one at La Piedad in the state of Guanajuato.

The first step in the corn program was to collect more than 1,000 samples of open-pollinated corn from all parts of the country. These were compared in field tests at a number of different centers with respect to yield, disease resistance, and time of maturity. Without waiting for further research, the best of these open-pollinated varieties were released for multiplication and distribution.

Simultaneously, work was begun on producing synthetic varieties and double-cross hybrids. A measure of the rapidity with which new varieties were released for general use is the report that by 1949, six years after the program had been launched, four open-pollinated varieties, eight synthetic varieties, and sixteen double-cross hybrids had been released.

One result of the systematic collection of many varieties was the creation of a "corn bank," maintained under conditions of temperature and humidity control, at the central station at Chapingo. The "bank" is constantly being enlarged by seed samples from all parts of Central and South America and provides an invaluable reservoir of foundation stock for future use by corn breeders throughout the world. It co-operates with similar "corn banks" elsewhere in Latin America, and with that of the Bureau of Plant Industry of the United States Department of Agriculture.

This development of new varieties of corn has not been the product of the work of geneticists working alone. Disease resistance has been as much of a factor in selection as has yield; the soils specialists have been working on the soils requirements of the new varieties, and entomologists have been developing or adapting methods of insect control.

Wheat: The major efforts of OEE with respect to wheat have been devoted to reducing the heavy losses resulting from fungus diseases. Because these diseases have been so destructive during the summer season, which is the season of rainfall and high humidity, wheat was grown during the cooler winter, when rainfall is unlikely and reasonable crops can be secured only by irrigation. Within the fist six years of operation, twelve new varieties of wheat were developed by OEE. These varieties can be grown either summer or winter. They are resistant to the major rusts and satisfactory in other ways.

Beans: The work with beans, the second most important food crop of Mexico, has been chiefly a matter of the testing and selecting of varieties for yield and for resistance to disease. Control measures for insect pests have also received considerable attention.

Other crops: Although corn, wheat, and beans have received the major attention, increasing attention has been given in recent years to potatoes and to vegetable crops. Potatoes are a staple in the diet of many Mexicans, particularly in the more isolated rural sections and among the working classes in the cities. Disease control and especially insect control have been demonstrated to be highly profitable.

The growing emphasis of OEE on the improvement of vegetables grows out of the initial commitment of the program to pay attention not only to the quantity but also to the quality of Mexico's food crops. Frequent criticisms have been leveled at the general emphasis in Mexico (not only by the OEE) on the production of cereals, at the expense of the food values to be found in greater amounts in fruits and vegetables. Improvement of these latter crops, plus popularization of them through extension, could appreciably improve the diet of the people of rural Mexico.

Soils studies: While it has been going forward with the improvement of the major food crops, OEE has also undertaken spot soil surveys to get general data about the soils of Mexico. These, supplemented by extensive trials of green manuring and measurement of the response of the selected crops to chemical fertilizers, round out the integrated approach when added to the work being done in breeding, plant pathology, and insect and weed control.

Nutritional assays: An example of the co-operation of OEE with Mexican governmental agencies is the arrangement with the Nutrition Bureau of the Department of Health and Welfare. Being interested in the nutritional quality of the varieties it is developing, OEE forwards samples to the Nutrition Bureau for analysis. These analyses are then considered along with OEE's own research results in deciding which varieties are to be released.

2. Although the highly integrated nature of the OEE research program, restricted to a few major food crops, has been emphasized in the previous section, separate mention should be made of the policy of *rapid release of research results.* In other Latin-American countries, research projects of technical co-operation have undertaken long-term projects of crop improvement out of which nothing of immediate usefulness has come year after year. Without minimizing the importance of long-term basic research, it is necessary to recognize the value of research pertinent to immediate problems, with rapid release of results as soon as some improvement is obvious, especially in programs of technical co-operation. One of the

purposes of such programs is to establish in the public mind the value of research, and this can be achieved only as sound results are released and publicized.

3. An integral part of the program is an apprentice type of trainee program. Each year OEE admits from thirty-five to fifty graduates of agricultural colleges to its trainee program. Of these, twenty to thirty are graduates of the five agricultural colleges of Mexico, and about fifteen are graduates of agricultural colleges of other Latin-American countries. The training given to all of these men is the same, but the length of time they stay in the program differs for the Mexican and non-Mexican trainees. All trainees work as apprentices in the research program, spending five days of each week working in the field plots and in the laboratories. Saturday of each week is devoted to seminars, lectures, and library study. This results in a very practical training in the actual techniques of experimental research.

The Mexican trainees are appointed for one year. Those who do satisfactory work during the first year are kept on for a second year. Some of the best trainees are granted scholarships after the second year for advanced academic study in the United States, and some are kept in the program in Mexico for longer periods.[6] The remainder of the Mexican trainees are aided in finding employment at the end of the second year.

The non-Mexican trainees are appointed for a period of fifteen months. At the end of that time, a few are granted scholarships for advanced academic study, and the remainder return for employment to their home countries.

Conversations with former trainees impress one with the success of this training program. When asked what he thinks are the reasons for the success of the trainee program, the present director replied:

(1) We try to select trainees who will work with their hands. These are not always the ones with the highest academic grades, although the best trainees are those who have done well academically *and* are willing to work with their hands. Some men without high intelligence but willing to work become good men, provided someone checks their work and their results.

(2) We impress on them that there is no way to reach the objectives of agricultural research except to start at the bottom. If that is done,

whether or not a man reaches his objective will depend on: (*a*) the accuracy of his knowledge, (*b*) his application to the job, and (*c*) his interpretation of results.

(3) We give them confidence. They learn that they can get results if they follow the rules and work. They develop confidence because they acquire a background on which they can rely.

(4) We give trainees responsibility, then we point out their mistakes pretty hard. Usually where they fall down is in giving a job to someone else to do. We have to impress on them that they must know exactly what is going on.

4. An important part of the program is the infusion of trained men into other government programs serving agriculture. This is made possible (1) by the eagerness of other agencies to get men whom OEE has trained, (2) by a rapid turnover of trainees, and (3) by keeping in touch with trained men and helping them into worthwhile jobs.

While a few of those trained are kept on the staff, most of them must find other employment. The office likes to see them placed in related programs like those of the Corn Commission, the General Bureau of Agriculture, the Plan Agrícola Mexicana, and the Institute of Agricultural Investigation. In a sense, trained men going from OEE into these other agencies continue to think of it as a sort of home and look to it for professional support in their careers. All official connection has ended, but the influence continues through personal friendship and through professional contacts.

5. Although integrated research and the training of agricultural scientists are the whole program of OEE, a related program has been undertaken by the Rockefeller Foundation: Co-operation in the Rural Extension Program of the state of Mexico. In 1952 the governor of the state of Mexico asked the foundation to collaborate in a general rural-development program. This program includes the establishment of an experimental farm, a reorganized bureau of agriculture, an active extension service operating in seven zones of the state, and one or more agricultural schools. It should be noted here that this rural-development program of the state of Mexico is much broader than just extension of the results of OEE research. Rather, it brings together and co-ordinates all efforts of the state of Mexico at rural improvement, including the building of schools and roads, the extension of health services, and the application of

rural credit, as well as extension teaching of specific changes of agricultural practice.

The Rockefeller Foundation agreed to participate in this program, but administratively the program has no connection with OEE. Instead, the foundation agreed to co-operate by making a grant of $100,000 for the first three years of the program and by having members of the OEE staff act as informal technical consultants. The director of the program is a Mexican and a former member of the OEE staff.

This program of the state of Mexico is mentioned here because it is, in three senses, a projection of OEE: (1) It receives financial support from the Rockefeller Foundation. (2) It is staffed almost entirely by Mexicans who previously had been on the staff of OEE, either as trainees or as regular members on the staff. (3) It carries the foundation out of the research field into the field of extension from which OEE excludes itself.

6. The Rockefeller Foundation follows a distinctive personnel policy for United States technicians. The personnel policy of the Rockefeller Foundation is quite different from that of IIAA and from that of FAO, each of which must accommodate factors external to a particular program of technical co-operation in its personnel policy. These other organizations generally recruit men with considerable career experience, and they cannot promise employment for more than a short period of years. By contrast, the Rockefeller Foundation recruits young men who have recently finished advanced postgraduate training with outstanding success, and it limits its appointments to persons who are willing to contemplate lifetime careers in agricultural research outside the United States.

The first principle of this personnel policy is that no United States technician is appointed to the staff of OEE "who is not regarded as first-rate when judged by American standards." The foundation combs the postgraduate ranks of United States universities for the most promising young agricultural scientists, then seeks to interest some of them in foreign careers. Its salary policy seems to be to offer to such young men somewhat higher starting salaries than they would be likely to receive elsewhere, but with smaller increments which result in somewhat lower salaries ten years or more after appointment than persons of the same age would receive under IIAA or FAO. This is acceptable to foundation personnel because of the professional opportunities and assured tenure that they enjoy within the foundation's program.

Two corollaries of this policy which may appear to be incidental are really of great importance. One is that the foundation gives careful consideration to the attitude of the wife of each man whom it considers for appointment. This is important in any personnel policy, but is particularly important in cases in which the family must live outside its native culture. Many excellent men, devoted to their foreign assignments, have been reduced in effectiveness by the unhappiness of their wives, and many have resigned and returned to their homelands because of this. In practice, in addition to careful screening in the United States, the foundation sends each prospective appointee and his wife to the proposed foreign assignment for a visit of one month. This allows them to know what their life would be abroad, and it allows those already on the staff to assess the prospective newcomers. (The foundation does not appoint any person about whom anyone already on the staff has misgivings.)

The second corollary is that persons accepting appointment under the foundation with the intention of making foreign service a lifetime career know that is is worthwhile to learn the language of the country to which they are sent. This is a tremendous asset. By contrast, appointees of IIAA and of FAO often feel that since they have no assurance of being in a country more than one or two years it is not worthwhile to learn the language. They rationalize this decision in many ways with the result that IIAA and FAO projects continue under the constant disadvantage of many of their people not knowing the language of the country in which they work.

This personnel policy of the Rockefeller Foundation has resulted in a stable organization of high competence. Of the sixteen Americans appointed to the staff by 1953, only three had left the service of the program in Mexico, apart from those who were transferred to the Rockefeller Foundation project in Colombia.

7. OEE makes full provision of the subsidiary facilities necessary to high-quality work. The most important of these are well but modestly equipped laboratories, a good research library, and adequate transportation.

OEE maintains administrative offices in Mexico City, and all technical personnel live in the city. They go out daily (when not on tour) to the research station at Chapingo, where the laboratories and farm equipment are simple but adequate for all of the tasks undertaken.

The library of OEE is both important and unique. It is an excellent research library, one of the best in Latin America. It is very well organized and is kept up to date with the most useful tools of library research. It adds much to the efficiency of the work.

With experimental work in progress in many parts of Mexico, OEE must be in a position to transport its personnel quickly and frequently. This is achieved by maintaining an adequate motor pool, as well as by using public transportation for some of the longer trips.

8. Close collaboration with other Mexican agencies of agricultural development is another characteristic of this program. Soon after OEE began operations, it had selected strains of corn ready for multiplication and distribution. Rather than complicate the structure of the program, the president of Mexico set up a Corn Commission for this purpose. Although this is a separate government agency not administratively related to the OEE, the collaboration between the two is very close. The latter releases improved strains to the commission and in addition advises on certain technical functions.[7] Later a Wheat Commission was set up by the Department of Agriculture, and improved strains of wheat, as well as of certain other crops, were multiplied and distributed by this agency.[8]

9. The salary policy of OEE for Mexican technicians allowed a strong start without embarrassing other agencies in the long run. When OEE first began operations, it offered appreciably higher salaries to its trainees than were being offered elsewhere in Mexico to men of the same qualifications. It was criticized for doing this; others complained that the foundation was monopolizing the most promising young Mexican agriculturalists. By 1953, however, other Mexican government agencies had upgraded their salaries for graduates of agricultural colleges above the 1953 level of salaries within the OEE. However, OEE can still recruit competent young Mexicans, despite its lower salaries, because of the high value able young men place on having had experience there.

10. OEE maintains close liaison with research scientists in the

United States. The same three men who made the initial survey have continued as consultants and have made repeated visits to Mexico to advise on the program. In addition, the foundation occasionally calls in other specialists for help on particular problems. Over and above this, the foundation brings each United States technician back from Mexico for the annual meeting of the scientific society in his field. This helps in two ways: it keeps him up to date by contact with professional colleagues, and it gives the program the benefit of the suggestions of many outside specialists through criticism of the scientific papers which members of the foundation staff submit to the various societies each year.

cost.—The total amount spent by the Rockefeller Foundation on its Mexican Agricultural Program, through 1953, was about $2,600,-000. It is anticipated that appropriations to the program will now continue at the present level of about $300,000 per year.

critique.—There are two standpoints from which it seems wise to try to evaluate the program of OEE. (1) Is it succeeding in its stated objectives? (2) Is its field of interest of major significance in the economic development of Mexico?

To the first question, the answer is "Yes." From its published reports, from the widespread favor with which its improved varieties are received, and from its obviously well-organized and well-staffed research operations, it is clear that OEE is succeeding in its research activities. Likewise, one has only to meet, talk with, and observe the work of young Mexicans who have been trainees to know that the program does, in fact, "train Mexican agricultural scientists." The trainee program has sent to other agencies a number of young men convinced of the value of research and confident that the productivity of Mexican agriculture can be greatly increased. This extends the influence of the program far beyond its own projects. It has led several Mexican commentators to state that this training function is the most important contribution of the whole program. Several of them feel that this training function is a much greater achievement than the concrete results of the research program, substantial as those are.

To the second question, the answer again is "Yes," for two reasons. First, when OEE was established, there was very little topflight agricultural research in Mexico. By carrying on a high quality of

research through an obviously competent staff and by rapidly releasing substantially superior strains of crops and tested cultural
methods, OEE has built respect for agricultural science and has
demonstrated and taught the techniques involved in it. As one man
put it: "It was necessary to demonstrate that the methods of scientific research would return big dividends when applied to problems of Mexican agriculture." Certainly that has been done. Second,
it will be recalled that although Mexico had achieved a rapid rate
of agricultural development in recent years, this development had
been chiefly on the more recently cultivated lands of the north and
with non-food crops. Little advance had been achieved with food
grains or in the agriculture of the central plateau and the mountain
valleys. Although some extension of cultivated area and of irrigated
area is still possible, Mexico must give much more serious attention
to raising production on the long-established farms on the plateau
and to improving the basic food crops. This does not necessarily
mean that the rate of increase of agricultural production will slow
down in the near future. It has taken time to evolve the methods by
which production can be substantially increased on lands long cultivated, but competent observers believe Mexico is now ready, and
has the fertilizers and crop varieties available, for widespread improvement. That this is now true results largely from the work of
OEE. It stepped into a crucial spot at which agricultural development was badly needed but not taking place. It has worked with
precisely those crops on which the agriculture of the central plateau
and mountain valleys must depend and has evolved strains of crops
and cultural methods that make the development of those regions
possible.

OEE would be the first to recognize that many other efforts are
likewise necessary "to raise the level of national food production."
It has chosen to keep within the field of research and training. It
has left the multiplication and distribution of seeds to other agencies, and, with the exception of its co-operation in the program of
the state of Mexico, the Rockefeller Foundation has kept out of the
field of extension. Only since 1953 has it begun making appropriations to aid in the upgrading of agricultural education in Mexico.
It has done nothing about agricultural credit, transportation, land
use, or general farm-management problems. These are all press-

ing needs, but it is clear that the limited objectives chosen by the foundation are in a significant field, and it is probable that its considerable success has been to a considerable extent the result of its self-imposed limits of attention.

Transferability of Features

In view of the outstanding success of OEE, it is in order to consider the extent to which some of its features could profitably be adopted in other programs of technical co-operation. Before discussing conclusions with respect to transferability, however, it is necessary to mention briefly two additional sets of factors that have contributed to the success of the program in Mexico and might or might not be matched elsewhere. One of these sets of factors has to do with conditions in Mexico; the other flows from the fact that the agency of technical co-operation is a foundation rather than a governmental body.

CHARACTERISTICS OF MEXICO.—The country in which OEE has been operating is a very dynamic one, for Mexico prides itself on its continuing revolution. It is concerned about agricultural productivity and when the non-political OEE quietly produces from its research something promising popularity, the political ferment of Mexico becomes an asset.

1. Political leaders can create new agencies (like the Corn Commission) or new programs (like the State of Mexico Agricultural Program) to build a popular program on the research findings. Where individual politicians might merely wish to do this in other countries, the current ferment facilitates it in Mexico. New agencies are created frequently. Reorganizations are common. The climate of public opinion is congenial for new developments. Thus the pattern of OEE operations is well suited to a dynamic situation like that in Mexico, leaving the question open as to whether a similar program could be equally successful in a country like Ecuador.

2. Mexico is close to the United States. This has been an advantage in several ways. It makes it relatively inexpensive to send prospective appointees down for a month's visit before a final decision on appointment is made by either party. It makes it relatively easy to bring technicians back annually for scientific meetings. It makes

it easy to obtain quickly any supplies or small equipment which may be needed urgently in an emergency.

3. A factor not peculiar to Mexico but which may have been a significant factor in the speed with which substantial research results were obtained is the fact that the crops chosen for emphasis are ones prominent in United States agriculture. Corn and wheat, especially, are temperate-zone cereals on which a great deal of previous work had been done; the foundation is able to recruit United States technicians who not only are trained as geneticists, pathologists, etc., but have been trained to work particularly with corn and wheat within their specialized fields. That this coincidence may be of some importance is hinted at by the relatively more modest success of the program to date in working with beans.[9] This program gives no answer to the question of what might be expected when dealing with tropical crops.

DISTINCTIVE ADVANTAGES OF A FOUNDATION.—The other set of qualifying factors in the transferability of features of the program of OEE, particularly to government programs, is the distinctive operational advantages of foundations.

1. A foundation can make long-term commitments to a project. A foundation may make its commitment for any period of years it may wish (consistent with the desire of the host government) and can omit a terminal date entirely at its discretion. This is a prime advantage. The necessity for a governmental technical assistance program, either bilateral or international, to depend on annual appropriations with, at best, assurance of support for a limited term only is a serious disadvantage. The Rockefeller Foundation has committed itself to stay in this program for a considerable time, thus giving stability to the program, in matters both of budget and of staff morale.

2. A foundation is free from the pressures of the United States political process. This is an advantage in several ways.

For one thing, the programs of a foundation can be more easily varied from country to country; there is much less bureaucratic pressure at the top for uniformity and no political pressure to do something for one country because it was done for another.

Second, its discussions on policy are private, not public. Its programs are not subjected to inspections by visiting congressmen who return to the United States to make public statements attuned more to the prevailing opinions or prejudices of constituents than to the impact such statements make when reported back to host countries, as they always are. The discussions of policy are private, among expert technicians, and only the board of trustees of a foundation has to be convinced that a policy is sound. Evaluations of its program can be entrusted to permanent officers with occasional evaluations by experts hired by the foundation itself. These can guide the trustees without the publicity inevitably involved in public processes.

Third, it can frame personnel policies on the sole basis of appropriateness for programs of technical co-operation. These do not have to be reconciled with policies and practices of a whole government.

TRANSFERABLE FEATURES.—1. A comprehensive research program devoted to a very few selected crops appears to be a good starting point and a good basis of continuing operations for a program of technical co-operation. Within the continuing debate whether to start with research, or with extension, or with agricultural education, there appear to be two strong arguments in favor of research:

a) Any modern agricultural development program must be based on public acceptance of the validity of a scientific approach to agriculture. It is therefore important to demonstrate that research *produces.*

b) Research is less in the public political process of any country than are extension and education. A good research program may incur the jealousy of other research men, but it does not center on itself the public attention which local politicians want to have centered on themselves. If a program of technical co-operation goes direct to the public in extension, it may get public credit for its contributions; but if it does the research and leaves to local agencies the process of extension, public credit will go to the local agencies, thereby building political support even for the research program itself.

Being out of the political spotlight, a research program with an associated training function can continue for some years as a continuing source of additional trained technicians and as a congenial haven for the professional refreshment of trained men who have gone out into responsible posts in other agencies.

It should be clear that such a research program needs to be comprehensive and well integrated, bringing to bear competence in all specialized fields related to the problems it tackles (e.g., genetics, pathology, soils science, entomology). It need not, however, try to tackle a wide range of problems. Restriction of the program to a few strategic crops (or classes of livestock) may be wise not only from the standpoint of economy but because it leaves many other research problems available for entirely local research agencies.

2. Apprentice training should be a prominent feature of any such research program.

a) Essential to all agricultural development within a country is the creation of a group of well-trained agricultural scientists. A training program like that of OEE not only produces men to staff that project but provides for the country many young men confident of the value of agricultural science and competent in some of its methods. The experience in Mexico indicates that such men become good extension workers as well as good research men, and they have a background which is valuable if they become teachers.

b) Such a training program can be launched without conflict with the established agricultural education within a country. The period of apprenticeship may need to be longer if the agricultural schools and colleges are poor and shorter if they are excellent. In either case, this apprentice training in connection with a research program can be an effective supplement to the existing facilities for agricultural education within a country, pending their improvement.

3. Exploratory and evaluation missions by topflight United States agricultural scientists should be more widely used. This technique has been used with great effectiveness by the Rockefeller Foundation. There is no reason why it could not be employed to a greater extent by IIAA. Such missions should always include one or more men normally employed in similar activities within the United States. They might also well include full-time advisory specialists of IIAA to provide effective cross-fertilization and comparison between similar technical co-operation programs in different countries.

4. The policy of the Rockefeller Foundation with respect to United States personnel is an advisable pattern for other such programs. It is a common complaint with respect to IIAA projects that it is difficult to get good men for two-year appointments. The problem

is broader than that, but the difficulty is real. There are some excellent men among IIAA personnel. Some of them are fully as competent as Rockefeller Foundation men, but the average is lower. In most cases, the really competent IIAA men are among those who have been in the field for a number of years; seldom are they found among those who go for two years and are not reappointed.

The difficulties of recruiting brilliant young men into the service of the United States bilateral programs might be eased if such men had some hope of making the work a career. In addition to the need for a longer term for such appointments, other provisions should be made:

a) A more liberal salary policy for *young* men. At the present time, the salary regulations of IIAA with special allowances for overseas service are quite adequate for older men (and are, in fact, so liberal that too many mediocre men seek such appointments for salary reasons alone), but they are not scaled so as to attract outstanding young men.

b) Much more attention needs to be paid to family situations. A number of IIAA technicians have wives made unhappy by living abroad. Some such applicants could be eliminated by more careful screening, even if IIAA could not adopt the practice of sending couples to their prospective posts for a preliminary period as the foundation does. Those who are appointed could be helped by more intensive briefing of both husband and wife regarding the special problems of living in the country to which they are appointed.

c) A revision of judgment about desirable qualifications for technical co-operation posts is in order. Thus far, more importance has been given to age and to previous successful experience in the United States than to potential native ability. Granted that there must be leadership of maturity and experience in each project, it is not clear that all the positions should be filled by older men. The flexibility of youth and the desire of competent young men to build reputations of achievement are desirable characteristics.

Here it should be pointed out that the type of field program should influence the type of personnel employed. Young men can best be utilized in a tightly knit, co-ordinated program such as the combined research and training program of OEE. More maturity and experience are required in more loosely organized extension and advisory posts, but wherever possible, for such posts, experience in foreign assignments of technical co-operation is preferable to long experience in the United States.

5. Finally, the experience of OEE emphasizes the value of protecting technical co-operation programs from the American political process. This may be a vain hope. Perhaps only foundations and other private agencies can experience the advantages of appropriate handling at the American end. But this would seem to be a sad conclusion to be reached by a nation that has prided itself on ability to adjust to new situations and to find methods of operation appropriate to new tasks.

The prospect, while not bright, is not hopeless. There are United States government agencies, such as the Federal Reserve Board and TVA, that have special status within the American government, but neither is a close parallel to what is needed for the administration of technical assistance programs. Perhaps some sort of special government corporation or other agency with power to carry over such reserves from year to year that it can make reasonable term commitments would help.

In the absence of some such new device, the health of governmental technical assistance programs will continue to be influenced by the degree of wisdom and restraint in public statements of the less-perceptive individuals among public figures in American life.

Appropriateness of the OEE Program

The program of OEE constitutes a successful adjustment of technical co-operation within a rapidly developing economy. In a country like Mexico the task is not to get development started but to supplement domestic programs by programs of high competence in neglected fields. Whereas in certain other countries it is important to locate a *servicio* in a prominent position and publicize its work, in Mexico OEE has succeeded partly because it has not sought the limelight but has performed a valuable function without fanfare.

This does not mean that a program, to perform this service, would have to be in research. Perhaps, in view of the need for, and inadequate provision for, rural credit, a program of supervised credit would be a good choice for a program of technical co-operation in Mexico. Perhaps in another country a totally different program would be better. But it is clear that to fit into a rapidly developing country a program of technical co-operation: (1) must be staffed by technicians of high competence, (2) must tackle a limited problem comprehensively, and (3) must fill an obvious gap between domestic programs. These characteristics the OEE program possesses.

7 THE CO-OPERATIVE AGRICULTURAL COMMISSION IN CUBA

Cuba is an island 700 miles long from east to west and 35 to 75 miles wide from north to south, lying about 100 miles south of Florida. It shows the same effects of proximity to the United States that one sees in Mexico: many United States business firms, many branch outlets for United States goods, a modern commercial capital on the north coast, and considerable income from the tourist trade. But it differs from Mexico in two important respects: (1) it is neither arid nor mountainous, so there is a much higher agricultural potential when measured against the total size of the country; (2) it is much less crowded with people in its more productive sections. Cuba has few of the very small agricultural holdings (under 5 acres) that are widespread in many Latin-American countries; when one speaks of small farms in Cuba, one means farms of the order of 30 acres in size.

In placing Cuba among Latin-American countries on the basis of its attitude toward technical co-operation, Cuba probably should be classed with Brazil, Mexico, and Argentina as a country which feels it is advancing fairly rapidly and is not badly in need of technical co-operation. Latin-American countries tend to compare themselves with other Latin-American countries, and in such comparisons Cubans feel they rate well. They welcome technical co-operation but against the background of this self-assessment of their own position.

The economy of Cuba is closely tied to that of the United States. On the export side, the dominance of United States markets is less than it used to be; 78 per cent of Cuba's exports went to the United States in 1935–39, but this had dropped to 60 per cent by 1952. Agricultural commodities made up 90 per cent of the total value of

127

Cuban exports to the United States in 1952, the most important commodities[1] being:

Sugar	$316,600,000
Molasses and syrups	34,200,000
Tobacco	26,300,000
Grapefruit	3,000,000

As for Cuba's imports, most of them come from the United States, and the percentage has been increasing: it was 68 per cent in 1935–39, 75 per cent in 1952. Because its agriculture is concentrated on sugar, Cuba has to import 30 per cent of its food. The chief food imports of Cuba (from all sources) in 1952 were:

Rice	$46,600,000
Lard	21,052,000
Wheat and flour	17,488,000
Beans	10,199,000
Canned milk	7,906,000
Raw cotton	4,942,000
Olive oil	2,099,000

Almost all of the rice comes from the United States, as does all of the lard, most of the wheat flour, beans, and raw cotton. More than 90 per cent of the wheat comes from Canada and most of the olive oil from Spain. The canned milk comes about equally from the United States and from the Netherlands.

As for the importance of Cuba in the total agricultural foreign trade of the United States, 8.3 per cent of United States imports in 1952 came from Cuba, and 4.6 per cent of United States agricultural exports went to Cuba.

The Dominance of Sugar

The economy and the agricultural thinking of Cuba are dominated by sugar. Because sugar is a plantation crop, its cultivation lends itself to large-scale organization that makes considerable use of modern methods. The sugar companies operate experiment stations and have introduced mechanical cultivation and many other modern techniques.

The preoccupation with sugar, while developing a major trade and bringing millions of dollars to Cuba, has had two adverse effects on Cuban agriculture.

1. It has concentrated attention on sugar to the exclusion of active

concern for the thousands of small farmers and for the many diversified crops for which the soils and climate of the island are suited.

2. It has put Cuba in a peculiar position with respect to the United States. By act of Congress, Cuba receives a quota in the United States domestic sugar market, much like a state or territory. Because Cuban sugar costs less than that produced domestically, the general United States economy would benefit from a bigger sugar quota for Cuba, but domestic sugar producers constantly urge a lower quota for Cuba. The uncertainty from year to year as to what the next year's quota will be keeps Cuba hoping and distracts her attention from the need to improve the production of other crops. As several Cubans and North Americans put it: "Cuba cannot stop dreaming of sugar. A larger United States quota, and a higher price, are her dream for a better future."

Meanwhile, thousands of acres formerly in sugar have reverted to pasture (but are still held by plantations in the hope of higher sugar production quotas in the future), and thousands of Cuban farmers with about thirty acres each get almost no public attention, continuing to cultivate year after year by primitive methods.

Technical Co-operation

Two substantial programs of technical co-operation in the field of agriculture are operating in Cuba. One is Project 39 of the Organization of American States (see chap. x). The other is the Cooperative Agricultural Commission, jointly operated by the governments of Cuba and of the United States. This second program began as a wartime complementary crops program concerned almost exclusively with an attempt to establish the cultivation and processing of kenaf fiber as a substitute for the fibers of Southeast Asia which were either unavailable or expected to be during the war. Thus neither of the programs of technical co-operation touches sugar, the main crop (and the sugar producers are quite competent to help themselves).

Being a Caribbean regional enterprise, Project 39 is only partly designed to help Cuba; yet its extension emphasis is aimed at one of Cuba's main agricultural problems—the many small farmers largely ignored by the governmental services of Cuba. The Cuban Ministry of Agriculture and Project 39 co-operate in a demonstration extension project just outside Havana, and it is hoped that this may set a pattern for extension services in Cuba and in other Caribbean countries. The extension agents in this demonstration area are employees of the ministry; already, therefore, this is an unofficial activity of the government of Cuba, and action was being taken early in 1955 to make it an official bureau within the ministry.

Until 1954 the bilateral program of the governments of Cuba and the United States, the Cooperative Agricultural Commission, was concerned only with kenaf; in 1954 it was reorganized to deal with problems related to nine crops, with a tenth project to handle miscellaneous problems. In addition to these, it had in progress at the beginning of 1955 an exploratory consideration of extension. There are four characteristics of the programs of the Cooperative Agricultural Commission that deserve mention here:

1. The kenaf program was valid until 1945 as a wartime measure and was continued after that time as a concentrated effort which could be of great significance to Cuban agriculture or could be virtually a failure.

2. The reorganized program, since 1954, is mainly research, with the training of Cubans as a prominent feature but handled differently from the procedure in other countries.

3. The exploratory examination of Cuba's need for extension is a close parallel to the program of Project 39 of the OAS.

4. The suitability of considerable areas of Cuba for rice has raised the policy question of the propriety of a program of technical co-operation, in which the United States participates, setting out to increase production of a product now imported in quantity from the United States.

THE KENAF PROGRAM.—In its effort to develop a dependable supply of fiber to replace Asian supplies in the Western Hemisphere, the Kenaf Program has had to face three basic problems, the first of which was the agronomic problem of finding or developing high-yielding strains of kenaf which would make cultivation of the plant in Cuba worthwhile. This problem was met with promising success, and the cultivation of kenaf was begun on a commercial scale.

The second problem was control of the diseases that attack the plant. These diseases were not serious in the early years of the project, but an anthracnose disease hit the crop very hard in 1951, destroying that year's crop and virtually destroying Cuban enthusiasm for kenaf. This problem was immediately tackled after the heavy losses of 1951, and though it has proved to be an involved and difficult problem, some progress has been made in developing resistant strains. Meanwhile, other diseases have been observed, and research has been undertaken to control them. At the end of 1954 it looked as though diseases would not prevent the cultivation of kenaf in Cuba, but the control of disease will continue to be a problem making continuous research in plant pathology necessary.

The third problem is that of finding economical methods for processing the fiber. The commission has a chemical division working on the retting of fiber and an engineering division trying to develop a machine for cleaning and washing the fiber after it has been retted. Both processes involve substantial technical problems. The commission's publications on retting have brought inquiries and visitors from a number of foreign countries. It is reported that Australia and New Zealand have adopted and gone ahead with the mechanized chemical process of fiber treatment developed by the Cooperative Commission. The task of designing and building a mechanical cleaner and washer has moved more slowly, but there was hope early in 1955 that the test machine was about ready for commercial use. Several unsuccessful attempts were made to get industrial firms interested in research on this machine, but each firm took the position that the potential market for such machines, even if they were quite efficient, would not be large enough to justify the investment in research. It is for this reason that the Cooperative Commission has been forced to continue the engineering phase of the attempt to introduce kenaf to Cuba.

How is one to assess this kind of program? There is no question about the wartime wisdom of trying to develop dependable supplies of fiber. A question does arise about the continuation of the project after the war was over.

As nearly as one can reconstruct what happened from the record, the agronomic trials were very promising by the end of the war. It appeared that the introduction of kenaf could play an important role in diversifying Cuba's agriculture. The disease problem had not yet appeared, and the difficulty of solving the processing problem was underestimated. Under these circumstances the project was continued, and the hopes for kenaf production were widely publicized. A support price was set for kenaf by the Commodity Credit Corporation. Both Cuban and United States investors (and speculators) began to produce kenaf seed and fiber on a wide scale. Disease destroyed most of the crop in 1951, and processing arrangements were not ready for the part that survived. These developments discredited the whole program, which was already under attack by Cuban sugar interests, who are reported to have feared that successful Cuban production of kenaf would lead to a requirement that sugar be exported in bags.

At this point, IIAA was inclined to drop the whole project, but its own investigating commission, after a trip to Cuba and interviews with Cuban officials, recommended that the project be continued.

Meanwhile, the project began to have some success in developing disease-resistant strains, and progress was being made in methods of processing. In 1954, FOA considered closing the project, but it also, after field investigation, decided to continue.

Since the reorganization of the program in June, 1954, work on kenaf is being continued but on a reduced scale, and the Cooperative Commission has undertaken new projects related to bananas, beans, cacao, coconut, coffee, pastures and forage, and potatoes.

In assessing the program, it can be said that, when the complementary crops program came to the end of the war with a promising new crop which might help achieve Cuba's badly needed diversification, continuing the project was sound. As the project developed, problems multiplied and became more complex, but the possibility of a major contribution to the economy of Cuba remained. With large investments already made in the program, it seemed better to go ahead than to quit. The one point at which a substantial criticism can be made is that, while agronomic, chemical, and engineering studies were going forward, apparently no major economic study was made as to the conditions of world supply, prices, and costs of production under which the production of kenaf fiber would be profitable in Cuba.

The lessons of this program for the administration of programs of technical co-operation are two:

1. It is much more risky and involved to introduce new crops than it is to improve the production of crops already grown in a country.

This additional risk is intensified when not only a new crop but a new industrial process as well is involved.

2. It is better for a program of technical co-operation, particularly in the field of research, not to concentrate on one new crop only. All programs of technical co-operation must be experimental, and some experiments are bound to fail. If a program puts all its eggs in one basket, it risks serious trouble in case it drops that basket. This is not to conclude that the kenaf program in Cuba has been a failure. The program may yet succeed, and its success may be of such magnitude that it will be worth all it has cost. But there are many other opportunities to improve Cuban agriculture which the Cooperative Commission passed by, prior to 1954, in its concentration on kenaf. It continued in its initial course through increasing complexity and in the face of rising realization that it was engaged in a "long-shot" gamble. It is very doubtful that another program should take such chances when more certain avenues to agricultural development are open to it.

THE REORGANIZED PROGRAM.—A heavy emphasis on research, including the training of Cuban colleagues for it, marks the reorganized program. When the decision to diversify the program of the Cooperative Agricultural Commission was made, the diversification was brought about within a program which remains almost entirely research. This appears to have been a wise decision. Whether the kenaf program finally succeeds or not, the research within the program appears to have been well organized and well executed. The results of the experimental work have been fully recorded, and a number of publications summarizing the work have been issued. The research technicians on the staff appear to be competent men. (Five of the North Americans have had five to sixteen years of experience in Latin-American countries.) With a going research organization on the job, it seems sound to continue with a research program.

Research is a prime need in Cuba. Until now nearly all of the agricultural research in Cuba has been on sugar: it is badly needed for other crops, for livestock, for soils, and for agricultural economics and rural sociology. Moreover, Cuba has a reasonably good agricultural college but no provision for postgraduate training. Employment in the public agricultural services is not popular among agricultural graduates. They prefer private employment, usually either by sugar companies or by implement or fertilizer firms. Those who would like to enter research are discouraged because the few governmental positions in this field are mostly administrative with little opportunity for field experimentation.

The Cooperative Agricultural Commission appointed nine Cuban agricultural graduates to its staff in 1952. These men were given training as assistant technicians in the program for one year. They were then sent to the United States on training grants, each for one year or more. On their return they were given more responsible positions in the research program. Two were lost to private employment (one is now in charge of a fiber-research program in the Philippine Islands). Two of the remaining seven have been loaned to the Agricultural and Industrial Development Bank of Cuba. The other five now have substantial research responsibility in the Cooperative Agricultural Commission, and four more Cuban technicians were appointed late in 1954.

The high priority given to this training function is attested both by Cubans and by North Americans in the Cooperative Commission. One Cuban government official, speaking of the older work on kenaf only, said:

We learned a great deal about the design and conduct of agricultural research. We have good young Cuban graduates who can learn from qualified North Americans. Some Cubans have formerly had foreign training, but they cannot teach very many *and they have not had experience.* Now we are starting to work on coffee. North Americans are not trained in coffee, but they are plant physiologists, soils specialists, horticulturists, and are well-trained in experimental methods; we can learn much from them.

Cubans in the program now list "a year's experience in this organization after graduation from agricultural college" as one of Cuba's great needs in agricultural development. North Americans in the program look on the training and freeing of Cubans to work on agricultural research as one of their most productive functions.

Thus the Cooperative Agricultural Commission is giving Cubans valuable experience in agricultural research, not through a trainee program—as in Mexico—but by bringing Cubans into prominent positions in the work of the commission itself.

THE PARALLEL EXTENSION PROGRAM.—The exploratory examination of Cuba's need for extension work is a close parallel to the program of Project 39 of the OAS. The Cooperative Commission maintains that its appointment of an extension adviser in 1954 came as a response to a request from the Cuban Ministry of Agriculture. In any case, Project 39 was established in Cuba before this entry into the field of extension by the Cooperative Commission. The approach of the two agencies is different, and it is conceivable that the two working in co-operation could hasten the development of a Cuban program of extension. From one standpoint, the approach of Project 39 is already superior: it combines work by home demonstration agents with the work of agricultural extension agents. From another, work in extension by the commission would facilitate a close connection between research and extension. From a third, it appears that development of extension through Project 39 would result in earlier absorption into the ministry itself.

Project 39 was established in Cuba first, therefore it is the Co-operative Commission which must be charged with "overlapping" if that is a mistake at this stage. Cuba, at its stage of development, probably will not benefit as much from two such closely parallel programs as it would from programs in more distinct fields.

8 THE PROGRAM OF ACAR IN BRAZIL

Probably the most significant technical co-operation program in agriculture in Brazil is the ACAR Program,[1] jointly sponsored by the state of Minas Gerais and the American International Association.[2] Its popular name comes from the Brazilian name of the joint organization: Associação de Crédito e Assistencia Rural. It is organized as a civil society, with a board of directors of four members, of whom two are appointed by the governor of the state of Minas Gerais and two by the American International Association. At the end of 1953, ACAR was carrying on a program of supervised credit, general extension education, and rural health from twenty-two local offices in the state of Minas Gerais, and eleven additional local offices were to be opened in 1954.

The Agriculture of Minas Gerais

Minas Gerais is a large Brazilian state located just north of Rio de Janeiro. It has an area of 592,112 square kilometers, or 228,615 square miles. The population of the state was 7,839,797 in 1950, of which 70 per cent was rural. The population growth of 33 per cent in the previous 30 years was appreciably less than the average for all of Brazil (50 per cent in the 25 years 1925–50). This reflects the fact that, although it is now recovering somewhat, Minas Gerais has suffered serious reverses in recent years. The disastrous slump of coffee prices in 1929 hit the state hard, and mining, which had been a major industry for many years, has not been developing recently. There is a very decided movement from rural areas to the towns and cities, where small to medium-sized industries are developing. The very importance of mining, coupled with an almost total lack of coal in Brazil, has resulted in serious deforestation of the rolling, hilly terrain of the southern third of the state, leaving a serious land-management problem. This adverse effect of removal of the forests

136

has been relieved to a slight extent by the residual roads and railways which originally were built to haul wood to the mines.

From Belo Horizonte north and west, the hills recede and the rainfall decreases from 40 to perhaps 20 inches per year. Northward, cultivation decreases steadily, but there is a considerable cattle industry, with major centers at Curvelo and Montes Claros. In this northern part of Minas Gerais, cultivated fields are few and far between, but there are thousands of scattered subsistence farms, with farm families living very simply, with minimum facilities, but with the rugged independence and self-reliance of settlers in the "Old West" of the United States. (The western panhandle of the state is reputed to be fertile and prosperous. It was not visited in the course of this study, and ACAR has no operations there.)

From Belo Horizonte south, the topography is hilly to mountainous with a rainfall of 40 to 50 inches fairly well distributed through the seven warmer months of the year. There are four generally recognized regions from Belo southward. The area in which ACAR does not operate between Ponte Nova and Campo Belo is the mining area, with little agriculture. The extreme south of the state, where, also, ACAR does not operate, is fairly high (3,000–4,000 feet) pasture land, with very few trees, almost entirely in large cattle ranches. The southwestern region around Lavras and Varginha, where ACAR does operate, has many valleys in general cultivation. This, before 1929, was a prominent coffee section, and the signs of abandoned plantations can still be seen on many hillsides. The southeast, or *Zona de Mata* ("Region of the Woods") has considerable general valley cultivation, almost all in small farms, with tobacco as the important cash crop.

For the state as a whole, just over 5 per cent of the total area was in crops in 1950. The area in major crops was as indicated in Table 12. The major cash crops are coffee and sugar cane, cultivated mostly on one-crop plantations, but with small amounts of each cultivated on thousands of small farms. Thus maize, beans, and mandioca are the major crops on the many small-scale farms. These are supplemented by an amazing variety of semitropical fruits—bananas, citrus, papaya, etc.—and by rice in the wet valley lowlands.

One qualified informant classified the farmers of Minas Gerais into three groups:

1. A relatively small but substantial number of big farmers with business connections in industry or in commerce. These farmers get the lion's share of government help, particularly in the use of government-owned mechanized equipment, either through political connections or friendship with officials. They can get credit from local banks whenever they wish. They reach out for, and adopt, new methods of cultivation and of livestock management.

2. A larger number of owners of big cattle ranches who make substantial profits despite inefficient and traditional methods of

TABLE 12

CROP AREAS IN MINAS GERAIS, 1950

Crops	Hectares
Maize	1,000,656
Coffee	559,524
Beans	442,500
Sugar cane	140,077
Mandioca	80,071
Bananas	17,026
Other crops	692,518
Total	2,932,372

management but who do not utilize their profits for better family living or for any other purpose except the acquisition of additional land.

3. A very large number of operators of small farms (under 250 acres) with little access to credit or to improved practices, producing primarily for consumption but selling some of each year's production to meet needs for cash. (The program of ACAR was developed primarily to meet needs of this third group, but, increasingly, in its general extension education, it reaches out to the two groups of larger farmers as well.)

The increasing urbanization of Minas Gerais and the introduction of more and more industry are having two pronounced effects on agriculture. With the rise of urban markets, there is a tendency for farmers having highway access to the cities to increase dairying especially and poultry enterprises to a smaller extent. Rising wage rates for industrial labor draw more and more agricultural laborers into the city. This, without compensating increases in prices of farm products, pushes farmers in the direction of more extensive cultivation, away from intensive crops which the cities need, and toward cattle-farming, in which the labor demand is least.

This urbanization is most pronounced in the capital city, Belo Horizonte, a "planned city" only 57 years old which has doubled in size in 20 years to its population of 300,000 in 1950, but the same trend is found in the towns and smaller cities. Pedro Leopoldo, a town of 8,000, perhaps 50 years old, now has stone-paved streets, city water, electricity, garbage disposal, cement sidewalks, and a few small industries. Sete Lagaos, a small village 20 years ago, has had the advantage of income from crystal quartz for which the world demand has grown rapidly. About 400 new houses were built there last year alone. Although Sete Lagoas is fifty miles from Belo, dairying is increasing rapidly to supply the city markets.

Older inhabitants insist that methods of crop production, on the whole, have changed very little in Minas Gerais in the past 25 years. They mostly feel that crop yields have declined and that soil fertility is decreasing, in a manner which would be expected with severe deforestation and very little use of fertilizer. Meanwhile, however, new crops have come in to a limited extent. Coffee has been reestablished around Varginha, and production patterns have changed along some of the few good highways, under the impact of growing towns and cities. The two exceptions to this general feeling of agricultural stagnation are recognition of the increasing use of hybrid corn and of fertilizers on progressive farms growing coffee, sugar cane, and tobacco.

Government Agricultural Services in Minas Gerais

Both federal and state programs for agricultural development are active in Minas Gerais. Federal programs for the country as a whole are large when measured either by expenditures or by number of technicians employed. The budget of the federal Ministry of Agriculture for 1954 was about $39,000,000, and the number of persons employed in all public programs for agricultural development in Brazil has been estimated to be 35,000. Since for each technician in these services there are at least six subordinate employees, there probably are about 5,000 technicians. About half of these technicians are graduates of agricultural colleges; many others are *peritos,* or graduates of non-collegiate, "practical" schools of agriculture.

Despite the size of budgets and the number of employees, however, these public programs are of limited effectiveness. Low pay is one serious drawback. Most technicians—whether in research, teaching, or direct developmental activities—receive such low salaries that it is taken for granted that they will accept additional outside employment. Most professors in agricultural colleges are on a part-time basis, and it is common for even the so-called "full-time" professors to teach also in other schools; or to perform services for farmers, such as surveying and pruning, for a fee; or to run private shops selling agricultural or other supplies. Research workers have private laboratories on the side, or teach in private schools, or have other non-agricultural employment.

An example of how little time must be devoted to official duties is found in the activities of one agronomist in a state office in Minas Gerais. In addition to his state position, he teaches twelve hours per week in a nearby college, he is sales representative for a seed and fertilizer firm, and he does a bit of surveying, on hire, for farmers. Inevitably under such circumstances there is the risk that governmental duties will take second place.

Another serious problem, reported by those working in agricultural development programs, is that the programs are not well co-ordinated. There are several agricultural development agencies at the federal and state levels of government, and federal agencies work independently of state agencies in all the states, including Minas Gerais.

FEDERAL PROGRAMS IN MINAS GERAIS.—The largest federal agricultural program in Minas Gerais, budget-wise, is the series of 29 *Postos Agropecuarios* which it operates in the state, with a total budget of about $175,000 per year. Their chief service is the multiplication of improved seed and seedlings. In 1952, the last year for which a report is available, these *Postos* (there were then 24, averaging 15 hectares) produced "227,708 kilograms of improved seed and 110,722 seedlings," according to the official report of the Ministry of Agriculture.

The second oft-mentioned service of the *Postos* to farmers is the provision, on hire, of mechanized equipment. For this service the farmer pays only for gas, oil, and driver's wage, the overhead being borne by the ministry. In 1952 the ministry reported that it had 104 tractors in Minas Gerais. In the country as a whole, with 575 tractors, fees were collected for only 25,582 hours of work for farmers, or only 44.5 hours per tractor per year (compare this to the 600-hour normal in the United States and the 2,000-hour average of the machinery pools of SCIPA in Peru). The total number of hectares on which operations were performed was reported as 10,518, or 101 hectares per tractor for the year.

The federal government conducts two research stations in Minas Gerais, one of which was visited during the present study. It is a small coffee station with only one technician, who is an excellently trained and experienced man experimenting mostly with fertilizers and shading.

STATE PROGRAMS.—The state of Minas Gerais apparently does not give high priority to agricultural development. Only 0.5 per cent of the state budget goes to agriculture, and agriculture must share the attention of one minister with three other sectors of the state's economy.

State agricultural programs are three: (1) the research program of the Instituto Agronomia at Belo Horizonte, with several sub-stations elsewhere in the state; (2) a teaching program, through the Universidade Rural; (3) the "development program" of the Secretaria de Agricultura.

Minas Gerais' competent teaching program rests in its Universidade Rural, with a school of veterinary medicine and animal husbandry at Belo Horizonte and a college of agriculture and home economics at Viçosa. The latter, developed under United States leadership for most of the time since its founding in 1913, is one of the best such colleges in Brazil and is the only college in Brazil teaching home economics. It graduated 20 students in 1952 and maintained a faculty of 37 members; an independent survey reported 119 students in 1953. A regular service at this college is a "Farmers Week," during which short courses are provided for visiting farmers—with 2,700 reported in attendance in 1953. A second agricultural college of good standing in Minas Gerais is the Escola Superior de Agricultura de Lavras, which is operated by the Presbyterian church in the United States and which graduated 14 students in 1952. It had 18 faculty members and 55 students in 1953. The personnel of ACAR is drawn about equally from these two colleges.

The development activities of the state Division of Agriculture are carried on through twenty-four local offices. These offices are divided into three sections, with a man in charge of each:

1. The commercial section sells small tools, plows, insecticides, milk cans, etc., to farmers, but most of the articles it handles are also for sale in commercial shops in the same towns. About $400 worth of such supplies were sold in a month in each of two offices visited during the course of the study.

2. The veterinary section calls on farmers on request, mainly to vaccinate and inoculate livestock. In the first 26 days of May, 1954, the one veterinarian visited had vaccinated 420 animals on four trips out of his headquarters.

3. The agronomy section helps farmers to prune and spray trees, apply fertilizer, run terrace lines, etc.

None of these employees has a vehicle with which to visit farmers in carrying out his responsibilities.

Perhaps the most significant current activity of the government of Minas Gerais from the standpoint of agricultural development is its emphasis on road-building. Main highways are being improved between Belo Horizonte and Curvelo, Belo Horizonte and Rio, and Belo Horizonte and São Paulo. The construction of connecting and feeder roads is facilitated by the fact that one of the state banks lends money to municipalities (counties) for the purchase of road construction and maintenance equipment. Even so, the roads to individual farms are still poor.

ATTITUDES TOWARD AGRICULTURAL DEVELOPMENT.—Efficiently organized and administered, the resources which Brazil puts into agricultural agencies could be highly productive. But one finds a general feeling that the combination of low pay, part-time employment, and sprawling organization greatly impairs the efficiency of most agricultural development agencies. Another major deterrent is the general knowledge that other public policies indicate that the federal and state governments are not seriously committed to a policy of intensive agricultural development.

If this summary of domestic development programs seems critical, it should not obscure the fact that Brazil has many agricultural technicians who would like very much to help develop the agriculture of their country. These men have had good training, and many of them are doing competent work. At the same time, they justifiably feel that they are a part of inadequately administered programs. These programs, they say, seem to have grown up "because we ought to have agricultural development programs" or "because a respectable way to increase the number of posts available for political appointees is to create additional and larger agricultural programs." What Brazil needs, according to them, is a serious, integrated attempt at agricultural development, with high priority in political thinking.

The bias against agriculture in the Brazilian economy is reflected in price policies designed to encourage industry and to hold down the cost of living of urban workers rather than to stimulate agricultural development. It is reflected in the relative prestige of the various governmental agencies and ministries. It grows partly out of the differential returns to capital in industry and agriculture at the present stage of the general development of Brazil. There is a great boom in urban real estate, with reported returns to capital up to 75 per cent, and rapid expansion of many secondary industries, with returns of 15 to 50 per cent. These make capital extremely scarce for agriculture, where returns are smaller at current prices and costs.[3] Operators of big farms with personal connections in commerce or industry can borrow for agricultural production at local banks at from 12 to 24 per cent interest. Other farmers find it very difficult to get production credit at all.

It is a significant reflection of a point of view inimical to agricultural development that the name of the state in which ACAR operates is Minas Gerais, meaning "general mines." Though mining is much less important to the state as a whole than is agriculture, soil erosion has been accelerated and other complex problems of land management have been created by deforestation to fill fuel demands of the mines and industries. The mines dominated state politics for many years, and urban-industrial dominance in political affairs persists to the present.

Significant Features of ACAR

The program of ACAR began experimentally, its form and activities resulting from the conviction that, under conditions prevailing in Minas Gerais, a program of supervised credit, similar to that developed within the Farm Security Administration in the United States would lead to better farm living and to increased agricultural production. The North Americans who participated in the program in the beginning, both in Brazil and in the New York office of the AIA had all had experience in the Farm Security Administration. In addition, both the first field director of ACAR and his successor had had experience in the supervised credit program of IIAA in Paraguay.

The program of ACAR in Minas Gerais was in its sixth year at the time of this study. The original three-year contract was renewed for another three years in 1951. The program has encountered problems of adaptation which the Farm Security program did not have to face in the United States. It has engendered considerable enthusiasm in Brazil, as is attested by the number of requests that AIA help set up similar programs in other parts of Brazil. At the same time, it has been severely criticized by a number of observers, mainly North Americans, the chief criticisms being two: (1) that AIA could better have co-operated with the state of Minas Gerais in improving existing programs rather than having set up a new one, and (2) that the costs of the supervised credit program, particularly the overhead costs, have been excessive for the number of families reached effectively by the ACAR program.

Each of these criticisms is discussed later in this chapter. For now, it is sufficient to state that the ACAR program has a number of features and a record of experience which make it very significant in the history and operation of programs of technical co-operation in agriculture in Latin America. The features of the ACAR program which make it significant and worthy of detailed study may be listed here, summarizing and anticipating the findings of this study:

1. It is one of only two technical co-operation programs that have made substantial use of the technique of supervised credit in Latin America (the other being a co-operative program between the government of Paraguay and the IIAA).[4]

2. In comparison with other technical co-operation programs in agriculture, it has centered its attention much more directly on *farm family welfare*.

3. ACAR has proved the effectiveness of the supervised credit approach under appropriate circumstances. This is shown by: (*a*) the

increasing financial "net worth" of borrower families, (b) changed family health habits and dietary patterns, (c) increased diversification of production, (d) introduction of soil conservation practices, and (e) proof of the credit-worthiness of the class of farmers served by the program, when periodic technical advice accompanies loans.

4. ACAR has the most complete records, well-designed for use in evaluation, of any extension program encountered during the study. This superiority is in the family records of borrower families. Reports on its general extension activities are similar to those of other technical co-operation programs, but its record of total costs is much more complete even there.

5. ACAR introduced the home demonstration agent concept to Brazil and has proved the value of such a service under Brazilian conditions.

6. ACAR has concluded that there is a class of farmers in Minas Gerais too poor to be helped by the supervised credit approach and has ceased working with such families.

7. There is no indication that combining supervised credit and extension education in one program has had an adverse effect on either activity.

8. The experience of ACAR has revealed, or underlined, certain basic issues involved in the success or economy of programs of supervised credit: (a) Is there a dependable and adequate source of loan funds? (b) What is the geographic dispersion or concentration of family farms for which supervised credit is an appropriate approach? (c) How adequate is road access to these farms? (d) How significant are the supervised-credit type of family farms in the agriculture of the region? (e) Are research facilities adequate as a source of tested improved practices? The experience of ACAR has been made more valuable with respect to these issues by the fact that there are considerable differences among the four regions in which ACAR operates in Minas Gerais.

9. The past five years have not been a fair test of the cost of a supervised credit program in Minas Gerais because of the inadequate supply of loan funds.

10. The popularity of ACAR's approach, as measured by requests from other parts of the country for aid in launching similar pro-

grams, is a significant indication that ACAR has brought a ferment into a lagging agricultural development program.

11. The achievements of ACAR are sufficiently impressive fully to justify the amount of resources provided by the AIA and to justify continuing this support for at least another five years, at a somewhat higher level.

12. The emphasis of ACAR, from the very beginning, has been to train Brazilians to assume all posts of responsibility. At first, three North Americans were on the staff, and at no time have there been more than four. Of the total staff of ninety-four at the time this study was made, only three were not Brazilians.

Organization

The organization of ACAR is very simple. The director is responsible to a board of directors, which meets periodically to confer on the program and to make policy decisions. Within this context, the director has full responsibility.

The operating unit of the program is the local office. Eight of these were established in 1949; by 1952 the number had increased to twenty-two. Each of these local offices has three employees, an agricultural agent, a home demonstration agent, and an office secretary. They have one vehicle with which to make farm visits and to attend meetings. It is somewhat of an inconvenience for the agricultural agent and the home demonstration agent to have to use the same vehicle, but this necessity is helpful in requiring integration of their separate activities.

The area served by ACAR is organized into four regions. For each of these regions there is a regional office, in which there is a regional agricultural agent, a regional home demonstration agent, and an office secretary. The duties of these regional agents are supervisory, with a strong emphasis on training local agents. This training function is particularly important in view of the high turnover of ACAR personnel, which is discussed more fully below (see p. 167). At the end of 1953, each region included five (in one case, six) local offices. Four of the eleven additional offices being opened in 1954 in the present regions were established to make a better proportion of six local offices per region.

The central ACAR office in Belo Horizonte has, in addition to the director: three assistant directors for field administration; three technical advisers (an agriculturalist, a home demonstration specialist, and a credit technician); and four administrative staff members (a business manager, an accountant, a keeper of personnel files, and a supervisor of materials). These, together with eight clerical and subordinate employees in the central office, complete the ACAR staff, a total of ninety-four.

Finance

There are two phases of financing a program that includes supervised credit among its activities. One is financing the program itself, including the supervision of loans. The other is providing funds for loans.

In ACAR, the operating costs of the program are provided jointly by the government of Minas Gerais and the AIA. The first three-year contract, for the years 1949–51, provided that AIA would contribute $75,000 annually and that the government would contribute $25,000 the first year, $75,000 the second year, and $125,000 the third year. The renewal of the agreement for the next three years, 1952–54, provided that AIA would contribute $75,000 the first year, $60,000 the second year, and $45,000 the third year and that the government would contribute 4,000,000 cruzeiros the first year, 5,000,000 cruzeiros the second year, and 6,000,000 cruzeiros the third year.

The most important feature of these comparative contributions is the steadily increasing Brazilian contribution in conjunction with diminishing financial participation by the AIA. Actually, the increased Brazilian contribution is greater than that indicated, for, in 1953, the Secretaria de Agricultura began appropriating 3,060,000 cruzeiros per year for an expansion of the program into new areas. In effect, at the present time, the AIA provides three North American personnel, and the government of Minas Gerais bears virtually all other expenses of the program.

The other phase of financing ACAR's program is the provision of loan funds. Unlike the Farm Security Administration, ACAR has never had its own loan funds but has had to depend on the cooperation of an established Brazilian bank. This may be fortunate from the standpoint of launching a program which can be completely transferred to Brazilian support and administration. However, it means that ACAR really had a double task: (1) to establish a program involving supervised credit, and (2) to educate at least one Brazilian bank with considerable resources in the soundness of such loans and to work out, with the bank, satisfactory techniques of co-operation.

This second task has proved to be more difficult than the first. The bank with which ACAR first negotiated proved not to have sufficient confidence in the supervised credit approach. ACAR then turned to another bank which, skeptical at first, soon became convinced that the program was sound. This is a state bank, which previously had financed only municipal (county) loans. Co-operation between this bank and ACAR has continued to be good, but a second difficulty arose when the number of loans recommended by ACAR increased rapidly, and the resources of the bank proved inadequate, in view of other governmental responsibilities of the state bank.

This inadequacy of the loan funds available through the co-operating bank became a serious obstacle for ACAR, beginning in 1952. Farmers were increasingly eager to receive supervised credit, and ACAR was approving a greatly increased number of loan applications. When the bank was unable to grant the additional loans recommended, this reacted both on the size of the supervised credit program and on the confidence of farmers in ACAR.

The effects of this credit squeeze on the number and size of ACAR loans is depicted in Chart VI. The "optimum number of loans" in this chart is based on ACAR's experience that fifty loans constitute a reasonable case load for a local office which is also conducting general extension activities and a health program. The chart shows that ample loan funds were available in 1949, 1950, and 1951. In 1951, the number of borrower families (561) was just over an average of 50 loans for each of the 11 offices then open. By 1952, the number of offices had increased to 22; however, that was the year in which the bank began to refuse a large number of loans for lack of funds. One result was that the average size of loans dropped; with limited funds the bank granted small loans but not large ones.

In 1954, a new agreement authorized the granting of loans by the Bank of Brazil on applications approved by ACAR. This is in addition to the continuing relationship to the state bank. It is hoped that this arrangement will work out satisfactorily, thus removing the problem of the availability of adequate loan funds.

Activities of the Program

The four activities that make up the program of ACAR are: (1) supervised credit; (2) general farm and home extension education; (3) medical care and health education; and (4) distribution of materials.

It is the estimate of ACAR's administrators that 40 per cent of ACAR's attention is given to supervised credit, 40 per cent to gen-

CHART VI

Optimum Number of Loans

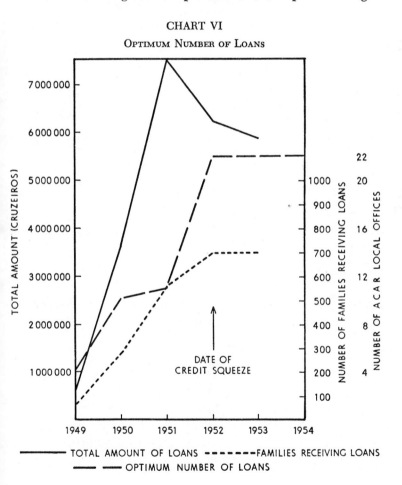

—— TOTAL AMOUNT OF LOANS   ======FAMILIES RECEIVING LOANS
—— —— OPTIMUM NUMBER OF LOANS

eral extension for non-borrowers, 10 per cent to the medical program, and 10 per cent to the distribution of materials. One way to check this distribution of emphasis among phases of the program is to review the records of local offices. This was done by the writer in six local offices, and two of those records are reproduced in Table 13. These findings appear to corroborate the ACAR estimate of comparative emphasis; however, the categories of the table are not parallel to the program breakdown given in the ACAR analysis.

TABLE 13

RECORD OF ACTIVITIES OF TWO LOCAL OFFICES
FEBRUARY–MAY, 1954

ACTIVITY	UBA OFFICE 2				SETE LAGOAS OFFICE			
	Feb.	Mar.	Apr.	May	Feb.	Mar.	Apr.	May
Visits to borrowers.......	13	25	20	24	17	25	21	36
Visits to non-borrowers...	15	16	24	32	27	29	44	21
Meetings by farm agent or home agent alone:								
No. meetings..........	9	18	15	28	22	4	11	36
Attendance............	139	191	184	444	226	47	34	269
Meetings by farm and home agents together:								
No. meetings..........	1	1	1	4	10	0	0	3
Attendance............	7	40	6	260	175	0	0	48
Medical meetings:								
No. meetings..........	1	1	3	1	4	4	5	4
Attendance............	51	72	175	50	534	549	473	819
Farmer visits to office....	31	27	40	50	30	30	36	55
Out-of-office visits*......	90	80	108	170	113	116	91	125

* Unscheduled program contacts outside of the office.

Supervision of credit apparently received even less than 40 per cent of the attention of these particular local agents during the four months represented by the table.

If this report were to describe each of these activities at a length proportionate to the amount of time given to each by the ACAR staff, the account of general extension activities would be about as long as that of supervised credit. That this is not the case results from two factors. First, there is little that is unique about the program of general extension; similar programs are being carried on in a number of countries in Latin America. Second, ACAR has more

complete records on borrower families, and this allows a more detailed analysis of the supervised credit program. The medical program is substantial but simple and quickly described. The distribution of materials is an important function, but it is subsidiary to the
other phases of the total program.

With respect to this combination of operations, a former officer
of the AIA made a comment that is worth quoting:

> The space given to supervised credit [in the first draft of this case study]
> is way out of proportion to that given extension education, medical activ-
> ities, and distribution of materials. The latter three are important, and
> they are also necessary supplementary enterprises to supervised credit.
> Without them, or something like them, supervised credit is too expensive
> per family served. If we are ever to get anything approaching adequate
> credit retailed to thousands of medium and little farmers in undeveloped
> areas, the distribution of the credit must be handled by an agency that is
> also distributing one or two other lines. I would never have gone through
> school (selling his products) if W. T. Raleigh had tried to sell only lini-
> ment to farmers with aching muscles. He had to load his wagons with all
> kinds of pills, spices, and extracts so that he could keep his cost of distribu-
> tion per unit within reasonable bounds. . . . On the recognition of this
> principle, and the designing of organizations to put it into effect, depends
> the whole future of transferring loanable funds out of the cities, which
> is where they accumulate, to thousands of scattered farmers, who can ef-
> fectively use at any one time just about as much credit as it costs to get a
> check to them and see that it is used properly. The distribution of loan
> funds can and should be done by an agency which distributes education,
> medical services, veterinary services and supplies, recreational services,
> etc. *To get one good organization serving rural people (ought to be) the
> goal for most of the underdeveloped countries.* Rich and bureaucratic
> U.S.A. has the wrong pattern for less affluent countries, because it splits
> up its services to farmers among several different organizations. ACAR
> has combined some—four—and in so doing has demonstrated something
> worthwhile.[5]

The comment is sound. ACAR has demonstrated that supervised
credit is a productive technique for agricultural development in
Brazil, but it must be combined with other techniques in a multi-
service rural program.

The Program in Operation, 1954

What was the program of ACAR in 1954? It will be described
here under the four headings mentioned in the foregoing section.

GENERAL EXTENSION EDUCATION.—At local offices both the agricultural agent and the home demonstration agent carry on ACAR's general extension education program. They operate chiefly through individual visits to farm families, but increasingly they have turned to serving groups of farmers in meetings. The sample record of activities of two local offices presented in Table 13 indicates the approximate number of general extension contacts per month in 1954. Whereas in the case of supervised credit an estimate of achievement can be made from the progress reports of individual farm families, in the case of the general extension program one has to rely on records of contacts, either in farm or office visits, and on records of attendance at meetings.

The range of improved practices recommended by the general extension program is broad but is limited by the availability of dependable research results. Recommended agricultural practices include the use of insecticides to control sauva ants (leaf-cutting ants common in Brazil) and insect pests of plants and livestock; the use of fertilizers, soil conservation practices, crop rotations, controlled use of irrigation water; and substitution of improved seeds—including hybrid corn—for unimproved varieties. Recommendations for better home practices include the improvement of the drinking-water supply; building of latrines; planting of home gardens; aids to health and hygiene; preparation of foods; child care; the making of furniture and mattresses; and sewing. Following field demonstrations, it is the practice of ACAR to lend equipment to one farmer after another so that they can try in their own fields the practices that they have seen demonstrated.

In recent years some attention has been given to the training of group leaders. However, though the general extension program has operated increasingly through group meetings, ACAR has not, so far, taken the initiative in organizing formal societies of farm men and farm women for rural improvement. In this respect it has fallen behind the general extension service of SAI (Servicio Agricola Interamericano of the government of Bolivia and the IIAA) in Bolivia and, to a lesser extent, of SCIPA in Peru. On the other hand, in program-planning and in supervision of field agents the general extension program of ACAR is at least as good as that in Bolivia, and it is better than that in Peru. Furthermore, ACAR has a larger staff of home agents and a stronger program for rural women.

A measure of the growth of the group emphasis in the extension program of ACAR is its report for its first four years of operation.

Year	Meetings	Attendance
1949	23	242
1950	458	14,447
1951	1,330	40,233
1952	2,959	70,434

SUPERVISION OF CREDIT.—As of June, 1954, ACAR was supervising 600 loans to as many farm families. This is considerably below the number it could be caring for if adequate loan funds had been available since 1952.

In the course of this study the writer visited eight of the twenty-two local offices of ACAR, studying the records of a sample of all borrower families and verifying these by visits to the farms and homes of one or two borrower families being supervised by each of the local agents. The families visited were chosen jointly by the writer and the local agent. The local agent was consulted in the selection partly to help choose representative families and partly to choose some to whom road access was relatively easy. That this latter consideration was not pushed very far is attested by the difficulties encountered in reaching several of the farms. Four of the farms visited are described briefly to give a more concrete understanding of the type of farmer with whom ACAR deals and the purposes for which loans are made.

Farm A: Francisco Luiz Lemos[6] lives with his wife and six of their ten children on a 97-acre farm in the rolling, cutover brushland north of Curvelo. Neighbors are scattered on farms carved out of the brush at spots where the soil is deep enough to give some promise. They are connected to the outside world by what in the United States would be considered an unimproved lane. This runs for about 10 miles before connecting with a country highway, and the closest railway station is 20 miles away.

Only 29 acres of the farm are cultivated, and they are planted to corn, beans, cotton, rice, and sugar cane. Normally, the family has about 20 pigs and 10 to 15 head of cattle. Of the pasture, about half is cultivable. The family lives in a frame house with a dirt floor, the house that Lemos built 18 years ago, lighted only by tiny, homemade tin lamps burning kerosene in a twisted cotton wick. Lemos is a competent carpenter. He not only built his house, but he also builds the oxcarts which are the family's only vehicles. He built a sugarcane press, with rollers and gears carved out of wood, powered by oxen. The pattern of farming is summarized by Lemos' statement: "We sell what is left over." In other words, production is primarily for consumption; there is no specific cash crop but they sell whatever pork, crude sugar, corn, or cotton the family does not need.

The family's net worth was calculated to be Cr. 118,000 in 1954, when it received an ACAR loan of Cr. 12,000. This loan was made in connection with a farm and home plan for the year providing for experimentation with hybrid seed corn, establishment of a home garden, vaccination of cattle against foot-and-mouth disease, culling the pigs, as well as for other activities indicated in the breakdown of the way the loan was to be used:

Purchase of two oxen	Cr.	5,000
Hired labor		2,700
Purchase of feed		500
Purchase of seed		500
Cultivation		1,000
Improvement of hog pasture		1,500
Construction of privy		500
Miscellaneous		300
Total	Cr.	12,000

Farm B: Anatolio Clarindo Leite, forty-two years old, and his wife and six children live on their 150-acre farm 20 miles from the town of Sete Lagoas. The terrain is very hilly and stony. To reach the farm, we had to ford several streams and push the jeep over boulders and up two stony hills.

Only 22 acres of the farm is cultivated. Two-thirds of this is in corn and nearly one-third in cotton. Beans are interplanted with half of the corn, and about an acre of rice is grown each year. The house is located in a small ravine surrounded by a small patch, perhaps an acre, of alluvial soil. It has a brick floor throughout and wooden windows. The cooking is done on a small open fire on a concrete table. A canal runs by the door, bringing water from a stream half a mile away. It irrigates the sugar cane and family garden and is used for drinking water and in cooking. There were two bicycles in the house when we visited the family.

The house and garden are at some distance from the fields and pastures. When asked why the house had not been built where the fields are, Leite and his wife replied, "That would be too far from our parents." Both had been born nearby and had always lived in the locality. They felt that their life had been about the same, with no changes in farm or home practices, until ACAR came.

The net worth of the family was calculated to be Cr. 72,000 in 1953, when their received an ACAR loan of Cr. 14,000. The loan was to be used for the following purposes:

Purchase of eight heifers .... Cr.	9,000
Hired labor	3,250
Purchase of feed	100
Purchase of seed	600
Purchase of chickens	50
Construction of privy	200
Construction of fences	800
Total .... Cr.	14,000

When asked how ACAR found him, since he lives in such an isolated spot, Leite replied that he had heard about ACAR from a town friend who had attended a meeting at which the program was explained. He walked the twenty miles to Sete Lagoas, found the ACAR office, and made arrangements for the agent to visit his farm. He met the agent at a town on the road four miles away and guided him from there to the farm.

Of the program, Leite said: "ACAR has helped me because I needed more cattle to use my pasture but did not have the money with which to buy them or with which to extend cultivation. With the help of ACAR, both through our loans and our planning, we have put in a filter for drinking water, we have all taken worm medicine, we have established this garden. Now we plan to plant some coffee and some oranges for home use. We are going to cultivate some of our pastures as soon as we finish clearing it of brush."

Farm C: Joaquim Nicodemus Matias is twenty-eight years old, his wife is twenty-six. They have a boy four years old and a girl six. They own 3 acres planted to coffee and 15 acres of pasture. In addition, they rent 15 acres, of which 10 acres are planted to corn and 2.5 acres each to beans and rice. The family has 2 cows, 1 heifer, 3 pigs, and 30 chickens. They live in an adobe house with rough board floors and a tile roof.

To reach the Matias farm from the town of Varginha in south-western Minas Gerais, one travels ten miles through lovely rolling hills, mostly in pasture. Although it is chiefly a dairy region of large farms, interspersed among them are a number of small farms and a few plantings of coffee. On the way to the farm, it is necessary to cross the Rio Verde in a rowboat and then walk about two miles.

The Matias family's net worth was Cr. 31,100 in 1954 when it received an ACAR loan of Cr. 7,000. The loan was to be used for:

Purchase of two heifers	Cr. 4,000
Repair of house	1,500
Building a corn crib	500
Building a pigpen	600
Constructing a privy	400
Total	Cr. 7,000

Along with this loan, the family was helped by the ACAR farm agent and home agent together to work out a family plan for the year, which included fertilizing coffee and other crops, the control of erosion, planting rice in the bottom land, and improving the farm garden.

This loan is smaller than the average, but the local ACAR agent feels that the family is fairly typical of borrower families in this region. He feels that it represents the kind of family with which ACAR should use supervised credit—the families with small farms scattered among the larger, more prosperous farms of the region. Because such farmers were suspicious at first, ACAR began by working with those on somewhat larger farms. Now families like this are becoming interested, but they require a great deal of super-vision in the beginning. For example, ACAR agents visited this farm seven times between January 1 and June 19, 1954.

Farm D: José Felipe Costa is a tobacco farmer living about 5 miles from the small city of Uba, in the southeastern region of Minas Gerais. His farm of 120 acres includes 30 acres of woods, 42 acres of pasture, and 48 acres of cultivated fields. He grows 35 acres of corn, 10 acres of tobacco, 2 acres of rice, and 1 acre of mandioca and has 5 cows, 2 pigs, and about 100 chickens. Thus, the family raises much of its own food in addition to the cash crop of tobacco.

Costa and his family have had three ACAR loans, one in each of the past three years. Costa is alert and progressive. He is using his ACAR loans well, and progress has been remarkable. Note the increase in net worth.

Year	Net Worth	Size of ACAR Loan
1951	Cr. 26,000	Cr. 30,000
1952	59,800	16,000
1953	74,300	27,000

During this period, Costa has built three houses: one for his family and two for laborers. The family has added a home garden, 4 papaya trees, and 8 citrus trees. Costa has built a tobacco drying shed and a tobacco store so that the family can now process its own tobacco instead of selling the leaf. This approximately doubles the sale value of the crop.

The 1954 loan is being used for:

Purchase of fertilizers	Cr. 12,000
Hired labor	6,750
Building a laborer's house	5,000
Building a tobacco store	3,000
Purchase of a water filter	250
Total	Cr. 27,000

Size of Farms: The area of land cultivated and in pasture varies widely among borrower families in the ACAR program, as indicated by the records, a sample of which is summarized in Table 14, studied in eight local offices. The table does not include figures on the total size of farms, since that would include brushland and woods for which there is no clear classification, and which in any case is of secondary importance. In very few cases do such lands provide current income, although they do, to varying degrees, provide some opportunity for extending cultivation.

Both the averages and the variations revealed by the table are significant. In cultivated areas, these 232 farms receiving ACAR loans vary from 0 (on a farm that is entirely pasture and woods) to 57 hectares, with the average being 12.7 hectares, or about 32 acres. In pasture area, these farms vary from 0 to 236 hectares, with the average being 38.4 hectares, or 96 acres.

Whether the variations among local offices are caused by differences in ACAR operations is not indicated by the data, but it is hard to see how they could result entirely from differences in the localities.

Rough observation in the field encouraged the conclusion that a supervised credit program could be more economically administered in the Uba region than in the Curvelo region. In Uba there are no large farms; thus the small farms are closer together than they are farther north. The higher percentages of cropland in Uba were anticipated, as was the uniformity among Pedro Leopoldo, Curvelo,

TABLE 14

SIZE OF FARM ENTERPRISE OF BORROWER FAMILIES

LOCAL OFFICE	NUMBER OF LOANS	CULTIVATED AREA (HECTARES)			PASTURE AREA (HECTARES)		
		Smallest	Largest	Average	Smallest	Largest	Average
Pedro Leopoldo..	33	1.0	25.0	9.5	0	162.3	33.0
Curvelo.........	50	4.5	34.0	17.7	16.8	170.7	70.8
Sete Lagoas.....	26	2.9	14.0	7.5	3.0	59.9	21.8
Lavras..........	17	6.0	22.0	11.6	9.0	31.6	26.0
Varginha........	31	0	17.0	5.9	7.0	236.0	65.7
Viçosa..........	14	8.3	36.0	22.2	0	18.6	7.7
Uba 1..........	42	5.0	57.0	15.3	2.0	52.0	22.1
Uba 2..........	19	6.0	20.0	11.6	1.0	26.0	11.2
Total.......	232	....	....	12.7	....	....	38.4

and Sete Lagoas. But the two extremes in Varginha and Viçosa were not, and these would require further investigation.

Financial Status: Another significant characteristic of borrower families in the ACAR program is their financial status. In general, one would expect these families to be in modest circumstances, since —patterned after the Farm Security Administration—the program's purpose was to serve farmers who could not get production credit through normal banking channels. At the same time, one would not expect to find loans currently being made to destitute families, in view of ACAR's statement that it had found that some farmers have too few resources to make progress, even with the help of supervised credit. Both of these expectations are borne out by the sample records examined in the local offices, as indicated by Table 15; but those farmers having "too few" resources to be considered by ACAR have very few resources! Translating these figures into United States dollar values reveals that the family with the lowest net worth among ACAR borrowers had assets of only $92 while that with the highest net worth had assets of $15,225. The average net worth of borrowers in each of the eight local offices visited varied from $1,233 to $4,080.

A more complete impression of the distribution of the financial status of borrower families may be gained from the classification of families according to net worth shown in Table 16. This is based on the sample of family records studied in local offices. For greater comprehension, the classes have been arranged to correspond to dollar equivalents at the June, 1954, free rate of exchange.

TABLE 15

FINANCIAL NET WORTH OF BORROWER FAMILIES, 1954

LOCAL OFFICE	NUMBER OF LOANS	FAMILY NET WORTH (CRUZEIROS)		
		Lowest	Highest	Average
Pedro Leopoldo..	33	5,500	542,900	134,952
Curvelo........	50	37,700	412,000	134,700
Sete Lagoas.....	26	18,500	141,000	73,962
Lavras.........	17	45,900	239,900	133,950
Varginha.......	31	19,300	913,500	224,885
Viçosa.........	14	37,500	267,500	172,498
Uba 1.........	42	12,600	598,500	244,770
Uba 2.........	19	76,750	248,000	146,131

TABLE 16

RANGE OF NET WORTH OF BORROWER FAMILIES, 1954

NET WORTH		PERCENTAGE OF TOTAL NUMBER OF FAMILIES
Cruzeiros	Dollars	
Under 30,000.........	Under 500	17.0
30,000– 59,999......	500– 999	14.8
60,000–119,999......	1,000– 1,999	18.2
120,000–179,999......	2,000– 2,999	20.5
180,000–239,999......	3,000– 3,999	10.2
240,000–299,999......	4,000– 4,999	5.7
300,000–600,000......	5,000–10,000	11.4
Over 600,000.........	Over 10,000	2.2
		100.0

Size of Supervised Loans: The one policy restriction on size of ACAR-recommended loans is that on the maximum amount. They must not exceed Cr. 50,000 (about $830 at the June, 1954, current exchange rate). A summary of the actual loan amounts of the sample families is given in Table 17.

Two facts emerge from this analysis. First, loan amounts are not determined by the maximum limit but actually are carefully decided on the basis of immediate need and productivity. Second, the amounts loaned are lower (on the average) for the more scattered subsistence farms of the north than for the more intensive farms in the southwest and southeast.

TABLE 17

SIZE OF ACAR LOANS, 1954

LOCAL OFFICE	SIZE OF LOAN		
	Smallest	Largest	Average
Pedro Leopoldo......	Cr. 2,000	Cr. 50,000	Cr. 15,703
Curvelo............	5,000	40,000	19,800
Sete Lagoas........	2,000	22,000	9,812
Lavras.............	10,000	50,000	24,217
Varginha...........	6,000	50,000	28,100
Viçosa.............	3,000	25,000	12,000
Uba 1.............	8,000	50,000	28,600
Uba 2.............	15,000	27,000	21,667

The size of ACAR loans can be measured further by the analysis in Table 18, in which 1954 loans are classified according to amount, for the sample offices that were visited.

Increase in Net Worth: Two measures of the increase in net worth of borrower families are presented here. One is the calculation made by ACAR on the basis of the first year of operation, 1949/50. This shows that the average net worth of 102 borrower families before receiving an ACAR loan was $4,423, whereas at the end of the year in which the family received a loan it was $5,374, an increase of 21.5 per cent.

The other measure is the series of four charts (VII to X) presented below, compiled from the records of the eighty-one borrower families, each of which has had at least three loans from ACAR.[7] Certain features of these charts deserve emphasis:

1. There is a general upward trend observable in all of them, indicating a rise in net worth for families securing several ACAR loans.

2. There is a marked difference among local offices in the resources of farm families for which ACAR recommends and supervises loans. The office in Pedro Leopoldo works with more poor families (at least it grants repeated loans to more poor families).

3. Although Uba is in the region where there are apparently more borrower families growing cash crops and easily accessible by road,

TABLE 18

FREQUENCY OF SIZES OF LOAN, BY LOCAL OFFICES
(IN NUMBER OF LOANS IN SAMPLE)

SIZE OF LOAN	OFFICE							
	Pedro Leo- poldo	Curvelo	Sete Lagoas	Viçosa	Lavras	Var- ginha	Uba 1 and 2	Total
Under 6,000 Cr.	7	1	3	1	0	0	0	12
6,000–11,999	13	3	2	2	2	2	3	27
12,000–17,999	4	1	1	0	0	2	2	10
18,000–23,999	3	2	2	1	1	1	3	13
24,000–29,999	1	0	0	1	1	0	4	7
30,000–35,999	0	1	0	0	1	1	2	5
36,000–41,999	2	2	0	0	0	1	0	5
42,000–47,999	0	0	0	0	0	1	0	1
48,000–50,000	3	0	0	0	1	2	2	8

Curvelo is the region where appreciable gains in net worth are more consistent (Curvelo is the region of lower general agricultural productivity, with isolated subsistence family farms).

4. The office at Pedro Leopoldo, which shows the most modest gains, is the one in which administrators of ACAR indicated (before these charts were compiled) that they have been least successful in getting and keeping good agents. The personnel turnover there has been very high.

In interpreting these charts, it should be kept in mind that only those borrower families that received repeated loans are represented. Not included are those that, after one loan, felt they could proceed with extension education only. There may be a tendency to give repeated loans to families that do not do too well at first, in an attempt to get them more satisfactorily under way.

MEDICAL ACTIVITIES.—Very early in the development of ACAR, a co-operative arrangement was made with the Health Department of the state of Minas Gerais. The Health Department had doctors and nurses who were supposed to care for rural people, but in many areas they were not in effective contact with the people needing service. On the other hand, ACAR had contact with increasing

CHART VII

CHANGES IN NET WORTH OF FAMILIES RECEIVING SEVERAL
ACAR LOANS: UBA No. 1

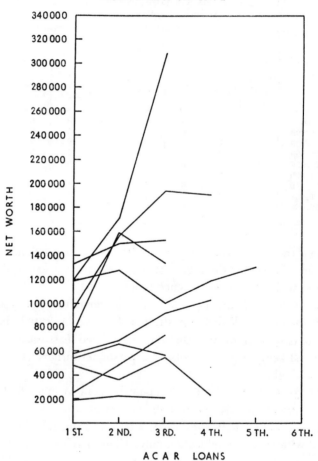

numbers of rural people but did not have medical personnel on its staff.

Under these circumstances, the Health Department agreed to set up a clinic in each of the towns near which ACAR was serving farm families and to provide the services of a doctor and nurse. Some of the clinics are open only at stated hours on stated days. On its part, ACAR agreed to provide transportation for the doctors and nurses whenever that was necessary, to urge farm families to use the

CHART VIII

CHANGES IN NET WORTH OF FAMILIES RECEIVING
SEVERAL ACAR LOANS: UBA No. 2

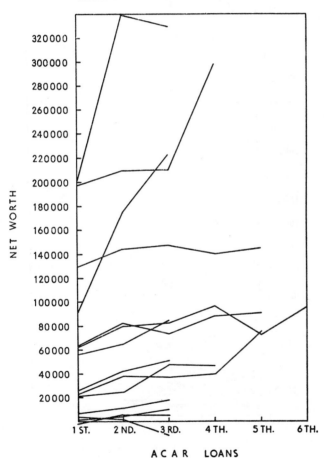

ACAR LOANS

clinics, and to organize rural meetings for health lectures and other public health education. Vaccinations, inoculations, dental treatments, and lectures are the major items in the program.

In the AIA report for 1949, the first year of the ACAR program, there appears the following paragraph on this phase of the program:

CHART IX

CHANGES IN NET WORTH OF FAMILIES RECEIVING SEVERAL
ACAR LOANS: PEDRO LEOPOLDO

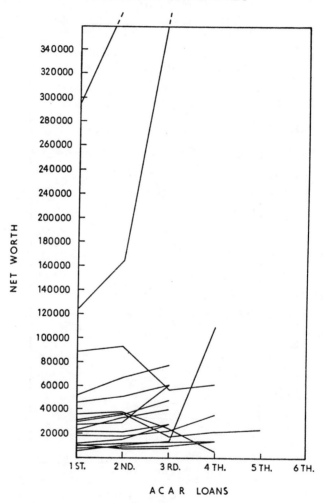

The State Department of Health of Minas Gerais set up clinics for examinations, immunizations, and sanitary engineering and privy building in every community where ACAR operates. ACAR furnished transportation and other facilities for a full-time doctor and nurse supplied by the States. 5,320 vaccinations were made, and 1,064 tests for intestinal parasites, with 1,312 people treated. In addition, the doctor conducted a sanitary campaign and distributed over 400 pieces of material and gave 113 lectures dealing with better hygiene, nutrition, and health.

CHART X

CHANGES IN NET WORTH OF FAMILIES RECEIVING SEVERAL
ACAR LOANS: OTHER OFFICES

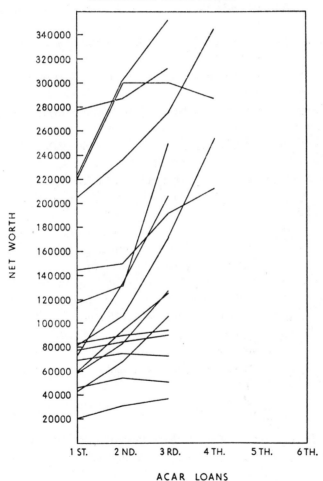

ACAR LOANS

In 1953, according to ACAR estimates, approximately 22,000 people received medical treatment through the program. This is both a substantial increase from the number reached in 1949 and an achievement of significant size. Improved health is a major need of rural Minas Gerais. Here is an excellent example of co-operation between two public programs, the resources of which are complementary. At little additional cost to either, a significant rural service has been achieved.

DISTRIBUTION OF MATERIALS.—A subsidiary but important part of the ACAR program is the distribution of materials. The agency provides materials to local agents who need them for demonstrations and to farmers, sometimes by sale, who desire them.

The normal way for ACAR to begin operations in a new area is for the local agent to conduct a series of demonstrations for farmers in the region—showing them how to kill leaf-cutting ants, deworm hogs, use insecticides on their crops, install a simple, low-cost, sanitary privy, or vaccinate cattle. Frequently these techniques have not been heard of or seen previously. Once demonstrated, some of the necessary materials—many of which are unavailable on a commercial basis in their area—are distributed free. Preliminary visits to farms are conducted in a similar fashion, with the home technician, for example, giving the housewife a free packet of seeds or a small sewing kit.

This distribution of materials is not confined to the introductory phase of the ACAR program but is a continuing part of the regular program. Demonstrations continue in such practices as soil conservation, the construction of trench silos, construction of home furniture, etc. In all of these, materials are used, distributed, or sometimes loaned. It has been one of ACAR's major aims, however, not to displace commercial sellers of these products but to stimulate the use of new products, formerly unavailable, and to provide a temporary source of supply until commercial sellers are able to meet local needs.

Major Problems

ACAR appeared, in 1954, to have three major problems: (1) an inadequate source of loan funds, (2) a high rate of personnel turnover, (3) uncertainty about the future interest of the AIA in the program.

The problem of inadequate funds has already been discussed. The administrators of ACAR hope that the new agreement with the Bank of Brazil will remove this difficulty. It is important to the confidence of farmers in ACAR that there be funds available to make the loans which ACAR agents recommend. The supervision of credit is a possible tool of agricultural extension only where credit is available.

ACAR loses up to 25 per cent of its agents after one year of service; the figure is somewhat higher for home agents, as many of them leave the service to marry. It is lower for farm agents, but many of them leave to become farmers or to accept higher paying employment. The situation could be relieved to some extent by higher salaries within ACAR, but the problem would remain.

The problem of personnel turnover faces all programs of agricultural development which have good in-service training, and so far in Latin America it is programs of technical co-operation alone that have such in-service training. From the standpoint of the general agricultural development of a country, this turnover of personnel is not a loss; instead, it constitutes a training function, putting out better-trained agricultural technicians into the country's agriculture. But it does constitute a problem for the specific program that trains them, and uneven turnover in different sections of a program impairs the comparability of records.

Uncertainty about the future interest of the AIA in the program bothers all of the Brazilians in ACAR, who know that AIA is putting less into the program each year. They are of the opinion that at the end of the present contract AIA will withdraw entirely, and this is a cause of considerable uneasiness.[8]

AIA has proposed that the present North American director of ACAR be succeeded by a Brazilian and that the composition of the governing board be altered to give Brazilians a majority of the members. Both moves are opposed by the governor of Minas Gerais and by the present Brazilian members of the board. The governor maintains that if a Brazilian is made the director, political pressure will be brought on him (the director) to alter the program, and that if a majority of the members of the board are Brazilians, they may change it. This is not a diplomatic tactic: it is a well-founded judgment. One of the unique contributions of programs of technical co-operation is the relative freedom of a foreign administrator from local pressures. This aid, in the case of ACAR appeared in 1954 to be about to be withdrawn by AIA, and that fact was adversely affecting morale within the program, despite the fact that the personnel of ACAR has been largely Brazilian from the outset. Two of the assistant directors are Brazilians. Both are competent men and handle practically all of the internal administration. But they have neither the prestige nor the personal position to stand up against political presure as it is essential that the director must.

A fourth problem, although not pressing at the moment, is appearing on the horizon. That is the limited adequacy of research into the agricultural problems of Minas Gerais. The ACAR technicians feel that the present recommendations of government research stations are adequate with respect to crop varieties and cultivation practices but that much more dependable information and research is needed on insecticides and disease control. As an extension service like this catches on, it quickly exhausts the contributions of prior research, and increased and improved research is needed if the extension program is to be soundly based. The Mexican Agricultural Program of the Rockefeller Foundation makes this its primary task. SCIPA in Peru, and SAI in Bolivia are in a position to undertake needed research, but ACAR is wholly dependent for research on other agencies.

Outgrowths of ACAR

It is significant that many Brazilians in official positions are so impressed by the achievements of ACAR that they have urged AIA to start similar programs elsewhere in Brazil. Two such outgrowths are already established. One is in Minas Gerais, where the secretary of agriculture has begun making additional appropriations of three million cruzeiros per year to finance eleven additional ACAR offices. Some of these are to be located in the present ACAR area; others are to be in a new section of the state.

The second outgrowth, called ANCAR, is a program patterned on ACAR but sponsored by the federal Bank of the Northeast to cover a large part of the dry northeastern section of Brazil. For this, the following appropriations have been provided:

Bank of the Northeast in 1954	Cr. 1,000,000
Bank of the Northeast in 1955	2,000,000
Bank of the Northeast in 1956	3,000,000
Bank of Brazil in 1954	2,000,000
Federal Ministry of Agriculture, each year	5,000,000
Federal Ministry of Education, each year	2,000,000

AIA has agreed to provide consultation by its North American personnel. Each of the first twenty-five local farm agents of ANCAR is receiving forty days of training by ACAR, part of which is on-the-job training with ACAR local agents. ACAR is also training home agents for the project.

Up to 1954, AIA had received several requests to open still other programs in Brazil. These requests came not from directors of agriculture but from governors and senators who were dissatisfied with their own agricultural services. In reply, AIA said, up to 1955, that it would consult about such new projects but could not contribute resident personnel or participate in administration.

Conclusions

To what conclusions does this study of the work of ACAR lead? What inferences may be drawn from the ACAR program with respect to the wider field of technical co-operation in Latin America? In attempting to answer these questions, it may be well to summarize what the program of ACAR has not done and what it has accomplished. Subsequently, an attempt will be made to judge the broader significance of features of the program.

WHAT ACAR HAS NOT DONE.—The whole NPA study of technical co-operation in Latin America supports the thesis that economic development in general, and agricultural development within it, cannot be achieved through any one program. Rather, it depends on a variety of factors, including many public programs. This study of ACAR underlines that fact, as can be demonstrated by several specific observations.

1. To date, ACAR has not modified the agricultural services provided by the government of Minas Gerais.

The example of ACAR has demonstrated the practicability of a number of improvements that the government of Minas Gerais could make. But the government of Minas Gerais has not introduced reforms into its own services incorporating the features of ACAR which are responsible for its success. Whereas ACAR has demonstrated that a Brazilian staff can be trained and equipped to conduct a creditable program fostering agricultural development, the government has not raised the inadequate salaries of its personnel. It has not provided vehicles for field agents. It has not introduced home agents into its services. It has not improved the quality of its supervision, nor has it introduced a program of in-service training. The example of ACAR, however, was probably a factor in two recent developments in the agricultural college at Viçosa. One of these is an increased emphasis on extension education. The other is the launching of a course in home economics.

Frequently, it has been argued that AIA, instead of setting up ACAR, should have worked with the Division of Agriculture of Minas Gerais to improve the state's existing agricultural services. The initial objective in establishing ACAR was to test the fruitfulness of an extension program utilizing supervised credit in Brazil. This would not have been possible within the Division of Agriculture because the same factors which result in limited efficiency of the existing activities of the division would have hampered a trial of such a new program. Also, supervised credit requires more facilities than present activities of the division provide, including workable co-operation with a bank with adequate loan funds, and at the outset these facilities could not have been commanded within the division.

In the same way that an extension service must demonstrate improved practices, not just talk about them, before farmers are convinced, so a new type of public program usually has to be demonstrated before a government can be persuaded to make such a project part of its regular program.

2. Nothing has been done by ACAR about the pressing need for improved agricultural research.

Both the state of Minas Gerais and the federal government of Brazil have research programs. Some of the work done by these is excellent; yet there are many serious gaps. There have been enough tested improved practices in the fields of varieties of seeds and of control of livestock diseases to give ACAR an adequate supply of recommendations. However, the supply is running low. The ACAR agents feel particularly the lack of adequate information about insecticides and fertilizers, and the need for more and better research will increase continuously as extension programs develop.

That ACAR has done nothing about research is not a criticism of it, for no one program can do everything. It is mentioned precisely to emphasize this latter fact. No matter how good any one program may be, its efficiency can be lowered quickly if other factors in agricultural development are not simultaneously strengthened.

3. After six years of operations ACAR still has not inculcated in Brazilian officials a full comprehension of (*a*) the range of necessities for efficient supervised credit and (*b*) the need to incorporate supervised credit as one technique among many in an efficient rural program.

It is one thing to demonstrate what can be achieved through supervised credit in a particular setting, and that has been done. It is another, equally important, to get across a full understanding of what is required in order to make such a program work and to see the technique of that program, however valuable in itself, in proper perspective. That this second step has not yet been completed is indicated by the fact that when Brazilian officials talk of undertaking a similar program elsewhere, they often seem to presume that supervised credit is the whole answer. They seem not to have caught the fact that ACAR's efficiency is in its broad program, of which supervised credit is only one instrument.

4. The ACAR program has not appreciably increased agricultural production in Brazil.

If ACAR were judged on the basis of annual statistics of total agricultural production—even in the municipalities (counties) in which the program has operated—the probability is that no effect could be discerned. This, again, is pointed out not in criticism but in the interest of an accurate understanding of what has been done and of how technical co-operation operates. The focus of ACAR's attention has not been on aggregate agricultural production but on farm family welfare.

There is considerable evidence that ACAR has had a substantial effect on the levels of living and on the agricultural resources of the families with which it has worked. This has involved increased production, but not yet on a scale to affect aggregate statistics appreciably. Whereas ACAR has demonstrated an effective process, that process would have to be extended and continued for a number of years to have a cumulative, widespread, and, eventually, a self-generating effect on Brazil's total agriculture.

WHAT ACAR HAS ACCOMPLISHED.—Some of ACAR's most significant effects are intangible. They have to do with changed attitudes toward agricultural development, not only those of the farm families with whom ACAR directly co-operates and of its employees, but also those of an ever-increasing number of other Brazilians who have observed the program and found it good. Changing attitudes and improved mutual understanding are found in all phases of the activities, as reflected by this summary of accomplishments.

1. The value of supervised credit in raising agricultural production and the level of farm living on Brazilian farms of a certain size and type has been demonstrated by ACAR, and supervised credit has been set in perspective within a broader program of extension education.

The question raised by ACAR when it was organized has been answered in the affirmative. Supervised credit is an effective tool of agricultural development under certain Brazilian conditions. In making its experiment, ACAR has learned much about the type of Brazilian farm and family that will respond to such a program.

Also, it has discovered that techniques other than supervised credit ought to be, and can be, used by the same rural program. It has learned that a program of general extension education can be as effective with farmers who do not need credit, or who can themselves command it, as supervised credit can be with another type of farm family. The increasing requests of many farmers for extension education is one proof of this; the confidence which the field agents have in general extension methods is additional evidence. Furthermore, in the ACAR areas of Minas Gerais, supervised credit has built public confidence in general extension.

2. Certain basic issues discovered or underlined by ACAR are involved in the success or failure of programs of supervised credit in Minas Gerais.

Five significant questions must have careful consideration in deciding whether or not to embark on a program of supervised credit:

a) Is there a dependable and adequate source of loan funds?

b) What is the geographic dispersion or concentration of family farms for which supervised credit is an appropriate program?

c) How adequate is road access to these farms?

d) How significant are the supervised-credit type of family farms in the agriculture of the region? (This is a good question, but it can be misconstrued. In Minas Gerais, such farms are in the minority, but they are strategic in view of the need to pull farmer attitudes out of traditional patterns of agriculture. One Brazilian non-ACAR observer emphasized the fact that ACAR's demonstration of what can be done on small farms is "shaming" operators of bigger farms into more progressive attitudes.)

e) Are research results in agriculture adequate to support a rapidly developing extension service whether supervised credit is used or not?

3. The ACAR program has demonstrated the value of the family-welfare orientation for a program of agricultural extension.

On this score, ACAR is the outstanding program encountered in the whole of the study. It not only has introduced home agents to Brazil but has made the co-ordinated work of farm and home agents an element of its entire program. It is significant that most ACAR loans include some funds specifically for home improvement, either in improved houses or arrangements for potable water or for sanitation. The results in improved family living—including a wider variety of home-grown foods on most farms—fully justify this combination of emphases and demonstrate what it can accomplish.

The leverage that supervised credit gives to insure early reflection of increased income in improved farm family welfare is important. Farm and home planning is possible in general extension, but, without credit, adherence to the plan depends on family decisions uninfluenced by any desire to qualify for a subsequent loan. For this reason, progress in farm family welfare is slower under general extension in Minas Gerais than it is within a program of supervised credit.

One of the Brazilian members of the governing board of ACAR was asked: "Is the emphasis of ACAR primarily on the welfare of the farm families touched by the program, or is it primarily on the general agricultural development of Minas Gerais?" His reply was: "It is on family welfare, but that emphasis has a consequent effect on agricultural development. That is the way it should be. To start at the other end might mean a more rapid increase in production, but not much of this would result in better family living at an early date. Moreover, emphasizing agricultural production would mean working with wealthier families. If that were done, the smaller farms would not be affected, as those farmers would assume that the new methods were beyond their means. Helping operators of small farms to improve both their production and their level of living, however, induces those on large farms to make changes, too."

4. Co-operation with ACAR has substantially increased under-standing of what progressive agriculture is, and the organization has increased general realization of the role that can be played in agricultural development by effective public programs.

Minas Gerais is a case in point of the need to educate farmers away from a traditional, and into a dynamic and progressive, practice of agriculture. That ACAR is succeeding in this is observable among both borrower and non-borrower families touched by its program. In addition, the number of requests for similar programs and the high esteem in which ACAR is held by many Brazilians are testimony to the effect of the organization is building public confidence in extension programs for agricultural development. It has done this by creating a staff of Brazilian technicians with the attitudes, the conditions of employment, and the equipment and organization necessary for an effective program.

5. The ACAR program has demonstrated a technique for effective technical co-operation in agriculture in a large, complex country with a federal government.

This contribution is inherent in the method of organization. There are two significant elements in this. One is the fact that it is a program in co-operation with a state government rather than with the federal government of Brazil. The second is the fact that it is organized as a civil society, with two representatives appointed by the governor of Minas Gerais and two AIA appointees on its board. This type of organization gives freedom from local political pressures while giving effective Brazilian representation.

6. ACAR records are unusually complete, both records of family progress and of extension project costs.

A general criticism of programs of agricultural extension is that they have inadequate records of their accomplishments; and it is a general criticism of projects of technical co-operation that they do not give a full accounting of their project costs. The first of these criticisms is easier to make than it is to justify, simply because "accomplishment," when applied to an extension program, is an elusive concept, hard to define and harder to measure. It is hard to define because, although changed practices constitute progress, they are achievements of a lower order than those changes in the thinking and behavior of people which result in their taking the initiative in reaching for new knowledge and in actively seeking better techniques. The changed practices can be counted, but the more important changes in thought and attitude are very difficult to measure. Moreover, an extension program is seldom the only influence on a farmer; therefore it is very difficult to assess the degree of credit due the program of extension when a new practice is adopted.

In contrast to these difficulties, ACAR has an easier task in recording the progress of borrower families. It records previous practices in preparing a loan application and subsequent practices in the course of supervising the loan. Furthermore, the nature of its records allows net worth to be used as a measure of progress. With these advantages, it has succeeded in amassing a large number of accurate records of family progress.

The usual lack of complete accounting of project costs in bilateral governmental programs of technical co-operation grows largely out of having to meet political pressure in both countries. It is not evasion but compliance with administrative necessities that prevents easy computation of total costs. At this point, again, ACAR has an advantage in that the external co-operating partner is a private organization. Having this advantage, the organization's complete and coherent cost records are a major contribution to a study of the costs of other technical co-operation programs of this type.

7. The ACAR experience has demonstrated the effectiveness of a Brazilian staff in a program of agricultural development with only a minimum of participation by foreign technicians.

From the beginning, the project has been staffed almost entirely by Brazilians. This Brazilian staff has been provided with: (*a*) full-time jobs at reasonable salaries; (*b*) the necessary equipment, including vehicles, with which to work; (*c*) a non-political atmosphere in which to work, with the assurance that promotions will be based on performance and that tenure will not be interrupted by political favoritism; (*d*) a continuing program of in-service training; and (*e*) appropriate organization and administration.

This does not mean that the ACAR program could have been developed without technical co-operation. Lacking that, the features of the program listed above could not have been achieved at this time in Minas Gerais. The North American technicians—although never more than four—have been an indispensable ingredient. They have provided ideas, a confidence that the program could succeed, experience in this type of work, and a director who is somewhat isolated from local cultural and political pressures.

SIGNIFICANCE OF ACAR EXPERIENCE.—Useful pointers for administrators of other technical co-operation programs in agriculture may be found in the discussion of these things that ACAR has and has not done. In addition, certain features of the program should be stressed which have even broader significance for technical co-operation in general.

1. The most significant achievements of a program of technical co-operation are often something other than those intended when the program is set up.

The intention of ACAR was to test the appropriateness of supervised credit as a technique within a program of agricultural extension. This intention has been fulfilled and the new programs now being established in Brazil can build on ACAR's experience. But it is probable that other results of the program are of greater significance.

First, ACAR has built public confidence in the ability of families on small farms to shift to dynamic, more productive agriculture. This is changing the general feeling that only wealthy men on large farms can be progressive. It has encouraged the Brazilian government to have faith that the farmers of Brazil's big northeastern bulge can, with guidance, transform their small farms. It has stimulated farmers themselves to seek the opportunity for an expanding life for their families on their small farms.

Second, ACAR has demonstrated to graduates of agricultural colleges that there is a satisfying career in working with rural families in a general extension service. This can be of enormous significance in developmental programs. Formerly, a graduate in Brazil could farm, or be employed to manage a large farm, or accept low-paid employment for part-time work in a government service of limited efficiency. Now, some of these young men are discovering that there is a pattern of public service that can combine a reasonable family income for the technician and a partnership with farm people in which technicians can have a feeling of sound achievement as they see the level of rural living rise.

Third, although the records that ACAR has kept are a by-product, they now constitute a very valuable asset in the understanding and further planning of other similar programs.

2. Programs of technical co-operation often look expensive in the beginning although they are really cheap in the long run.

Programs of technical co-operation can be wasteful, either through poor administration or through being so mistakenly conceived that they get few, if any, results. Even well-conceived and efficient programs, however, usually appear to be expensive in the beginning. They can be judged rightfully only in the light of all of their repercussions and cumulative effects over time.

There are several reasons why programs of technical co-operation appear to be, and often are, expensive in the beginning. They must grapple with problems at those stages of agricultural development when experimentation as to methods is necessary, and experimentation is usually costly. They must work where conditions are unfavorable and facilities are lacking. They usually must be located where roads are inadequate, where public transportation is slow, where telephones do not exist, and where other subsidiary services are inadequate. Perhaps even more important, they face situations in which only as the attitudes of the people change can technical changes be widely adopted. Attitudes are likely to change slowly; thus, in the beginning, even efficient programs that are affecting attitudes appear to be moving very slowly.

These considerations are relevant to the criticism frequently leveled at ACAR by North American observers that it has been unduly expensive. Moreover, ACAR has been judged on the basis of fewer fields of achievement than it has deserved. Some critics have divided the total cost of the program by the number of borrower families and have concluded that the cost per supervised loan is exorbitant. But ACAR's work on supervised credit has been less than one-half of its program. Its contributions in the field of general extension education, in demonstrating an effective pattern for a combined farm and home program, and in improving rural health are substantial. To these should be added its accomplishment in raising the confidence of rural Minas Gerais in the possibilities and techniques of agricultural development. When all of these achievements are recognized, and the validity of reasonably imputing the costs of the program to all of them is recognized, the program has not been unduly expensive.

The third factor creating the impression that ACAR has been expensive is the fact that the financial accounting is complete and detailed. It is easy to find out what it costs and how its expenditures are divided. This is not true of most other programs.[9]

3. The ACAR program shows that such an effort need not be nation-wide in the beginning to have wide influence at an early date.

Today, the example of ACAR is influencing public plans for agricultural development in distant parts of Brazil; yet ACAR has never operated widely. Even in Minas Gerais, it operates in a small minority of the municipalities of the state. Significant success in the early years is much more important than the geographical extent of the project.

This observation should not lead to a generalized principle. Under other circumstances, in other programs, the conclusion seems inevitable that a large-scale program has advantages over one of limited scope. It may be that in Brazil—a big country with many agricultural development agencies—there has been a particular advantage in being small and relatively inconspicuous in the beginning. This allowed the program to get established without too much jealousy and opposition.

Two factors have combined to give ACAR's localized program national influence. One is its success. The other is a good public relations program. Regularly, ACAR has issued readable reports and has distributed these to influential people throughout Brazil. This has made Brazilians aware of what is going on and has stimulated duplication of the example elsewhere. Publicity with respect to programs of technical co-operation can be harmful when it magnifies the part played by foreign technicians. But intelligently handled, it is an indispensable phase of educating influential people in the possibilities for, and in the techniques of, agricultural development.

4. An apparently insignificant and irrelevant factor may play a large role in the success of a program of agricultural development.

After this account of the ACAR program was in draft form, the writer was discussing it with the man who had been the field director of the program in its formative years. When he had finished, the field director, grinning, said, "You haven't even *mentioned* ants; ACAR was *made* by ant-control!"

There is no feature of the landscape of Minas Gerais more prominent than the millions of mounds of red soil, two to five feet high, built in tens of thousands of fields and pastures by termites. Only a running battle can keep them under control, and the battle is usually lost. The mounds are built swiftly and soon get so big that it is easier to cultivate around them than to break them down. Another almost universal pest in Minas Gerais is the sauva ant. These leaf-cutting ants can strip crop plants in minutes and can destroy the crops of a large area in a few days. ACAR introduced the use of chlordane to exterminate this pest, and the chemical proved to be effective in combating the mound-building termites as well, although they are much harder to eliminate.

In introducing an effective control for these two destructive pests, ACAR built public support by a method that recurs frequently in successful programs of technical co-operation—a dramatic, simple method of overcoming an obvious, simple need. This dramatic technique apparently need have no greater importance to the main emphasis of a program than the role of ant control in total agricultural development. What such a technique does is to establish the personnel of a program as men and women who can get results by applying new knowledge to old irritations.

The remark of the field director was an overstatement; nevertheless, his point is exceedingly important. Programs of technical co-operation have to be so devised that they overcome a great variety of problems. Some of these problems are physical and biological;

others concern trade, credit, social customs, and public policies. At the same time, the arguments that sell programs to rural people are not always the sophisticated wisdom of the total approach. The immediately effective arguments are more likely to be one, or a few, forceful demonstrations that knowledge can overcome ancient ills— like ants.

5. Technical co-operation needs to be a long-term process, even in some individual projects.

Launched in 1949, ACAR has learned a number of fruitful lessons and has started useful processes, but the task of technical co-operation in this particular project has not been completed. The AIA's apparent intention to withdraw from ACAR in 1955 was regrettable. Programs of technical co-operation are sometimes criticized for hanging on too long, but in this instance the case is just the opposite. The AIA role from the first has been near the minimum to insure the unique contributions of a program of technical co-operation. Much more than technical competence on the part of a local staff is necessary to insure continuation of a program begun as technical co-operation. Both political support for a program and a well-matured local concern for its autonomy are prerequisites to successful continuation of a program under entirely domestic auspices.

The appropriateness of the ACAR program under Brazilian conditions has been demonstrated. Public demand for the multiplication of such programs is strong, but new programs are not yet well-established. Under such circumstances, this is no time to withdraw the peculiar advantages of the process of technical co-operation.

9 THE BILATERAL AGRICULTURAL SERVICIO IN ECUADOR

Ecuador is the smallest of the Andean countries of South America. Like Peru, it has three natural regions: the coast, the highlands (at 7,000 to 11,000 feet), and the eastern slopes of the Andes toward the Amazon. Unlike Peru, however, the coast is humid and largely in forests, and the eastern slopes of the Andes are virtually untouched; only a few rough roads penetrate the eastern range of the mountains, and what cultivation there is on the eastern slopes is scattered subsistence farming in isolated villages. The two significant regions are the highlands and the coast. Ecuador has few discovered mineral resources.

Of the 3,500,000 people living in Ecuador about 50 per cent are Indians who do not speak Spanish and who live largely in a culture of their own. The common definition of an Ecuadorean Indian is economic: "He wears native dress and no shoes; when this changes, he is no longer an Indian." It has been estimated that 40 per cent of these Indians live as semi-serfs on large, highland haciendas. A law on the books for the past twenty years requires that they be paid cash wages, but most of them derive their chief income from the small, hillside plots, the use of which they receive as compensation for their labor, several days of each week, on the land of the owner of the hacienda. The 60 per cent of the Indians who are not attached to haciendas live in Indian communities. Most of them own small farms, but their plots, through inheritance, are becoming smaller and smaller. Many of them pursue part-time handicraft industries, chiefly weaving and the manufacture of panama hats. Those who do not may be worse off than the Indians on haciendas.

In the highlands the major agricultural enterprises on the large haciendas are cattle and sheep plus substantial acreages of wheat, barley, corn, and potatoes. On the small holdings of Indians the

181

crops are chiefly corn, beans, potatoes, barley, and wheat. The high-lands comprise a largely self-sufficient agricultural region; very little food is imported, while 500,000 quintals of barley and a similar quantity of wheat are sold annually across the boundary into Colombia. The capital city, Quito, is in the highlands; it is there that many of the owners of haciendas have their homes, and the cultural, educational, and political life of the highlands is largely concentrated there.

The coast, formerly largely unutilized because of diseases and the preference of both Indians and the descendants of Spanish colonists to live in the highlands, has been developing at an increasing rate in recent years. It has been an exporter of rice for many years. When the world price of rice fell below Ecuadorean costs of production in 1948, a concentrated effort, backed by Development Bank loans said to total $50,000,000 between 1948 and 1952, raised banana production from nearly zero up to a point where Ecuador is now the world's largest exporter of that fruit; its exports of bananas in 1954 were valued at $21,000,000. In the same year, other major exports from Ecuador's coastal region were:

Crop	Value of Exports
Coffee	$20,000,000
Cacao	18,000,000
Rice	15,000,000

In addition to these export crops, the coast produces considerable cotton, all used within Ecuador, and enough food crops to feed the population of the coast. Only a little wheat and some fruits from Chile are imported.

The farms of the coast are both large and small. Bananas are a small-farm crop there. It is estimated that they are produced by 140,000 separate growers, of whom only 25,000 have more than 5 acres in bananas, and that the United Fruit Company produces less than 5 per cent of the crop.

Although agricultural production is being constantly extended on the coast, most of the cultivable area is still in virgin forests. Roads are badly needed; the relatively flat terrain makes road-building there much easier than in the mountains. And, of course, it is a major advantage that much of Ecuador's potential agricultural land is near the sea, making export relatively inexpensive.

The chief city of the coast and the main port for Ecuador is Guayaquil, a rapidly growing commercial city with its face toward trade and the sea. It is the political competitor to Quito; power in national politics tends to alternate between the two.

Into this small country of two nearly separate agricultural regions,[1] the Office of Foreign Agricultural Relations (OFAR) introduced a complementary-crops mission in 1942. It established an experimental station at Pichilingue, on the coast, where the initial interest of the program was in rubber and pharmaceuticals, and at later dates three branch experimental stations were established in the highlands. As the wartime need for these crops lost urgency, experimentation was begun on other crops, chiefly bananas and cacao at Pichilingue and wheat at the highland stations.

This program has been focused on agricultural research; very little has been achieved in the way of extension or of agricultural education. There has been no program of Reimbursable Facilities. Enthusiastically supported by the president of Ecuador between 1948 and 1952, the research program steadily lost favor under the succeeding regime.

A new chief of field party was appointed in January, 1954. The program has been reorganized, and the government of Ecuador has doubled its appropriation in the hope that an effective program can be developed. However, the remarks made about the program in this study are for the period prior to 1954.

Why the Program in Ecuador Should Have Succeeded

Although this program must be characterized as one of very limited accomplishment through 1953, it is important to note that there are at least two reasons why it should have succeeded.

1. Ecuadorean agriculture is very similar to that in Peru and somewhat like that in Bolivia, where programs of technical cooperation have been successful.[2] Ecuador has very substantial agricultural resources; yet it needs almost everything in the way of research, extension, and agricultural education. Although there are hundreds of thousands of small plot-holders still living in the Indian tradition, not all small farmers are of this type: Ecuador has thousands of small farmers with some freedom to innovate. Ecuador also has many, at least several hundred, well-educated operators of large

estates with complete freedom to innovate. Many of these, to be sure, in the highlands, are not seriously interested in greater productivity, since they have "sufficient" income, and estate ownership, with them, is at least as much a matter of prestige as it is of production. But many of them, particularly on the coast, are really commercial farmers. A few hundred may seem a small number, but it is quite large enough for a good start, especially in a country the size of Ecuador. The Ecuadorean government cannot be said to be deeply concerned about agricultural development—for the most part it must be classified as indifferent—but it did have a president from 1948 to 1952 who was enthusiastic about bilateral technical co-operation and who secured for the program far more opportunity than the program was able to utilize.

2. A second reason why the program could have been expected to succeed was that it had continuity of United States personnel. OFAR appointed its technicians for periods of three years each, subject to reappointment, and with the wise provision for nine months of postgraduate study in the United States after each six years of foreign service. The crippling effect on technical co-operation of the necessity for short-term appointments has been pointed out in other sections. Here has been a program that did not have this disadvantage.

Reasons for Failure

Despite the factors mentioned previously, the OFAR program had only scattered achievements, through 1953. On what grounds is this judgment based? (1) With the exception of the dairy-improvement program, technicians within the program itself do not claim any achievements other than the accumulation of experience in "research in progress," nor is there any record of achievement. The dairy program succeeded because it was well planned and directed by a competent man and because of the well-organized and active Ecuadorean Holstein-Friesian Association. (2) Ecuadoreans in domestic programs for agricultural development felt neither enthusiasm for the program nor jealousy of it; they simply saw no significance for Ecuador in it. (3) Morale among United States technicians in the program was very low. All technicians except two among those interviewed were eager to blame other technicians within the program for its failure. (Significantly, in view of obvious failures in leadership, they are reluctant to blame the United States director of the program. This reluctance is not based on fear; it is based on affection.)

There were several reasons for the lack of enthusiasm among Ecuadoreans:

1. They remembered that in 1942 a large share of the $5,000,000 borrowed by the government of Ecuador from the Export-Import Bank went into a wartime complementary crops program with no visible favorable results to the country.

2. The program included no extension except in dairying. Activities confined to the laboratory and experimental plot do not awaken enthusiasm among the general public, especially when no results of experimentation are publicized.

3. Ecuadorean technicians were not incorporated in the program except a very few in very minor posts.

4. No effort was made to inform the public of what was going on. As late as 1952 the Congress of Ecuador was reluctant to make appropriations to the program because many of the congressmen had never heard of it.

What seem to have been the reasons for the failure of this program? The easy answer is twofold: interagency rivalry in Washington and poor field leadership. That is the summary answer usually given. These were undoubtedly important factors, and in one sense all other failures may be said to flow from them, but for the guidance of future programs it is well to try to analyze in just what ways these two factors have brought about mistakes in this program in Ecuador.

1. The program has been badly oriented. As a wartime complementary crops program, interested chiefly in rubber and pharmaceuticals, it was not directed toward the general development of Ecuadorean agriculture. Such a program could not even be expected to improve the production of the crops in which it was primarily interested until after research results began to demonstrate what could be done. The *initial* orientation of the program cannot, therefore, be criticized. What can be criticized is the failure to change. (The Peruvian program began similarly, but a shift of emphasis was under way as early as 1945.)

2. The center of activities for the program was far removed from the capital. The major activities of the program were at Pichilingue, on the coast, perhaps 100 miles north of Guayaquil, until 1953. This place was not easily accessible until recently. It still is isolated by swollen rivers throughout the rainy season. One has to make a special trip to see it at any time. This fact has meant that Ecuadoreans have not known much about the program and have not seen what little there has been to see. It is poorly located for utilization in connection with education and extension, no matter how satisfactory its location may have been for the original war-time purpose of the program.

3. The focus of attention throughout has been exclusively on research. Starting with an interest in rubber and pharmaceuticals, the research interest of the program has broadened to include appreciable work on wheat and, in later years, on insect pests, but still the emphasis is on research. Little or nothing has been done to investigate the problems of getting improved techniques into practice. Substantial progress has been made since 1948 on dairy improvement extension in the highlands, but that is the sum total of the extension activities of the program. For brief periods, the program co-operated with the three Ecuadorean Practical Schools of Agriculture, but in each case the program of co-operation was dropped, in one case because "the principal of the school was transferred" and in the other two cases for undiscovered reasons. Recently, a new program of co-operation has developed between the Practical Schools of Agriculture and the station at Pichilingue in which students of the schools spend one month each working with United States technicians on simple problems at the stations. Apart from this, there has been no training program in connection with the research.

4. United States research technicians have had no Ecuadorean counterparts. There were five Ecuadoreans on the staff at Pichilingue in 1953 who had been there several years. They were men who had been trained in the Practical Schools of Agriculture; they were not college graduates. A common complaint of United States technicians is that "there are no trained Ecuadoreans in agriculture." It is true that there are relatively few, but the program could have selected some of those who did exist and, by making them real

colleagues in the research program, it could have trained them to be increasingly competent in agricultural research. This has not been done. That it has not been done is blamed on the orientation of the program as a project of OFAR: "It was never the intention to make this an Ecuadorean program but to continue it as a foreign operation of the USDA."[3]

That the failure here was not just the emphasis on research is obvious from the outstanding success of the Rockefeller program in Mexico. But in Mexico the OEE, while confining its own organized activities largely to research, had leadership concerned about the allied activities of extension and education. It took an active part in urging the establishment of the Corn Commission and felt a responsibility for getting research findings publicized and distributed quickly. It was the *exclusive absorption* of the Ecuadorean program in research, coupled with the lack of a sense of urgency about getting improved methods into practice, that was its mistake.

5. It has worked mainly with tropical crops. By and large, those bilateral research programs that have concentrated on temperate crops appear to have been more successful than those that have worked with tropical crops. No one seriously disputes this conclusion, but experts vary in their interpretation of it. Some maintain that tropical crops are inherently more difficult to deal with; others argue that if equal ability were applied to tropical crops, equal improvement could be achieved. In any case, the program in Ecuador worked chiefly on rubber and pharmaceuticals in the beginning, and on bananas, coffee, and cacao later. Meanwhile, its demonstrable achievements seem to have been greatest with wheat.

6. The program has not been systematically organized and sustained. Very few reports have been issued. Few summarizing publications have been prepared. Records of experiments have been lost. Apparently the same simple trials have been conducted at different periods within the life of the program, and few records kept of any of them.

In the case of wheat experiments, however, adequate records have been kept of all trials. (The same man has conducted all of them, and he is a man who realized the importance of keeping adequate records even when apparently neither Washington nor his field director required him to do so.) Nevertheless, no published reports of this work have been issued, although the project has run eleven years.[4] Again, at this point, the predilection of this program to conduct research without being concerned about its early application in local agriculture is obvious.

One further point: several United States technicians reported that they could recall only one general staff meeting, and that was in 1952.

7. In recent years, this program has suffered greatly from interagency rivalry in Washington. From its inception in 1942, this was a program of OFAR under the Department of Agriculture. From the same year, the IIAA had been conducting programs of technical co-operation in Latin America. In 1951, in the process of reorganizing and integrating all programs of technical co-operation, IIAA was charged with administering the programs previously conducted by OFAR. This was greatly resented by OFAR, and the resentment persisted to impede work under IIAA, because personnel of the program (in Ecuador as elsewhere under similar conditions) remained employees of OFAR, even though the director of the program (still, himself, in Ecuador, an employee of OFAR) now became administratively responsible to IIAA in Washington.[5] The agricultural program in Ecuador had only OFAR personnel through 1953. OFAR in Washington, in 1953, was still overriding requests of its field director in Ecuador that one of its technicians be withdrawn as incompetent, presumably opposing the move because a replacement would be appointed by IIAA instead of by OFAR. (The technician whose withdrawal was recommended had been in Ecuador ten years, and for five of those years the director is reported to have been trying to have him withdrawn.)

Apart from such specific instances of conflict, the fact that IIAA, but not OFAR, stressed orientation of its programs to the current needs of recipient countries is probably partially responsible for failure adequately to reorient the agricultural program in Ecuador.

8. The field director (chief of field party after IIAA took over) was not up to his job. Although obviously the failure of the program in Ecuador cannot be attributed to the field director alone, a different man might have operated a much more successful program. This is borne out by the fact that the difficulties with which he had to contend plagued programs in other countries as well, and the field

director in Ecuador knew about these other programs, knew how their orientation had been changed, and knew that the situation in his own program was considered unsatisfactory. Other difficulties could have been overcome by different decisions and more effective leadership. The interagency struggle was no worse in Ecuador than elsewhere in Latin America. Directors of programs in other countries did reorient projects which began as wartime complementary crops programs. Research could have been methodical, and it could have been redirected to some Ecuadorean needs. And there were administrative weaknesses within the Ecuadorean program itself which can be ascribed only to weak leadership.

Everyone agrees that the field director (replaced in January, 1954) was a competent tropical agriculturalist. Everyone liked him as a person. But he was ineffective in the difficult job of *directing* a program of technical co-operation in a country where problems are big but not bigger than elsewhere. His task was made much more difficult by the interagency rivalry in Washington.

(The writer has carefully considered adding the judgment that the United States technicians in the Ecuadorean program have, for the most part, been mediocre men. But he is not at all sure that they have been less competent, on the average, than men in more successful programs. This program gives occasion for a reservation that must be made about longer terms for United States technicians in such programs. On the whole, it appears that the men who have been longest in the Ecuadorean program are less competent than those appointed in the past five years. If terms are to be long, appointees must be capable. Long terms are excellent where the standards of appointment are as high as they are in the Rockefeller program in Mexico. If appointments are not uniformly good, however, adequate means for eliminating the less competent technicians are essential.)

Epilogue

It should be stressed again that this report is of the program in Ecuador prior to 1954. Since January, 1954, under a new chief of field party with field experience with SCIPA in Peru and in other countries, the program has been entirely reoriented. The annual report of the agricultural *servicio* for 1955 reveals quite remarkable progress. This Servicio Cooperativo Interamericano de Agricultura (SCIA) now works with an extension service in 15 offices, all field agents of which are regular employees of the Ecuadorean Division of Agriculture. The activities and accomplishments of this extension service appear to compare favorably with those in other Latin-American countries. Imports of insecticides and fungicides, for use primarily on potatoes, have increased about 70 per cent (from $300,000 to $530,000) in the two years this extension service has been operating. The cultivated area of the experimental farm at Pichilingue has been increased from 60 to 700 acres. While much of this increase has gone into bananas, substantial areas have been put into coffee nurseries and into multiplication plots for clonial cacao.

The program of research has been continued, but emphasis is now on crops of major importance to Ecuador: potatoes, cacao, coffee, bananas, wheat, and corn. The *servicio* has released 12,000 pounds of corn seed for distribution. Research in bananas has so impressed growers that the Banana Growers' Association began a $200,000 research and extension program in 1956, channeling two-thirds of this amount into the budget of SCIA. The other one-third will be spent on an extension program by the association, advised by SCIA. Fifteen new bulletins and 155 news articles were released in 1955 as part of the SCIA information program. Agricultural education is being served under a contract with the University of Idaho.

The Ecuadorean appropriation to SCIA, doubled in 1955, was increased by another 220 per cent in 1956. In addition to this, Ecuador has increased appropriations to its wholly domestic Division of Agriculture and has begun revising policies and procedures within that agency.

10 PROJECT 39 OF THE ORGANIZATION OF AMERICAN STATES

The OAS has three agricultural programs. One is the Inter-American Institute of Agricultural Sciences located in Turrialba, Costa Rica.[1] The second is the Pan-American Anti-Aftosa Center in São Bento, Brazil.[2] The third is Project 39, which is discussed in this chapter.

Project 39 was launched in August, 1951. It is operated under the auspices of the Inter-American Institute of Agricultural Sciences by a director who is responsible to the director of the institute. This project, entitled "Technical Education for the Improvement of Agriculture and Rural Life," is the largest of the technical co-operation projects of OAS. As originally planned, this project was designed, in the first instance, to supplement the training facilities of member countries by international courses in subjects related to agricultural development, and, growing out of this, to help enable certain regular training facilities of member countries to serve internationally. The means adopted to these ends were:

1. The establishment of three zones: Northern,[3] Andean,[4] and Southern,[5] each with a staff of technicians serving the member countries within its zone.

2. A series of international short courses at zone headquarters to give intensive training in specific subjects of current importance to agricultural development in member countries.

3. Setting up a "demonstration area" in connection with each zone headquarters, to be used (a) for practical training in connection with international courses and (b) to demonstrate "the effectiveness and value of solving problems of rural life in an integrated manner."

4. Granting fellowships for study in the fields of agriculture and home economics.

These initial intentions have been followed in general, but there have been variations between zones, and the apparent value of the

191

various activities of the project was different, at the end of 1954, from what had been anticipated. This later perspective can be summarized by stating: (1) that some international courses can better be held at other institutions of member countries than at those nearest to the zone headquarters; (2) that national courses are an important complement to the international courses; (3) that the demonstration areas, although not serving the same purpose in all zones, are an essential and important phase of the project; (4) that short-term advisory visits by OAS technicians to member countries within each zone have proved to be very valuable and should be recognized as a major contribution of the program.

Northern Zone

The Northern Zone headquarters was moved from its temporary location in San José, Costa Rica, to Havana, Cuba, on January 1, 1953. It is housed in the same building as the Cuban Ministry of Agriculture. It had a staff of eight technicians, in addition to the director, at the end of 1954. They were in the fields of rural sociology, home economics, extension methods, land-use economics, horticulture, farm management, forestry, and agricultural engineering, and they came from Puerto Rico, Costa Rica, Cuba, and the United States.

The Northern Zone is developing a demonstration area in the vicinity of Bejucál, about twenty-five miles out of Havana. In this area the Cuban Ministry of Agriculture employs an agricultural engineer, an agricultural inspector, and two home demonstration agents. The area was set up unofficially as a bureau of the ministry, and negotiations were under way in January, 1955, to get it recognized officially as a functional unit of the ministry, which until then had had no extension service. The OAS technicians act as advisers to this Cuban staff, in addition to conducting independent studies within the area to make it more valuable as a teaching aid in the short courses of Project 39. The activities of OAS technicians in the demonstration area are also viewed by the zone director as an important part of their own education in the agricultural problems of the zone. Thus far, the most effective extension work within this demonstration area has been in home improvement, under the direction of the OAS technician, who is a Puerto Rican.

The Northern Zone sponsored three short courses in 1953 and five in 1954. These were in the fields of extension, home economics, tropical forestry, horticultural production, and agricultural economics. Only two of these were held at Havana. Three were held in Puerto Rico, two in Mexico, and one in Panama, as shown in Table 19. This illustrates the shift of Project 39 away from the idea of holding all courses at the zone headquarters in favor of holding each at the location within the zone where the best facilities are available.

TABLE 19

INTERNATIONAL SHORT COURSES: NORTHERN ZONE

Subject	Duration (Months)	No. of Students	No. of Countries Represented	Location
1953				
Home Economics........	6	13	8	Puerto Rico
Agricultural Extension...	1	21	9	Havana
Tropical Forestry.......	1	32 (7)*	14	Puerto Rico
Total..............	....	66	....	....
1954				
Agricultural Economics..	2	30 (3)	12	Mexico
Home Economics........	2½	16	11	Puerto Rico
Agricultural Extension...	1	22	10	Panama
Tropical Forestry.......	1	24 (3)	9	Mexico
Horticulture...........	1	21 (1)	11	Cuba
Total..............	....	113†	....	....

* The numbers in parentheses record the number of students from outside the Northern Zone. They are included in the total.

† Of the 113 students in 1954, 84 received stipends from Project 39.

The Northern Zone has not gone very far in the direction of short advisory visits to member countries. A rough estimate of the time spent outside of Cuba by the entire staff adds up to about eighteen months for the year 1954, and most of these visits were in connection with arranging short courses. This means that about 80 per cent of staff time was spent within Cuba, despite the fact that six of the eight short courses were held in other countries. Such concentration perhaps was justified during the year when the demonstration area was being set up; but in view of the need to follow up the students who have participated in courses, and of the needs of member countries in the zone for counsel in the fields in which Project 39 has technicians, a higher percentage of time devoted to country visits may be wise in subsequent years. In 1953, six fellowships were awarded for postgraduate study outside the zone.

TABLE 20

REPRESENTATION OF COUNTRIES IN SHORT
COURSES: NORTHERN ZONE

	1953	1954
Costa Rica..............	8	9
Cuba...................	16	21
Dominican Republic.......	0	2
El Salvador.............	4	5
Guatemala..............	2	9
Haiti..................	3	7
Honduras...............	4	12
Mexico................	5	17
Nicaragua..............	5	8
Panama................	4	12
Puerto Rico............	8	4
Total...............	59	106
Outside the zone.........	7	7
	66	113

Andean Zone

The headquarters of the Andean Zone was located in the building of the Peruvian Ministry of Agriculture in Lima throughout 1953 and 1954. Plans call for it to be moved to the National College of Agriculture at La Molina, eleven miles outside Lima. At the end of 1953 there were four OAS technicians, in addition to the director. They were in the fields of forestry, agricultural engineering, land use, and home economics. During 1954 a sociologist joined the staff. Three more posts had been approved: in plant physiology, soils, and extension methods.

Three international courses were conducted in the Andean Zone in 1953. One, a two-month course in tropical forestry, was attended by eight regular students plus nine final-year students of the Peruvian National College of Agriculture. The eight regular students came from Bolivia, Colombia, Peru, and Venezuela. Six of them were chiefs of section in the forestry services of their respective governments, and the other two were officials in such sections.

The second international course was in the field of nutrition and home economics extension. It was a three-month course, with sixteen students from four countries: Bolivia (5), Colombia (2), Peru (7), and Venezuela (2). Two scholarships were offered to Ecuador but were declined. It may be significant that the larger numbers of students were sent from the countries which, with other technicial assistance, have started programs of extension in home economics. This course has led to requests for similar courses to be given in Colombia and Venezuela.

The third was a course in grain storage, with nineteen students from five countries: Bolivia (4), Colombia (4), Ecuador (1), Peru (6), and Venezuela (4). Of these students, fourteen came on fellowships provided by Project 39. Two were sent by the Colombia–United States bilateral *servicio,* one was sent by SCIPA (Peru), and two were sent by the Development Corporation of Venezuela.

In addition to these international courses, two national courses were held in 1953. A five-week grain-storage course was held in Colombia for thirty-one students, and a two-week short course on rice classification (grading) was held in Peru. Although the original intent was to offer only international courses under this project, the demand for courses in particular countries has proved high enough and sound enough that these have been brought within the terms of reference of the project.

In 1954, again, three international courses were held, but the total number of students in them increased substantially (from fifty-two to seventy-seven). A larger increase occurred in the number of national courses, of which eleven were held in 1954 for a total of 374 students. In all but two cases the full stipends for students in the national courses were supplied by the national government concerned.[6] These short courses of the Andean Zone for 1953 and 1954 are summarized in Tables 21 and 22.

The second major activity in the Andean Zone is consultation of project staff with government officials on specific problems. Requests for such consultation have come for help in home economics from Colombia, Ecuador, and Venezuela, on forestry problems from Bolivia and Peru, and on grain-storage problems from Colombia and Peru.

The Andean Zone granted sixteen scholarships in 1953 for regular postgraduate study outside the zone. Fourteen of these were for study at the Inter-American Institute at Turrialba; the other two were for study in the United States. In addition, six girls were sent to Puerto Rico for six months as special students in home economics, and one was sent to study extension information at Turrialba and in the United States.

TABLE 21

INTERNATIONAL SHORT COURSES: ANDEAN ZONE*

Subject	Duration (Months)	No. of Students	No. of Countries Represented
1953			
Tropical Forestry....	1	17	4
Home Economics.....	3	16	4
Grain Storage.......	1¼	19	5
1954			
Tropical Forestry....	1	25	4
Agricultural Extension	3	27 (5)†	6
Home Economics.....	3½	25	4
Total...........	....	129	....

* All conducted in Peru.

† The number in parentheses represents students from outside the Andean Zone. They are included in the total of 27 for that course.

TABLE 22

NATIONAL SHORT COURSES: ANDEAN ZONE

Subject	Duration (Weeks)	No. of Students	Location
1953			
Grain Storage...............	5	31	Palmira, Colombia
Rice Classification...........	2	10	Lima, Peru
1954			
Agricultural Extension........	1	70	Medellín, Colombia
Agricultural Extension........	1	40	Palmira, Colombia
Agricultural Extension........	1	25	Chinchiná, Colombia
Home Economics.............	6	21	Quito, Ecuador
Agricultural Economics.......	2	16	Palmira, Colombia
Grain Storage...............	4	14	Lima, Peru
Grain Storage...............	1	35	Bogotá, Colombia
Agricultural Extension........	5	45	Palmira, Colombia
Agricultural Extension........	3	30	Bogotá, Colombia
Agricultural Extension........	1	18	Maracay, Venezuela
Plant Physiology.............	1	60	Medellín, Colombia
Total.....................	....	415	....

Southern Zone

The Southern Zone headquarters was established at Montevideo, Uruguay, in 1952. The program in this zone got started quickly, and two international courses were started within that year. Seven technicians were on the zone staff at the end of 1954. In addition to the director, there was one specialist each in the fields of extension methods, pasture management, rural sociology, land-use economics, extension information, and home economics. Two of these were Chileans, one was from Peru, one was from Puerto Rico, and three were from the United States.

With the exception of Paraguay, the countries of this zone all have relatively progressive sectors within their agricultural economies, and they are countries which have not been notable for co-operation among themselves. At the same time, there is a great need in each of them for establishing, or for greatly improving, programs of agricultural extension. As a result, two differences characterize the program of Project 39 in this zone. One is the greater importance of national, as distinguished from international, short courses. The other is the relatively greater importance of the demonstration area in the program. In view of the second of these, a third activity has developed: the addition of longer-term in-service training, under the supervision of OAS technicians, in the demonstration area itself.

These characteristics of the program in the Southern Zone are summarized in Tables 23–26. Table 23 shows that two international courses have been held in each of the first three years of the project. National short courses (Table 24) have increased, with none in 1952, three in 1953, and five in 1954. A total of 310 students took part in these short courses (Table 25), representing all five member countries within the zone. In addition to these, thirty-nine trainees had in-service training of from one to twelve months each in the demonstration area near Montevideo. The countries from which these trainees came and their fields of study are summarized in Table 26.

Nine academic scholarships were granted during these first three years. Five women received scholarships to study home economics in Puerto Rico, and four students received scholarships to study, one each, in Mexico, United State, Chile, and Turrialba, Costa Rica.

The demonstration area has played a pivotal role in the program of the Southern Zone. It has been effective in demonstrating to member countries what can be accomplished by a well-conceived program of extension in agriculture and home economics. Through it OAS technicians have become familiar with problems of agricultural development within the zone, and in the process they have directed the in-service training of selected trainees. It has provided

TABLE 23

INTERNATIONAL SHORT COURSES: SOUTHERN ZONE

Subject	Duration	No. of Students	No. of Countries Represented	Location
1952				
Agricultural Extension and Rural Sociology	2 months	38	5	Uruguay
Soil Management and Conservation.......	3 months	41	7	Chile
1953				
Extension and Farm Management.......	2 months	31	4	Uruguay
Management of Native Pastures..........	2 months	34	5	Argentina
1954				
Farm Management....	53 days	35	6	Chile
Pasture Management..	53 days	26	5	Uruguay, Brazil

TABLE 24

NATIONAL SHORT COURSES: SOUTHERN ZONE*

Subject	Duration (Days)	No. of Students	Location
1953			
Home Economics.........	8	7	Brazil
Agricultural Extension.....	10	15	Chile
Extension in Home Economics..	12	7	Uruguay
1954			
Agricultural Extension and Home Economics........	13	35	Brazil
Pasture Management......	15	12	Chile
Home Economics..........	26	6	Brazil
Home Economics..........	12	18	Brazil
Home Economics and Agricultural Extension.......	10	8	Uruguay

* No courses offered in 1952.

valuable teaching materials both for the international and for the national short courses. As a result of a soil survey made in the demonstration area by OAS, Uruguay requested FAO to send a mission to help make a soil survey of the entire country. Also as a result of work there, Chile asked that a similar demonstration area be set up within its borders. The Chilean government is providing all of the funds for this, and an OAS technician visits the demonstration area in San Vicente, Chile, every second month to give counsel and guidance.

TABLE 25

REPRESENTATION OF COUNTRIES IN SHORT
COURSES: SOUTHERN ZONE*

Country	1952	1953	1954	TOTAL
Brazil..........	10	21	71	102
Chile...........	23	25	34	82
Uruguay........	22	21	22	65
Argentina.......	10	17	4	31
Paraguay.......	12	10	8	30
Total.......	77	94	139	310

* Including both international and national courses.

TABLE 26

IN-SERVICE TRAINEES: SOUTHERN ZONE

COUNTRY	No. OF TRAINEES						
	Home Economics	Extension	Agricultural Economics	Soils	Rural Sociology	Pastures	Total
1952							
Uruguay......	1	1	....	....	....	....	2
1953							
Uruguay......	2	1	5	1	....	....	9
Paraguay	....	2	....	....	....	....	2
Brazil.........	1	....	....	....	....	....	1
Chile.........	....	....	1	....	....	....	1
1954							
Uruguay......	2	2	2	5	2	1	14
Paraguay......	1	4	....	....	....	....	5
Brazil.........	3	1	....	....	....	....	4
Chile.........	....	1	....	....	....	....	1
Total.......	10	12	8	6	2	1	39

Home economics extension and farm youth clubs have been prominent phases of the program in the demonstration area, and three
community committees have been organized to plan community
activities. These committees include representatives of farmers, farm
women, youth clubs, banks, schools, and businessmen. The demonstration area covers 64,000 hectares (about 160,000 acres) of farm-
land.

In the Southern Zone, 34 visits, totaling 183 days, were made by
technicians to other countries of the zone in 1954, mostly in connection with choosing trainees for training courses, or following up
those who had been trained. Technicians spent a total of 194 days
outside Uruguay participating in eight training courses. Four visits,
totaling 49 days, were made to Chile in connection wth the demonstration area being established there by the Chilean government.

The budget of Project 39 for 1954 was $516,000.[7] Of this amount,
$372,000 provided for "salaries and subsistence"; $90,000 for travel;
$30,000 for equipment and supplies; $10,000 for contractual services;
$4,000 for printing; and $10,000 for contingencies. The personnel
provided for within this budget are indicated in Table 27.

Discussion

When one analyzes the activities of Project 39 from the standpoint
of the elements of agricultural development, it is at once obvious
that this project limits itself to trying to influence a single one of
these elements—agricultural education. Therefore, if one were to
ask, "Supposing there were no other technical co-operation programs
in operation, has OAS made the right choice of emphasis?" one's
reply, whether a net "Yes" or a net "No," would have to include the
comment, "It only touches one phase of agricultural development,
whereas simultaneous action with respect to many others is imperative if any real result is to be achieved." But there would be no
point in asking such a question to begin with, for other programs of
technical co-operation, with greater resources, already existed when
this project was developed, and their continuation was assumed.
Project 39 was viewed, rightly, as one among many programs; thus
the pertinent form of the question is: "Has Project 39 chosen a
significant, though limited, field of action supplementary to other

domestic and technical co-operation programs, and is it set up in such a way that it can reach its objectives effectively?"

In trying to answer this question, it is necessary first to take account of the limitations on its freedom of action, as viewed by OAS itself. These are implicit in the presentation by the secretary-general of the OAS to its Co-ordinating Committee: (1) the program must be one of modest cost; (2) it must be equally available to all member states; and (3) it must avoid competition and conflict with the technical assistance programs of other agencies.

TABLE 27

PERSONNEL FOR PROJECT 39: 1954 BUDGET

PERSONNEL	ZONE			
	Northern	Andean	Southern	Head-quarters
Program director............	....	....	....	1
Zone directors............	1	1	1	....
Specialists..............	8	7	5½*	2
Part-time technicians and assistants†	7	5‡	12	2
Executive secretary........	....	....	....	1
Clerk-typists.............	4	2	2	4
Messengers..............	2	1	....	1
Chauffeur................	....	1	....	....

* The fractional figure results from one man working six months.
† These are part-time technicians to help in specific short courses.
‡ These were never appointed.

In addition to these considerations, it is also necessary to recall certain needs and relationships within the field of agricultural development itself:

1. Improving the technical competence of agricultural personnel in these countries is an urgent necessity. Yet the institutional provisions for agricultural education are inadequate, and, more important, schools and colleges are so integral a part of the whole cultural complex of each country that changing them is a slow process at best. For the same reason, foreign participation in educational institutions is not always wholly welcome.

2. For the most part, training for extension work is most effective

when conducted as in-service training, developing competence to meet new problems as those problems arise.

3. Relatively speaking, most of these are small countries. All of them have need for specialists in many fields, but to maintain high-quality institutions in each of them for training every needed type of technician would be expensive. Some joint provision for much of such training is more economical than any attempt to make similar provision country by country.

Each of these factors supports the decision of the OAS in its choice of objectives for Project 39. Without ruling out the possibility that it might have found other worthwhile fields of action, it seems clear that it did find a good one, particularly in its short courses and in its consultative services. If it retains flexibility and responsiveness to emerging needs in choosing the subject matter for its short courses, it can reinforce and supplement the in-service training given to the staff of the infant extension service in each country.

It should be recognized that Project 39 was developed within a definite policy for technical co-operation which OAS people have come to know as the "Lleras Doctrine." "This policy would consist, basically, in making . . . the program of technical assistance entrusted to OAS a program of technical education, so designed as to put within reach of all countries of the hemisphere opportunities for their citizens to perfect certain techniques and knowledge, by the creation of a considerable number of technical centers in the institutes, universities, or research centers of the several countries."[8] This policy would require close co-operation between Project 39 and national colleges of agriculture. Such a development is working out satisfactorily in the Andean Zone, and the other two zones are trying to work out equally satisfactory relationships.

Since the Lleras Doctrine was accepted, two new developments have taken place. One is the establishing of university-to-university contracts under IIAA. The other is the increasing of demands on the zone headquarters of Project 39 for short advisory visits by OAS technicians to member countries. The first of these will not appreciably affect postgraduate education in the near future, except at La Molina, but it should give a considerable boost to undergraduate education in many national colleges of agriculture. The second is opening a broad additional field of service, particularly appropriate for OAS.

In view of these two recent developments, it is likely to be wise for Project 39, while continuing to work closely with the college of agriculture nearest to each zone headquarters, to place its major emphasis for several years to come on a full program of international and national short courses and on increasing its program of advisory visits to member countries.[9] It fills a great need in each of these fields. The demand for its short courses shows that they are needed and profitable. The project is in a particularly strong position to offer advisory services because:

1. It has staffs of competent technicians specializing in the problems of each zone.

2. Its technicians are based where they can make repeated follow-up visits to help carry through programs that member countries may wish to establish or strengthen.

3. Many of its technicians are so fluent in Spanish that they can function effectively even on initial visits.

4. There are technicians in the government services of each country who have had training in the short courses of Project 39.

Because zone headquarters are located in or near colleges of agriculture, the technicians of the project can continue to help develop these as international centers for postgraduate training. It would be unwise for them to accept routine postgraduate teaching assignments in those colleges, however, as that would tie them down for much of each year, thus unduly limiting the number of advisory visits they could make to member countries. Other types of technical co-operation—university contracts and grants-in-aid from private foundations—can help develop postgraduate teaching, but these cannot provide regional advisory services as well as OAS can.

IMPORTANCE OF DEMONSTRATION AREAS.—The question of the importance of the demonstration area in each zone to the purposes of the project has been a matter of considerable debate. Early in the project two different statements of the purpose of these demonstration areas were made. One defined this purpose "as an instrument in the field training of . . . workers who attend the courses at our training centers."[10] The other declared that the purpose was "to demonstrate the effectiveness and value of solving problems of rural life in an integrated manner." As the project has developed, and as its various needs and the needs of other projects have pressed on the resources of OAS, there has been some opinion that the demonstration areas are an unnecessary phase and should be eliminated.

In the early stages of this study, the writer, too, was doubtful about the necessity for demonstration areas. It was thought that in the Andean Zone, where no demonstration area was actually established within the first two years of operation, the program seemed to be progressing satisfactorily without it. It was thought also that using the demonstration areas "to demonstrate the effectiveness and value of solving problems of rural life in an integrated manner," might bring into this project an emphasis on research, rather than extension, which would be more appropriate for some other agency.

Subsequent visits to the Northern and Southern zones and another visit to the Andean Zone after the demonstration area had been established resulted in a revision of that judgment. The demonstration area is an important part of Project 39 in each of the three zones and ought to be retained. It has proved to serve two important purposes in each zone. One of these, of great value, is to force the technical staff of the project to acquaint themselves intimately with one agricultural region of the zone. This serves both (1) to give each technician a firm grounding in the zone, learning in the process what adaptations of previous experience are necessary in view of local conditions, and (2) to bring about an integration and reconciliation of the views of technicians in different fields, through their working together in the demonstration area.

The second important contribution of the demonstration area is to provide practical field experience for trainees in the international courses and, equally important, to provide pertinent local teaching materials for use in these courses. These two are closely interrelated. Students need field work, but it is important that they get this where their teachers are on home ground directing study and practice in a plan with which they (the teachers) are already thoroughly familiar. Whether each zone formally has a demonstration area or not, students in international courses need practical training in the field in connection with many courses, and all OAS technicians need field experience in the zone. What the establishment of a demonstration area really amounts to is a regularization of these activities and a decision to concentrate several of them in a single "Area."

Although these positive functions are performed by the demonstration areas of all three zones, there are differences in the way the areas are organized and in the conduct of their respective programs. These differences grow partly out of differences between Cuba, Peru, and Uruguay, but they also grow partly out of differing needs in establishing Project 39. This second factor has special importance in the Southern Zone, and it is probable that the demonstration area has been more largely responsible for the success of Project 39 there than it has been in the other zones. In the Andean Zone, member countries were already convinced of the value of extension and wanted opportunities for training. In the Southern Zone, the value of extension had to be proved, and the demonstration area has become the spearhead of influence by the project as a whole.

In considering the recent proposal that the demonstration areas be eliminated, one factor for consideration is their cost. Figures were not secured for the Northern Zone, but the Cuban government pays most of the salaries of extension workers there, and Project 39 pays only transportation for its own technicians plus the contribution of technicians' time, a modest supplement to the salaries of Cuban technicians, and a moderate amount for equipment and expenses. In the Andean Zone, the project's share of the cost of the demonstration area was $2,806.93 in 1954, plus the time technicians spent in the area. In the Southern Zone, the total expenditures on the area for 1954 were about $9,000, of which $2,000 went for the purchase of a jeep, leaving a balance of $7,000 spent on operating expenses. To a much greater degree than in the other zones, this demonstration area in the Southern Zone provides a major in-service training program in extension methods; therefore, much of any saving if the demonstration area were to be dropped would have to be used to provide alternative forms of training.

DEMONSTRATION AREAS AS RESEARCH.—In the initial outline for Project 39, the purpose of the demonstration areas was defined as being "to demonstrate the effectiveness and value of solving problems of rural life in an integrated manner." This is a valid objective for a research study because so far it is a hypothesis rather than a proved fact. It is true that most extension projects have been improvised in the absence of prior detailed surveys of human and cultural factors and of natural resources. Although knowledge of all such factors can be of great value to an extension service, it has not been proved that they should always precede establishing the service itself. No one will ever know all about them; how much is "enough to begin with" is an unanswered question.

The established purpose of Project 39 is technical education. Therefore, the validity of the demonstration areas must be established on the basis of their contribution to teaching. This does not mean that there is no place for experimental projects designed to search for more effective patterns of rural extension based on more thorough knowledge of natural, cultural, and regional factors. However, Project 39 has wide opportunities open to it apart from such experimentation, and it is doubtful that the two programs should be combined. The Department of Economics and Rural Life of the Inter-American Institute in Turrialba has been conducting valuable studies pertinent to this subject. Meanwhile, the demonstration areas have proved to be a valuable integral part of providing training opportunities to citizens of member countries. They ought to be continued with that emphasis.

DURATION OF PROJECT 39.—The project was organized to run for five years and hence will reach its termination date in 1957. Should it be extended?

First, it should be recognized that this project, in its present form, is of necessity an interim project that should not be continued indefinitely. Its validity, at least in part, grows out of the present inability of national colleges of agriculture to provide the types of training needed in the new extension activities of member countries. That Project 39 is filling this gap effectively is attested not only by the use being made of it by member countries but, more important, by the testimony of extension agencies as to the value of the training some of their employees have received through its courses. This testimony is uniformly favorable in many countries.

Will this function of Project 39 have been fulfilled by 1957? It is most unlikely that it will. For one thing, extension services are just getting under way in a number of countries, but so far there is no college of agriculture in all of Latin America where training in extension methods has even been begun.[11] Project 39 is stimulating interest in this, but the translation of interest into programs is a slow process. For another, there is, and will continue to be for some years, a need for regional co-operation and cross-fertilization of ideas in agricultural extension. The zonal organization of the project is admirably suited to this purpose, and should be retained. Furthermore, a project like this one does not reach full effectiveness for several years after it is begun. Project 39 has developed as rapidly as could be expected and is now well established and becoming increasingly effective.

For these reasons, it would appear to be highly desirable that a decision should be made soon to renew it for a further period of perhaps three years, with the decision about its continuation beyond 1960 left in abeyance for the time being. Not only is it making substantial progress in the task assigned to it, but it fills a key position in the total pattern of technical co-operation in Latin America. The development of bilateral programs and those of FAO, as well as the increase in national programs for agricultural development, make Project 39 of even greater importance in the next few years.

Subsequently in this report, reference is made again to the strategic importance of Project 39. In this, its trizonal organization is a major factor. Therefore, the emphasis within the project should continue to be that of having strong teams of technicians at three zone headquarters in different parts of Latin America. The project's effectiveness would suffer were there any decision to centralize the staff at fewer centers. If any reorganization has to be considered on the basis of economizing administrative costs, it would be better to consider amalgamating the central office of the director (now in San José) with the office of the Northern Zone, rather than to reduce the number of zones or to pull technicians out of them.

ADMINISTRATION.—Two phases of the administration of Project 39 are pertinent to its effectiveness: its internal organization and its relationship to OAS.

As for the first, the present organization appears to be well adapted to the purposes of the project. The project has a director, with headquarters in San José, Costa Rica. He is responsible to the director of the Inter-American Institute of Agricultural Sciences at Turrialba, Costa Rica, forty miles away. Each of the three zone directors is responsible to the director of the project. The zone directors meet periodically with the project director for over-all project administration; within each zone, the zone director is in charge.

The second phase of the administration of Project 39 presents a more difficult problem. The resolution launching the OAS program of technical co-operation in 1950 was passed by the Inter-American Social and Economic Council (ECOSOC), which continues to be responsible for the program. This body, which meets in Washington, D.C., is made up of one representative of each member country. Representatives on the council are normally the same persons who are the representatives of member countries to the OAS itself. They are, therefore, political appointees, some of whom, as individuals, have had considerable technical experience in one field or another, but none of whom could be said to have broad experience in technical co-operation as such.

To administer the OAS program of technical co-operation, the council set up a Coordinating Committee on Technical Assistance (CCTA). The secretary-general of OAS is the chairman of CCTA, and the other members are "a representative of the Pan American Union and the highest ranking official, or his representative, of each of the cooperating agencies."[12] It is thus largely a committee of administrators, each of whom is a specialist in one field (agriculture, statistics, Indian affairs, etc.) with the representative of the Pan American Union being responsible for programs of technical co-operation outside the particular fields of the "specialized agencies" of OAS.

CCTA has a number of responsibilities embracing both the administration of projects *and* the formulation of recommendations to ECOSOC regarding projects to be undertaken and the allocation of funds among them.[13] These recommendations go to a Committee on Technical Cooperation, consisting of five members of ECOSOC itself, for consideration and recommendation to the full meetings of the council for action.

There is an inherent problem in any arrangement for the administration of technical programs by a political body. This inherent problem is accentuated in the administrative organization of OAS by the fact that recommendations regarding project selection and fund allocation are made first by a body of administrators of dis-

)arate kinds of programs, then acted upon by a political body, with 10 carry-over of common membership except the employed secretariat of CCTA and the secretary-general. Within the committee, each member, other than the chairman, brings recommendations for)rojects in his own specialized field, and he brings financial requests or projects already under way under his administration. None of hem has particular competence to pass on the proposals of others; ll of them have to compete for inadequate resources.

Under the circumstances of such organization, it appears that CCTA and its secretariat have discharged their responsibilities with ntegrity and ability. However, the inherent problem of the liaison)etween technical administrators and a political body might be nore adequately resolved by a different organizational relationship. [wo possibilities seem to deserve consideration. One would be to nerge CCTA and the Committee on Technical Cooperation into a ingle body, with the secretariat of CCTA becoming the secretariat)f this new committee. If this were done, the (politically appointed) nembers of the present Committee on Technical Cooperation would)e participating parties in discussions of proposed projects and of)udget allocations. The members of what is now CCTA would present proposals and argue the case for budget needs but would not)e solely responsible for the recommendations going from the new)ody to the council. In addition, the members of the Committee on "echnical Cooperation could then go before ECOSOC well-informed)y their prior participation in formulating the recommendations they re to present.

Another possibility would be to divide the present responsibilities)f CCTA, giving the responsibility for examining proposals for projects and for allocating funds for projects to the Committee on Technical Cooperation,[14] leaving CCTA as a purely executive body to dminister the projects approved by ECOSOC on recommendation)f the other committee. If this were done, the present members of CCTA should be made consultative members of the Committee on "echnical Cooperation and should, as heretofore, present project)roposals and budget requests for consideration by the Committee.

Neither of these proposals would eliminate the problem, but either vould appear to be preferable to the present arrangement.

OAS Tasks and Contributions

There are two considerations to be taken into account in discuss
ing the OAS programs of technical co-operation in agriculture. One
of these is the question of what tasks within the agricultural develop
ment of the Americas can best be achieved through Pan-American
programs operated by OAS. The other is the contributions that can
be made to strengthen the organization by its having a strong
program of technical co-operation, in the field of agriculture as well
as in other fields. Although this monograph must give major atten
tion to the first, the second is not beyond its purview. As pointed
out in the Introduction, technical co-operation is always *instru*
mental; it is not the ultimate objective. For the most part, and
rightly, this study concerns choices within technical co-operation
from the standpoint of impact on agricultural development. But in
many cases, once the question of "what kind of technical co-oper
ation" has been decided, the question of "under what auspices" re
mains. In some such cases, such a clear difference in impact on agri
cultural development follows from the choice of auspices that a de
cision on that score alone is in order. (Even so, there may be cases
in which a political consideration may properly override a technical
advantage.) In other cases, it apparently makes little difference what
the auspices of a particular program of technical co-operation are.
In such an event, the desirability of strengthening an international
organization by giving it substantial functions in the technical field
becomes an important consideration.

It appears from this study that technical co-operation in agricul
ture is a valid activity of OAS and that it strengthens the fabric of
the organization itself. All American countries look on it as their
own. Technicians of many countries are effectively employed in it.
The organization of Project 39 into three zones not only answers to
the regional varieties of Latin America, but it results in having tech
nicians based where they are accessible to member countries. And
its program of short courses, advisory visits, and fellowships give it
the necessary flexibility to serve well both the needs of individual
member countries and the needs for regional co-operation in agri
cultural development.

11 THE PROGRAM OF FAO

This chapter differs from the preceding seven case studies in that it summarizes the total program of the FAO throughout Latin America. This different treatment is made necessary by the nature of FAO activities in the field of technical co-operation. With few exceptions, the organization does not administer programs. Rather, it (1) provides individual experts[1] on request to member countries; (2) provides fellowships for technical study abroad; (3) participates in regional international programs and organizations; and (4) offers periodic short courses in subjects of international agricultural interest. FAO does, on occasion, provide the equipment necessary to demonstration projects (as in logging) or to get a new laboratory established (as for the production of vaccines), but most of its program of technical co-operation consists of advisory experts and the provision of opportunities for training.

Certain characteristics of the organization and of the circumstances which affect its program in Latin America need to be kept in mind.

1. FAO is an intergovernmental agency, created by governments to serve governments. It must take its directives from the legislative actions of its own biennial conference, or international governing body, and it can deal only with governments or with the governmental institutions of its member countries.

2. FAO, in most of its programs of technical co-operation, is part of the Expanded Technical Assistance Program of the United Nations, and is therefore subject to the policies, procedures, and budget allocations of the Technical Assistance Committee and the Technical Assistance Board of the United Nations.

3. The programs of technical co-operation of FAO in individual countries must be relatively small, since its total budget for such programs is only of the order of five to seven million dollars per year

for the entire world, and there is political pressure for FAO to offer technical co-operation to a large number of member countries.

The Expanded Technical Assistance Program was launched in 1951, and the expenditures of the Expanded Technical Assistance Program of FAO in Latin America for the years 1951 through 1954 are given in Table 28. As shown, the national programs, including the provision of experts and the granting of fellowships, are by far the greater portion of the program. The regional programs, each serving several countries, accounted for less than 5 per cent of FAO-ETAP expenditures during these years. Total expenditures in Latin

TABLE 28

FAO-ETAP EXPENDITURES IN LATIN AMERICA, 1951–54*

	1951	1952	1953	1954	Total
National programs....	$383,866	$729,128	$871,178	$861,616	$2,845,788
Regional programs....	9,244	12,628	52,198	37,402	111,472
Total............	$393,110	$741,756	$923,376	$899,018	$2,957,260

* Compiled from data supplied by FAO, Rome, June, 1955. See country-by-country table in Appendix. The figures in Table 28 include British Guiana, Jamaica, Surinam, and Trinidad in addition to the countries covered by other sections of this study. The total spent in those countries (1951 through 1954) was $137,039.

America were approximately $900,000 in 1953 and 1954, or about one-tenth of the amount spent by IIAA on agriculture programs in those years.

4. The programs of FAO in Latin America have been considerably affected by the fact that United States bilateral programs were well established and of considerable size before the Expanded Technical Assistance Program of the United Nations was begun. For this reason, it is particularly important not to take this account of the work of the organization in Latin America as being representative of its program in other parts of the world.

National Programs: Experts and Fellowships

Within the first four years of the Expanded Technical Assistance Program, FAO had national programs in seventeen of the countries covered by this study. The only countries in which there were no such programs were Bolivia, Cuba, and Argentina. These national programs include two activities: the provision of the services of experts, and the granting of fellowships for study outside the country.

THE DEVICE OF THE FAO EXPERT.—The major device of FAO programs in Latin America is the provision of the services of an expert, for a designated period, on the request of a member country. The organization appoints an expert with the required background of experience and training, and the member country provides office space, secretarial assistance where needed, and local transportation. The expert is assigned to one of the governmental agencies of the member country, and usually the member country designates one of its own technicians as a counterpart to him, although in some instances an expert works with a whole agency without any one person being designated as his counterpart. The responsibility of the expert is defined before he is appointed. This responsibility may be to study a particular problem and make recommendations to the member country, or to act as a day-to-day adviser to the agency to which he is assigned, or to train technicians in a specific technique, or to conduct a demonstration of new methods, or to undertake any other task which is approved in advance by the member country and FAO. For this reason, the unifying factor in the activities of the organization is, not concentration in particular fields related to agricultural development, but the method of operation: the provision by FAO of individual experts to work with established agencies of the member country on problems related to food and agriculture. There are widely differing opinions as to the relative value of this device when compared with the use of technicians-from-abroad in a special joint agency with its own funds, such as the *servicio;* this issue is discussed in chapter xv.

FIELDS IN WHICH FAO HAS BEEN ACTIVE.—Although the unifying factor in the programs is the method of operation rather than subject-matter fields, a study of the assignments of FAO experts to Latin America for the years 1951–54 does show striking concentration in certain fields. According to information supplied by the ETAP Unit of FAO in Rome, 163 of the organization's experts served in Latin America within the years 1951–54.[2] A summary of this information, classified according to the subject matter of individual assignments, is presented in Chart XI. From this chart, it will be seen that five fields were most prominent in FAO technical co-operation activities:

	No. of Experts
Forestry	34
Livestock and veterinary medicine	33
Fisheries	22
Crops and soils	16
Agricultural economics and statistics	16

The other 41 experts were scattered among 15 additional fields related to food and agriculture.

This concentration of emphasis is very different from that in the United States bilateral programs. Although there has been some work on forestry by the latter, FAO has been much more prominent in this field. One reason for this is the policy of IIAA to give primary attention to food crops. Another may be the greater ease of recruiting foresters for such positions from countries other than the United States. Scientific forestry is well advanced in Europe, and 23 of the FAO experts in this field have been Europeans, while only 4 were recruited from the United States.[3]

Of the experts in the field of livestock and veterinary medicine, half have been veterinarians, and they have been especially welcome because Latin-American countries so often lack veterinarians. Honduras, Haiti, El Salvador, and Paraguay, for example, have none except those brought through technical co-operation. Because veterinary medicine is currently a very lucrative profession in the United States, all agencies of technical co-operation find it hard to recruit veterinarians there. The IIAA cannot appoint technicians from other countries; therefore FAO understandably has its program weighted toward finding them elsewhere. The only United States veterinarian who has served under FAO in Latin America completed three successive assignments to different Latin-American countries.

Another point of interest is the relatively large number of FAO experts in the field of agricultural economics and statistics. Their presence is probably the result of two factors. One is the recognition by the Latin-American countries of their need for technicians in this field. The other is the fact that the IIAA programs have recruited very few agricultural economists, and the energies of those recruited have been absorbed mainly within the *servicios* to which they have been attached. By contrast, the agricultural economists appointed by FAO have been available to member countries to work directly with established agencies of their ministries of agriculture. A prominent part of their work has been in helping to improve arrangements for the collection and use of agricultural statistics.

It is to be expected that FAO would receive many requests for experts in the fields of crop and livestock production. It has some,

CHART XI

FAO EXPERTS BY FIELDS, LATIN AMERICA

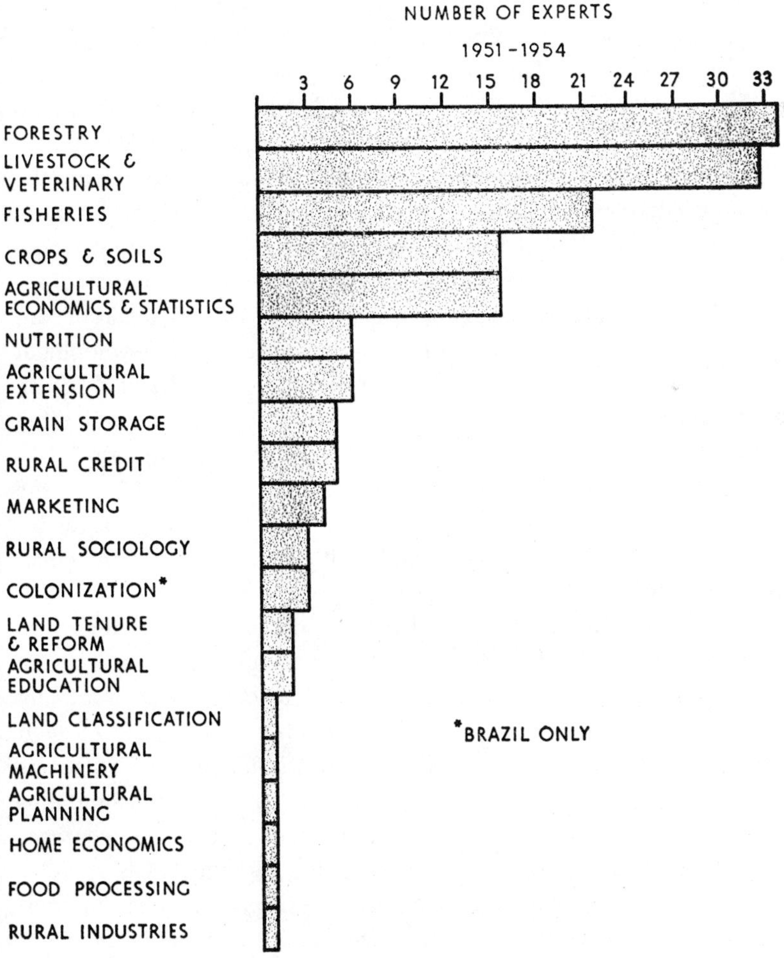

NUMBER OF EXPERTS

1951–1954

	3	6	9	12	15	18	21	24	27	30	33

FORESTRY

LIVESTOCK &
VETERINARY

FISHERIES

CROPS & SOILS

AGRICULTURAL
ECONOMICS & STATISTICS

NUTRITION

AGRICULTURAL
EXTENSION

GRAIN STORAGE

RURAL CREDIT

MARKETING

RURAL SOCIOLOGY

COLONIZATION*

LAND TENURE
& REFORM

AGRICULTURAL
EDUCATION

LAND CLASSIFICATION

AGRICULTURAL
MACHINERY

AGRICULTURAL
PLANNING

HOME ECONOMICS

FOOD PROCESSING

RURAL INDUSTRIES

*BRAZIL ONLY

but it appoints fewer than might be expected. This probably is at least partly the result of the greater activity of IIAA in these fields and also the result of the fact that some member countries have a number of competent experts in these fields.

Another significant fact about the fields of operation of the organization is the wide range of other problems on which member countries request help. It is worth noting that so far only two experts have been appointed in the field of agricultural education, and only one in the field of home economics. Also, despite the frequent remark that international agencies are in a stronger position than IIAA to advise on land tenure and land reform, only two experts have been appointed by FAO in this field.

It will be noted that the organization has sent six nutrition experts to Latin-American countries. This is another field that has received relatively less attention by agencies other than FAO.

INTENSITY OF USE.—Chart XII depicts the extent to which the various countries of Latin America have made use of the facilities offered by FAO. What this distribution means is a question which the data gathered in the course of this study cannot answer. Four of the five countries making the most use of the organization are those with governmental institutions for agricultural development much above the average of Latin America: Chile, Brazil, Mexico, and Columbia. The fifth, Ecuador, is a country in which the United States bilateral program was singularly ineffective through 1953.[4] Three of the five countries making the most use of FAO are the three countries in which the organization has its regional offices for Latin America: Mexico, Brazil, and Chile. How much, if any, effect has this had?

It is probably significant that two countries in which there are long-established IIAA agricultural programs large in relation to the size of the countries—Costa Rica and Peru—have made relatively little use of FAO. In both of those countries, the chiefs of field party of IIAA were considered by their Washington headquarters to be competent men whose judgment was to be trusted, and this probably made it easy for the country concerned to get whatever additional technical co-operation it wanted through IIAA.

On the whole, the relative sizes of FAO programs in different Latin American countries seem reasonable. The more alert countries, with better-developed institutions, have reached out for the organization's assistance and are probably in the best position to utilize the kind of help it gives. At the same time, FAO has sent many experts to the countries whose agriculture is least developed, as it ought to do, even though less is accomplished in these countries. FAO sends experts only on request, and the countries that have had the fewest experts are those that made the fewest requests.

DURATION OF FAO ASSIGNMENTS.—In comparisons of FAO programs with those of other agencies, the point is frequently made

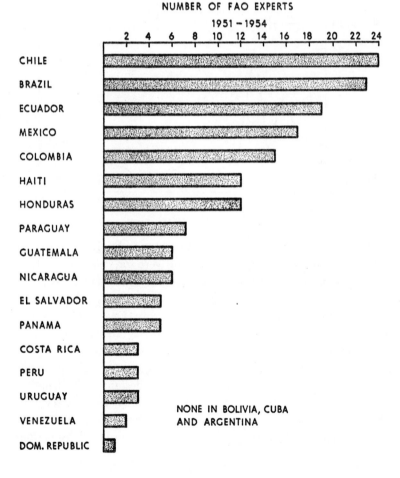

CHART XII

FAO EXPERTS BY COUNTRY, LATIN AMERICA

NUMBER OF FAO EXPERTS

1951 – 1954

that the former suffer from the short period for which experts are assigned. Since this is a criticism made with great frequency by Latin Americans, it is one that deserves attention.

What are the facts? Charts XIII and XIV summarize the facts with respect to the duration of individual assignments for the 114 assignments completed by the end of 1954. Chart XIII shows the number of assignments of each length, by three-month intervals. Chart XIV combines these into four classes and gives the percentage of assignments falling into each class. From it, one sees that 29 per cent of

CHART XIII

DURATION OF ASSIGNMENTS, FAO EXPERTS, LATIN AMERICA
1951–54, BY MONTHS

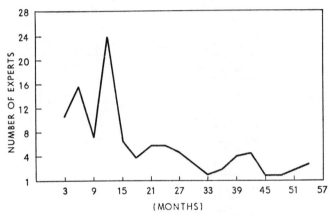

FAO assignments were for less than eight months, 33 per cent were for eight to sixteen months, 19 per cent were for seventeen to twenty-eight months, and 19 per cent were for more than twenty-eight months. Six FAO assignments to Latin America each, by extension of the initial term, lasted four years or more. One involved a marketing expert in Chile; the other five involved forestry experts, three of them in Chile and one each in Brazil and Mexico.

There are at least three factors affecting the length of assignments. The first is that member countries designate the length of initial appointment in their requests for technicians. The second is the fact that the Expanded Technical Assistance Program operates on an annual budget, the size of which is determined by national contributions which are not known in advance, so that the organization cannot make long-term commitments. The third is that FAO tries to make a limited budget go as far as possible, and assignments for longer terms would reduce the number of appointments possible at a given budget level.

No general rule is possible for the length of assignments. Some very short assignments have produced valuable results. One of the best examples of this is the one-month assignment of an expert to Mexico in 1951 to advise on a pineapple disease that had suddenly

CHART XIV

DURATION OF ASSIGNMENTS, FAO EXPERTS, LATIN AMERICA
1951–54, BY PER CENTS

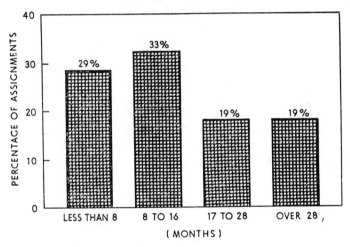

become serious. The expert was able within the month to prescribe control measures and to train operators in using them, with the result that a very valuable crop was saved. Other situations arise in which a brief period of consultation or training is adequate. For the most part, however, technical co-operation requires much longer terms of service for individual experts, and this is as true for FAO as it is for other agencies. It is probable that in most cases the organization's experts would be more effective if appointed for terms of at least two years. Two-year appointments are now made in some cases, and there is increasing opinion within the organization itself that two years should be the normal minimum period of appointment for its experts. This opinion seems sound.

NATIONAL ORIGIN OF FAO EXPERTS.—Whereas the IIAA can appoint only citizens of the United States to posts in its program, FAO can and does recruit experts from all parts of the world. The national origin of the organization's experts serving in Latin America between 1951 and 1954 is shown in Table 29. The United States

TABLE 29

NATIONAL ORIGIN OF FAO EXPERTS IN LATIN AMERICA, 1951–54

North America				50
United States	45	Canada	5	
Europe				72
France	15	Denmark	11	
Netherlands	11	United Kingdom	11	
Italy	7	Germany	5	
Switzerland	4	Austria	3	
Czechoslovakia	2	Greece	1	
Belgium	1	Spain	1	
Latin America				17
Argentina	7	Uruguay	1	
Mexico	1	El Salvador	1	
Chile	1	Brazil	1	
Paraguay	3	Venezuela	2	
Asia				8
China	6	India	2	
Australia				6
South Africa				1
Undesignated				9
Total				163

provides a larger number of FAO experts than any other one country (45), but more come from European countries taken together (72), and 17 are appointed from Latin America itself to other countries within the region.

There are three factors that make this possibility of FAO appointing experts from any member county an advantage. One is the fact that in certain specialties other countries are as advanced as the United States, and certain countries approximate more closely the climatic and other agricultural conditions of the countries in which experts are appointed to work than does the United States.[5] The second factor is the greater availability of certain types of technicians in other countries. Several European countries have many agricultural technicians who served former colonial areas. (They are not uniformly welcomed in Latin America; some countries dislike personality traits that they claim have been developed by colonial service. At the same time, there are individual experts with colonial experience who are considered to be exceptions to this criticism.) Also, the economic demand for highly trained technicians within the United States makes certain types of experts difficult to secure. (This appears to be particularly true of veterinarians and tropical foresters.)

The third advantage of FAO being able to recruit experts from many countries is chiefly psychological. It makes technical co-operation seem more mutual when a country using technical co-operation personnel in one field is simultaneously supplying them in another.

The Example of Honduras

Although there may be other Latin-American countries in which FAO has been equally effective, the one with which the writer is best acquainted is Honduras. Honduras is a small country with considerable agricultural potential for its size; yet it is greatly underdeveloped except in banana culture on the costal plain. Within the past five years it has made significant progress in organizing for agricultural development, and FAO has played a prominent role in this.[6]

The role of FAO in the development of the agriculture of Honduras has been fivefold. First, an agricultural economist, on a six-month assignment, made an intensive study of the problems of agriculture in the country and submitted a report which has been the basis for much subsequent planning. Second, FAO provided three forestry experts, two for a few months each and one for two years. They made a survey of forest resources and assisted the Ministry of Agriculture in organizing a forestry division when the ministry was established in 1952. Two Hondurans were granted fellowships to study forestry abroad, and FAO provided the equipment for a forest-research laboratory.

Third, FAO provided a total of five veterinary experts within a period of three years. Honduras still has no veterinarians of its own, but five students are now studying abroad on government scholarships and will begin to return in 1957. Meanwhile, the FAO veterinarians have helped set up an animal clinic at San Pedro Sula and a veterinary laboratory in the capital city, Tegucigalpa, with facilities for diagnosis, testing, and vaccine production. Much of the equipment for this laboratory was provided by FAO. There is a *servicio* in Honduras, STICA, operated by the government of Honduras with the co-operation of IIAA. STICA has an extension service, but since FAO has veterinarians in Honduras, the former depends on the latter's experts and does not bring in veterinary personnel. Both organizations agree that the co-operation between them in animal health and hygiene is good.

Fourth, a succession of three FAO experts has helped the Development Bank develop a grain storage and marketing program.[7] These experts first worked out plans for small grain stores, of which the Development Bank is now building nine and plans to build seventeen to twenty more in the next two years. The expert on the job at the end of 1954 was helping the bank develop a minimum-price grain-purchase program to eliminate some of the large speculative market fluctuations which have been normal in the past. Simultaneously, he had persuaded the bank to create a Department of Agricultural Statistics and was training the five or six young Hondurans who had been appointed to it.

Fifth, from Paraguay, where he had experience in an IIAA *servicio*, came an expert in supervised credit who in two and one-half years helped the Development Bank set up a supervised credit program in six localities of Honduras. The program reputedly is continuing satisfactorily under personnel trained by this expert. FAO recently sent two other experts to Honduras, one in fisheries and one in nutrition, but their projects are very new.

APPARENT REASONS FOR SUCCESS.—This program in Honduras is not described because it is typical of FAO programs in Latin America. On the contrary, it may be that it is the best. It does, however, indicate that the methods used by the organization can be effective under appropriate circumstances. What are the apparent reasons for its success?

First, Honduras is a small country, and the number of FAO experts has been higher for the size of the country than anywhere else in Latin America except Haiti.

Second, following the initial survey of the agricultural potential and problems of the country, FAO experts have worked in four selected fields; and within those fields there has been continuity of policy and personnel over a period of four years, a continuity which will probably last at least two years more. Not all of the individual experts have stayed for long periods, but one stayed forty months and another forty-four months. In the field of veterinary medicine, asignments have been shorter, but replacements have provided continuity.

Third, where necessary in order to get on with a job, FAO has made grants for laboratory equipment.

Fourth, with both FAO and IIAA operating in a single small country, there has been an agreed division of labor and satisfactory co-operation between them. This appears to be true despite the tendency for both to claim credit for some of the same specific developments.

Fifth, the record of the government of Honduras has been unusually good in living up to its agreement to provide local facilities for FAO experts. The experts have not been hampered there, as they have in many other countries, by lack of counterparts, or of office facilities, or of timely transportation.

The FAO Pattern in Latin America

Earlier in this chapter, several summary analyses of the technical co-operation activities of FAO were presented. These give the total picture during the first four years of operation of the Expanded Technical Assistance Program, but they do not depict the size and variety of the organization's activities at any one time. In the present section, the activities of FAO as of December 31, 1954, are summarized. FAO had 53 experts working in 14 Latin-American countries. As shown in Table 30, there were only 5 countries in which more than 3 of the organization's technicians were at work. There were only 3 countries in which as many as 3 experts were at work in a single field of specialization: 5 foresters in Chile, 4 foresters in Brazil, and 3 veterinarians in Honduras.

It is this dispersion of activities among countries and among fields of operation that makes the concept of an "FAO technical co-operation program" quite different from the "programs" of other agencies. All Latin-American countries have a right to call on the organization for experts in any of the fields related to food and agriculture with which it deals (unless, of course, the UN Technical Assistance Committee were arbitrarily to limit the fields of operation). With a modest budget for technical co-operation, there is no way in which FAO can change these circumstances of dispersion under which it must operate. Therefore, the organization is right in classifying the sending of experts to a country as separate

TABLE 30

FAO-ETAP Experts at Work in Latin-American Countries
December 31, 1954

Country	Fields of Work and Number of Experts	Total Experts
Chile	Forestry (5), Fisheries (2), Marketing (1), Veterinary (1), Agricultural Statistics (1), Nutrition (1), Range Management (1)	12
Brazil	Forestry (4), Soils (1), Irrigation (1), Fisheries (1)	7
Honduras	Veterinary (3), Marketing (1), Agricultural Econ. (1), Forestry (1), Fisheries (1)	7
Ecuador	Livestock (2), Agricultural Statistics (2), Fisheries (1), Agricultural Machinery (1)	6
Paraguay	Forestry (2), Agricultural Education (2), Fisheries (1)	5
Mexico	Forestry (1), Range Management (1), Fisheries (1)	3
Panama	Veterinary (2), Fisheries (1)	3
Colombia	Nutrition (1), General Agriculturalist (1)	2
Costa Rica	Livestock (1), Fisheries (1)	2
Haiti	Livestock (1), Agricultural Extension (1)	2
Venezuela	Dairying (2)	2
Peru	Agricultural Extension (1)	1
Nicaragua	Agricultural Economics (1)	1
Total		53

assignments rather than as a "program" or a "mission" as these are conceived by other agencies.

With this dispersion of effort, it would be even less valid to try to measure the effectiveness of FAO by changes in aggregate agricultural production than in the case of bilateral programs. The organization does not have a "program" of its own; it concentrates on assisting domestic programs and does this only at a few points among the many factors of agricultural development in any one country. This does not condemn it; it only describes it. The best FAO has been able to devise in the way of criteria to measure the success of its experts are two: Did the member country approve of the expert sent to help it? Did the member country live up to its part of the bargain in providing local facilities for the work of the expert? With the present budgetary limit on size of operations, it is difficult to see what other measure could be applied. There does, of course, remain the question as to whether the method of technical co-operation is the best the organization can achieve under the circumstances. This cannot be objectively answered but deserves consideration.

Validity of the "Individual Expert" Device

So long as FAO has world-wide responsibility and relatively limited resources, it has no option but to continue to use the device of the individual expert for the greater part of its technical co-operation activities. In practice, the sucess of this device ranges from excellent to very poor. The major strength of the device is that it results in technicians working very closely with the personnel of established agricultural agencies within the country. The factor which can be either strength or weakness, depending on local conditions, is that it takes as given the prevailing pattern of administration and personnel policy of national agencies. This is a strength where local conditions are relatively good, but it is a weakness where local administration and personnel policies are unstable or poor. The major weakness of the device of the individual expert is that it provides only one among so many factors essential to agricultural development, even in a limited sphere, that its chances of success are limited.

These factors indicate that, in general, the device of the individual expert is more effective, the more stable and adequate is the national agency for agricultural development to which the expert is attached. It is less effective in the least developed countries with the least stable agricultural institutions, particularly when assignments are of short duration. Where an FAO expert is assigned to a backward country for a long period, he himself provides some of the continuity which otherwise is missing and the lack of which would be likely to vitiate his work. This argues for longer periods of assignment of experts, particularly in countries with the less developed agricultural institutions.

Another way to compensate for the lack of stability in the less developed countries is to appoint several experts in the same field of specialization, both simultaneously and for overlapping terms of service, thereby concentrating enough strength in a specific field to make substantial achievement possible. This has been accomplished in Honduras, but not in several other countries where national institutions are weak or unstable.

No matter what the country may be, or what measures are taken to compensate for the weaknesses inherent in the device of the individual expert, success requires the appointment of a really outstanding man for each and every assignment. In a *servicio*, an outstanding chief of field party can utilize the services of competent but not outstanding technicians. The *servicio* itself provides working conditions in which a normally competent man can be effective; and where it is necessary for a technician to establish close relations with another agency, the chief of field party can be of considerable help. Where each man is largely on his own, however, as every individual FAO expert is, he must be of high competence. Of the organization's experts met in the course of this study, several have made outstanding contributions; at the same time, it is obvious that quite a number have not been able to break through the difficulties of local circumstances under which they are required to work. Proposals to make the FAO device of the individual expert more effective are outlined in the final section of this chapter.

EXCEPTIONAL PROCEDURES.—That some administrators, at least, within FAO are fully cognizant of the differential appropriateness of the individual expert adviser and of the operating program (like a *servicio*) under different circumstances is revealed by their comments in conversation and by departures of the organization from its normal procedures in certain instances.

In Bolivia, FAO was asked for, and supplied, an expert on land reform. He was to be an adviser only. He made recommendations, whereupon the Bolivian government asked him to administer the recommended reforms. He demurred, saying that he was only an adviser. The government replied by stating that the next morning the adviser would have a staff and a fleet of vehicles. People losing land began coming to him and saying, "You are giving away what is not yours." He replied, "I am only an adviser." Actually, however, he did administer, for a brief period, this program at the request of the Bolivian government. The government wanted a disinterested outsider in whom it had confidence to make the difficult decisions.

In the Amazon Basin of Brazil, FAO was asked to provide experts in forestry. The objective, as seen by FAO, should have been to establish a federal forestry service. But to do this, they felt, required a *demonstration* of what such a service could do and how it might operate. Consequently, the organization provided the necessary equipment for the demonstration and is carrying it out according to the line of reasoning frequently used with reference to *servicios*. Thus, while FAO normally provides only individual experts, it does, on occasion, develop programs of the "operating" type.[8] One FAO administrator commented that "our programs tend to become operational when they are successful."

That this procedure in Brazil contributed to the desired results is indicated by the intention of the Brazilian government now to establish a Forestry Research Institute for the Amazon Basin, as part of a very large program for the development of the region. This total Amazon program is to receive 3 per cent of all federal revenues for a period of twenty years.

Fellowships

In the years 1951 through 1954, FAO-ETAP granted 77 fellowships for study outside the homeland of the recipient. In each case, the recipient was an official of his government before appointment and returned to government service after his period of study was completed. In general, fellowships have been awarded only in the fields in which FAO had one or more experts in the country, and the granting of a fellowship was part of the effort to secure continuation of the work that the expert had begun or strengthened.

The fellowships granted by FAO-ETAP are summarized in Table 31. Apart from the 20 fellowships for a four-month course in nutrition in Guatemala, the largest number of recipients studied in the United States (27), with nearly as many (21) going to Europe. Some 11 persons studied elsewhere in Latin America, and 6 went to Australia, Asia, or Africa.

It might be expected, in view of the policy of granting fellowships to provide for carrying on the work of experts after their departure, that the number of fellowships granted in forestry and fisheries, particularly, would have been much larger. For two reasons, no fair comparison can be made from the data available. First, there are other sources of fellowships. Governments can be encouraged to provide fellowships in a particular field. One place where this has happened is Honduras, where the government has sent 5 students to Europe to study veterinary medicine. Second, the budget for fellowships is small; therefore, needs in many fields of specialization must be considered.

TABLE 31

FAO-ETAP FELLOWSHIPS GRANTED TO LATIN AMERICANS, 1951–54*

COUNTRY	FIELD OF STUDY												TOTAL NUMBER	PLACE OF STUDY					
	Agr. Engineering	Agr. Extension	Crop Culture	Livestock	Farm Management	Soils	Fisheries	Nutrition	Agr. Econ. & Stat.	Forestry	Entomology	Other		Australia	Asia	Africa	Europe	Latin America	North America
Brazil	..	2	..	..	..	..	..	1	1	..	..	2	6	..	..	1	2	2	4†
Chile	1	..	3	4	2	..	1	3	1	..	..	..	15	3	..	..	6	1	8
Colombia	..	..	..	1	..	..	..	..	3	..	..	..	4	..	..	..	1	..	3
Costa Rica	..	..	..	..	..	..	..	2	1	..	..	..	3	..	..	..	..	2	1
Ecuador	..	..	1	4	..	..	1	4	..	1	..	2	13	1	..	..	3	6	4
El Salvador	..	..	..	1	..	1	..	1	..	..	..	..	3	..	..	..	1	2	1
Guatemala	..	..	..	..	..	..	..	3	..	1	..	..	4	..	..	..	1	3	..
Haiti	..	..	2	..	..	..	2	2	..	2	..	1	9	..	1	..	4	2	2
Honduras	..	..	..	..	..	..	..	4	..	2	..	2	8	..	..	..	2	6	..
Mexico	..	..	..	2	..	..	..	..	1	..	..	..	3	..	..	..	1	1	1
Nicaragua	..	..	..	..	..	..	..	4	1	..	..	..	5	..	..	..	..	4	1
Peru	..	..	1	..	..	..	..	2	..	..	..	..	3	..	..	..	..	2	1
Uruguay	..	..	..	..	..	..	..	..	..	..	1	..	1	..	..	..	..	..	1
Total	1	2	7	12	2	1	4	26	8	6	1	6	77	4	1	1	21	31‡	27

* Compiled from information provided by the ETAP Unit of FAO, Rome, June, 1955.

† In some cases, a fellow studied on more than one continent.

‡ Twenty of the 77 fellowships were for a four-month nutrition course given by INCAP in Guatemala.

The largest number of fellowships (25) of FAO in the years 1951–54 were for twelve months of study. If to this number are added the number for ten months (7), the number comes to 32 for a full academic year of study. Some 20 fellowships were granted for the four-month nutrition course in Guatemala. The other 15 fellowships were for various periods of three to nine months each.[9]

Regional Programs

In addition to its technical co-operation with national governments, FAO has had a part in seven regional programs related to agricultural development in Latin America. None of these is a project exclusively of FAO; each of them is an example of co-operation between it and other international agencies.

These seven regional programs are:

1. Caribbean Commission, for which FAO provides three experts in the fields of home economics, pulp and paper technology, and economics.

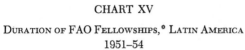

CHART XV

DURATION OF FAO FELLOWSHIPS,* LATIN AMERICA
1951–54

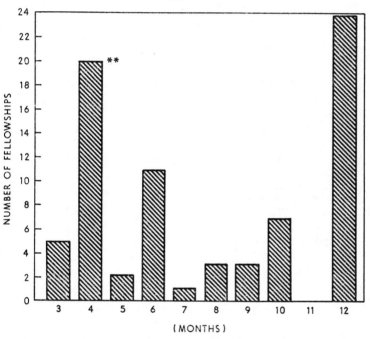

(MONTHS)

* Compiled from information supplied by ETAP Unit, FAO, Rome, June, 1955.
** All for nutrition course of INCAP, Guatemala.

2. Central American Locust Control, for which FAO provides an entomologist.

3. Central American Integration Project, for which FAO provides a veterinarian, an agricultural economist, and a forester.

4. Andean Indian Mission, for which FAO has provided two experts.

5. Latin American Center for Fundamental Education (CRE-FAL), for which FAO has provided four experts: one in agricultural extension, one in agricultural co-operatives, and two in home economics.

6. Central American Foot and Mouth Disease Protection, for which FAO has provided two experts.

7. Institute of Nutrition for Central America and Panama (INCAP), for which FAO has provided one nutritionist.

TABLE 32

SHORT-COURSE TRAINING AND SEMINARS

Subject	Location	Duration (Months)
1951		
Agricultural Statistics Tabulation Methods..............................	Brazil	....
Agricultural Development Planning....	Chile	3
Agricultural Statistics...............	Costa Rica	3
1952		
Fisheries...........................	Chile	2½
Application of Statistical Techniques...	Ecuador	4
Agricultural Credit..................	Guatemala	1
Soil Conservation and Management....	Chile	4
1953		
Land Problems......................	Brazil	2
Range and Pasture Development......	Argentina	3
Agricultural Extension*..............	Peru	4
1954		
Fisheries Development...............	Mexico	4
Agricultural Extension*..............	Peru	1
Rural Co-operatives.................	Puerto Rico	4
Range and Pasture Management†......	Argentina	1½
Farm Management...................	Uruguay	3

* In co-operation with SCIPA, Peru.
† Chiefly OAS; FAO had a minor part.

In addition to the regional programs, all of a continuing nature, the organization sponsors international short courses and seminars related to agricultural development. Thirteen of these were held in 1951–54 for periods of one to four months each. In addition, several conferences of about a week each were convened by FAO in different parts of Latin America.

Those training courses that lasted one month or more are shown in Table 32. A few of these were sponsored by FAO alone, but most of them were sponsored jointly by FAO and OAS.

Conclusions regarding FAO

1. The Regular Program of FAO contributes substantially to agricultural development in all countries. The international meetings and conferences of FAO have become increasingly important as forums for the discussion of agricultural problems shared by many countries. The regional organizations and "working parties" that it sponsors have furthered international co-operation both regionally and by crop interests. The regular visits of FAO officials to member countries have a stimulating effect on official thinking with respect to agriculture and are instrumental in increasing a profitable exchange of information between countries. (In this respect FAO visits are particularly helpful to the smaller nations that have fewer agricultural attachés or information officers of their own scattered about the world.) The publications of FAO fill an important role. The "Agricultural Series" and the "Development Papers" are particularly helpful to those countries having difficult problems of agricultural development, while the world-wide statistics published by FAO are helpful to all member countries.

2. The international status of FAO makes it less suspect of political motives than are bilateral governmental agencies. It might be thought that FAO would never be subject to such suspicions; however, in some Latin-American countries this suspicion attaches to some United States technicians even when they are serving under FAO. In one case, a forestry mission of FAO was accused of being a United States agency even when no United States personnel were in the mission, apparently because the regional representative of FAO happened to be a United States citizen. In other countries, there is a marked preference for FAO technical co-operation precisely because it is international, and this appears to be the usual case.

3. FAO is free, within quite wide limits, to appoint its personnel from any country, wherever good technicians can be found. Apart from the obvious advantage of being able to recruit the best men, regardless of citizenship, this is a good way to stress the mutuality of helpfulness in technical co-operation. The similarities of agricultural resources between a Latin-American and a European or Asiatic region in a certain respect may make the exchange of experts between such regions advantageous. Moreover, some observers feel

(and this is justifiable in some cases but is rationalization in others) that European agricultural scientists are broader in their training than the "highly specialized" Americans.

The limitations on FAO's freedom of choice with respect to the nationality of technicians are not severe, but they are real. Its multiple-currency income is one; sometimes when FAO is short of the currency of the country from which the most competent expert could be recruited, it has to turn to a country where it has accumulated funds. Differences in salary level among prospective sending countries is another. In general, FAO tries to strike a balance between the earning power of a particular "expert" in his home country and the need to avoid too large discrepancies between the salaries of the various members of a single FAO mission. If FAO must choose between an American who commands a high salary at home and a lower-salaried but nearly as competent technician from another country, it frequently feels it must employ the latter. Another factor in the nationality of FAO technicians is availability.

Despite these limiting factors it remains true that FAO does have the advantage over United States bilateral programs of being able to appoint technicians from many countries. In a sizable mission this can have the added advantage of compensating for the national bias with which any one technician may come to the program.

4. In view of the inherent advantages of an international agency in programs of technical co-operation, from the standpoints of political neutrality, wider choice of technicians, and equality of status of participating nations, many people (this writer among them) wish that the programs of technical co-operation of FAO might be expanded. In contemplating such expansion, however, certain basic obstacles and limitations must be recognized, and certain changes of policy on the part of FAO appear to be desirable.[10]

There are two outstanding problems in connection with strengthening the technical co-operation activities of FAO in Latin America. One is the problem of securing a fulcrum for effective influence by FAO on priorities in technical co-operation; the other is finding a way to enlarge its budget while safeguarding its international character.

FAO, in order to be more effective in technical co-operation, needs a more influential voice in educating officials of underdeveloped countries in the priorities of technical co-operation. In talking with officials of FAO, whether at headquarters or in the field, one is impressed by their insistence that they are the servants of member nations and that, as such, they can step in only when invited and only in conformity with job descriptions drawn up by the recipient governments. There are two strong arguments for accepting these limitations without question. One is that there is no point in urging on a country a type of co-operation for which it is not enthusiastic. The other was well expressed to the writer by a high official of the organization. "It would be immodest of FAO (with $5,000,000 for 50 countries) to look at each country and try to decide where it needs help; it is far better to find an operating head of a domestic agricultural program with ability and imagination and back him up with technical aid." With this, the writer fully agrees. But as matters stand now, administrators have little room for initiative in finding such men.

This should be corrected by the next biennial conference of FAO. That conference should recognize that in many countries some of the more serious obstacles to agricultural development are not the lack of specific techniques (for which such countries now often call on FAO) but lack of understanding of what is really needed. The conference should so change its instructions to administrators that the latter feel a responsibility to advise member countries on priorities in agricultural development and to suggest specific aid. This can be done without in any way impairing the right of any host country finally to determine what FAO may or may not do to help it.

At this point, a comparison with the relationship of the Inter-American Institute of Agricultural Sciences to OAS is instructive. The Inter-American Institute, like FAO, is the servant of an international agency. But, unlike FAO, it has wide autonomy in deciding what its program is to be. It offers to member countries what it thinks they need, and each country is free to accept or reject this particular service. It is true that this agency initiative is easier when the program of technical co-operation is like that of OAS than when the program consists largely of experts sent to individual countries, as in the ETAP of FAO.

Whether FAO actually has considerable latitude in recommending programs to member countries is debatable. Certainly one gets the impression that its technicians feel it has little such latitude. If it is to make its maximum contribution to agricultural development in member countries, it needs to be confident that it has both authority and responsibility to recommend programs to member countries, not just the duty of responding to ready-made requests.

The second problem in connection with enlarging the programs of technical co-operation through FAO is the need to keep the organization truly international in its source of funds. The United States now contributes 30 per cent of the budget for the Regular Program. This is less than the 33 per cent now contributed by the United States to the general budget of the UN, and the contribution to the Regular Program could probably be substantially increased without endangering the international character of that program. But the United States for three years contributed 60 per cent of the total budget for the Expanded Technical Assistance Program; in the fourth year this was reduced to 57.7 per cent. This ETAP budget controls the magnitude of programs of technical co-operation, and it is doubtful that the percentage contributed by the United States could be appreciably increased without destroying the truly international character of the programs of technical co-operation of FAO. This means that the only way substantially to increase the technical co-operation budget of FAO is through a general rise in the contributions of all countries, or at least of a substantial number of countries other than the United States. Since many of the member countries now have limited agricultural productivity, any increase they make in their contributions to ETAP may be argued to be at the cost of domestic programs. It would still be wise for even the "poorest" countries to treble their contributions to ETAP in order to allow the contributions of wealthier nations to rise without increasing the percentage those contributions are of the total. There is a kind of vicious circle here in that FAO needs larger programs of technical co-operation in order to be efficient, but it is difficult to get increased contributions (particularly from the poorer countries) prior to demonstrating the value of enlarged programs.

An inevitable limitation on technical co-operation activities of FAO is that the agency cannot provide funds to match or to supplement local funds for a project budget. This would remain true even if the ETAP budget of FAO were trebled, and a greater increase than that is not sufficiently likely to merit discussion for the next few years. Other expansions of expenditure deserve much higher priorities than cash contributions to project budgets. Specifically, the effectiveness of FAO programs would benefit by having more of the agency's funds put first into providing secretarial help and travel facilities for technicians and their counterparts and after that into an increased force of technicians.

If FAO is to be expanded or made more effective at its present size, certain changes of policy appear to be desirable. Among those most to be recommended are the following.

1. The policy of requiring from a host government payment of a per diem to each FAO-ETAP technician working in its country should be dropped.[11] Two arguments are used to justify the policy of per diem pay. One is that the recipient government ought to meet part of the cost of each project of technical co-operation and therefore the per diem for each technician is a legitimate form for part of this local participation. The other is that per diem payment by the host country reduces the cost per technician, thereby allowing more technicians to be appointed.

To understand this issue, it must be realized that such a per diem is, in reality, a supplemental salary. It is intended to be, not the actual cost of board and room, but an extra inducement to get technicians to accept assignment in a foreign country and a recognition that technicians leaving their homeland for a period of time usually retain obligations at home. Rather than establish salary scales covering these needs, the agency prefers to set a salary related to normal homeland income, then add a per diem to supplement this salary through host governments.

It is right for FAO-ETAP to require local participation in the cost of a project, but wrong to insist that part of this shall be per diem pay to each technician. The handicap imposed by this practice, while chiefly psychological, is substantial. Often the per diem pay to the technician is larger than the total salary received by the local officials with whom he works. This irritates local technicians and annoys governments. To many it looks like what it is in fact—not per diem as that term is normally used but a supplemental salary.

FAO is also quite right in pointing out that for it to assume this supplemental salary would increase its cost per technician. The question is whether such a change in policy, together with adoption of the proposals made below as to more appropriate forms for local financial participation and as to length of term of appointment of technicians, would increase or decrease the lasting effect of projects. It is the writer's judgment that the proposed changes would substantially increase the effectiveness of FAO-ETAP programs. The present per diem policy is misunderstood and is a needless obstacle, since there are more productive forms for local financial participation to take.

2. FAO-ETAP should assume the cost of secretarial help, office supplies, and all travel expenses of its experts. In the first two years of ETAP, a second requirement forced recipient governments to provide not only office space but office supplies, secretarial help, and travel within the country for each technician. This requirement was justified on two counts: (*a*) that if ETAP had to meet these expenses, the number of technicians it could send out would have to be reduced, and (*b*) that for ETAP to provide such facilities would greatly increase its administrative task in view of the large number of widely separated projects in which it is involved. The handicap imposed by this requirement resulted both from breach of contract whenever a local government did not, in fact, make the provisions it had agreed to make and/or from delay in making such facilities available. Providing travel for technicians is likely to be unsatisfactory by a government not accustomed to providing frequent travel facilities to its own agricultural officials. It would be much better for all such costs to be met by ETAP and for local governments to be required to make their contributions to the costs of the projects in other ways.

3. A clear distinction should be made between the survey adviser, the operating adviser, and the training adviser as different devices of technical co-operation, and greater use should be made of the device of the operating adviser. The provision of advisers as a device of technical co-operation has not had a fair trial, with few exceptions, in Latin-American countries. On the one hand, FAO has argued the superiority of this type of technical co-operation over the device of the operating program or *servicio*. It has cited considerations both political and normative for this position. It has held that,

as a creature of many governments, FAO cannot take responsibility for any program within a single country. It has urged the normative position that it is wrong for an outsider to be an administrator; for such outside administration "creates an island within a country amounting to a violation of national sovereignty." But while extolling the superiority of the device of "advisers" in technical co-operation, FAO has not given that device a fair trial. This is not the fault of the agency alone; many of the decisions which prevented a fair trial were made by recipient countries.

What is an adviser? Although the distinction is not always clear-cut, there are two general types. One is the survey adviser, who studies the task assigned to the person or ministry he is supposed to advise and then submits a report on what should be undertaken, or on how the job should be done, or both. The other is the operating adviser, who works closely with a person or an agency on its assigned task, making frequent, usually oral, suggestions and helping out in substantive ways short of administrative control.

Both of these types of adviser have their place in technical co-operation, and both are sound devices for FAO to use under its circumstances of budget and responsibility. Both are being used in Latin America, but in the case of each there is an unfulfilled condition to success which limits the effectiveness of each.

For the work of the survey adviser to be effective, two special requisites beyond the technical competence of the adviser are essential: (1) he must have been in the country long enough to get a thorough grasp of local problems and conditions, and (2) there must be reasonable grounds for hope that his report will receive careful consideration once it has been made. For the operating adviser to be effective, the chief requisites beyond technical competence are: (1) effective rapport, without a language or other cultural barrier between the adviser and the person or persons he is advising, and (2) sufficient freedom to experiment on the part of the official or agency being advised. Without the first, the effective communication of suggestions is impossible; without the second, successful communication of suggestions is only frustrating. Although length of experience in the country is advantageous for the operating adviser, it is less important for him than for the survey adviser, as the errors of understanding of the operating adviser come to light piecemeal and can be corrected in his day-to-day contacts with local technicians.

The unfulfilled condition for complete success of survey advisers in Latin America has been adequate length of appointments. The unfulfilled condition for complete success of operating advisers has been budget provision to allow some freedom to experiment.

It must be recognized that there has been some tendency in the past (it is decreasing now) for host governments to prefer the first type. Thus in sending out survey advisers, FAO has been "giving member countries what they want." But there is increasing disillusionment with surveys standing alone and increasing recognition on all sides that a day-to-day advisory working relationship is in many cases more fruitful. This does not mean that reports are not valuable, and the present FAO practice of requiring monthly reports to Rome, periodic memoranda to officials in the host country, and a final report by each technician on termination of his appointment to a country is sound. But such reports are and ought to be a phase of orderly operations rather than the chief end of the programs.

4. To these two types of advisers should be added the category of training advisers. Their important function is to train local technicians in a specific technique, whether of laboratory technique in relation to the manufacture of vaccines or of statistical treatment of experimental data. The most important condition to the success of such missions, in addition to technical and teaching competence, is adequate organization of the training program itself.

Each of these three types of FAO technicians has a distinctive task despite the fact that a particular technician may be called upon to perform more than one function. In so far as possible, this combining of functions should be foreseen, so that adequate steps are taken in advance to expedite his work. However, no such pre-planning should be binding, for it may be found after a technician arrives that his talents and temperament are better suited to some variation of his original assignment.

What are the facilities that each of these three types of FAO technicians needs, and which of these can profitably be required of recipient governments? In all three cases, office space, office supplies, secretarial help, and domestic travel should be provided by FAO.

Beyond these basic requirements, the needs of the three types of technicians differ. It is important that the survey adviser and the training technician have local counterparts who may absorb as much as possible of the knowledge and skill of the technician while he is there. The cost of such counterparts should be undertaken by the recipient government in advance (as is now the case), although it is often wise to delay selection of the counterpart until the FAO technician can participate in the selection. In addition, when a training technician is assigned to a country, the project agreement should require the local government to make a cash deposit in advance to cover the cost of the training facilities that will be required, including stipends for trainees if those are to be required.

The type of FAO technician which might prove to be of greatest value if adequately tried is the operating adviser, one who works daily as an adviser and consultant to the local administrator of a domestic program but without administrative authority. His task is not to produce a written guide to a particular phase of agricultural development, not to train men in a designated technique, but to serve as professional colleague, consultant, and adviser to the administrator of a significant domestic program related to agricultural development. Two conditions need to be met if this type of advisory co-operation is to be given a fair trial. First, the minimum period of appointment for such technicians should be two years. Second, the host government, for the experimental period of the adviser's stay and for at least two years afterward, should make a substantial cash deposit available to the administrator with whom the adviser is affiliated.

Of course, if an operating adviser is provided for a new activity, which is itself experimental, the need for special provision for such experimental pocket money does not arise. But the task for which an operating adviser is usually requested is to help upgrade an existing agency or activity, and it is in precisely this circumstance that existing budgetary provisions are likely to be most rigid. Frustration is likely to result unless provision is made for a small fund to finance innovations.

It is at this point that FAO decries (while several of its administrators and technicians also envy) the independence of action of a bilateral *servicio*. It is one thing to argue that administrative authority should remain in the hands of nationals; it is quite another to ignore the fact that delegated administrative discretion in using a free reserve fund for experimentation with new methods is an important element in improving public programs related to agricultural development. In a few instances, it may be possible to improve a program by the reallocation of budget funds at the previous level of appropriation, but even where that is true, it normally entails tedious procedures of securing approval for reallocations. Additional funds must be found for experiments that may or may not succeed, anticipating using the demonstration value of successful innovations to justify larger and reorganized appropriations in the future.

If a recipient government wishes the services of an operating adviser, then FAO has the right and the responsibility for ascertaining that the recipient government is serious in wishing to improve its own program. One test of this, as well as an essential element in the success or failure of such a mission, is the willingness of the recipient government to appropriate an experimental fund to be administered jointly by the local administrator and the FAO adviser. This fund should be at least as large as the annual salary of the administrator to whom the adviser is attached and could well be as large as the salary of the adviser. Neither amount would be large in relation to the need; but it would at least make some minor experimentation possible.

If the device of the operating adviser is to be given a fair trial, each such adviser must be appointed for a term of at least two years. No shorter period is a fair test. Within the first year the adviser will learn far more than he can teach. During the second year he can correct some of his early mistakes and make a more creative contribution.

The present administrators of FAO agree that most appointments should be for periods of at least two years. However, they point out that, under existing budgetary arrangements, FAO cannot commit itself to two-year appointments for more than a relatively small number of its technicians in ETAP. The annual allocation of funds (to FAO) on a very uncertain voluntary basis makes commitments for longer than one year impossible. The difficulty is a real one, but the solution is not one-year appointments. Rather, it is either longer-term commitments by member countries or a decision by the FAO biennial conference to set up a substantial reserve, or "carry-over," fund to make longer-term commitments possible within the present practice of annual appropriations.

5. Apparently, two common misconceptions about technical co-operation have limited the effectiveness of many of the projects of FAO-ETAP. These are: (1) the idea that a foreign technician has some special quality that equips him, on arrival, to demonstrate and teach "improved" techniques with respect to some phase of agricultural production and (2) the idea that it is the sole function of technical co-operation to introduce and/or teach specific techniques.

Although occasionally a foreign technician can, on arrival, demonstrate and teach an improved technique, this is the exception rather than the rule. Usually, the foreign technician must go through a period of trial, adaptation, re-trial, and readaptation before discovering, in co-operation with local technicians, what a real improvement under local conditions would be. The foreign technician's most valuable attributes on arrival are: (1) his basic training, (2) his flexibility and determination to learn, (3) his misgivings about the adequacy of any proposals he may have or be able to develop, and (4) his recognition that a country's need for help at a particular agricultural point does not necessarily mean a deficiency of ability, or of integrity within the social values of the culture, or of desire to improve. Because of the central importance of these attributes, the best-qualified foreign technician is likely to be slow in making definite recommendations.

The second common misconception is that the sole function of technical co-operation is to introduce and/or teach specific techniques. There are circumstances under which training only is required. FAO-ETAP has engaged in some training programs and has provided some training technicians. Where such a simple transfer of a specific technique is sufficient, these projects have been successful. But here, also, such cases are the exception rather than the rule. For the most part, technical co-operation must be a "partnership-over-time-in-institutionalization"—not so much a technique as *a pattern of solving problems* within agriculture. This intimate partnership is what makes the real assets of the foreign technician fully fruitful, but it cannot be achieved within the dominant present pattern of single technicians called in for a short time, each to do a specific job. Again, the fault for this is not to be laid primarily on the employees of FAO, many of whom fully realize the limitations under which they operate. Basically, it is what member nations ask of FAO and the instructions their representatives formulate in the biennial conferences that are at fault.

It should be recalled that these recommendations with respect to the program of FAO are combined in this section with the judgment that FAO is already playing an important role in agricultural development and with the recommendation that the size of its program could well be trebled in the immediate future. Every agency has its own limitations, within which it must find an effective pattern of operation. FAO is in the new and growing field of international organization and has special problems because of that. One conclusion of this study is that FAO has weakened its own program by policies undertaken to make meager resources go as far as possible. Such policies should be revised in the interests of more lasting effectiveness. Meanwhile, member countries should increase their contributions to the agency so that its programs can be enlarged.

PART **III**

ANALYSIS AND CONCLUSIONS

12 AGRICULTURAL DEVELOPMENT

It was pointed out in chapter iii that one of the major obstacles to this study was the lack of an agreed explanation of how an agriculture becomes more productive. Some of the explanations that have been advanced in recent years were mentioned there: a *knowledge* theory (that what is chiefly needed is information about improved agricultural techniques); a *capital* theory (that what is chiefly needed is capital for implements, seeds, fertilizers, insecticides, etc.); a *public administration* theory (that since agricultural development requires a variety of public programs, the first requirement is administrative improvement in these public programs); and a *general economic climate* theory (that advance in agriculture depends largely on the availability of markets, roads, education, health facilities, and favorable monetary, price, and general economic policies).

Although it is not a purpose of this study to try to develop a definitive theory of agricultural development, three types of data unearthed by the study would be pertinent to that task.

1. The tasks undertaken by programs of technical co-operation reveal a number of the kinds of activity that different agencies and different national governments believe to be essential to agricultural development.

2. The many domestic programs of Latin-American governments likewise indicate the activities those governments consider to be pertinent to agricultural development.

3. The obstacles to greater achievement that have been encountered by both types of programs point to other factors of agricultural development of which account would have to be taken.

This chapter summarizes the evidence of the study relevant to the topic of the nature of agricultural development in two ways. The first of the following sections presents four basic comments on agricultural development which the evidence of this study appears to support. These comments by no means constitute a proposed substitute for the theories of agricultural development which others have advanced. They are, rather, the additional considerations which the data of this study reveal to be relevant to the search for such a theory.

The second section presents a list of the elements of agricultural development, as revealed by the current activities for, and obstacles to, agricultural development in Latin America. These, again, do not add up to a theory or explanation of agricultural development, but they constitute a kind of "check list" for assessing the current needs of a particular region at any given time if agricultural development is to be accelerated.

The third section of this chapter might be termed speculative. It draws attention to a distinction between two kinds of resources for agricultural development, under the heading of "Economic and Self-generating Resources," a distinction suggested by the differing experiences of the many countries of Latin America in this field.

Basic Comments on Agricultural Development

The facts brought to light by this study support four basic comments on the nature of agricultural development:

1. A vital phase of developing a more productive agriculture is learning to make choices, learning to take responsibility for the results of choices, and learning how to use money.

2. Agricultural development does not depend on farmers alone but is one product of the whole way of living, the whole culture, of a nation or of a region.

3. Agricultural development and rural welfare are interrelated, with the cause-and-effect relationship moving in both directions.

4. Either an external crisis or a strong, widely felt internal impulse to progress appears to be necessary as an incentive to national effort toward agricultural development.

1. *A vital phase of developing a progressive agriculture is learning to make choices, learning to take responsibility for the results of choices, and learning how to use money.*

The agricultural systems of Latin America are ranged between two extremes: (*a*) traditional agriculture, in which both the combination of crops and the methods of cultivation remain virtually unchanged from generation to generation, and (*b*) progressive agriculture, in which changes and adjustments are made more or less frequently in response to shifts in demand, or in costs, or in technology, and to the fact that one change usually has repercussions which require additional changes. Obviously, there are many gradations as an agriculture moves away from the traditional type. Examples of many stages can be cited both in different regions of the Americas and within single regions. On the holdings of Indians in the highlands of the Andes there is very little change; agriculture is almost wholly traditional. Within a few miles of them one may find haciendas drawing heavily on recent discoveries and making frequent changes in agricultural practices. In parts of the United States, with wide and rapid dissemination of new agricultural knowledge, and detailed cost accounting on tens of thousands of individual farms, there are continuous changes in crop patterns and methods of cultivation; yet in other sections, or even within the same locality, one finds patterns of farming that are relatively traditional. In much of Brazil there is great sensitivity of acreages of cash crops to price changes, but such farms are interspersed by others (particularly some of those producing cattle, corn, and beans) which remain much the same from decade to decade. Part of the distinction between the two is the difference between small and large farms, but not all; as pointed out in chapter viii, it is customary to distinguish between progressive large farms and stagnant large farms, the difference being in sensitivity to market changes and to new knowledge rather than in size.

For the most part, underdeveloped agricultural regions are those in which traditional agriculture is dominant. Farmers grow the same crops, in the same ways, using the same implements, generation after generation. This is true in the Andean highlands; it is true in most of Central America; it is true in many parts of Brazil. And people who live largely by tradition develop ways of acting, ways of thinking, and even whole systems of values that are quite different from those in a choice-making, constantly changing, largely commercial economy.

Changes occur in agriculture, even in the most traditional pattern, but these changes come about infrequently and slowly, with ample time for adjustment to other phases of the life of the people.

Progressive agriculture, however, is not simply another slowly evolving pattern of farming but a *rapidly* changing pattern in which each change calls for additional changes, quickly. A new crop makes new demands on the soil. Concentration on a new crop results in multiplication of the pests and diseases of that crop. Even the races of disease fungi and viruses keep evolving so that control measures effective yesterday are not effective today. Thus, whereas the farmer in a traditional agriculture can do as his father did, a farmer in a progressive agriculture cannot do even as he himself did three years ago.

Traditional agriculture depends only very slightly on the market. Tools may be purchased in a traditional economy, and sometimes draft animals, and renters may have to pay cash rent, but for the most part the economy of the farm is self-contained.[1] However, as agriculture becomes more progressive, it becomes dependent on many materials available only by purchase, and the prices of these are determined, in part or in whole, by factors elsewhere in the economy. Agriculture has to compete with other industries for capital. Wage rates become more important. The market prices of the crops produced replace in importance the utility of those particular crops to the farm family in consumption.

For many of those farmers who have been accustomed to farming by tradition, the use of money is a new practice and requires new types of judgment. While those who are trying to stimulate agricultural development would like to see most new cash income go into new capital investments or into improved family living, there is a strong tendency for much of it to be used in pursuit of social values already established. The "rational" use of money in a largely traditional economy (where economic, social, and religious life are intimately interwoven) is quite different from the "rational" use of money in a choice-making, commercial economy. The transition from the one to the other takes time.

The opposite of traditional is "choice-making." The process of decision-making is at a minimum in any traditional culture or method of production. Thus, encouraging farmers to move from traditional agriculture to progressive agriculture requires the development of a wholly new habit of thinking, a new way of living. One way to characterize an early stage of agricultural development is to state that it has the task of substituting a dynamic, constantly changing agriculture for a traditional pattern.

It is a common fallacy to think that there is a "modern agriculture" which can be substituted for a "primitive agriculture" and that then the job is done. This is not true. Rather, the movement is from a static combination of agricultural practices to a continuously changing pattern of production. This is elementary to agricultural scientists, but it is commonly ignored by governments launching programs of agricultural development. The task never ends. It becomes more complex. It requires more and more public institutions related to agricultural development. Each step forward introduces new problems. Farmers must not be induced to make "a change" in farming but to shift from an attitude of tradition to one of continuous choice-making in economic and political fields as well as in the narrow realm of farming practices, realizing that all of these vitally affect agricultural production.

It is the high importance of this major and difficult shift from traditional to choice-making ways of thinking and acting that gives much of their importance to programs of extension education for farm men and women. Such programs confront people with alternatives: a new variety of corn or the old, a new type of plow or the old, an unfamiliar fertilizer or none at all. Constantly confronting people with alternatives stimulates choice-making and aids people during their adventurous experimenting.[2]

Similarly with programs of supervised credit; it is not enough to make credit available; people must learn how to use credit. Accustomed to borrowing to buy food during a lean season, they have to learn that credit can be *productive* when used to finance new methods of farming. Supervised credit both teaches the use of credit in production and (when combined with home extension education) helps people learn how to use enhanced income to achieve better levels of living.

Perhaps it should be repeated here that this difficult transition from the traditional to choice-making is only a *stage* in agricultural development. Many regions of Latin America are beyond this stage, and a few farmers are beyond it in most regions. But there are many and very large parts of Latin America where this process has hardly begun. We must, therefore, recognize as basic to agricultural development the necessity of farmers' learning to make choices, learning to take responsibility for choices, and learning to use money. And the importance of this fact must have high priority in selecting criteria for evaluating programs of technical co-operation.

2. *Agricultural development does not depend on farmers alone but is a product of the whole way of living, the whole culture, of a nation or of a region.*

Farmers of many tropical coasts and mountain valleys of Latin America are debilitated by malaria, hookworm, and other diseases. If these diseases are to be effectively controlled, governmental action on a wide scale is necessary. The illiteracy of many rural people can be overcome only by school systems beyond the power of farmers, acting alone, to provide. If fertilizers are to be available in the inland parts of Brazil at reasonable prices, roads and railways must be built. The prices farmers must pay for agricultural requisites and the prices they are to receive for their products are determined to a considerable extent by the price and monetary policies of their governments and by the earnings of urban workers employed in other industries.

In many parts of Latin America, there still lingers a social attitude against manual labor as a respectable activity. Men in "the professions" command much higher prestige than agricultural technicians. These are phases of the *general culture* of a people; yet they vitally affect agricultural development by deterring many competent men from becoming agricultural technicians. Such circumstances cannot be changed appreciably by farmers alone.

In some manner, any tenable theory of agricultural development must take this factor of the nature of the whole culture into account. The general culture can greatly facilitate or disastrously hamper any strictly "economic" or any exclusively "rural" program for agricultural development which may be undertaken.

3. *Agricultural development and rural welfare are interrelated, with the cause-and-effect relationship moving in both directions.*

In theory, this conclusion is seldom challenged; in practice, only one-half of it appears to be honored in most discussions of requirements for agricultural development and in most programs. No one wants agricultural development just for itself. Agricultural development is always sought as an instrumental means toward a further end. This further end in some instances seems to be only a matter of national prestige or national "power," but it usually includes a concern for the level of living of people, rural people among them. What is so often ignored in practice is that phases of rural welfare often are causative factors leading to greater agricultural development. Yet this fact is corroborated by the experience of programs of technical co-operation throughout Latin America.

The higher the present level of living of a farmer, the greater is his capacity to respond to programs for agricultural development. Better education, better health, increased mental and physical alertness, all increase a family's capacity to respond and to innovate. This is a phase of the general phenomenon that development is cumulative; the more a person or an economy develops, the greater its capacity for further development. We have seen this principle operating in the programs in Peru and Brazil and, at the other extreme, in Haiti. It is the operators of medium- to large-sized farms who have responded most rapidly to the programs of SCIPA in Peru, while the poorest farmers have responded least. Administrators of the ACAR program in Brazil found the poorest farmers unable to benefit from its program of supervised credit. In Haiti, the absence of any substantial group of farmers with an already reasonably adequate level of living appears to be a factor in the relative lack of success of extension programs there.

This fact explains one of the problems of agricultural extension services. The more progressive farmers in a region welcome the help, and may monopolize the time, of extension agents. Working exclusively with such farmers does result in the greatest immediate increase in total production. Only by consciously allotting part of his time to the less responsive, less progressive farmers can an extension agent redress this tendency to monopoly and get the process of development started among those not yet reinforced in their growth by a rising trend in the level of living.

The *prospect* of a higher level of living is a powerful incentive to agricultural development for many people. Economists express this by stating that the "standard of living" (what a family aspires to) needs to be higher than the "level of living" (what the family actually has) for economic development to take place. As farmers begin to believe that a better life is possible for themselves and their families, their interest in new agricultural practices, leading to greater income, increases. This process can be discerned in what is happening in the Bejucál project of OAS in Cuba, in the interest of farm families in the ACAR program in Brazil, and in the few other places where home demonstration agents have become an effective part of programs of extension education.

Studies of the aspirations of rural people and of the organization of rural society are of considerable value to the administration of extension programs. Sometimes such studies uncover motivations that can speed agricultural development directly. At other times they reveal forces which must be overcome or neutralized if people are to move ahead. Still further, they may reveal legitimate aspirations which, though not agricultural or home "economic," can still be honored and achieved through activities which an extension service can organize or encourage. This is particularly true of desires for better recreational facilities. If people can gain confidence that they can reach their aspirations through their own efforts, this is of great importance to agricultural development, whether every instance of such success is agricultural or not.

There is undoubtedly a considerable lag between increased income to farmers and higher levels of living, in the absence of specific emphasis on family welfare. Farm women probably are more responsible for levels of family living than are their husbands. Just as farmers must see changed farming practices demonstrated, so farm women must see changed home practices demonstrated and must be encouraged to believe that higher levels of living are possible. Although women may have more influence on welfare than men, both need to be educated and convinced (preferably through the same program in order to assure consistency of information and emphasis).

Everyone agrees that the significance of agricultural development is as a means; the end is, or includes, the general welfare. Rural welfare is a part of the general welfare and therefore is a part of the general objective to be served by agricultural development. But rural welfare is simultaneously an important element fostering agricultural development and is thus a "means" as well as part of the "end."

4. *Either an external crisis or a strong, widely felt internal im-*

pulse to progress appears to be necessary as an incentive to national effort toward agricultural development.

Latin-American countries vary greatly in the strength of their domestic efforts toward agricultural development. Mexico has, for many years, been sponsoring programs of land reform, establishing agricultural banks, building irrigation systems, and extending educational and health facilities to rural people. Colombia has her Coffee Federation, her big agricultural co-operative, relatively good agricultural colleges, widespread rural schools. Brazil established numerous agricultural services but allowed most of them to remain mediocre, apparently bemused by the supposed magic of industrialization until aroused to fresh interest in agriculture by the realization that a backward agriculture was retarding her general growth. Bolivia did virtually nothing about agricultural development so long as there was a good market for tin, and until a socially minded government, determined to improve the lot of the common man, came to power. Haiti still slumbers.

How are these differences to be explained? An adequate explanation is certainly beyond the scope of this study. However, the differences among countries cannot be explained by differences in physical resources, or by differences in available capital, or by differences in access to knowledge. There are differences in these respects, unquestionably. But it apparently requires a drastic external pressure or an internal atmosphere of crusade, the roots of which seem to be social or political or humanitarian at least as often as they are economic, to support wide national efforts at agricultural development.

Of this, too, it would seem that an adequate theory of agricultural development must take account, and it is taken up again later in this chapter under the heading "Self-generating Resources."

Elements of Agricultural Development

This section attempts to catalogue the many elements in the total culture of a region which are observed to contribute to agricultural development. There is no significance either in the exact number of these elements or in the order in which they are presented. The number of them could be increased or decreased by varying the degree to which they are subdivided or grouped.

There are three general groups into which these requirements seem to fall. First, agricultural development depends on a number of *attitudes*. Second, agricultural development requires a *series of services*, either public or private, providing facilities necessary to agricultural production. Third, agricultural development depends on *social traditions* and a *legal framework* which support, and provide means for, the frequent changes necessary in a progressive agriculture.

ATTITUDES.—The attitudes could be variously classified, for those that affect agricultural development are different for farmers, technicians serving agriculture, businessmen, bankers, government officials, editors, teachers, and the general public. Here, the discussion centers on three groups of people whose attitudes are particularly determinative of the rate of agricultural progress at the present time in Latin America: farmers, the political elite, and the general public.

Attitudes of farmers: Several attitudes of farmers have considerable effect on the rate of agricultural development. One of these is confidence that it is possible to improve agriculture. Another is willingness to take responsibility for the results of choices, knowing that frequently a change will be less productive than was hoped, either because of insufficient information or through lack of skill. Attitudes with respect to consumption are important. If farm families are satisfied with their present levels of living, they have little incentive to increase production, but if they desire better homes, better health, better standards of living in general, they have such an incentive.

The confidence of farmers in public programs relating to agriculture is important. They are good judges of the sincerity and intent of public programs. If they look on government as primarily exploitative, they are suspicious of any government program. When they are convinced that a public program is well conceived and genuinely seeks to further their welfare, that program begins to be effective.

Attitudes of the political elite: The political elite are those citizens in a country who have substantial political influence, whether because of official position or because of influence with officials or on general public opinion. One may argue that in a mature democracy, with universal suffrage and many channels of news and information, the political elite includes everyone, but such a stage has not been reached in most of Latin America. The percentage of the total population included in the political elite, as defined here, varies widely among Latin-American countries. In a few countries, it includes nearly everyone; in a few, it is limited to a small ruling group; in most, it does not include more than perhaps 10 per cent of the adult men of the country. In the Andean countries, the Inca tradition was aristocratic and authoritarian, and so was that of the Spanish who came to Latin America: aristocratic, authoritarian, and feudal. Even where revolution against these feudal backgrounds has gone furthest, the attitudes of the political elite are of great importance in view of lagging education, continuing economic inequality, and the political immaturity of the masses.

The attitudes of the political elite of a country with respect to agricultural development are important because it is these people who largely determine the priorities of government programs and the legal framework within which agriculture must operate. Do they really want increased agricultural productivity, or are they absorbingly interested in industrialization? Do they realize the necessity for, and have faith in, public programs for agricultural development? Are they far-sighted in realizing the value to the country of investments in land improvement, in education, in public health, and in roads, or is their main interest in keeping taxes low and in directing all capital into private firms and personal haciendas at the expense of investment in the kinds of "social overhead investment" mentioned above? Do they believe in the educability of farmers and the wisdom of decisions which farmers may make for themselves, or do they believe that agricultural practices must be changed by decree or by compulsion if production is to rise? Are they committed (or resigned) to the spread of political participation to the whole population (including all Indians in the Andes countries), or do they seek to perpetuate an aristocratic society and government? The attitudes of the political elite with respect to each of these issues are important elements in the agricultural development of each country.

Attitudes of the general public: Since in most countries of Latin America a transition from aristocratic government to more widespread political participation is either in process or incipient, the attitudes of the general public are increasingly important as an element in agricultural development. Public opinion is increasingly a force, even before the general public has political power. Existing aristocracies in many instances make concessions to public opinion, often in an attempt to retain the aristocratic pattern. Where this is true, and it is true in many countries, the attitudes of the general public with respect to a productive agriculture, and the degree of understanding among the general public of the political steps involved, are an important element in agricultural development.

SERVICES AND PUBLIC PROGRAMS.—The second group of elements of agricultural development is composed of services and public programs that are continuously essential to agricultural development.

Programs of research: Agricultural development requires new knowledge. This new knowledge comes as the result of study and research. For the most part, such study and research must be a public function, carried on either by universities or by governments. This research is needed in a variety of fields, including agricultural resources, crops and livestock, farming practices, institutions for credit and marketing, methods of extension, rural organization, and rural aspirations and value systems. Each of these has its own contribution to make. No one of them can make its maximum contribution without simultaneous development of the others. There is a tendency, historically, to regard the first three as the core of agricultural research. These undoubtedly are basic, but their value to agricultural development is limited without the others. The newer fields of research in agricultural economics, extension methods, rural organization, and rural values are particularly important in the early stages of agricultural development, partly because of the new attitudes that must be fostered and the old ones that need to be honored. Yet there is *very* little research being carried on in any of these newer fields in Latin America.

There is an unjustifiable tendency to assume that methods of extension and school education which are effective in one country will be equally effective in another. Where technicians from one culture work in another, in programs of technical co-operation, there is particular need for systematic study of the human agent in agricultural development.

Programs of agricultural education: In a traditional agriculture,

education is a simple procedure. It need consist only of the indoc-
trination of the young in the practices of their elders. But in an
agriculture that is constantly changing, education must equip people
to *understand, evaluate, choose,* and *take responsibility.* Within the
field of agriculture alone, education must equip people to make
biologic choices between varieties of crops and types of livestock,
economic choices in the allocation of limited capital among land,
labor, equipment and fertilizers, and *political* choices as these affect
public policies that have repercussions on the agricultural industry.

This requires a type of education quite different from that required merely to transmit traditions. Moreover, in a progressive
agriculture, agricultural education of the young must be both for
future farmers and for technicians to carry on all of the varied
services and programs that contribute to agricultural development.
Latin America is very weak in this element.

Programs of rural extension education: Extension is out-of-school
education in matters of rural interest. Most farmers in Latin America
have had relatively little schooling, and what they have had was not
specifically adapted to problems of agricultural development. In
such cases, extension services are especially important. But in any
productive agricultural economy, agricultural knowledge keeps
changing; thus even farmers who have had good schooling need to
keep learning. In the United States, it is usually those farmers who
have had agricultural training in high schools and colleges who
subsequently make the greatest use of extension services. They realize the value of extension because they realize the importance of
continuing to learn.

Extension in home economics has similar value. It has special significance because of the interplay between farm family welfare and
agricultural development.[3] The demonstrably greater response of
farm family welfare to extension programs in which both agriculture
and home economics are emphasized testifies to the importance of
extension in home economics.

Programs of general education: Although education of farmers in
the techniques of agriculture is important, other education is equally
important to agricultural development. At the most elementary
level, technical education is dependent on prior ability in reading
and in arithmetic. But for really productive agriculture, farmers

need to be full citizens of their localities and of their nations. This requires an adequate general education. In a traditional society social attitudes and behavior are determined by tradition just as fully as are patterns of cultivation. In a progressive society (and only in such a society can agriculture be really productive in any national sense) social attitudes and behavior must increasingly be governed by understanding and by choice. This argues for increasingly adequate general education at progressively higher levels.

Moreover, it is not for farmers alone that general education is a factor in agricultural development. Since certain attitudes of the political elite and of the general public are important to agricultural productivity, the amount and quality of general education for these groups have important repercussions on agriculture.

Programs of rural public health: An important element of agricultural development is the physical and mental vitality of rural people. To a considerable degree, this is a function of health. Response to new ideas, as well as energy in manual labor, is far higher among healthy people than it is among those suffering from intestinal parasites and from endemic diseases. Therefore, adequate programs of rural public health are an important element in agricultural development.

Programs of irrigation and drainage: One of the major factors, both in extending the cultivable area within a country and in increasing production on existing farms, is water and the management of soil moisture. In many instances, projects of irrigation and drainage are beyond the power of individual farmers, requiring large-scale operations, often extending to thousands or tens of thousands of acres. Under some circumstances these large-scale projects can be undertaken by private enterprise; yet all countries seriously interested in agricultural development find some public projects of irrigation and drainage to be advisable. The considerable extension of irrigation in Mexico has been a substantial factor in her recent development. Other countries are now putting large investments into this important element of agricultural development.

Land clearing is a similar task. It can more frequently be accomplished privately than can irrigation and drainage, but it must be achieved in one way or another and is often a justifiable public activity, especially in the beginning.

Transportation and communication programs: Only as agriculture moves away from the subsistence pattern can regions capitalize on their comparative advantages in production. Only as agriculture uses more materials that must be purchased, often from distant suppliers, can it become more productive. As these changes take place, agriculture becomes increasingly dependent on good transportation and communication. Just as valleys well suited to fruits must have access to markets, so must plains well suited to extensive cultivation of grains. This is one of the major current needs in most Latin-American countries. Mountainous topography is a big disadvantage, making transport expensive in many region Long distances and an unfortunate early pattern of disconnected and dissimilar railway systems are major problems, for example, in Brazil.

Credit programs: As agriculture becomes less traditional and more progressive, it needs increasing amounts of capital and requires credit for varying purposes and periods of time. It is characteristic of underdeveloped economies that the institutional provisions for agricultural credit are inadequate. Here again, one meets the proposition that improving the situation with respect to one aspect of agricultural development requires simultaneous improvement along other lines. The high interest rates at which some credit is available in traditional economies reflects, in part, the low level of technology and the uncertainty of repayment. An increase in agricultural productivity, as well as new skill in the handling of money, is necessary to credit-worthiness, while credit is needed to increase productivity. "Supervised credit" is one solution to this problem but not the only one. Latin-American governments have established various types of agricultural banks, but agricultural development still is held back in many regions for lack of adequate credit facilities.

Programs assuring equipment: Whereas traditional agriculture is normally self-contained, a progressive agriculture is dependent on an increasing array of specialized equipment and supplies which must be purchased. Farmers in a developing agriculture need an increasing variety of implements, fertilizers, building materials, fencing, fuels, power, insecticides, vehicles, etc. It is one task to discover dependable new agricultural practices and another to make these known to farmers, but such activities are frustrated if farmers do not have the necessary materials with which to work.

The provision of such agricultural requisites within the United States is almost entirely a function of private business. In any well-developed, mature economy private busines can be relied on to discharge this function, and competitive markets are the best method of allocating resources to the production of agricultural requisites in accord with demand.

Both the fact that private enterprise has pretty well kept up with (and has often itself produced) new agricultural knowledge in the United States and the fact of the conviction that this function of providing agricultural requisites *ought* to be left to private trade have resulted in underestimating the importance of this element of agricultural development in Latin America. However, the lack of an existing network of commercial outlets for agricultural requisites, the lack of confidence by merchants that the demand for new agricultural requisites will justify investment in inventories, and the limited size of many national markets all combine to make this a substantial problem.

It is in this context that programs to provide agricultural requisites other than through normal commercial channels—or public programs to develop normal commercial channels—become a major element in agricultural development in Latin America.

Programs to facilitate marketing: The situation here is similar to, but also different from, that with respect to agricultural requisites. The marketing of agricultural produce is normally a task for private enterprise. Yet it is unlikely that commercial opportunities in agricultural marketing will be recognized as rapidly as the need for better marketing becomes a crucial element in agricultural development. Such opportunities as exist may be seized upon by merchants in order to reap unusual profits by exploiting increased production, particularly where transportation and communication are not highly developed. Where this happens, agricultural development is retarded by denying farmers as high a price for their product as the ultimate market justifies, thereby greatly weakening a major incentive to still greater production. The rapid dissemination of accurate market information can help at this point. Co-operative marketing by farmers has been another check on such exploitation in advanced economies, but it involves special skills and aptitudes that are not quickly acquired.

While minimizing exploitation of markets for farm products is one problem of agricultural development, a greater necessity is some physically efficient channel for marketing, regardless of price relationships. Proper storage facilities are among the needs in this direction.

Programs to control pests and diseases: Like irrigation, the control of some pests and diseases is a phase of agricultural development which farmers cannot provide individually. The only effective control measures for foot-and-mouth disease, for locusts, and for many other pests and diseases require joint action over wide regions. Even many of those measures that a farmer can undertake on his own farm require the services of veterinarians, either publicly or privately employed.

Programs of price and wage policy: If all markets were left free, this would not be a necessity for agricultural development. When they are not, the way prices and wages are affected by public economic policy does affect agriculture, and such policies need to be so regulated that they do not put agriculture at a disadvantage.

Programs of rural organization: This need does not arise out of conditions peculiar to Latin America but is intensified by special circumstances there. In any culture, there are many rural problems that need to be handled by the group action of farmer organizations. Some of these problems are purely agricultural; others are more related to rural welfare, as in the case of community health and recreation. Yet farmers are not inclined to organize nearly to the extent that their own welfare justifies. They are accustomed to working alone. For this reason, public programs fostering and supporting rural organization can be an important element in agricultural development.

Programs for co-ordination: In view of the large number of public programs seen to be contributory to agricultural development, somewhere in the pattern there needs to be provision for considering all public programs together, both to prevent unwarranted overlapping and to see that vital gaps are not left unfilled. The importance of such over-all consideration and planning is sufficient to justify listing this as an additional element in agricultural development.

Co-ordination is a better word than integration to express what is needed. Many of these public programs should be administered independently. But the need for an over-all look at what is happening remains, even though it may be better to limit the power of such a generalized consideration to recommendations and to education of public opinion.

SOCIAL TRADITIONS AND LEGAL FRAMEWORK.—The third group of elements of agricultural development is made up of certain factors in the cultural and legal framework within which the agriculture of any given region is carried on. These may vary considerably within a single country if different cultures are relatively distinct—as are the Indian and the "European" cultures of Ecuador—or if laws with respect to land tenure vary from state to state—as they do in Mexico. Such traditions and laws constitute important "rules of the game" for agriculture. Among these, traditions change under the impact of changes in values and in ways of living, but they change slowly. This slowness is not all bad, for it has the positive conservative function of holding the society together, preventing serious disruption by new forces. It conserves the old while time and experience are proving whether or not the new is better. But meanwhile this slowness does retard whatever of the new is really better. Laws can be changed more quickly than can cultural values, but this does not mean that changes in legislation are easier to achieve. Cultural changes seep through a society and are hard to combat, but once an intrenched interest has political power, it can control legislation, thereby using the force of government to maintain its position. Farmers need to be full citizens in order to participate in bringing about legal changes which will facilitate agricultural development.

Four features of this institutional framework in which agriculture is carried on seem to be outstanding in their effect on agricultural development: the system of land tenure, social determinants of the size of the labor force, social factors affecting population mobility, and the status of farmers in the political process.[4]

The system of land tenure: The rate of agricultural development in any region is profoundly affected by the system or systems of land tenure prevailing there. For the maximum rate of agricultural development, certain characteristics are desirable in the land-tenure system:

1. It should encourage putting each field to its most productive use. (Large hereditary holdings, many of which are not taxed, in cultures in which the mere ownership of land carries more prestige

than efficient management, keep much land from its most productive use in many parts of Latin America.)

2. It should provide adequate incentive to maintain and increase soil productivity. (This requires either an assurance of continuity to renters or some arrangement to compensate the renter for increases in soil productivity brought about at the renter's expense during his tenancy, as is done in Cuba.)

3. It should make it possible for farms to change in size: (*a*) in response to changes in technology (new implements or sources of power may increase the optimum size of the farm unit), and (*b*) in response to changes in the size of the labor force, considered together with current employment opportunities inside and outside of agriculture.

4. It should provide for mobility into, and out of, farm operation. It is important that young men who wish to be farmers have an opportunity to get into farming, for this desire to farm is an important factor in good farm management. It is equally important that no one be committed to farming just because his father was a farmer. The system of land tenure should provide both a way in and a way out. (The widespread impression that an appreciable percentage of renters among farmers is a bad sign often ignores this need. Renting is a good way for a new farmer to try out his managerial skill. Where rental agreements are equitable, it is often a good way to accumulate working capital and the down payment for land purchase.)

5. It should be compatible with welfare goals of a social and political nature. (A common argument against land reforms that break up large holdings into small farms is that these lead to an immediate drop in production. Actual cases can be cited to corroborate this argument. But the same reforms may be defended on the grounds that they represent social gains by giving many more people independence of action and a feeling of becoming full citizens of the nation. This, too, is corroborated by actual cases, as in Mexico and Bolivia, and is a valid argument. Landownership apparently is a significant factor in rural welfare for every family that experiences it, quite apart from the economic efficiency of farming. Therefore, efficiency in production is not the only objective to be sought in a system of land tenure.)

Finding the best combination among these (often conflicting) desirable characteristics of a system of land tenure is difficult, and this constitutes part of the complexity of the problem of land reform. Despite this complexity, the systems of land tenure in any region are an important element in agricultural development. Widespread distribution of landownership, when attained through a flexible system with a feasible way in and way out, appears to be best in an overall sense. This seems to be true even though (*a*) it increases the task for agricultural extension since it greatly increases the number of farm operators who must make production decisions, and (*b*) it may often lead, in the transitional stage (before the many new owners have become adept) to a lowering of current production. These latter considerations highlight the importance of accompanying land reform by other measures, particularly an effective extension service and appropriate credit institutions. They commend the example of Bolivia, which, in its current land reforms, is drawing heavily on the experience of other countries (particularly Mexico) in similar programs.

Social determinants of the size of the labor force: For Latin America as a whole, population is increasing at the rate of about 2.5 per cent per year. This is about double the average rate of growth in the world as a whole, and it has a strong influence on agricultural development. It constitutes a rapid increase in the size of the labor force and a rapid increase in the need for food. Since none of the countries of Latin America is highly industrialized, the new opportunities for employment in industry each year are fewer than the net increase in the size of the total labor force. This means that the absolute number of persons engaged in agriculture cannot be reduced in the near future but will increase, even though a reduction would be economic, in some regions, from the standpoint of price relationships within agriculture.

It is likely that this increase in the agricultural labor force is a retarding factor in agricultural development when that development is defined as an increase in output per unit input. It may, however, be a factor facilitating agricultural development in certain regions, when agricultural development is defined as an increase in the total agricultural product, because of the increased labor inputs which become possible.

Whatever the direction of its effect in a particular region, the size of the agricultural labor force is a social factor significant in agricultural development.

Social factors affecting population mobility: One of the recurrent and persistent dreams of several Latin-American countries is that of being able to move many Indians from the highlands of limited productivity into the undeveloped lowlands. Formerly, the prevalence of malaria and other diseases on the coastal lowlands and in the Amazon Basin kept people up in the mountains. In Bolivia, for example, 50 per cent of the population lives on the arid *altiplano*, at elevations above 11,000 feet, and another 45 per cent in mountain valleys, mostly above 5,000 feet. Only 5 per cent live on the more humid eastern plains which comprise half of the country.

In recent years great progress has been made in conquering the diseases of the lowlands, and the agricultural potentialities of much formerly unused land in the lowlands have been proved. Yet people do not rush from the crowded highlands to the undeveloped plains, and part of the reason, in addition to the anticipated health hazard, is social and cultural. Being established in the highlands, people are reluctant to leave. Not only are their families there, but their cultural values have grown up around highland living (as witness the fact that for many mountain people particular mountains are their gods).

These factors that inhibit population "place mobility" are a real factor in agricultural development, though their force is sometimes exaggerated. Thousands of Indians have moved to the coastal plain of Ecuador in response to opportunities for employment there. Indians have moved farther and farther down the valleys of Ecuador, Peru, and Bolivia as malaria has been pushed out of the valleys ahead of them.[5] Also, recent studies in Venezuela, as yet unpublished, show that the concentrations of population in the Andes region of that country are more the result of patterns of transport and communication that of other aspects of the culture.[6]

The status of farmers in the political process: Previous sections of this chapter have discussed the fact that as agriculture moves away from the traditional toward a progressive and more productive pattern many of the decisions which vitally affect agricultural productivity are made through the political process. In view of this, it is important to agricultural development that farmers have a full voice in political affairs. They have this in a few countries of Latin America but not in most. Whenever the dominance of an aristocracy, or the personal concept of government,[7] persists, only the big farmers, and often not many of them, have an effective political voice. In many countries, small farmers have no vote. Often those who have a vote for representatives in the legislatures have only a choice between two candidates both of whom are residents of distant cities. In the state of Minas Gerais in Brazil, for example, where the greater part of the state has little industry but is strongly agricultural, representatives need not be residents of the districts they represent and usually are not. Cities have a natural advantage in political affairs which can be mitigated only by universal suffrage for rural people, combined with the requirement that candidates be chosen from among local residents by local processes. Any other system compounds the political disadvantage natural to rural people because of their dispersion.

SUMMARY.—Agricultural development, the process through which a people's agriculture becomes more productive, is dependent on many elements within the total culture of those people. Some of these are attitudes, others are services and public programs, still others are phases of the social traditions and legal framework within which agriculture is carried on. The elements of agricultural development that emerge from this study are repeated here in outline form:

ELEMENTS OF AGRICULTURAL DEVELOPMENT

I. Attitudes
  A. Of farmers:
    1. confidence that agriculture can be improved.
    2. willingness to take responsibility for choices.
    3. desire for higher levels of living.
    4. confidence in public agricultural programs.
  B. Of the political elite:
    1. desire for increased agricultural productivity.
    2. confidence in public programs.
    3. realization of value of public investments in transportation, irrigation, and agricultural programs.
    4. confidence in the educability of rural people.
    5. desire for extension of political participation.
  C. Of the general public:
    1. realization of importance of agricultural development.
    2. understanding of the process of agricultural development.

II. Services and Public Programs
   A. Programs of research.
   B. Programs of agricultural education.
   C. Programs of rural extension education.
   D. Programs of general education.
   E. Programs of rural public health.
   F. Public investment in irrigation and drainage.
   G. Public investment in transportation and communication facilities.
   H. Programs with respect to rural credit.
   I. Programs to insure adequate availability of agricultural requisites.
   J. Programs to facilitate the marketing of agricultural products.
   K. Programs to control pests and diseases.
   L. Price and wage policies.
   M. Programs fostering rural organization for voluntary group action.
   N. Co-ordination of public programs related to agriculture and rural life.
III. Social Traditions and Legal Framework
   A. Systems of land tenure.
   B. Social determinants of the size of the labor force.
   C. Factors affecting population mobility.
   D. Status of farmers in the political process.

Economic and Self-generating Resources

When we speak of resources for agricultural *production,* we are thinking of land, labor, and capital instruments such as seeds, fertilizers, implements, draft animals or tractors, etc. These, we say, must be "economized." If an acre of land is put in one crop, it cannot simultaneously be put into another. If a tractor is used all day in plowing, it cannot be used throughout the same day to power a feed grinder. If a farmer has $1,000 of production capital, he cannot devote all of it to the purchase of seed and also use all of it for paying labor and for buying fuel. He must "allocate" limited resources among various uses, trying to do this in such a way that the combination is optimum (the most productive combination achievable under the circumstances).

In trying to assess the resources of any country for agricultural *development,* we too frequently limit our investigation to these resources for agricultural production: land, labor, and capital. The burden of the conclusion stated in this section is that there are really two kinds of resources for agricultural development. One kind includes those resources commonly considered with respect to agricultural production (and which must be economized). The other includes those resources that facilitate changes over a period of time (and that need not be economized because they turn out to be self-generating, being augmented rather than consumed in use).

It is the actual history of recent agricultural development, and of numerous programs to bring it about, in Latin America, that forces us to recognize the large role played by *attitudes* in the process of changing technology and increasing agricultural production. Attitudes, far from being consumed in use, actually tend to reproduce themselves and to reinforce each other. The confidence of one farmer in the possibility of greater production through changed practices tends to build this confidence in other farmers. The well-founded vision of one persuasive political leader that the lot of the common rural man can, and ought to be, improved can be contagious, reproducing itself in other leaders and in a widening group of political followers.

The writer was first impressed with this important fact about agricultural development not in Latin America but in India. In India, in 1950–55, agricultural production has increased 15 per cent, in a land of 50,000,000 tiny farms, with a heavy density of population, among people largely illiterate, and with capital very scarce. Assuming that one-half of this increase may have been due to unusually good weather, the record still is astounding. Yet the programs that have wrought this change, while much larger, are not substantially different from programs tried fifteen, twenty, and thirty years ago, with only occasional results. In that earlier period, the standard reply to any suggestion of change, even after intellectual assent to its value, was: "It is not our custom" or "We don't do it that way."

What could be responsible for this difference in response? The only way the writer can explain it, and he was there in both eras, is in terms of a dramatic change in the attitudes both of rural people and of the political elite. The only adequate explanation for the permeation of this change throughout the land is in the personalities and doctrines and examples of the leaders of the struggle for independence, notably Mahatma Gandhi. For years, Gandhi and his followers went from village to village throughout the country, blaming all of the ills of the country on British colonialism, thereby undercutting the prevalent attitude that each person's lot was his divinely ordered fate and building a general confidence that, if allowed to order their own government, the *people* could build a substantially better life.[8]

The point here is that the spirit and the confidence inspired in the Indian people—both peasants and political leaders—do not have to be economized. They reproduce themselves. They spread, like a constructive infection, through a population. They *exhilarate* a people, thereby alerting them to opportunities for greater productivity, inspiring them to undergo technical training to fit themselves to participate in a national renaissance, releasing them from old traditions to an expectation of changes, alternatives, responsibility, and better days to come.

This analysis of what happened in India appears to be corroborated by the evidence of this study in Latin America. On the walls of filling stations and schools and along the roadside fences of Mexico, one continually sees the painted slogan "For the Revolution!" That revolution is now forty years old, but it still, though at a reduced heat, kindles the imagination of Mexicans. Much more recently, the MNR movement has brought something of the same spirit to Bolivia, giving the Andean Indians a feeling both of hope and of responsibility. These attitudes, again, need not be economized; instead, they are cumulative.

Although the foregoing examples are political, this phenomenon is not limited to the political field. One sees a similar process at work within the organization of SCIPA in Peru where, despite some obvious technical weaknesses of the program, a morale of pride and confidence in a new kind of public service has been engendered and is contagious. The same process can be seen in Ecuador, where the enthusiasm of one man and his faith in the process of technical co-operation were largely responsible for keeping bilateral technical co-operation alive through lean years of little accomplishment until a change of policy gave it a more effective form. These self-generative resources can be observed multiplying in Brazil, both among the farm families served by ACAR and among Brazilian political leaders who are now confident that similar programs can be helpful in other parts of Brazil.

If this analysis has validity, what are the implications of it? It says, in effect, that *the resources for agricultural development in any particular region are not limited.* No amount of creative attitudes can, of course, increase the acreage of a region; but a confidence in agricultural development, armed with techniques of scientific investigation, can find new uses for semi-arid or swampy land and can discover new techniques for getting much more from land already cultivated. No pitch of national enthusiasm can substitute for rational "economizing" of the material resources for agricultural production, at a given level of technology and at a particular moment in time, but the self-generating resources can motivate people to develop skills in economizing and can open their minds to a consideration of new alternatives.

For programs of technical co-operation, this analysis seems to say that *the most productive programs of technical co-operation are those that work at tasks of increasing the output from economic resources in such a way that the self-generative resources for agricultural development are enhanced.*

No one would suggest that the overt tasks of technical co-operation should be shifted from wrestling with the economic resources for agricultural production to an overt attack on attitudes as such. Whatever effects technical co-operation can have on the self-generative resources arise in two ways: (1) through demonstrations of the higher production possible through improved technology and improved allocation of economic resources and (2) through the manner in which technical co-operation is conducted, the personal outlook, temperament, and influence of individual technicians. The continued loyalty of Latin-American technicians to the OEE in Mexico long after they have completed their training is evidence of the reality and power of these self-generating resources which need not be economized. So is the increasing confidence of commercial farmers in the program of SCIPA in Peru.

Another way to state the implications of this analysis for technical co-operation is that *by working on the economic resources of a region with imagination and enthusiastic confidence, it is possible to strengthen other resources of attitude which are augmented as they are used.* These new attitudes, in turn, can send men and women of every region into that disciplined research, persistent education, espousal of sound public investment, reconsideration of land tenure systems, and many other activities that further agricultural development.

13 THE ACHIEVEMENTS AND ROLE OF TECHNICAL CO-OPERATION

In this summarizing chapter of the study's general conclusions about technical co-operation in Latin-American agriculture, one would wish that of the two main topics—*achievements* and *role*—the former might be discussed quantitatively. If a monetary value could be put upon achievements, one's answer to the question "Has it been worth what it cost?" could be straightforward and unambiguous. However, for reasons stated in chapter i and illuminated by case studies, that cannot be done. All that can be done is to outline the kinds of achievements that technical co-operation has to its credit in Latin America and to mention the number of countries in which different results have been substantial. It is left to the reader to assess the value of these achievements, against the two touchstones of the nature of agricultural development and the nature of technical co-operation. The writer's own over-all assessment, measuring achievements against what they have cost, is stated in chapter xix.

Achievements of Technical Co-operation

Many, but not all, of the variations to be found among programs of technical co-operation in Latin America have been illustrated by the case studies. However, the programs in several countries other than those discussed would be equally instructive as case studies were there time and resources for studying them more intensively and space in this volume to report them.

The program in Paraguay illustrates the problems of operating in a country with weak domestic programs for agricultural development. It illustrates how a concentration of effort in the early years of a program on establishing an experiment station in a country without agricultural research can lay the groundwork for subsequent extension activities. It includes one of the most active and apparently successful youth-club projects to be found in Latin America.

271

Bolivia has one of the biggest IIAA programs in agriculture. This country until recently had weak domestic programs for agricultural development, but the present government is vigorously engaged in introducing widespread social and economic changes, and this produces a ferment conducive to progress. Bolivia has the spirit but faces crucial problems of method and of the reconciliation of many staggering needs for simultaneous action. The country director of IIAA in Bolivia has had, to an unusual degree, the confidence of the Bolivian government, and therefore he has had more opportunity to discuss general economic policies with high officials than has been the case in most other countries. This Bolivian program, in addition to being broad and well balanced within the field of technical co-operation, has been one of the few examples in Latin America of a combination of technical co-operation with economic aid.

The 1954 agricultural program of IIAA in Brazil was large, in terms of United States appropriations. Since this program, in its present form, is new, it is too early to begin to assess it. Several features of it, however, merit study. There has been considerable difficulty in getting it organized. More than any other bilateral program, it is set up (although in the *servicio* form) to aid domestic programs through the provision of adviser-technicians and grants of supplies and equipment. It has the unusual feature of a Brazilian co-director of the *servicio* who has been in the organization for several years and who has unusual prestige and influence on the program.

It will be recalled that Brazil has many domestic programs for agricultural development, and the sprawling independent nature of these is more of a problem to agricultural development than lack of programs.[1] This is part of the general difficulty of working with rapidly developing countries, a difficulty that IIAA has not been very successful in overcoming. Brazil, therefore, merits continuous observation and study.

In Chile, the situation is different yet similar. Separate IIAA programs in health, agriculture, and education have operated, some of them fitfully, for several years. In 1954 these were brought together for an "Area Development Scheme" in the area around Concepción in an attempt to find a more successful mode of operation in an alert and progressive country. The scheme is too new to allow any conclusions about it.

El Salvador presents an example of a research program started by the OFAR which has been fruitful and has endured, and to which has been added an extension service entirely financed and administered by the Salvadoran government, with only advisory help from IIAA. It is instructive as a case in which (until 1955) IIAA operated without using the device of the *servicio*. Then a *servicio* was established. Some claim that IIAA pressed for this change; others insist that it was made at the request of the Salvadoran government. This *servicio* is to administer the continuing research program, and there is some support for its taking over extension education as well.

Honduras, Colombia, Costa Rica, Venezuela, and Uruguay are the other countries with significant experience with respect to IIAA programs. These countries were visited briefly, and aspects of their experience are mentioned in this and succeeding chapters in connection with specific problems or opportunities in technical co-operation.

EVALUATION AND UNDERSTANDING.—It was pointed out in the Introduction that, although this study was undertaken with a mandate to be evaluative in character, the nature both of the process of agricultural development and of the available data imposes rigid limits on the extent to which *quantitative* evaluation of programs of technical co-operation is possible. It was likewise pointed out that *understanding* the process of technical co-operation and delimiting its role in agricultural development under various conditions is particularly needed at the present stage.

The conclusions in this chapter are therefore of both types— evaluation and interpretation. These conclusions are based on the total study, involving fifteen countries, but all of the conclusions are illustrated by one or another of the case studies presented in Part II. Subsequent chapters analyze further the more important aspects of technical co-operation and of the relationship between it and agricultural development.

1. *Programs of technical co-operation are having a substantial effect on the rate of agricultural development in Latin America. This*

conclusion is substantiated by evidence in five fields: (*a*) the level of agricultural production of specific crops and on thousands of individual farms; (*b*) the introduction of new types of programs for agricultural development; (*c*) the improvement of existing Latin-American programs for agricultural development; (*d*) a change in the attitudes of farmers and of the political elites with respect to agricultural development; and (*e*) the training of agricultural technicians.

Levels of Production: The greatest increase in production in a single crop, traceable to technical co-operation, has been in the case of corn. The OEE in Mexico, through extensive collections and field trials, found the best varieties of open-pollinated corn for different regional conditions and released these for general use. This, alone, has resulted in very appreciably increased production on thousands of farms. The organization then developed hybrids that yield up to 60 per cent more than the best open-pollinated varieties, and these have been widely disseminated by the Mexican Corn Commission and have been introduced into several other countries. Synthetic varieties, not requiring the purchase of new seed every year (as is the case with hybrids) yield up to 30 per cent more than the best open-pollinated varieties, and the distribution of these has been responsible for very considerable increases in production in many regions.

Cuban Yellow Corn, first developed (not through technical co-operation as defined here) in Cuba, has been picked up by United States bilateral programs and widely distributed, particularly in Peru and Bolivia. Technical co-operation did not produce the seed, but it provided the channels of distribution by which production has been substantially increased in new regions. This seed was successfully introduced at Tingo Maria, Peru, and it was demonstrations of Cuban Yellow Corn at General Saavedra Experiment Station, Bolivia, that influenced realization of the enormous agricultural potential of the eastern plains of that country.

Similarly spectacular results have been secured with respect to potatoes, although on a less wide geographic scale. This increase has been secured chiefly through the control of diseases and through the use of fertilizers. Technical co-operation introduced both the methods for securing larger yields and the insecticides and fertilizers necessary to improved practices. Under this stimulus, commercial suppliers of these materials are increasingly taking over the function of supply.

Another substantial crop increase has been the increased production of tomatoes. In Peru, tomatoes formerly were only available at high prices for a restricted season each year. Today the price is only a fraction of what it was, and tomatoes are available in quantity for a much longer season.

These examples, while among the most widespread in their effect, are only illustrative of a large number of contributions to aggregate production through improved varieties, fertilizers, pest and disease control, increased facilities for irrigation, and improved cultivation practices.

Introducing New Programs: A second contribution of technical co-operation has been in establishing new types of programs for agricultural development. Extension education did not exist in Latin America except in a few spots like the state of São Paulo, Brazil, before technical co-operation began. In co-operation with IIAA, extension services were started in Peru, Costa Rica, and Paraguay in 1943, and since that time most of the other countries of Latin America have established such programs. These programs vary greatly, and the relationship of technical co-operation to them varies as well. The program in the state of Mexico is a domestic program, strengthened by a grant of $100,000 from the Rockefeller Foundation and by informal consultation with the personnel of the OEE. In Colombia the domestic extension service has recently been reorganized in an attempt to strengthen the element of education within it. IIAA in Colombia helps with a pilot extension program in one district as an experiment and a training ground for extension agents to work elsewhere in the country. In some countries extension education is now firmly established and well organized; in a few the programs are lagging. In all, however, technical co-operation has been the biggest factor both in awakening countries to the value of extension education and in getting such programs organized and launched.

Home demonstration agents have been introduced into several Latin-American countries through technical co-operation, and in no other instance do they exist. Although this phase of extension has lagged behind that devoted primarily to agriculture, it is spreading and proving to be effective. The two agencies that have done the most in this field are IIAA and AIA. The latter has done the more *intensive* job both in Brazil and in Venezuela. IIAA has introduced the home demonstration idea and practice into Peru, Bolivia, Haiti, Paraguay, and Honduras. The OAS includes home economics in its regional training programs in each zone. A university contract between Purdue University and the Rural University of Minas Gerais is building the first full college course in home economics to be established in South America. Most of these new programs in home economics extension and teaching have been strengthened through drawing on personnel trained in the University of Puerto Rico, in addition to using North American technicians as advisers and trainers.

Supervised credit programs were first introduced to Latin America through technical co-operation. This was done first by IIAA in Paraguay and later by AIA in Brazil and Venezuela and FAO in Honduras. More recently, small experimental programs have been set up in Peru and Bolivia. In Brazil this type of program has been adopted for the large, wholly domestic program for the northeast region of the country.

Projects of reimbursable facilities, introduced by technical co-operation, have tided countries over the transitional period between the creation of new rural demands for agricultural requisites and the development of adequate commercial channels through which these needs can be met.

At the time technical co-operation began, there was comparatively little agricultural research being carried on in Latin America. There were relatively good programs in Brazil, in Colombia (in coffee and sugar), and in Peru. There was considerable research being carried on by plantation corporations and by growers' associations in Cuba, Mexico, Honduras, and Peru. Today, however, there are governmental programs of agricultural research in every country covered by this study except Haiti and the Dominican Republic. Some of these are feeble; others have gained strength rapidly. Technical co-operation does not deserve all of the credit, but it does deserve much of it.

Improvement of Existing Programs: Another substantial effect of technical co-operation has been the encouragement of domestic agricultural programs. All countries had some agricultural programs, but in many countries they were scattered or buried in ministries with many other responsibilities. Since technical co-operation began, Haiti, Honduras, El Salvador, Bolivia, Paraguay, and Peru have established ministries of agriculture. Many of the administrative practices of domestic agencies old and new have been modified under the influence of technical co-operation. Field agents in a few countries have received vehicles with which to do their work. Salaries have been raised. Better equipment has been provided for research stations. New, wholly domestic agencies, other than ministries, have been established, such as the Corn Commission in Mexico, the National Economic Council in Honduras, and the Association for Rural Credit and Welfare of Northeast Brazil.

Perhaps the least effect of technical co-operation is to be observed with respect to formal agricultural education at the high-school and college levels. The Rockefeller Foundation has had a substantial effect on agricultural colleges in Colombia and some effect elsewhere. FAO and OAS have done very little directly with the colleges, although OAS is beginning to have an effect on them. IIAA has laid the groundwork for some effect on secondary agricultural education in Peru, through the teacher-training work of the education *servicio*. Not until the advent of university contracts, however, had IIAA found a way to be effective in the field of agricultural education. Purdue, Michigan State, and Arkansas have had co-operative relationships with colleges in Colombia, Brazil, and Panama since 1951. More recently (since 1953) contracts have been negotiated to work with agricultural colleges in Mexico, Costa Rica, Ecuador, and Peru, but these relationships were only in the preliminary stage when this study was made.

Changes in Attitudes regarding Agriculture: A fourth effect has been on attitudes of farmers and of the political elite with respect to agricultural development. Tens of thousands of farmers, to whom extension education or supervised credit has come for the first time, are turning from a traditional to a progressive attitude toward farming. Perhaps equally important, technicians in public programs related to agricultural development are finding new and satisfying careers in working effectively with farm people, through new outlooks and freer conditions of work both in *servicios* and in rejuvenated government agencies. In several countries the attitude of many of the political elite is changing with respect to agricultural development and with respect to the ability of farmers to take the initiative in adopting new practices.

Training Agricultural Technicians: Technical co-operation has greatly increased the number of trained agricultural technicians in Latin America. Partly this has been achieved through formal training programs, both in Latin America and abroad.[2] Partly it has been accomplished through informal in-service training and through the increment of professional experience gained by Latin Americans employed in *servicios* or working as counterparts to FAO and IIAA advisers.

A common complaint of administrators of programs of technical co-operation is the high turnover of local staff. This is a disadvantage to program continuity, but it arises, in most instances, from the fact that experience in these programs so increases the competence of technicians that they are in great demand. Staff turnover, therefore, while being a problem for those programs, represents a valuable increase in the resources of competent agricultural technicians in each country. This is a significant achievement in itself. In Mexico, Peru, Brazil, and Cuba, particularly, the high turnover in staff personnel can be attributed to the increased competence which participation in these programs develops.

After the field work of this study was completed, the writer was invited to participate in a conference, sponsored by FAO and OAS, in Costa Rica on the organization of agricultural research in Central America. The participants were the directors of research and their assistants from Nicaragua, Guatemala, El Salvador, Honduras, Costa Rica, and Panama. All of these officials are young men serving in research programs initiated within technical co-operation, and every one of them has received most of his advanced training and experience within such programs.

Repeatedly, Latin Americans expressed the opinion that this training of technicians, however formal or informal, is the most valuable product of technical co-operation. Only part of the value of this training is in the scientific techniques which it imparts. Other valuable parts are professional attitudes, habits of effective administration, and the creation of pride in professional opportunities and in their new role in the development of their countries.

2. *Some of the results of technical co-operation are roughly measurable, but many important effects, though observable, cannot be measured.* In the foregoing section, few statistics of the changes brought about by technical co-operation were presented. There have been estimates of the increases in production brought about by technical co-operation in Mexico, Peru, Brazil, Bolivia, and Venezuela, but these are always open to the criticism that there is no way of knowing just how much of such increases was the result of the programs and how much was the result of other factors, public or private. What can be stated with confidence is that these increases occurred while technical co-operation was trying to achieve them and that there has been a demonstrable influence by programs of technical co-operation on many of the other agencies or developments which may deserve to share the credit. It seems a fair inference that programs of technical co-operation have played a substantial role in the recent agricultural development of Latin America, but even in fields where quantitative measurement might seem feasible (such as increased crop yields) the question of other possible contributing influences leads to so much debate that the effort at quantitative evaluation does not seem justifiable.

With respect to other contributions, quantitative measurement is impossible. How much will it have been worth to Brazil to have the technique of supervised credit successfully established in its country? What is the monetary value of getting community organizations of farmers started in a few villages of Haiti? Obviously, such contributions cannot be represented quantitatively; yet they are important contributions to agricultural development.

The point is frequently made that programs of technical co-operation are, or ought to be, *educational.* They ought to increase the capacity of a people to solve problems for themselves and to organize effectively for common ends. They should not do things for people but should help people to help themselves.

This should be kept in mind whenever the question of evaluation arises. Can education be quantitatively evaluated? What is the monetary measure of the achievement of a particular United States university in a particular ten-year period? If the major goal of technical co-operation is increasing capacity for self-generated development, then a change in attitude is of first importance, and this kind of change is most difficult to measure. Even where such changes might be measured, the problem of imputing credit for them to specific agencies or factors would remain practically insurmountable.

3. *The needs for agricultural development are broader than existing programs of technical co-operation, and the number of elements of agricultural development affected by technical co-operation is different for different agencies of technical co-operation.*

Chapter xii classified the elements of agricultural development into three fields: that of *attitudes* with respect to agriculture and rural people, that of *services and public programs,* and that of *social and legal frameworks* within which agriculture operates. It is now possible to note which of these elements are being affected by programs of technical co-operation in Latin America. A schematic summary of this is presented in Table 33, which, it should be observed, does not include any reference to the element of social traditions and legal frameworks. In this table, the column just to the right of the list of elements indicates the relative concentration of effort of Latin-American governments on the various services and public programs related to agricultural development. This is a generalized summary, with no attempt to differentiate between the programs of individual countries. It will be noted that these programs touch nine out of the fifteen services and public programs listed as elements. Little or no emphasis is given by domestic programs to four elements: home economics extension, availability of agricultural requisites, rural organization for group action, and organizations to assure a balanced pattern of public programs.

The next four columns to the right indicate the elements of agricultural development which are affected by the programs of the international agencies and by programs of the foundations and of religious agencies. The programs of FAO are not concentrated on any one group of the elements of agricultural development but occur at whatever points national governments ask for help, and the range of these requests is broad. Those of OAS, however, are concentrated at three points: agricultural education, training of workers for extension programs, and disease control.[3] The effect of the programs of both international agencies on attitudes is chiefly on those of the political elites (including the technicians in domestic governmental programs). For the most part, these programs do not immediately involve farmers; therefore they do not have much direct effect on farmers' attitudes.

TABLE 33

CONTRIBUTIONS THROUGH TECHNICAL CO-OPERATION TO ELEMENTS
OF AGRICULTURAL DEVELOPMENT

ELEMENTS OF AGRICULTURAL DEVELOPMENT	ADEQUACY OF DOMESTIC PROGRAMS	FAO	OAS	Foundations	Religious Agencies	Bolivia	Peru	Haiti	Paraguay	Honduras	Costa Rica	Ecuador	El Salvador	Cuba	Colombia	Chile	Brazil	Mexico
Attitudes:																		
a) Farmers	....	....	...	xx	x	xx	xx	x	xx	xx	xx	...	xx	...	x	x	...	...
b) Political elite	....	xx	xx	xx	...	xx	xx	...	xx	xx	xx	...	xx	xx	x	xx	x	x
c) General public	....	...	...	x	...	x	x	...	...	...	x	...	...	...	x	...	...	...
Services and public programs:																		
a) Research	+	x	...	xxx	...	xx	xx	...	xx	x	x	xx	xxx	xx	...	...	x	...
b) Agricultural education	+	x	xx	xx	xx	...	x	...	...	...	...	...	x	...	xx	x	xx	xx
c) Extension (agricultural)	±	x	xx	x	...	xxx	xxx	x	xx	xx	xx	x	xx	...	x	x	...	...
d) Pest and disease control	+	x	x	xx	...	x	x	x	x	x	x	x	x	x	...	...	...	...
e) Availability of equipment and supplies	−	...	...	...	x	xxx	xx	x	x	x	xx	...	...	...	...	...	...	...
f) Irrigation and drainage	+	...	...	...	...	x	x	xx	...	x	x	...	...	...	...	...	...	...
g) Extension (home economics)	−	...	xx	x	...	x	x	...	x	x	...	...	...	...	...	...	...	...
h) Rural organization for group action	−	...	x	...	...	x	x	x	...	...	...	...	...	...	...	...	...	...
i) Credit	+	x	...	xxx	...	...	...	x	x	...	...	...	...	...	...	...	...	...
j) Price and wage policy	+	...	...	...	...	x	...	...	...	...	...	...	...	...	...	...	...	...
k) Balanced pattern of public programs	−	x	x	...	...	x	...	...	...	...	...	...	...	...	...	...	...	...
l) Marketing	±	x	x	...	...	...	...	...	...	...	...	...	...	...	...	...	...	...
m) Roads, railroads	+	...	...	...	...	...	...	...	...	...	...	...	...	...	...	...	...	...
n) General education	+	...	...	x	x	...	...	...	...	...	...	...	...	...	...	...	...	...
o) Public health	±	...	...	x	x	...	...	...	...	...	...	...	...	...	...	...	...	...

+ = receiving considerable attention   x = an influence
± = receiving relatively little attention   xx = a decided influence
− = few, if any, programs   xxx = a special emphasis

* The ordering of countries by columns in this part of the table has been purposely arranged to put together the countries in which IIAA programs have a similar range of projects, ranging from Bolivia and Peru on the left to Brazil and Mexico on the right. IIAA had no agricultural program, in 1953 and 1954, in Venezuela, Uruguay, and Argentina. The agricultural programs of IIAA in Panama, Nicaragua, Guatemala, and the Dominican Republic were not visited in the course of this study.

The two elements that have received special emphasis in the programs of foundations are research[4] and rural credit. Agricultural education has also received considerable attention, chiefly through grants-in-aid and fellowships for foreign study. Foundation programs have had an influence on attitudes both of farmers and of the political elite. This influence is chiefly on the political elite in programs of research, but in the rural program of ACAR it has been considerable with respect to both farmers and the political elite.

The agricultural programs of religious agencies have been small. They have had some effect on agricultural education;[5] they have done a little extension education;[6] and they have made seeds and implements available to a few farmers. They have some influence on the attitudes of farmers, but they have little influence on the political elite or the general public with respect to agricultural development.

Turning to the bilateral programs of IIAA, four significant facts are indicated by Table 33.

a) In those Latin-American countries which, by the measure of per capita income, are usually considered less developed, the programs of IIAA have touched a greater number of the elements of agricultural development than have the technical co-operation programs of other agencies.[7]

b) In the more rapidly developing countries of Latin America, IIAA's programs in agriculture are much more limited in scope and are chiefly programs of research and agricultural education.

c) The programs of IIAA have a much greater immediate impact on the attitudes of *farmers* than have the programs of other agencies; simultaneously, they have a substantial effect on the attitudes of the political elite and, in many countries, some effect on the attitudes of the general public.

d) Even with the wide influence of IIAA programs on many of the elements of agricultural development in the "less-developed" countries of Latin America, there remain several important elements with respect to which IIAA has very few projects. Chief among these are roads and railways, marketing, credit, price and wage policy, and rural organization for group action.

The reasons for the variations in IIAA programs in different countries appear to be somewhat complex, but among them the following can be identified.

a) In the more rapidly developing countries there are more and stronger domestic programs for agricultural development. Under such circumstances, a program of technical co-operation with a single emphasis has a reasonable chance of success because it has the support of domestic programs working in many other fields.[8] By contrast, in the less developed countries, with fewer and weaker domestic programs, programs of technical co-operation are forced to tackle a greater variety of problems. If they did not, programs undertaken would be likely to fail for lack of a way to meet other but neglected needs.

b) IIAA has probably tied its own hands, so far as the more rapidly developing countries are concerned, by being too rigid in its negotiating procedures and too doctrinaire in its insistence on use of the *servicio* device for agricultural programs.[9] If IIAA had allowed greater negotiating freedom to chiefs of field party and had been willing to make greater use of the device of the adviser-technician,[10] it might have been more helpful to the more rapidly developing countries.

c) There have undoubtedly been some variations in IIAA programs between countries because of different outlooks and emphases of chiefs of field party. Some have had predilections in the direction of research, while others have tended toward irrigation projects or toward extension. Counsel from IIAA headquarters undoubtedly has tended to minimize program differences resulting from this factor, but it cannot, and ought not to, totally prevent them.

d) Some program differences between countries reflect genuine differences in country needs. No two countries have the same needs; therefore programs of technical co-operation ought to be different for different countries.

4. *The major responsibility for agricultural development must rest on the people of individual countries.* Within this responsibility there are three discernible components: (*a*) public policies conducive to agricultural development; (*b*) public programs to foster agricultural development; and (*c*) a wise choice of projects to be undertaken within the process of technical co-operation.

Each Latin-American country feels and wants this responsibility. Each has undertaken a variety of programs in order to discharge it. The ministries of agriculture, agricultural banks, development corporations, agricultural colleges, research stations, and one-crop associations that are to be found throughout Latin America are evidence of this recognition of responsibility to provide public programs to foster agricultural development.

In the field of policy, also, most countries are active. To be sure, some of the policies adopted fail to achieve their intended purpose, and agriculture has to compete in the field of economic policy with other national interests. All national governments, however, are aware of the impact of economic and fiscal policies on agricultural development. Similarly, every country makes choices with respect to projects of technical co-operation: their fields of operation, the operational devices to be employed, and the agencies to be invited to participate.

These responsibilities of national governments are sufficiently important that chaper xiv is devoted to the first two of them, and chapter xv analyzes the choices involved with respect to technical co-operation.

5. *A considerable scope of choice is open to agencies of technical co-operation as to the fields in which they will agree to operate and as to the operational devices they will employ.*

The previous case studies illustrate the wide variety of fields of operation in which technical co-operation is being carried on: research, extension, supervised credit, reimbursable facilities, agricultural education, irrigation design and construction, economic studies, etc. They also illustrate a wide variety of operational devices: the *servicio,* adviser-technicians, fellowships for advanced study, short courses, demonstration farms, etc. Each of these fields of operation and each operational device has strengths, limitations, and special problems. Sections A and B of chapter xv present an analysis of these.

6. *The most effective combinations of processes (necessary to agricultural development) into single programs of technical co-operation are different in different countries and at different stages of development.*

This is a conclusion which would be anticipated from the variations among countries in resources, problems, and existing programs for agricultural development. It follows from variations within single countries as well. Under some circumstances, a more or less traditional pattern of extension education, as practiced in the United States, can function well standing alone. Under other circumstances, such a program may be less successful than would a multipurpose rural program of adult education. In some places supervised credit for some families can profitably be combined with general extension education for others in a single program, while in other localities supervised credit would be relatively ineffective. No rigid rules can be deduced from experience to date about such combinations of processes into programs, but certain inferences about the adjustment of programs can be made, and these are brought together in chapter xvi.

7. *The effectiveness of programs of technical co-operation is conditioned by a number of local circumstances over which the sponsors have no control.*

The great variety of local factors that influence the effectiveness of programs of technical co-operation has been illustrated in the case studies. One of these is the range in sizes of farms: results come more rapidly where there is at least a liberal sprinkling of medium to large-sized commercial farms throughout a region and much slower where there are small farms only. Another conditioning factor is the looseness or rigidity of the local culture: generally speaking, progress is faster in the more individualistic societies and slower in the tightly knit Indian communities of the Andes, Mexico, and Central America. A third is the ease or difficulty of transport and communications: the ease of movement in the irrigated coastal river valleys of Peru makes extension education much more productive per unit of effort there than it is among the rough mountains and deep valleys of the *Yungas* in Bolivia, with their few roads. A fourth is the stage of development of domestic programs for agricultural development: Mexico, with its agricultural colleges, widespread sales organizations for implements, fertilizers, and seeds, agricultural banks, and irrigation programs is a much easier environment in which to get results than Haiti, with its weak programs for agricultural development. A fifth external factor is the prevailing attitudes toward agriculture and toward progress itself: Bolivia, with its government's determination to achieve widespread development of its people, and Mexico, with its continuing revolution, give an impetus to programs which in certain other countries is almost entirely lacking.

All of these factors are *external* to programs of technical co-operation and vitally affect their success. In a few countries, of which Costa Rica is perhaps the best example, almost all of these national factors are favorable; in other countries, like Haiti, nearly all of them are adverse.

8. *The effectiveness of programs of technical co-operation is affected by administrative practices within them.*

Administrative patterns are different for each of the agencies of technical co-operation; thus they must be separately considered. Generally speaking, those of the foundations appear to be the most satisfactory, as would be expected since foundations have the greatest freedom of action in setting these patterns. The administrative patterns of IIAA programs vary somewhat in the field, but the major administrative problems of IIAA arise with respect to relationships between the chief of field party and the United States director of operating mission, or "country director," and with respect to IIAA headquarters administrative practices in Washington. FAO and OAS each has its distinctive pattern and problems. The administration of agricultural technical co-operation is the subject of chapter xvii.

9. *Quality of personnel is a major factor in the effectiveness of programs of technical co-operation, and some of the elements in this "quality" are distinctive to individual programs.* This is a conclusion to which almost every study of technical co-operation has come, and it is corroborated by the present study as well. Technical co-operation has to cope with many facets of human personality, in an unusual association of persons of different nationalities, operating in a field where there are few set rules to follow. These circumstances make heavy demands on human ingenuity, adaptability, skill, perseverance, and ability to communicate. These qualities are hard to find in combination and difficult to gauge in advance. Technical co-operation, because of its international character, is a process where personal failures cast long shadows of misunderstanding and resentment. "Personnel" is the subject of chapter xviii.

The Role of Technical Co-operation

Several elements of the role of technical co-operation in agricultural development can be deduced directly from the achievements of programs in Latin America as summarized in the foregoing section.

1. *Technical co-operation can aid in raising agricultural production by introducing and developing improved agricultural techniques.*

The introduction of techniques from other countries must be cautious. Many techniques that are very successful in one country are of no value in another. Yet there are many techniques that can be successfully transferred from one country to another, and programs of technical co-operation have used this technique with appreciable effect on agricultural production. In other cases, technical co-operation has itself developed new techniques. This, although expensive both in money and in time, is safer and more "germinal," since it sets up within countries the machinery for more research on new and different problems in the future.

Technical co-operation is not the only process through which transfers of agricultural techniques from country to country can be made, but it can be effective where other processes are not. Individual progressive Latin-American farmers adopt techniques from abroad, sometimes unaided. Techniques are carried home by students who study abroad and even by the migrant laborers who move from region to region (including the hundreds of thousands of Mexican *braceros* who cross into the United States for seasonal employment in agriculture). New ideas about agricultural technology flow into Latin America through books, advertising, and commercial salesmanship.

Technical co-operation can and does introduce agricultural techniques from abroad, but its contributions are greater in developing new techniques within each country (research) and helping to achieve the translation of knowledge of such techniques into farming practices on hundreds or thousands of farms (one phase of extension education). This merges with the second element in the role of technical co-operation.

2. *Technical co-operation can facilitate the creation of new domestic agencies for agricultural development and can increase the effectiveness of older agencies.*

One way in which it can do this is through advice and counsel alone. (This, dominantly, is the method used by FAO.) The technician-from-abroad can counsel with national officials, either helping them to recognize the need for a particular program or helping them to organize and launch one for which they already feel the need. Another way is through a combination of counsel and of an offer to help finance the program in its initial stages. (This, for the most part, is the method used by IIAA.)[11] Frequently a government recognizes the potential value of a new program but does not give it sufficiently high priority to be ready to finance it. In such a case technical co-operation actually shares in the allocative function by making an offer of partial financing if the host government is willing to provide the remainder of the funds for the initial period.[12]

It is not agricultural and home practices alone but types of public programs as well that must often be demonstrated before the value of them is accepted. This certainly has been true of home demonstration programs in Latin America. It is also generally true of programs of agricultural extension education. Most governments recognize the need for research institutions, but many do not realize what form research establishments need to have in order to be effective. Such programs usually have to be demonstrated before the value of them is recognized, and this demonstration of the value of new types of public programs can be an important contribution of technical co-operation.

3. *Technical co-operation can increase greatly the supply of competent agricultural technicians in a country.*

It can do this partly through sending technicians abroad to study; it can do it by working with agricultural colleges within each country; it does it most of all through in-service training, counterpart experience, and operating experience in co-operative programs.

4. *Technical co-operation can provide for some of the available competent technicians of each country a more productive and stimulating professional atmosphere in which to work.*

It is one thing for a country to have a substantial number of competent technicians in fields related to agricultural development and rural welfare. It is quite another to have the institutional arrangements that allow them to work productively. Sometimes what is needed (particularly if the national technician is young) is simply the reinforcing judgment of a foreign technician who has greater prestige because of the position which he occupies. More frequently what is needed is protection from political dismissal, or adequate salaries for full-time work, or administrative leadership that understands technical problems and encourages initiative by subordinates.

Without technical co-operation, these conditions for effective professional contributions can be achieved only by the (usually slow) evolution of an entire governmental structure. With technical co-operation (particularly where the *servicio* device is employed), "temporary islands" can be created in which competent national technicians can produce to capacity while gaining further competence. Although the contrast between the conditions of work within these islands and in the regular agencies of the host government frequently causes some jealousy and resentment, this contrast (and even the jealousy and resentment) have proved an effective stimulus to constructive changes within the regular agencies themselves.

5. *Technical co-operation can inject a "detached participant" into a program of agricultural development.*

It has been pointed out that many aspects of a culture affect agricultural productivity. Many of these are often not apparent to one who has grown up completely within that culture. Even when a person recognizes cultural or legal obstacles to agricultural development, he is often deterred from tackling them because his own emotions, or financial interests, or those of his family or of his intimate friends, are involved. Also, a person working in his own culture is often subject to dismissal if he proposes policies that persons with more political power feel are against their interest.

A foreign technician in a program of technical co-operation is in a much more independent position to identify obstacles to agricultural development and to shape programs to remove or circumvent them. He has the advantage of seeing this culture, which is new to him, more objectively because he comes from outside it. He is constantly comparing agricultural problems in the host country with those in his own country and is stimulated by the differences. Furthermore, he is far away from his own relatives, and what he does will not affect their interests. He is expected, professionally, to be objective about problems and usually is not penalized by his own agency for being so.

Of course, a foreign technician in a program of technical co-operation must be sympathetic about difficulties and tactful in his discussion of them, and he may make serious mistakes unless he is subject to local correction; but this does not change the fact that he occupies an advantageous position in programs of agricultural development precisely because he comes from another culture and is in a relatively independent position. This contribution, also, can be made outside the context of formal technical co-operation by foreign experts employed by a local government or private agency, but programs of technical co-operation greatly increase the number of persons in a country who are qualified to make this contribution.

6. *Technical co-operation can increase the resources immediately available for particular programs related to agricultural development by financial contributions to their budgets.*

Most countries of low agricultural productivity have many other problems equally pressing; therefore, the limited resources of their governments must be divided among many programs. Moreover, until the fruitfulness of programs related to agricultural development has been demonstrated, governments are reluctant to allot substantial resources to them.

A program of technical co-operation can step into this situation with double effectiveness. First, resources offered from abroad through technical co-operation for a particular program constitute an outside addition to local appropriations for that type of program. Second, if increased financial contributions by the host government for a particular program are a part of the agreement for the program of technical co-operation, then the policy of the host government is influenced in the direction of giving higher priority to programs of agricultural development in the allocation of its scarce financial resources.

7. *Technical co-operation can appreciably increase the "self-generative" resources of a country for agricultural development.*

Too frequently, technical co-operation is thought of as a "pump-priming" operation. But the false concept which this term implies is not so much in its sugestion of a brief preliminary boost as it is a misunderstanding of what technical co-operation does to "prime the pump." Any suggestion that a small injection of specific new techniques will, in itself, transform the agriculture and rural life of a country must be repudiated. Such a suggestion is an insult to the very considerable and effective efforts that most Latin-American countries have been making, for many years, on their own behalf. It also ignores the great number of different elements involved in agricultural development, no few of which can substitute for gross deficiencies in the others. Agricultural development is an enormous task, with many facets.

But it must also be recognized that relatively limited efforts at technical change can have enormous and self-multiplying effects in agricultural development when they are so chosen and so conducted that they enhance the "self-generative" resources of a people for development. This is where the "trigger-action" of technical co-operation can come in. It is not in any material increment in the "economic" resources of a country, however small or great. It is, rather, in the effect that small efforts in tackling economic problems (in a way that changes attitudes, develops confidence, and fires imagination) can have on the self-generative resources of a people for development.

How long technical co-operation can valuably perform this function will vary from country to country, and the forms that technical co-operation should take will vary, depending on how rapidly these self-generative resources are growing. The potential contributions of technical co-operation will be great enough over at least the next ten years in Latin America that no early thought of termination, but only of flexibility, should be entertained.

8. *Technical co-operation can foster the establishing of international facilities for agricultural development.*

It has been pointed out that some of the problems of agricultural development (for example, the control of pests and diseases) require international programs and that some countries of Latin America are too small for each to provide, economically, all of the specialized facilities needed for agricultural development. Here lies another major opportunity for programs of technical co-operation. Although it would seem to be reasonable to expect adjoining countries with joint problems to work out co-operative enterprises among themselves without outside participation, this frequently does not happen. Ancient antagonisms between adjacent countries are strong in parts of Latin America. "On principle" certain countries will not co-operate with each other, even when co-operation is clearly to the advantage of each.

An international agency of technical co-operation is often a good solution to this problem. Sometimes such an agency can itself operate an international program, as, for example, Project 39 of the OAS. At other times an agency of technical co-operation may be able to take the intiative in bringing different countries together in a co-operative activity that they have failed to undertake themselves though the need may be long-standing.

Summary

From this summary of the achievements and analysis of the role of technical co-operation, when viewed against the conclusions of the previous chapter with respect to agricultural development, the writer draws three major conclusions:

1. *Technical co-operation has proved to be an effective method of accelerating agricultural development in Latin America.*

This is to be seen in increased production, in increased technical training, in new and improved public programs, in increased financial resources for public programs, in changed attitudes with respect to agricultural development and rural welfare, and in international (regional) facilities for agricultural development.

2. *The most important contributions of technical co-operation lie in what it does to the self-generative resources of a country for agricultural development and rural welfare.*

In a country where these are weak, technical co-operation can provide a temporary *substitute* for these, in the confidence, determination, and imaginative attitudes of technicians-from-abroad. This can be brought to bear both directly—in projects undertaken by technicians-from-abroad—and indirectly, through providing local technicians with a more productive atmosphere in which to work. How long this need for technical co-operation as a substitute for local self-generative resources will continue varies from country to country. It has been fulfilled and passed in many countries of Latin America but still exists, even after twelve years, in such countries as Haiti and Paraguay.

The period in which technical co-operation provides a substitute for local self-generative resources merges into one in which these resources are awakened and increasing. In this second period, technical co-operation accelerates and stimulates the growth. It provides constant collaboration on emerging technical problems. It has a special responsibility in this second phase to keep a strong emphasis on the importance of augmenting the self-generative resources as a corrective against a constant tendency to regard economic resources as of sole importance. Agricultural development is now at this stage in most Latin-American countries. We are well into the period in which technical co-operation should be of maximum effectiveness.

3. *Technical co-operation can never be more than supplemental; the major burden of agricultural development is being, and must be, carried by each country for itself.*

Our review of the many elements of agricultural development and of the fields in which there are projects of technical co-operation shows that technical co-operation by no means covers the whole range of needs for agricultural development. Some elements of agricultural development could receive more attention from technical co-operation than they have. These include rural credit, home and family welfare, and community organization for local group action. Others appear to be beyond the reach of technical co-operation. These include most of the social and legal arrangements within which agriculture must operate (land tenure, population mobility, structure of taxation, size of the agricultural labor force, etc.). They also include public programs in the field of price and wage policy. On some of these matters, technical co-operation can provide stimulation and counsel, but it can never go as far in the institutionalization of desirable changes in them as it can in other fields.

Both in the needs for agricultural development that technical co-operation cannot effectively tackle and in providing the bulk of the support for all public programs, each country must carry the major burden for its own agricultural development and rural welfare. The findings of this study that point to needs for re-examination of such domestic efforts by Latin-American governments are summarized in the next chapter.

14 CONCLUSIONS ABOUT NATIONAL POLICIES AND PROGRAMS

Three of the conclusions stated in the preceding chapter are: (1) that the major responsibility for agricultural development must rest on the people of each country; (2) that the needs for agricultural development are much broader than programs of technical co-operation in agriculture; and (3) that factors external to programs of technical co-operation in each country influence the effectiveness of these programs. All point to the fact that there is much that technical co-operation cannot do and that must depend on policies and programs worked out by the people of each country. To try to delineate what the people of each country ought to do about these responsibilities is not central to the purpose of this study, but the least that should be done is to indicate the areas in which national policies and programs appear, from evidence accumulated by this study, to be particularly in need of attention.

There are two groups of policies of national governments that have substantial effect on the rate of agricultural development. One of these includes public policies regarding the legal framework within which agriculture operates and regarding economic relationships between agriculture and other sectors of the national economy. The other includes policies regarding public programs for agricultural development.

General Economic Policies and the Setting for Agriculture

PUBLIC INVESTMENT IN COMMUNICATIONS.—Roads and railways are absolutely basic to agricultural development, and they require very substantial investment. They are essential for bringing agricultural requisites and public services of education and health to individual farms and for taking agricultural products away. It is easy to understand why the development of roads and railways has lagged in many parts of Latin America. The rugged topography of many regions makes construction and maintenance difficult and expensive. However, those countries allocating substantial resources to developing a better network of transport and communication are also the ones that are moving ahead more rapidly than the others.

From the standpoint of agricultural development, farm-to-market secondary roads are at least as important as main highways between cities. The latter are more likely to receive attention, because they are of primary importance to increasing industrialization and to national unification. In a few countries, governments have begun to give serious attention to secondary roads, as in parts of Mexico, Brazil, and Venezuela. In many regions, however, agricultural development is seriously hampered by lack of secondary roads.

The new Santa Cruz–Cochabamba highway in Bolivia is a striking example of the transforming influence of improved communication. The new highways now being built into Paraguay from Brazil, Argentina, and Bolivia may soon bring similar changes.

PRICE POLICIES AFFECTING AGRICULTURE.—This is a broad and difficult field to which the present study can only draw attention. In some countries, governments are trying through public programs to increase agricultural production, while simultaneously pursuing price-control policies that severely limit the profitability of producing the very agricultural products they would like to see increased. In other cases, as with wheat in Colombia, the prices of certain agricultural products are heavily subsidized in the interest of national self-sufficiency, when freer markets would result in a greater total national product through growing better-adapted crops and depending for other agricultural products on international trade. Wage policies for urban industrial workers likewise affect the availability and the pricing of labor in agricultural production. This is quite apparent in Minas Gerais, Brazil.

THE RATIONING OF FOREIGN EXCHANGE.—Many Latin-American governments practice rationing of foreign exchange in one way or another. In some cases, this affects the profitability of producing agricultural products that the country is in a position to export. In other cases, it makes prohibitively expensive or prevents the importation of fertilizers, insecticides, implements, tractors, and other requisites essential to greater agricultural production.

This is one of the points at which the passion of a government to industrialize rapidly may operate to the disadvantage of agriculture. In making decisions in this field, governments need to be careful that they do not favor urban industry simply as a symbol of progress in circumstances where an equal stimulus to agriculture could result in a greater increase in the national product.

PUBLIC INVESTMENT IN IRRIGATION.—Generally speaking, the value of public investment in irrigation works has been better recognized in Latin America than has the value of investment in farm-to-market roads. Mexico, Venezuela, Brazil, and many other countries sustain large irrigation programs. Yet in many regions agricultural development could be considerably advanced by increased investments in wells, dams, and canals to extend the irrigated area of agricultural land.

LAND TENURE, TAX STRUCTURE, POLITICAL PARTICIPATION.—There are many other general public policies that affect agricultural development profoundly: pattern of land tenure, tax structure, degree of participation of farmers in political life. They are matters in which comment by outsiders is not always welcome, although several countries have solicited counsel in the first two, usually from United Nations agencies. Promoting such evolution within them as will stimulate agricultural development is thus mainly a matter for domestic initiative and consideration.

Policies regarding Agricultural Programs

Within the field of public programs, there are a number of points at which attention needs to be given to policies with respect to organization, function, personnel policies, and budgeting matters.

1. *It would be logical for each country to examine its ministry of agriculture to see whether it is well fitted, administratively and politically, for its task.* Several questions are pertinent to such an examination:

a) Are technicians within the ministry employed on a full-time basis? In too many instances, appointments to ministries of agriculture are for part-time work, and it is taken for granted that each technician will undertake subsidiary employment outside the ministry in order to supplement his income. This inevitably leads to a division of attention and to the feeling that the work of the ministry is not highly important.

b) Are the salaries of technicians such that positions in the ministry attract first-class men? One function of adequate salaries is to make it possible for technicians to give full time to their work, but another, equally important, is to attract competent technicians to positions in the ministry. There are many opportunities for employment of agricultural technicians in private companies and in agricultural programs outside the ministry in most countries. In many instances, technicians prefer not to work for the government, because they can get more adequate salaries elsewhere. Although there are a few competent technicians who look on their employment in a ministry of agriculture as their chief vocation, many employees look on such appointment either as a political reward or as temporary employment until they can secure better salaries elsewhere. The situation with respect to salaries has improved recently in some countries, notably Mexico and Peru, but in most countries it still is not conducive to rapid progress.

c) Do technicians in a ministry of agriculture have career protection from frequent political changes? All of the services related to agricultural development, whether they be in research, teaching, extension, rural credit, etc., require experience as well as initial training. It is only when technicians are protected from frequent political changes that they have the opportunity to stay in a position long enough to achieve expert competence in it.

There is, of course, another side to this. In many countries, personnel with little or no technical training or experience have been appointed to ministries, and many of them are now protected against replacement by civil service regulations. An efficient service would protect employees from political changes but require continued technical growth and competence, with dismissal as the penalty for stagnation.

d) How is the power to appoint and dismiss personnel distributed within the ministry? Usually, to achieve the most efficient service, this power needs to reside in the administrator in immediate charge of each branch of the ministry. In many countries, one finds that only the minister of agriculture has the power to appoint personnel within the whole ministry, and in some cases, the minister himsel: does not have that power but must accept whatever appointment. are made by the office of the president. Under such circumstances political appointments are inevitable, and there is no opportunity for the administrator in charge of a particular branch of the ministry to select men who are technically competent. Furthermore, if each administrator lacks the power to appoint personnel, he feels less re sponsible for their performance and cannot remove men who are in competent. To the extent that the power to appoint resides in the minister, he should appoint only from among persons recommended as technically competent and acceptable by the head of the agency or the bureau in which the employee is to serve.

e) How much initiative and latitude do the minister and the ad ministrators of bureaus within the ministry have in recommending the budgets for their respective organizations? If they are to develop effective programs, they need to have an effective voice in budget allocations. In the absence of such influence on the budget by tech nicians, too many budget provisions are likely to reflect political de sires. For example, much too high a percentage of the total budget of each bureau or agency may be devoted to salaries. This increases the number of persons who can receive (political) appointments but it means that those who are appointed seldom have adequate facilities or funds with which to work. Another frequent mistake is to allocate funds for new buildings but not for adequate equipment to go in them or for sufficient operating budgets. Competent person nel and adequate buildings are important, but these are productive only when they are supplemented by adequate budgets for the equipment, the transportation, and the other facilities necessary to productive work. Ministers and administrators of bureaus are in the best position to make productive budget allocations among person nel, buildings, equipment, and services. Budget *flexibility* likewise is important in order that emergent problems can be tackled promptly

f) What provision is there for continuity of policy and program within the ministry? It is inevitable and right that ministers of agri culture should be political appointees; but the impermanence of such appointments greatly retards agricultural development unless there is provision for continuity of policy. One solution for this is a national agricultural plan for a period of years, to which the government, as such, commits itself. Another is an agricultural policy committee of which the minister is a member but on which other experienced members, each appointed for a designated term of three to five years, also sit. In the absence of some such device, policy and program tend to shift with each change of ministers, and little work of a long-term nature can be accomplished. Honduras has such an agricultural policy committee, but it was recently established, and the current minister of agriculture has been in office several years; therefore, continuity of policy with a change in ministers has not yet been tested.

2. *The question of the extent to which public programs for agricultural development should be decentralized should be explored in each country.* Certain public programs undoubtedly need to be kept on a national basis, and several Latin-American countries are small enough that unified programs may in all cases be best. There are, however, many instances in which decentralization would contribute to the effectiveness of programs. Throughout this study the part played in agricultural development by a willingness of farmers to assume responsibility has been emphasized, and the need to vary public programs to fit regional conditions has been stressed. Each of these is difficult to achieve where all of the agricultural services of a country are centralized in a national government.

Some decentralization is normal in federal governments like those in Mexico and Brazil, and some has been achieved in recent years in Peru, Chile, and Colombia. Such decentralization may need to take different forms in different places. One solution is to grant greater taxing power to local governmental units, then give these local units responsibility for more public programs. This not only achieves desirable decentralization of agricultural programs but widens political participation and strengthens local responsibility for local problems. Another is to institute a system of grants-in-aid by which the national government can help to support programs administered by states or by municipalities (counties). Still another may be to grant broad regional autonomy to field administrators of federal agencies and bureaus. (This is a method now being tested in Chile in the Plan Chillan and in Brazil in the Amazon Development Authority.)

Whatever the method, however, greater local responsibility for public programs would, in many places, speed agricultural development.

3. *In many countries there is considerable need to eliminate overlapping and duplication by various agencies of agricultural development.* This is true even in countries where most programs are nationally operated. At the present time in Brazil the great need is for elimination of overlapping between the federal and state agencies. In Colombia it is between the Ministry of Agriculture, the various strong one-crop associations, and the Caja Agrario Crédito, all of which are prominent and effective agencies in agricultural development. In too many countries the tendency has been for the government to establish more and more new agencies for agricultural development, without establishing effective co-ordination between them. This process needs to be carefully studied in each country and adequate steps taken to eliminate overlapping and duplication.

4. *Each country wishing to speed agricultural development should itself grant fellowships for postgraduate training of some of its technicians in appropriate institutions abroad.* In the long run, each of the larger countries will need to have its own facilities for postgraduate training in each of the fields of the agricultural and social sciences. In the short run, it is quicker and cheaper to get well-trained agricultural specialists by sending selected technicians abroad for advanced study.

Within such a national fellowship policy, which should be in addition to the fellowship programs of each of the agencies of technical co-operation, there are certain elements that ought to be included. One of these is the assignment of fellowships annually to selected members of the faculty of each of the agricultural colleges in the country. Fellowships to faculty members help to build better training facilities *within* the country, so that in the future fewer men and women will have to be sent abroad. These fellowships should be appropriately divided among the plant sciences, the animal sciences, agricultural economics, rural sociology, and agricultural education. So far, the tendency has been to send most students for training in the first two of these fields. No country in Latin America has anywhere near an adequate supply of men in agricultural economics, rural sociology, or agricultural education, but these are equally important in agricultural development. (This emphasis on the assignment of fellowships to the agricultural colleges does not mean that there should not also be selections from the government bureaus and ministries.) Additional fellowships ought to be offered annually in home economics.

The second necessary element in such a national fellowship program is provision for appointments on the basis of merit and professional promise. To achieve this, a non-political selection committee is usually necessary.

A third important element in such a fellowship program is a wise balance between fellowships for study in the United States and for study in other Latin-American countries. Effective postgraduate training can be secured at the Inter-American Institute of Agricultural Sciences in Costa Rica and at the University of Puerto Rico, and postgraduate courses in certain fields are offered at the National College of Agriculture in Peru. As other centers of postgraduate education in agriculture are developed in Latin America, some of the students who receive national fellowships for study abroad should go to the other Latin-American institutions, where conditions are similar to their homelands and where Spanish or Portuguese is the medium of instruction. Others should continue to be sent to United States institutions, where they will be exposed to different problems and to different techniques of investigation and teaching.

We may point out that although no example exists of a fellowship program of this type in the field of agriculture, the program of the Bank of Mexico illustrates that it is possible for a government to have a domestic fellowship program that greatly increases the number of highly trained technicians within the country. The governments of Venezuela and Honduras, also, have sent a number of agricultural technicians abroad to study.

5. *Each agricultural college needs to have a program of research and a program of extension education in combination with its resident teaching.* It is important to combine research with resident teaching in order to build a faculty of men who are themselves actively engaged in trying to solve problems related to agriculture and in order to expose students to, and train them in, the methods by which agricultural problems are solved. It is important to com-

bine extension education with resident teaching in order to keep the feet of the faculty on the ground through intimate contact with farmers and their current problems and in order to give students close contact with a type of public program that particularly needs college graduates for its personnel and that can offer them challenging careers.

To meet this need for combining research and extension education with teaching in agricultural colleges, it is not necessary that only agricultural colleges be responsible for agricultural research; nor does it mean that colleges should be responsible for agricultural extension work to the extent that they are in the United States. Many sections of Latin America need multipurpose rural development programs that include elements of public health, home and family welfare, rural recreation, and village social organization along with agricultural extension. For such a multipurpose program, additional public agencies need to be involved as well as agricultural colleges. Consequently, there is a good argument for having such programs administered by ministries rather than by colleges.

Even in cases where a nation's extension services and multipurpose rural-development projects are administered by a national or state agency, however, there still is need for an extension service in connection with each agricultural college. This extension service need not cover a large region of the country so long as each college is intimately involved in a program with farmers in such a way that some of its research program is geared to immediate rural needs and its classroom materials are consistent with the subject-matter needs of agricultural development in the country. In most cases, an area with a radius of thirty to seventy-five miles from the college is sufficient for this purpose. Also, extension services conducted by ministries are likely to become stereotyped, whereas small independent extension programs of colleges can be experimental, constantly seeking more effective methods and more appropriate types of organization.

6. *Colleges of agriculture need to have full-time faculties.* The idea that part-time professors can make up a satisfactory faculty of agriculture arose out of a concept of the agricultural college which embraces classroom teaching only. Even for that concept, part-time faculties are inadequate, for keeping up with new agricultural

knowledge is a full-time job. But with the broadening of agricultural education to include laboratory and field experience, and with recognition of the need for combining research and extension with teaching, full-time faculties, adequately compensated, become essential.

It is poor economy for any country not to have the kind of agricultural colleges which only full-time faculties can provide. This is so important that several competent observers have proposed that provision for a full-time faculty should be required in any case where technical co-operation through a university-to-university relationship is contemplated.

7. *Each country needs to review the role of the practical schools of agriculture.* In many countries these schools are looked upon as training for technician posts in ministries of agriculture. Such an opinion may have been adequate in the past, but it will not be adequate in the future as agricultural development progresses and as the technicians in each ministry need to be more highly trained.

What function, then, can such schools fill? This is a debatable question, and it is a difficult one to outline for all of Latin America because the schools that carry the name "practical" differ widely. Some are elementary schools, enrolling boys who have had only four years of primary education; others are secondary schools, with entrance requirements the same as for the high schools. Some have well-equipped buildings on adequate-sized farms; others are located in dilapidated old hacienda buildings with little equipment or land. Some are led by imaginative principals with alert teachers; others are staffed by indifferent time-servers.

Certain propositions for discussion can be advanced to start the re-examination of the function of these schools in which every Latin-American country ought to engage:

a) Even poor Practical Schools of Agriculture (at the elementary level) are better than none in regions where there are not enough schools for all rural youth; but the human potential of the boys in the schools is too valuable for any nation to waste by allowing its institutions to remain of low quality.

b) At the secondary level, pupils need general education whether they are getting vocational training or not. Every country with a substantial rural population needs rural secondary education that

(1) offers a broad general education for citizenship to all students; (2) provides a framework for vocational progress[1] to those students who will not continue into a university; and (3) provides opportunity to meet university entrance requirements.

The future of any secondary Practical School of Agriculture not meeting these three criteria is very questionable no matter how lavishly it may be housed or equipped. Perhaps the best model illustrating these characteristics in Latin America is the Pan-American School of Agriculture, operated by the United Fruit Company in Honduras.

c) A number of the existing Practical Schools of Agriculture could become institutions of pivotal importance in agricultural development, were they adequately integrated with all-round regional development programs. All countries would do well to study the new school being developed by the state of Mexico at Chalco as a part of its State Agricultural Program. The school is new, but it is well integrated with the whole rural development program of the state.

If Practical Schools of Agriculture are to become significant institutions in regional development, the question of the agency under which they are to be administered is important. Where this is a ministry of education, these schools are usually weak in technical agriculture and in integration into regional development programs. Where it is a ministry of agriculture, they are usually weak in general education, and even in educational techniques within agriculture. In some cases, they can be more effectively administered by a new type of state development agency of the government. (This may be a good place for experimentation through technical co-operation, preferably with a private foundation as the external agency.)

8. *Each Latin-American country should establish a national co-ordinating committee for technical co-operation in agriculture.* So long as programs of technical co-operation continue, there will be a need to integrate these with the national public programs for agricultural development in each country, and the selection of projects of technical co-operation should grow out of the specific needs of each country. It would be well if such a co-ordinating committee could have representatives from the national ministry of agriculture, from some of the state ministries of agriculture, and from the agricul-

tural colleges. It might be well, also, to have one representative from each of the ministries of health and education. Such a committee could meet periodically to examine the total program of the country for agricultural development and to make suggestions as to the most fruitful projects for technical co-operation. It could also make recommendations with respect to selection among the agencies of technical co-operation so that the most appropriate agency might be invited to help with the most appropriate tasks.

PART IV

TOWARD IMPROVING
TECHNICAL CO-OPERATION

15 MAJOR CHOICES IN TECHNICAL CO-OPERATION

Choices with respect to programs of technical co-operation are made through negotiation between national governments seeking to balance and strengthen their own programs of agricultural development, on the one hand, and agencies of technical co-operation, on the other. At the country level in such negotiations, each party has a given range of choice. In the case of national governments, this range of choice is determined primarily by three factors: (1) estimates of the relative *needs* of the country with respect to elements of agricultural development; (2) the appropriateness of the process of technical co-operation to the needs; and (3) the *readiness* of the government to entertain technical co-operation, by a specific agency, through an acceptable device, in a particular field of operation. Meanwhile, each agency of technical co-operation has its own range of choice determined by its nature (public or private, national or international), its policy decisions, and the organizational devices through which it is willing to operate.

There are, then, three major areas of choice with respect to programs of technical co-operation in agriculture: (*a*) fields of operation, (*b*) organizational devices, and (*c*) agencies. Each of these is separately discussed in this chapter, drawing together the experiences of the programs examined in the field, many of which were described in the case studies. Choices in the three areas, however, cannot always be made separately, as, for instance, when an agency operates only in certain ways within certain fields. A composite summary of such restricted choices is attempted in the following chapter, under the title "Adjustment of Programs to Country Needs."

A. Fields of Operation

What is really being examined in this section is the appropriateness and effectiveness of the process of technical co-operation when applied to various types of agricultural programs. There follow observations based on this study as to the limitations of each field of operation and the mistakes into which one or more programs of technical co-operation have fallen.[1] The *need* for particular programs and a country's *readiness* for them are factors brought into consideration in chapter xvi. The approach in this section is to outline the functions, strengths, limitations, and special problems of programs in each field of operation.

While recognizing that a program of technical co-operation in one of these fields should be expected to make its contribution primarily by developing an effective public program within it, one should be alert to concomitant effects of each type of program on attitudes of farmers, of the political elite, and of the general public. These attitudes cannot be the primary target of programs of technical co-operation, but it should be clear from the case studies in Part II that some projects have had a pronounced effect on attitudes affecting agricultural development and that such an effect is of major importance.

Likewise, one should keep in mind possible repercussions on the social and legal framework within which agriculture must operate. These, like attitudes, cannot be primary targets in programs of technical co-operation, but if certain types of projects do influence the social and legal framework, either positively or negatively, this fact should be recognized in choosing projects.

RESEARCH.—The *function* of programs of agricultural research is to identify and to find solutions for problems arising in the process of agricultural development and to discover fruitful new means to agricultural progress. In the case of research projects within technical co-operation, there is an additional function of great importance—the training of local technicians in experimental methods. The obvious reason for such training is to equip these local technicians to carry on with agricultural research in their own countries; but in practice it has been found that such training plays a large part in equipping local technicians to take part in phases of agricultural development other than research, thus serving as a phase of general agricultural education in the country.

The *strengths* of programs of research in technical co-operation are the following:

a) Research projects provide a reservoir of locally tested agricultural improvements.

b) Research projects can tackle emergent problems arising in the course of projects of extension.

c) Research can discover productive uses for unemployed resources.

d) Research projects of technical co-operation can work quietly without attracting much political attention and are therefore somewhat freer to go about their task without interruption than are programs more in the public eye.

e) Research projects, when well chosen and properly publicized, can build public confidence in, and support for, agricultural development.

Many farmers in Latin-American countries and even many leaders in the agricultural life of these countries are not aware of the considerable possibilities for increased agricultural production within the limits of their economic resources. By demonstrating what can be done with the crops commonly grown, how the soils can be improved, and how insect pests and diseases can be controlled, a project of research demonstrates the *possibilities* of agricultural development that have to be established in the public mind before agricultural development can go very far.

Along with the strengths of projects of research, our study illuminates three mistakes sometimes found in projects of research:

a) Since many problems that researchers must investigate require study over a considerable period before solutions are found, research workers are accustomed to long-term projects and can easily ignore the need to get some of their results to the public quickly. This need is particularly strong in countries not highly developed agriculturally, because research by itself cannot bring about agricultural development. Other public programs, such as extension education, need to get started promptly, and these must be based on sound research findings.

b) The "research temperament" may neglect to make intimate contact with extension programs, whether these are carried on by the local government or through a program of technical co-operation. This temperament is an important component in the success of a research program. Research workers need to become engrossed in their work, but there is always a danger that this may cause them to neglect the need for maintaining intimate contact with extension programs.

c) From this same absorption in research problems comes a strong tendency for research workers to think of their problems in terms of the laboratory rather than of farms. Each study undertaken turns up a number of unexpected related problems that could well receive additional or separate attention. It is valid for new research projects to grow out of preceding ones. However, if this excludes turning to new problems that immediately concern farmers and that delay further progress through the extension program, the tendency can become detrimental. Especially in the early stages of agricultural development, research facilities ought to be available for tackling promptly the emergent problems delaying farmers.

d) Several projects of research have not met their responsibility to contribute to the upgrading of agricultural education through training technicians in experimental methods.

EXTENSION EDUCATION.—Programs of extension education have three functions. The most important of these is to educate farm men and women in changed farm and home practices and to help them incorporate this new knowledge in agricultural production and in home management. A second is to educate rural youth in phases of rural living. A third is to alert research organizations with respect to pressing agricultural and home problems so that these may be studied and solutions found.

The strengths of projects of extension within programs of technical co-operation are:

a) Extension programs work with present farm managers and their wives, thus at the precise point at which decisions have to be made if agriculture and home practices are to be changed. In working with farm youth, extension educates for the future, while in working with their parents, it is co-operating in the current modification of agricultural production and farm family living. Some observers feel that the example of their children in 4-H clubs is more effective than any other extension technique in convincing rural fathers of the value of changed practices.

b) Extension projects increase the confidence of farmers that they can help themselves, whereas before they may have believed that there was no alternative to traditional methods of farming or that anything that might be done to improve agriculture must be done by the government. A project of extension education can change these attitudes and build that confidence of farm families in themselves which is a very important factor in agricultural development.

c) Projects of extension education can develop a widespread public demand for agricultural development and for the other public programs necessary to it. Generally speaking, farm families in Latin America have relatively little direct influence on political decisions.[2] Under such circumstances their governments do what all governments do: they respond to those sectors of the public that make demands upon them. By demonstrating that a public program of agricultural extension is effective in raising the level of rural living, projects of agricultural extension aid in building a demand by the rural population for increased appropriate government action in the direction of agricultural development. They also influence merchants to stock new agricultural requisites, thereby building up the commercial supply lines on which agricultural development depends.

d) Projects of extension education increase the awareness by the political elite of the potentialities of rural people. In most countries, the urban elite tends either to ignore rural people (especially those on small farms) in thinking about national development or to assume that any development in the agriculture of the country is going to have to be conceived and directed by the elite itself. Sustained and increased agricultural development, however, comes about only where a great deal of the initiative comes from rural people themselves. When the political elite of a country discovers that there is great capacity within rural people themselves for initiating and organizing activities leading to greater agricultural productivity, the country is in a much stronger position to move ahead.

With all of its strengths, the power of extension education alone is frequently overestimated. Even programs of extension that are well conceived and successfully initiated may be quickly limited in their effectiveness if a number of other needs for agricultural development are not simultaneously met. If a region heretofore largely self-sufficient and isolated from outside markets is helped through extension education considerably to increase its production of a particular crop, the extension process itself may be quickly discredited if access to outside markets is not simultaneously established. A considerable increase in the production of a particular crop may increase the incidence of a disease of that crop to a disastrous extent unless research facilities are adequate to solve disease problems as rapidly as they develop. Farmers may be educated to the value of a new insecticide, but this knowledge is useless to them unless the insecticide is available. Extension education is important but is only one among many needs.

There are three *special problems* of projects of extension education. The first of these is that successful extension education frequently requires an intimate knowledge of the values, customs, and habits of a people. Some people argue that for this reason projects of extension should not be undertaken as a part of technical co-operation but only as a part of wholly domestic programs. This is a doubtful proposition, first, because more than knowledge of the values and customs of a people is involved in successful extension education, and technicians who have had experience in other countries can contribute much in the way of extension methodology. It is questionable, second, because precisely at the point of understanding the relevance of local customs and habits, a sensitive person from completely outside the culture can be of great help. It is normal for a person to be less competent in recognizing the significance of customs in the midst of which he has lived from birth than is a trained person from the outside. Frequently, also, local people overestimate the degree to which a cultural trait is unchangeable.

The second special problem of projects of agricultural extension is their tendency when successful to outrun research. Because so much research has been done on agricultural problems in other countries, and because in a particular country there are so many improved practices not yet generally followed, one very frequently hears the statement, "We already know so much more than our farmers practice that it will be a long while before extension catches up with the results of research." It is significant that this statement is rarely heard once an extension program begins to become effective. When an extension project catches on, it very quickly is faced by new unsolved problems unless there is an adequate continuing and expanding research program.

The third special problem of extension projects is the tendency to spread too thinly over too many interests or over too much territory. The tendency is strong to do what was done in Peru, namely, to establish extension agents at major centers all over the country. The initial procedure in Bolivia appears to have been better, namely, to group extension agents around regional offices where they are close enough together to make contact with most of the farmers in the region and to make supervision and in-service training feasible and economical.[3] While the tendency to spread out over too much territory is strong and ought to be resisted, the territory covered by an extension project does need to contain a reasonable number of immediately responsive farmers with whom each agent can work. Concentration can be carried too far, but the real danger is that it will not be carried far enough.

AGRICULTURAL EDUCATION.—There are four different activities within the field of agricultural education that require separate discussion: (*a*) agricultural education in colleges and universities, (*b*) pre-college agricultural education, (*c*) fellowships for students to study abroad, (*d*) agricultural short courses.

Colleges and Universities: The *function* of agricultural education at the college and university level should be to help young men learn to think about the problems of agriculture. Much college education in agriculture falls far short of achieving this function. In Latin America as in most other countries, agricultural education at the college level has more of the characteristics of vocational training than it has of the emphases necessary to awaken the mental powers of young men whose careers are to be related to agriculture.

Latin America needs much more and much better agricultural education at the college level than it now has. There are quite good agricultural colleges in a few countries, but most colleges lack first-hand contact with current agricultural problems in their countries. Their curricula include little agricultural economics or agricultural engineering and no rural sociology. They are dependent on part-time professors who have to earn a considerable share of their livelihood at other pursuits. There are two unfortunate effects of having few professors simultaneously engaged in research: it makes it unlikely that students will be attracted to the field of agricultural research as a career, and it encourages professors to teach the same information year after year, thus giving the impression that agricultural knowledge is a past accomplishment rather than a continuing pursuit.

These limitations of agricultural colleges in Latin America make agricultural education a fruitful field for technical co-operation, provided that appropriate forms for this co-operation can be found.

There are two *strengths* of projects of technical co-operation in agricultural education at the college level:

a) They build for the future by strengthening Latin-American institutions that can be continuing seedbeds for agricultural development throughout the years to come. Well-conceived agricultural education can be as "germinal" as any project in agricultural development. To exploit this possibility, however, the emphasis must be on thinking and on experimentation rather than on training in current patterns or present knowledge.

b) Agricultural colleges are already an accepted institution in most countries of Latin America.[4] In this field the problem is not to create new institutions but to co-operate productively with those which already exist.

The *limitations* of agricultural education at the college level as a field for technical co-operation at the present time are three:

a) Education in agricultural colleges does not touch the present managers of farms. It prepares for the future, but this alone does little or nothing to change agricultural practices in the present. Unless current agriculture begins to change, college graduates go into a traditional agriculture that may not welcome their abilities or new knowledge.

b) Considerable effort is wasted because of shifts in occupation after students have completed college. Even where students go through college at family expense, many of them later change their minds about what they want to do, or they are confronted by offers of more lucrative employment in other fields and therefore desert agriculture as an occupation. In many agricultural colleges of Latin America, the government grants scholarships that cover both tuition and living costs for many or all of the students. This draws into agricultural colleges a considerable number of young men who have no particular interest in agriculture, and it is therefore natural that many of them will scatter to other fields after they have received their degrees at government expense.

c) In most instances, secondary-school education does not prepare *rural* boys adequately for college entrance. This means that the great majority of students in Latin-American agricultural colleges are city boys who have had no previous experience in agriculture and who therefore are not in a position fully to understand the problems about which they learn in college.

There are two *special problems* with respect to projects of technical co-operation in college education. One of these is that each country is sensitive about its culture and for this reason is reluctant to have any foreigner associated with its university education in other than the most routine capacity. Any suggestion that technicians-from-abroad may be helpful in reorganizing curricula or in otherwise reorienting education is likely to be resented. The other special problem is that countries of Central America and some of the countries of South America are too small to be able to afford advanced agricultural education in all of the fields in which each country needs technicians with advanced training. This need not affect undergraduate colleges, because every country needs them, but it does indicate that in many cases postgraduate education in agriculture should be on a regional basis so that several countries have advanced education in a particular agricultural specialty available to them in a single college.

In view of the importance of college agricultural education and of the special problems connected with improving it, four techniques have been found appropriate for projects of technical co-operation. One of these is the university-to-university arrangement in which the technicians-from-abroad come from a similar agricultural college in the United States,[5] making the relationship one between two academic institutions rather than between an academic institution on one side and a government agency on the other. The second appropriate technique is provision for apprentice and observation training for students of Latin-American agricultural colleges in research and extension projects of technical co-operation. The most effective form of this seems to be the arrangement whereby students of agricultural colleges go regularly for brief periods of time to observe the work of extension agents or to observe and get a little practical training in experimental methods. The third effective technique employs fellowships for faculty members to get advanced training abroad. The fourth locates projects of technical co-operation in the fields of extension and research near agricultural colleges, so that the work of these projects becomes known to students and faculty members, thereby increasing their interest in, and understanding of, agricultural development.

Pre-College Agricultural Education: The function of pre-college agricultural education is to give practical training in progressive farming and in the processes of a dynamic agriculture at the secondary school level to boys who are not going to continue to college.[6]

The *strengths* of pre-college agricultural education are that it may be a good type of secondary education for skilled farm workers and it can be used to train operators of mechanized farm equipment.

The *limitations* of pre-college agricultural education as a field for technical co-operation, are more numerous:

a) It is of relatively little value to students who are to be farmers in the absence of well-established programs of extension education, inasmuch as a constant flow of new information is essential if these farmers are to practice what they have learned about the frequent changes required in progressive, decision-making farming.

b) This kind of education is inadequate for students who are to become agricultural technicians in ministries or who are to find their careers in other public programs devoted to agricultural development. At the present time most of the personnel of ministries of agriculture in several countries have had only this type of secondary education, but this is not an adequate pattern for the future. Such technicians need the education of agricultural colleges, and if they are to go on to this, a broad general secondary education is more appropriate to their need.

c) The task of improving this kind of education is very formidable, since the schools are scattered in many parts of each country, and results per unit of effort are likely to be slight.

There are several instances of a technician-from-abroad making a significant contribution to the improvement of pre-college agricultural education, but this appears to be possible only when there is already considerable eagerness on the part of the principals of these schools to improve and/or when a technician has an opportunity to participate in the normal-school training of teachers for the secondary schools or for the Practical Schools of Agriculture.

DEVELOPING NEW LANDS.—The *functions* of projects to develop new lands for agricultural production are, first, to increase the available agricultural resources of a country and, second, to train technicians in development techniques.

The *strengths* of such projects are, first, that all countries in Latin America need more productive agricultural land and, second, that projects of land development consist of straightforward engineering operations and therefore are not subject to the cultural obstacles which may hamper extension. In addition to these, projects of land development have the further virtue that they are visible and may be dramatic, an important feature in a country where confidence in agricultural development has not yet been well established.

The *limitations* of projects of land development within programs of technical co-operation are four:

a) They have little educational value for the wide rural public.

b) The training given to technicians is less transferable to other fields than is the training given in connection with projects of research.

c) Land-development projects may distract attention from the need to transform techniques of production in the older agricultural regions.

d) Such projects require considerable capital outlay, and this can tie up an appreciable share of the resources of a program of technical co-operation, unless the capital costs are made available from a different source.[7]

Four techniques of land development have been successfully used within programs of technical co-operation. One of these is the clearing of land by large mechanical equipment on contract for the owner. The second technique is surveying for and designing small-scale irrigation projects to be constructed either by groups of farmers or by the government. The third is the actual construction and operation of irrigation systems. The fourth technique is demonstration farms to test the agricultural potentiality of land that might be worth developing. Each of the techniques has been successfully used in one or more countries.

SUPERVISED CREDIT.—The *function* of programs of supervised credit is to meet the need of those farm families who desire credit but for whom the availability and effectiveness of credit are dependent on associated extension education.

There are four *strengths* of programs of supervised credit:

a) They can draw into progressive agriculture farmers who have not had access to credit or experience in its use.

b) They can demonstrate to laggard operators of larger farms the productivity of agricultural knowledge combined with the enlarged resources available through credit.

c) They can demonstrate to the political elite of a country the productivity of appropriate amounts of capital applied to small farms.

d) They combine farm and home planning, placing major emphasis on family welfare.

The *limitations* of programs of supervised credit are:

a) They are expensive unless combined with other programs such as general extension education, rural health, etc.

b) There is a danger that where they are successful they may be looked on as a panacea rather than as one effective technique within a broader program of extension education.

c) Like projects of extension education, they can get into difficulty by outrunning research unless public programs for the latter are adequate.

There are two *special problems* of projects of supervised credit. One is the problem of securing adequate loan funds. This can prove to be a major difficulty, as it was in the program of ACAR in Brazil. It is important to the success of projects of supervised credit that adequate provision for loan funds be made at the very beginning. The other special problem is that the supervision of farm loans is a specialized skill requiring careful training. One reason for the success of the ACAR program is the intensive initial and continuing in-service training of its agents.

Where projects of supervised credit are contemplated, it is probably wise to begin with relatively small pilot projects until the suitability of the technique for the chosen region has been demonstrated. In selecting regions in which supervised credit is to be tried, it is important to make sure that there is an adequate number of farms of the appropriate size, reasonably accessible by road, and that conditions are also right for the other program emphases, such as general extension, which are to be combined with supervised credit.

REIMBURSABLE FACILITIES.—The *functions* of projects of reimbursable facilities are, first, to make agricultural requisites available as rapidly as farmers are ready to adopt new practices requiring them; second, to stimulate and demonstrate effective commercial demand for these agricultural requisites; and, third, to make available, on hire, large mechanized equipment of the kind not yet widely available in a region.[8]

The *strength* of projects of reimbursable facilities may be stated in either of two ways, both valid. One way to state it is that they provide a quick way to secure the requisites that must accompany extension education in order for agricultural development to proceed. The other is to state that the education of commercial firms in their role in agricultural development requires demonstration that a growing demand exists for certain new products.

There are three *dangers* of such projects:

a) They may hold on too long, thus usurping a role that private business could play.

b) They may bring criticism for favoritism or commercial failure onto programs of extension education to which they are related.

c) In cases where agricultural requisites are offered for sale through the local offices of an extension project, this may distract the attention of the extension staff from its main task of extension education, unless these local offices are so organized that the office secretary can handle the sale of materials.

Two *special problems* of such projects are: (*a*) they require a quite different type of administration from that needed by other projects of technical co-operation; (*b*) some of them require a substantial investment in stocks and equipment.

DEMONSTRATION FARMS.—The *function* of demonstration farms (as usually conceived) is to demonstrate how much agricultural production can be increased by the simultaneous application of many improved practices to the operation of a single farm.

The *strengths* of demonstration farms are, first, that they are a visual evidence of agricultural possibilities and, second, that they can demonstrate to a government the potentialities for agricultural development of the regions in which they are located. This second strength is a specialized function of demonstration farms, and in practice it is the only function they can perform satisfactorily.

There are four *weaknesses* of demonstration farms as projects, whether of technical co-operation or within domestic programs for agricultural development:

a) Generally speaking, farmers do not copy the practices they see demonstrated on such farms. The major reason for this is that they see too many new practices at the same time. A commercial farmer must change practices a few at a time. *The demonstration farm does not indicate priorities.* Also, seeing so many new practices at once, farmers are likely to conclude that such farming requires financial resources or managerial ability beyond their own.

b) The influence of demonstration farms is limited by location. Farmers must come to the farms in order to be impressed, and thus such farms are less effective than demonstrations of single practices, widely scattered on individual farms.

c) Demonstration farms are expensive in relation to the results achieved except when they perform the special function of demonstrating the suitability of a new region for development and settlement. In that case, they are very valuable.[9]

THE AREA APPROACH.—The *function* of the "area approach" in technical co-operation is to demonstrate by simultaneous programs of agricultural education, health, industrial productivity, etc., what can be achieved in a particular region by integrated public programs for all phases of regional development. This is a new emphasis in technical co-operation. The only such project actually in operation by the end of 1954 was in Chile, and the time has not come when conclusions can be drawn from it.

The *strengths* which it is hoped that the area approach will have are three. First, it should encourage the concentration of each program emphasis, such as agriculture or public health, in a more effective area. Second, each phase of the program should support all of the others: by an integrated program it ought to be possible to remove obstacles that are not in the direct field of one program by appropriate action in another phase of the total project. Third, if such a project is successful, it should build public confidence in the possibility of similar regional developments elsewhere in the country and give officials and technicians of the host country the necessary experience to repeat the regional development pattern.

The major *weakness* of the area approach will likely be that of engrossment in immediate-action programs to the exclusion of more long-range research and specialist training. By highlighting, in a host country, the virtues of concentrated regional development, the process of technical co-operation may obscure the necessity for basic and germinal attention to each of the component fields without which multiplication of regional programs will be impossible.

B. *Operational Devices*

This section turns to the question of the choice of operational devices through which projects of technical co-operation in agriculture can be carried on.[10] There are seven of these devices, each sufficiently important to warrant discussion: (1) the *servicio,* (2) the adviser-technician, (3) fellowships for academic study abroad, (4) observation tours and leader grants, (5) short-course training in the host country, (6) university contracts, (7) grants-in-aid.

THE SERVICIO.—A *servicio* is a bureau established by legislative or executive action of a government for the express purpose of carrying on a program of technical co-operation with an outside agency.[10a] This outside agency in most cases is the United States government. There is no difference in form, however, between the many *servicios* in which the outside agency is the United States government and the two examples at the present time in Latin America in which the outside agency is a private organization, OEE and ACAR.[11]

In most cases, the terms of reference of a *servicio* are much broader than its actual program. Although the agreements vary in their provisions, in general a *servicio* is set up to undertake whatever projects within the field of agricultural development are mutually acceptable to its director and to a minister of agriculture. The actual program in each case is the summation of the individual projects undertaken by the *servicio,* each project being approved both by a minister or other official of the host government and by the outside agency.

The *servicio* is an administrative device—not a program. It has been likened to a flatcar onto which it is possible to load different projects, carry each one to the point where it should be transferred to another agency of the host government, and unload it at that point, thus making room for other needed projects.

Another useful figure of speech applied to the *servicio* likens it to a marriage in that its legal foundation provides the nominal framework, but its quality is a product of mutual respect, mutual adaptation, mutual planning, and joint work. This is a good simile because it emphasizes the large role that constructive human relations play in the success or failure of the work of the *servicio*.[12] The legal device provides the framework within which it is possible to build a constructively co-operative program, but there is no magic guaranty in the legal arrangement except as a high order of intelligence, sympathy, and understanding are applied to it.

The first strength of the *servicio* is that it establishes an administratively integrated binational technical staff to undertake selected projects related to agricultural development. There are other relationships in which technicians of two or more nationalities work together but not within the context of administrative authority that characterizes the *servicio*. When an individual adviser works with a regular agency of the host government, there is interplay between him and the local technicians of the agency; but there is no administrative necessity even to compromise on program, for all of the administrative authority is in the hands of the officials of the host government. In the *servicio*, on the other hand, the administrative authority is so ordered as to make imperative a reconciliation between local and outside viewpoints in the selection and administration of projects.

The second strength of the *servicio* is that it offers an opportunity to demonstrate new administrative patterns for agricultural programs. A *servicio* is never an adequate substitute for the constant improvement of the normal practices of public administration within the government of any country. At the same time, it does offer an opportunity to launch programs within new patterns of administration without waiting for the slower evolution of administrative practices within the host government. By doing this, a *servicio* may even hasten the evolution of practices of public administration in other parts of the host government, through demonstrating the advantages of a changed pattern.

This opportunity to establish different patterns of administration is part of the third strength of the *servicio*, namely, the opportunity which it affords for well-trained local technicians to make fuller use of their talents. We have pointed out that there are many well-qualified technicians in Latin-American countries who have not found within the existing agencies of their governments fruitful opportunities to use their talents for the development of agriculture. In some cases, this results from the widespread practice of replacing the personnel of a ministry with each annual change of the minister. In other cases, the reason is that less-qualified directors of agencies fear the consequences of outstanding achievements by subordinate technicians in their agencies and therefore do not give well-trained young men adequate opportunity. In still other cases, the reason is simply that general administrative practices are so rigid and cumbersome that effective work within them is difficult. For these reasons, a *servicio* can be a very effective device of technical co-operation even when almost all of the technicians within it, other than the director, are drawn from the host country. In such a case, the director makes his contribution primarily through the working climate which he makes possible rather than through any technical superiority in agriculture.

A fourth strength of the *servicio* is that it may increase the resources devoted by a particular government to agricultural development. Normally the financial contribution of a host government to a *servicio* is not subtracted from the appropriations that government is already making to its own activities related to agricultural development. The offer of an outside agency to make cash appropriations for the program of a *servicio* is an incentive to a government to increase its allocation of appropriations for agricultural development.

Fifth, the *servicio* type of organization contributes substantially to the continuity of projects of technical co-operation. If such projects are undertaken through some other device, one at a time, each by special agreement, it is necessary to renegotiate for each new project. However, once a *servicio* is established to operate in the field of agriculture, it provides a bureau that can continue any particular project until it is mature for transfer by agreement between the director and the minister to whom he is responsible.[13]

This continuity of a *servicio* has a particular value in countries where there are frequent changes in the office of minister and where in many instances the minister of agriculture is not a trained technician. Of course, any incoming minister of agriculture has the authority to require termination or modification of projects being carried on by a *servicio*. Normally, however, he is wise enough not to do this precipitately but only after thorough discussion of the issue with the director. Within this process of discussion, the director has an opportunity to argue the value of the project, and the net result is that projects carried on by *servicios* do in fact have far greater continuity than projects of technical co-operation in which the technicians-from-abroad have only the status of advisers.

Against the strengths of such a device for technical co-operation must be set certain dangers. In most cases, these dangers are inherent in the very characteristics of the *servicio* that give it strength.

The first of these dangers is that particular projects may be kept within the device longer than necessary. This is usually ascribed to an alleged desire of the *servicios* to hold on to projects; however, retention of well-established projects by a *servicio* happens just as frequently at the insistence of the minister to whom the director is responsible. It is true that a *servicio* often wishes to retain a project because it brings credit to the organization. But it is also true that a minister often insists that a project remain within a servicio, either because he is uncertain that it could be adequately financed if transferred or because he wants it to retain its greater administrative freedom. To him, the project is equally a part of his ministry whether it is in the *servicio* or in one of the other agencies.

Because of this inherent danger, it is frequently argued that use of the *servicio* device postpones the reorganization of the regular agencies of the host country. It is pointed out that the establishment of a *servicio* may be an escape from the problem of administrative reorganization of the regular agencies.[14] It certainly is an escape and can often be justified on the grounds that it allows badly needed programs of agricultural development to get under way quickly without waiting for the slow processes of reorganization of the regular agencies. But it should be recognized that a *servicio* can also have an effect in the direction of reorganization by demonstrating in action a kind of administrative pattern that it would be wise for other agencies to adopt.

A third danger in the *servicio* is that of weak liaison, a tendency resulting from two factors. The first is that the *servicio* becomes engrossed in its own program and may forget about the need for maintaining proper relationships with other agencies; the second is that, being somewhat outside of the usual pattern of organization of the ministry as a whole, the *servicio* is not automatically drawn into the normal interplay between regular agencies.

A fourth danger is in its opportunity to outfit itself with more elaborate equipment than is necessary or even desirable under the circumstances. Since the director is a North American who can order equipment from the United States, and since he has been accustomed to using a considerable amount of equipment in similar work in the United States, many *servicios* get not only automobiles but most of their office equipment from the United States. In some cases, this goes as far as the installation of short-wave radio equipment for intercommunication among extension offices scattered about the country.

Not all of this use of equipment is bad. Unless technicians, even highly competent ones, have adequate facilities with which to work, their achievement will be very limited. Many countries have field agents of the ministry of agriculture and wish to call them members of an extension service, but in cases where none of these field agents has any means of transport, it is premature to speak of them as carrying on extension education.

On the other hand, several *servicios* are undoubtedly over-equipped. In few instances is the difference in efficiency between a locally made office desk and one imported from the United States adequate to justify the difference in price between the two. (If office furniture is too unsatisfactory for *servicio* use in a particular country, it would probably be a worthwhile phase of technical co-operation to help design satisfactory furniture made from whatever material is available locally and then to stimulate the development of this type of equipment by local orders.)[15]

The use of too elaborate equipment, especially if the equipment is imported, leads to a feeling that the materials available locally are not adequate to the tasks of national development; people both within and outside the *servicio* get the impression that only through the use of such elaborate equipment can the work of agricultural development be satisfactorily carried on.

A sixth inherent danger is the tendency toward jealousy on the part of local technicians in other agencies of the country's government. One reason for using the device of the *servicio* is to enable it to have personnel and administrative practices different from the routine practices of the regular agencies of the government. This gives local technicians working within it better conditions of employment, freer operation, and better equipment with which to work than their fellow citizens in the other agencies of government, and this very often leads to considerable jealousy on the part of the latter.

ADVISER-TECHNICIANS.—The second major operating device of technical co-operation in agriculture is the adviser-technician, that is, a single technician-from-abroad in the position of adviser to one of the regular agencies of the host government. Such a technician has no administrative authority, and he must accomplish his mission entirely by advice and influence.

The *strengths* of the device of adviser-technicians are three:

a) This device fully protects the self-respect and autonomy of local technicians. It is they who continue to have charge of the program, and it is they who get the credit for whatever advance is made. For this reason, the adviser-technician device is preferred by many Latin-American officials.

b) Since the adviser-technician is free from routine administrative responsibilities, he can give full time to study, counseling, and teaching.

c) Working completely within established agencies, although progress is usually slower, leaves domestic agencies with no subsequent problem of transfer.

Although the strengths of the device of the adviser-technician are sufficient to warrant its use under many circumstances, there are several limitations:

a) The effectiveness of the adviser-technician depends entirely on influence, for there is only limited opportunity to demonstrate the validity of some of his proposals. Technicians within a *servicio* have more opportunity to try specific new ideas without convincing local officials ahead of time that they are sound.

b) A second closely related limitation is that the adviser-technician often must work with an official or with an agency that has little or no administrative or budgetary discretion within which to try new ideas and methods. Even when discussion alone will persuade a local official that a particular new method ought to be tried, nothing will come of the suggestion if neither the local official nor the adviser-technician has a measure of administrative freedom. This is likely to be the case in the established agencies of governments. Where the agency to which the adviser-technician is related is itself new and in a trial period, however, it is likely to have freedom enough for experimentation.[16]

c) A third limitation of the adviser-technician device is not inherent but has usually appeared in practice, namely, that adviser-technicians normally are assigned for much too short a period. A year is the minimum effective period for experience in the agriculture of a region; thus, until a technician has been through an entire year in a particular country, he is not in a strong position to advise with respect to crops. Certain livestock problems can be mastered more quickly, but most of them, too, are related to the climate and the agricultural seasons. If an adviser-technician is to be able to revise his previous ideas on the basis of experience in the country, he needs time in the country after this first year has elapsed. This means that the minimum effective period for an adviser-technician is usually two years. Unfortunately, many of them have been appointed for one year or less, and some of them for only three or four months.

Since sound proposals must be demonstrated before they are acceptable, the device of the adviser-technician is more effective in research than it is in extension education for the reason that many research techniques can be demonstrated in a laboratory or on field plots at little or no extra expense whereas most demonstrations in the field of extension education require the provision of additional equipment for the development of subsidiary activities or the retraining of personnel, and these require both extended experience in the region and additional funds.

FELLOWSHIPS FOR ACADEMIC STUDY ABROAD.—Not much is being said in this monograph about the use of technical co-operation funds to send students abroad to study, for that is the subject of another study within this series.[17] The importance of such programs must be mentioned, however, in discussing the choice of operational devices for technical co-operation in agriculture.

The *strengths* of fellowships for academic study abroad are:

a) They afford the quickest and least expensive way to get advanced training for Latin-American technicians.[18]

b) Study abroad not only speeds the academic training of specialists, but it greatly stretches the imagination of students by giving them firsthand experience of the measures for agricultural development in a country or countries quite different from their own.

The *limitations* of fellowships for foreign study as a device in technical co-operation are not severe but do exist:

a) The postgraduate training in any country is against the background of the problems of that country. This has value to students from abroad, but many students find it difficult to make the transition back to their homelands, adjusting to different conditions from those under which their training took place. One frequent feature of this transition is learning to carry on programs with less elaborate equipment and other facilities than they found abroad.

b) An excellent command of the English language is essential to postgraduate study in the United States. Although this is an obstacle, overcoming it is an achievement that becomes an asset in subsequent careers because more scientific literature related to agriculture is in English.[19]

The *special problems* of fellowship projects are, first, that postgraduate training abroad is not very productive unless there are creative opportunities for students to use it either in domestic programs or in projects of technical co-operation after they return, and, second, since several different agencies of technical co-operation grant fellowships for study abroad, there is particular need in such projects for co-ordination of the programs of the various agencies.

OBSERVATION TOURS AND LEADER GRANTS.—A frequent device of technical co-operation in agriculture is financing observation tours for technicians to travel for a period of one to three months in one or more countries where similar activities are being carried on.

There are two *strengths* of the observation tour as a device of technical co-operation.

a) They stimulate the imagination of technicians by exposing them to new techniques used in their own field of activity in other countries and to types of agriculture with which they have not been previously familiar. Among these new experiences there will be some that they can transfer directly back to their work in the home country. More frequently, they see techniques that they know will not work at home, but they are stimulated by these to search for adaptations or even to develop completely new methods after their return.

b) Since observation tours are relatively inexpensive and the period that technicians are out of the country is short, it is possible to use the device repeatedly with different technicians (perhaps sending different ones to different countries), so that the experience of local technicians as a group is greatly broadened.

The *limitations* of observation tours are that they are too brief to be of major importance in increasing knowledge and, second, that they are often poorly planned, since trainees do not go into regular courses but must have special arrangements made for them by busy people in the countries visited. This second limitation might be eased by having a single tour program once a year in a particular country like the United States for trainees from all Latin-American countries or at least enough of them to make special arrangements feasible. Unless this is done, with trainees drifting in one or two or three at a time to projects in the United States where the personnel are all busy at their regular tasks, observation tours do not fully exploit the possibilities of this device of technical co-operation.

Whereas observation tours are normally arranged for technicians within agriculture, leader grants are arranged for high officials of departments of agriculture or for other influential citizens in host countries.

The *strengths* of the leader grant as a device of technical co-operation are three:

a) A leader grant not only increases the knowledge of influential citizens with respect to agricultural development but helps to correct many mistaken impressions of the United States. The knowledge that anyone, no matter how well read, has of American agriculture without having seen it is quite different from the understanding that results from visiting the country's agricultural agencies and farms of many varieties, sizes, and types. The kind of person to whom a leader grant is normally given has influence in his home country, not only within the field of agriculture, but in the relationships between agriculture and other sectors of the economy and in the political process. These are all important to agricultural development; and the broader understanding that a person can get by travel, where his program is specially arranged to increase his understanding of agricultural problems, has proved to be of great benefit.

b) Leader grants can increase the understanding by high officials of what their subordinates are, or ought to be, trying to do. This can have a very constructive influence in helping them reorganize their own work after they return home.

c) By arranging leader grants for groups of officials, either from one country or from a number of similar countries, acquaintances and understanding among officials with similar interests can be increased. In the same way that a single technician studying abroad has difficulties when he goes home in securing approval for new experimentation or in securing the acceptance of transferable ideas, an individual official who travels abroad has the same problem. If, however, a director of agriculture, an official of an independent producer's association, an editor, and a college professor of a country have all had the same experience together, there is a much greater likelihood that their separate but supplementary efforts will enable them to utilize their experience effectively after their return.

There is one substantial *limitation* of the leader grant as a device of technical co-operation, namely, the rapid turnover among officials. So long as the current practice persists in Latin America of appointing a new minister of agriculture at frequent intervals, often every year, and so long as it is common for a change of ministers to mean a substantial change in the personnel of the ministry, the education of responsible officials in the necessities of agricultural development must be repeated at very short intervals. Leader grants should not be abandoned because of this. Men who have been directors of agriculture and who are replaced by a subsequent administration usually remain influential in agricultural leadership in their own country; thus their experience is not lost. At the same time, the probability of a rapid rate of turnover among agricultural officials ought to be taken into account in assessing the value of leader grants as a device of technical co-operation.

SHORT-COURSE TRAINING IN THE HOST COUNTRY.—The *function* of agricultural short courses is to give specific training on a limited subject in a Latin-American setting. Such courses may be national for trainees from a single country or regional, bringing together trainees from a number of countries.

There are several *strengths* of agricultural short courses as projects of technical co-operation.

a) Short courses can be well adapted to regional conditions because normally the program of each short course is specifically designed.

b) By holding short courses on the same subject at appropriate intervals, these can serve as a kind of in-service training for Latin-American technicians.

c) Through short courses it is possible quickly to give some training at critical points at which agricultural development is impeded.

d) Short courses are relatively inexpensive.

e) Where short courses are regional, they bring together technicians from several countries who face problems that are similar but that differ just enough to provide provocative contrasts.

f) When short courses are held at agricultural colleges, they can stimulate those colleges to interest in new fields of study, experimentation, and training.

The *limitations* of short courses are that they can be superficial unless carefully planned and that they are not very successful unless the superior officers, under whom the trainees are to work after the courses, really understand what the trainees have learned and make it possible for the new ability to be used effectively.

A *special problem* is that sometimes national suspicion prevents the full utilization of regional (international) short courses. This is a limitation only in the case of a few Latin-American countries, but for these countries it is a serious problem. One country has repeatedly refused to send students for short courses in an adjacent country with which it is not on good terms.

An important characteristic of short courses as a device of technical co-operation is that they are well adapted to co-operation between agencies. Thus in several short courses FAO and OAS have worked together. In the extension short courses at Lima, FAO and SCIPA have co-operated. In other courses, OAS has co-operated with local colleges. This is a good field in which to bring agencies of technical co-operation closer together.

UNIVERSITY-TO-UNIVERSITY CONTRACT.—The university contract is a comparatively recent development as a device of bilateral technical co-operation.[20] It is a contract between the United States government and a United States university under which the university agrees to carry on technical co-operation in a specified country and the government agrees to pay the cost.

A particular type of university contract, namely, the university-to-university arrangement, offers more promise than the contracting of a total technical co-operation program to a United States university. In such an arrangement, the United States university undertakes to establish an exchange between itself and a Latin-American college or university dealing with similar subject matter. Such programs in agriculture are between a college of agriculture in the United States and a college of agriculture in Latin America. The essence of such an arrangement is that the two colleges agree on the fields in which the United States university will provide professors who will serve for a stated period, usually two years, in the Latin-American university. There is no standardized number of professors for a contract; rather, the number is negotiated between the two colleges concerned. While professors from the United States college are teaching and helping with research in the Latin-American college, faculty members of the latter are receiving postgraduate training in the United States university under the same contract. Some participants hope that these relationships may develop into programs in which exchange professors from Latin-American colleges teach during the time they are in the United States, but that development has not yet taken place.

There are several *strengths* of the university contract as a device of technical co-operation in agriculture:

a) Such a contract enlists the total technical resources of a United States university, and the Latin-American college can call on its North American counterpart for specialized services not yet available in its own country.

b) The university contract is an acceptable device for technical co-operation in agricultural education and research at the university level. It has been noted previously that other devices of technical co-operation are subject to suspicion by Latin-American colleges, especially the *servicio*. The same sensitivity does not exist, however, with respect to university contracts. Within such a contract, professors from United States colleges are accepted as academic colleagues. They do not have administrative authority but are free to paritcipate fully in the teaching and research activities of Latin-American colleges.

c) University contracts facilitate the enlistment of competent technicians for limited periods. One of the real difficulties in enlisting competent men in agriculture for posts in technical co-operation is that such appointments take them outside the normal pattern of American employment. For this reason, many men who would be quite willing to go abroad for a period of two or three years if they would have an assured professional position on return to the United States are reluctant to take assignments in technical co-operation. This problem is avoided by the university contract, because those who go abroad retain their regular positions on the faculty of the college where they have permanent positions. For them, assignment abroad for two or three years is a regular part of their responsibility to a university.[21]

d) University-to-university arrangements result in fairly equal mutual benefit to the co-operating parties. Although participation in any program of technical co-operation greatly enriches the experience of United States technicians in it, there is usually no institutional arrangement at the United States end for fully utilizing this experience and for making it more widely available. In the case of university contracts, however, United States technicians returning from assignments in technical co-operation automatically go into precisely those careers where the experience they have gained can be most valuable and most widely disseminated. After a United States university has engaged in a program like this for five or six years, a sizable group of its faculty members have had experience in the program. Not only the teaching and research of these particular faculty members but the group activities of the faculty of the United States college are enriched by this experience of working in another country on problems similar to those being studied at home.

Over against these very considerable strengths of the university contract as a device for technical co-operation, there are two *limitations* of the device that should be noted:

a) There has been some tendency, quite strong in 1954, for the Foreign Operations Administration of the United States government to make university contracts under which universities undertake functions entirely outside their normal field of operations. While a United States college may be admirably suited to the task of helping a Latin-American college to develop, its competence is fairly rigidly limited to education and research. University contracts that obligate universities to co-operate in programs abroad involving regulatory functions and participation in the determination of government policies are in fields for which universities in the United States do not take responsibility and for which they are not well equipped abroad.

b) Although American colleges are rich in experience in education and research, their experience has occurred within American culture, *and they have not experienced the specific and unique tasks of technical co-operation.* With respect to agricultural extension, for example, there is a tendency for members of faculties of United States colleges to feel that the appropriate type of agricultural extension in all countries is that which has grown up in the United States under the land-grant-college system. There is a tendency for them to look with suspicion on any plan to combine supervised credit, for example, with general agricultural extension, probably because of the administrative division in the United States between the Extension Service and the Farm Home Administration. Similarly, they tend to feel that projects of reimbursable facilities should not be connected with an extension service because in the United States the extension service has seldom sold agricultural requisites to farmers; they have been taught to believe that this function should always be fulfilled by private business. Likewise, they tend to believe that extension services should always be under the control of agricultural colleges rather than under government ministries. This has been the pattern in the United States, and few people would wish to change it there. However, it ought to be remembered that the United States pattern of extension has remained acceptable within the United States only because other government programs have done what extension does not. Other countries cannot afford as many programs as can the United States, and a different pattern of adult education for rural people may be better under other circumstances.

It is not programs of extension education alone that must assume different forms from country to country. Similar problems of adaptation should be anticipated in the fields of college teaching and research. Because of the nature of secondary education in Latin America and because of attitudes with respect to manual labor, curricular and extracurricular activities in Latin-American colleges of agriculture usually need to be different from those common in the United States. Current tasks of agricultural research, also, are specific to Latin America.

The point here is not that United States college professors are inflexible and cannot adjust to new necessities in new countries; rather, it is that the necessity to find new forms in the countries in which technical co-operation is operating means that the colleges do not have any special competence for such programs which is not possessed by other United States technicians who may have come out of one of the other government programs related to agricultural development. It is probably a wholesome experience for a United States college to participate in a program abroad where concepts need to be different, but this may benefit the college more than it does the cause of agricultural development in the country in which the program operates.

GRANTS-IN-AID.—Within the context of technical co-operation, the grant-in-aid has been used so far only by the private foundations. One could argue that there is an element of this device in the *servicios,* since the United States government makes a cash contribution to the budget of each one. However, in that case the contribution is combined with technicians-from-abroad in an operating program and in a setting in which the granting agency retains some administrative control. The grant-in-aid standing alone is discussed in this section.

The *strengths* of the grant-in-aid as a device for technical co-operation are four:

a) Grants-in-aid can greatly strengthen the work of competent Latin-American technicians by providing equipment and/or project funds. This is an effective device to increase the contributions of many Latin-American technicians who are quite competent to do good work but who are not in an administrative or institutional framework where they have adequate funds.

b) Grants-in-aid are acceptable in colleges and universities reluctant to accept the *servicio* as a device for technical co-operation. Very often grants-in-aid from a foundation can greatly strengthen the effectiveness of a university-to-university arrangement that may be supported by the United States government in a bilateral program. Such grants can do this through providing equipment with which both the Latin-American and United States faculty members can work during the period of the contract. They are also very helpful to Latin-American colleges where there is no university contract in strengthening the resources for agricultural education and research.

c) Grants-in-aid supplement the resources available for a particular program related to agricultural development.[22] It is not just the amount of the grant alone that increases the resources available. By requiring matching funds from the government for a grant-in-aid, an agency of technical co-operation can increase the amount that the government itself puts into the chosen program. Furthermore, in many instances the government or college will accept a grant-in-aid under an agreement that, after the program has been launched with outside financial help, the institution or the government will continue the program with its own funds.

d) Grants-in-aid can direct attention to neglected problems by offering financial aid for a new project.

Against these, there are certain *limitations* of the grant-in-aid device which need to be recognized:

a) Grants-in-aid do not carry experienced technicians with them and therefore are entirely dependent upon the ability of the technicians of the agency receiving the grant. Where funds alone are the limiting factor, they are a good device; where broader experience and the interplay among technicians of two national backgrounds are important, they are of limited effectiveness.

b) A grant-in-aid does not normally upgrade patterns of administration. In other sections of this report it has been emphasized that it is not techniques alone, or even financial resources alone, but effective patterns within which these can be used as well that are important to agricultural development. A particular project receiving a grant-in-aid may bypass present patterns of administration by relieving technicians from the limitations of prevailing administration, but the grant-in-aid does not itself change these patterns of administration for tasks in days to come.

C. *Agencies*

The third major choice in programs of technical co-operation in agriculture is the choice of agencies. Four major types of agencies have been active in this field in Latin America: IIAA, OAS, FAO, and private foundations. An analysis of the comparative advantages and distinctive features of these four types of agency is of interest from three standpoints. From the standpoint of Latin-American governments, an estimate of the comparative advantages of the various agencies is helpful in deciding (where there is a choice) which agency is best suited to a particular task. From the standpoint of each agency, a study of its position vis-à-vis other agencies is important in policy determination, and each agency is continuously making these comparisons. From the standpoint of the United States political process, an assessment of different types of agencies can contribute to defensible decisions as to what proportion of resources assigned to technical co-operation should be designated for bilateral programs and how much should be apportioned to each of the international agencies.

The comments made in this section take as given the characteristics, policies, and resources of agencies as these existed in 1954. A few of these seem to be inherent in the nature of each agency, but many of them could be changed. For example, FAO might, but is unlikely to, decide to use the device of the *servicio.* The United States could decide drastically to shift the proportion of the resources it puts into bilateral and into international programs. These and other changes are worthy of consideration, and, if some of them were made, the comparative advantages of agencies would then be different, but speculation based on such developments is beyond the scope of this study.

To what conclusions regarding the choice of agencies of technical co-operation, then, do the data accumulated in this study lead, taking as given the characteristics of these agencies in 1954?

IIAA.—The main advantages of this agency in programs of technical co-operation in agriculture are three:

a) It has the largest financial resources of any single agency of technical co-operation.

b) It is in the strongest position among the public agencies of technical co-operation to participate in *servicios.*

c) It is in the strongest position to engage United States institutions in technical co-operation.

In the fiscal year 1954, the contributions of IIAA for agricultural technical co-operation in Latin America totaled about $10,000,000. This is about eleven times the expenditures on agricultural programs of the OAS;[23] it is eight times the expenditures of FAO on programs in Latin America;[24] it is about fifteen times as large as the appropriations of private foundations for agricultural programs in Latin America.

IIAA's strong position in regard to *servicios* is partly a matter of the extent of its resources, but it is also partly the result of the greater ease of creating such *servicios* between a host government and one outside government than between a host government and an international agency. Both IIAA and the international agencies have, so far, been subject to frequent fluctuations in resources, but IIAA, though limited at this point, has been able to make somewhat longer-term commitments than have FAO and OAS. OAS, further, has the (probably wise) policy of engaging only in international training programs, and this automatically rules out participating in *servicios* with particular national governments. Furthermore, the flexibility necessary in adapting programs and organizational devices to differing country needs is more easily achieved by an agency responsible to one government, as IIAA is, than by an international agency of necessity responsible to many governments under uniform policies and procedures. By no means all projects are best served by the *servicio* device, but IIAA has an advantage for those which are.

IIAA's capacity to engage United States institutions in technical co-operation is of importance both to many projects in their field operations and to the process of increasing understanding within the United States of the aspirations and problems of people of other nations. In the field, many projects need the "technical backstopping" of mature scientific agencies. IIAA can gear to this need the resources of the federal government, of many universities, and of state services (as has been done in the case of public health). Its record has improved steadily at this point; co-operation among United States domestic agencies on tasks of technical co-operation has increased with the years.

An additional service performed by IIAA is that of allowing the United States to participate as fully as it desires in programs of technical co-operation without jeopardizing the international character of international organizations. Although the United States might wish that the programs of the international agencies were larger, it would not be wise for the United States to put more funds into those agencies unless all other co-operating governments also increased their contributions. Meanwhile, the needs for technical co-operation in Latin America are far greater than the resources of other agencies; therefore, the only avenue open for expressing the willingness of the United States to co-operate to the extent that programs of technical co-operation may be productive is through IIAA.

Against these strengths must be set certain *limitations.* Some of these are inherent in the character of the IIAA as a governmental agency; others are operational and could be changed if the policies of IIAA were revised.

The first inherent limitation of the IIAA is that it is suspected of national political motivations. It is no disadvantage for a program to be suspected of the long-range political motive of expressing the desire of United States citizens to see standards of living raised throughout the hemisphere. It is a disadvantage to these programs, however, when they are suspected of being instruments of short-run political and commercial policies of the United States, or when they are viewed as inadequate substitutes for trade policies and policies of international investment that would allow Latin-American countries to develop more rapidly under their own power.

The second inherent limitation of the agency is that its policies are subject to general political approval in the United States, whereas a private foundation is in a position to determine its policies solely on the basis of their effect on the general welfare in the countries where programs operate. It is necessary for IIAA annually to secure appropriations from the United States Congress, and this means that the policy of the institute has to respect the general climate of political thinking within the United States, and it is forced to tailor its program of technical co-operation abroad to current United States opinion.

There is probably a third inherent limitation of the agency: an inability to make financial grants-in-aid. To do this would require a considerable change in policy that, even if it could be achieved, would inevitably increase the present confusion of technical co-operation with programs of economic aid.

There are two other program limitations that may not be inherent but are limitations within the present policies of the institute. One of these is that the programs are subject to frequent changes of policy resulting either from changes of political administrations in Washington or from changes in personnel at high levels within the agency. The second operational limitation is that the institute cannot make long-term commitments for programs of technical co-operation. Under the Act for International Development, this limitation was mitigated by the power given to IIAA to make appropriation commitments for a period of three years and contract agreements for a period of five years. This was an improvement over the earlier policy, and it was also better than the policy under the Foreign Operations Administration after 1953, when commitments, again, could not be made for more than one year at a time.

OAS.—The one great strength of this agency can be stated in different ways. One way is to say that the organization is accepted as "its own" by each American republic. Since each of the republics participates as an equal in the Economic and Social Council of OAS, each of them feels that it has a full voice in the programs.

Another way to say this is that the feeling of reciprocity is strong in the programs. Technicians appointed under the technical assistance program of OAS come from most of the Latin-American countries. There is no predominance of technicians from any one country in the staffs of these programs. OAS has been able to recruit very competent personnel from a number of Latin-American countries to serve in its regional programs of training which are the heart and the greater part of its agricultural technical-assistance programs.

A third way to state this is that through the organization the American republics can join in building a program of mutual assistance for the general welfare throughout the hemisphere. The financial participation of all countries may not be equal, but the fact remains that the organization is considered by all of the countries of Latin America to be an acceptable and appropriate agency for co-operative hemispheric programs.

There are only two *limitations* on the programs of the organization. The biggest of these is limited financial resources. The programs of OAS are new and only now proving their effectiveness. Certain countries still do not participate financially at all (although all have a voice in policy through membership in the Economic and Social Council), and the financial contributions of the rest, excluding the United States, are comparatively small.

The other limitation is the friction and jealousy between certain Latin-American countries which prevent the appointment of technicians from nearby countries. This is by no means always true, but there are many instances in which a Latin-American country prefers a technician from North America or Europe to one from a country near at hand. It is regrettable that this is true, because in many instances a technician from a nearby Latin-American country is the best qualified. He knows the conditions of the region; he is perfectly at home in the language; and the cultural barriers which stand in the way of success in some projects do not exist for him.

Because of these strengths and limitations, it appears that OAS has a comparative advantage in three types of programs of technical co-operation. One of these is in the provision of regional services, either for research or for short-course training. (The opportunities for substantial contributions through such services have been demonstrated by the regional training centers of Project 39.) The second field of probable advantage, over IIAA, at least, is in programs related to land reform. Although a bilateral program can make some contributions to such reform, it is often viewed with suspicion. Meanwhile, there is considerable land-reform experience in Latin-American countries on which other countries can draw. The third comparative advantage of the programs of the organization is in the field of short-term advisers to member countries. This again is a technique that has been worked out within Project 39, where technicians attached to the regional offices of the project can make short trips to a particular member country to give advice on a specific topic. In such activities, the OAS technicians have a very great advantage because of their acquaintance with conditions in a particular region of Latin America, because of the lack of any language barrier, and because of the fact that they return after the advisory visit to a base near enough so that they can make another visit whenever necessary. The lack of follow-up is a major weakness of the device of the adviser-technician in technical co-operation. The fact that OAS can have competent technicians permanently stationed in regional headquarters in various parts of Latin America gives them a great advantage in the very short-term advisory relationship that is profitable under many circumstances.

FAO.—It is important to remember in discussing the comparative advantages of this agency in programs of technical co-operation that it has two sections. One is the regular program which is of basic value to all countries in the determination of agricultural policies and in the exchange of agricultural information. The other section of its program is technical co-operation as defined in this study. The division between these two is approximately the same as the division between the Regular Program of FAO and the Expanded Technical Assistance Program of the United Nations.[25]

The *strengths* of FAO are very similar to those of the OAS. It is not subject to the charge that it is operating in the political interests of the United States or of any other country. The feeling of reciprocity is strong, with each of the member countries feeling that the organization is its own. In addition, there is one special strength: its ability to draw on non-American experience in appointing technicians. FAO has been able to appoint a considerable number of foresters from the Scandinavian countries, France, and Australia, and it is able to recruit European technicians for tasks for which they seem best suited.

FAO has the same *limitation* as OAS in the limited resources at its disposal. It has two further limitations from which OAS does not suffer. One is its dispersed responsibility for all member nations throughout the world. While the diversity in agricultural problems in Latin America is great, the diversity of these problems throughout the world is even greater. In having to give its attention to programs in many parts of the world, it is not able to concentrate on Latin-American problems to the same extent as OAS. The second special limitation is the necessity for uniform policies throughout the world which prevent special adaptation to the needs of a particular region. Many different countries are represented at the biennial conference of FAO, which is bound by policy decisions of the Economic and Social Council of the United Nations. Each of these countries is at liberty to propose new policies, but each country tends to propose policies having special reference to the region in which it is located. Yet if one of these policies is adopted, it is applied generally throughout the world. Thus, the so-called French plan, which many informants insist really was instigated by a representative of the United States, and which was adopted by the council, has seriously limited the initiative of the officials of FAO in helping each country plan its programs of technical co-operation.

In view of these strengths and limitations, FAO has a comparative advantage in programs in which non-American experience is particularly helpful. Furthermore, in view of the dispersed nature of its administrative responsibility, it is probably wise for it to specialize in the use of the device of the adviser-technician, particularly if the policy changes proposed in the concluding section of chapter xi were to be made.

Because the programs of FAO are small in Latin America compared with its programs in other parts of the world and because its comparative advantages, although real, are not great, there is particular need for co-ordination between its programs and programs of other agencies. There are two points where such co-ordination appears to be important.

1. Although it has been recognized that FAO, in most instances, cannot administer operating programs of technical co-operation, a wide, inadequately tested, opportunity exists in the provision of operating advisers for domestic programs related to agricultural development. Obviously the projects need to be chosen in such a way that they do not conflict with the operating programs of other agencies. Responsibility for preventing such conflicts rests with all agencies.

2. Where FAO provides a survey or policy adviser to a country while one or more other agencies are conducting operating programs in a related field, fruitful co-operation can be developed between these programs. The recipient country may be more willing for an international agency to advise it on certain agricultural *policies* than it is to accept the advice of bilateral agencies, but the operating program of a bilateral agency may be in a stronger position to give effect to a recommended policy. There are numerous examples of such co-operation having been developed, and there are examples of each agency having gone its own way in ignorance of, or without regard to, what other agencies were doing. Examples of successful co-operation are the training course on agricultural extension given co-operatively by FAO and SCIPA in Peru and the

similar training course offered co-operatively by OAS and FAO in Montevideo. An example of lack of co-operation is the FAO advice given to Ecuador on extension in 1951 but not utilized locally, followed by the launching of extension activities by a bilateral *servicio* in 1953 without drawing on FAO experience.

FOUNDATIONS AND OTHER PRIVATE AGENCIES.—Among all of the agencies of technical co-operation, it is the foundations and similar private agencies that have the greatest strengths and the fewest limitations. The one major limitation is that their resources, though considerable, are limited. Despite their strengths, therefore, they are not adequate alone to carry on the amount of technical co-operation needed in Latin America at the present time.

Within their limitations of resources, the foundations have six *strengths* as agencies of technical co-operation.

a) A foundation can determine its policies without recourse to the public political process. It is therefore in a position to devise appropriate policies and need not enter into any compromises on these in order to secure public approval or public appropriations or in order to achieve administrative integration with domestic governmental agencies.

b) A foundation can make long-term commitments to programs of technical co-operation. This does not mean that it promises indefinite support to particular projects; for it is customary to enter into contracts having definite terminal dates at which time projects can be reconsidered. However, a foundation can commit itself to staying in the field of technical co-operation in a particular country for a considerable number of years. Such a policy recognizes the fact that the objectives of technical co-operation cannot be quickly achieved.

c) A foundation can establish career opportunities, even for periods of time longer than it may be willing to commit itself to programs in any particular country. A foundation that decides that it will stay in the field of technical co-operation in agriculture over a considerable number of years is in a position to recruit young men of outstanding ability, waiting for experience to give them the additional qualifications of maturity. Meanwhile, the promise of a productive career is a strong inducement to men of ability to accept appointments in this field.

d) A foundation can establish joint operating programs with *local* governmental units and with private agencies as well as with central governments. Although the bilateral agencies are able to establish *servicios* together with federal governments, it is very difficult for them to go past these governments to state governments and municipalities or to wholly private agencies within host countries. A private agency does not share this disadvantage. It can join in setting up an agency like ACAR in Brazil, and it can do this in co-operation with a state government or with another private agency. One of the great needs of many Latin-American countries is more decentralization of programs for agricultural development. Foundations and other private agencies, therefore, have a distinct advantage in being able to go directly to private agencies or to state and municipal governments.

e) A foundation need justify the results of its program only to its own board of trustees, not to the general public. Since the duty of board members is to become experts in the kind of programs which the foundation carries on, the programs of foundations need only be justified to informed persons and are not subject to frequent misinterpretation and changes of policy by people who do not understand their nature.

f) Since they are not governmental, foundations are not politically suspect, and host governments do not read political considerations into adverse decisions on requests. It is inevitable that in bilateral programs some projects will be approved solely because of political considerations. Also, once a governmental program has been established, it is very difficult for the outside agency to discontinue its co-operation without political repercussions. Foundations are accepted as being non-governmental and therefore have more freedom of action in undertaking and discontinuing projects.

Because private agencies have more strengths than any of the public agencies in technical co-operation, except for financial resources, it would seem wise that they should operate in agriculture at those points where public agencies have particular difficulties or are less acceptable than foundations. Five such cases appear to be of outstanding importance.

First, foundations are particularly well qualified to help in improvement of agricultural education at the college level. The bilateral governmental agencies have been relatively unsuccessful at this point, particularly up to the time when university contracts were established. Even university contracts have definite limitations on their effectiveness.[26]

A second comparative advantage of foundations is in using the device of financial grants-in-aid. So far, none of the public agencies has been able to use this device to any appreciable degree. The Rockefeller Foundation has used it effectively in the agricultural colleges of Colombia and of Mexico and in connection with the agricultural programs of the state of Mexico. Public agencies of technical co-operation are deterred from using this device because of the necessity for financial accountability to their governing political bodies, whereas foundations need justify their grants only to their own boards of trustees. In practice, foundations have a considerable influence on the judicious use of their grants because the receiving institutions know that the foundations will be operating for a long time. Each recipient institution hopes that the record of its use of one grant will make it eligible for similar grants from the same foundation in the future. Although the financial grants-in-aid made by the Rockefeller Foundation to agricultural colleges in Latin America have been chiefly in the field of higher education in agriculture, the experience of the Ford Foundation in the Near East and in Asia has demonstrated that there are many opportunities within the field of agricultural development for very effective technical co-operation through the device of the grant-in-aid.

Third, foundations are in a particularly strong position to undertake research projects, especially those in which results may not appear for a long time. Here again, their advantage arises from the fact that they can afford to wait.

Fourth, foundations have a comparative advantage in costly pioneer projects of potential promise but of uncertain outcome. Public agencies cannot afford to wait a number of years for demonstrable effects of their projects.

Fifth, private agencies have an advantage in establishing programs emphasizing farm family welfare among the poorer people of a country. They are not under the compulsion of public agencies to show an early impact on aggregate agricultural production. The programs of religious agencies have been particularly strong at this point, but all private agencies share the same advantage.

16 ADJUSTMENT OF PROGRAMS TO COUNTRY NEEDS

The evidence of this study clearly shows that no one program of technical co-operation in agriculture is optimum for all countries. Rather, the need for program variation is so great that if identical programs of technical co-operation were to be found in two countries, one might conclude that one of them must be wrong.

Moreover, no one program is optimum for a particular country over a considerable period of time. The changes being brought about in each country every year by domestic programs (both public and private) and the changes effected through technical co-operation modify the factors that should determine the projects for technical co-operation. This leads to a dual necessity with respect to program evolution in a particular country. Program emphases normally ought to change to correspond to changing conditions in the country; but emphases maintained for only a brief period are likely to have little lasting effect. Once undertaken, a particular project should not be dropped until its effect is reasonably likely to endure or until its failure is clearly established.

The discussion of the adjustment of programs to country needs is divided in this chapter into three sections parallel to those in the preceding chapter: fields of operation, operational devices, and agencies. This division is not rigid, however, for there are many decisions in which choices in the three fields must be simultaneously considered.

Fields of Operation

Since programs of technical co-operation are discussed here, the same three questions asked with respect to the irrigation projects in Haiti are of first importance in choosing fields of operation:

a) What does the country *need* to accelerate agricultural co-operation?

349

b) What does the host government *want* through technical co-operation?

c) What emphasis within limited resources will give the best returns in agricultural development, including the germination of greater achievement by future domestic programs?

It is with these questions in mind that the following general conclusions have been reached. With respect to the second question, one special remark is in order: a fine balance must be sought that both capitalizes on the enthusiasm of political leaders for particular projects and chooses and locates projects with strong probabilities of success and reproducibility. The enthusiasm of political leaders for a project is a strong asset. It is inevitable that each such leader may tend to favor his own part of the country or certain pet projects and that, from time to time, a government may desire a particular project for wholly political reasons, as happened in the case of Fonds Parisien in Haiti. Also, the influence of an agency of technical co-operation is weakened in a country if it gets the reputation of bending with every whim of political leaders. No definite rule can cover this problem. Alertness to it and a constant effort to strike a productive balance are the only guides.

1. *A research project makes a good starting point for an operating program (of the* servicio *type) of technical co-operation.*

Research is basic to agricultural development. Without it, the more successfully a program of extension is received, the more quickly it runs out of improved practices to recommend and the more frequently it runs into new problems needing careful study. Only in cases where there is already a good program of agricultural research in a country is it wise to omit research from the program of an agricultural *servicio*. A second factor making research a good starting point is the opportunity it offers to supplement available agricultural education by taking graduates of domestic agricultural colleges as trainee-apprentices for two years each. A third factor favoring projects of research is that research workers are trained to be cautious, and they are competent in the testing of techniques for adaptability to a particular region. Having such men among its personnel strengthens any *servicio*.

It has been pointed out that foundations have a comparative advantage in programs of research conducted through the *servicio* pattern. In countries where IIAA has a *servicio* devoted to extension, however, the decision may tip in the direction of undertaking a research program within that *servicio*, partly because this facilitates integration of research with an extension service and because some of the same personnel can conduct research and serve as extension specialists. IIAA's record in research is not uniformly good, but it has demonstrated that it can operate with competence in this field.

Whether such a research project should be confined to comprehensive research on a few chosen crops (as in Mexico) or should be guided more in its program by the immediate needs of an extension program (as in Bolivia) varies from country to country and from time to time. The former choice appears to be more appropriate in countries already alert to the need for agricultural development and having some agricultural research under way. The latter is more appropriate for countries where extension, as well as research, must be developed through technical co-operation.

The time may come when each of the smaller countries will be able to have research programs throughout the whole range of its agricultural problems, but that time is not near. Such a development would be too expensive. Rather, regional centers of *basic* agricultural research for contiguous small countries are advisable, together with a program of *applied* agricultural research in each country, closely related to an extension program and increasingly integrated with agricultural education.

2. *Projects of research have distinct advantages as a continuing base for a* servicio *program.*

In addition to its desirability as the initial project in a particular country, research has two advantages as a continuing operation. First, research projects are not in the public eye and thus do not compete for public favor with domestic programs. They can solve problems, train technicians, and discuss the whole range of agricultural development with farmers, officials, and politicians on an informal basis.[1] Second, when a research project trains men later employed in domestic programs, it provides them with a haven of professional interest and encouragement after they have gone into these other positions. This contribution can play a significant role in the agricultural development of a country.

3. *Most Latin-American countries can benefit from technical co-operation in the field of extension education, and, in most cases, the* servicio *is the best device for such projects.*

Extension is an essential element in agricultural development. To be successful, extension must embody both a philosophy and methods of operation that are usually more easily achieved within the autonomy of a *servicio* than by trying to upgrade a wholly domestic program with the aid of advisers alone.[2] Moreover, since extension education is a new concept in most countries, initial discouragements are likely to be great. Considerable trial and error is usually necessary. For this reason, a new extension program can benefit greatly from technicians who have participated in successful extension programs elsewhere. Not only do they bring methods—which may need considerable modification—but they are convinced that extension is important and must be made to succeed. An additional reason for using the *servicio* device in connection with extension is that building an extension service is a long-term task, and there is greater likelihood of program continuity in a *servicio*.

No public program for agricultural development touches so many decision-making persons, whose attitudes must be positive and well informed if development is to take place, as does extension. It cannot stand alone without research. It cannot go forward without an adequate supply of agricultural requisites. It is limited in effectiveness where adequate capital (usually in the form of credit) is not available. Still, it is the central educative process to facilitate bringing all of these together for changed patterns of agricultural production.

4. *Although most regions of Latin America can profit from specialized agricultural extension services, there are important groups of farmers among whom it is probable that only broad multipurpose rural development projects can succeed in raising agricultural production and levels of living.*

This is true among the Indian communities of the Andes, Guatemala, and Mexico, and it is true in Haiti. The Haitian mesh of agriculture, health, and education is so intricate that an integrated program of rural development can be much more effective than extension education limited to agriculture alone. In Haiti, also, there is no sprinkling of medium- to large-sized commercial farms where agricultural extension can take hold. In Peru, where extension has been effective with many farmers, there still is little evidence that agricultural extension without adult education programs in health, community organization, and general education can be generally successful in tightly knit Indian communities.[3]

The agricultural program of the state of Mexico has many of the features of such a multipurpose program, with agricultural extension, programs for family welfare, short-course schools for rural youth, rural broadcasting, and investment in rural roads and schools, all well integrated. The combination of activities within the program of ACAR is another move in this direction. It has been mentioned before that Latin-American countries may find the experience of the Near East Foundation, around the eastern end of the Mediterranean and of the Community Development Projects of the government of India helpful at this point.

5. *Somewhere in most programs of technical co-operation in agriculture there should be a strong project aimed specifically at increasing farm family welfare through home demonstration agents.*

Chapter iii discussed the fact that farm family welfare is a cause as well as an effect of increased agricultural productivity. In the absence of specific programs for farm women, much of increased farm income does not get translated into improved family living. Techniques are as important in improving the quality of family living as they are in increasing agricultural production, and the same process of extension education is the major public channel for carrying these techniques to farm families.

Home demonstration is a difficult field for programs of technical co-operation for two reasons. One is that the kind of activities with which such projects must begin are often quite different in Latin America from those common to home demonstration programs elsewhere in the world. The other is that in many Latin-American countries the status of women in the culture makes a different approach to the problem necessary.[4]

6. *Supervised credit is an excellent component of an extension project in technical co-operation, under appropriate circumstances, but should not be undertaken alone.*

It is appropriate where there is a substantial number of farm families with a modest but appreciable amount of land, freedom to make family choices, and already accustomed to the use of money.[5] The conditions necessary for success, the special problems, and the need for specialized training for personnel make supervised credit a somewhat intricate device. However, it can yield big dividends where it is appropriate and well directed.[6]

7. *Some provision for the sale of agricultural requisites in connection with projects of extension education is justifiable and helpful where commercial channels of supply are inadequate.*

In addition to the distinction that can be made between countries at this point, differences in the appropriateness of the technique are also prominent within single countries. The need for this service is widespread in countries like Paraguay, Bolivia, Honduras, and Haiti, but it is also strong in many parts of Mexico and Brazil. It is very doubtful that such a project should ever be the only or the major activity of a program of technical co-operation.[7] It is only where an extension service is active that there is the danger of agricultural development being obstructed by the lack of agricultural requisites. (Theoretically, circumstances might arise in which a domestic extension program is strong but the need for agricultural requisites is so great that technical co-operation limited to reimbursable facilities alone could be justified. However, no example of such circumstances has been encountered or seems likely.) Even where such sale of requisites in connection with projects of extension education is appropriate, major attention should be given to developing commercial channels for the supply of each commodity needed in agricultural production, so that the public program can be relieved of this task as soon as possible.

8. *Machinery pools, although effective under appropriate circumstances, should be considered only as adjuncts to* servicio *programs that are strong in other fields.*

Machinery pools are a good technique where there are a number of farms big enough for the use of tractors but where there is not yet a tradition of tractor-servicing and maintenance. For a lone farmer to buy a tractor for use in a locality where servicing facilities do not exist is hazardous and usually uneconomic. But to bring ten tractors and a repair shop into the same locality may be highly profitable and safe.

One or more machinery pools may be advisable primarily to clear land when a country has substantial uncleared arable land. That tractors are used for such a purpose does not mean they should always be used for subsequent farm operations. In many cases, with plenty of land available for pastures, horses or even oxen may be a more economical source of power for ordinary operations.

Despite their virtues, machinery pools should be undertaken only in certain circumstances. First, the method should be the *servicio*, since adequacy of organization is a primary factor in the success of the pools and since the investment makes relatively long-term operation important. Second, they should be undertaken only where they are a minor part of the total program of technical co-operation, because mechanization is not the heart of agricultural development. Machinery pools demonstrate the value of mechanization (in appropriate circumstances), but they are less effective in changing basic attitudes than extension education and less basic to future development than research or agricultural education.[8]

It is doubtful that funds for technical co-operation should ever be tied up in machinery pool inventory. A very small pool is almost certain to be uneconomic but may nevertheless be justifiable as a trial demonstration. A larger pool requires too much capital to be supplied from the limited funds for technical co-operation. In Peru, the government bought the equipment for SCIPA, using a loan from the International Bank for Reconstruction and Development. In Bolivia, the equipment came as a part of economic aid, related to, but not itself, technical co-operation.

9. *Demonstration farms are advisable only in testing the feasibility of opening a new region to settlement.*

The Pucalpa farm of SCIPA in Peru is a good example of a sound demonstration farm project. The farm's success established the suitability of the eastern slopes of the Andes for progressive cattle farming. It has also identified an unexpected parasite problem that must be solved before commercial ranching becomes widespread.

But demonstration farms as a frequent technique of *extension* are not sound. They present too many new ideas all at once. They never really duplicate the problems of a commercial farm. Demonstrations are much more effective when they present one recommended practice at a time on normal commercial or subsistence farms.

10. *Latin-American agricultural education at the college level*

needs technical co-operation. Foundations should be encouraged to co-operate with these colleges, and university-to-university relationships should be encouraged and continued. The device of the servicio *is not appropriate in this field.*

If technical co-operation should engage in projects that are germinal, sowing seeds for increasing domestic achievement in the future, one would think that the agricultural colleges are good places to begin. However, that often has proved not to be the case. Apparently there have been two reasons why agricultural education has not been a major field of technical co-operation to date. One is that the officials of bilateral programs have taken the attitude that although college education might be germinal, its period of germination is too long; they have preferred to emphasize projects promising to yield quicker returns. The other reason is that the colleges and universities of Latin America have prized their autonomy and have not rushed to embrace outside co-operation, except that offered by the foundations. The new university-to-university contracts have been welcome in cases where a *servicio* approach was not.

Meanwhile, the most effective contributions to training local technicians in connection with *servicio*-type programs of technical cooperation have been the supplementary training in experimental methods given by OEE in Mexico and the in-service training given to local technicians on the staffs of various *servicio* projects.

Three methods of technical co-operation with agricultural colleges have proved effective. The longest established, and still of great importance, is fellowships for faculty members to get advanced training. This raises the level of technical competence of the faculty and introduces new ideas as to teaching methods and college administration. The second effective method is grants-in-aid for equipment and, occasionally, for buildings and/or faculty salaries. The third, more recently developed, is the university-to-university exchange.[9]

Operational Devices

The advantages and disadvantages of the various operational devices for technical co-operation, as discussed in chapter xv, hinge on the precise nature of the task to be undertaken and the degree of adequacy of domestic programs in each field of operation. This means that few generalizations can be made on this subject. Those which summarize the conclusions of this study are the following.

1. *Every country in Latin America can benefit by having one program of technical co-operation organized on the* servicio *pattern.*

Despite its inherent dangers, the *servicio* has strengths of which every country should take advantage. These lie particularly in its opportunity to *demonstrate* new patterns of administration and its ability to insure *continuity* of new projects over a period of years sufficient to test their value. The other advantages of the *servicio* are important, but these two are sufficient to justify having one in each country.

2. *In countries with relatively new or immature domestic agencies for agricultural development, the terms of reference for an agricultural* servicio *should be broad, whereas in countries with long-established and active domestic agencies the* servicio *should have specific, fairly narrow responsibility.*

This conclusion is supported by the records of those *servicios* that can be called successful, and it is also corroborated by the difficulties which the device has met under other circumstances. In countries like Peru, Bolivia, and Honduras, the use of the device with broad terms of reference has facilitated prompt initiation of new projects at whatever points appeared to be the immediate bottlenecks to agricultural development. In Mexico, Colombia, and Brazil, on the other hand, *servicios* have been successful only when they concentrated on a particular field of operation, or in a limited geographical area, or both. Mexico never agreed to having an IIAA *servicio* (and IIAA has never established, in any country, one with narrowly defined terms of reference).[10] There is a new, broad IIAA *servicio* in Brazil, but it does not operate like others. Instead, it is primarily a central agency to make grants and provide adviser-technicians to domestic Brazilian agencies and programs. This may be more appropriate for Brazil, but it does not retain the advantages that IIAA *servicios* have in other countries or that ACAR (with its limited objectives and small geographic responsibility) has in Brazil.

The recent concentration of IIAA efforts in Chile in the limited geographical region of the Plan Chillan is a move in the direction suggested here. The agricultural *servicio* in Chile had broad terms of reference, but in practice its activities are largely confined to Plan Chillan.

3. *To strengthen an activity or an agency already well established*

in a country, the adviser-technician is often a better device than the servicio.

When an agency is already well established, usually, but not always, its value is understood, and the national government is ready to support it. What is most often wanted from technical co-operation in such cases is new skills or new understanding with respect to specific problems. The adviser-technician is a good device to this end.

National governments in asking for adviser-technicians should understand that few improvements can be introduced into established agencies without the expenditure of additional funds, or reorganization of the agency, or both. It is unrealistic to expect an adviser to make a worthwhile contribution simply by imparting new knowledge or techniques. Seldom are these the sole deficiencies of an agency. In requesting the help of an adviser, therefore, the national government should be prepared to make additional funds available to the agency with which he is to work and to give serious consideration to organizational changes which he may propose.

For a similar reason, adviser-technicians should normally be sought for a longer period of time than is usually the case. Just because an adviser-technician, rather than a *servicio*, is the operational device does not mean that the process of institutionalizing new ideas or techniques is any less important or any easier. It is frequently argued that the "transfer problem" does not arise when the operational device is the adviser-technician. The argument advanced is that whereas a *servicio* operates projects that at some point must be administratively transferred to domestic agencies if they are to become permanent, the adviser-technician, since he works with a wholly domestic agency, avoids this transfer problem. Actually, there is a transfer problem in each case but of different kinds. In the case of a *servicio* the transfer must be of an activity from one agency to another. In the case of the adviser-technician the transfer is from the *proposals* of the adviser to the *program* of the agency. In the case of the *servicio* the internal administrative problems of the new activity can be worked out within the *servicio* before transfer; in the case of the adviser-technician these must be solved at the time proposals are turned into program. Too often, this is after the adviser has left the country, and a frequent result is that the proposals are abandoned as "fine in theory but not applicable to our country in practice." Therefore, where the device of the adviser-technician is used, the duration of appointment should continue through and somewhat beyond the time when the new proposals have been successfully put into effect.

Each of the other devices of technical co-operation discussed in chapter xv has advantages and limitations. Each is appropriate for

TABLE 34

AGENCY OPPORTUNITIES IN AGRICULTURAL DEVELOPMENT*

Contribution	FAO	OAS	IIAA	Private Agencies
1. Introduce new techniques...................	x	x	x	x
2. Facilitate the creation and improvement of domestic agencies...........................	x	x	x	x
3. Increase supply of competent technicians.......	x	x	x	x
4. Provide local technicians with a more productive professional environment......................	....	....	x	x
5. Inject an "outside look" or "detached participant":				
a) as advisers............................	x	x	x†	x‡
b) as administrators........................	....	....	x	x
c) as training technicians....................	x	x	x	....
6. Increase financial resources for specific programs	....	....	x	x
7. Increase self-generative resources for agricultural development.............................	x	x	x	x
8. Establish international facilities for agricultural development.............................	x	x	....	....

* x indicates an opportunity and therefore a suggested emphasis.

† IIAA has provided advisers in relatively few instances, but there is no apparent reason why the number could not be increased.

‡ Foundations have not provided agricultural advisers in Latin America, but they have done so in other parts of the world.

specific tasks of technical co-operation. Each, therefore, can contribute to the optimum total pattern of technical co-operation in any particular country.

Agencies

It may be helpful to recall the potential contributions of programs of technical co-operation as they were discussed at the end of chapter xiii and to compare the opportunities of the various agencies with respect to these. This is shown in Table 34.

With respect to the first three contributions, all agencies have substantial opportunities and are appropriate vehicles. All can introduce new techniques, although private agencies and IIAA, since they often participate in operating programs, enjoy a somewhat greater opportunity to test and adapt new techniques which have been introduced. All agencies can facilitate the creation and improvement of domestic agencies, even though the techniques whereby they can do this vary. All can increase the supply of competent technicians through fellowship grants, through apprentice and in-service training, and through experience as colleagues in programs of technical co-operation.

So far as providing local technicians with a more productive professional environment is concerned, IIAA and the private agencies have a decided advantage. This is because they can enter administratively into *servicios,* thereby providing conditions of employment and standards of equipment for effective work which the domestic agencies are not yet ready to provide.

In considering the possible contributions of programs of technical co-operation in injecting experienced men from successful foreign programs into a national program for agricultural development, three different cases need to be considered separately: advisers, administrators, and training technicians.

Injecting experienced advisers into national programs can be done by all four agencies, but it is probable that FAO and OAS should make larger use of this device than the other two agencies, partly because it is more appropriate to their nature and partly as an arbitrary division of labor. However, there are many instances in which IIAA has resorted to *servicios* in cases where the provision of advisers could probably have been equally effective, and a continuing adviser can often facilitate the transfer of a mature project from a *servicio* to another agency. Again, because of the way in which they are set up, it is probably well for FAO to make larger use of the device of the long-term adviser-technician while OAS specializes in short-term advisory 'services, emanating from the regional centers of Project 39 in the Northern, Andean, and Southern zones.

For the most part, only IIAA and the foundations can inject experienced administrators from the outside within the context of technical co-operation. It is, of course, possible for a Latin-American country to employ a foreigner to administer one of its own programs but that is not technical co-operation within the definition of this study.

With respect to training-technicians, it is probably well for OAS, while occasionally sending them to help individual countries, to confine its training function chiefly to regional centers as is now done in Project 39.[11] The other three agencies are in a position to send training-technicians into national programs of agricultural development. However, in view of the decided advantage of the foundations for long-term projects, it probably is well for this function of providing short-term training-technicians to be filled by the public agencies.

Only IIAA and private agencies are in a position to increase the financial resources for specific national programs of agricultural development. Private agencies can do this through grants-in-aid, and both foundations and IIAA can do it through making contributions to operating programs in which they are partners. FAO and OAS do not now make financial grants to national programs, and it probably would be unwise for them to undertake such grants.

All agencies can increase the self-generative resources for agricultural development, and this contribution ought to have high priority among the objectives of each of them.

In encouraging the creation of international facilities for agricultural development, it seems that the international agencies have a natural advantage, and one is inclined to conclude from the evidence of the field studies that OAS is in the strongest position to establish such international facilities. It is acquainted with the particular conditions in Latin America, and it can concentrate on this task without having concurrent responsibilities under different circumstances elsewhere in the world.

In view of the comparative advantages of the different agencies with respect to specific tasks within technical co-operation, it is recommended—

1. That foundations and other private agencies increase their programs to the extent of their resources, particularly in the fields in which other agencies find it most difficult to work.

2. That all countries increase their contributions to the technical co-operation programs of OAS and FAO. Both of these programs need to be much bigger. The United States cannot increase its ap-

propriations without upsetting the international character of these organizations unless other countries simultaneously increase their contributions as well.

3. That the United States increase its contributions to OAS and FAO programs up to the limit of the percentages it was giving to each organization in 1953.

4. That the appropriations of IIAA in agriculture be increased by 5 to 10 per cent per year over the next five-year period. The performance of the IIAA programs to date and the experience now available for improving them justify this degree of expansion.

Size of Programs and of Individual Projects

The task of agricultural development is very large and the changes necessary to bring it about are both varied and revolutionary. To a very great extent, the rate of such development is determined by attitudes toward it. For this reason, programs of agricultural development which are big enough to help create a national mood of confidence and crusade are much more successful than programs which may be equally well conceived technically but which are small and inconspicuous. The large program may be mostly domestic, or it may be mostly a program of technical co-operation. Mexico illustrates the advantage of a whole people feeling that it is in the middle of a revolution, re-creating its own society in a new and better pattern, chiefly through domestic programs. In Bolivia, although the national feeling of ferment and change stems from domestic political and social sources, the confidence in the feasibility of *agricultural* development comes largely from a big program of technical co-operation. As for individual projects, size and success are much more closely related in some cases than in others. Size is a big advantage in projects of extension education, and of machinery pools.

Extension projects, although kept to the size for which adequate personnel can be found or trained, should be big enough to make a splash. The public attention paid to such programs is part of the reason for their success. It is one thing to work with a few farmers introducing a few changes; it is quite another to develop a feeling within a country that something significant is happening with respect to agricultural practices and that a general movement is going to change substantially the whole complexion of agricultural production. However, projects of extension education within programs of technical co-operation need not cover a whole country. As pointed out in chapter xv, it is well for such a project to operate in only part of a country, leaving other parts in which a totally domestic extension service can be developed.[12]

Considerable economies have been introduced into the machinery pools of SCIPA in Peru by the procurement of a large amount of machinery that can be moved from one part of the country to another, depending on the season, thereby increasing the usage of each machine per year.

Size of individual projects appears to be less important in the case of other fields of operation so long as the whole effort at agricultural development, domestic and co-operative, is big enough to create a national mood of confidence and creative change.

Sizes and Types of Farms

The speed of agricultural development is quite different on three common types of Latin-American farms, and the rate of development of the agriculture of a country is powerfully influenced by the proportion of each of these types in the total agricultural economy of the country. Generally, progress is most rapid on medium to large commercial farms or plantations, where the managers look on farming as a commercial enterprise, often keep financial records, and make choices on the basis of relative profitability. Progress is much less rapid on large holdings where the ownership of land is in itself a factor in social prestige, where medieval patterns of remuneration to labor still persist, and where income from the hacienda (even where relatively unproductive traditional methods of farming are employed) is adequate to support the owners' families in relative affluence, often in distant cities. Progress is least rapid on the much more numerous small farms, that, for the most part, are subsistence units on which farming is more a phase of an integrated way of living than it is a commercial venture. These differences in the rate of development of different types of farms are pertinent both to decisions within programs of technical co-operation as to where major emphasis should be placed and to attempts at evaluating the effectiveness of such programs.

More rapid progress can be achieved by programs that devote attention to the medium- or large-sized commercial farms. Success there has a substantial effect on aggregate agricultural production and, equally important, convinces influential persons of the value of good public programs for agricultural development. It can, in addition, lure owners of large haciendas following unproductive traditional practices out of their complacent underutilization of land resources into more productive and more profitable farming.

Some people argue that small farms will never be sufficiently productive to justify public programs, that these are marginal farms on which it is not profitable to expend public resources. There are four reasons why the argument is untenable.

1. A considerable portion of the arable agricultural land of Latin America is in pockets, in valleys, and otherwise unsuited to large-scale farming. The countries of Latin America need all of the agricultural production they can achieve, and this requires that *all* land, including that suitable only for small farms, be fully utilized.

2. The rate of population increase in Latin America (about twice the world average) is so high that in most countries industrialization cannot, in the near future, provide alternative employment for very many of those now gaining a livelihood from agriculture. Small farms, therefore, even where inefficient, must provide whatever level of living millions of people are to have in this generation.

3. National development, as well as agricultural development, requires an increasing integration of the whole population in a culture that is choice-making and flexible rather than traditional. This is an educational task of major importance and of large proportions. Hence, programs to help people on small farms achieve agricultural development have dual significance: they increase agricultural production on land resources which Latin America cannot afford to leave untouched, and they educate these rural people in choice-making, in the use of expanding technical knowledge, and in the development of social institutions geared to change and progress rather than to tradition and the status quo.[13] This type of education of rural people also can make for a much broader political base for Latin-American democracy.

It might be inferred from the foregoing discussion that large farms are always more efficient in the use of resources than small farms and that it is only the topography of Latin America, the increasing population, and the need to educate small farmers out of traditional habits which validate giving serious attention to small farms. But three comments about economy of scale in agriculture must be added. First, there are many circumstances under which a small farm may be more efficient than a large farm. Second, as agriculture becomes increasingly commercial (buying many supplies, selling agricultural products, and buying commodities for family consumption) a "small" farm may be a "big" agricultural enterprise. This is particularly possible in poultry farming, dairying, and in the production of vegetables and some fruits. Third, with the dispersion of industry to small cities, part-time farming becomes increasingly feasible and should be just as efficient in the use of resources as is full-time farming.

In planning or evaluating programs of extension education, therefore, two different criteria as to the type of farms with which it should work are both valid.

1. If extension education is working with medium to large commercial farms, it is working with those on which agricultural development is easiest to achieve, at the point where success will have the greatest immediate impact on national agricultural production, and with agriculturalists who can exercise considerable political influence for more adequate domestic public programs.

2. If it is working with small farms, it is working with those on which agricultural development comes slowly and is difficult to achieve. It is, however, working at a portion of the task that is of primary importance from the standpoint of long-term agricultural and national development but that is almost universally ignored by domestic programs. In the process, it is seeking to help the poorest people in the country and cannot be charged with "only making the rich people richer."

In the light of these two criteria, appropriate public programs for agricultural development are necessary for all sizes and types of farms. The place of projects of technical co-operation in this need will vary from country to country. In general, the total program of technical co-operation should include some projects particularly designed to stimulate production on large commercial farms (both because of the intrinsic need and in order to build political support for programs of agricultural development) and some projects specifically designed to stimulate production and to raise levels of living on the smaller farms.

Balance between Agricultural and
Other Programs

It is beyond the scope of this monograph to deal with the question of the balance between agricultural and other programs of technical co-operation in any country. It would be necessary to analyze the problems, opportunities, and specific contributions of programs in the fields of health, education, public administration, transport, communications, industry, labor, etc., in order to deal with such a topic realistically. At the same time, it is justifiable to state conclusions about the problem as they arise in the context of this agricultural study.

From 1943 through 1950, the relative emphasis given to agriculture within the program of IIAA remained at around 20 per cent of total United States contributions. Meanwhile, the emphasis given to health and sanitation declined from 80 per cent to 60 per cent, and this saving from programs in health was used to increase programs in education. Beginning in 1951, agricultural programs gained in relative importance until in 1952 agricultural programs were receiving 46 per cent of the total United States contributions, health 29 per cent, education 15 per cent, and the remaining 10 per cent was divided among the newer programs. In 1953 the diversification of the bilateral programs increased, with programs of public administration receiving 8 per cent of the United States contributions and industry and labor 11 per cent. Education dropped to 12 per cent, and even agriculture, which had been the biggest program in 1952, was reduced from 46 per cent to 38 per cent of the total program.[14]

What can be said about this trend in the relative strength of programs from the standpoint of facts brought to light in this study?

1. All programs of technical co-operation, in whatever field they may be classified, are aids to agricultural development. From the analysis of the elements of agricultural development, it is clear that the health and the general education of the population are important items in agricultural productivity. Likewise, agricultural de-

velopment is retarded in many cases because of poor practices of public administration. In many of the countries of Latin America poor transport and communications is a major deterrent to higher productivity. Agriculture needs many products that a rising industrialization can provide, and it also needs an outlet for excess labor in industries other than agriculture. Hence, all of the programs of technical co-operation, no matter how they may be classified, are of value to agriculture.

2. Although programs in all of the fields now covered by technical co-operation contribute to agricultural development, there are three strong reasons for having a substantial program of technical co-operation specifically in the field of agriculture in each country:

a) All Latin-American countries have substantial opportunities to increase agricultural production, and many of the resources available for this are not transferable to other industries.

b) With the rapid increase of population, the majority of wage earners in every Latin-American country must gain their livelihood from agriculture for many years to come.

c) If rural people are to be liberated from traditional to choice-making patterns of living, and integrated into the national life of each country, changed patterns of agriculture and rural life must do it.

The first and second of these reasons argue for distributing the attention of technical co-operation within agriculture throughout the range of the elements of agricultural development wherever the potential contributions of technical co-operation programs are greatest. They thus argue for programs of research, extension, reimbursable facilities, supervised credit, etc. The third reason argues specifically for programs of agricultural extension, supervised credit, and multipurpose community development.

3. It may be that the process of technical co-operation is better adapted to programs in some fields than it is to programs in others. The record of programs to date demonstrates that agriculture is a field in which programs of technical co-operation can be quite effective. Also, it is one in which the United States has had considerable experience and in which Latin America wants help.

4. Another sound argument for programs of technical co-operation in agriculture is the fact that rising agricultural productivity

requires changes of attitude and new knowledge throughout the whole population of a country. In the last analysis, attitudes will determine the rate of economic development. Where people have the will to develop, the flexibility to change, a thirst for knowledge, and a willingness to accept individual responsibility, economic development is going to take place in one way or another. To say this is not to underrate the need for the basic physical resources of land and capital and for all of the other elements of agricultural development that have been discussed earlier in this study. All of these, however, are *instrumental*. The character and the outlook of the people are of first importance. Since agricultural development requires these changes throughout the population of a country, it is an advantageous field for technical co-operation.

17 ADMINISTRATION OF PUBLIC PROGRAMS

One of the major findings of this study is that the trend in head-quarters administration of the United States bilateral programs appears to be away from those patterns that contribute to the success of programs in the field. This is a serious matter. Can the trend be halted and more appropriate administrative organization devised? Or will the inherent difficulties in administering technical co-operation prove insurmountable? The evidence of the present study indicates that technical co-operation is unusually difficult to administer but that great improvements could be made if the necessity were sufficiently felt.[1]

Distinctive Administrative Problems of Public Programs

Why is it that administration has been an especially troublesome problem for programs of technical co-operation? The experience of such programs in Latin-American Agriculture suggests four distinctive administrative problems.

1. *Being supplemental to domestic programs in each country, co-operative programs must vary widely in content and organization.*

The primary organizations for agricultural development in Latin America are the domestic agencies of Latin-American governments. This requires an unusual distribution of responsibility for policy and program determination of technical co-operation. IIAA's "total" program, for example, should be a collection of separate programs that differ both in content and in administrative structure. Though policies and procedures are usually formulated at the top levels of administration for subordinate officials to execute, technical co-operation requires that wide latitude be given to administrators in each country. The type of headquarters administration that ought to be evolved would:

(1) Select field administrators with a broad grasp of the process and function of technical co-operation.

(2) Delegate wide policy and operational authority to these field administrators.

(3) Make a continuous study (as a staff rather than a line function) of the process of agricultural development and discuss this frequently with chiefs of field party.

(4) Develop a concept and a structure for headquarters administration as a *service* agency to widely differing field programs and as an *interpretive* agency to explain technical co-operation to the government and people of the United States or to the member countries of international agencies.

(5) Eschew any temptation to dictate policies or to force administrative uniformity on field programs.[2]

The shortcomings of the administrative structure of IIAA have stemmed to a considerable degree from failure to evolve a pattern of country-to-country variation that would leave much of policy and administrative responsibility to chiefs of field party. From this standpoint, the earliest pattern was the best. In the early years of IIAA all headquarters administrators knew they were engaged in a novel activity, they realized that trial and error had to prevail, and consequently they delegated wide authority to chiefs of field party. As the programs grew, increasing size and complexity of the total program brought valid administrative changes, but other new factors of doubtful validity came to be thought important (such as the doctrine that all kinds of technical co-operation "ought to be integrated" and the other doctrine that the true orientation of technical co-operation should be "immediate impact on economic development"). These newer factors have been at least partly responsible for the trend in IIAA administration away from separate authority for agricultural chiefs of field party toward the less productive uniformity, "integration," and centering of policy formation in Washington.[3]

At this point, FAO administration has been better, perhaps partly because FAO programs in Latin America have been much smaller. FAO is often criticized for having not "a Program" at all but only "a collection of projects." To this, FAO rightfully replies that it would be presumptuous of it to have a program for a member country; rather, it should co-operate, on request, with domestic programs of each member country in whatever way member countries desire. This is sound, in that it recognizes the overriding need for country-to-country variation. If carried to an extreme, however, as it has been by some FAO officials, this attitude deprives member countries of the guidance FAO might give in considering the relative priorities of alternative projects.

OAS largely avoids this particular problem of administration in its agricultural programs of technical co-operation, since it does not work directly with national programs but offers certain international training courses which member countries are free to use or to ignore.

2. *Effective technical co-operation must be a long-term activity, but the fiscal patterns of supporting public agencies are all based on one-year appropriations.*

The distinction between the life-span of specific projects of technical co-operation and continuity of technical co-operation as an activity must be re-emphasized. Specific projects developed within the process of technical co-operation reach the point at which they no longer need this process. For some projects, such as the design of irrigation works or training in a particular technique of vaccine manufacture, this maturity may be quickly reached. For others, such as a research or extension program, it may require a number of years. But the process of technical co-operation, no matter what its specific projects at any one time, is one which, once begun, needs continuity for some years, and this need holds also for many specific projects.

Yet the appropriations for all public programs of technical co-operation are on a year-to-year basis. Congress annually decides what the total United States appropriation for technical co-operation is to be. Member countries commit themselves for only one year at a time with respect to international agencies. Consequently no agency of technical co-operation can make firm commitments for more than one year.[4]

This difficulty of annual appropriations is increased when appropriations are not made until, or even several weeks after, the beginning of the fiscal year to which they apply, as has happened repeatedly. Reports of IIAA programs are full of references to program interruptions because of late appropriations. Experienced field administrators find ways to mitigate the serious effects of these delays on staff morale, but the need for such mitigation should not arise.

Here, again, there has been a deterioration in the administration of the bilateral programs of the United States government. The IIAA was set up as a semi-autonomous government corporation to allow budgetary discretion that could alleviate, to some degree, the limitations of one-year appropriations. It was able to make program commitments for periods of up to five years and financial commitments for periods up to three years. The Act for International Development (1950), in order to facilitate program continuity, authorized Congress to make annual appropriations for technical co-operation, so that only one bill had to pass Congress annually instead of two (one to "authorize" an appropriation and a second actually to make it).

The Mutual Security Act of 1954 superseded the Act for International Development and did not contain the previous continuing authorization of annual appropriations. Moreover, the placing of both technical co-operation and economic aid under the Foreign Operations Administration, together with the then prevailing attitude favoring early termination of economic aid, once again placed technical co-operation in an atmosphere of year-to-year uncertainty and of likelihood of early termination.

It is not necessary to change the whole tradition of annual appropriations in order to give greater assurance of continuity to programs of technical co-operation. They once had this under the operations of IIAA as a government corporation and under the Act for International Development. It should at least be possible to regain this lost ground. In addition, if the people of the United States are as ingenious as they feel themselves to be, it ought to be possible to create appropriate administrative instruments for the process of technical co-operation, which they were largely responsible for launching.[5]

FAO and OAS also face this administrative problem of annual appropriations for a long-term process. Solution of the problem may be inherently more difficult for them, but at least the United States could, if it would, lengthen the term of its commitments to them. It would seem, also, that some authorization for reserves to complete three-year to five-year projects might be granted to international agencies of technical co-operation by their parent organizations.

3. *The headquarters offices are hampered because the primary needs arise in the countries where programs operate, whereas the pressures for various forms of administration arise in Washington or in the political councils of international agencies.*

The needs of United States bilateral programs are abroad, whereas the pressures for alternative types of administration are in Washington. It is difficult for field needs to be kept in view when the Department of Agriculture, the Department of Commerce, the Department of State, and the Budget Bureau are only a few blocks away, all adding their pressures to those arising from the political considerations and public sentiments represented in Congress. These pressures relate not to the field needs of programs of technical co-operation but to questions of interagency and interdepartmental prerogatives and relationships in Washington. Local exigencies are so insistent and so much better known by both administrators and legislators that they loom largest in considerations of how technical co-operation is to be organized and administered.

In the case of FAO, it is difficult for field needs in agriculture to win out when they conflict with organizational pressures of divisional offices within FAO, when the pressures from other UN specialized agencies are coupled with a passion for uniformity in TAB. This difficulty is less characteristic of OAS but is present even there, since its programs of technical co-operation in agriculture have to be combined with quite different programs of other specialized agencies, and since all of these are subject to final decisions in the politically constituted Economic and Social Council.

Administering programs of technical co-operation would be hard enough if the *operating needs* of these programs were represented by effective pressures at headquarters. It is doubly difficult when the field needs are far away and insistent administrative and policy pressures are near at hand. One frequently gets the impression that subordinate officials in headquarters offices, who are usually closer to field needs, often try to present a field viewpoint, but top officials are subjected to politically more powerful pressures from other agencies and bureaus. Technical co-operation would benefit greatly from an adaptation of the adage that it is the task of the politician to hear not those who speak but those who are silent. Technical co-operation needs a kind of administration that responds not to competing agencies at headquarters but to the widely varying needs of many supplemental programs operating half a world away. The circumstances out of which this difficulty grows cannot be changed. They can be alleviated only by much broader understanding, throughout the United States government and the international organizations.

4. *The administration of United States bilateral technical co-operation has suffered from a rapid succession of reorganizations in Washington and from a high rate of turnover among administrative personnel.*

From 1943 to 1950, United States bilateral technical co-operation in Latin America had a continuous organizational form in Washington in the IIAA. In 1950, following passage of the Act for International Development, the Technical Co-operation Administration was formed, but IIAA continued as the branch of TCA responsible for administering programs in Latin America. In 1953, with the passing of political power from the Democratic to the Republican party, TCA was superseded by the Foreign Operations Administration with combined responsibility for technical co-operation, economic aid, and military aid. This change was made for what may have been good reasons within Washington, but it had two adverse effects on agricultural programs in Latin America. It gave the appearance (to Latin Americans) of making what formerly had been technical programs in agriculture into instrumental arms of United States economic and military policy. It made the operations of the single agency (FOA) so much bigger that greatly increased standardization and more complicated procedures inevitably followed. In 1955 still another reorganization occurred, this time from FOA to the new International Cooperation Administration within the Department of State.

The point here is not that these frequent reorganizations could have been avoided, although it can be argued that the one from TCA to FOA in 1953 was motivated more by the political change within the United States than by the internal needs of the program. The point is that these frequent reorganizations have hampered field operations in agriculture in Latin America more than they have helped, by complicating field administration, by concentrating more and more policy and operational decisions in Washington, and by confusing Latin Americans as to the purposes of the United States in technical co-operation and as to the intent of the United States about continuing to support these programs.

A high rate of turnover among administrative personnel in Washington has had a similarly adverse effect. There were sweeping changes in 1953 when TCA gave way to FOA, and very frequent changes have continued since. A few of the top administrators in Washington have had previous field experience in technical co-operation, but most of them in recent years have been recruited either from programs of economic aid in Europe or direct from American life without any previous foreign experience.[6]

Early in this study, many observers made the statement that the political instability of Latin-American governments was a major obstacle to the success of programs of technical co-operation. It now appears that administrative and policy instability in Washington have been at least as great a problem, and today it is probably the larger difficulty. Latin-American governments have become accustomed to technical co-operation and have developed reasonably stable policies with respect to it. The same cannot be said of the United States.

Field Administrative Needs of IIAA

On the whole, considering the difficulties arising both from the inherent problems of field programs and from inappropriate administration at headquarters, the field administration of IIAA programs in agriculture appears to have been relatively satisfactory. Practices within the discretion of chiefs of field party vary considerably from country to country. In some countries there is a tendency for the chief of field party to make decisions and to delegate responsibility for assigned tasks to one or another member of the staff without much if any prior staff consultation. In others, the pattern is more that of joint discussion and decision, with the chief acting as chairman and giving considerable weight to recommendations by members of his staff before reaching decisions. Generally speaking, both United States and local personnel of *servicios* are happier about the second practice than the first. The second procedure also would seem to have more value than the first as an educational process. Local technicians grow in administrative competence more rapidly when they have a part in the reaching of administrative decisions from the very beginning. Despite the educational superiority of the second method, in practice some of the most effective programs have evolved in countries where the chief of field party has made decisions and has delegated specific responsibility without previous staff discussion.

Within a generally satisfactory record of field administration, five weaknesses are quite widespread.

1. *There is too little cross-fertilization of ideas and experience among technicians in different countries.*

Chiefs of field party meet periodically, usually for conferences with administrative officials from Washington. They are in a position to visit nearby countries when they wish. On occasion, too, United States technicians who are not chiefs of field party are allowed to visit projects in nearby countries. This is infrequent, however, and the conviction of technicians, almost universally, is that Washington frowns on such "diversions" and that even chiefs of field party do not encourage them.

Programs would be considerably improved by frequent and regular visiting and conferring among technicians in nearby countries. Country programs are strong and weak in different aspects. Technicians in Chile, Bolivia, Peru, and Ecuador should be better acquainted with the youth club work in Paraguay. Extension technicians in Chile, Paraguay, Peru, and Ecuador should see in action the superior in-service training of extension agents in Bolivia. Extension technicians in a number of countries could benefit from visiting and studying the multipurpose program of ACAR in Brazil. These are only examples of many gains to be made by a regular policy of intercountry visits and consultations.

2. *IIAA programs could benefit from a system of regular consultations with a top-level panel of technical experts.*

This is a system which the Rockefeller Foundation uses with great effectiveness. It has an agricultural consultative committee of three top scientists in its operational fields. These three men make frequent visits, on leave from their regular positions in United

States universities, to counsel with the field staffs of foundation programs in Mexico, Colombia, and Chile. The composition of this group has remained unchanged for twelve years.

Occasional visits from IIAA headquarters in Washington affect administrative matters more than they do technical problems. IIAA needs a panel of traveling experts in such fields as extension training, research design, social and economic surveys, farm power, and irrigation design. IIAA has many competent technicians in the field, but few of them are among the very best in each subject-matter field in the United States, and most of them are serving for relatively short periods. Their work could be greatly strengthened by consultation with panel experts serving over a longer period of years. Perhaps two or three such panels should be appointed, each to serve for a region of Latin America.

3. *There is need for a well-designed and sustained program of research into extension methods under Latin-American conditions.*

Although the IIAA program includes a project of extension in almost every country in which it is active in the field of agriculture, at no place in Latin America is any controlled experimentation in extension methods to be found. Programs vary considerably, depending on the judgment of technicians as to what methods are most effective under local conditions. This is inevitable and must continue to be the procedure on many matters. However, a number of the factors in extension education are of such a nature that controlled experimentation with respect to them is feasible; and only through such experimentation can experience be made cumulative and false starts be rectified. This need ties in with two previous points. An extension-methods expert on the recommended panel of consultants could be of great value in helping set the design for such experimentation and in correlating the experimental projects in different countries. Research in extension methods is also a phase of the staff function of a reoriented headquarters administration of IIAA: to make continuous studies of the processes of agricultural development and of technical co-operation.

If each Latin-American college of agriculture had an extension service for the surrounding countryside, some, at least, of the controlled experimentation in extension methods might be located there. The opportunity for this is even greater where the college has an exchange relationship with a United States college accustomed to conducting research on extension methods.

It is easy to understand why controlled experimentation has not been undertaken before this. Technical co-operation was begun under the impression that it would be much simpler than it has proved to be. Also, there has been a pressure on public agencies to show results quickly, and this pressure pushes research into methods out of limited budgets. Third, even in countries with long-established public programs for agricultural development, research into extension methods has been very slow to develop.

4. *Regular monthly staff conferences should be made a feature of each general-purpose agricultural servicio in which IIAA co-operates.*

Such conferences should include both United States and local technicians, as is the practice in Haiti and Honduras. It is too much to expect that technicians stationed in distant parts of large countries attend every month, but all of them should attend at least quarterly. Such conferences have added value when they are held at various points in the different agricultural regions of each country rather than in capital cities.

The need for conferences does not depend on whether the chief of field party seeks group decisions on administrative matters or not. If technical co-operation is primarily educational (as it should be), such monthly staff conferences are a very important phase of technical co-operation itself. In addition, no initial "orientation" can be adequate for newly arrived United States technicians; they need in-service training quite as much as local extension agents do.

5. *IIAA needs to make better provision for the professional growth of technicians appointed for more than one term of service.*

The background of this need is more fully discussed in the next chapter, but provision for meeting it is an administrative matter. Part of the professional growth of technicians in these programs is a matter of cumulative experience. Another contribution to such growth is the combination of occasional visits to programs in nearby countries and the regular field-staff conferences already discussed. In addition to these, each technician returning on his first home leave should get some additional formal training in a United States agricultural institution. To make this possible, it is proposed that each technician who wishes reappointment, and whom IIAA wishes o reappoint, be given an option as to term of field service and ength of home leave. He might then elect to take his first home eave after two years of service and to receive six months of such eave, of which four months would be spent in an approved program of study in preparation for his second term of service. He might, however, elect to have his first term of service extended to three years, in which case he would receive twelve months of home leave, of which nine months would be spent in an approved program of study. It is true that this would increase somewhat the cost per year of field service of each technician, but the increased professional competence should more than make up for this. The difference in cost between the two options would be reduced by the saving in family home-leave travel between the three-year and two-year terms of field service.

6. *Greater attention should be paid to the relationship between the perquisites of United States and domestic employees of each servicio.*

Salary differences are understood and do not often lead to much resentment, but the differences in perquisites do. One local official of a *servicio* pointed out with great bitterness that when he and his United States counterpart go on tour: "We cannot even stay at the same hotels. He receives more than twice the *per diem* that I receive." Such differences of treatment would be serious enough if domestic employees of *servicios* were all junior men. Frequently, however, men with considerable seniority and previous experience in domestic agencies become members of *servicio* staffs. In several instances, former directors of agriculture who had been dismissed to make room for new political appointees have, because of their technical competence, been appointed to *servicio* staffs. When such a man finds that his perquisites are much below those of even young United States technicians, new to the country and not knowing the language, bitterness is very likely and quite understandable.

7. *The director of each* servicio *in which IIAA co-operates should always be a United States technician.*

From time to time there is talk about the advisability after some years of operation of having a technician of a host government as the director of a *servicio*. In other cases, the proposal is that there be joint directors, one United States technician and one technician of the host government.

Against the former proposal it may be said that a *servicio* is established in the first place as an agency of co-operation between two governments or between a government and a private organization of technical co-operation. Consequently, each party ought to be represented by one major official. As the *servicio* is normally organized, the national minister of agriculture has the final say on any project and on the over-all policy, while the director of the *servicio* is in charge of day-by-day operations. This has proved to be a good, workable arrangement. If a technician of the host government is made director, the *servicio* thereby loses the advantage of having a distinterested administrator who is not subject to local political and social pressures.

The argument used in favor of the appointment of local technicians as directors or joint directors of *servicios* holds that it is well to begin the administrative transfer of the *servicio* to the host government in preparation for IIAA withdrawal. This argument reveals a mistaken understanding of where the transfer problem lies. It is the *individual projects* that need ultimately to be transferred to another agency of the host government, not the *servicio* itself. As an interim operational device, the *servicio* exists only to administer technical co-operation in authorized fields. It need *never* be transferred as an agency. After all of its projects have someday been unloaded to other agencies, the *servicio* itself can be shunted onto a siding and cut up for scrap.

There is no reason why a project undertaken by a *servicio* should be retained by the *servicio* as long as the *servicio* lasts. As a matter of fact, the opposite case is true except in a few instances. It is right to develop local administrators who can take over projects completely, but it is not correct to assume that the administration of the *servicio* as such should pass increasingly into the hands of local technicians. Authority is well and reasonably divided as originally conceived. That division of authority should remain as long as the *servicio* exists.

Administrative Needs within University Exchanges[7]

From the standpoint of effective field operation, there are four administrative needs in connection with university-to-university exchanges in agriculture.

1. *The administrative responsibility for university exchanges should rest with the two universities involved in each case.* The relationship of the chief of field party and country director to such a program should be purely advisory.

One major reason for the exchange being an acceptable vehicle of technical co-operation in higher education in agriculture is that it occurs between two academic institutions. For the chief of field party or country director of IIAA to be given, or to assume, administrative control over the exchange itself or over the United States personnel within it is to destroy this important value of the device. So long as the arrangement is entirely between the two universities involved in each case, the administrative position of the dean of the Latin-American college is unimpaired. To bring the chief of field party or country director into the administrative procedure has the appearance of invading the autonomy that most Latin-American universities prize.

Three arguments are frequently advanced for giving the chief of field party or country director supervisory control over the operation of such an exchange. The first is that IIAA pays the bill, and these officials are responsible for all IIAA programs in the country. The answer is that by contracting with a United States university to enter into such an exchange, IIAA thereby delegates or ought to delegate responsibility for administration to that university. The second argument is that university appointees are new to a country, unacquainted with what needs to be done, and need the guidance of IIAA officials. The answer is that there can be counsel without administrative control and that, in any case, this is a temporary need when an exchange is first launched. A better way to effect the orientation of new university appointees, once the program is under way, is to overlap the terms of appointees. The third argument is that these exchanges need servicing in such procedures as getting university appointees moved to and into the country and in making adequate living arrangements for them. The answer is that such facilities can be extended to university appointees without any administrative control over the exchange as such.

2. *University exchanges would be more effective if United States technicians were appointed for a period of three years instead of two.*

Throughout this study, stress has been placed on the fact that experience in technical co-operation is an important phase of the competence of each technician. In the normal programs of IIAA, although technicians are appointed for two-year terms of service, there is ample provision for re-appointment of technicians who do well and who wish to continue. In the case of university exchanges, re-appointment of a technician is unlikely, since he comes from a regular university position in the United States to which he is expected to return. Yet the need for experience in the process of technical co-operation remains. A new appointee must spend most of the first year learning. He develops increasing confidence and competence in the second year. A third year can be the most fruitful and would greatly strengthen the university device as a whole.[8]

3. *The terms of individual United States technicians in a university exchange should be staggered.*

Under a system of overlapping terms, new appointees could be aided by others who had been in the assignment longer. Several times in Latin America, a whole group of technicians sent at about the same time, each person for a two-year term, has been succeeded by new technicians also arriving as a group, again for two-year terms. Such a replacement system greatly lengthens the newcomers' period of initiation and partly wastes the experience of the outgoing technicians. Staggering of terms seems such an obviously advantageous practice that it is difficult to understand why it has not been universally adopted.

4. *Every United States technician in a university exchange needs to know the language of the host country.*

Knowledge of Spanish or Portuguese is important for all technical co-operation personnel in Latin America but especially for technicians in university exchanges. The only cases in which it is even partially satisfactory to forego learning the language occur when the United States technician is certain before he arrives that the Latin-American professor who will be his counterpart speaks English fluently. Even in such cases, not knowing the language is a severe handicap, for few students in Latin-American colleges know English. Spanish is not a difficult language to learn, and North Americans who learn it are rewarded in better personal relations during their term of service.

The importance of learning the host country's language affords an incidental argument for three-year terms instead of two-year terms. If the technician is to serve for three years, he thinks it more worthwhile to learn the language, even after reaching Latin America, than he would if he were staying only two years.

Note on the Organization of Project 39

The most important feature in the administration of Project 39 is its regional organization with offices in Havana, Lima, and Montevideo. Each of these offices is in charge of a zone director responsible to the project director in San José, Costa Rica, but with wide latitude in the determination of the program within his zone. This is as it should be, for the problems of the zones differ greatly, and the chief strength of Project 39 is its ability to service the various needs of the countries in each zone. Moreover, by locating its technicians in the three zone headquarters, Project 39 can quickly and thriftily send advisers to countries wishing special help, and its technicians are able to specialize in the particular problems of each zone. It would be a great mistake if any change were made in the direction of strengthening the central headquarters at San José at the expense of the zones. The greatest structural weakness of the Inter-American Institute of Agricultural Sciences, from the standpoint of serving all of Latin America, is its location in one spot in Costa Rica. When an organization has a headquarters with resident programs of instruction, it is difficult for its personnel to visit member countries frequently. The same difficulty would beset Project 39 if it were centralized. The present organization is sound, and Project 39 has an increasingly large role to play in the agricultural development of Latin America. When the present project terminates, it should be renewed for at least three more years, with its present organization into three zones.

Co-ordination of Public Programs

It has been stressed throughout this report that each program of technical co-operation should be integrated with domestic agencies rather than with other agencies of technical co-operation or even with other programs of technical co-operation (such as health or education) under the same agency. At the present experimental stage of technical co-operation, it is advantageous to have several different public agencies, each seeking to discover more effective techniques. It would be a mistake to try to integrate them, though it is right to encourage consultation so that duplication of similar efforts can be avoided.

There is one point at which greater co-ordination of the programs of the different agencies should be attempted, namely, the granting of fellowships for study abroad. At the present time, fellowships are granted by IIAA, OAS, FAO, and foundations. Their policies vary; each should at least be fully aware of what the others are doing.

18 PERSONNEL

The most frequent refrain in discussions of technical co-operation is this: "Success boils down to quality of personnel." There are two valid reasons for the predominancy of that point of view.

In the first place, public programs of technical co-operation being young and experimental, the principles that underlie successful programs are still being formulated. Consequently, the men and women who have been relatively more successful in them are those who "have good judgment" about what to do and how to do it. This state of affairs, however, need not continue indefinitely. As past and present programs are analyzed, principles begin to emerge, and we begin to have a body of knowledge that can be studied, taught, and learned. If, in addition, a career service can be created in the field of technical co-operation with men and women trained for it, much of what has been "personal judgment" in the past can be professional competence in the future.

Second, technical co-operation is an activity by and for human beings. Its technical and economic aspects are aspects of a relationship among people. To hear some people discuss it, one would infer that technical co-operation is an autonomous exercise in which people are an unfortunate obstacle. On the contrary, technical co-operation is essentially a human activity. It arises because of certain human aspirations; it depends for its validity on the nature of people; both its means of success and its obstacles lie in human characteristics.

Of course, this "humanness" of technical co-operation is not unique to it; the same could be said of all human activities. Domestic activities have the same human characteristics to build on and to deal with, but these operate within a single, generally accepted set of customs, ideals, and social values. In technical co-operation, the problem is made more complex because the people involved come from different cultural backgrounds. This increases their opportuni-

ties and intensifies their problems. It carries them outside old pat
terns into a realm in which personal discretion, sensitivity, and
judgment are unusually important precisely because the rules are
few or, more serious, conflicting.

Thus, both because the programs are new and experimental and
because the human relations involved are varied and intercultural
the "personal factor" is unusually important in technical co-operation. It therefore deserves special consideration and analysis.

Background of Present Personnel

Although many of the characteristics of persons that affect their
efficiency as technicians in programs of technical co-operation are
personality traits difficult to analyze and impossible to express quantitatively, several facts are rather easily discovered and stated.
Among the latter, six are frequently mentioned in discussions of
personnel policy and recruitment: (1) age at the time of appointment; (2) previous academic training; (3) number of different
countries in which the person has worked; (4) years of experience
in the country of present assignment; (5) years of experience in
technical co-operation; (6) nature of experience prior to first appointment in technical co-operation.

A sample survey with respect to these six facts was conducted
among persons employed in Latin America in 1955 by IIAA, FAO,
and OAS. In the case of IIAA, the sample consisted of 46 technicians (from a total of about 250 in Latin America) serving in Chile,
Costa Rica, El Salvador, Honduras, and Paraguay. For FAO, the
sample consisted of 15 technicians serving in Honduras, Paraguay,
and Uruguay (from a total of about 55 for all of Latin America).
In the case of OAS, the sample included all technicians in Project
39. The results of this survey follow.

AGE AT FIRST APPOINTMENT.—Chart XVI shows that there is a
marked difference among the three public agencies in the age of
technicians at the time of their first appointment. FAO has the most
even distribution of men of all ages. OAS is a young men's organization at the present time. IIAA appoints fewer men under the age
of thirty than either of the international agencies. The greatest
number of new appointments by IIAA is in the age groups between
thirty and forty; there are relatively fewer appointments in the

forty-to-fifty range, with a marked rise again at ages of fifty and above.

The significance of these differences is not evaluated by this study, but the following comments may be made. Project 39 is in a good position to use young men effectively because it operates in three zone units, in each of which an experienced zone director can co-ordinate and direct the activities of the technicians under him. It would seem that IIAA should also be able to use young men in

CHART XVI

AGE OF TECHNICIANS AT TIME OF FIRST APPOINTMENT*

FOR IIAA, FAO, AND OAS

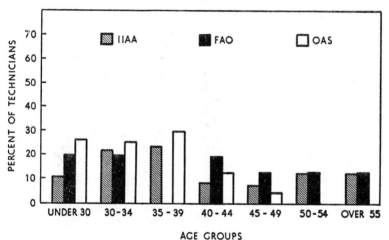

* Nature of sample (technicians in service, June, 1955): IIAA—technicians in Paraguay, El Salvador, Chile, Honduras, and Costa Rica (46 men); FAO—technicians in Uruguay, Honduras, and Paraguay (15 men); OAS—all technicians in Project No. 39 (23 men).

its *servicios*. The method of operation of FAO (through individual adviser-technicians) would appear to require older men in most instances. However, the fact that FAO has recruited a number of younger men means that it has the opportunity, if it can retain their services, of building up a corps of men experienced in the process of technical co-operation, each with experience in several different countries. OAS, also, if Project 39 is renewed for another five years, is in a strong position to build up a corps of technicians experienced in the specific problems of each region of Latin America.

The age distribution of IIAA appointees is not explained by this study, but the following hypotheses may be advanced:

a) IIAA is known to have placed greater emphasis on experience prior to appointment than on amount of formal training related to agriculture.[1] This tends to rule out most men under the age of thirty.

b) Generally speaking, men in their thirties are more ready to accept foreign assignment than men in their forties, for family reasons. It is easier to make satisfactory school and social arrangements in Latin America for children below the age of fourteen than it is for older children. Moreover, wives of technicians are usually more

CHART XVII

PREVIOUS ACADEMIC TRAINING OF TECHNICIANS[*]
FOR IIAA, FAO, AND OAS

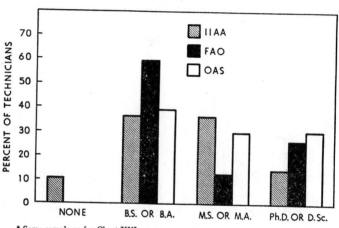

* Same sample as for Chart XVI.

ready to consider living abroad if they and their children are young than they are after they have reached the age of thirty-five to forty and their children are entering adolescence.[2]

c) Both family considerations and the emphasis of IIAA on previous experience in agricultural programs may explain the relatively high percentage of appointments of men above the age of fifty.

PREVIOUS ACADEMIC TRAINING.—Chart XVII depicts the differences in the formal academic training of the technicians of IIAA, FAO, and OAS. From this chart it is clear that OAS has put the greatest emphasis on previous academic training. FAO ranks second on the basis of those with Doctor's degrees, but if those with Master's and

Doctor's degrees are grouped together, IIAA ranks second. Taking those with Master's and Doctor's degrees together, OAS has 61 per cent of its technicians in this category, IIAA has 52 per cent, and FAO has 40 per cent.

IIAA is the only public agency that appoints some technicians without a Bachelor's degree. In some of its *servicio* projects IIAA needs technicians for whom non-academic qualifications are thought sufficient. This is particularly true of such technicians as well-drillers and machinery maintenance personnel.

There is considerable debate, particularly in IIAA, about the value of advanced academic training. There are several field administrators who argue against the appointment of men with advanced degrees. When pressed for examples, they point to technicians who seem to have few qualifications other than academic degrees. In no case does an administrator persist in maintaining that a particular man with an advanced degree would have been more competent if he had not had the advanced training. On the other hand, there are many observers who contend that IIAA is weak because of having few highly trained men. They argue that the tendency of IIAA to appoint "practical men" gives it a staff lacking in ability to analyze problems thoroughly and results in its undertaking many ill-conceived projects that end in failure.

The conclusion to which this debate points is that other qualifications, personal and professional, are very important in the choice of personnel for technical co-operation assignments. Advanced academic training alone is seldom if ever sufficient. At the same time, there is increasing need for continuous analytical study within technical co-operation and of the process of technical co-operation itself. To meet this, more personnel with advanced academic training—in addition to the other qualifications of a successful technician—are required.

FOREIGN EXPERIENCE.—Chart XVIII compares the records of IIAA and FAO with respect to the number of countries in which individual technicians have served. (OAS technicians are appointed to regional international centers rather than countries.) Roughly two-thirds of the technicians of each organization have worked in only one country. IIAA technicians with experience in more than one country have almost all served in only two countries. Only 2 per cent of the IIAA technicians in the sample have served in three different countries.[3] Of the FAO technicians, 13 per cent have served in two countries, 13 per cent have served in three countries, and 7 per cent have served in four.

It should not be inferred from the inclusion of this analysis that experience in a large number of countries is always an advantage. Length of experience in a single country is often a more valuable qualification. However, in the case of FAO technicians, where one-year appointments are the general rule, there does appear to be an

CHART XVIII

NUMBER OF COUNTRIES IN WHICH EACH TECHNICIAN HAS SERVED*
FOR IIAA, FAO, AND OAS

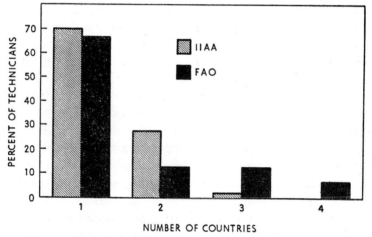

* Same sample as for Chart XVI.

advantage in a technician's having had experience in a number of different countries.

It should be remembered that the FAO program of technical co-operation had been in operation only four years at the time this study was made and that the number of FAO technicians in Latin America has been rising. It may be that in coming years the proportion of FAO technicians with experience in more than one country will rise. IIAA has been in operation longer; thus there is less reason to anticipate a change in the proportion of IIAA technicians with experience in more than one country unless there is a change of policy with respect to this.

One attitude has been encountered so frequently among IIAA personnel that it should be reported. This point of view argues that there is an optimum length of service for an individual technician in a single country, usually estimated at four to five years. The argument advanced in support of this is that a man does not reach full effectiveness until the third year, but that after the fifth year his enthusiasm is fairly well spent, whereupon transfer to another

CHART XIX

NUMBER OF YEARS IN PRESENT COUNTRY* (INDIVIDUAL TECHNICIANS)

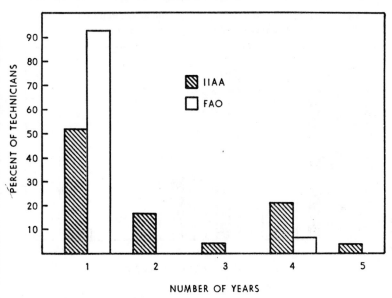

NUMBER OF YEARS

* Same sample as for Chart XVI.

country, with a different set of problems, has the effect of stimulating him to new interest and fresh enthusiasm.

YEARS IN PRESENT COUNTRY.—Chart XIX shows the number of years that individual technicians of FAO and IIAA have been in the country in which they were working at the time of this study. As would be expected from the nature of FAO operation, 93 per cent of its technicians had been in their present countries one year or less. The single exception (in this sample) had been in the same post for four years.

By contrast, 48 per cent of IIAA technicians had been in the same country two years or longer, and 26 per cent of them had been in the same country four or five years. This contrast underscores the fact that, within present policies, FAO depends on one-year appointments, whereas IIAA relies largely on the device of the *servicio*, in which longer periods of service by individual technicians are utilized in staffing a succession of specific projects. It also illustrates the fact that, although appointments are for two-year periods, a substantial number of IIAA technicians have been reappointed.

YEARS IN TECHNICAL CO-OPERATION.—Against the background of

CHART XX

YEARS OF SERVICE OF TECHNICIANS WITH PUBLIC AGENCIES OF TECHNICAL CO-OPERATION,* IIAA, FAO, AND OAS

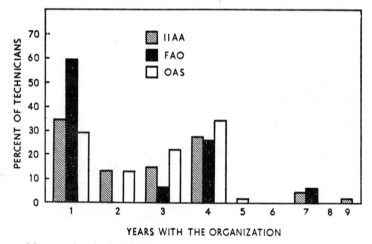

YEARS WITH THE ORGANIZATION

* Same sample as for Chart XVI.

one-year and two-year appointments and reappointments, what are the results on personnel continuity in practice? Have the agencies begun to build a core of personnel with several years of experience in technical co-operation?

Based on the same sample as the four preceding charts, Chart XX presents a summary of technicians' years of service in the agencies. FAO has a much higher percentage of technicians who have been with the organization one year or less (60 per cent, compared to 35 per cent for IIAA and 30 per cent for OAS). For longer periods of continuous service, however, the difference between agencies decreases. Some 57 per cent of OAS technicians have served three years or longer, compared to 52 per cent of IIAA technicians and 40 per cent of those of FAO. For personnel who have served four years or longer, the differences are still smaller. Some 37 per cent of IIAA personnel fall in this category, compared to 35 per cent for OAS, and 34 per cent in the case of FAO.

Again, it must be remembered that the technical co-operation programs of FAO and OAS are younger than those of IIAA. OAS appears to hold the greatest promise of staff stability. FAO, if it is to continue to rely heavily on the device of relatively short-term adviser-technicians, needs a larger staff of men with considerable experience in technical co-operation. IIAA, using the *servicio*, can utilize a higher percentage of technicians with limited foreign experience, but has, in fact, despite its two-year term of appointment, done reasonably well in building up a staff of experienced men.[4]

PREVIOUS HOME EXPERIENCE.—From the analysis of these technicians' experience prior to entering technical co-operation, the more striking disclosures are the following:

a) There is a marked contrast between the previous experience in agricultural research of the technicians of OAS and those of the other two agencies. Some 36 per cent of OAS technicians have had previous research experience, compared with 15 per cent in the case of IIAA and 13 per cent for FAO.

b) OAS leads also in the percentage of its technicians who have had college teaching experience. Some 41 per cent of OAS technicians have taught in agricultural colleges, whereas 27 per cent of FAO technicians have had such experience but only 17 per cent of those serving under IIAA. If the IIAA technicians with experience in high-school vocational agricultural teaching experience are added to these (and the duplications excluded) the total comes to 27 per cent, the same as for FAO.

c) OAS has the highest percentage of technicians with previous experience in agricultural extension (23 per cent). Only 7 per cent of IIAA technicians have been county agricultural agents, another 7 per cent have been extension subject-matter specialists, and 9 per cent have had experience in the Farm Home Administration (or its predecessor, the Farm Security Administration). If these are consolidated and the duplications eliminated, a total of 17 per cent of IIAA technicians have had experience in one or another of these fields. No FAO technician in this sample had had extension experience.

d) The large majority of the technicians of all public agencies of technical co-operation come from previous public employment; only a few are drawn direct from commercial employment. This would be anticipated and is probably desirable. Men who have not had experience in public programs in their homelands are, other things being equal, probably less well equipped to participate in such programs abroad. IIAA has at times almost made a fetish of "being practical," and it has drawn more technicians from the ranks of farm managers and others previously in private employ. Nevertheless, field observation discloses that where the programs of IIAA have been most successful, the men most responsible for them had considerable previous experience in public agricultural agencies. There are a number of instances where men without previous public experience have made major mistakes.

These comments and Tables 35, 36, and 37 are presented here, not because there are objective criteria as to what type of men the agencies ought to have selected, but only as a record of what has happened. The writer would anticipate little criticism of the records of FAO and OAS on this score. FAO tries to find men to meet specific country requests, and since these requests vary widely, the background of FAO technicians would be expected to vary correspondingly. OAS, with its single, concentrated program in the field of short-course training in specific subjects related chiefly to extension services also has a staff with the type of background training that would be expected.

In the case of IIAA, criticism is more likely. Those who have argued that IIAA has seriously underestimated the need for research will maintain that this record supports their contention. In view of the reputation of IIAA for trying to bring about spectacular results quickly, and in view of frequent assertions that the county agent is the model of what the United States can contribute through bilateral technical co-operation, it is surprising that so few IIAA technicians had field extension experience prior to appointment. Light was thrown on this by the comment of a high (headquarters) IIAA official, "We cannot use men from the old-style U.S. Extension Service; they are too inflexible in their ways." This same official im-

TABLE 35

PREVIOUS EXPERIENCE OF IIAA TECHNICIANS*

Type	Number of Technicians	Percentage of Total†
Soil Conservation Service................	9	20
College instructors or professors..........	8	17
Agricultural research....................	7	15
Vocational agricultural teaching (high school)............................	5	11
Farm manager (including self-employed)..	5	11
Farm Home Administration.............	4	9
Private forestry.......................	4	9
No previous employment................	4	9
Extension specialist....................	3	7
County extension agent.................	3	7
Geodetic Survey.......................	1	2
United Nations Relief and Reconstruction Administration......................	1	2
Well-driller...........................	1	2
Vocational home economics teaching (high school)............................	1	2
Government engineer, general...........	1	2
Agricultural Adjustment Administration..	1	2
Private agency of technical co-operation...	1	2
European Economic Administration......	1	2
Private fruit company..................	1	2
Military government...................	1	2
Bureau of Indian Affairs................	1	2
State plant quarantine authority.........	1	2

* Same sample as for the charts in this chapter and for Tables 36 and 37.
† The total number of technicians in this sample is 46; several technicians had previous experience in more than one field.

TABLE 36

PREVIOUS EXPERIENCE OF FAO TECHNICIANS

Type	Number of Technicians	Percentage of Total*
College instructor or professor...........	4	27
Government agricultural administration...	2	13
Government forestry service.............	2	13
Commercial forestry....................	2	13
United Nations Relief and Reconstruction Administration......................	2	13
Agricultural research...................	2	13
Medical practice (hospital)..............	1	7
Government statistician.................	1	7
Farm Home Administration..............	1	7
Veterinarian..........................	1	7
Farm manager.........................	1	7

* The total number of technicians in this sample is 15. Information regarding previous employment was not given for one technician. Several technicians had experience in more than one field.

plied that men with experience in the "action agencies"—Soil Conservation Service, Farm Home Administration, Agricultural Adjustment Administration, etc.—have shown greater competence in the field of technical co-operation. While no quantitative data can be advanced to support the statement, field observation in this study leads to the conclusion that there is some justification for the official's view. With few exceptions, most of the outstanding men in IIAA have either had previous experience in several different United States agencies or had varied experience in foreign countries.

TABLE 37

PREVIOUS EXPERIENCE OF OAS TECHNICIANS

Type	Number of Technicians	Percentage of Total*
College instructor or professor............	9	41
Agricultural research....................	8	36
Agricultural extension...................	5	23
Government agricultural administration...	4	18
Farm manager.........................	1	5
Government forestry service.............	1	5
Machinery maintenance.................	1	5
Agricultural engineer (design)...........	1	5
Meteorologist.........................	1	5
Commercial employment................	1	5

* The total number of technicians in Project 39 (excluding an administrative assistant) is 22. Duplications (inidvidual technicians with more than one type of experience) account for the sum of percentages equaling more than 100.

At the same time, another conclusion from field observation is that IIAA is weak in extension organization and techniques. In only two of the countries visited—Paraguay and Bolivia[5]—is adequate competence in this field obvious. Some of IIAA's other extension projects have made substantial contributions, but this has occurred despite quite glaring weaknesses in extension practice or because of particularly favorable external circumstances such as the availability of well-trained local technicians or the progressive outlook of a substantial number of farmers.

Most men whose sole experience has been in the Extension Service in the United States have one specific attitude to overcome in working in technical co-operation in Latin America—the belief that the process of extension education must always be separately organized, having nothing to do with credit, or with the distribution of agricultural requisites, or with such activities as machinery pools.

It is necessary to distinguish between the *process* of extension education and its *organization*. There are circumstances under which it should be separately organized but others where it should not be.[6] What has to be achieved is a flexible attitude and a habit of probing to find the most effective organizational relationships under each given set of circumstances.[7] Further, it is important that this flexibility be achieved by men with substantial previous extension experience, because the programs of IIAA badly need more men who have expert competence and experience in this field.

STABILITY IN PRIOR WORK.—From time to time, it is said that the agencies of technical co-operation have a high percentage of personnel who are of low competence at home or who are misfits running away from unsatisfactory situations. Such a statement obviously combines several factors, each difficult to measure.

As one check on this, data were collected about the number of jobs each technician in the sample had held previous to his appointment in technical co-operation. This data is not such that it can be quantitatively presented here, partly because of uncertainty about its completeness and partly because the fact that a man has changed jobs frequently does not necessarily denote instability. In some cases, frequent changes in jobs for a young man reflect outstanding competence. What can be reported here is that the data do not support the charge of a high proportion of men with unstable professional backgrounds. They do the opposite. They demonstrate the presence in these programs of a large proportion of men who previously have had stable and continuous careers. There are, however, a number of individual technicians who are of limited competence in technical co-operation. There are also a limited number who are emotionally unstable or notably immature. IIAA personnel do not uniformly represent the best that the United States possesses (as they should), but they are probably a representative cross-section of United States talent in the field of agriculture.

In several instances a man has done an outstanding job in technical co-operation far above what those who knew him previously in the United States expected. This is eloquent evidence that the task of technical co-operation is distinctive, that it is not simply a foreign extension of a previous career but something quite different, calling for special talents and special combinations of abilities.

Elements of Professional Skill

When one turns to a final consideration of what talents appear to be necessary to high-quality personnel performance in technical co-operation, previous investigations into the characteristics making for success in similar fields are warnings that no blueprint would be valid. Studies of extension agents in the United States, for example, have shown personal attitudes, individual temperament, and "a way with people" to be more important in many instances than specific skills or breadth of formal knowledge. It is likely that the same is true to some extent in technical co-operation. There is, however, one enormous difference. The United States extension agent is in his home culture. His "way with people" which comes so naturally is, to a great extent, a fine adjustment to the cultural pattern within which he has lived from birth. Personnel in technical co-operation, however, work in a foreign culture.

Sensitivity to people's moods and prejudices and an easy naturalness with people are important ingredients in success in technical co-operation. They bear full fruit, however, only when they operate on top of all the systematic knowledge one can gain about people, about how changes occur in ways of living, and about the specific role of technical co-operation. The bedside manner of a physician and the confidence he inspires in the patient as a person are undoubtedly important factors in rapid recovery, but they are no substitute for a profound knowledge of physiology and of the pharmacopoeia. Technical co-operation has suffered from two false assumptions: the first is that a post in technical co-operation is not different in kind but only in geographical location from one in the same technical field at home; the second is that in whatever adjustments need to be made to a foreign culture, a good bedside manner is sufficient.

Some would argue that any discussion of professional skill in technical co-operation must recognize the very different roles that different technicians are called upon to play. They would point out the wide disparity between the responsibility of an individual adviser-technician on problems of agricultural school curricula and that of a machinery-maintenance technician in a *servicio*. Or they might cite the considerable difference in function between the administrative and diplomatic role of a chief of field party, on the one hand, and the technical task of an irrigation engineer, on the other. Despite these differences, there are two reasons why a discussion of the elements of professional skill can profitably treat all technicians together:

a) Whether a particular technician is an administrator, a field man, or an adviser-technician, he represents the total complex of technical co-operation to many of the people with whom he comes in contact. Few farmers or government officials come into intimate contact with a whole staff. Most of them deal chiefly with one or two men. Consequently, whatever the job description for a particular technician, he gets informally drawn into many aspects of professional and personal life far removed from the subject matter of his official assignment. No matter how narrow his special task, the mere fact of his employment in technical co-operation necessitates his understanding the total process of which he is a part.

b) In view of the distinctive nature of the task of technical co-operation, it ought to be rare for an administrator not to have had considerable previous experience as a technician in technical co-operation. The writer knows of no exception in Latin America to the generalization that the better chiefs of field party all had other field experience before being appointed to an administrative post. This, plus the fact that individual technicians need to understand the special problems of their administrators in technical co-operation, justifies a single discussion of the elements of professional skill. The differences between job requirements with respect to these elements of professional skill are differences of degree and of opportunities for application. They are not differences of kind.

1. *Professional skill in technical co-operation requires technical competence in at least one field related to agricultural development.*

It is this qualification with which job descriptions are almost exclusively concerned. A man must be a plant pathologist, or an irrigation engineer, or a rural sociologist, etc., in order to qualify. Standing alone, technical competence is completely inadequate. Nevertheless, it is indispensable.

Increasingly, specialization entails advanced, expert skill, not just normal competence. There are three reasons for this. One has been stated earlier: the fact that an agriculture is "underdeveloped" does not mean that its problems are simple. Second, many technicians are much more on their own in technical co-operation than they were at home; although a soil conservation man, for example, may be in a large *servicio,* there usually is not another technician in his own specialized field. Finally, many Latin-American countries increasingly have their own technicians who are highly trained in these fields. Even where the technician-from-abroad has greater practical experience and inventive ingenuity, there is a tendency to judge him by his breadth of theoretical knowledge and by his "scientific" approach. He needs to be able to hold his own in professional consultations with well-trained Latin-American colleagues.

2. *Professional skill in technical co-operation requires a thorough understanding of the requirements for agricultural development.*

This is one of the points at which intuitive good judgment has had to be depended upon thus far. Although a number of technicians have dealt with this problem long enough to begin to formulate it (chaps. xii and xiii of this study are based, to a considerable degree, on their insights), there has been no systematic attempt to facilitate the gaining of this understanding by the whole body of technicians, except in a few, isolated, on-the-field, in-service conferences. As a result, too many technicians overrate the importance of their own narrow specialty, or become discouraged when their efforts bear little fruit because other requirements for agricultural development are being neglected, or propose new projects that are ill-timed in view of the relative priorities of attention that different aspects of agricultural development should receive. The broad view, as well as a restricted specialty, is an essential element of professional skill in technical co-operation.

3. *A knowledge of the elements of teaching and learning is a third important requirement.*

In a sense, all of technical co-operation is education. Were all technicians experienced teachers, whether in the classroom or in an extension service, it could be assumed, rightly or wrongly, that they had some knowledge of education. But they are not. A review of the tables on pages 395–96 will indicate how many technicians have been drawn and should be drawn from other professional backgrounds. Technical co-operation involves skills of teaching that they may not previously have been called upon to exercise, and it involves a learning process that they need to understand, whether this be by a farmer, or by professional colleagues, or by politicians who determine appropriations for public programs, or by members of the general public who need a new attitude toward agricultural development.

4. *Professional skill in technical co-operation requires at least a rudimentary understanding of cultural differences and of the relationships between technology and other phases of a people's way of living.*

There are two points at which such understanding is important in technical co-operation. One is that cultural factors often appear as obstacles to specific agricultural changes. The other is that agricultural development both constitutes and demands substantial cultural changes.

Every technician in programs of agricultural development has been impressed by the close connection between certain professional problems and local attitudes, customs, and superstitions. Those technicians who have some knowledge of cultural differences and of the interwoven patterns of a people's way of life are more likely to develop expert competence in their jobs. Without cultural awareness, the technician is unlikely to take an objective view of customs strange to him.

Custom, tradition, taboos, and standards of good taste characterize all cultures. Generally speaking, these are more rigid in the less developed countries. (This is almost a tautology: less developed economies change less, and their values tend to cluster around what is old and tried.) Therefore, in countries where programs of technical co-operation are carried on, the technician needs to be able to comprehend the whole way of life into which he comes.[8]

In this connection, one common adage that must be challenged is the statement, "It is the task of technical co-operation to give technical help, but this must be done without disturbing the local culture." Uncritical acceptance of this as a dogma would immobilize technical co-operation. *Every* technological change is a cultural change. Some have such a slight effect on values that they seem practically neutral, but many such "neutral" changes have a substantial cumulative effect. One tractor in a region where there has been none causes very slight cultural repercussions, whereas a complete shift to mechanized power drastically changes the demand for farm labor, the nature of agricultural implements, the willingness of farm boys to remain on the farm, and many other features of a people's way of living. Since the introduction of the first tractor (through a public program) usually is a trial looking toward a general shift, the whole ultimate shift in values is implicit in the first trial. Other changes of considerable importance to agricultural development are themselves changes of values, as, for example, the change from looking on landownership primarily as a matter of prestige to viewing it as a commercial investment.

In general, technical co-operation must concern itself chiefly with changes that, in the first instance, are reasonably neutral in their cultural effects, leaving to wholly domestic programs the task of tackling problems of agricultural development in which local values are immediately challenged. Instead of the false assumption that cultural values are not involved in technological change, the tenable position is that technical co-operation normally must be content to work with changes the cultural impact of which is gradual. If this principle is to be followed, however, the technician needs a considerable knowledge of the local culture to distinguish between projects that are suitable for technical co-operation and those that are not. Moreover, the way in which projects of technical co-operation are administered and the private lives of foreign technicians are as likely as technical matters to involve cultural clashes.

5. *Proficiency in the use of the local language is an essential tool of professional skill in technical co-operation.*

This has been mentioned before, but it cannot be stated too strongly. Fortunately, Spanish is the official language in all but two Latin-American countries.[9] It is not a difficult language to learn. Many technicians learn to use it well, but the general emphasis on language proficiency is inadequate. To a great many Latin Americans, failure of a foreigner to take the trouble to learn the local language is an indication that he is not really interested in the country, and that he does not see enough value in it to make him want to be a part of it. Conversely, the very fact of a foreigner's using the local language, even imperfectly, means to Latin Americans that he recognizes the right of each people to its own ways, and wishes to participate in the life of the country.

To some readers, this section on the requirements of professional skill in technical co-operation may seem either academic or utopian. Many will argue that all a man or woman needs is technical knowledge or experience coupled with adaptability and good common sense. Surely it is not the intention here to imply that a person must be a full-fledged anthropologist, educator, psychologist, and saint in order to do a creditable job in technical co-operation. At the same time, technical co-operation, because of its bicultural or multicultural nature, has to operate largely without benefit of those grooves of custom and tradition that so largely guide a technician within his native land.

To gain a reasonable understanding of these novel elements with which a technician is called upon to cope is not a Herculean task. For anyone who has the adaptability, common sense, and concern for people that must in any case be part of his preparation for an assignment, it is a pleasure. From the standpoint of agencies of technical co-operation, since these requirements are essential to fruitful service on the part of technicians, it is short-sighted not to make it possible for technicians to achieve them. The only real obstacles in the way of achieving a reasonable degree of competence in these phases of professional skill are lack of sufficient realization of their importance and failure of headquarters agencies and field administrators to make adequate provision, both of time and of opportunities, for acquiring it.

Morale Factors

Along with professional skill, the performance of technical co-operation personnel is conditioned by two important morale factors. One is the attitude of the technician's wife toward her husband's career and the adequacy of provisions for their family life. The other is the stability or instability of the home-base backing for technical co-operation.

Except in the case of relatively short appointments under FAO, it is taken for granted that normally a technician's family will accompany him. This means that service under an agency of technical co-operation entails family living in a foreign environment. Too often this is translated to mean "living under conditions of hardship." Whether that is a fair translation depends chiefly on the attitude of the husband and wife. Certainly life abroad is different, but to people with curiosity, sensitivity, and an interest in people it can be a considerable enrichment of life. For children, also, while educational opportunities are different, a period of living abroad is in itself a valuable education that they could never receive growing up in only one country.

A few places in which technicians are asked to live, of course, have many fewer physical amenities and fewer opportunities for contact with other persons of similar interests. Under such circumstances, whether or not a family is happy will depend largely on such factors as the self-sufficiency of the family, the degree to which it feels that technical co-operation is an activity worthy of personal sacrifice, and its desire to share, to the extent possible, in the life of the people among whom it lives.

In general, interest of the wife in learning the local language and pursuing other activities independently are important factors in family contentment. Wives have a greater task of adjustment than their husbands, since they do not have professional duties to absorb their time and are, therefore, thrown more on their own resources.

In view of the major importance of family welfare, it is probable that greater attention should be paid to family situations in personnel recruitment. In chapter vii the procedure of the Rockefeller Foundation at this point was mentioned.[10] That procedure is not feasible, in its entirety, for public programs of technical co-operation, but more attention should be paid to giving families an advance notion of the opportunities and problems of careers abroad.

The second major morale factor is the stability or instability of home-base backing for technical co-operation. As pointed out in chapter xvii, technical co-operation has always had to live in an atmosphere of uncertainty, and this uncertainty seems to have increased in recent years. To be effective, technical co-operation must deal with long-term processes and must itself, in many instances, continue in the same projects for a number of years. Those interested in the political repercussions of technical co-operation have recognized, as well, that a country cannot afford to start an activity which it irresponsibly drops after hopes have been raised but before substantial results have been achieved.

Despite these insights, technical co-operation still has to operate without assurance of stability either of continuation or of scale of operations. It is not conducive to good morale in the field for technicians to feel that what they have begun may not be completed or to feel that, having tried to achieve new skills to meet professional responsibilities in technical co-operation, there is no assurance of their being able to continue in it beyond a current one-year or two-year term.

This is not a matter that can be rectified by any improvement in recruitment or in training. It can be solved only by a firm acceptance of responsibility in technical co-operation by the people of the United States, at an assured level of participation, over a longer period of years, and with some device for cushioning the disruptive effect of dependence on annual appropriations.

PART V

OVER-ALL ASSESSMENT

19 OVER-ALL ASSESSMENT OF PUBLIC PROGRAMS

The limited possibility of assessing the results of technical co-operation in quantitative terms does not eliminate the necessity for making decisions about whether, and at what level, technical co-operation should be continued. Public decisions are being and must be made on these matters. The factors that should be taken into account in these decisions are many and complicated; they cannot be simplified. Yet the public decisions finally arrived at, whether for one year or for many, must be based on a summation of judgments with respect to these many factors.

The propositions stated in this concluding chapter are the writer's own over-all assessments that he believes should guide such decisions with respect to both bilateral and multilateral governmental programs.[1] Because the evidence presented by this study is both quantitative and qualitative, it can be combined only in general propositions.

1. *In general, programs of technical co-operation in agriculture in Latin America have justified the investment in them, and they should be continued.*

If it were possible, but it is not, to measure the actual increment in agricultural production brought about in Latin America because of programs of technical co-operation, it seems probable that the monetary value of that increment in production would be found as great as the monetary resources that have been invested in technical co-operation. But the increment in agricultural production to date is only a minor portion of the achievement already realized by these programs. To rely on that measure alone would ignore the future value of the many new ministries of agriculture, extension services, research institutions, irrigation installations, and commercial channels for agricultural requisites that have come into being, stimulated by, even created by, the process of technical co-operation. In addition, the careers of most of the Latin-American technicians who have received training through technical co-operation are still ahead of them. They are young men. The investment in them can be expected to bear fruit only in the future. If technical co-operation were confined only to such training, much of it might be presumed to be lost. But when technical co-operation also participates, as it does, in helping create productive institutions in which the trained men may work, it is reasonable to presume that most of the training will pay off, in one way or another. Over and above these achievements is the potential future production in the regions newly opened up to agricultural production, partly through programs of technical co-operation, particularly in Peru and Bolivia.

Without question, many projects have failed, and numerous incidents within projects can fairly be judged, in retrospect, wasteful. But mistakes must be expected in such new types of programs, and most of the few serious wasteful moves resulted from circumstances that the understanding of agricultural development and technical co-operation now available can prevent from recurring.

Programs of technical co-operation in agriculture in Latin America should prove to be more productive per unit of expenditure in the future than in the past, both because experience teaches and because development is cumulative. A unit of technical co-operation appropriately applied in a rapidly developing country is more immediately productive than one appropriately applied in a less rapidly developing economy. In most, but not all, of the countries of Latin America, the stage has been set for more effective technical co-operation in the future, and the need for it is still great. This need is the greatest in those countries that so far have shown the least response.

It is the writer's judgment that United States bilateral technical assistance in agriculture should be continued in Latin America at the present level, or with an increase in appropriations of up to 10 per cent per year, over at least the next ten years.

2. There has been a marked increase in the efficiency of programs of technical co-operation over the years.

Those conducting the programs have learned from their mistakes and have extended the operation of methods that have proved to be sound. If what has been said about the uniqueness, difficulties, and pitfalls of the process of technical co-operation is sound, then one would expect a rather extended period of trial and error to be inevitable. One of the hopeful facts about technical co-operation is that programs have evolved as experience has been gained. The experience of Ecuador is eloquent proof that an initial, even prolonged, period of stumbling in technical co-operation can be succeeded by a productive period drawing on experience gained in other countries.

This hopeful history does not mean that the era for imagination and innovation has passed. One of the dangers now faced by technical co-operation is that it might become more rigid and standardized, along lines seemingly proved to be good. Countries are constantly changing. Many facets of agricultural development have so far stubbornly resisted modification. Many problems remain unsolved. It would be a tragedy now to limit technical co-operation to what it has learned to do well, thereby denying it the opportunity for (costly) attempts to solve those problems with which it has failed so far.

What technical co-operation needs now is a flexibility within which it can draw on its past without being bound by it. Granted such flexibility, it is likely that much better forms and methods can be found in the near future than have so far evolved.

3. *Notwithstanding the increasing efficiency of programs of technical co-operation, two recent trends in the administration of United States bilateral programs have retarded the advance and ought to be reversed.*

One of these is the trend to more "economic" criteria in judging proposed projects. The other is the reduction of the authority of chiefs of field party and the increased authority of Washington officials in project selection.[2]

The first of these trends apparently came about through the decision to consolidate, in Washington, the administration of technical co-operation and of economic aid in a single agency. Since the appropriations for economic aid were so much bigger than those for technical co-operation, it was inevitable that the latter should receive greater consideration in policy formation. What happened in fact was that criteria presumed to be valid for projects of economic aid have been increasingly applied to projects within technical co-operation as well.

This increasing application of conventional economic criteria reveals an insufficient appreciation of the importance of the self-generating resources for agricultural development.[3] It fails to give adequate value to the germinal concept of technical co-operation: the real value of technical co-operation is less in its immediate impact on production than in the increasing capacity of people in each country to solve their own future problems.

Urging a reversal of this trend is not to say that technical co-operation should not be "technical" or that projects having an early impact on production should not be chosen. The presence of some such projects in each country is of great importance, primarily because it helps establish confidence in public programs for agricultural development and enthusiasm for expanded efforts. But the major criterion in project selection should be the probable effect of each project on the self-generating resources for agricultural development. If this is done, projects will still deal largely with improving efficiency in the use of economic resources for agricultural production and for farm family welfare, but they will be chosen from among such projects primarily on the basis of their relative *potential effect in augmenting the self-generating resources* for agricultural development and rural welfare.

The second mistaken trend is that away from delegated authority to the chief of agricultural field party in each country and toward the concentration of authority, particularly in project selection, in Washington. The error in this recent trend is partly that the program in each country should be suited particularly to the distinctive needs of the country and partly that, in order to work effectively with the minister of agriculture of a country, the chief of field party needs to have policy and administrative discretion. Under the recently prevailing situation, he is increasingly considered to be a technical subordinate to a usually non-agricultural country director (called "Chief of U.S. Operating Mission") and competent not to make policy decisions but only to forward project suggestions to Washington. This major handicap is increased by the fact, now widely recognized by Latin-American officials, that in Washington project proposals are both delayed and subjected to inappropriate criteria in many cases. In practice, only those chiefs of field party who have been in a country since long before the change in policy or who have unusually able and influential country directors are able to compensate for the ill effects of the current policy.

This major criticism of these two current United States policies is not made without knowledge of the inherent and complicated problems of administering a world-wide governmental program of technical co-operation. (An attempt was made to outline and understand these in chap. xvii.) But in trying to reconcile many conflicting administrative and policy desirabilities, the decisions that gave rise to these two recent trends sacrificed the greater needs in order to satisfy lesser considerations. The pressures contributing to those decisions came only partly from within the Foreign Operations Administration. They came also from ill-advised pressures of other agencies of the government and from ill-informed public opinion within the United States. With the information now available, it ought to be possible to reverse both trends.

4. *Even if programs of technical co-operation had not seemed to "pay off" so far, broader political considerations would demand that they be continued and be made more effective.*

This conclusion is based on observations and data that were incidental by-products of field work in this study. It goes beyond the internal aspects of technical co-operation and agricultural development. Still, it is so much an outcome of what has already been done through programs of technical co-operation that it demands consideration in any decisions about the future of such programs.

The United States stands in a peculiar, contradictory position in the minds of many Latin Americans, particularly in the minds of the political elite of each country. The power of the United States is resented and feared, particularly in the parts of Latin America closest to it. The prosperity of the United States is envied throughout Latin America. The technology of the United States is respected and coveted even while many Latin Americans, often in compensation, argue that "you North Americans think only about efficiency; we Latin Americans place a higher value on friendship."

The political ideals of the United States, especially those given expression in the early years of our country, are, for the most part, shared or wistfully regarded, though among the ruling aristocracy of some countries they are written off as Anglo-Saxon and unsuited to a culture with its roots in Spain and in the high Indian civilizations of the Americas.

It was into this ambiguous situation, in which cries of "Yankee imperialism" were both frequent and strident, that technical co-operation was introduced. The war-orientation and the "complementary crops" phase of the early programs did not touch rural people broadly, and, among political leaders who knew about them, these programs seemed adequately explained by United States self-interest narrowly and selfishly conceived. As the programs expanded, however, and were oriented more and more to the distinctive needs of each country, the attitude of many Latin Americans toward them began to change. As programs widened out to work directly with thousands of farmers and with hundreds of Latin-American technicians, the impression of United States ideals being put into practice with neighbors gained ground. Here was the belief in the value of each individual expressed in helping Latin-American farm families learn to improve their own lot. Here was democratic administration intent on encouraging technical colleagues to develop their own powers and on giving them freedom in which to work.

To be sure, the trend toward viewing technical co-operation as proof of a new era of neighborly helpfulness between the Americas has not been even and uninterrupted. It has been set back by examples of personal callousness and by occasional arrogance. It has been retarded by baffling contradictions between what seemed to be the friendly intent of technical co-operation and certain United States trade policies that seemed to fit more readily into an older period of economic imperialism or isolationism which many hoped was dead.[4] It has been interrupted by major fluctuations in United States interest in technical co-operation and by occasional swells of public sentiment that technical co-operation should be curtailed as an unwarranted drain on the taxpayer. These setbacks, however, have been counterbalanced by the opportunities opened up through programs of technical co-operation and by the obvious friendship, concern, technical competence, and hard work of many United States technicians.

Technical co-operation, to much of Latin America, has become a primary symbol of United States integrity with respect to its own social, political, and economic ideals. It is an indication that the United States means business with respect to sharing opportunities and building the basic fabric of a peaceful, friendly world. The United States can greatly strengthen this impression by giving to technical co-operation: (1) continuity of support, policy, and administration, (2) priority in the recruitment and assignment of some of its most competent personnel, and (3) adequate protection from the commercial and military policies that must be other phases of relationships among nations.

It is because of this symbolic role of technical co-operation with respect to United States sincerity and integrity in inter-American affairs that the United States could not afford, at this stage, to decrease or let fail the new co-operative venture between countries (which it created) even if results to date had been disappointing.

5. *Technical co-operation can be both a highly creative profession for those who engage in it and an enriching experience for important sectors of the public of the United States.*

This conclusion, in itself, is not an adequate justification for continuing programs of technical co-operation. At the same time, the first part of it can be an important factor in securing competent personnel for these programs, and the latter part recognizes an incidental effect that may become a major asset within the United States.

Participation in programs of technical co-operation can be a highly rewarding experience. Obviously, it is not for everyone. There are many United States technicians in Latin America who are unhappy or frustrated, partly because of the circumstances in which they find themselves but more because they fail to recognize their opportunities, within whatever limitations. For people who like to tackle novel problems, for those who like to combine learning with teaching, for those interested in learning why there are differences between cultures and countries—technical co-operation offers intriguing opportunities for technical achievement with opportunities for personal growth in human understanding and friendship, and for family experience outside the confines of the culture in which one happens to have been born. It often throws an interesting and instructive light on problems still unsolved within the United States. Obviously, no opportunity can combine these advantages without exposure to contrasts that may lead to tensions—tensions in which the more adaptable persons grow and in which the weakest may break.

Many technicians with experience in technical co-operation like it so much that they want to make a career of it. Although a few have been in United States programs for many years, current policies hold no guarantee of career possibilities. It would strengthen technical co-operation if they did. But even within present limitations, technical co-operation can be one of the highly rewarding "frontier" experiences of American life, and the career possibility is not entirely lacking.

Technical co-operation also enriches the experience of many citizens of the United States who never participate in it personally, except by supporting it through taxation. These primarily are the faculties and student bodies of participating universities, friends and families of technicians who learn of it through correspondence, those who read published accounts about it, those who come in contact with citizens of other countries who come to the United States (through technical co-operation) to study, and policy-makers and administrators within the United States government.

One of the handicaps of the United States in its new role of international prominence and responsibility is its limited understanding of other peoples. Such understanding can be increased in various ways, but one of the best is to work together with people of other countries on tasks of mutual concern. This kind of co-operation is frequently disillusioning, because it is knowledge gained with the sleeves rolled up, in the heat of everyday labor, and frequently with pride intruding from both sides. But it is more realistic and therefore more valuable because of this. Reports of technical co-operation activities, the participation of returned technicians in United States institutions and agencies, and the increased understanding by the government of the everyday problems of the people of other countries, in their fields and factories and offices and homes, are important contributions to the maturing of the United States in international affairs.

A STATEMENT BY THE NPA SPECIAL POLICY COMMITTEE ON TECHNICAL CO-OPERATION

The NPA Special Policy Committee on Technical Co-operation has considered, without necessarily passing on details, *Technical Co-operation in Latin-American Agriculture,* by Dr. Arthur T. Mosher. Like other research associates of the NPA Project on Technical Co-operation in Latin America, Dr. Mosher has based his monograph on firsthand observation of bilateral, multilateral, and private programs of technical co-operation in agriculture in Latin America. His detailed account of the way the public and private agricultural programs work, what they have and have not accomplished, and his conclusions on ways to increase their effectiveness should prove useful to policy-makers, administrators, and the public generally.

Real progress has been made in many areas in Latin America toward increasing agricultural productivity and raising the living levels of rural people. But the vast majority in Latin America and in many other parts of the world are still following traditional practices and making a meager living on their farms. Technical co-operation can and should be used to spread knowledge and skills that will help these millions of rural people help themselves in achieving a better life. Dr. Mosher's study was confined to Latin America, but we believe that many of his findings offer guide lines to other parts of the world.

We take pleasure in recommending to the NPA Board of Trustees, therefore, that *Technical Co-operation in Latin-American Agriculture,* by Dr. Arthur T. Mosher, be published as a research monograph of the NPA Project on Technical Co-operation in Latin America.

MEMBERS OF THE COMMITTEE

LAIRD BELL, *Chairman*, Bell, Boyd, Marshall & Lloyd
THEODORE W. SCHULTZ, *Director of Research*, Chairman, Department of Economics, University of Chicago

JAMES M. BARKER, Skokie, Illinois
WILLIAM L. BATT, Philadelphia, Pennsylvania
ALFONSO CORTINA, Mexico City, Mexico
MARRINER S. ECCLES, Chairman of the Board, First Security Corporation
HERBERT EMMERICH, Director, Public Administration Clearing House
CLINTON S. GOLDEN, Solebury, Pennsylvania
R. G. GUSTAVSON, President, Resources for the Future, Inc.
OSCAR HELINE, Marcus, Iowa
JAMES H. HILTON, President, Iowa State College of Agriculture and Mechanic Arts
ERIC JOHNSTON, President, Motion Picture Association of America, Inc.
RT. REV. MSGR. L. G. LIGUTTI, Executive Director, National Catholic Rural Life Conference
CLARENCE E. PICKETT, Honorary Secretary, American Friends Service Committee
GALO PLAZA, Quito, Ecuador
SERAFINO ROMUALDI, Inter-American Representative, AFL-CIO
MRS. RAYMOND SAYRE, Ackworth, Iowa
MISS ANNA LORD STRAUSS, New York, New York
H. CHRISTIAN SONNE, President, South Ridge Corporation
GEORGE K. STRODE, Whitingham, Vermont
RALPH TYLER, Director, Center for Advanced Study in the Behavioral Sciences
LEO D. WELCH, Director, Standard Oil Company (N.J.)
DAVID J. WINTON, Chairman of the Board, Winton Lumber Company
MRS. LOUISE LEONARD WRIGHT, Midwest Director, Institute of International Education
OBED A. WYUM, Farm Program Consultant, Farmers Union
ARNOLD S. ZANDER, International President, American Federation of State, County and Municipal Employees, AFL-CIO

★ ★ ★

JOHN MILLER, *Assistant Chairman and Executive Secretary of the National Planning Association and of the Policy Committee*

418

APPENDIXES

APPENDIX A

NPA PUBLICATIONS POLICY

NPA is an independent, non-political, non-profit organization established in 1934. It is an organization where leaders of agriculture, business, labor, and the professions join in programs to maintain and strengthen private initiative and enterprise.

Those who participate in the activities of NPA believe that the tendency to break up into pressure groups is one of the gravest disintegrating forces in our national life. America's number-one problem is that of getting diverse groups to work together for this objective: To combine our efforts to the end that the American people may always have the highest possible cultural and material standard of living without sacrificing our freedom. Only through joint democratic efforts can programs be devised which support and sustain each other in the national interest.

NPA's Standing Committees—the Agriculture, Business, and Labor Committees on National Policy and the Committee on International Policy—and its Special Committees are assisted by a permanent research staff. Whatever their particular interests, members have in common a fact-finding and socially responsible attitude.

NPA believes that through effective private planning we can avoid a "planned economy." The results of NPA's work will not be a grand solution to all our ills. But the findings, and the process of work itself, will provide concrete programs for action on specific problems, planned in the best traditions of a functioning democracy.

NPA's publications—whether signed by its Board, its Committees, its staff, or by individuals—are issued in an effort to pool different knowledges and skills, to narrow areas of controversy, and to broaden areas of agreement.

All reports published by NPA have been examined and authorized for publication under policies laid down by the Board of Trustees. Such action does not imply agreement by NPA Board or Committee members with all that is contained therein, unless such indorsement is specifically stated.

H. M. Horner, Chairman of the Board, United Aircraft Corporation

Eric Johnston, President, Motion Picture Association of America, Inc.

Fred Lazarus, Jr., President, Federated Department Stores, Inc.

Murray D. Lincoln, President, Nationwide Mutual Insurance

David L. Luke, Jr., President, West Virginia Pulp and Paper Company

James G. Patton, President, National Farmers Union

Clarence E. Pickett, Honorary Secretary, American Friends Service Committee

Walter P. Reuther, President, United Automobile, Aircraft, and Agricultural Implement Workers of America, AFL-CIO

John V. Riffe, International Representative, United Steel Workers of America, AFL-CIO

Elmo Roper, Elmo Roper & Associates

*Theodore W. Schultz, Chairman, Department of Economics, University of Chicago

Herman W. Steinkraus, President, Bridgeport Brass Company

Charles J. Symington, Chairman of the board, The Symington-Gould Corporation

Robert C. Tait, President, Stromberg-Carlson Company

John Hay Whitney, J. H. Whitney & Company

David J. Winton, Chairman of the board, Winton Lumber Company

J. D. Zellerbach, President, Crown Zellerbach Corporation

NOTES

NOTES

NOTES TO PREFACE

1. See my "The Role of Government in Promoting Economic Growth," in *The State of the Social Sciences,* ed. Leonard D. White (University of Chicago Press, 1956), pp. 372–83; "Latin American Economic Policy Lessons," *American Economic Review* ("Papers and Proceedings" issue), XLVI (May, 1956), 425–32; and "The Economic Test in Latin America," Sidney Hillman Lectures, Cornell University, March, 1956.

2. See Kathryn H. Wylie, "Food Consumption in Mexico," *Foreign Agriculture* (United States Department of Agriculture, August, 1955). The average daily per capita calories for 1935–39 are given at 1,680 and for 1953 at 2,490.

3. For one such program see Arthur T. Mosher, *Technical Cooperation in Latin America—Case Study of the Agricultural Program of ACAR in Brazil* (National Planning Association, December, 1955).

NOTES TO INTRODUCTION

1. These last are countries also studied by the whole NPA research staff or by the writer.

2. These studies were made by Dr. Cesar Cisneros, professor of economics, Quito University, Ecuador, and now on the staff of the Organization of American States in Washington.

NOTES TO CHAPTER 1

1. Some of these are considered in the study by John Deaver, *The Roles of the Export-Import Bank and the IBRD in the Transfer of Productive Techniques into Latin America* (National Planning Association–University of Chicago Studies," TALA 55-030, July 29, 1955).

2. These are discussed by Simon Rottenburg in *The International Transfer of Technique: United States Firms in Latin America,* to be published by the University of Chicago Press.

3. James Maddox, *Technical Assistance by Religious Agencies in Latin America* (Chicago: University of Chicago Press, 1956).

4. A very helpful brief summary of cultural features of Latin America which are particularly pertinent to the subjects of agricultural development and technical co-operation is to be found in Brunner, Sanders, and Ensminger, *Farmers of the World* (New York: Columbia University Press, 1945), chapter ix, "Extension Work in Latin America," by Charles P. Loomis. This chapter is helpful both in its discussion and in its numerous references to other source materials.

5. The spectacular recent increases in agricultural production in Mexico are cited in chap xi.

NOTES TO CHAPTER 2

1. This account concerns only agriculture, and it omits a great deal of detail about the history of these agencies of technical co-operation. A much more complete historical sketch is to be found in Glick, *The Administration of Technical Co-operation,* to be published by the University of Chicago Press.

2. This is the program still widely known as Point 4. At different times, the Institute of Inter-American Affairs (IIAA) has been independent, then a branch of the Technical Cooperation Administration (1950–53), then a division of the Foreign Operations Administration (1953–55), and, since 1955, a division of the International Cooperation Administration. The name "Institute of Inter-American Affairs" has stuck throughout these administrative reorganizations in Washington and will be used throughout this study to denote United States bilateral programs in Latin America.

3. Creole Petroleum Corporaton; Shell Caribbean Petroleum Company; Mene Grande Oil Company, C.A.; Socony-Vacuum Oil Company.

4. Bolivia is excluded from this calculation, since the greater part of U.S. contributions to that country was really economic aid, not technical co-operation, but the appropriations for the two are lumped together in the statistics.

5. The history of this rivalry would make an instructive study but has not been intensively investigated as a part of the present study.

6. One experienced administrator in this field, formerly a high official of OFAR, said to the writer in conversation: "Looking back now, it seems to me that there were two major weaknesses of the programs of OFAR. (1) They never really represented the best in U.S. agriculture. We hired men away from other programs to serve under OFAR, but we failed to utilize the organized resources of U.S. bureaus and colleges. (2) The programs did not put nearly enough emphasis on training nationals as technicians. The need for this should have been obvious to us. For example, when the OFAR program in Ecuador was started, there were only two Ecuadoreans with a college education in agriculture."

7. See p. 188.

8. *Yearbook of Food and Agricultural Statistics,* Vol. I: *Production,* Vol. II: *Trade; Yearbook of Fisheries Statistics; Yearbook of Forest Products Statistics.*

9. FAO is not primarily an agency of the United Nations, since it has its own independent charter, governing body, and list of member nations. However, in view of the existence of FAO, the UN did not set up a specialized agency in the same field, but FAO performs the functions of a specialized food and agriculture agency of the UN.

10. *Report of the Secretariat of the Inter-American Economic and Social Council on Technical Assistance Activities in Latin America* (Washington, D.C.: Pan American Union, 1954), Agenda, topic 2, item *c,* p. 66.

11. "Expanded Programme of Technical Assistance for Economic Development," Seventh Report of Technical Assistance Board to Technical Assistance Committee, Economic and Social Council, UN, Official Records, 18th sess., New York.

12. Material supplied by IIAA and summarized in *Statistical Base Book for U.S. Bilateral Programs in Latin America* ("National Planning Association–University of Chicago Studies," TALA 55-021, May 2, 1955), Table 2, line 5.

13. In Uruguay, IIAA really had no program, although an appropriation of $1,600 was shown for it. Similarly, FAO listed programs in Bolivia and Guatemala for 1954 but showed only $1,000 devoted to each. Eliminating these three leaves seventeen country programs for IIAA and sixteen for FAO.

14. This figure includes 252 technicians of IIAA, about 50 of FAO, and about 33 in the two agricultural projects of OAS.

NOTES TO CHAPTER 3

1. For examples of such statements see pp. 48 and 108.

2. London: Oxford University Press, 1953, pp. 117–204.

3. Another, and much more comprehensive, summary of thought and experience with respect to economic growth is to be found in W. Arthur Lewis, *The Theory of Economic Growth* (London: Allen & Unwin, 1955). This important book came to the writer's attention just as this report was going to press. As its author states in his Preface, "The factors which determine growth are very numerous, and each has its own set of theories. What I have done is to make not a theory but a map. So many factors are relevant in studying economic growth that it is easy to be lost unless one has a general perspective of the subject" (p. i).

All that can be said here about the conclusions of this study and those of Mr. Lewis in his study is that they are consistent. The conclusions of this present study are drawn from field obervation in Latin-American agriculture only, while Lewis roamed a wider field and discussed in far greater detail the total field of economic growth.

NOTES TO CHAPTER 4

1. Roberto F. Letts, writing in 1924, stated that the coastal rivers discharge 80 per cent of their volume in three months of each year (*Aprovechamiento de las Aguas del Peru*, as quoted in *The Peruvian Economy* [Washington, D.C.: Division of Economic Research, Pan American Union, 1950], p. 40).

2. The material in the table is quoted in Washington Patino, "SCIPA (in Peru) and Point Four" (Lima, 1953; mimeo.), p. 13. Official exchange rates within this period were: 1942–48, soles 6.50 = $1; 1950, soles 15.43 = $1; 1951, soles 15.18 = $1.

3. Estimate of Andrew J. Nicholls in *Development of the Peruvian Extension Service* (Washington, D.C.: U.S. Department of Agriculture and Department of State, August, 1952).

4. By a combination of 1, 2, and 3, SCIPA is confident that potato production can be increased from two to fourfold in different sections of the *sierra.*

5. This is largely a study of SCIPA as it was operating in 1953. For a historical summary of its activities and development, see "Development of the SCIPA Program" (Lima: SCIPA Information Department, January, 1954; mimeo.)

6. Summarized *ibid.*, pp. 20–21.

7. For a more detailed account of this extension project, see Andrew J. Nicholls, *Development of the Peruvian Extension Service* (Washington, D.C.: Office of Foreign Agricultural Relations, August, 1952).

8. While this is a frequent argument advanced for postponing home-economics extension, it is of very doubtful validity, in view of the factors discussed in chap. xii, pp. 250–52.

9. "Development of the SCIPA Program," p. 25.

10. These demonstration farms, although discussed here under a separate heading, are administered as part of Facilities and Services for Agriculturalists.

11. To some analysts, this reduction in the number of families employed is a social cost that should be incurred only very gradually. To others, of equal competence, the actual displacement of agricultural labor is the necessary first step to increased industrialization. In either case, the families displaced had to find new employment, and this is an example of the readjustments individuals have to make in any dynamic, progressive economy.

12. Cf. p. 48.

13. Under such circumstances, a program is likely to reflect the interests and emphases of the minister and the chief of field party. In the case of SCIPA, inasmuch as there have been thirteen ministers of agriculture in Peru in the past ten years while the same man, John R. Neale, was chief of field party during the entire period (except for 1951), it is understandable that Mr. Neale has been primarily responsible for the form that the program of SCIPA has taken.

As a matter of fact, the easiest way to describe the program of SCIPA briefly is to say that it is the institutionalization of John R. Neale "playing by ear" on the problem of developing the agriculture of Peru—"playing by ear" not haphazardly but out of the background of his own experience and without any written score to follow, since the agriculture of Peru must be developed within the unique culture of Peru, and the needs of that agriculture have not, as yet, been scored.

14. From analyses of office records made by field investigators of this study.

15. From monthly report of SCIPA for December, 1952.

16. P. 40.

17. Buitron, chief of the Section of Labor and Immigration, OAS, served as a member of the field party of TALA in its study of Peru.

18. These circumstances are those that need to be developed in the ministry of agriculture of each country, a matter discussed more fully in chap. 16.

19. These consisted of interviews with randomly selected farmers in which they were asked what they knew about SCIPA and about the Ministry of Agriculture, what services they receive from each, and what services they would like to have but cannot get.

20. In Paraguay, jealousy between *servicio* personnel and the local agents of the Paraguayan Supervised Credit Organization, formerly intense, has been substantially eliminated by the practice of inviting the latter to serve as members of the local agricultural committees organized within the *servicio* program.

21. See pp. 352–53.

22. This discretion was withdrawn by FOA in Washington early in 1955 by the so-called "Operation Blueprint" requiring not only uniform procedures in all countries but the approval of each project by Washington as well. Re-establishing field discretion with respect to new projects is a primary need of these programs.

NOTES TO CHAPTER 5

1. This quotation is from Selden Rodman, *Haiti: The Black Republic* (Devin-Adair, 1954), p. 28, and the foregoing sketch of Haitian history borrows heavily from this source.

2. Some observers claim the élite holds much land but only speculatively. If true this does not change the argument here; for they would still lack real interest in agricultural productivity, and only such an interest can result in an understanding of the problems of agricultural development.

3. The use of "IIAA" rather than "SCIPA" at certain points in this chapter conforms to a recent division of authority between the *servicio* "SCIPA" and other IIAA technicians in Haiti. Part of the U.S. Field Party in Agriculture works through SCIPA and part of it works with ODVA.

4. In addition to these, a few minor irrigation projects have been taken over by the Haitian government.

5. Cf. p. 51.

6. It was reported to the writer that better progress has been made with animal-drawn implements at Aux Cayes, a region not visited in the course of this study.

7. A few months later, SCIPA was concerned lest this success backfire. This crop had the unusual advantage of very high soil moisture, and new diseases may have come in with the seed.

8. With 2,500,000 acres of arable land and 3,800,000 people dependent on agriculture for a living, Haiti has only about two-thirds of an acre of arable land per rural person.

9. This term, which throughout this study is used to denote that portion of a population having substantial political influence, can be misunderstood with respect to Haiti, where it is customary to use the term for the socially prominent, with ancestry going back to leadership in the early days of Haiti's independence from the French. Like all aristocratic classes, that social elite deplores but recognizes the swelling of its ranks by the rise of new families of wealth or of contemporary political power. Thus

the use of the term in Haiti is now approaching the meaning of the word in this study.

10. From George H. Hargreaves, "Irrigation and Drainage Problems in Haiti" (Salt Lake City Congress of Irrigation and Drainage Division, ASCE, September, 1954).

11. No new projects of irrigation have been undertaken by SCIPA since October, 1952.

NOTES TO CHAPTER 6

1. We use the term "real" to distinguish such revolutions from those which merely involve transfers of power within privileged classes.

2. Department of Economics, University of Chicago, 1953. See also Moore's "Agricultural Development in Mexico," *Journal of Farm Economics,* XXXVII (February, 1955), p. 72.

3. These initials are from the name of the agency in Spanish: Oficina des Estudios Especiales.

4. *The Mexican Agricultural Program* (Rockefeller Foundation, 1953).

5. For an instructive account both of agricultural conditions in Mexico and of the OEE program, see E. J. Wellhausen, "Rockefeller Foundation Collaboration in Agricultural Research in Mexico," *Agronomy Journal,* XLII, No. 4 (April, 1950).

6. In 1955 there were seventy Mexican technicians (including trainees) on the OEE staff. Ten of these had had more than two years of training in the program. Two were men with Ph.D. degrees who had been in the program more than five years.

7. The Central Station of the Corn Commission at Cortesar, near Celaya, put out 1,740 tons of seed in 1953. So far, the Corn Commission has subsidized this multiplication program. It provides single-crosses to growers to produce double-crosses to be returned to the Corn Commission for distribution. Since the Corn Commission has no salesmen and no decentralized distribution system, the possibilities for increasing the use of hybrid corn have not been fully exploited. Some opinion favors a revised policy by which the Corn Commission would provide only single crosses and would encourage the growers who produce double-crosses to go into the business of selling double-cross seed direct to farmers. (Already this is done to some extent without authorization.)

8. In 1954 the Wheat Commission was abolished and the task of multiplying wheat seed was given to the Extension Service (Plan Agrícola Mexicana) and to the two banks (Banco de Credito Ejidal and Banco Agrícola). These banks give out seed from their warehouses for multiplication, and extension agents designate the fields from which seed is to be brought back to the banks for distribution.

9. There are two other factors that may be responsible for the more modest success with beans. One is that relatively less attention has been paid to this crop by OEE. The other is that insect control is a major problem with beans in Mexico, and the Mexican practice of interplanting corn and beans prevents application of the insect-control measures that bean culture requires.

NOTES TO CHAPTER 7

1. The statistics on trade are taken from *Cuba as a Market for United States Agricultural Products* (Foreign Agriculture Report No. 81 [USDA Foreign Agricultural Service, September, 1954]).

NOTES TO CHAPTER 8

1. The substance of this chapter has been published separately as *A Case Study of the Agricultural Program of ACAR in Brazil* (National Planning Association, Washington, D.C., December, 1955).

2. The American International Association for Economic and Social Development (AIA) is a philanthropic organization, located in New York City, sponsored and supported by Nelson Rockefeller and his brothers. It launched an agricultural program in Venezuela in 1947, and in 1948 it surveyed the possibilities for a similar program in Brazil. After considering several possibilities, AIA accepted an invitation of the governor of Minas Gerais to co-operate in establishing a program in the state, and ACAR was organized.

3. This statement may have to be revised in view of a study now being made by Clifton R. Wharton, Jr., at the University of Chicago, on rates of return on capital invested in agriculture in Minas Gerais.

4. A third, smaller program of supervised credit was started in Honduras with the help of a technician provided by FAO. Started in only six localities, it is reputed to be working well.

5. Letter of James Maddox to the writer.

6. The names of these farmers are fictitious, but the cases are real.

7. Four of these cases do not appear on the charts because inclusion of them would require an impractical scale.

8. This fear, which was strong in 1954, had receded by 1956. Every indication in 1954 was that AIA would withdraw in 1955, but it reconsidered in 1955, and in 1956 it was expanding operations widely in several parts of Brazil.

9. In this discussion of the expense of the ACAR program, no comparison has been made of its cost with that of other programs of technical co-operation in the field of agriculture in Latin America. Such comparisons are seldom fair, because programs differ so greatly in size, objectives, type, and obstacles or "resistance." If such a comparison were made, ACAR would rate very well. The annual amount put in by AIA has never been above $75,000, and at least half of this has represented the cost of providing North American personnel. Other programs of comparable size have had much larger foreign contributions, and in them the proportion of total costs borne by the recipient government has been lower.

NOTES TO CHAPTER 9

1. Only one narrow-gauge railway connects the coast and the highlands; it is out of commission, because of the line being broken, for frequent stretches running into weeks each year.

2. Ecuador has many fewer trained agricultural technicians than Peru but has nearly as many as Bolivia.

3. There may be a valid case for long-continued research in Latin-American countries by the USDA, but that is not technical co-operation within the definition of this study. Since this program in Ecuador, at least after 1951, was supposed to be oriented to Ecuadorean needs, such a policy of exclusively United States personnel is clearly untenable.

4. One of the steps taken by the new chief of field party early in 1954 was to get a competent outside expert to review the work which had been done on wheat. He is reported to have advised that considerable valuable data has accumulated, and arrangements are now under way to get this published.

5. OFAR advanced arguments against the integration of its programs in IIAA which sound reasonable: that agricultural programs abroad should be related to the Department of Agriculture in Washington; that OFAR can select more competent agricultural technicians than can IIAA; that the USDA can give technical backstopping to agricultural programs abroad. However, its arguments are not substantiated by facts in the field. Its personnel are certainly no more competent than men with similar assignments under IIAA. Technical backstopping is not discernible. And IIAA has unquestionably tried to orient programs in the directions (*a*) of being truly co-operative and (*b*) of contributing rapidly to local agricultural development. The one country in which an OFAR program changed directions at an early date and became well oriented to serving local agricultural development is El Salvador.

NOTES TO CHAPTER 10

1. The Inter-American Institute at Turrialba was organized as an international agency in 1944. It became a specialized agency of the newly organized OAS in 1948, along with seven other inter-American agencies. The institute at the time of its organization was intended to become a center for research in the tropical problems of Latin-American agriculture and a center for postgraduate training for Latin-American technicians. Its location in Costa Rica was decided after a survey of a number of sites offered to the institute by different countries in Latin America. Although it has been handicapped from the beginning by lack of sufficient funds, it has done substantial work in the field of research, and its postgraduate teaching has made important contributions. It is administered through the Council of the OAS and by a seven-member Administrative Committee appointed by the Council. The director and a staff committee at Turrialba are responsible for operations. Although its program has been of substantial help to Latin-American countries in agricultural development, the institute itself does not fall within the definition of programs of technical co-operation under consideration in this report, except as an administering agency. It administers Project 39.

2. The Anti-Aftosa Center has not been covered by this study.

3. Costa Rica, Cuba, Dominican Republic, El Salvador, Guatemala, Haiti, Honduras, Mexico, Nicaragua, Panama, and the United States.

4. Bolivia, Colombia, Ecuador, Peru, and Venezuela.

5. Argentina, Brazil, Chile, Paraguay, and Uruguay.

6. It should also be noted that practically all of these national courses were held at, and in co-operation with, national colleges of agriculture.

7. *Programa de Cooperación Técnica de la Organización de los Estados Americanos para el año civil, 1954* (Washington, D.C.: Union Panamericana, 1954), p. 34.

8. Memo of Alberto Lleras, secretary-general of OAS, to the Coordinating Committee on Technical Assistance, June 12, 1950.

9. The writer is aware that both the offering of national short courses (for students of a single country) and the practice of making brief advisory visits to member countries by the zone technicians of Project 39 have been criticized by the Coordinating Committee on Technical Assistance of the OAS as being outside the established terms of reference since "such activities constitute direct technical assistance to one member-country." He is, nevertheless, convinced that both practices, within limits, are sound and should be encouraged. At this stage of agricultural development, it is not wise to be doctrinaire. While the emphasis should rightly be on *international* short courses, both to spread benefits and because this is the rightful long-term field for a program of OAS, it would seem foolish not to capitalize on the interest in more such training aroused in particular countries by building on it while enthusiasm is active, particularly where a country is ready to bear most or all of the cost other than the time of technicians. As for advisory visits, Project 39 has a comparative advantage over other agencies for reasons given in the text, and such advisory visits serve an important subsidiary purpose in helping each country realize the benefits it does and can secure through enlarged participation in the programs of OAS.

10. Executive Committee, Turrialba, June 14, 1952.

11. The Inter-American Institute of Agricultural Sciences at Turrialba opened the first such course in July, 1956.

12. ECOSOC Resolution of April 10, 1950.

13. *Ibid.*, sec. 4.

14. *Ibid.*, secs. 4a, 4c.

NOTES TO CHAPTER 11

1. "Expert" is the official FAO designation for the technician-from-abroad within a program of technical co-operation.

2. The writer cannot vouch for the accuracy of this total. In at least one country, Honduras, the number of experts serving that country in this period was put at fifteen by records in Honduras, while the total shown in the information from Rome was only twelve.

3. FAO administrators point out that this ratio is partially the result of the high demand (relative to the supply) for foresters within the United States, resulting in salaries much higher in the United States than in Europe. Another explanation is that the chief forester of FAO is European and may have favored the appointment of European foresters.

4. The programs of IIAA in agriculture have not been strong in any of the five countries making the most use of FAO. FAO certainly is not responsible for weak United States programs; however, it may be that the device of individual experts is better adapted than the *servicio* to rapidly developing countries which already have many domestic institutions for agricultural development.

5. Clearly, the United States is not the only source of technical proficiency, nor is it at the peak of technical development in all fields.

6. The role of IIAA has been at least equally prominent in this development but in different fields of activity. The co-operation between the two agencies appears to be good.

7. In Honduras, the Ministry of Agriculture is responsible for matters related to agricultural *production,* the Development Bank for matters related to agricultural *marketing.*

8. It is argued by some that the example of *servicios,* operating bilaterally, has been used by certain Latin-American countries to push FAO in the direction of conducting such demonstration projects.

9. The duration of one fellowship granted by FAO was not designated by the ETAP Unit, FAO, Rome.

10. On seeing an early draft of this section, two high officials of FAO protested that FAO is powerless to make such changes and that the criticism implicit in this statement should be laid at a different door. Perhaps it should be made clear that "FAO" in this report is not a collective noun denoting the persons who at present are the employees of FAO but the organization as a whole. As the policy body of FAO is its biennial conference, it is that body which has to make policy changes.

11. This provision was relaxed somewhat by the "Biddle Plan," which reduced the liability of a host country to 40 per cent of the per diem of each technician and which required that this be deposited in advance with the resident representative of the U.N.

NOTES TO CHAPTER 12

1. This is not always true. There are many cattle farms in Brazil which are completely traditional in their operations but which do sell their crop on the market. Other examples could be added. But this does not invalidate the argument of this section that as agriculture enters the market more and more, adjustments between agriculture and other sectors of the economy become increasingly important.

2. This statement of this function of extension education should not be interpreted as a conclusion that extension education is "more important than" research or roads or schools. All that is being said here is that extension education is particularly valuable in helping people move from traditional to choice-making habits of thought and action.

3. See Committee of Allahabad Agricultural Institute, *Experiment in Extension: The Gaon Sathi* (Bombay: Oxford University Press, 1956).

4. It should be noted that these factors are discussed here because they appear to be particularly important in Latin America. The list might well be different for some other part of the world.

5. The co-operation of the International Health Division of the Rockefeller Foundation, over the past 30 years, has been a very large factor in this conquest of lowland and tropical diseases in many countries of Latin America.

6. Special study of the Consejo Bienestar Rural, a joint dependency of the Venezuelan government and of the American International Association.

7. See George I. Blanksten, *Technical Co-operation and Foreign Policy,* another in the NPA series, to be published by the University of Chicago Press.

8. Although this dramatic change is here ascribed to the nationalist leaders, it obviously had its roots much deeper in history. One of those roots was the fact that schoolboys and college students had studied in English, reading the liberal essayists of Europe, for 150 years. A second root was the large number who had studied the Bible in missionary schools or privately and had been strongly attracted by Christian ethics. A third was the increasing mobility of population and permeation of new ideas brought about by improved transport and communications. A fourth was the number of Indian leaders who had studied in Europe and North America.

NOTES TO CHAPTER 13

1. See chap. ix.

2. These programs are examined, in another monograph in this series, by Howard R. Tolley and James G. Maddox.

3. This is the field of the Pan American Anti-Aftosa Center of OAS, in Brazil.

4. This has been *biological* and *physical* research; foundations have not taken up research in the social sciences (which is also necessary to agricultural development) except in the case of the Consejo Bienestar Rural, in Venezuela, in which the American International Association co-operates. The only other institution making a real effort in the field of research in the social sciences related to agriculture and rural life in Latin America is the Inter-American Institute of Agricultural Sciences at Turrialba, Costa Rica.

5. Chiefly in the College of Agriculture conducted by the Presbyterian Church (U.S.) in Lavras, Brazil.

6. Mostly in Mexico, Ecuador, and Bolivia.

7. Except the programs of FAO. The difference here is that IIAA programs operate through *servicios,* whereas FAO provides adviser-technicians to wholly domestic agencies.

8. It may be noted that all of the successful limited-emphasis programs of foundations are in the rapidly developing countries of Mexico, Colombia, Chile, Venezuela, and Brazil.

9. See the case of negotiations with Mexico, recounted in Philip M. Glick, *The Administration of Technical Co-operation.*

10. These devices are analyzed and compared in chap. xv.

11. It also is the method employed by AIA, and by the Rockefeller Foundation with respect to its research programs in Mexico and Colombia.

12. There is considerable disagreement as to whether, when an agency of technical co-operation offers to share in the financing of a new program, the host government should be required to promise in advance to make the program permanent. This writer's judgment is that the question of such guarantees is of minor importance, and insistence on such a guarantee can actually impede a program. If the program is successful, it is reasonably certain that the host government will want to continue it. If it is not successful, it probably should be dropped or drastically reorganized.

NOTES TO CHAPTER 14

1. This should not be limited to training in skills (which can usually be more efficiently learned in apprentice training) but should prepare the pupil to continue his own vocational growth through self-education and through taking advantage of programs of edult education, including extension education.

NOTES TO CHAPTER 15

1. Inclusion of these observations as to characteristic mistakes is not a logical necessity to the choices being discussed here, but this chapter still seems to be the best place to summarize them.

2. The landed gentry in a country have political power and hold a substantial proportion of the total agricultural land, but they are far outnumbered by people operating medium and small-sized farms.

3. In Bolivia, the good initial policy has not been maintained, and a number of widely spaced offices have recently been opened.

4. There was no agricultural college in 1954 in Paraguay, Nicaragua, Panama, or El Salvador and no government agricultural college in Honduras.

5. See R. E. Buchanan, *University Contracts for Technical Cooperation.*

6. There is little point in including training in traditional methods of agriculture in school programs. These can be much more quickly and effectively learned through working on farms.

7. It will be recalled that in Peru land development is on a pay-for-service basis. In Haiti, on the other hand, a number of irrigation construction projects have been paid for out of *servicio* funds.

8. As pointed out in chap. xii, these are functions of private business both in the United States and in Latin America. Projects of reimbursable facilities within public programs of technical co-operation have, therefore, been frequently criticized. It is important to realize in considering this question that such projects are intended to be *temporary*, serving as a supply line for agricultural requisites only until commercial outlets become available. On the whole, the record of these projects is quite good for "going out of business" with respect to particular articles as soon as commercial sources develop.

In many parts of Latin America there is an added obstacle to the development of commercial supply lines for agriculture, over and above the normal reluctance of merchants to stock new and unfamiliar articles before a reasonable market for them has been proved. This is the size of national markets, coupled with considerable economic nationalism. The United States has the advantage in that it can absorb the total output of many firms of optimum operating size in each industry. This has the dual advantage of making domestic production of most of its needed agricultural requisites economic, and of creating conditions of competition among the firms. By contrast, many Latin-American national markets are small. Many countries cannot economically produce their own tractors, insecticides, vehicles, implements, etc., under competitive conditions. Freer international trade would help, but for the time being projects of reimbursable facilities within programs of technical co-operation with importing privileges from the United States are substantial contributions to the rate of agricultural development.

9. Cf., for example, the discussion of livestock demonstration farms in Peru, pp. 56–58.

10. These devices for technical co-operation are more fully discussed in Philip M. Glick, *The Administration of Technical Co-operation.*

10a. See also Kenneth R. Iverson, "The 'Servicio' in Theory and Practice," *Public Administration Review*, XI, No. 4 (Autumn 1951).

11. The administrative and budgetary arrangements within a *servicio* have already been discussed. See pages 47–49, 76, 109.

12. Human relations are an important factor in all devices of technical co-operation, but they are particularly important in *servicios* because of the necessity for joint administrative decisions and because of the presence of an outsider as the chief administrative officer.

13. This implies a delegation of authority by the outside agency (usually the United States government) to its chief of field party to negotiate such project agreements in consultation with, but not subject to ratification by, its headquarters office. Such delegation has not always been made, but it is an important ingredient in sound administration of technical co-operation.

14. There are cases in which this is probably true, as in El Salvador, where an agricultural *servicio* was established in 1955 after a bilateral program had been carried on without a *servicio* for a period of twelve years.

15. In Paraguay until 1953 the agricultural *servicio* used locally made office desks of beautiful Paraguayan hardwoods. These were replaced by desks shipped from the United States, for which the shipping charges alone were greater than the purchase price of Paraguayan desks.

16. The Banco Nacional de Fomento, the recently established Ministry of Agriculture, and the National Economic Council of Honduras, with all of which adviser-technicians of FAO have apparently been able to work quite effectively, enjoy this greater freedom.

17. James Maddox and Howard Tolley, "Training Programs within Technical Cooperation" (in preparation).

18. Simultaneously, the development of postgraduate facilities in Latin-American universities ought to be pushed. The logical first step is to send faculty members abroad for advanced study.

19. In Chile the agricultural *servicio,* DTICA, has made a contract with the Cultural Institute to teach English to selected Chilean technicians in order that language may not be a handicap when the occasion for foreign fellowships arises. By such planning in advance, this language problem can be adequately met.

20. See Buchanan, *op. cit.*

21. Although university contracts make recruitment easier under present conditions, the use of them for this specific purpose is only justifiable as an emergency measure. As discussed in chap. xviii, conditions of employment under regular bilateral programs should be so ordered that equally qualified men are available in adequate numbers to IIAA.

22. Cf., for example, the case of the State of Mexico Agricultural Programs, pp. 114–15.

23. OAS expenditures were set at $914,900 in 1954, according to *Report of the Secretariat of the Inter-American Economic and Social Council on Technical Assistance Activities in Latin America* (Washington, D.C.: Pan American Union, September 15, 1954), p. 32.

24. FAO expenditures were set at $1,237,700 in 1954 (*ibid.,* p. 26).

25. FAO has the authority to conduct programs of technical co-operation within its Regular Program, but, both because of the other demands on FAO and because of the special resources available for technical co-operation through ETAP, in practice nearly all of the regular budget of FAO goes to its Regular Program, and practically all of its program of technical co-operation is a part of the Expanded Technical Assistance Program of the United Nations.

26. See pp. 335–37.

NOTES TO CHAPTER 16

1. This is not in conflict with the judgment expressed elsewhere that wide publicity to certain projects can increase public understanding of the processes of agricultural development. Such publicity can be given to other projects carried on by a *servicio* while research continues as a basic project without fanfare.

2. There are, nevertheless, a few examples of considerable progress in extension education where advisers have worked with domestic programs. One is in El Salvador, and the procedure is now being followed in Ecuador. Likewise, Project 39 is making substantial contributions through its training courses in extension methods.

3. In discussing this point, Dr. Allan Holmberg has quite rightly pointed out that there are other reasons for lesser results among Indians in Peru than the character of their culture. One of these is that class consciousness is such in Peru that non-Indian extension agents prefer to work with those farmers in their areas who are not Indians, and extension agents are frequently derided by friends in the towns where they live for "going out to see the Indians." These factors limit in practice the success of SCIPA's effort to allot much of its energies to working with Indian communities.

4. Programs for family welfare are a point at which the experience of

Puerto Rico can be of great help. The University of Puerto Rico has developed a strong Department of Home Economics. The Extension Service of Puerto Rico has a strong home demonstration division. Effective home demonstration work is being done by Puerto Rican women in Cuba and Brazil. This resource could be more widely utilized.

5. New programs embodying supervised credit were launched in Peru and Bolivia in 1954, under contract with International Development Services, Inc. These should help to resolve the question whether being already accustomed to using money is essential to the success of supervised credit or whether supervised credit can make a substantial contribution to this transition. They should also throw light on the question of how much freedom from community control families have to have in order to benefit from supervised credit.

6. Cf. pp. 136–80.

7. The only technical co-operation program in which this function has been undertaken by itself is the technical-assistance program of the Cooperative for American Remittances to Everywhere, Inc. (CARE), and even that case was a subsidiary program giving rather than selling agricultural requisites. Its operations in Latin America have been very limited.

8. That even large machinery pools can be uneconomic when poorly managed is demonstrated by those of the Ministry of Agriculture in Brazil. These provide services at a ridiculously low rate to a few favored farmers, at a heavy cost to the people of Brazil (see pp. 140–41).

9. This whole question of college education and of university contracts is fully discussed in R. E. Buchanan, *University Contracts for Technical Co-operation*. See also pp. 333–37.

10. The possible exception, PCEA, a *servicio* in Peru for agricultural research only, was liquidated after two years.

11. This should not be construed as a criticism of the justifiable and valuable national short courses conducted by Project 39 on a supplemental basis.

12. See pp. 314–15.

13. It might be added that at this point the *resource* problem and the *welfare* problem of public programs merge very intimately. The small farms of Latin America contain a great deal of land that should be used as productively as possible. They are also the source of support for large segments of the population in each country, and at present yield only a meager living. These two considerations both point to the need for effective public programs to stimulate agricultural development on small farms.

This important distinction has grown out of the search for sound farm policies in the United States. The resource problem is to adopt public policies that encourage full utilization of agricultural resources of land, labor, and capital. The welfare problem is to assure a socially acceptable level of living for farm families. This distinction was first made by T. W. Schultz in *Redirecting Farm Policy* (New York: Macmillan Co., 1943).

14. This comparison of sizes of programs in different fields is of programs of IIAA only. It does not take account of expenditures on agricultural programs by OFAR, which were separately financed and administered up to 1951.

NOTES TO CHAPTER 17

1. Administration is such an important aspect of technical co-operation that a separate major study of it has been made within the NPA series (Philip M. Glick, *The Administration of Technical Co-operation*, to be published by the University of Chicago Press). The present chapter therefore contains only a short description of what seem, from the standpoint of programs in agriculture, to be the major administrative problems.

2. Although such a pattern of administration is unusual in public agencies, it is not unlike the current trend to decentralization of administration in many large business corporations.

3. Another factor may have been the frequent argument of headquarters administrators that "we are responsible to Congress for the funds appropriated for this agency; therefore we must determine policy and control operations." This argument has considerable validity, but it would still be possible for a competent headquarters administration to explain and defend the need for decentralization in technical co-operation. This is not abdication of responsibility but the only way effectively to discharge it.

4. In practice, it can commit itself to somewhat longer continuation for a few selected projects by deciding that those projects will be protected in any general appropriations cut unless there is definite action to terminate one of them.

5. See *Organization of U.S. Government for Technical Cooperation* ("NPA Technical Cooperation in Latin America Series" [Washington, D.C., May, 1955]).

6. Similarly, appointments to the very important post of director of U.S. Operating Mission in Latin-American countries, in 1953 and 1954, included a retired admiral, a paving contractor, a utilities lawyer, and a lawyer-rancher, none of whom had any previous contact with technical co-operation, but all of whom were personal or political friends of the director of the Foreign Operations Administration.

7. See R. E. Buchanan, *University Contracts for Technical Co-operation*, for a detailed study of such exchanges and of the administrative problems within them.

8. The writer is aware of the plea of some U.S. universities that they cannot spare good men for three years. This argument has validity, but the *field needs* for program effectiveness call for three-year terms.

NOTES TO CHAPTER 18

1. OAS has placed more emphasis on formal agricultural training than either of the other agencies. See Chart XVII.

2. The fact that FAO has made relatively more appointments of men in their forties than has IIAA may be explained partly by the fact that it can appoint technicians from any member country. Three of the five FAO appointees in this age range in the sample were from Latin-American countries. In addition, since most FAO appointments are for one year

only, it is more frequent for FAO technicians not to be accompanied by their families.

3. This calculation includes only the countries in which technicians have served under IIAA. A few of them have had other foreign experience under MSA, UNRRA, or in private employment.

4. This conclusion is based on the numerical summary; it does not take into account the important question as to whether the more or the less effective technicians have been retained by IIAA.

5. Further study might result in adding Honduras to this list.

6. See chap. xvi.

7. Another predilection of men from the U.S. Extension Service is to feel that only when extension is administered by a college is it "right." As pointed out earlier, in no Latin-American country is this the present practice.

8. An instructive series of case studies discussing specific proposed changes and cultural response to them is presented in E. H. Spicer, *Human Problems in Technological Change* (New York: Russell Sage Foundation, 1952).

9. The official language in Brazil is Portuguese, and in Haiti it is French.

10. See p. 116.

NOTES TO CHAPTER 19

1. Only *public* programs are discussed in this concluding chapter, since it is only with respect to these that public decisions must be made.

2. There are other pressing needs for policy and administrative changes in Washington. It is to be hoped that the reader has read the discussion of these in chap. xvii.

3. Discussed in chap. xii, pp. 267–70.

4. A recent regrettable example of this was the ambiguous amendment to Public Law 480 of 1955 by which technical co-operation was forbidden in any case in which it might help a country increase (even for home consumption) a crop of which there exists a current world "surplus." The ambiguity offers loopholes, but it also characterizes the thinking behind the amendment.

INDEX

INDEX

Adviser-technicians, 237, 328–29, 343, 357, 358, 360; operating, 226–27, 236–41, 283; survey, 236–41; training, 236–41, 361
Advisory visits (OAS), 193, 202, 203, 343
Agricultural development, 33, 245–70
Agricultural education, 256–57, 277, 281, 302–3, 315–18, 348; college, 315–18, 355–56; pre-college, 318
American International Association, 14, 136–80, 276
Andean Zone (OAS), 193–96
Animal-drawn implements, 87, 355
Argentina, 198, 213
Artibonite, 81
Attitudes, 90, 99, 120, 128, 138, 172, 173, 175, 177, 254–56, 268, 311, 312–13, 319, 352, 362, 367–68

Bejucál, 130, 191, 252
Bolivia, 194, 213, 253, 263, 264, 265, 269, 272, 274, 276, 277, 295, 315, 354, 357, 362, 396
Brazil, 136–80, 198–99, 217, 251, 252, 259, 266, 269, 272, 277, 278, 295, 296, 300, 354, 357
Budget policy, 90, 328
By-products of technical co-operation, 176–77, 310

Caribbean Commission, 229
Chile, 199, 200, 217, 272, 322, 357
Colombia, 196, 217, 253, 273, 275, 276, 277, 300, 357
Committee on Technical Cooperation (OAS), 208, 209
Community development, 69, 92, 93, 96, 97, 114, 302, 352–53, 367
Coordinating Committee on Technical Assistance (CCTA), 208, 209
Costa Rica, 216, 217, 273, 277, 278, 285
Credit, 61, 85, 91, 103, 143, 259, 281, 293

Cuba, 127–35, 192–93, 213, 263, 274, 278
Cultural missions, 105

Damien farm, 82
Decentralization, 174, 299, 347
Demonstration areas (OAS), 192, 197–200, 203–6
Demonstration farms, 56, 58, 319, 321–22, 355
Dominican Republic, 217, 276

Economic studies, 49, 132
Ecuador, 181–90, 217, 262, 265, 269, 277, 411
Education (general), 257–58, 366
Ejido system, 101–3
El Salvador, 217, 273, 277, 278
Engineering services, 58, 59, 319
Expanded Technical Assistance Program (UN) 21, 211–42
Export-Import Bank, 82, 185
Extension education, 50–52, 67–68, 83–87, 94, 145, 257, 275, 312–15, 329, 352, 365–66, 377, 396–97

Family welfare, 144, 171, 173, 174, 250–53, 257, 293, 320, 348, 353
Farmer organizations, 50–51, 80, 152, 200
Fellowships, 113, 134, 193, 195, 197, 221, 227–28, 300–301, 329–30, 356, 384
Fisheries, 222
Fonds Parisien, 77–79
Food and Agriculture Organization, 20, 26, 28, 211–42, 280–81, 287, 359–62; administration of, 370, 372, 373; advantages of, 344, 345; limitations of, 344–46; personnel of, 385–97
Forestry, 211, 214, 218, 221
Foundations, 7, 12–15, 100–126, 136–80, 281, 346–48, 384; advantages of, 121–22, 346–48
Future Farmers Clubs, 85

World Food Supply

An Arno Press Collection

Agricultural Production Team. **Report on India's Food Crisis & Steps to Meet It.** 1959

Agricultural Tribunal of Investigation. **Final Report.** Presented to Parliament by Command of His Majesty. 1924

Bennett, M. K. **The World's Food:** A Study of the Interrelations of World Populations, National Diets and Food Potentials. 1954

Bhattacharjee, J. P., editor. **Studies in Indian Agricultural Economics.** 1958

Brown, Lester R. **Increasing World Food Output:** Problems and Prospects. 1965

Brown, Lester R. **Man, Land & Food:** Looking Ahead at World Food Needs. 1963

Christensen, Raymond P. **Efficient Use of Food Resources in the United States.** Revised Edition. 1948

Crookes, William. **The Wheat Problem.** Revised Edition. 1900

Developments in American Farming. 1976

Dodd, George. **The Food of London.** 1856

Economics and Sociology Department, Iowa State College. **Wartime Farm and Food Policy,** Pamphlets 1-11. 1943/44/45

Edwards, Everett E., compiler and editor. **Jefferson and Agriculture:** A Sourcebook. 1943

Famine in India. 1976

Gray, L. C., et al. **Farm Ownership and Tenancy.** 1924

Hardin, Charles M. **Freedom in Agricultural Education.** 1955

High-Yielding Varieties of Grain. 1976

[India] Famine Inquiry Commission. **Report on Bengal.** 1945

Johnson, D. Gale. **Forward Prices for Agriculture.** With a New Introduction. 1947

King, Clyde L., editor. **The World's Food.** 1917

Marston, R[obert] B[right]. **War, Famine and our Food Supply.** 1897

Mosher, Arthur T. **Technical Co-operation in Latin-American Agriculture.** 1957

The Organization of Trade in Food Products: Three Early Food and Agriculture Organization Proposals. 1976

Projections of United States Agricultural Production and Demand. 1976

Rastyannikov, V. G. **Food For Developing Countries in Asia and North Africa:** A Socio-Economic Approach. Translated by George S. Watts. 1969

Reid, Margaret G. **Food For People.** 1943

Schultz, Theodore W., editor. **Food For the World.** 1945

Schultz, Theodore W. **Transforming Traditional Agriculture.** 1964

Three World Surveys by the Food and Agriculture Organization of the United Nations. 1976

U. S. Department of Agriculture, Agricultural Adjustment Administration. **Agricultural Adjustment:** A Report of Administration of the Agricultural Adjustment Act, May 1933 To February 1934. 1934

U. S. Department of Agriculture. **Yearbook of Agriculture, 1939:** Food and Life; Part 1: Human Nutrition. 1939

U. S. Department of Agriculture. **Yearbook of Agriculture, 1940:** Farmers in A Changing World. 1940

[U. S.] House of Representatives, Committee on Agriculture. **Oleomargarine.** 1949

[U. S.] National Resources Board. **Report of the Land Planning Committee. Part II.** 1934